Bomoki's Gate

Look for these other great titles!

Dar Tania – October 2016, a 100 page story
Malcor's Story – November 2016
Bomoki's Gate – April 2017
Bruce & Syliri, A Forsaken Isles "100 Page Story" – August 2017

For more information about the stories set in the Forsaken Isles, its characters, author, or whatever else inspires you to contact Dar Malcor:

Send me an email and join my email list
at darmalcor.weebly.com

Edited by Tony Reynolds, Brian McClean, and Benjamin Duffy

Library of Congress: 2017902999

ISBN: 978-0-9981076-6-0

Table of Contents

Preface and Synopsis So Far

Bomoki's Gate follows Malcor's Story but does not need to be read in order to understand or appreciate Bomoki's Gate. In Malcor's Story, Malcor left his home village of Klenna to become a paladin. Tanian paladins, also called knights, face two ritual challenges. The first tests their ability to withstand and endure pain and suffering through faith, coupled with healing. The second is to defeat a mighty foe.

Joining the Order of Water, so named because its knights are expected to be adaptable, Malcor broke the two-day record for the first rite, enduring five sleepless days of combat and fighting. This rite, a mix of combat training, endurance test, and starting skill assessment, also occurred under the healing prayers of the Temple to see how much healing a paladin could take. There is a limit. Part of the rite is to learn and master that limit.

The Order's leader, who turned out to be his aunt Dar Kendra, paired him with a veteran battle priest named Tembri. An augmentor-type battle priest, Tembri is able to change the outcome of his spells to better serve his allies. Together with the Order of Water, they left for the southern island of Khasra to render aid to a Tanian trading partner there called Ori. Ori had come under attack by a lich. Morbatten chose this lich to be Malcor's second rite – to defeat a mighty foe.

A lich is a sorcerer who strikes a deal with a god of necromancy to prolong their life through the consumption of others' life force. When they at last die, usually a violent death, their soul and those consumed by the lich, return to the god of necromancy. There is only one god of Necromancy and to say his name, Orcus, is to invite his attention in the world. As such, Malcor's people refer to Orcus as The Necromancer, or the Jade God.

To reach the lich, Malcor joined a party of Imperics, so named because the people of Ori worship the god Imperius. They reached the lich's mountain fortress and battled their way in. Through this quest, Malcor learned that he possessed the same affinity for the shadow dragons as his father Dar Kell.

In the course of this adventure, The Necromancer learned of the lich and sent its avatars, commonly referred to as hellhounds, to capture the lich. The Order blocked the hellhounds but could not prevent the lich from succumbing to the Jade God. Malcor and the Order faced the possessed lich. Wounded and nearly dying, Malcor communed with Takhissis and learned that the lich's soul gem could be retrieved and thus save his Order's victory.

Though Malcor successfully captured the lich's soul gem and swayed the battle from defeat to victory. he felt that because he did not face the lich, he had failed. Amidst great fanfare, Malcor and the Order returned the lich's soul gem to Morbatten and saved the Imperic nation of Ori. Promoted to the noble R'Dar title by the god emperor, Malcor returned to his paladin training. Feeling he did not deserve this, and increasingly challenged to master his inner shadow dragon powers, Malcor turned to isolated study and meditation when not in training. The human king of Morbatten, Dar Rojo, commanded Malcor to join the Nineteenth Legion marching to reinforce their armies in the Valley of Bloodstone when the first snow falls.

Though just four months have passed since Malcor first became a paladin, he now finds himself marching to the heart of The Necromancer's power. Plagued by thoughts that he might be an imposter, or at least undeserving of his acclaim and position as a holy knight, Malcor joins the Nineteenth Legion commanded by Verit, a hero appearing in Malcor's Story. Feeling trapped between pressure to fulfill a prophecy he does not believe in – that he is to become king, and his hopes that might be deserving of being a paladin, Malcor learns that faith requires sacrifice. While not all sacrifices are worth the price, Malcor must come to terms his role in the Sister Prophecy, which is what the Tanians call the prophecy about the next king.

One thousand seven hundred years have passed since Dar Tania rose up as Tiamat's first priestess. Malcor enjoys the rich paladin traditions established by Dar Tania and Captain Sean. With an eye single to the Goddess' will, paladins fight by divine inspiration and with holy powers. Unlike their Pha Rannic brethren who fight for the absolutist cause of Good, Tanian paladins fight to preserve the world as their Goddess' throne world. After all, dragons created the world, not Pha Rann. The god emperor Alerius, an eldar dragon and patriarch of the fire breathers, has assembled the colored dragons living in the mortal realms together as allies to advance Tiamat's claim that the world belongs to Her.

Morbatten's dragon religion thrives in their consecration-based worship which captures the faith and actions of all in Tania as power given to the Goddess. Only on this world of Tehra, which sits in the exact center of the multiverse, does the faith and worship of mortals increase a god's powers. Because of this, worshippers are defended and the gods fight a dynamic war of might, magic, and dominion against each other – sometimes with culture, and doctrine, and yes, swords as well. Tiamat's dominion is the colored dragons and a throneplane carved out from Hell itself. Tiamat's doctrine is to return Herself to Tehra and usher in an eternal paradise. Based on this doctrine, the god emperor Alerius has organized Morbatten as a human empire ruled by Temple priestesses acting as avatars of the Goddess. There are male priests too, though they are a new revelation from just three decades ago.

In contrast, the Necromancer, also known as Orcus, the Jade God, is an abyssal power that, like all other eldar, views Time as a disease. He views Tehra as the source of that disease and believes that by freezing it all into undeath, Time will cease and the state of the multiverse will return to how it was before Time: boundary-less, infinite, and exactly how Orcus wants it. Orcus' dominion consists of necromantic controllers that raise and continue undeath. He also claims two abyssal realms adjacent to the nexal gate of Chaos. This makes Orcus very powerful in Tehra, as he can step through the nexal gate to Tehra if open. In the First Cascade, such a gate opened. The first hellhound, Bomoki, has tended that gate ever since.

There are many gods active in Tehra, as well as other realms touching Tehra, but this world of Tehra is unique. Sentient creatures of any race native to Tehra can rise up, ascend, and become gods. When a mortal who worships or is consecrated to a deity ascends, the Tehran's new dominion is magnified into their god's dominion; think of a chess pawn becoming a Queen, from a divine perspective.

It's a lot like writing the Forsaken Isles' stories. In Dar Tania, we met the first priestess. In Malcor's Story, we met the legacy that Dar Tania created. Bomoki's Gate continues Malcor's Story. I'd like to thank and note the contributions of those who worked with me on this project.

Tony Reynolds, many thanks for your support and ideas. The Battle Priestess Sonnet is perfect. To read the sonnet out loud, with a drum instrumental, it's amazing. Your editing work makes this story a thousand times better. I'd also like to thank Darko Tomic, the artist who did such an excellent job on the cover art.

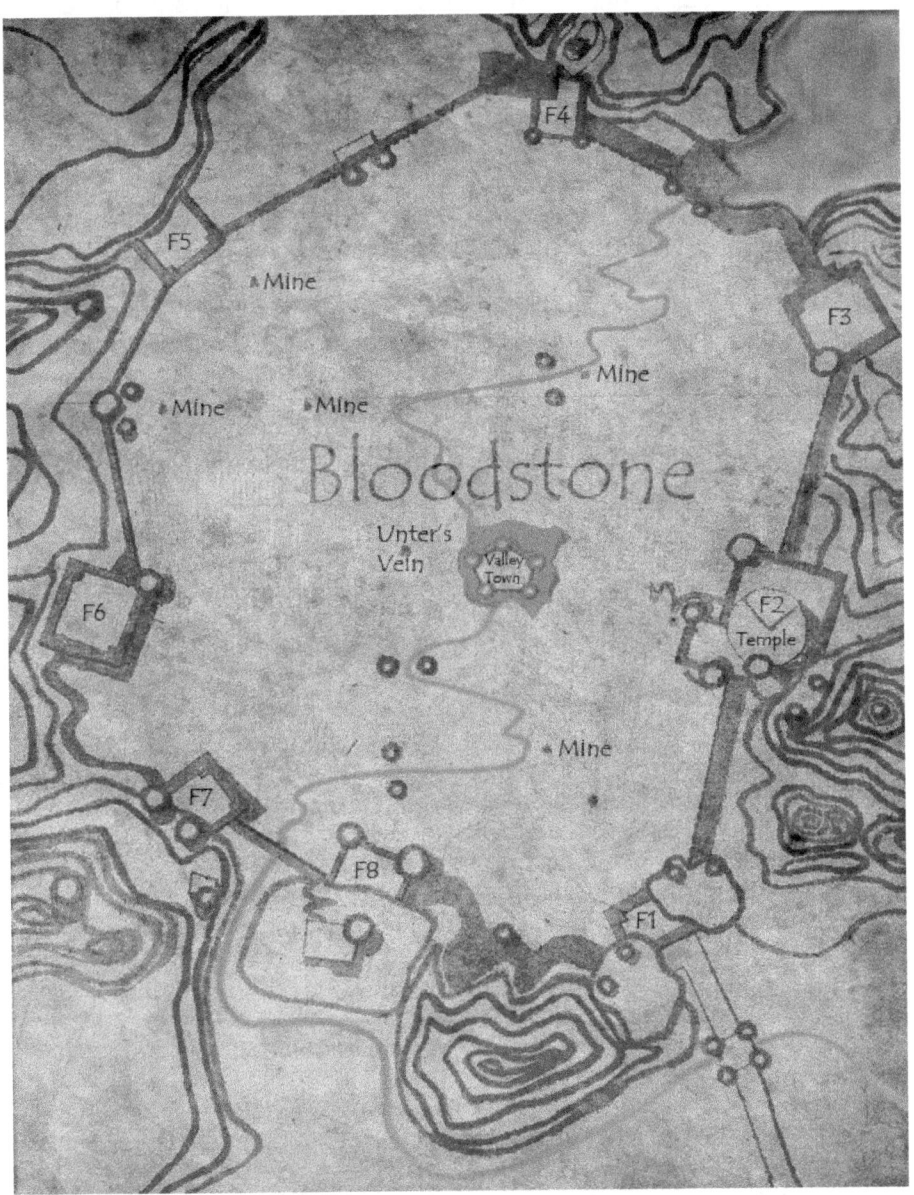

Chapter One – Cor'tanos the Shadow Patriarch

Seline entered the command tent and saluted Legion Commander Verit. "Seline du Quattrain, Knight of Fire, reporting for duty!" She snapped a formal salute and waited for Verit's to acknowledge her. The commander stood hunched over a table littered with maps and scrolls. Four runners stood with additional scroll tubes. Verit's battle priestess, Seline recognized her as R'Dar Fion, signaled for Seline to wait a moment.

After several moments, Verit wrote a few sentences and signed his name. He passed the scroll to one of the runners, who took the scroll and sprinted out of the tent. Verit cracked his knuckles and turned to see Seline. "Lady Seline, your reputation precedes you." He gestured to the pile of scrolls. "Somewhere in this mess is a glowing recommendation from Dar Niss. She said you, and I checked with the Temple, ranked first in your class in all disciplines. That's impressive. I'm hoping you have some skill with this bureaucratic stuff?" His hand swept the table again.

"Commander Verit, I do. My father, the Duke of Quattrain, wanted to ensure I'd be ready to take the throne."

Verit raised his eyebrow and Seline saw him take in the Order of Fire insignia. "It would seem that either your or the Goddess have different plans than ruling Quattrain then." Seline nodded with a wry grin. "Perfect. Lady Seline, I'm going to take a break. Please see what you can make of this mess. Fion will assist."

The priestess shot Verit a lethal glare but the commander had already left the tent. Seline set to work. Dar Niss had warned her that Verit had already asked her if Seline had skills that would help organize the legion. Three hours later, when Verit returned, Seline knew she had done a good job. Fion explained that Seline had organized a pile of work that Verit would need to handle personally. Another larger pile represented issues that could be delegated to someone Verit trusted. The last pile was for small items and issues did not matter. Fion picked up a card. "For example, this is a warm greeting and blessing for your success from the Merchant Guild."

Verit chuckled and said, "Fion, I trust that you and Seline will handle this going forward? What a relief."

Fion elbowed Seline, "I told you he'd try and get out of this."

The two ladies had established an easy rapport and Seline hid her smile. Verit picked up the several messages they had indicated he needed to handle. "This first one," Verit read aloud, "says that, because no new bloodstone mines have been found, less than a quarter of veteran candidates than predicted enlisted. It gives me an option to double pay to any of the current Legion's troops to stay with us." He rubbed his eyes. "This only works if we double their past five years' pay as well. We may as well inflate wages for everyone. No. We won't do this. Rather, I won't do this." He crumpled the parchment and threw it into a brazier to burn.

"My lord," Seline began. "If you want a break, I'm curious to ask – Niss, did she say if I should take tactical command?"

Verit began laughing. Not a loud or mocking laugh, but his words came as a relief to Seline. "You're Order of Fire, Seline. Yes. You'll be in the thick of it. But, there are no undead to fight here – just piles of parchment."

"Thank you, my lord."

"Verit. When it's just us, call me Verit." He turned to Fion. "This new class of paladins, so formal. Did you talk to Malcor about this?"

Fion replied, "I spoke to his battle priest. Tembri told me to tell you that Malcor still calls him by formal title as well."

Verit whipped his head back to Seline, "I command you to not be formal with me, except in front of the legion. Understood? And, when you have a chance, see if you can get Malcor to relax."

Outside the tent, the ground trembled. A sudden rushing of wind pulled at the canvas wall from all directions. Fion answered Seline's questioning look. "The aforementioned Malcor. He is still training with the shadow patriarch."

"So, it's true. I heard that Malcor would be in the Nineteenth Legion." Seline looked to Verit, "So, you're the Verit who fought the Khasran Lich."

Verit bowed and asked Fion, "When did they start training?"

"Midnight," Fion answered. "They've been at it continuously. I've had runners take food and drink to Malcor, but they all report that Cor'tanos gives him no time. They've been at it for twenty hours now."

The entrance to the tent brushed open and Malcor entered. He saluted and bowed. "R'Dar Verit," Malcor began.

"Malcor, it's just us. Call me, Verit. That's an order. Again." Verit noted the tremble in Malcor's clenched fist salute.

Verit studied Malcor more closely. The young paladin looked strung out and near a breaking point he desperately tried to hide. Cor'tanos, the dread lord of the shadow dragons, stood to the side in the shadows of the large command tent. Verit had grown accustomed to the red dragons and the presence they carried with them. This dragon though felt so different. Where the reds often felt overwhelming or triggered delusions of grandeur, this one just felt arbitrary and cold, as if at any minute, violence would happen thoughtlessly.

Verit willed himself to look calm. He had just listened to Malcor's report of training with Cor'tanos. It sounded needlessly brutal and violent. "So, when you shadow dragonshift or shadowstep as a human, you are still unable to recognize the real world? That's what I'm hearing you say."

Malcor's eyes glazed over a bit and Verit felt Malcor's shade from the lantern and lamp light writhe and twist. It unnerved Verit. He had to force that calm again. "Commander, my report is that I have extended my use of shadow, but" and the knight sighed so deeply it almost sounded a sob. "You are correct. I'm not making excuses."

"Nor should he have to," Cor'tanos interjected. "His progress exceeds his father's."

Verit noticed Malcor flinch at the dread lord's words. Verit asked, "Mastery? Progress? He is still a liability to the entire Legion. I have yet to see anything that says it won't be worse in Bloodstone. He needs mastery now."

Cor'tanos surged forward snarling and hunched down eye to eye with Verit. From just inches away, Verit felt the skin on his face chill and freeze. Verit forced a smile and continued, "He, you, this blessing you have given to him is, at this time, a curse to me and those I command. Powerful undead and the Jade God have dominion over shadows. You are this close," Verit held up two fingers in Cor'tanos' face, "to being undead yourself, dread lord. Prove me otherwise."

Cor'tanos smirked and stepped back. Frostbitten skin tore and blood ran down Verit's face from his forced smile and he hand-signed to his battle priestess for healing. Without missing a beat, he pressed on. "We need Malcor as a knight and we need him as a shadow dragon. So far, the knight restrains the dragon and vice versa. In the middle, I see the berserker who fought through the Khasran wilderness to topple a lich. I have yet to see mastery."

"He will show you. Now!" Cor'tanos roared. Malcor watched this exchange stoically, but leaning against a tent pole. For a just a moment, Verit thought he saw something akin to concern for the boy in the dread lord's expression but it passed. They left the tent and walked out to the large field behind their post. Cor'tanos pointed to the moon and said, "Malcor, you have a good mix of moonlight and darkness. Show your mastery!"

Malcor stretched out his arm and explained, "Before, I was trying to extend my shadow. Cor'tanos has taught me to instead wrap myself in shadow." In the faint moonlight, darkness rose up around Malcor like tattoos inking over his skin and then armor and clothing. His voice, now more a whisper, continued, "Extending my own body like this is similar to the enlargement blessing we use in combat."

He pointed his finger at a stone about five steps away. Though Verit did not see it, he felt movement and then a molten hole the diameter of Malcor's index finger appeared in the center of the stone. The hole stabbed into the ground behind the stone as well in a perfect line between Malcor's finger and the dirt floor.

"Very good," Cor'tanos cooed. "More. Show more!"

Malcor summoned his sword which quickly became painted in shadow from his hand. He prayed to the Goddess and flames burst from the blade, though the flames had an odd grey tint to it. "The shadows become an extension of my desires," and his arm pulsed into a dragon claw. The claw form rippled from his shoulder to his fingers and back. Verit noted that it was not a uniform claw as if either by will or exhaustion, the boy could not completely transform his arm. "When ready, Commander," Malcor said.

Verit nodded and so Malcor began a basic sword dance, like the katas used in training. It was an attack and defense drill used by knights just learning sword work, similar to other kata used earlier in sparring. Verit countered and joined the dance. It occurred to him that Malcor had been in the knighthood less than a handful of months. As the kata moved through its slowly building tempo, Verit saw that Malcor's other arm started to dragonshift.

Verit leaned back to parry during one of the moves. Right at that moment, Malcor's other hand reached out and grabbed Verit's shadow and pulled Verit off balance as if a real hand had yanked him. Though he quickly recovered his balance, Malcor's head dragonshifted and he found himself looking into the maw of a shadow dragon. Malcor breathed shadowfire just to the side of Verit's head. Appearing like grey lightning outlined by white flames, it shot past Verit's head.

Malcor helped Verit recover his footing and stepped backwards. In the tent wall behind Verit, a burning hole in the silk tent about a man's width in diameter glowed as the burning ring spread. "That was a restrained breath attack," Malcor said as his dragon head returned to his bald and forge-scarred human one.

Cor'tanos chortled. "You see, doubting commander? He has mastered this. Control of the total dragonshift can wait for the long march to Bloodstone."

Malcor held his form of two dragon arms. Verit summoned his shield and said, "I'm still doubting, dread lord. I doubt you can pull a hellhound off balance." His shield and sword erupted into flames that he slammed into Malcor trying to use his shield to sweep Malcor's legs and open him up to a sword attack.

The sudden light made Malcor's shadow arms waver and he barely dodged the shield sweep. "That was intentionally slow. Our enemies in Bloodstone can summon light." At a hand sign, Verit's priestess Fion ignited the multiple points of bright daylight all around. Verit stabbed into Malcor's center. "And fear," he grunted as he turned Malcor's parry into another attack that cut his face. "And they can use shadows. Who's to say that they won't be able to control Malcor?"

Malcor leapt clear of a sweeping firesword attack and dove outside the the bright ring of daylight. Verit followed and Malcor noticed the Commander's earring sparkle blood red. From that bloodstone gem, magic shadows, just like Malcor's grey fire, leapt out into a five feet high by thirty long wall. The ends of the wall, like a double-headed serpent, struck at Malcor with the dark fire twisting into snake heads. "And shadows are a type of necromancy! C'mon, Sir Malcor - must I kill you here? Show your mastery!"

Verit pressed his attack with Malcor barely able to deflect and parry. His wounds began to accumulate and his shadowform wept black blood. Barely keeping up, Malcor attempted to strike Verit from outside the flowing River of Time. Staying where he was, Verit parried and deflected as Malcor took his fight out of the River. It put Verit on the defensive but never once did any of the attacks land. Verit noticed that Cor'tanos watched the fight with great interest. It was clear that the dread lord wanted to help. Verit wondered, *Is he waiting for Malcor to pray to him? Perhaps I should let Malcor win rather than pressing him to that point. No, that is not the paladin way. Malcor, I must trust, will remain faithful to the Goddess.*

Verit parried a counterattack that stung his hand with its force. If and when the boy's prayers shifted from Tiamat to Cort'tanos, *Would the Queen notice? Cor'tanos surely will. No, I must trust Malcor's love of being a paladin.*

Verit's hand shot up as Malcor launched an attack from above. His hand caught Malcor's neck and he threw the boy from the River back to the ground in the real world. Stunned, Malcor struggled to breathe. Thrown from the River of Time so abruptly, he felt only asphyxiating anxiety.

The dragonshifted parts of his body began cracking away like dried mud. Malcor struggled to regain his balance as his slid through the grass and freezing mud. Verit saw Malcor still had fight left in him even though he was wounded terribly and beyond exhaustion now. It reminded him of Malcor's rites in the Order of Water and also the final battle in Khasra.

From behind Malcor, Verit saw Tembri, Seline, and others running up. "Look Malcor, you have an audience now!" Verit cried. "Like Cor'tanos said, show me more! Bloodstone won't let you rest." Using his bloodstone earring again, shadowfire erupted into a column that rose up around Verit into the sky. Malcor leapt at Verit his arms shifting into dragon claws even as Verit heard the boy call upon his sword's powers. Verit grinned and called on his own sword, "*Nightmare of Chaos* - hear me rage!"

"*Coming Undone!*" Malcor gasped, and their swords met in a shockwave that rippled out and washed over nearby tents smashing them to the ground. Something caught Mal's sword at the point of impact and then snake-like tendrils of fire shot out from their steel-on-steel edges. The fire from Verit's sword, the snake wall of shadowflame, and glowing daylight of the command tent eliminated any shadows and Malcor hung pinned in the air by burning knives piercing through him. Verit pulled back and the spikes retracted to drop Mal to the ground. All along *Nightmare of Chaos*, fragments of the edge began to crackle and sheer away.

Malcor coughed up blood, his body wracked through by pain everywhere. Wrapped in shadow, but just barely, he felt so close to death. Blood dribbled out from the shadows cracking off his body. He heard the Goddess laughing at him. How had he never figured out that there would be those able to pull him from the ethereal back into the flow of time? Malcor choked for air, "How?" If Verit heard, he did not answer.

He shook his head, trying to clear the bright images burning there. Shadowvision and bright lights did not mix well. He almost signaled for healing, but no. So far, he was letting Verit set the rules. If he signaled for healing, so would Verit. His mind darted back to memories of his first rite and he realized, he had no more healing left in him. His training with Cor'tanos had drained all the available clerics. The training's pace was just one day, not five.

Malcor's body barely moved and struggled to stand. He knew Verit was looking at him, watching him, daring him. From a distance he heard

Tembri's voice, but his head swam. In the midst of wondering if he could go on, Cor'tanos' voice chided him. "Did you think being a shade is easy? I pushed you harder than this earlier and you fought and fought for mastery. Don't you dare give up! If your body fails, use the shadows to move it."

Malcor lifted his head and saw Verit, just as he imagined. Verit's eyes dared him continue the fight. *Why won't my legs move?*, he wondered. *I must not fail!* He tried to use the shadows but they would not respond to his desires. Cor'tanos mocked him now. He knew if he looked, he'd see the shadow dragon ridiculing him. Malcor knelt up trying to stand. It made his entire body tremble.

Feeling Coming Undone in his hand, he curled his fingers around and wrapped them to the blade with shadows. He prayed to the Goddess for strength. She seemed to ignore him and so he called to Cor'tanos instead and remembered their training, the first time he met the dread lord, and his father Kell. It strengthened him a bit. Cor'tanos felt it, that glimmer of faith in him rather than the Queen and exulted. In this marvelous world, Malcor's tiny spark of faith filled him with power and he returned a portion to the boy as an answer to that prayer. Malcor saw Verit's face darken and knew he'd made a mistake.

A hand sign from Verit cut Tembri's healing prayer. Tembri could feel Verit's sword straining for blood and victory, like a leashed attack dog. Verit circled Malcor like a predator, swinging what remained of his sword. Though wounded, Tembri saw no immediately fatal wounds but without aid, Malcor would die. The key thing though was the boy's demeanor. Tembri saw that drained look as if undeath itself had emptied him of blood and vitality. He knew Malcor was probably praying, or reciting scripture, or studying Verit looking for an opening. The dread lord watching met Tembri's eyes and it struck him that the dread lord cared for this young paladin, and then the feeling passed.

Next to him, Seline came up and gasped when she saw Malcor's condition, appearance, and the rivulets of blood raining down his arms, back, and legs. Malcor tried to stand, using his sword as a support, he barely made it. Tembri felt something then, something odd, and he shifted to the River's edge. He saw his charge standing in a stream of darkness. Before him in that black nightmare, Verit stood aflame in the Queen's many colors of favor. On the other side of the River, Cor'tanos stood. At the moment Malcor's prayer shifted to an ask for help from Cor'tanos, Tembri saw the dread lord's shadow reach across the River and wrap around Malcor. Their shadows touching in this place, both Cor'tanos and Malcor seemed to energize.

In the real world, Tembri watched Malcor inflate as vitality and energy flew into him. Tendrils of shadow wrapped around Malcor's body and, using the shadow for control, Malcor re-engaged battle with Verit. Across the way from where Tembri had arisen from time's flow to see, Cor'tanos winked at him. The shadow patriarch then leapt into the sky, dragonshifted, and flew away from the River with a hungry shriek.

Malcor took a deep breath and re-joined Verit in combat. His wounds remained, but he fought on solid footing as he unleashed a series of attacks that drove Verit back. Though Verit parried, Malcor's strength vibrated through their sword strikes, igniting the air with fury and gray lightning and black fire.

When Verit tried using a particularly strong attack/parry to trigger the same fire attack he used before, Malcor spun his sword and cut the tendrils of fire. *Coming Undone* continued to chip away at *Nightmare of Chaos*. Verit compensated by saving the blade for definitive strikes and used more of the bloodstone earring's magic and punch-kick attacks.

Though the wall of fire kept seeking Malcor, he moved fast enough to dodge it. So long as he pressed his attack on Verit, the wall remained too slow to respond and react. Verit needed concentration to control it and Malcor kept the commander distracted.

Seline gasped suddenly realizing that the two combatants had kept to the sword kata the entire time even as they improvised and added new attacks and magic. "How does Malcor do that?" she asked Tembri. "I just barely got good enough at it in my last couple of training sessions to see where I might improvise, but I was also trained well before the knighthood. Mal, he was a -"

"An armorer, yes." Tembri said. "But he is also gifted with an almost instinctive understanding of combat. That doesn't mean any of us couldn't go toe to toe with him and win. It just means that you have to fight him as if he were someone like Verit or Kendra, at all times. In this case though, Verit is also a gifted and talented warrior in his own right. If Malcor were not near death, I can't tell who wins. Malcor is obviously exhausted. Look how he uses the shadows to strengthen his body!"

"I never thought someone like Malcor, someone at my level, could stand against someone like Verit," Seline marveled.

Their fight raged for several minutes, back and forth as fire and shadow tore at each other. At last, Malcor struck at Verit with such force that Verit almost lost his sword grip. He jumped backwards to dodge the follow up, and Malcor's right foot kicked out with all his might. He missed Verit by many steps, but then Verit winced and grabbed his thigh as the shadow kick connected with Verit's momentary shadow in the raging light.

Malcor had moved Verit to a position where their combat created just enough shadow for Malcor to use his own shadow as a weapon. A small molten hole and a cauterized lance wound speared through Verit's left thigh. "Got you at last," Malcor said. He then collapsed unconscious, dropping to the ground like a curtain falling in the wind.

Tembri ran up to check on him, but Verit called him to back off. "No," the commander growled, "no one sleeps during war. Malcor! Our fight is not yet done! Stand and fight!" His words spoken as the *Voice of Command* made Malcor's body twitch. "Stand and fight!"

Malcor struggled upright and drunkenly moved to attack but this time, Tembri caught Malcor in a head lock. "Verit, the boy is unconsciously obeying you. As his battle priest, I ask you to stop. Or at least, tell me your purpose so I may help."

Verit sheathed his sword but as he did so, *Coming Undone's* magic shattered the blade. The commander winced seeing the cracks growing through the pommel and dropped it while walking over to Malcor. Mal struggled to attack and obey but when Verit saw the boy's unfocussed eyes, he nodded. "I see."

"Commander, he is loyal and more than anything desires to serve and prove himself. I, however, with the same desires, do not see how continuing this proves anything."

Behind Tembri, the onlookers nodded in agreement though were careful not to meet Verit's eyes when he looked at them. Seline stood her ground, "Captain, this far exceeds my own rite from the looks of it. Please, help me understand so that I too may help."

"It's easy. I wish to test his mastery of the shadows. In the past, he loses all self-control and goes berserk when the shadows take him." Verit, who partially held Mal by his face, let go and said, "Sleep, knight." Mal collapsed into Tembri's arms.

Addressing the group, Verit said, "Listen to me now. Though this young knight is a primary objective for us, I have another I wish to add to your thinking. We go to Bloodstone to fight, to serve, to live. Surviving is another primary purpose, and I – as your commander – will be damned if we throw our two primary objectives against each other to our detriment! We have almost two months of travel to the valley. We will use that time to continue training." He looked at Malcor while speaking, "To figure out how to use this shadowdragon as a blessing, a weapon, a tool to break our enemies. Seline, send out word. In three days' time, we receive a very important guest, and on that third day, we head out. Ensure all is ready for a noon departure. Also, Seline, please have a mage send you back to Morbatten. You are to ensure that the dog soldiers join us on schedule."

As Verit walked back to his tent, he said, "Tembri, bring me Sir Malcor when he recovers. We have much to do. And, Tembri, Malcor owes me a new sword. During the journey, I'll make arrangements with the Mage's Guild to allow him to teleport to the forge and make a replacement."

Tembri nodded and carried Malcor away to their hospital tent. Verit remained standing in the field destroyed by his fight with Malcor. Only the pommel of *Nightmare of Chaos* remained. Verit knelt and closed his eyes. Clasping his holy symbol of Tiamat, he prayed and asked, "Shall Malcor be punished for seeking divine aid of Cor'tanos?"

No answer came. Verit stood and breathed deeply as he felt his numerous wounds. R'Dar Fion approached and sent healing prayers his way. "Most of my armor requires repair too," Verit said to her. The hole through his leg ached even with healing. Malcor had just missed his bone and major arteries. "I wonder if that was on purpose." Fion shrugged and helped Verit remove his damaged plate mail. "Fion, I need you to combine with me. There is a question I must ask the Queen."

Combining her might to Verit, Verit knelt and repeated his prayer. When no answer came, Verit said, "Fion, how many other clerics are available to combine with me?"

"None, my lord. I held myself back in case you needed me, but throughout their long training, the shadow lord and Malcor exhausted all of the priestesses as well as the contracted adventurers."

Verit's eyes widened. "All of them? Everywhere in Klenna?" When Fion nodded, he sat down on the frozen ground. "This one day then is close to his First Rite."

Realizing this, his answer came at last as a whisper in his mind. "Malcor is pressed all about by shadows. No atonement. I require that you give the knight Malcor a reason to remain human, to remain mortal. This is where Kell's madness began. He will realize his error and castigate himself. The pain of today's combat is sufficient. Give him reason to live."

Chapter Two – The Eighteenth's Relief Army

Calvin leaned back on Soldier Fort's battlements while several columns of soldiers marched out for Bloodstone. The red banner with a central black circle left blank for their campaign number snapped in the breeze. They squinted from snow blowing into their eyes. Up here, the wind made it so much worse. *They will pass through Klenna*, he thought. He threw a rock into the gravel watching it bounce and clear the snow from its impact. *I wonder what they'll say about Malcor.*

The cadence of soldiers' footfalls gradually faded as they passed out of sight and then the clip-clop of horses approached. He looked up and groaned, suddenly wishing he was anywhere else. The banners and heralds of a high priestess bade him bow. The high priestess did not even look at him, but the sight of her forced him to re-evaluate his scale for judging a woman's beauty. The high priestess looked beyond beautiful. If he were only a knight, she would no doubt take him with her. The wind whipped the banners and it was not until the heralds had passed him that he saw the people he did not want to see. She was already waving at him. Lady Seline pulled out of line and urged her mount forward to Calvin. Behind her mounted unit, more infantry followed. Calvin saw that Ayden also broke ranks and ran forward to join him. He put on a brave face.

Seline had changed, even more than the last time he saw her. Always intense, her eyes now glowed a faint red and several red tribal tattoos danced, barely noticeable, along her temple and ears. Her armor glinted with red glowing Temple verses, which only made him more aware of his own lackluster and shabby appearance. He tried to look unimpressed, but when Seline jumped down from her saddle and hugged him, his composure broke. "Lady Seline, you look like a knight of legend." Something about her touch made his skin tingle, like how he felt as a young boy her presence.

She stepped back and spun around for him. "Why, thank you! And you look like one of those officers unimpressed by anything. How is the myrmidon training working for you?"

He shrugged. "It is what it is. It's nothing like being a knight, but I'm learning and trying to adjust my expectations."

Ayden calling out to him interrupted his next sentence about how he was thinking of leaving entirely. As Ayden ran up, Calvin introduced the two. "Oh, you two know each other?" Ayden asked somewhat confused. She tugged at her hair where it grew over her facial scars. Calvin wondered if she felt as inadequate as he did around Lady Seline, and then it occurred to him that the Order of Fire had recruited Ayden. *Why is it that everyone moves up except me?*, he complained inside.

Seline answered Ayden, "Yes, Calvin and I joined the initiates together in the Order of the Shield. We went through the first several rites together. By the way, I need to catch back up to Dar Niss. Calvin, should you come to Bloodstone, please find me. I will keep a commission open for you." She winked at him, waved goodbye to Ayden, and then she was gone.

"Are you going to Bloodstone too?" Calvin asked Ayden.

"Yes, aren't you? I figured you would be -" Ayden noted Calvin's lack of insignia that would tell her he had joined anything. "You're too skilled to stay in training," she said.

Calvin pointed to the blank Legion Star on her chest. *She already has an officer's commission. No wonder Seline knows her.* He sighed, "No, I decided to stay back and train some more. Your unit will be going through my hometown, and I – I guess I am not quite ready to face my family. I need more time."

"I understand, but you know. Most myrmidons don't even make it through the first rite. I certainly didn't. There is no dishonor. You are going to be one of the elite few who has. I'm sure your father will under -"

"No, no he won't. He's the mayor. All the people there, they all saw me with Malcor. They knew we left together to become knights. Plus, it wasn't just Malcor and me going off to become knights. The king talked to us, in front of everyone. The dread lords went all dragon and danced. Nothing like that has ever happened in Klenna. They'll probably be expecting something equally spectacular." He pointed to his armor. "I can't go back like this. They'll see me as a myrmidon standing next to Malcor the paladin. You do know about Malcor right?" he asked raising an eyebrow.

"Well, like most, I have heard the name. I haven't met him yet though. I didn't realize you two were friends." Stories about a new paladin defeating the Khasran Lich had spread far and wide starting about two months ago.

"And right there Ayden, that's why I can't go this time. Let this be Malcor's moment. You have heard stories about him. So have I. They're everywhere. What stories are told about Calvin of Klenna?" He laughed mocking himself. "None except that he washed out of the knighthood, he was Malcor's friend, Malcor rose while his friend fell. Some friend, though, as I haven't heard or seen anything of him since we entered the Temple."

"Oh Calvin, no one talks like that. The stories about Malcor and the Order of Water, they're too real to be true. There's no way someone just joining the knighthood could do all that. Can you even imagine?"

Calvin eyed her dubiously. "Says the girl who has yet to meet Malcor. Ayden, I watched him dance with the king and the knights. It is funny, growing up, I never would have thought that he'd be so much better than me at everything." He picked up a handful of stones and skipped them across the courtyard. Behind Ayden, more infantry streamed past. "Well, not everything, though he is a different class of warrior than I turned out to be. Hey, why is the legion star blank? You're the Nineteenth right?"

Ayden looked at it and held it forward. "We won't be official until we reach Bloodstone. The high priestess there will formally name us the Nineteenth. At least, that's what I hear. Most of us call us the Nineteenth, though our captain, I hear, is really particular about it. Someone told me that he calls us the Eighteenth's Reinforcements." One of the groups waved at her to join them. Ayden looked over her shoulder at the passing column of dog soldiers and said, "I hope to see you again, Calvin. Shall I tell him you said hello - your father?"

Calvin shook his head and hugging her, replied, "Good fortune to you, Ayden. May Bloodstone bless you with glory."

Hugging him back, Ayden kissed his cheek. "And may you find what you are looking for." Ayden turned and ran back to her column. Though frowned upon, breaking ranks to say goodbye to family and friends was tolerated in those who were going on long campaigns. Bloodstone, though almost an institution for hero-making, consisted of five year long campaigns. One by one, others broke ranks to hug, kiss, and speak good-byes. Some received gifts or tokens, while others grimly continued on with no one to see them off. Ayden looked back one more time and saw Calvin walking back to the Soldier's Fort. She wondered if he had hoped to see his friend. She wondered when she would meet this Malcor. Would the difference be what Calvin feared?

She turned to a young man walking beside her. "Have you heard about a new paladin, name of Malcor?"

The young man laughed. "Who hasn't? I mean, you mean the one that fought the Khasran Lich right? Oh yeah. I wonder if he'll be joining the Nineteenth too. Right timing for him. What do you think?" They speculated as they walked and Ayden, listening to the conversation through Calvin's perspective, felt a deep empathy for him.

The road twisted its way down from the Soldier's Fort and eventually met with the northern route. A caravan of supply wagons and strong draft horses waited just off the road. As her column cleared the intersection and turned westward, the supply line pulled out behind them. Apparently, it would accompany them all the way to Bloodstone. Looking at it, she guessed it must be three miles long.

They marched all day and Ayden grew accustomed to the stares of other travelers clearing the road for them. Sooner than she would have guessed, the trumpets signaling camp blew and she realized some number of hours had passed with her watching the back of the soldier in front of her. She struggled to remember exactly when she blanked out.

She missed her solitary walks in the high mountain passes around Soldier's Fort. With no leaves to crunch underfoot, she had come to appreciate the quiet grind of gravel and the sound of her own breathing. Marching like this in a group felt different. *We're moving from here to there. That's it.*

By nightfall of the second night on the road, they had made excellent progress and could see Klenna. Ayden's group picked a camp and sent a runner to the supply wagons. With military efficiency, tents and supplies appeared as if by magic. A dog soldier, a conscripted Tanian who then decided to stay in the army, set up their campfire and began cooking a hearty stew for the group. As was their way, the dog soldiers cracked jokes and asked how they all felt about going to Bloodstone. Ayden learned that their cook had been to Bloodstone two times. "Third time is the charm, so they say," he grinned. "I just know that this will be the one where I earn a commission."

Dog soldiers usually represented people lacking skills, interest, or qualifications for specialty work. The cook seemed battle-hardened and war-ready though. They made up the bulk of a legion having up to ten thousand of them. After military service, they would most likely become farmers or servants. Three Bloodstone campaigns guaranteed him a commission equivalent to Ayden's starting one. Ayden thought about the criteria and finally asked him, "Sir, in all your tours, no war party has asked you to join?"

The soldier, who had introduced himself as Bruun, chuckled and nodded. "I was asked and did join, but we fell prey to a cascade or other misfortunes. Cascades are a nasty business. All kinds of demons and divine powers clashing. Seems to only happen in Bloodstone though. The commanders of my party fell in battle. Such has been my luck all these days. But, this time will be different." He looked at Ayden and then raised his eyebrow, "You look as if you've had a bit of a scrap or two getting here as well."

Ayden's comrades looked sidelong at each other. Many had wanted to ask herbut none had dared after noticing her officer rank. During the long march out of the capitol, speculation about her facial scars ranged from a childhood accident to more fantastical attacks by monsters. The scars looked most like a clawed creature had raked her face.

Ayden smirked, "It's not something I enjoy talking about. But, since you made such a delicious stew. My home was along the frontier and one winter we were attacked by gnolls. I was nine years old. It was past midnight and we were all asleep. Their claws shredded through our home's walls as if they could see where we slept by the fire. They killed my father. Took my mother. I was too weak and scared to move. All I could do was pray for help. The Queen answered my prayer and I found my father's sword. I saved my younger sister and brother by killing two of them. I guess the gnolls were satisfied with my parents. I never saw them again. In the fight, after it was over, I had these cuts that go from my abdomen up along my chest and neck to my face. They're ghastly, I know."

The soldier grunted and said, "As a nine year old, you fought off those dog-headed goblins? Impressive."

"More impressive had I saved my parents." She handed her empty bowl back to Bruun for more. Tania fed its troops well.

"But still, you were a kid. Even if on the frontier," Bruun said. "I see you're a myrmidon? So you'll be one of our officers."

Ayden waved her hand to dismiss the notion. "Until we get to Bloodstone and are consecrated as the Nineteenth," she pointed to the empty star badge on her shoulder that they all had, "we're just reinforcements for the Eighteenth. Anyway, by the time we alerted the rest of the outpost, the gnolls were gone. Our cleric could not heal me though she did save my life. I suppose I never put my father's sword down."

Another soldier commented, "So that's where they came from. We thought it had to be something like that. Though we guessed robbers."

Ayden took another serving of stew back from Bruun and leaned back. "Robbers. Rapists. Monsters. I've heard it all. Truth to tell, as I get older, I kind of like the scars. They remind me that the Queen is there for me, even when I was too young to appreciate Her." She drew her sword. "That was my first kill. I dedicated my life to learning blade technique." She stabbed it into the snowy mud. "Your turn, Bruun. Tell me about the cascade. I'm not familiar with that term."

"You've heard stories though right? About how in Bloodstone, gods and demons pile up on top of each other? As one appears, a countering whatever appears and it escalates as each god summons allies to fight whichever enemy just appeared. Ghastly things. Being in divine presence is enough for me. Being in multiple presences all full of combat, it's beyond my ability to describe. Even now, I just have flashes of memory. I was thrown hundreds of paces away and unimportant as a mortal, was overlooked as the battle shifted away from me. At least, that's what they told me when I was found."

Conversation gradually turned to other topics and then, like blowing a candle out and falling into darkness, the camps quieted. They continued talking about Bloodstone just more quietly. Horses whinnied and snickered around them. Soon, the sounds of sleeping soldiers and quiet conversations became the normal tone.

Against that white noise, a lone figure seated high on a heavy war horse walked slowly and carefully through the camps. Like them, he had the empty star banner. He had come from Klenna. On the charger's back sat a young paladin in gleaming armor. The dim cooking fires cast the runes emblazoned on it in reddish hues. The young man was bald and Ayden noted where faint burn scars had removed his hair. Against the colored sky overhead, a glint of silver flashed and a falcon cried. When he drew closer to their camp, Ayden and the others felt an uncomfortable presence press into them. "Is it a dread lord?" someone whispered.

"Can't be," someone answered. "He wears knight's armor, no dragon markings."

Ayden, against every instinct in her body to kneel, struggled to stand. It felt right. "Ho there," she called. "Care to grab a bite before you pass on, sir? The knights are hours ahead." Her voice sounded lonely and weak, but something about this paladin compelled her to offer, and shamed her for not kneeling to him. The paladin turned his horse and stopped at Ayden's camp.

As the knight dismounted, Bruun moved forward with food ready and took the charger's reins. "Sir, it is our honor to have you join us. I'm Bruun, and this lass here," he pointed to Ayden, "is Officer Ayden." Until that moment, it had not even occurred to Ayden that she wore officer markings. No wonder the conversation had focused on her so much. *And here I thought they just liked having a girl in their group*, she chided herself.

"Yes, yes, please, here sit..." a chorus of voices rose up around him. The knight smiled and took the food. His horse tolerated being led away. Sitting, Ayden noticed that the back of his neck bore scars that had not been magically healed. Looking at them, they must run beneath his armor. The scars looked fresh and gnarled his skin. The young knight saw her eyes tracing the scars and shrugged. Normally, she would feel self-conscious about her face, but it seemed petty given how damaged he was. He looked over the group \ and Ayden saw his eyes find the banner over her small tent. "I see you, like me, are bound for Bloodstone. I am Malcor. What are your names?"

One by one they introduced themselves, some of their voices faltering as they realized who had joined them. Slowly, the camps around them joined to listen, to see this Malcor of the stories. Finally, unable to endure it, someone blurted out, "Tell us Sir, are you the Malcor we have heard about who went to Ori?"

He nodded half-smiling. "I am."

All at once, voices called out for him to tell his version, to set the stories straight: did he really fight a lich, a hellhound? What is the Order of Water? …and it went on and on. Watching him, Ayden heard Calvin's words run through her mind. She remembered Seline. Calvin would have felt so out of place. She imagined him standing here with Malcor. Calvin had been accurate in the difference. Malcor had not just risen compared to Seline; he had transcended. The difference between Calvin and Seline, and then Seline to Malcor, and she traced it in her mind. She saw that, like Calvin, she existed not just on a lower rung, but a completely different scale from the paladins. Malcor sat down by Ayden and complimented their setup. "I see this group knows how to work the logistics officers. Great setup."

The din around the campfire slowly faded and Malcor at last indicated he would tell his story. "Yes, I really did fight a lich. However, our legion commander R'Dar Verit took the main brunt, as did the rest of the knights in my Order. I was technically there, but my mission was different. Also, I never met a hellhound, nor did I fight a hellhound. I must be very clear here. My unit fought a lich and several hellhounds. I did not."

Disappointed looks fell his way as he continued, "My role in all of these stories was as an initiate. I was supposed to fight a lich, and for a few brief moments I did. The lich barely touched me and, without Takhissis' intervention through my battle priest, I would have died right then and there. R'Dar Verit, my battle priest Tembri, Dar Kendra - these are the names you should hear in these stories."

He noted Ayden's blade in the snow and slowly pulled his own sword out. "You really should not leave your sword in the ground like that," Malcor said quietly. Unlike most paladins' swords, Malcor's lacked adornment and decoration, except for fine gold draconian scripting worked into the edges.

It also lacked a point, ending instead in a blunt square. Rather than tapering, the blade widened slightly giving it a club-like appearance. He stabbed it into the snow next to Ayden's. He watched it and then, withdrew both. Giving Ayden her sword and re-sheathing his own, Malcor said, "So, let me tell you instead the story you have not heard. Our southern trading partner, Ori, had come under attack by a lich from the eldar times. The lich had assembled an army of goblins and other creatures that by themselves would not threaten Ori let alone the few of us assembled here at this camp. Backed by this lich though, eventually, the Jade God became involved. You see, everyday, they'd fight the living, and then at night, the lich would raise the dead, who then continued the fight. In some ways, it was like what Bloodstone is. My role was to fight a mighty foe. At the time, I did not realize it, but am told that I defeated several vampires and a greater revenant on my way to confront the lich. I don't want to bore you though. The part I remember most was…"

He told the story of how his group was trapped in the storeroom and more gathered around them from neighboring camps. Sitting so close to him, Ayden felt a near-divine presence ebb and flow of energy between herself and Malcor. She saw the others affected by it as well. When strong, it filled her with a desire to follow this knight. When it ebbed, she felt a warmth of regard that her life mattered in the grand scheme and that, while she might not see what role her life played in it, this knight and those like him did and would stand with her. Close to him, she felt energized and alive. She felt safe, perhaps even saved by this knight. It felt glorious and she saw Malcor in her imagination's eye as he laid out the real story.

Malcor had stopped talking as people asked him questions but Ayden blushed when she noticed him looking at her. That through-the-soul gaze made her shudder. He turned away to respond to a question and she heard him continue, "I was much honored to meet the God Emperor and his sons but credit for the lich cannot rest with me. Besides, this is Tania! Such feats, these belong to all of us."

An accented voice challenged that and all eyes turned to an Imperic lady. "I am Sako and I was part of Malcor's party. Though the Order did exactly what Malcor has said, it was Malcor who found and captured the heart of the lich's power – its soul gem. Having that, it ended the war. Ended the lich. Enabled defeat of the Jade God's influence which could have been very bad."

At her words, Mal dropped his eyes and the weight of renewed regard from those gathered in the camp returned to him. "My new friends, this is Sako. She and an Imperic priest Noboyuki are our guests during this tour. Is Noboyuki with you?" Sako shook her head. Malcor turned to the group and thanked them. "Never mind, I feel I have disrupted your evening routine.

Thank you for the food. Remember, all of the things, the stories, what we discussed, what you imagine might have happened, was all done in the Queen's name and for Her Glory forever. I am Hers. We are Hers forever."

The camp echoed his "forever". As he left, those nearest touched him and Ayden, fearing she would miss this, lunged forward to touch him too. She expected his armor to feel warm and was surprised at how cold it felt. Hours later, after he had left and the conversation surrounding him had faded, the chill in her hand remained a mystery.

The next day dawned to more of the same camp routine. When Klenna finally appeared the day after, Ayden felt only relief. Training, brutal as it had been for months, was not all day long marches nor was it absolute routine. It would be another six week march to Bloodstone and winter would deliver more cold days and nights before they reached their destination high atop even colder mountain fortresses. Eight fortresses carved by undead in the living rock circled the Valley of Bloodstone.

Chapter Three – Festival at Klenna

Klenna greeted Verit's command team decked out with bright flags snapping in the wind. The villagers threw flowers at them, probably dried all summer long for this very purpose. Posters declared a celebration at the shrine that night.

Ayden found the shrine that evening brightly lit with torches and large bonfires. Food and drink flowed everywhere. A podium in the courtyard had been erected and on it, a banner proclaimed the local armory as the celebration's sponsor, courtesy of the House of Sai. Another banner welcomed Malcor home.

Ayden assumed the man standing at the podium was Calvin's father but as she drew closer, she noticed another man dressed as the mayor and then the paternal resemblance to Calvin struck her. The other man looked around greeting villagers and welcoming the soldiers alike. His gaze, however, also looked for someone else. At last, Ayden saw his face light up and he drew his wife up to the podium with him. The man pointed Malcor out to her, and then they both waved calling to him.

As if by magic, the crowd parted in a straight line to Malcor. He grinned and waved back. Captain Verit, Tembri the battle priest, and the Imperics from camp followed Malcor to the podium. Though Malcor's parents bore no physical resemblance to him at all, they greeted their son with obvious family warmth. Malcor introduced Captain Verit and the others. While Malcor handled introductions, Ayden saw the mayor give up looking for Calvin. For a moment, he lingered near Malcor, hesitating. He left.

Ayden pulled Seline's arm and pointed back to the shrine. From the shrine, a priestess walked out. Dressed in a shimmering white gown and robes, she almost looked transcendent except her white hair did not burn with fire. Since Malcor's Coming of Age ceremony, more and more of the transcendent priestesses had been coming through town. Her lips, even from this distance, looked pale and cold where a transcendent priestess' lips would be ruby red. A silvery bird of prey jumped from her arm into the sky. The priestess walked straight towards them. Ayden could not remember a priestess like this.

The priestess paused on the edge of Malcor's circle until Malcor noticed her. His face came alive and he reached out for her hand. "Dad, Mom, this is R'Dar Ora." Ayden and Seline both chuckled realizing now how much effort Malcor had put into being proper. The priestess completely undid any sense of formality. Malcor began telling the story about how Ora had saved him from the House of Tor.

Ishan asked her, "So, you've known our son since he became a paladin?"

The priestess smiled and said, "Yes. Technically, a day before he became one. His Order asked me to help with his rites and imperial ceremonies."

Ishan's wife, Michelle, looked completely unnerved by being around so many heroes so Ishan asked for her. He pointed to Malcor's hand, which still clasped Ora's, and asked, "Are you two?"

Malcor began to answer but paused. Before it became awkward, Ora answered, "Malcor is a paladin and I love his faith and worship of the Goddess." She squeezed his hand. Overhead in the dark night, the silver falcon screeched. "If you don't mind, I'd like to speak with him?"

The mood proved festive and the people turned to dancing and singing as the entire village celebrated their son Malcor's return. At some point, the crowd pushed Malcor to the stage with cries for a speech. Ayden noted a number of local girls attempting to flirt with Mal and failing horribly. *Even without his crush on Ora, didn't they know a paladin when they saw one?* If Malcor noticed, it did not show at all. Again, Ayden felt stunned by how differently Calvin would handle the same situation. For some reason, she had a momentary vision of Calvin flirting with Ora and she burst into laughter.

Whatever Ora had said to him, Malcor looked a bit shaken. He climbed to the stage and cleared his throat to speak. "My friends, people of Klenna, my family. Thank you for this. Thank you very much! I never guessed that when you carried me here months ago that I would return to so much love and warmth. It humbles me. As my dreams have come true, I have tried to give back and am pleased that the armory has prospered. I understand there have even been fights about extra work?!" At this comment, the crowd erupted in laughter as smiths shoved each other back and forth.

"*Extra* work, who would have thought it?" More laughter exploded in pockets around the courtyard. "I understand stories have flown far and fast. I caution you to hear those stories and know that they do not accurately or adequately touch what happened. Bards exaggerate and manipulate words to rhyme or serve a rhythm's beat and tempo. They fail to do justice to my friends and the Order I serve, who took the brunt of the heroics noted in those stories. I can only hope and dream that someday I will fill the measure of those stories.

"In the coming days, more soldiers will arrive to prepare for Bloodstone. You know the stories and legends of that place. I will take Klenna with me in my heart and never forget my home, never forget you."

As Malcor spoke, Ayden felt her memories drawn to her own family. Unlike most of her thoughts of that time, these were warm thoughts. She remembered a loving family, playing in the winter snow, and autumn leaves. She remembered bonfires with the villagers and chasing her friends through forest meadows and paths. She hardly noticed at first but suddenly, she became aware of the priest accompanying Malcor. He stood right next to her. His large muscled bulk, how she did not notice this earlier, had escaped her somehow. He bore many scars and wounds and had the air of a veteran. He turned and smiled at her briefly.

For just a moment, she almost smiled back until she noticed a parchment floating in the air just to Tembri's other side from her. It glowed softly with magic and a feathered quill wrote words in ember Temple script. Ayden tried to recall what little she knew of the strange Temple language, *draconian*. The top of the scroll was easy enough to read. It noted today's date and the year of the Emperor's reign. It also noted Malcor's name and something else, the book of *something*. Tembri's right hand danced in the air as the quill wrote to the same cadence as Malcor's speech.

Tembri's left hand suddenly moved through a dance of gestures and he tapped her shoulder. Suddenly, the words on the scroll burst into meaning. *The New Book of Shadows as dictated by Malcor Kell'tayris, adopted son of Cor'tanos of Shadow and Ishan of Klenna, son of Kell and blessed prodigy of Takkhissis*. It continued on to say, *"In his first homecoming in this year 6,791, Kell'tayris blessed his human family with the Queen's words proclaiming Her Love and Warmth. And these are his words witnessed by the people of Klenna here in the presence of Captain Verit, Captain of the Nineteenth Bloodstone Guard and Tembri, a battle priest, both in service to the Order of Water.*

Her eyes grew wide and she wanted to ask, but Tembri shook his head. "I shall enter you as a witness. Revelation and prophecy is how the Queen gives us scripture. Right now, Malcor is wrapped in Her arms and we are commanded to listen. Speak of this to no one. Only the scripture of the worthy is entered into Canon and Malcor is still very young in proving his worthiness."

Malcor continued to speak of his rites, of meeting the dread lords, his visions in the River, and Ayden noticed the entire group had stilled as if under a trance. Malcor at last drew to a close saying, "I left Klenna with the dreams of my youth, to be a knight. However, I have not forgotten that dream. Attaining a dream is not the end of it. The vision was to travel all over the world, to serve the Queen as a knight. I have but reached part of my dream. This dream first came to me here at the forge, in the arms of Klenna. Now, in the arms of the Queen I will continue to dream, to focus on each part, and to serve with honor, to do the Queen's trust in each of us justice. To humbly serve in whatever capacity I am asked, until death and glory take me."

Moments of silence drew out and the spell lifted. It broke slowly at first then swelled as one villager after another began to applaud. Malcor stepped back and so the mayor could re-commence the celebration. Tembri's scroll and quill vanished and he seemed almost about to touch her and remove the gift of translation, but he hesitated. In that moment, Ayden wiped a tear from her eye and said, "Thank you. I struggled with learning to read. It has never come so easily to me. I'm Adyen."

"Tembri, at your service. Very well, my lady Ayden. May the Queen's blessing of reading languages continue with you. But know this, should you ever break the Queen's will, the spell will be removed and you will be required to pay a price."

"A price?" she whispered.

"Yes," Tembri said, closing his eyes for a moment and thinking. "The price will be an undoing of the scars across your lips. The healing that bound them will be undone and you will suffer pain the rest of your life."

Ayden touched her lips as the memory of the gnoll's claws tearing across her body came back. "How will I know the Queen's will? I am not a priestess nor am I paladin. I would rather return this gift than ignorantly break Her Will."

Tembri beamed as if she had said something very wise. "I like you, Ayden. I can see why the Queen favors you with this gift. Very well. Since you already understand your own limitations, I pronounce this. The gift shall fade but should you ever require it in the future, a prayer to the Queen and infliction of pain on those lip scars shall return it until the pain is healed." He reached out and touched her lips while his right hand clasped the dragon symbol hanging from his cloak. Ayden felt a tingle and imagined she heard a female voice whisper to her. Then, Tembri turned and walked away with an over-the-shoulder wave. Her own fingers touched her lips. This priest, he was completely different from any of the priests or priestesses she had ever encountered before. Unlike the lofty priestesses, he felt grounded. Tembri seemed unconcerned with the tokens of power the other male priests bore. Except for his physical size, he looked like any normal Tanian.

Ayden waved good-bye to his back and turned to go find some food. Many of the food stalls and banners and pinions had words written in either Tanian, draconian, or just pictographic emblems. She found she could read them all so long as her lips pained her. She giggled and stopped at a food stand selling a sautéed noodle and chicken entrée. The music had picked up and she knew that very soon, the knights would do their combat dance. How could they not? Stories of Malcor's Ceremony and the dance of the king, his retinue, and the many dread lords had spread far and wide during Malcor's training.

After an hour, the mayor called for a performance. Malcor led the dance setting a much easier and slower tempo than King Rojo had. A young girl joined Malcor at one point and though Ayden could tell they were not the same family, the girl clearly adored Malcor. A villager pointed and said something about Klara. *That must be her name*, Ayden thought. Taking the girl's hand and helping her through the paces, Malcor called for children and other villagers to join in and only after they left exhausted did he pick up the tempo. Soon, only Malcor, with the girl on his shoulders, and Temple functionaries remained in the dance, with everyone else clapping and stomping their feet along.

The three paladins put Tembri in their center and when they signaled in unison, Tembri triggered a column of fire that blasted heat out to the paladins and warmed the onlookers. The fire melted the courtyard sand and snow within its radius. To the amazement of the crowd, from that red glassy pool, Tembri pulled up coiled serpents that writhed and twisted around the paladins. With her new literacy, Ayden saw the serpents making symbols and suddenly her perspective shifted and she imagined she watched from a height looking down. Verit's symbols clearly meant *Water*, the Queen's domain for purification. Seline's showed *Fire*, the Queen's domain for justice. Malcor's showed *Shadow*, and there was no meaning yet, just a question resembling the rune for destiny or fate. At the center of these symbols, Tembri whirled in the kata and she saw his symbol in crystal clear detail – *The Queen*.

Ayden realized something that had long been in her mind. Her feelings for Calvin passed. Aloud, during a roar of fire, she said, "My next love, it will be epic." No wonder he did not want to come back. His father would most likely want to see him and have the village see him there in that holy trinity of fire. Were he there, like Ayden, the fire would kill him.

Ayden caught up a cup from a villager handing out drinks and taking a big sip, she raised her hands and danced. In that moment, feeling the heat and reveling in how liberated she suddenly felt, she did her best to keep up with Malcor and the others. In no time at all, a group of young men vied for her attention and she forgot about her facial deformities and Calvin.

At last, when the dance ended and after much applause, Ishan's family raced over to catch up. The knights and other dancers left Malcor to spend time with them. As Malcor walked away, Seline smiled and said to Verit,

"So, that is Malcor. I would enjoy hearing your stories and, as your Second Lieutenant -"

Verit interrupted her, "Lady Seline, you will be First Lieutenant."

"Excuse me?" she choked.

"You heard me right," and so saying, he pinned a star to her chest bar. In the center of the star, the draconic symbol for *First* appeared floated amidst dueling dragons encircling the medallion.

"Well, I assumed that the Order of Water -"

"That was a mistake. Our Order has no significance to Bloodstone. You and Malcor are both under my command and I decided, in counsel with Dar Niss and others, that you shall be First."

She bowed low. "And I shall serve with all my heart."

"But? You're about to ask about Malcor?" She nodded. "He has some challenges that are to be his primary concern and quest. I doubt I will make him Second."

Seline's eyes widened, "So he will not be commissioned at all?"

"He is a knight of the Order of Water on special assignment; that is his commission. Seline, I want you to assess the soldiers and see if you can identify the one attribute each of them possesses and present a plan to form squads."

Seline pulled him aside from those standing nearby. "If I may, my lord," she broached the topic of the legion's size. "All my studies, a legion is supposed to be twenty-thousand strong. Will we grow to that number?"

Verit found a stick and drew in the dirt. "Yes, a classic legion is twenty thousand soldiers, not including logistics support. However, our legion will be about half strength by the time we reach the valley. We anticipate that a third to half of the Eighteenth will stay on. With some luck, we'll have a full legion, but I'm not counting on it. The lack of any new bloodstone discoveries in the past five years has hindered recruiting and interest." He drew a square and then a large circle. "This square is the command team. Myself, you, Tembri, Malcor, and a few others. We'll lead the legion directly." To the side of the large circle, he drew smaller ones. "These will be special unit squads, to be led by an officer. They'll have special duties."

Seline pointed to the large circle. "As First, do you want me to command the dog soldiers?"

"Indirectly, yes. We'll find capable leaders amidst their group and I expect Captain Pember of the Eighteenth will have some recommendations." He drew an intermediary circle between the command team and the legion. "We'll put them here. They will report to you and I directly. Your primary focus will be the special unit teams. When we get to Bloodstone, you'll see what I mean. During relative periods of calm like this, the legion is there just in case. The greater need is to be able to scramble smaller teams and reinforcements throughout the valley and fortresses. I expect, and have received reports that the Sixth Fortress is in rough shape. That'll be a primary focus for the legion."

Verit stood and brushed dirt from his knees while kicking through the sand. "My time will be spent mostly between the Temple and Valley Town. What I sense we need is the ability to deploy smaller teams quickly. Study the maps and think on this: how do we best deploy our strong unit teams – which will be strengthened by at a least a cleric or mage and adventuring parties, around the edges of a scattered legion deployment?"

Seline thought for a moment and then her eyes widened. "I see," she lowered her voice. "You want to use the legion to entice attack, or at least draw out opponents."

Verit smiled at her. "Don't tell anyone, except the unit officers and only after they earn your trust. Because of this strategy, I want to limit special unit command to a First and Second. The legion itself will have a traditional structure once you make your recommendations for force disposition and command. Also, Dar Ana sent me a letter expressing some frustration with Pember's overly cautious nature. It's important we do not disappoint that high priestess especially. Early victories will be key to winning Ana over and securing more recruits."

Seline did a quick mental check. What Verit called the command team would be him, his battle priestess, a Mage's Guild liaison probably, herself, Malcor, Tembri, special unit First and Seconds, and then however many marshals Verit required over the dog soldiers in the actual legion. No doubt, there would be others as well. She shook her head. "The command team will be too large to effectively work with the special unit teams. I have experience from Quattrain with small patrol-sized groups. May I command the special unit teams? This will allow us to communicate and keep objectives separated between them and the legion."

Verit agreed, "On condition that you remain strategically focused on the special unit teams. Typically, as First, you would command the dog soldier marshals. In this case, I will command them directly. For you to be my eyes and ears and voice with them, you cannot yourself lead one. You're able to do this?"

Seline pushed the thought of the conscripts, for hire, and new soldiers in the legion out of her head. Bloodstone would feast on them if Verit's command team did not juggle this correctly. "It will be as you say." She smiled broadly and commented, "Dar Ana is going to love us." When Verit caught the double-meaning, Seline knew that she and Verit would get along just fine.

From there, talk turned to news of Bloodstone, what they had heard of veterans amongst their group, and other things. "One thing I want to be clear for this campaign. I do not want the knights to become a clique. In my first campaign, the commanders pretty much kept to themselves. Over time, the rank and file started keeping to themselves too. As a result, they began trading on favors amidst cliques. Loyalty disintegrated outside of the cliques. I do not want that to happen here. When Malcor rejoins us, we'll talk about this more. However, I plan on assigning a squad to each of us. If we can, we'll evenly spread veterans through the groups. We'll have to train for Malcor, and it's too risky to keep that knowledge limited to just command." Seeing the questions in Seline's eyes, he added, "You know how some dragons can humanshift, while other Tanians are able to dragonshift?" She nodded. "Have you seen a human dragonshift?"

"No, just stories, Captain," and she began to wonder about Malcor.

"Malcor can dragonshift, but he also tends to berserk. Luckily, unluckily, the dragon clan he has become a part of also lends itself to berserking. We think. Also, he has yet to resolve his human and dragon parts. That is his challenge. It makes him unreliably powerful. The Nineteenth's mission during the long trek to Bloodstone is to integrate Malcor and make him an asset to Tania."

"Earlier, when I met him, and again when he spoke, he had a feeling of a dread lord," she wondered aloud.

Tembri, who had just walked up to join them, nodded. "His dragon aura will get stronger. It won't affect those of us in the Temple, but until he resolves and learns to control the dragon part of his soul, it will affect the morale of those not blessed by the Goddess like we are with resistance to dragonterror. His clan of shadow dragons, they don't cause normal terror either. Their fear eats away at the spirit, resulting in a cold feeling of paralysis, indecision, and lethargy. If the paralysis is not removed, eventually the person will turn into a shadow."

Seline's eyes widened. "I have read about shades – err, shadows. But, the books always noted they are incredibly rare. Tania has never-"

"That's not entirely true," Tembri interrupted her. "Shades were common during the Kell Conflict. They were used as weapons and spies. You see, Dar Kell is a shadow dragon shifter."

Seline looked between Tembri and Verit and then she nodded, "So *Tania* knows about shades, but the truth was kept from people like me. I see. Suddenly, the Kell Conflict – it looks very different to me now."

"Indeed," Verit said taking a sip from his cup. "Shades. Well, here comes Malcor." Malcor joined them and Verit continued, "Mal, we were just talking about shades. Seline here labored under the impression that shades are mythical. By the way, this is Lady Seline. A R'Dar from the Dutchy of Quattrain, actually part of their royal family. However, she is fast on the way to earning the title in her own merit. She will be our First."

Seline watched Malcor as Verit said this. If he felt put out by not being named First, he showed no indication. *Maybe he knew already?*

Malcor addressed her. "Lady Seline, it is an honor to meet you. So far, my training has not allowed me much opportunity to meet others outside my Order." His voice, his eyes, they bored into her and left her feeling self-conscious and naked.

Seline swallowed and answered, "Though I have met many, no one in our class comes close to the stories already told about Malcor." She spoke this hoping for a reaction, but Malcor gave none except a self-deprecating half-smile.

Malcor approached them with a small girl on his shoulders. "Legion Commander, Lady Seline – may I introduce my very good friend Klara?" He put her down on the ground.

The small girl with exceptionally bright blue eyes looked up at them and curtsied though she kept her grip tightly on Malcor's hand. Seline smiled at Klara and took her other hand. "You're very special you know, Klara. Not many have had the honor of holding Sir Malcor's hand or dancing with him."

Klara giggled and then reached out to take Verit's hand. She did the same with Tembri. "You're all very big and scary," she said. "But please, take care of my brother."

Verit said that he would and then signaled Tembri to let Seline and Malcor get to know each other. Watching them walk away, Malcor pointed to the valley, "I was going to head down to the Armory with Ishan to see some of the improvements House Sai has invested in. Would you like to join me?"

Together, they walked down talking about their rites. "I don't remember seeing you on the mountain with the white dragon," Seline said.

"I was there, but they sent me alone. I had to climb the peak."

"Alone, really? I was with a group of maybe thirty and all we had to do was wait. Even then, several of us died just from the cold."

"Tell me Seline, was Calvin in your class?"

"Yes, he and I stood together for warmth on the mountain. We encountered each other several times after that. I have heard that you and he are friends. He talked about you a lot, often wondered if you'd show up in our classes."

Malcor sighed, "Yes, we grew up together but my life in the forge and his life as the mayor's son kept us worlds apart. I like to think of him as my friend. Tembri and the Order has been teaching me around combat training. The thought of a class sounds nice. It all gets jumbled in my head sometimes."

As they wound their way down the hill from the shrine, the Armory's lights illuminated their destination, wavering in the heat from its many fires. Before it, the taverns served as the bright points. "It is odd to see the Armory illuminated. Even when we had to work extra, there was only ever just enough light to work by."

"Malcor, there's something you should know, about Calvin. We had a field test, a simulated battle. We had to protect members of the Mage's Guild and my command captured Calvin's. He was removed from the knighthood shortly after it. Though I have been told it was not because of that, I do feel responsible. Because he was your friend, if you're angry about it, let's have it out now. I don't want either of us on the road for six weeks to Bloodstone and then in Bloodstone with this between us."

Malcor shrugged as if to say it did not matter. "Tell me what happened and what you know about Calvin. I'll tell you right now that Dar Shara cautioned him against joining the knighthood. She said it would bring him suffering." Mal rubbed his hand over his head. "I don't think Calvin and suffering go together well."

Seline told him everything about her interactions with Calvin. Just when they reached the Armory, Malcor said, "Calvin must really be struggling. Here in Klenna, he was always the best. Best tutors, best grades, best girlfriends, best sports awards, best on and on and on. To be removed, beaten by his mentor in front of everyone, I imagine that was the first time he failed, or at least failed in public view. With a lady like you watching, he must still struggle with it."

Seline, wanting to lighten the mood, quickly asked, "So you had the not-best girlfriends, Sir Malcor?"

Malcor laughed. "The previous owners of this armory were cruel taskmasters. I never had time. They worked us from dawn till collapse. When I had time, the burn scars and my low status made it hard for me to catch any of the ladies' eyes. But, surely, if I did, Calvin always seemed to win them over before I had a chance."

Seline stopped and looked at him, catching his arm. She was surprised at how cool his armor felt through her gauntlet. "You're a good friend, Malcor."

"I don't know. I never really had the time for friends." He laughed, "Of course, if winning a beautiful lady had been a requirement for paladins, I'd no doubt be stuck in the forge still and Calvin would have bards exaggerating his adventures!"

Ahead of them, a new shop section of colored glass and open windows greeted them with bright lantern light.

Chapter Four – Malcor Turns the Forge

They turned the corner and Ishan waved at them from the Armory's new retail and shop entrance. Two of the older smiths sat nearby and they greeted Malcor enthusiastically. Not wanting to have a formal evening with his father and former co-workers, Malcor removed his armor.

Ishan helped him and said, "Look Mal, Sai R'Dar and that amazing priestess of yours left us this falcon to watch over things. It's magical! Sometimes it talks to the group, and even defends us from thieves."

Mal recognized it from his interactions with Ora and remembered the one she gave him at the shrine. Her words echoed in his mind, "It'll follow you unless you tell it to leave. It will allow me to see you when I miss you." The falcon cocked its head at him without blinking. After a moment, it leaped down and landed on Ishan's shoulder.

A gentle voice sounded in the room somehow centered on the magical bird. "Malcor, welcome home. We trust that you will find the Armory thrives since you freed it from House Tor and entrusted it to House Sai. R'Dar Ora has also tended to the employees and their families. You should find everything is well. After your review with Ishan, if you have any other instructions, please provide them to the Cystoran Falcon."

A brief pause and Ishan pointed to the shop area. "We've never had a shop before, but with the improvements and Sai's instruction to train and improve, many of the smiths have started side projects that we sell here on commission. Check this out." Ishan walked over to a glass display case wherein lay any number of jewelry mounts, clasps, and other works of gold, silver, and alloyed metals. "We have yet to get a stable source of gemstones – we pick them up as adventurers come through, and Sai does not want us to become a gem shop."

Malcor picked up a medallion necklace and pendant, waiting for a thumbnail sized gem. "Who did this one?" When Ishan told him, Mal laughed. "I never would have thought! And he did this after working hours?"

"Indeed. When Ora introduced us to this commission structure, we had only a few takers. But the first commission, when it sold, paid ten gold coins. Ten." Ishan looked at Lady Seline and explained, "Ten gold here in Klenna is basically an annual wage for a family of ten. After that, the race was on. House Sai also has sent us commissions from their other businesses. Though we don't display them here for sale, we pulled this one out to show you. I mean, it's nothing compared to your sword, but still. What do you think?"

One of the other smiths walked behind the counter and opened a metal chest with magicked hinges and an elaborate lock. From within, he lifted up a mace of dark steel and iron but engraved with cursive draconian along the handle and flanges in gold. "This is a blank for magic to be added back at Sai's estate in the capitol. This commission paid enough to fund all of our operations all year. Though, we're only doing blanks for Sai. Since you left, we can't figure out how to actually infuse them with magic."

Malcor hefted the mace, which was almost perfectly balanced. He handed it to Seline who took some practice swings. "Must be for a cleric?"

Mal nodded, "Ishan, this is really good work. But, I'm afraid to tell you - the balance is not quite there for combat."

Ishan and the others' eyes widened, "Oh no, it's not? It's supposed to be. We don't know the intended purpose but we have had a few sent back for a number of reasons. Balance, standard thickness of the metal, alloys being just off, stuff like that. Where is the issue?" Ishan leaned in to look, trying to see what Malcor saw. The other smiths did too.

Mal pointed about three fingers' width below the head. "Here I would say. In a serious battle, the shaft will fracture here. This weakness will prevent it from holding strong magic. For lower level stuff, it'll be just fine." He eyeballed it and asked about delivery schedule. He added, "You know, we could fix this. May I, Ishan?"

He held onto the mace, occasionally balancing it in either hand as they continued through the Armory into the work area. They came to where Mal and Ishan had worked together for years. Like the forge set up in his quarters back with the Order of Water, Sai had upgraded the forge to the magical green gems. "Seline, you're welcome to stay. This won't take long and I could use the help. It gets hot in there," he said pointing to the crucible where metal would liquefy.

Ishan and the two smiths looked at Malcor who said, "The forge – so, here is what I need: gold, mithril, and black diamond." As he gave instructions, he removed his armor's gambeson. The smiths ran off to bring tools and materials.

With his tunic off and in the flickering light of the forge, Seline winced to see the jagged scars along Malcor's spine up his neck. She noted the black teardrop wound in his left arm. With each observation, she imagined the combat that must have occurred to create such damage. Without thinking, she walked up and touched the scar along his back just aside from his spine. "Tembri wasn't with you?" she asked.

"No, most of my Ori experience, I was on my own. We had a cleric, but Noboyuki is not a Tanian battle mage. And, the fighting was without end." Malcor rubbed the raised edges of the scars that came up behind his ear.

Noticing Seline's attention to his son, Ishan came over and looked and choked. "My son, my boy, you – this reminds me of when you were burned. I hurt to see it. You have been in danger, more than I can imagine."

Malcor looked at them and grinned, "True, but I'm okay, and this is what serving the Goddess requires sometimes. Most of these I don't remember. I went berserk. The team had to tell me later." Poking the one Seline had touched, he continued, "Those were from what I thought were wraiths but turned out to be revenants. A force wall cut me off from help. Frankly, I'm surprised I don't have more scars. Natural healing can't be healed over magically, so Tembri tells me I'll have these the rest of my life."

Malcor pulled on a leather shirt, thick and heavy and designed to shield from the forge's heat. "Seline, we need to torque this part of the handle to restore balance. It'll mar the handle so they'll have to add a design over it. We need to heat it and twist. I'll need you to join me in there for that part."

The smiths set to work and Seline marveled at how easily Malcor stepped into the flow of the work with them. Ishan's wife, Michelle, brought in food and drinks and set them down. Michelle commented to Seline, "It's amazing how they work. Mal has always been like that, but we were never able to get teams to make anything of quality."

Seline asked a few questions about the process. Mostly, she found herself mesmerized by the flames and the shadows cast all along the walls. It reminded her of a dance. She snapped out of the reverie though when Michelle poked her arm. "He is quite handsome, isn't he?" referring to Malcor. "The local girls either couldn't get past the burn scars, or were too busy chasing the more socially popular kids."

Seline stammered a bit, "Um, to tell you the truth, I was more caught up in the flow of their work, but now that you mention it, I suppose he is."

The older lady chuckled and elbowed her, "Were I young and beautiful, I'd be right after a catch like that."

Seline grinned and felt grateful for the shadows that hid her blushing. "As paladins, we can't even allow ourselves to think that way. While Malcor will no doubt be very desirable for the priestesses like R'Dar Ora, neither he nor I will ever, could ever. It just can't." She shrugged.

"Tell me, Lady, do you know if the Temple is treating Malcor well? His wounds-"

"The Temple provides everything we need. I had thought that all training occurred at the Temple, but have learned that there are exceptions. Like with Malcor. I'm actually envious. To have accomplished the rites and experienced the world through a quest like he has, I can't imagine it. Every day, I woke up and studied, trained, lived and breathed the knighthood. To have also had time to do a quest like he did. And look at him now."

"Are you a knight?" Michelle asked. "Excuse me, but Malcor always talked about being a paladin. The difference is that... well, I don't even know. In the welcome speeches, the term gets used as the same thing?"

Seline smiled at her and they stepped back a bit from the loud work. "I am a knight and a paladin, like Malcor. A knight is a specially trained officer, a commander of sorts that has training to ride heavy war horses. They have a special charter to govern, lead, and have authority to settle disputes amongst the people if no other authority is present. Knights can have a rank that exceeds a R'Dar in authority, but it is an imperial authority. So, for example, Malcor's and my rank exceeds the mayor's here. But, so long as there is not an imperial issue happening in Klenna, we defer to the mayor. So, that is a knight."

"I see. So, all paladins are knights. Only some knights are paladins. I think I understand, though I don't see Malcor as a governor." Michelle laughed. "But, when he speaks to us, it takes my breath away."

Seline had a turn to laugh now. "Yes, that caught me by surprise too. I've just barely met him. I doubt Malcor has had much time to study law. His title as knight, I'm guessing, is more honorary right now. I grew up in the Dutchy of Quattrain and had to study Tanian law since I was a child."

"Oh, I did not realize." Michelle looked more closely at Seline. "Pardon another question, my lady, but paladins and knights, are they royalty?"

Seline shook her head. "Nothing in Tania is ever so clean cut. Knights can come from any lot in life, though there is a clear path to become a R'Dar through mighty deeds. No, most knights begin to specialize in either law and governance, or they continue in war training." Seline thought for a minute about Ayden and added, "Not all knights train with heavy chargers. One of our command seems to have forsaken that to focus instead on small unit tactics in place of law, and infantry weapons instead of horses."

Michelle turned and watched her son working in the forge for a while. "I can't see him riding horses into combat."

In that moment, Seline noticed Malcor's shadow on the wall had become noticeably dragon-like. She wondered if Michelle saw it too. Seline pointed to her holy symbol and held it out for Michelle to see. "A paladin is also a knight, but has a Temple commission and serves the Goddess. Where a knight might continue to learn governance and law, or pursue war skills, paladins pursue faith and doctrine. It allows us to fight by divine inspiration, and do other things. I don't see Malcor riding a horse either."

Sweat poured down Malcor's arms as he wrestled the mace near the cradle, twisting and turning it. Every now and then he would hit the weak spot with one of the large hammers passed to him by Ishan. The leather gear he had donned smoldered threatening to burst into flame, only it did not because of the divine fire resistance that came with being a paladin. The tap-tap-smash of the hammer felt slow but from the straining of his arm and back muscles, Seline could tell he hit the mace far harder than the sound suggested. Ishan and the others waited, occasionally stirring the fire, operating the bellows at instruction from Malcor, or adding material to the crucible where the new metal slowly glowed and would eventually melt.

At last, the crucible became liquid and Malcor turned to Seline. "It's time, please join me in the cradle." Malcor summoned his armor into being around his body, and stepped into the cradle amidst a shower of golden and green-tinted sparks. Though the air ignited around him and the others gasped, Seline stepped into the cradle to a similar flash of her air and the heat of burning. Seline could not resist looking at Ishan and the others' expressions to see them standing in the forge. Malcor had been tap-tapping on the handle where he thought the balance had been off, but now he handed the head of the mace to Seline.

She took it and both braced themselves as Malcor squared his feet and then twisted the handle. Seline strained in the other direction. Sweat ran down their bodies, hissing and sizzling in the forge's cradle. After several minutes, Malcor said it was no good. "We'll have to be very fast with this." He signaled for a vise and a series of clamping tools to be placed nearby. The smiths ran to bring him the equipment.

"With this heat, with how hot the metal is, you and I should have been able to nudge it just enough to create a weakness I could then reshape. It's no good. I can see it." He shoved the mace back into the green gemstones. "We'll have less than a minute to do this before those tools begin to soften. As such, we'll need to be very fast." He explained what they were going to do while the mace slowly began to glow molten hot.

When the smiths had brought all they needed, and used poles to push them as close to the forge as they could, Malcor stepped out and passed tools to Seline. First, they set up a vise and squeezed the mace's head securely into it. Then, they clamped the handle and both of them twisted. Seline watched, looking for that telltale sign she knew Malcor would be searching for. When she saw nothing, she wondered what exactly he looked at so intently. Though she strained with all her might and prayed to the Goddess for more, she felt dwarfed by the might exerted next to her. Glancing sideways, she noted how Malcor's entire body strained, and then the black pools of his eyes caught her. He stared at the mace handle just below the head but at the same time did not. She had seen this before with Dar Niss and a few of the higher ranked knights and clerics. She had felt it during her encounters with Dread Lord Blade. All at once, she envied and craved this man next to her and she put her entire self into twisting the mace handle even as the vise began to glow red.

"Got it," was all he said. He quickly removed the mace and dropped the clamping tools outside the cradle. The vise did not make it. While they unclamped and saved the more delicate tools, the vise turned white hot and like candle wax began to slowly pull down on itself. Mal picked it up and put it outside where the others quickly struggled to put out fires around the ground where the vise's heat ignited debris all around it. Even the dust in the air kindled and crackled.

Their work complete, they stepped out of the cradle and out of the forge area before their heat would cause problems, like the vise where explosions of steam billowed up as the smiths doused it with water. Even outside in the chilly night, dust and debris around them ignited like a crown of sparks rising up into the stars. High above them, the celebration continued at the shrine though the moon showed it well past midnight. "Thank you," Malcor said. "That type of work is so much easier when you don't have to worry about burning. I'm still amazed that paladins, mages, and magic in general does not lend more of a hand to activities like this."

"The changes we made," Seline questioned. "Will they be enough?"

"Absolutely. The weakness in the metal, you can see it. We removed it entirely. I'd say that part is now the strongest."

Seline shifted back and forth and finally said somewhat annoyed, "You can see it? See what? What are you talking about?"

Malcor looked down from the sky and for just a moment his look became vulnerable. "Are you mocking me? No, I see you aren't." He looked back up at the sky and then on a whim, he reached out for her hand.

Though her gauntlet still smoldered, the touch of his hand shot ice through her arm and she cried out, "So cold -" before her vision shifted. Suddenly, she found herself standing by the River. Dar Niss had talked to her about it and she experienced it briefly during her initiation into the Order of Fire. Her vision, sight, sound, smell… all of it altered and became sweeter, even sensuous. Around them, the busy work in the forge next to them washed downstream and faded but flickered back to their present location on the bank.

Malcor let go of her hand. "I wasn't sure this would work with you." He drew his sword and held it out to her gaze. "Look, in this place, the sword's small imperfections become obvious. Only perfection can survive here. Even though we have stepped out of the River, it corrodes and eats away at everything. Except those magically protected or perfect. The mace, from this viewpoint, was so flawed that only a conscript would be able to use it. I kind of wish I had shown you this before, but in my Order, everyone can, well, we do this all the time. We even train there. For the mace, the imperfection glowed with decay compared to the rest of the weapon."

Seline drew her own sword. Holding it out next to Malcor's blade, she immediately noticed a vast difference in potential. Draconian script flowed along Malcor's blade and she read its name. "Coming Undone?" she asked. Her unnamed sword, the best she had ever had, sparkled here outside of Time. Motes of light fell away from it. *No*, she realized. Her sword aged and it was disintegrating before her very eyes. *Coming Undone* gleamed like a mercurial reflection of the lights and auras all around them in this place. "This was the best sword I have ever had and now I see it as ugly," she grimaced. "Your sword is beautiful."

Malcor took her blade and pointed to a spot she had passed over before. "This is where your sword will ultimately break. Though it can be fixed, its core materials at this point would not support very much magic. If you want, we can work on a new one."

She looked up at him and suddenly remembered the stories of the *Apprentice's Sword*, which she just saw up close. "You'd help me make a new one?"

"As time allows," he said. "But, I feel the River pulling you back."

As they stepped back into the River, for just a moment, Seline saw a light-swallowing dragon shape rear up behind and around Malcor. The stabbing cold hit her again and then Malcor let go of her hand back in the real world. Ishan was just stepping out of the armory and had called their names. He held the mace and said that it was perfect. "It felt perfect before," he winced. "We actually saved it to show you because of that. But, it's even better now. Thank you."

He walked up to Malcor but stopped about three steps away feeling the residual heat, "You're still that hot?" he marveled.

They laughed, "Yes, the Queen has been good to me. We are expected to endure dragon fire, so why not a forge?" He held out his hand, "How did it temper?"

"Perfectly. Check it out," Ishan said tossing him the mace.

The rest of the evening passed in a blur. Though exhausted from travel and the party, they eventually found themselves walking back up to the shrine as Ishan filled Malcor in on family and business. Like his mother, Ishan seemed uncomfortable asking about the scars but finally did. Malcor shrugged it off but when Ishan kept pressing, Malcor finally told him about the battle before the golden door against the wraiths. "I did not know they were revenants until I had been cut off from the group."

Same as when Malcor spoke to the entire village, Seline found herself hanging on his every word and could imagine the battle in her mind's eye. She saw Ishan's concern replaced with awe as the story progressed. It felt exultant. That spirit carried them back to the shrine where the celebration continued with sleeping children and others collapsing while the heartier Klennans continued. The bonfires throughout the shrine kept them warm. When dawn lit up the eastern sky, Malcor, Tembri, Verit, and Seline stood in the center of the courtyard and offered the day's first prayer in unison.

Some of the villagers awoke and joined them sleepily. When the sun burst over the distant mountains, Verit looked all around and barked out an order. "Soldiers of the Eighteenth Replacement Army! Assist with clean up and then report back to camp at high noon for first training." As one, they turned and began picking up debris assisting where they could. It took a few moments for the orders to sink in. With their commanders already in action, and in spite of exhaustion, the entire army got to work.

At high noon, most of the army units had reached their designated spots in the training field. The knights stood at attention in gleaming armor, their heavy war horses snorting in the bright sunlight. A wind began blowing and the clouds overhead suggested snow would fall soon. Five were not present and Verit took their names and demoted them a full rank.

Verit walked the rows and called out those names and then said, "Bloodstone will not be an all night celebration amongst friends. Bloodstone is not happy to see us. Tanian forces there will not be happy to see us. They will view all of us as novices, beginners, a liability in a place so deadly. The undead there do not rest and they remain active during the day. It is our job to be ready whether we feel rested or not, whether we are hungry or not, whether we feel like fighting or not. Today is the first test. Today we demoted some of you to the rank of private. Any demotion below private and you will be given punished by lash, or dismissal."

Verit took a deep breath and continued, "We have a six week trek ahead of us. We have an uphill climb to Bloodstone where winter is already in full swing. The trip will be winter cold, snow, rain, whatever the Goddess sends our way. If we cannot survive cold, we will not survive Bloodstone.

"I am Captain Verit. This will be the Nineteenth Legion. Lady Seline step forward. This is Lady Seline, my First. In my absence, you will obey her. R'Dar Tembri, step forward. This is Tembri, my Second. He is a veteran of Bloodstone. He serves Sir Malcor. Malcor step forward. This is Sir Malcor, a member of my Order. Though Bloodstone is our destination, it is not our objective. Malcor?"

Malcor stepped forward into an open space between Verit and the legion. He crouched down and then leapt into the sky. For a moment, he hung in the air and then inky darkness blotted the sun where Malcor had just been. From that darkness, giant wings snapped into the wind and the young black-looking dragon, sinuous and almost fragile looking, climbed between the Nineteenth and the sun. Seline realized it was not a black dragon because his darkness did not reflect daylight.

Malcor moved through the sky like nothing Seline had seen. He climbed and then dove only to pull out and sweep over the heads of the legion. Verit and Tembri watched the reactions of the group while Malcor climbed again. "Brace yourselves, here comes the terror."

Malcor dove spearing down towards them again and this time, an unease that tingled fingers and toes grew into a cold-numbing despair. Everyone felt it differently. Seline had to drop her guard to feel it and though she felt the exaltation of the dragon, the aching cold through her gauntlet reminded her what the others must be feeling. At the forge, the chill she felt when touching Malcor, this explained it.

All around them, entire units had fallen as if stupefied. Others hugged their sides and stared at the ground. A few ran away from the wyrm, breaking rank and fleeing. And, then Malcor was gone and the sun warmed their skin again. Malcor flew until he crossed behind a cloud and only when he could no longer be seen, did the Nineteenth try to regroup. Verit passed some observations to Seline for follow up with those who had broken rank.

Black lightning forks of energy pulled all the body warmth out of a cluster of legionnaires near Verit as Malcor reared up from their own shadows. All but five of the group collapsed unconscious. Ayden stood on shaky legs as the others dropped to their knees. One began to vomit.

"Excellent," Verit said to Ayden. "We have special work for you. Malcor, we have what we need. Tembri, help restore my army. All of you, remember this! This terror comes from a YOUNG DRAGON! In Bloodstone, this is what a hellhound feels like. They attack with fear first."

The Nineteenth took the rest of the day to recover from Malcor. The next day, the commanders met with the five who had not fallen. Verit pointed to one, a lady priestess and said, "My Lady Sofen, I am pleased to have you with us." Verit separated Sofen from Ayden and the three other fighters.

"We are going to make you squad leaders of the Nineteenth," Verit said pointing at them. "Here is the issue with Sir Malcor. In combat, he is a berserker. As a dragon, he cannot control that berserking. To make it more interesting, unless there is light, shadow dragons cannot see well enough to navigate the real world. Their world becomes two dimensional. Berserking makes this all worse because Malcor will struggle to identify friend from foe. In addition to us, you four will be marked with a series of tattoos along your face and hands and arms. Shadow dragons can see quite well in the dark but lose their sense of distance when interacting with the real world. You will help orient Malcor to where we need him."

Ayden asked, "Should Malcor should be treated as a dread lord?"

Tembri answered saying, "No, Malcor is not a dread lord. Dread lords are dragons allied with Morbatten through the god emperor. They are actual dragons. Some are powerful with magic and can shapeshift into human form. Actual dragons are dread lords."

While discussing how Malcor should be treated like any other paladin, Ayden asked a clarifying question they all danced around. "Captain Verit, Malcor is part of command, but is not an officer. Does this change when he becomes a dragon?"

"No," Verit said flatly. "I alone command the Nineteenth. No exceptions." Verit walked up to her and looked at her closely. "Except if the Goddess tells you otherwise." He added, "R'Dar Tembri will handle the markings here in Klenna." Verit then commanded them, "You are my leaders. Begin organizing your squads."

Chapter Five – Organizing the Nineteenth

Ayden immediately knew what she needed to do. While the others set out for their own groups, Ayden sought out Bruun, the squinty-eyed veteran who had not yet earned his commission. She found him tending the knights' horses and making ready to check on the supply trains. For just a moment, she felt anxiety and wondered if he would follow her, but then strengthened by some feeling of calm, she called out to him. "Bruun, Captain Verit has made me a squad lead. You will join as my First."

Surprised but immediately pleased, he nodded and then bowed, "With all that is mine, I shall serve."

At his words, Ayden almost jumped up and down and clapped her hands but resisted though a giant smile crept across her face. "I want the best of the best Bruun. You've been to Bloodstone. Let's get anyone else who has been there or who you think has the mettle to not just survive but excel. I want them all. There are four others gathering recruits. I want to beat them to the best."

By late afternoon, Ayden and Bruun had assembled seventeen members into their group, six of whom had already been to Bloodstone. Ayden was relieved that Bruun had not served with any of them and appeared to have no direct friendship or motivation for picking them. Ayden could not hide her smile that hers was the first squad to arrive at the field. Verit sparred with Tembri on the far side of the field. Ayden used that time get to know her unit.

Like her, most were myrmidons or soldier veterans of experience. Like Bruun, none had received a commission yet. Two had left the Temple under instruction to learn the arts of war before re-applying to the priesthood and she made note of them as they had each passed the initial Temple rites. The real surprise was with Bruun, a Tanian but not a worshipper of Tiamat.

In surprise, one of the others asked "Why?" before Ayden could. Bruun shrugged, "Wasn't part of the family, I guess. We were part of the Merchant Guild and that's almost a religion unto itself." He laughed and rubbed his fingers together as if handling a gold coin. "The family needed soldiers so I was enlisted. Eventually, I found my way to one of the battlefield gods. We call him "Joust" as a kind of a joke as most battles are not nearly so structured or fair, but it's what we pray for, a fair fight and the right to win or die with honor."

Ayden thought about it. She had heard the god Joust several times in her own training. "Joust worshippers, so you actively seek out equal, level combat to test yourselves right?" Bruun nodded. Ayden tucked her hair back over her ear. "I respect that, but we're going to Bloodstone to win. And, that means we want every advantage possible. We won't have a problem with that right? I want to win."

"No, none at all. There is no equal combat with undead. They're already dead." Bruun and the others chuckled. They referred to a joke Ayden had heard as well. She joined them before she got serious. "Listen up, you all saw Malcor yesterday right?" Across the field, Captain Verit was donning his armor and other squads had started to arrive. She gestured to Verit and the arriving groups. "I want our squad to be the first to withstand Malcor. That is our first goal." Lady Seline rode up and heard Ayden finish. "Our second goal is to impress our command team with our diligent follow through on all commands."

Seline joined Ayden's unit and they walked over to Verit and Tembri. Verit looked closely at Bruun when Ayden introduced him as her First. "You were one of the five demoted for being late. Explain yourself, Private. Bruun, correct?"

Bruun bowed and without any tone of excuse said, "Captain, the supply train horses spook easily. This is my third campaign and the third time a Captain has made it a point to test the troops, though not with a dragon. I thought it worth the rebuke to ensure the horses did not run away." The four other demotees stepped forward in support. Ayden realized they were all Bloodstone veterans and all in her command. She suddenly worried if Verit would think less of her.

To her relief, Verit said, "Very good of you, Bruun. Though next time you decide to act independently, you will notify Ayden. She will set tasks for you five. When accomplished, at her discretion, your rank shall be reinstated." He walked across the ranks of soldiers before him, eyeing them, judging them.

Verit moved to stand before the army that had gathered behind Ayden's unit. He signaled to R'Dar Fion and his voice magically amplified. "My job as Legion Commander is to ensure that our mission is completed. It is not my job to ensure any of you survive. That is your job! Specifically, it is your teammate's job to ensure your own survival and so on. Your lives rest within your team. When we give an order, I expect execution and follow through as if your very life depends on it. If you do not understand my orders, that is your, not my problem." Malcor noted that as Verit spoke, he made a hand sign for Fion to ready a healing spell.

Verit called Ayden's unit forward. "You are Ayden, correct?" She nodded. "You are one of my Officers." He pointed to a member of her team. "Take your sword and run him through."

Without hesitation, Ayden drew her sword in a flawless draw-attack technique. The man stepped back to dodge but confused at the sudden violence of the otherwise normal discussion. Ayden's sword speared through the fighter's tunic. The man gasped in pain and confusion, wide-eyed and in shock as Fion's healing spell caught and held him alive.

"My orders will never be confusing. They come from the Goddess. We have six weeks to get to Bloodstone and for you to "get" me and my command. Squad leaders, do what Ayden did to a member of your team." Again that hand sign. Some ten or so broke rank and ran away as their squad leaders cut into team members. Ayden withdrew her sword and the wound closed. Suddenly, a wall of fire erupted from the direction of those retreating. It pressed the deserters back to the field. A mage came up behind the wall and Malcor grinned to see it was Sako with Noboyuki.

"My orders will both endanger and protect your life. There is no desertion in Bloodstone. There is no room for cowardice. Retreat is by express command only. You must condition yourselves to trusting in my commands even if it looks like you may die. Even if every fiber of your soul screams out, *Dear Goddess, I am going to die!*, you must learn to put that fear aside, and trust us. This is war. We are going to war against an enemy that is relentless, eternal, and ever-hungry. In Bloodstone, if you run, you become undead and therefore our enemy. You will be killed at the first sign of flight. Deserters, you have a choice here in Klenna though – demotion or lashes."

All but one of them chose demotion and rejoined their original teams. Verit ordered ten lashes. As each lash fell and stripped flesh, Tembri healed the wound just in time for the next wound. All watched, grimly. When they had reformed their ranks, Verit continued. "We have guests joining us. These are comrades of Malcor's. A skilled thief with some mage talent – Sako. And Noboyuki, a cleric of the god Imperius. You may recognize their names from the stories told about the Khasran Lich! Seline is my First. Tembri is my Second. You will consider the Imperic Noboyuki as my Third. These others," he pointed to Ayden and the squad leaders, "are your squad leaders, your Officers. For today, I want sparring exercises. At sunset - Command Team - we will spar with them and see how the Nineteenth does. I want assessments ready to look at tomorrow. Start now."

Bruun tapped Ayden's arm and said, "We need to be the first. Let's go." Ayden nodded and gave the order as her unit broke away and paired off.

She was pleased to see the veterans had skill and familiarity with martial training. During a pause, Seline stepped in and challenged her. Replacing their swords with wooden training swords and dropping their armor, they started slow and then increased their tempo. Ayden called for the others to do likewise and soon her squad began showing off trying to one up each other. Unspoken was the risk that they'd be removed from the best team.

Ayden focused on Seline. Fortunately, Seline and Ayden were both about the same number of years into their training and Seline's Temple studies actually impaired her martial training. Ayden began scoring points but felt no surprise that a paladin would redouble her efforts in such a situation. Just as Ayden thought she might be able to win, Seline began scoring points and so back and forth they went until Verit called for a break.

Servants from the supply train brought forward barrels of water and hearty snacks. Just before they rotated partners and began again, Seline praised Ayden's skill and noted that she would be moving to spar with one of the other squad leaders. "I look forward to picking this up again, Ayden. My training has all been sword and shield. I like how, without the shield, you do things I have not yet tried."

For a few minutes, Ayden got her group started and was about to spar with Bruun when Tembri stepped forward and asked if she would like to be his partner. For that entire session, Ayden failed to score even a single point though she had a few times where she thought she would. Tembri barely moved and at one point joked with her, "You don't get to be my age by dancing around the battlefield!" As Ayden desperately tried to score a point, Tembri moved to the side to avoid her attack. He scored on her again. "You're doing well, Ayden. Stay focused. I'll tell you, unless you get very lucky, you're not going to hit me. Next break, you'll be going up against the cleric Noboyuki."

Sure enough, break came and went and Ayden found herself facing off against the cleric. Noboyuki bowed low and they began. Like Tembri, he had an economy of movement but was not familiar with Tanian sparing and fighting styles. She scored a few points on him before he really got the hang of it. "My other opponents were sloppy compared to you, Miss Ayden," he said.

Exhausted but feeling quite good, Ayden looked up to see Malcor walking her way for the next rotation. She sighed. "I must be a mess," she mumbled to herself tucking hair behind her ear. She became instantly self-conscious when Malcor called out to her for a match. Like her, Malcor had sweat soaking through his clothing. Throughout the day, clouds had been rolling in and when the sun dimmed, it got cold.

"Interesting to see the stamina of everyone here," he said as he swung the wooden sword back and forth. "How are you holding up?"

"Well enough," Ayden said stretching and picking up her sword. "I feel like you all have me on the attack. It's easier to conserve energy when defending."

"Let's change that," Malcor said as he hammered his sword sideways into her making a grand sweep through the air. It was an easy enough attack to block as he put no finesse into it, but when her sword intercepted his, the force of the blow jarred her hands and she danced back. Malcor pressed forward unleashing obvious attacks letting her be on defense. As strong as his first hit had been, Ayden marveled that each time she blocked, the force increased. Soon, her hands felt numb and unresponsive as did her arms and shoulders. "I'm not going to pull my blows if you fail to block these," he added as she just barely deflected another attack.

She tried to turn her deflection into a counterattack and just barely managed to prevent his next attack. She tried harder to move to the offensive but then their fight took them through several of the others' fights. Bruun tried to give her a field advantage by "accidentally" blocking Malcor with a trip. It was no good. Like the wind or a wave or some other force of nature, Malcor pressed forward. If he noticed Bruun, it did not slow or pause the attacks. *A full day of combat and now this*, Ayden thought when her sword splintered to pieces.

Without pausing, Malcor tossed his sword aside and pressed forward hand to hand style. Like with the swords, he started slowly and obviously followed the paladin combat dance. It made it easy for her to block, but even unarmored, his hands, forearms, and legs felt like she was blocking metal weapons. The exhaustion and numbness did not help either.

Malcor increased tempo and switched from the dance kata to more of a boxing style. She could tell that he had little familiarity with it beyond the basics, where she had trained to a proficient level in most types of combat. Telling herself she could do it, she tried to turn his apparent lack of skill to her advantage. She quickly scored a few hits, even bloodied Malcor's face a bit, but when he finally landed a blow, it knocked the air out of her lungs and she could barely breathe. His other fist blocked a kick she aimed at his groin, stars danced before her eyes and she fell backwards. By the time she regained her balance and breath, a healing spell had washed over her. Fatigue still weighed on her but less urgently. She could feel her arms again. From across the way, Tembri, like a statue, blocked his attacker and had somehow managed to heal her at the same time. *Amazing*, she thought.

Malcor grinned seeing her renewed vitality. "Very nice," he said as he continued to press forward. Renewed and feeling good, Ayden redoubled her efforts and almost landed some counter-attacks before they called for a break. As they walked over to get a drink, she noticed his eyes dancing over the other members of her group. When his eyes lingered on one of her team, she looked to see what had caught his attention and wondered if it was how heavily the man breathed.

At the water barrel she asked him, "The soldier back there," she thought quickly to remember his name. "Farant, I think. I saw you looking at him. What caught your attention?"

Malcor wiped water from his chin and then washed sweat off his face. He looked back at the man and then at Ayden. "Just a feeling. There is something about him that seems off to me. Did Seline or Tembri – No, they would have said something to me about it. For now, put it out of your mind. By the way, I heard you trained with Calvin. How is he doing?"

"Okay enough. He feels bad about leaving the Temple. He often speculates as to how you're doing, but when the stories came out about your Ori adventure, he kind of went silent. I think he's a bit jealous."

Malcor looked west at the lowering sun and listened to her. "He knew it would be difficult. Did you originally apply for the Temple as well, Ayden?"

"Me? No, I was pushed into the military by my village and never felt I had what it takes to be a knight or a priestess. Seline and some of the others from the Temple sometimes came and watched our training exercises." Ayden shrugged. "To be honest, I kind of like being free to fight my way. It serves the Queen just as much as when you fight Her Way, right? Plus, I'm not limited by some creed. If you're not careful, I punch below the belt!"

Malcor laughed. "Yeah, I was glad you missed that one." They laughed.

Across the way, Verit signaled the break's end and so they all pressed on until it felt as if everyone had fought everyone. When at last Verit dismissed all but the Command Team and squad leaders, Ayden grabbed Bruun and noted she needed to know, who on their team actually wanted to be there. "All but three," he whispered and then left to catch up with the others.

"Wait, I need to know anything you know about the one named Farant," she called to his back. He nodded and waved that he would do it.

Sweat soaked and quickly cooling, cooks and squires brought food and chairs to them on the field. Dinner had never tasted so good. The exhausted fighters ate, and talked. Lingering over drinks, Verit asked each of the squad leaders to assess themselves. When each had finished, he asked the Command Team to add anything that had been missed.

Interviewing them, Verit asked them how they came to be fighters and if they actually wanted to be squad leaders. When it came time for Ayden, she told her story briefly about the gnoll attack and how her village had enlisted her immediately in the military. "I fight for the Queen in my own way and live to serve. She will strengthen my weaknesses as She sees fit."

The paladins nodded and Tembri winked at her. She suddenly realized she had been the only one to express any level of religious faith. After her, Sako and Noboyuki told their stories. Verit went last. "I joined the knighthood young. When I learned about the Order of Water, I applied and was rejected for many years. Only after a dragon quest – that is, a mission to convert a dragon to the Queen – did the Order consider me. My quest to Ori with Malcor was my first mission with the Water. Though I have two Bloodstone campaigns completed, this will be my first under Dar Kendra's command."

He paused quietly for a moment and then Malcor spoke, "Verit stood alone against one possessed by the Jade God. Had it not been for the Captain, I most certainly would be dead or worse. The success of my mission was secured by Verit facing the Jade God and the possessed lich."

Tembri nodded. "It's true. We hung by a thread of fate with only piles of treasure blocking us from being crushed or turned undead." He chuckled. "I never thought I'd refer to piles of gold and wealth as a defense."

"Please gentlemen -" Verit started to say but even Sako and Noboyuki added their own views of the quest. Malcor had yet to hear that part from any but official reports.

"I wish we had some of the others here who saw it all first hand, but I will do my best," Tembri interrupted. "It's my turn to embarrass both Verit and Malcor now. The sceptre of the Jade God is powerful. It takes control and infuses what it takes with lethal power. It magnifies whatever powers are already there. It can kill. It can transform any living being into a hellhound in the blink of an eye. It can summon other hellhounds and given time or the proper conditions, bring its master to our world. At first, we were lucky. The wand took an ogre, not a very good host for a necromancer as there is not a lot of magic potential there to amplify. Once taken, only divine power or very powerful magic can defeat it. Though Malcor and I stood against the ogre, the lich watched from the doorway and was eventually seduced by the Jade God.

"When the Order arrived, Verit stood first against the sceptre-possessed ogre. Our mission took us away to seek the container for the lich's soul. What I have heard is that the lich and the wand came together leaving the ogre as an undead monstrosity. Though the rest of the Order arrived to help, Verit faced that monstrosity and killed it. I will never forget the sight of Malcor attacking the lich, while Verit – with his hands mind you – ripped and pulled the wand out of the ogre's spine. In all of our records of the Ori conflict, Verit was the first to strike a blow. Everyone else lost their souls before they could strike. And then, he faced the lich taken by the Sceptre of the Jade God and rallied the Order to stand against it."

Verit waved his hand and tapped his cup to speak. "You do me honor, R'Dar Tembri. Let's not forget that without Malcor's capture of the lich's soul, we'd all be dead. What is often lost in these stories is that more than half the Order, including me, fell to the lich. And, as it readied to summon its master, Malcor captured its soul. The sceptre cannot inhabit a body lacking free will. The original creature's will is what gives the Jade God and that artefact what it needs to act in this realm."

"What happened to the lich's soul?" Seline asked.

Tembri answered, "It is being held by the god emperor. Though an eldar lich could be a great ally to Morbatten, the risk is too great. They will figure it out but for some time, I suspect they will leave the lich's soul trapped in its container. Great magic can be wrought with such a thing, even if the lich disagrees. In the end, all serve the Queen."

Over the next several days, they organized the teams into squads. Bruun proved to be a godsend. The time spent getting organized, gave many of them time to recover from the exhausting war games. Ayden used the time to get to know her team. The day of ultraviolet tattoos had been awful. Though many of them had normal tattoos, the magical inks used burned long after normal pain would have subsided. Several passed out and required healing.

Ayden took the pain stoically but later, when alone, she collapsed sobbing and writhing in agony. At some point, she passed out. Some of her unit were less discreet and though everyone went through it, Verit delayed departing Klenna a full extra week to allow for recovery. If the Command Team felt anything from their own marking, they never showed it.

Ayden found herself spending more and more time with her squad, and when not, with the Command Team. She noted that Command started using her to convey orders to the other squad leaders and even the master of the supply train. Malcor fascinated her and she noticed that Seline shared her fascination. It caught her by surprise that even the Imperic lady,

Sako, would watch Malcor. There was something about him. At first it annoyed her, until at last one day she realized that Malcor, when not carrying out orders or in training, spent all of his time either talking with Ishan, playing with Klara, or reading from the scriptures. A silver bird of prey always lingered over his location too. He was alone, by choice.

During one of these moments, Ayden saw Seline walk over and talk to him while he read. He simply pointed to the book and did not answer the question. His isolation struck her. After a moment, she left. By contrast, Verit stood at the center of all legion activity. His energy sometimes was all that kept them going.

During a restful day, Ayden and Bruun happened to see the first signs of a southern caravan coming their way. More supplies, resupplies, and non-soldiers had been sent to join the Nineteenth. "Verit said they'd be here tomorrow and after a day's rest, we would move on," she said to Bruun who nodded. "Supposed to be a mix of dwarves, some elves, and some halflings even. Mostly human though."

Bruun waited a moment and then said, "You know some of them will be spies right? There always are. This core group here is made of those with unquestioned or proven loyalty. For the most part, these other groups are pilgrims, fortune seekers, adventurers under commission with the Adventurer's Guild, or spies. Remember that soldier from the other day, the one you said Malcor keyed off? Turns out he's a member of the Thieves Guild. I couldn't get close enough to get anything other than that, but he didn't hide it when I asked him. If he were here on official business, Verit would know. There's a good chance that he wants the adventure. Said his name's Farant."

"Farant, okay. Let's keep an eye on him. Back to the spy thing. I mean, really? Why? Spying seems a bit extreme. What are they spying for and for whose benefit?"

"Think about it. Bloodstones are rare and Morbatten controls them absolutely. The only way you can get one is to find it in Bloodstone or take it off a dead corpse. Tania only allows the finder to keep them as a form of payment. Spies come looking for news of a fresh find. Selling information is easier than selling actual bloodstones. Though smuggling is harshly punished, it would seem Tania allows enough to escape its watchful eye to create a healthy black market, which in turn drives up the value of registered stones."

"Ha, that's brilliant. Have you ever seen one?"

Bruun shook his head. "Well, not up close. My units never made it far enough into the tunnels or were near enough a major combat to even have a chance. But Verit has one. I think Tembri does too but am not sure."

"No, Bruun! I've studied our Commanders and never noticed any bloodstones!" she exclaimed.

"Look closely at the symbol of Takhissis he wears as an earring. You'll notice an obvious diamond, but there is a cluster of rubies around it, much smaller. One of them is a bloodstone."

"I've seen that. It's a beautiful piece of jewelry. But a bloodstone -"

"Think about it, Ayden. Paladins aren't allowed to have personal wealth. A knight wearing something like that, it'd have to be sanctioned by the Temple and it'd have to be significant. If you look at it just right, you'll see that it shines even after you close your eyes." Seeing her questioning look, he added, "Stare at it and then close your eyes. You'll see a point of bright red where the one stone is set even after you close your eyes."

Ayden looked just as Bruun told her. When she closed her eyes, she continued to see a faint red afterglow for one of the rubies. "Thanks for showing me that. Though now, I'll be looking at everyone this way."

As the days passed full of preparations for the legion to move out, Ayden could not but help notice Verit's bloodstone every time she worked with him. She found herself using Bruun's technique to see if other Command Team members had one. She felt certain that Tembri must have one too. "Tell me, Ayden, are you looking for the special red stones?" he asked her one day after she had stared at him and then closed her eyes.

She blanched and then quickly recovered, "Yes. It seems like you might."

"Here," he said. "Let me show you something different." He pulled his tunic to the side so she could see the many coiled dragon tattoo that covered his right shoulder blade and most likely his back as well. "Here is mine. I mixed it into an ink and had this symbol tattooed here. While it diminishes the power of the bloodstone, it cannot be taken away from me nor can I lose or misplace it. Look at it."

When she did, the tattoo left that odd image in her mind's eye though not nearly so bright as Verit's gem. "Lord Tembri, when you, what I mean is, may I –"

"Go ahead," he said. "It's just a normal tattoo. Usually the stones amplify an item's abilities, whatever they are. I wanted to use mine to make a statement and rather than amplify something like an item, which could be lost, I chose to do this. It amplifies me. As a battle priest, the issue I face every battle is not being able to withstand the divine power the Goddess wishes me to send to Her Paladins. And unlike a Temple cleric, that power does not renew me. It consumes me. Using my stone like this helps me endure and by so enduring, I am a more capable servant."

"How big?" she asked her fingers tracing over the faint ridges of the dragon mouth inked in red and black.

"The tattoo covers most of my back. Oh you mean, the stone." She nodded. "It was about the size of a horse's head. Too large to be placed on an item, unless Tania wanted to equip a siege weapon. At about the size of a marble and larger, they have names like 'ball', or in my case, 'tower' – meaning that a stone that size would typically be placed within a tower-sized building. Instead, I powdered it to make ink dye."

She really wanted to ask what it amplified but she felt she had been nosey enough. She pulled her hand back and instead expressed her thanks. "I have always heard stories of the bloodstones, but to touch one. Thank you."

He caught her hand, "Ayden, it's amazing you were even looking for it. How did you know?" She told him about Bruun. "Ah yes, our professional non-officer veteran. That makes sense. Since the two of you both know how to spot them, I'd like to ask that you both walk through the new groups and see if any of them have bloodstones. There are myths that the stones attract other stones and fortune-seekers do all kinds of things to get into Bloodstone and find them. The problem is that they break rank in their desire to find them. Well, that and they also then could represent quite powerful adventurers and I'd like to know that as well."

She nodded but the warmth of his hand still holding her own made her pause. His hands were so calloused, even more so than her own. In the chilly day, it felt warm and that warmth enveloped her as if she stood in summer sunlight. He kissed her hand, "I'll see you again soon Ayden." The warmth stayed even after he had walked away.

Tembri walked away from Ayden grinning. It had been a long time since he had met someone like her. Ayden had the perfect mix of strength and vulnerability. He stretched. Waiting around all the time, and then the waiting more, it still got to him. "Malcor and I need to do some really hard training. I'm getting bored," he said to himself. He quickened his pace to the Shrine At Klenna. "I bet Malcor is there, or making a new sword for Verit." Verit had been relentless in ensuring Malcor stayed on that task.

Chapter Six – Seline and The River

Seline found herself alone with Tembri one evening after dinner. "You seem troubled, Lady Seline, with regards to Malcor. Might I guess that you feel a bit off put by the fact that Malcor can access the River, and also dragonshift, and you cannot?" He caught her careful non-expression.

She said, "Envy? Well, perhaps. Dar Niss has told me about the flow of Time. I have seen it with her and Blaze, and now with Malcor. But, I cannot just go to it whenever I want. I feel like I should be able to by now."

She turned to follow Tembri back down to the encampment. Tembri said, "Someday you will. Be careful. Don't judge yourself by someone like Malcor. He was truly a prodigy before he ever joined the knighthood. His work, even I had heard about the Apprentice's Sword. Imagine if he had joined the knighthood at an earlier age. We cannot afford to judge ourselves by these once in a generation children. You'll start questioning yourself and that isn't what the Queen wants."

"It's not just that," she sighed. "Growing up, even here in my Temple training, I always felt like I was ahead of everyone else. Here though, suddenly it is like I'm not good enough. This must be what Calvin feels like. Oh Goddess, it is!"

"Not true. Verit placed you in command right? He wouldn't do something like that lightly. And it places you ahead of Malcor." Tembri chuckled. "Knowing what you do about Mal, you think that went down well with him?"

She shrugged. "If it bothered him, I sure haven't heard it yet. Did it?"

"Indeed. A lot. In his view, being a knight is an entirely different focus than what I think your view is. To him, it's reassurance that he is on the right track. He sees this through his powers' growing as well as the more obvious trappings, like being made a leader. Being part of the Command Team, but not having a leadership rank, trust me, it messed him up. But, I have total confidence that, if you gave him an order right now, he'd put his heart into obeying it. Like the River."

"Like the River, what?" Seline pressed.

Tembri put his arm around her shoulders and gave her an encouraging hug. "Just like the River, your growth has to flow. When you're drowning in Time's flow, all you know is the struggle to survive, to be, to eat, to be warm, to feel secure, to feel like your life has meaning even when everything and everyone around you is dying before your eyes. When you are able to step out of the River, you'll understand these things differently.

That understanding makes it easier to move in and out of the River, but right now, since all you know is the River, it is harder.

"It's the same for Malcor. All he has ever known is *not being* a knight. As such, he struggles with it in ways you do not. You were born to rule, to lead. Since you were young, I'd guess, you've had support. Malcor was ridiculed and blocked every step of the way by House Tor. The king finally ordered Malcor to kill his employer to set him free. They'll probably have to order Malcor to comply with prophesy." Tembri smiled at Seline. "It all came naturally to you, my lady. That's what he grew up knowing - resistance. It's frankly amazing that he isn't an untrusting sociopath."

Their talk continued like this until they came back to Klenna. They struck an odd couple – the battle-scarred priest walking next to the much smaller and lithe she-knight in her gleaming plate armor. A head popped out of a tavern and Ayden waved at them to join her team for drinks. They did.

Ayden realized her interest had changed to infatuation with Tembri. When he saw her waving and nodded, it did something to her. She eyed Seline talking with him, and thanked the Goddess that knights had rules preventing the paladins from courting anyone; they could only accept the courtship of a priestess. She wondered if a male priest could take a female knight? *Naw, there were plenty of stories but it always went the other way. Plus, what if the knight became pregnant? Pregnant priestesses are common enough*, she thought. *Maybe like them, a knight would work within a shrine or Temple for a while?*

While talking, a mercenary at a nearby table, mentioned he had served with Tembri in an earlier Bloodstone campaign. Tembri had raised an eye and after a few moments, they figured out the when and who commanded and the details of the mission. Soon, questions from the group drove the story of their mission. Tembri deferred to the veteran saying, "Ben, right? Go ahead and let's hear your tale."

Ben nodded and picked up his tankard of ale and swept his hand across the dining hall. Everyone went silent. "It was early morning. The night patrols had just come back from torch duty-" he looked around and then explained, "Torch duty is a nightly task for the valley crops. Bloodstone is so infused with undeath that mists and shadows from the day's death toll creep along seeking out any last remnants of life. The crops and animals there have to be protected from this mist. Simple fire does the trick."

He took a long drink and stood up on his chair. "Anyway, one of the patrols did not come back. They asked for a rescue squad and I volunteered. I get paid extra for stuff like that," he laughed. "So, me and five others head out with torches in each hand. We get about five hundred steps out and we find a pack of ghouls ripping into a horse, but no sign of the rider. No sign of the patrol either. The ghouls immediately turn and attack us even as the horse is beginning to turn." He looked around again. "Uh, I should explain. any living thing that dies in Bloodstone comes back as undead unless you decapitate it before it turns."

Someone called out, "Get on with the story, you drunk!"

Ben growled at the voice, scanning to see who had said it. He continued, "Too many ghouls. Most of them looked like us. Dirty and worn armor and weapons, except they showed the teeth, fang, and claw marks of their death. One of the ghouls, which could have been a wight actually, leaps at us ahead of the others and is carrying some magic items. This both excites us because, you know, magic is bounty for mercs like us. His first attack scatters us and we have to drop torches and draw weapons to defend. Meanwhile, the death mists are touching us whenever it can. One of my buddies is taking it bad with the wight and..." Ben waved his hands sprinkling his fingers through the air. "Just like that, every single one of them burns away. I felt this warm almost sexual feeling, you know how your Goddess is, and then this guy," he pointed to Tembri, "comes walking in." The speaker flexed his arms and chest parodying Tembri's physique.

"It's freezing cold and he's just like this, no shirt, tattoos, armored battle skirt. He's holding his mace and his other hand forward. This wall of colored light blows over and past us. The burning ghouls burst apart in sparks and the death mist pushes back. The horse just falls over dead. I've seen some powerful clerics turn undead, but to disintegrate an entire pack of them?" He raised his tankard to Tembri and tossed it back. Everyone else did as well. Somewhere, a mandolin began playing, attempting to catch the cadence of Ben's story.

"Allow me to interrupt," Tembri said standing up. He thumped his tankard on the table to get everyone's attention. "You're describing what any priest of any allied god would have done. And you're downplaying your own role, Ben. Fine, the Goddess intervened, but your group would have beaten the ghouls, and the horse reanimating as a zombie. The next part is where your group really pulled it together though."

Now it was the veteran's turn to grow bashful. "Well -"

Tembri talked right over him, not giving him a chance to speak at all. "No, really. You see, Ben's squad had attracted the attention of, what we call in the Temple, higher order undead like wraiths and vampires. We tracked them through dawn to a tunnel. With sunlight to our backs, we decided to check the tunnel out. Just behind the daylight, they had set an ambush."

The vet jumped up on the table and began flexing again, even bumping up against Tembri. With everyone laughing, Tembri finally let the veteran speak. "Oh muscled one, okay okay, enough. And again, you're not telling it correctly. So Tembri here had made us invisible to undead. So, we walk right into their ambush and they can't even see us! A vampire and the patrol's freshly-turned vamps are all twisting and thrashing about in total silence waiting for us. We had asked Tembri to not burn them away so we could claim bounty. We went after the boss." Tembri almost interrupted him, "Fine, I went after the boss. It was a tough fight and one of the mercs almost died, but we won." The vet looked over at Tembri, "I heard a mining crew found a bloodstone vein there later."

Tembri nodded, "They did but the vein never panned out. No actual stones of quality were found and then the tunnels started shifting as they do."

Ayden eyed the veteran. He seemed to be one of those adventurers she had grown up hearing stories about. Always in the thick of things, unafraid, and always seeming to make things work out. As the conversation shifted, Tembri leaned over and whispered to her, "Fun story, but he glossed over the fact that the entire patrol died and was not recoverable, or that he led an expedition back to the tunnels before the mining crew and lost more than half of them. He's reckless. Though Tania needs people like him, we need cool-headed officers more. I hope that if you take anything from that story, it's that there are tales and then there is the part of the tale that is never told."

"Did you go back with his expedition… oh muscled one?" she asked with a funny smile.

Tembri flexed his bicep under her hand, "No, the Goddess has more important things to do than help mercs treasure hunt. They went back with a hired cleric. I heard about the aftermath."

Seline leaned in to better hear. She waited for a pause and then asked, "By the way, I've been meaning to ask you about Calvin. Have you heard anything from him?"

Tembri perked up. "Yes, Malcor once asked if Calvin had registered for the Nineteenth. I checked and found no one by that name."

Ayden sighed, "No, not at all Seline." She turned to Tembri. "Malcor and Calvin grew up here. They were friends," she explained. "When he came to the Fort, he was – like many of the paladins – quite dejected. The instructors have gotten used to helping them get out of their funk but Calvin never quite did. He talked about you by the way. Said there was a lady who had so thoroughly trounced him he could not recover. I could tell it bothered him quite a lot."

It was Seline's turn to sigh. "He trounced himself. He was so close, but in training - even in lectures, he never seemed to be quite there, like his thoughts and desires were somewhere else. I could never figure it out."

"He feels competitive with Malcor," Ayden observed more of a statement than a question.

"No doubt, which is odd because Malcor does not really seem competitive with anyone." Seline took a sip of her wine and wondered if Malcor just hid it really well. "How can you be a knight and not have ambition?"

"True," Tembri said. "He drives himself. To be more correct, the Goddess drives him. You've both felt it in yourselves, and I'm sure you've seen it in him. Not many are touched by the Goddess that way. Malcor has rarely spoken to me about his life before. I know about his family life. That's it."

"Maybe that's it," Seline said. "Calvin, if he was driven, it does not show. The closest I ever came was in the rite on the emperor's mountain. We stood together and it was weird."

Tembri raised an eyebrow. "Weird?"

She blushed. "I could tell he was not thinking about the rite."

Tembri chuckled and Ayden giggled. "Oh," she said. "You mean he-"

Seline blushed and Tembri's chuckle turned into laughter. "A knight enduring the second rite without a focus on the Goddess, no wonder. Look, everyone has to set their own course, but pretend Calvin had stayed in the knighthood. Do you know that more than half of all paladins leave after just one year? They fall in love and can't endure the vows, the lifestyle, or the rigor. There is also a lot more pain than glory in the beginning. Even Malcor, he's always alone meditating and studying. His intensity threatens to burn him out. And, I worry about his isolation. I hope you can both help with that."

Seline asked, "What about the Order of Water?"

"You mean myself and Verit? We're the only ones. Water is not like Fire. We are small in number and the camaraderie suffers because of it."

Chapter Seven – The Halfling of Legend

Tembri put his arms around both of them. "By the Goddess, this talk is too much." He gave them both a warm hug. "Lady Seline, if ever you need it, I am yours to command. Ayden, as your commander, I have a simple order for you. Keep an eye on this lady knight here. And Seline?"

"Yes?" she asked from being crushed by his huge arms.

"Calvin was not, is not, worthy of someone like you. Tell me about Kaia."

Ayden looked up and pushed back from him. "Kaia?"

Without hesitation, Seline responded, "I met him on my way to the Temple. My family insisted I travel with an escort. Everything was by the numbers. However, one night when we were still quite some days out, I had a dream and a voice called to me from the darkest darkness I could imagine. I felt helpless and naked. I tried to stand up, but all I felt was this darkness. I knew it was a dream and then I heard this voice in my head. The voice identified itself as Kaia and told me I could be one of Tania's great heroes. The voice then tracked my life from birth and without mercy laid bare the failings of my ancestors, the weaknesses of my parents, times when alone, I felt weak and humiliated. It was horrible. With each word I saw images in the darkness and relived each awful second." She looked at Ayden, "You probably think I'm crazy but I'm not."

Tembri said, "Kaia has come to many of us. I foresee he will visit Ayden as well."

"I could tell Kaia was driving me to despair or anger or tears. I vowed to give him nothing. But his words continued and I prayed to the Goddess for help. That seemed to annoy him and the darkness lashed out at me like a whip, and it hurt. Each time I prayed, the darkness attacked me and I fell to my hands and knees but refused to betray anything about how this all made me feel. That was when Kaia said it again. "You are trying to hide your human feelings, but I love your stubborn pain. It is delicious to see your nakedness and your form and the form of your naked rage. I have changed my mind, you could be one of the GREATEST heroes of Tania. But it will cost you." The voice then asked me what I wanted.

"Foolishly, I asked for him to die. That seemed to amuse him. I remembered stories about Kaia, the odd Halfling who helps young heroes. I kept wondering why he kept hurting me instead of helping. Those stories are so wrong. He mocked me. He said he would give me my greatest dreams but only at a price. We negotiated and I accepted his price."

"What did you get and what price?" Ayden asked.

Seline blushed and muttered, "I'd rather not say."

"That's okay," Tembri interrupted. "Ayden, when Kaia comes for you, remember this. He came to me when I was eighteen. He offered me strength in exchange for what he called a "favor of patience". I realize now what that was and what it meant." He let them sit up from the hug and grinned at them both. "Still, two beautiful women having dinner with me now, it seems like a dream."

Ayden ran her fingers on his arm, "You sure got strength. What did the favor of patience mean? What was it?"

Tembri looked up at the ceiling for a moment. "I was recruited to the Order of Fire, Seline's Order. As I was joining, Kaia came and told me not to accept. That was the price – not joining the most prestigious and fearsome paladin Order in the empire. Three years later and three years of service as a for-hire contractor priest to wherever I was needed, I found my way into the Order of Water. It was years still after that before I became an actual battle priest serving with an actual knight. Patience indeed!" He reached forward and took a long drink.

Almost tentatively, Seline asked him if the trade had been worth it. "The strength has come in handy more than a few times. But, my career and rank would certainly be much farther along now had I not endured this favor. To this day, I'm still not sure why or what the motives were in the trade – strength for patience, or what the halfling got out of it. I consider myself patient, but to watch my friends and peers progress so much farther than me, was hard. Of course, with Malcor now, it seems worth it."

Seline blew her hair out of her face and sat back, frustration radiating from her. Tembri was about to continue when Seline interrupted him. "Look Ayden, if or when Kaia comes for you. You just need to know that he'll offer you something you really want. But, and this is important, there's a price for it. Tembri's was a career delay of years waiting in limbo. While it might seem worth it now that he is who and where he is, I can tell you as someone still stuck early in this deal, it is torture. The price now, looking at it right now, is so much worse than it seemed when I was talking with him. The deal I got was not worth it. I think I'd still have made the Order of Fire, or at least been happy in whatever Order I entered. The price though. It's sometimes too much. Also, Calvin got a shield. He doesn't even know or care to learn how to use it." Seline stood up, brushed her hair behind her ear, and without another word, left.

Ben leaned over and said, "Knights," he said raising his glass. "So busy with their advice and words."

Ayden smiled and on a whim asked, "How about you, sir? Have you met the Halfling of Legend?"

Ben nodded, "Indeed I have. It was at the start of my first visit to Bloodstone." She prodded him to tell but he pointed to his empty tankard. Tembri ordered another and the vet continued. "We were just leaving Haven. The snow was thick but the roads clear. We made camp near a supposed safe area. That night, we were attacked by a series of archery volleys from a particularly well-organized warband of orcs. I took a small group to scout out how many and where they were attacking from. ***

"We found them. There were only about thirty or so. Not enough to slow us down at all, but they had a leader, a vampire, keeping them in check. Plus, their gear was, well, awesome. Magic bows, intensely magicked arrows. Silenced armor. Stuff I would expect us to have, not them." He drew out his sword and handed it to Ayden and Tembri. "This was the vampire's sword. My deal was power to kill the vampire. The price was stupid. Kaia told me exactly what would happen and exactly what I would do. So I did what he told me I would do anyway.

"I killed the vampire. Don't know how, but somehow I did." He tapped his armor, "This was its armor. It went exactly like the Halfling said. I went back but two of my unit did not make it. They died and turned before we could do anything. Because my mission was to scout not engage, the same-as-Verit commander of the unit, court-martialed me after demanding apologies and questioning my judgment. Kaia wanted me to be proud of defeating the vampire and keep my cool while defending my actions but to never touch my weapons even to defend myself.

"With each verbal attack and with each cool and logical defense, the knight became more and more enraged. At last, he drew his sword and attacked me. I thought I was going to die. A second before his blade was to cut into my head, Kaia appeared and blocked it. I remember how wide the knight's eyes went. You see, apparently the knight had made a deal too, something about not striking Kaia. The Halfling said simply, "You dare attack me?" The knight fell back from us."

Tembri at this point said, "I've heard this story. It was seven years ago right? An up and coming hero in the Order of Earth," he looked at Ayden and added, "it's a siege equipment unit for catapults and wall smashers, on his way to Bloodstone ran afoul of Kaia. I wonder what his trade with Kaia was."

The veteran smiled, "I don't know. I've heard the same stories but I was also there. I would guess the price and the gift were something about his mental stability. When he fell back from Kaia, a madness entered him that not even the most powerful clerics could cure. I heard the insanity ran in his family."

"Ah, and that would have disqualified him from not just the knighthood but anything other than farming or infantry. I see now."

Ayden asked, "I don't get it. Insanity, why couldn't the clerics heal it?"

"Because he was born with it. The Goddess can cure wounds or inflicted insanity. But what is created cannot be changed except at great price, even for a god. It's a wrinkle in the creation process and the fabric of the world." He pointed to a curled knot in the table's surface. "This wood has a knot. It was created that way. Healing magic will not make the knot go away. Even if we cut it out and then heal it, it will heal back to the knot. The same thing happens with infants born missing limbs or something like six fingers, even blindness. Because it is their natural state, healing only takes them back to their natural state. Ironically, a blind infant gifted with magical sight, if healed, would lose the magical sight. The same thing you see with Malcor. His wounds healed naturally, as such, no amount of healing will restore his skin."

Outside, Seline leaned back against the wall. She felt hot and fevered. Listening to them, she recalled vividly her own experience. She had been offered a magic sword, but had refused. "What good is a sword if I can't use it well?" She had asked for the ability to wield any sword of any size or weight or shape as if it weighed no more than a dagger. The price had been absolute chastity. She had already expected that going into the knighthood. What she had not expected was how being denied something made her more aware of it. She also, in that moment of bargaining, had forgotten that knights could partner with clerics. Usually, she would throw herself into training or study or anything to distract her feelings, but there were times when it was almost unbearable. Her meeting and initiation with Dread Lord Blade and some of her interactions with Dar Niss, they obviously felt attracted to her, and whatever attraction she had for them magnified. *Was it worth it? I hope so*, she wondered.

Farther back in the alley, a group of men watched her and discussed whether they should take her. She was gorgeous and the armor, even though it marked her as a knight, would be worth a fortune. She seemed drunk with too much ale. They nodded and two of them walked forward. She looked up, not quite right in her eyes. She felt their evil intent. When she saw their faces and saw their lust, the part of her that longed for intimacy shut down. Grateful for the distraction, she leaned forward and smiled at them. "How can I help you?"

The two and then the other six behind came forward and circled her. She felt a malignancy from at least one of them and wished she could step from the River and see which one carried it. The leader answered her, "Nothing. Everything. A beautiful young lady like you can help all of us with everything. You should be more careful, alone on a night like this." A dagger dropped into his hand as from behind them, a weighted net sailed up and over their heads to land on her.

Seline stood, unmoving. The rising thrill of combat and a blood-boiling surge of strength filled the part of her that moments ago ached with longing and visions of desire with Tembri, the veteran, anyone who would have her. She thought about dread lord Blade and, as the net landed around her with sharp hooked barbs pulling into her armor's crevices, her armor and body ignited in a sphere of dragon fire. The net cindered and the hooked barbs melted to liquid slag. She pointed her hand at the leader and called her sword into her hand.

She began to speak in draconian, but changed to Tanian Common so they would understand her words. "In the earliest days, the children were unruly choosing to fear rather than worship the Goddess. She smote them with fire and ice and lightnings. With great thunderings, the God Emperor raged amongst them until the unruly fell to their knees, or just fell and died in their fear. Their cries for mercy became hymns of praise. When they see the Goddess, they see now eternity."

By the time she finished reciting the key scripture held by the Order of Fire, the leader's flesh had burned away to skeleton, and that fell to pieces. She spun into the others and her sword left cauterized wound tracks that held them agonizing in pain but unable to bleed out and die. Only one managed to attack her by throwing his dagger. It hit the burning aura around her and liquefied to splash against her breastplate and drip away. By the time the dagger fell, the assailant's head stopped rolling. And then, Tembri was there. His priesthood lashed out and held the three of them left on the edge of death. "Seline, we'll take these as prisoners."

She extinguished her aura and watched the last traces of wet blood bubble and hiss and then powder around the attackers. "They attacked me. Idiots."

Ayden drop kicked two of them while others pinned the third. She tied them quickly and looked up, "I'll take them to Verit. We don't want this kind in our legion. I doubt Klenna wants them either."

Chapter Eight– Valley of Bloodstone

Dar Ana sat on her throne in the Temple At Bloodstone. Situated in the central chapel beneath a rotate-able stained glass dome, the colored glass filled the chapel with the colors beloved by dragons. Red especially dominated the theme. The glass mural showed a mix of the guardian dragon, Crimson Burning, confronting the Consort Dragon who betrayed Tiamat. It then morphed into the story of Tiamat, showing her dual aspects of Tiamat the Nurturer versus Takhissis the Warrior. Sunset barely shimmered through the gathering storm clouds on the western horizon. From her throne, Ana looked out to the sky through the clear glass windows barely colored to show the Goddess in her dragon from. A paladin reported about yesterday's activities. She interrupted him, "Tell me about the miners."

The paladin stopped talking, paused to collect his thoughts, and reported, "They continue under constant attack. So far, lower level undead such as zombies and skeletons. The reinforcements we sent five days ago helped enough to let the miners tunnel in. As the dwarf Unter speculated, their tunnel connected to older mineshafts. Draconian writing dates those tunnels to at least a thousand years ago. They have sanctified their camp and will wait out the night. Tomorrow at dawn, they will enter the tunnels again."

She leaned forward and stood. The knight kept his eyes carefully on the stone steps leading up to her. Like all the high priestesses, Ana exuded sensual beauty. Unlike other high priestesses, she wore the minimum tokens of her rank, which left her almost nude. Her bare feet padded down to him and she asked, "What arrangements have you made to ensure this expedition does not end like the last one?" She referred to an event about a month ago where the entire mining team had been lost except for two dwarves. "Unter. He was one of the survivors, correct?"

The paladin tried to think but his thoughts lingered on her closeness, her scent. Somewhat choking, he finally replied, "Yes. Unter. He was one of the two survivors. For extra security, we tested some of the mercenary clerics – they passed strong enough - and assigned a contingent to them. Also, we have provided double the normal guards. There is a mage in the group in touch with our mages here. The knights at Valley are ready to ride out on a moment's notice. Another group is ready to provide relief during the day."

Ana touched his head trailing her fingers through his hair as she walked past him to a large bloodstone sphere an arms' length across just past him. Her touch gave him goosebumps. She tapped the tower bloodstone and whispered to it in draconian. From its red tinted depths, a mist billowed out to fill the sphere and then within it, the image of the mining party appeared. Magical light spheres burning with daylight gleamed at eight points around their central magical fire. Some twenty dwarves sat around the fire as they checked and re-checked their tools, mapping gear, armor, and weapons. The paladin joined her and observed, "They appear in good spirits."

Ana whispered again at the stone. The image swirled amongst two women each wearing the robes and armor of clerics. They carried battle staves and maces. Though one was not a cleric of the Goddess, if they passed her knights' scrutiny they must be strong, well - strong enough for patrol work.

"We've had merc priests before. Tell me about this female." Ana pointed to her.

"The lady is a priestess of Krentismar. She did exceptionally well, controlling four vampires. Her name is Helena. The other two were not able to reach that level of control to even a single vampire. However, they showed an ability and willingness to combine with the Krentismar cleric."

Ana touched the sphere and whispered. In its crimson depths, the priestess looked up at Ana and smiled. Through the sphere, her words came saying, "I'm ready to do whatever is required, High Priestess."

"She heard me. Very good. You've done well, Captain." Ana turned and kissed the paladin's forehead. "You are dismissed. Let me know if anything occurs. This is the best chance we have had to find a new vein of stones in a long while. I hate to relieve the Eighteenth without a find. We'll attribute this to them if it pans out."

The captain watched as she sashayed up the steps to her throne. He knew he had turned bright red at her lips' touch. He bowed and left before she turned and saw his discomfort. It'd be a long night and the image of her red hair parting around her back, how her girdle just barely hid her, the feel of her lips on his skin… would stay with him all night. At his promotion to captain, the Order of the Shield had told him serving Dar Ana would be difficult. It would be a long night indeed. He sighed.

* * *

Down in the valley, one of the dwarves strolling the perimeter with a torch cursed. In spite of the day globes, a grasping snake-like mist occasionally made its way through. It had just brushed his leg. "Damn wights," the dwarf growled as he stabbed his torch into the mist. It burst apart without a sound but the lethargy in his leg continued. By dawn, and in spite of all they could do, every single one of them would have some degree of lethargy from this mist.

The priestess Helena came up behind the dwarf whispering a prayer to her god, the god of this world known by the human name Krentismar. The lethargy faded and the dwarf smelled a forest fresh after rain before the decaying stench of the valley overwhelmed it. "My lady," he bowed.

"Not wights. Leftover spirit energy from so many deaths, undead killed, resurrections, and healings. Thousands of years and millions of lives recycled here creates this. It's an abomination. Wights are physical, most often evil people who died while obsessed with some evil purpose."

"Aye," the dwarf muttered. "Still I'd give that and more for a stone or two!" He stabbed his torch at another mist swirl and swore.

The priestess continued her walk around the perimeter, blessing those affected. Out and away from them, in the darkness, she knew eyes watched her. She knew they were there. She blew those watching eyes a kiss. If Dar Ana still watched, that would impress her. The border of their camp had been sanctified and she felt pleased that, except for some of the mists, her boundary held. Passing Unter, she noted the excavator flipping through a log and referencing something. "Divining the secrets of the tunnels?" she asked.

Unter looked up and grunted. "Just a record of my work here. The tunnel we dug, I need to give it name and mark. I'm hoping for something more creative than Stone mark eighteen." He looked around, scanning the darkness around their almost too bright encampment. "If I hadn't been out here for years, the quiet darkness right now would really be messing with my head," Unter grumbled.

Helena nodded. "It is unnerving, but you should get some rest. Tomorrow will be here before we'd like and it will be an important day for you."

Unter's intensity increased. "Your god has told you it will be?" he asked hopefully.

Helena shrugged. "Each tomorrow is a blessing. Our life's most important work lies ahead. Now, please. Rest."

Unter slammed his diary shut and laid down while grumbling about vague clerical pronouncements. "Augur it, priestess," he called out to her back.

Bloodstone never slept, but her team needed to rest. Tomorrow, they would re-enter the tunnels and try to expand their map. If they got enough, they might be able to correlate it to other map fragments held by the Temple At Bloodstone. It might tell them where to find already known veins, or it might tell them of other treasures, even dangers. The dwarves chuffed at the delay but even Bloodstone cautioned patience. In a few hours, daylight even if clouded and dark in winter, would dispel the mists and give them a slight advantage. Tania had learned to use every advantage, no matter how small, in the many centuries of occupation here.

From a ridge, far from the light, a humanoid sat on a rock. He watched. A ram's skull rose up and leaned over his shoulder. It watched too. He patted it, pushing it back. He did not recognize the people's faces and their way of talking felt off but he heard and understood everything. "Too long. It's been too long to find the surface," he groaned to himself. "So much time if their language is now this."

Behind him, a handful of undead swayed side to side, waiting for a command. "I wonder how they will do."

At a hand gesture, three zombies lurched forward towards the camp. The guards saw them coming but refrained from stepping out of the circle of light. The humanoid noticed how they did not leave the drawn circle in the dirt. The zombies went right up to it, but would not cross it either. One of the guards went right up, just a step from the zombie. Eventually, one of the clerics came over and sent them away. Seeing the zombies turn and begin to walk to him, he sent them a command. "Attack the line in the dirt. Try to break the line."

The zombies struggled, continuing to walk towards him, and then spun to head back to the camp. He saw the guards laugh, making a joke. This time, the lady priestess came over to watch. When the zombies dropped to their hands and knees and shuffled forward, the priestess said, "Get torches. Step out of the circle, and end the zombies."

The guard did so and the watcher noted how the priestess had to pull the guard back in, while the zombies ignited and burned. Another hand flick sent two ghouls pattering to the camp running on all fours. The ghouls leapt at the guard who just barely saw them. The ghouls crossed into the boundary and their skin burst aflame. Seeing they would soon die, the watcher sent a wraith. A vampire nearby asked, "Great Bomoki, do you wish for me to test their strength?"

The humanoid answered, "No, I'm curious is all. I do not recognize the people, the dress, or the customs. The wraith will fail." Bomoki looked at the vampire and grinned. Half his face smiled anyway. The other half showed gritted teeth and decaying material where ligaments would have attached the jaw to the upper teeth. "You would fail too, my pet."

The wraith hit the guard who immediately collapsed. Like an alarm, the guard's fall stirred the camp into action. They retaliated with magical weapons, spells, and the lady priestess commanded the wraith to burn. Though the wraith did not burn, it tried to flee the priestess. As the attackers struck at its back, the wraith reached out a hand to Bomoki, who did nothing. "That will happen to you if you go. Do you wish to go?" Bomoki asked.

The vampire replied, "I wish to serve you."

"Then, let's take these with a greater force that ensures our victory." Bomoki stepped up and back from where he had watched. The vampire and other undead parted for him and then followed as the earth opened to swallow him into a tunnel that had not been there a moment before.

Chapter Nine – Dar Rojo Joins the Nineteenth

The next two days passed in a blur for Malcor as he regained his strength. Though still too weak to help, he sketched out Verit's new sword design and had Tembri requisition needed components. When he could finally stand, he stumbled out to find Verit and noted that he could rebuild the sword, but it would be lighter. Verit clapped Malcor on the shoulder and told him, "That's fine by me, Malcor. Thank you!"

Finally able to move, Malcor noticed that Tembri and Ayden had begun spending most of their free moments together. Watching Tembri hold Ayden's hand in a moment of thought about how to approach Verit's new blade, it struck him that Tembri and Ayden looked good together. Ayden, like Tembri, rolled along with required actions either getting the tasks done or requesting help. In the midst of their growing encampment, Malcor had finally had a chance to see how the Temple and the military operated outside his own very specialized Order of Water. The delays, the blaming, the inaction of so many had bewildered him at first until he realized he had been spoiled by Dar Kendra's well-run brotherhood.

Cor'tanos never returned though Tembri often thought he saw weird shapes in the shadows around his ward. Each night, they restrained Malcor in case he woke up with Verit's command still ringing in his mind. But, he did not. On the third morning, Seline entered Malcor's field tent to wake him but found him ready for the day ahead. The ordeal with Cor'tanos and Verit had taxed him far worse than any of the rites she had done to get into the Order of Fire. His eyes held a haunted look even though he smiled and spoke with her cordially enough. She asked him questions about his rites but his answers were slow and disjointed. Tembri finally arrived and sent her away.

Later, at evening dinner, Verit asked Malcor, "How are you feeling?"

"Dangerous, sir!" Malcor said with enthusiasm. Seline remembered though how gaunt and ragged his skin had looked earlier when he pulled on a shirt.

"Excellent. You hear that team? R'Dar Malcor is feeling dangerous. How about your team, Ayden?"

"Dangerous and ready for anything, Captain."

Tembri answered, "Blessed and favored."

Each answered and then Verit continued, "We will be hosting someone important on this trip. May I introduce to you King Rojo, King of Morbatten, and Goddess-blessed protector of the Empire?"

The door flap opened and Rojo entered the room as they each dropped to their hands and knees. He stole the light with him as he entered but the grin on his face made it somehow seem okay. Seline had never seen the king this close. Every part of her rose up wanting to excel. She felt the same with Verit, but with Rojo the feeling magnified. The king touched Verit, who introduced his Command Team. "This is Seline, my First. I have put her in command of special unit teams. Tembri is my Second."

Seline ordered everyone to stand. "Dar Rojo," she said. "We cannot express how glad we are to have you with the Nineteenth."

Rojo bowed to her. "I am travelling with you on different business. Seeing this group, my heart leaps for the heroic deeds you will do. Truly, I will be with the Nineteenth in spirit." He walked past Malcor and stopped. "Ah, Sir Malcor, we seem destined to meet in Klenna. I understand your training is moving quickly." Malcor nodded as Rojo made his way through the group.

An hour later, the King asked the other squad captains to be brought in including the leaders of the mercenary and supply trains, as well as the dog soldier marshals. Verit had anticipated this and when all had crowded into the field tent, Rojo addressed them as a group. "This past summer, I visited Klenna to fulfill a prophecy set during the Kell Conflict. At that time, I vowed I would be here again when the snow first falls. There is another prophecy, this from far before our times, during the Ancients." He referred to the tribal history of Tania when Alerius stood at the head of a totem over the barbarian tribes he had spent thousands of years transforming into Morbatten. "This prophecy concerns the Bloodstone Valley, our destination, and the future of the empire."

Rojo looked up at the tent ceiling and when he looked back at them, Ayden met his eyes. She tried to keep her facial expression unaffected but she felt deeply, as if the King stared into her soul. Her desires and fears all spread out there before him, like a lover for those things that might arouse interest, like a criminal seeking to hide things she felt undesirable. Tembri touched her leg and she felt a bit better.

Rojo's voice became somewhat wistful and even distant as he continued, "In the dark times, when chaos raged in the heart of *Morbat*, The Mother strengthened Her Son and said, "You shall be my mighty spear to drive chaos out." The Son, with that weapon, battled chaos and threw the Necromancer into the Valley of Blood. But woe shall fall on the children for the sacrifice and the price paid to remove the Necromancer, for the harm caused to *Morbat*. Mother wept when She saw the few surviving and charged the Son to safeguard them. There, by the pool of the Necromancer's blood, the Mother vowed, "Let this blood remain as a reminder to the Necromancer that I am Mightiest. Through me, My Children are Mighty." Rojo let his voice quiet and then spoke in his own voice.

"We have become mighty and once again become a target for the Necromancer. Dar Verit and Sir Malcor have fought this evil and won a victory against the Khasran Lich, but the real battle against necromancy is to happen in Bloodstone. There is a link between the Valley of Bloodstone and our great empire. It draws the undead to us. It pulls them against us. They are the grindstone on which we sharpen our fighting spirit into a mighty weapon the Necromancer cannot even comprehend.

"So, what is our mission? Our mission is to serve this prophecy. To find the gate in Bloodstone Valley. Finding it, controlling that gate will make us a great weapon." Rojo looked around meeting their eyes with that uncanny gaze. His gaze lingered on Malcor. "Do not think of it as a sword, or a spear though prophecy names Tania as The Spear. The great weapon in this prophecy is our faith and love of the Queen. It is you, me, all of us. It is the dragons and the gods that stand for this world." This time he looked directly at Malcor and added, "It is time for the Heretics to come back to their Mother. To that end, we go to consecrate the Heretics, if they will come back to their Mother."

Most of this talk went right over the heads of everyone present. Even Malcor struggled to grasp its meaning, but he checked his sense of purpose and felt the Goddess' approval. Nearby, Seline did the same and felt it too as a deep sense of rightness and an excitement to make it happen. The King also had a presence about him that hurt her, almost physically. She felt herself slowly smolder and had to push images of herself and the king away and focus on his words. She clenched and unclenched her hand wishing she could retreat from the River – this feeling she assumed was the river - and at least temporarily end her agony.

The silence hung in the air just long enough for each to feel it and then Verit announced, "And the Nineteenth will be ready, my King!" His fist in the air, he cried out and the others joined in. The heavy weight on Seline lifted as the King's attention turned away from Malcor. She wondered why it had affected her so but given her emotional state earlier and all that happened, she tried to focus on the moment. This moment of purpose etched itself into her being. She looked for Malcor and saw him looking at Cor'tanos. The shadow dragon patriarch stood half-smiling back in the shadows, at the edge of the group. For just a second, Seline imagined she saw a hungry look in the dread lord's face, and then it passed.

Servants began bringing in food and drink. Soldiers trained in the Tanian art of drumming, uncovered an array of large and small drums. Outside, all around them, large drums the size of wagons began to beat a slow rhythm. Then, one by one, the drummers brought their smaller and higher pitched drums into play. Within minutes, the booming syncopation of drums filled the air.

Across the room, Verit bowed to the king and said, "Dar Rojo, all is ready for the Nineteenth to depart. On your order, sir."

"Tomorrow in late morning, we will set wagon to road and begin our journey. The legion looks ready. Tell me, how fares your planning with my squire?"

Verit blinked and then recovered, "Your squire? Oh you mean R'Dar Malcor. He continues to grow in his mastery of the shadows. I am impressed with his advancement as a paladin. I'm sure you have heard of my fight with him."

Rojo's smile told Verit that he had. "It is hard to believe that just a few months ago I crossed blades with Malcor here in the summer Coming of Age Ceremony. He should be the next king." Verit's eyes went wide and Rojo continued, "Except for Cor'tanos' interference, the Sister Prophecy, or maybe the former owner of the Klenna forge? It depends on how you look at it, I suppose."

Rojo watched the group for long moments, seemingly lost in thought. Verit remained bowed and silent. At last, Rojo waved for a drink. A priestess brought him a steaming cup of tea and Verit caught an acrid whiff of medicinal herbs. Rojo took a sip and then pointed to Malcor. "Jeri," he said to the priestess, "look at the young knight there and then this other lady knight," indicating Seline. "Tell me what you see."

Verit noted that Jeri had the look of all high priestesses, eternal youth and sublime beauty. She radiated strength and then he noticed her hair. Like all favored and transcendent priestesses, her hair glowed a crimson red yet it just barely sparkled with gold. He had never seen this one before. In the lantern and magical lights, something glinted and he saw just enough to realize skin colored tattoos had been interlaced all over her body. The draconian script told the tales of war and he realized she must be the king's battle priestess. She briefly turned her attention back to Rojo. "My lord," she began to say. Under that shortest gaze, Verit felt his entire life pulled into the flow of Time around her, and it stuttered in the downstream lull of her might. He kept his composure and smiled back, bowing.

"My dear Rojo, the boy is heavy with prophecy but he is torn between his love of the Goddess and his fascination with the heretics. His aura is conflicted and the shadows are being manipulated by Cor'tanos to pull him away from the Mother." She looked at Seline. After a moment, she licked her lips and smiled broadly. "That one has paid a dear price to the Halfling. She burns with passion and desire. She is self-conflicted and in that burning desire she longs for love and lust and glory and power. She knows of the River but has yet to break free. Both are powerful. The boy," Verit saw her eyes glass over and her voice altered slightly becoming more serpentine…

"The young man Malcor stands between the banks of the River. He is pulled to the Goddess and is also seduced to the shadows on the other side. He must make a choice, a decision of consequence and pain. That choice-"

Rojo nodded, "That choice will break him of his willingness to serve Tania as king. I had hoped to speak with him on the road but can see, it is pointless at this time. I will train with him, for his dragon self."

Jeri nodded confirmation. "It will break him of confidence, but he may still serve if the heretics come home, or he breaks free of them. But, no, the Goddess tells me there is another path. The father could sacrifice himself for the son. That path brings both a homecoming for Cor'tanos and the kingship secured."

Rojo sipped his tea and took Jeri's hand so that she stayed by them. "Verit, tell me, in a fight who would you choose – Kell or Cor'tanos, as your opponent I mean?"

Verit answered without hesitation. "Cor'tanos. To die fighting such a worthy foe and mighty enemy would be an honor. To fight Kell, even assuming equal favor by the Goddess, would be to ensure my own destruction."

Jeri looked at him now and he felt that heavy regard. "So, you see them both as your destruction but Kell is perhaps more destructive?"

"Indeed my lady. As I see it, both choices are suicide but one grants me an afterlife. I have no doubt that Kell, even were I to somehow win, would destroy my soul."

Rojo indicated for Verit to sit by him and the two began to discuss Bloodstone, war stories, and the plans ahead. Dar Jeri continued watching Malcor, her eyes occasionally darting to Tembri and the dread lord Cor'tanos watching from the shadows. After some time, Verit turned and studied Dar Jeri more carefully. Amused, the king asked him what had caught his attention.

"It's nothing, my liege. Apologies. I was distracted."

"Do tell, Captain. Jeri has drawn the gaze of many here in the empire. I'm curious. Was it her beauty that caught you? Her presence?"

Verit looked at her again and found Jeri smiling at him with a sly smile. "My king, I have served with many of the Dar priestesses. Dar Jeri," and he inclined his head to her, "she reminds me of the dread lords. No offense intended, my lady. And I thought that I knew of them all."

Rojo finished his tea while Jeri answered, "Offense? None taken at all. We all crave the day when we can fly as dragons."

Jeri reached out her hand and touched Verit's. Her fingers felt warm and cold at the same time. Verit felt himself regarded from outside of time and he knew.

"Dar Jeri, you are a dread lord." Scared to move his hand, he froze instead and bowed his head.

Rojo and Jeri watched him silence. "Very good," the king said. "Tell me Captain, what else?"

Verit moved up and out of the River. There, from its banks, he saw a radiant golden aura rise up from the priestess born on wings of sunrisen gold from which sparkles of shimmering light rained down into Time's current. There, on the banks of that place, Verit dropped to his hands and knees in worship. The gold dragon's head rose up around the human form of the priestess and looked into his very soul. Her bright laugh echoed around him with a carefree sense of endless mirth. "Captain," her voice holding a flirtatious note, "your heart is all service and valor and pride, but like all Tanians, you have a dark fascination with Mother."

"Oh my lady, I am overcome with your glory!" and the Captain trembled beneath her gaze.

Her human form unraveled and the titanic form of a slender gold dragon reared back and then dipped down to look in Verit's eyes as her magic lifted him up to her view. "Tell me. Why do you serve the Mother?"

Verit withered under her gaze and tears began flowing from his eyes so overcome was he. "The Mother," he stammered, "She... she is the only hope to secure the world from the Jade God and other powers of darkness."

Jeri pressed in on his last words, "But you are a dark paladin serving a Goddess who rules from Hell. Is she not Darkness itself?"

Verit struggled for air as his body twisted in the magic winds holding him up. "No dread one, the Mother, my goddess, she is the fulcrum on which darkness can become light itself. Heaven, like the All Father Dragon, they left us alone against all the powers of Hell and the Abyss. Only the Goddess left patriarchs and Her Powers intact in the world. Worthy causes, like saving the world for Her, Her Children, for me and my children, require sacrifice. How can 'good' be good when its only action is to react to evil? I serve the Mother because I want to be a mighty tool to save the world for those I love. For the dragons, for the humans, for everyone. If that drenches the world in blood and pain, so be it. I will pay that price and carry the burden of murder and trampled innocents until the end of my days and eternity after."

It all came gushing out of him in that torrent of awestruck majesty that required a totality of conviction and truth. Jeri gently returned him to the River. Suddenly, they were back in the tent. Verit, on his knees, sobbed freely and Rojo touched his shoulder. "Jeri is special to our cause. She sees deeply. The Nineteenth has a worthy Captain in you."

Jeri leaned down and kissed Verit's cheek. "Recover yourself and know that Mother loves you, Captain."

Wheels creaked and ground into the frost and ice splintered ground. The road stretched before and behind and the wagon train seemed endless. Ayden passed her time moving to and fro the column's length, but really she just wanted to be at the head of the column. That's where Dar Rojo led from his heavy war horse. Though riding a horse day after day was still riding a horse, it felt more glorious by the king.

They had traveled for two weeks now passing through and near settlement after settlement. Within Tania, the settlements appeared as small farming communities. Each had either prepared food for the army or had sent it to the capitol ahead of their departure. The roads throughout Morbatten, even those departing Klenna for the wilderness, stood firm and well-maintained. Increasingly, ice and wintery weather slowed them, but the quality of the road was less a problem than the weather. They only stopped to camp. Each day, new groups joined the Reinforcement Army with adventuring groups and supply wagons making up the bulk of the newcomers. Already, the convoy stretched several miles made up of thousands of walkers and nearly a thousand large wagons.

A few days prior, the Soran army joined them nearly increasing their size by a third. A dour but charismatic knight of the Sun God Pha Rann led. He introduced himself as Sir Alan and had quickly squared off against Verit in challenge for leadership of the legion that had stopped just shy of battle. It had ended with King Rojo reaffirming Verit's leadership.

Verit declined making Sir Alan part of the Command Team, and when Ayden met the Cuthbert knights in Alan's group she immediately understood. They tended to range far away from the war train, preferring their own company to the Tanians. One of them had challenged her faith in the Queen. She had responded as ordered, and kept her silence. A few of the legion did not and bloody fights broke out as either the zealots so offended those challenged that they drew weapons and attacked, or deliberately provoked them. Ayden could not believe that a group so obsessed with absolute righteousness could be so bloodthirsty.

Talking about it with Tembri during a quiet moment, he clarified it for her. "The Order of Cuthbert believes that evil, in any form must be opposed or else, by their definition, they condone it. As such, any god that is not part of Cuthbert's pantheon is challenged. Some welcome the challenge. But, for the most part, I think they do it as a form of worship. If you pay attention, you can tell which of them do it as a matter of devotion versus the others who do it because it's an expected part of their worship."

"Sir Alan's challenge of Verit, was that real?" she asked.

"Yes. Because of the Winter War and Tania's long history opposing them, whenever the zealots join Bloodstone, their leader always challenges the Legion Commander. In the past, there have been fights to the death. Sir Alan is known to us. Verit would have beaten him easily. In some ways, it's too bad Rojo prevented it."

With Morbatten growing more and more distant behind them, the road continued but became magically supported by earth elementals moving through the ground underneath. Bound there ages ago and renewed by Tania through its mages and the Temple, they smoothed the way for the train. It had caught Ayden off guard there at the front of the train to see twisted cobblestones, ruined bridges, and frozen mud puddles suddenly smooth over and become firm. The elementals kept the road intact for about a hundred paces ahead and behind the train.

Though the Reinforcement Army grew in size as they continued to acquire non-combatants and others in the form of pilgrims, adventurers, trading caravans, and refugees heading in either direction, the elementals maintained that safe distance. The opportunity to walk the Blood Highway to Haven even drew a few spectators from villages and outposts.

Tembri caught Ayden relaxing in the back of the train watching the road disintegrate behind them at one point. While he joined her in the wagon, she asked and he explained it to her, "The elementals are bound to a special sceptre in Verit's possession. He'll give it up to Dar Ana in Bloodstone as part of our official commission as the Nineteenth, but for now, it's what keeps this road intact. The Eighteenth will use that sceptre to return in spring after we sort out how many of them will join us."

"Watching it, it seems like one of those legendary things you would hear songs about," she said pointing to a tree that had just settled back into the side of the crumbling road. She leaned against him enjoying how warm he felt. "You should dress more warmly," she chided him.

He waved at the snow drifting down. "I'm warm-blooded, besides my Order and faith keep me warm. The roads are not legendary because not all mages in Tania are. You have great ones, like Reznor, like Dread Lord Blaze, like Sai, and the Vampire Generals. Then you have everyone else. They pay for their training in the Mage's Guild by binding elementals like this into our empire. I had a civics class where they showed how much was spent just on just road maintenance before this practice. Now, it's just the effort to keep the elementals happy. Everything works this way actually, from the lights to Tania's water system, to the roads, to strategically important buildings and structures, just with different elementals."

Ayden took his hand in her own. "Like the Temple and shrines. I saw that in Klenna. By the time we left, the damage from our training had all been repaired."

"Healed actually, if you want to get technical. The earth elementals are able to tap into stored spells like *Stone Mend* to quickly repair and reshape created things like a bridge or road. Created structures actually makes them quite mad. We pay the ones in front to pull the road together. The ones in back are paid with the pleasure of destroying it all. Fun, huh? There are two such sceptres and the Legion Commanders juggle them so that one group of earth elementals is always paid to destroy the road. It's not an even trade, but it is a lot cheaper and easier to give them precious metal and gems than building and maintaining an actual road this long."

Ayden nodded but cared less about how magic worked and more about how close she felt to Tembri. "Why don't we have any mages in our army?"

"We have quite a few actually, just not any you have ever heard of. For example, Mal's friend Sako is a mage. The Mage's Guild is monitoring us from Tania. If we need one, they'll send one. Every war train has a dedicated group of mages to support us. Mages don't do well with travel and weather though. Most don't do well at all in combat. In fact, I'd say there are less than a handful in all the empire that are truly effective in combat."

"The Order of the Shield guards them right?" she asked thinking about Calvin and Seline.

He nodded, "Of those, there are only maybe three that could fight in Bloodstone or with the Order of Water and not become a liability. They're a very rare breed, Ayden. Like you, they are very hard to find. Enough about this though, what's on your mind?"

"I'm wondering what Haven is like and whether we will have any time together there. You spend all your time in exercises with Malcor. I assume Bloodstone will be worse."

Tembri hugged her tight and kissed her forehead. "Bloodstone is always worse."

A swirl of snow in the wind gusted around them in that moment and Ayden shuddered. "That was ominous. Is it so much worse that even the winter is bothered by it?"

A charger clad in gleaming silver and gold came into their view. It carried a mounted cleric of Pha Rann. The priest scowled at them and then pointedly looked back at the end of the roadway dissolving behind their wagon. He crossed the roadway and stayed in their sight as if daring them to continue being in love, offended by it. Ayden giggled and then started laughing. Amused, Tembri asked what and she pointed to the priest, "I don't get it." She called out loudly, "Why the sour face?"

The priest's expression soured even more and he rode forward. He locked gaze with her and said, "You're a squad leader to the Command Team. Ayden or something? Did I get that right? You're a leader and you're hanging out back here with Lord Tembri who is also on the Command Team. It's wrong. It sets a bad example."

Ayden was about to answer when Tembri said simply, "The Goddess does not see it that way. Love is part of life. You should try it."

The abruptness of the command jolted the priest who took his sour face and left as the wagon rolled past him. Tembri chuckled. "I've never seen a Pha Rannic priest ever stand up to confrontation. It's the knights you have to worry about."

"Tembri," Ayden asked. "The legions. I imagined they'd be bigger. Is this really it?"

"Well, we stretch about five miles right now. It's not like we're small, but we're not at full strength either. It was not until Rojo confirmed us as an official legion that I finally got it. A real legion occurs every five years when Bloodstone is active or at war. In between, major reinforcements are still sent at five years. The god emperor and Dar Ana felt a legion is required based on prophecy and revelation. When we reach Bloodstone, Verit expects half of the Eighteenth to re-enlist with us. That'll bring our dog soldiers to a full ten thousand count and complete the Command Team." He tapped his fingers and added off-handedly, "Though we'll be the nineteenth legion, it's interesting that the five year legions span almost a thousand years. That should tell you how valuable Bloodstone is to the empire."

Miles rolled underneath their cart as they watched the land and sat together for warmth. Dragonshifted, Malcor soared back and forth over the train. Ayden marveled at how much larger and more powerful Malcor's dragon form had become. To that Tembri shrugged, "Humans that can shapeshift into dragons do so with their own power, where a normal dragon ages and grows. Malcor is becoming more sure and confident in his powers. He'll continue growing as a function of faith and confidence rather than age. I understand his father, Dar Kell, is titanic."

Chapter Eleven – The Miracle on the Road

Though they kept guard, and Ayden frequently led her squad on night patrol, bandits, monsters, everything and all possible disturbances left them alone. Though Malcor spotted a few possible raiding parties, those parties quickly retreated from moderate sorties or fled from the midnight dark dragon flying overhead. Their biggest problem came from newcomers not adequately prepared for the cold onset of winter. Even then, the supply wagons and caravans joining them brought supplies. Whenever they passed a frontier settlement, the people came out to the greet them.

The settlements along the roads all had Tanian names, but so far outside of the empire, the villagers lived in fortified walls of wood or stone. The center of these outposts each held large granaries storing wheat, corn, and other dryable or storable food. This allowed the wagons to resupply and kept the animals nourished. The commanders of these groups always waited for them and spoke with Verit. Sometimes, Verit sent Seline and the special teams to investigate outposts, or to let them know the Reinforcement Army would be arriving. Only once did Ayden notice anything amiss. The commander had passed away and the outpost could not determine who would take over. Rather than store provisions for the Bloodstone Legions, two factions had emerged which traded or sold their stored food for weapons.

Verit had not liked that. He ordered the paladins and combat-trained clerics of Tiamat to capture them all. "Do not hurt the innocents." Ayden remembered watching them vanish from a nightly patrol. Though she knew their mission, the pang of jealousy she had felt almost made her reconsider entering the knighthood and trying out to be a paladin. Tembri's wave good-bye raised her spirits.

"He could probably take the entire outpost by himself," she said to his back. Though only twenty paladins and an equal number of clerics had left, Ayden knew the settlement would fall quickly. Two days later, the Army reached the settlement. Two groups of men and women had been tied hand and foot in a line. They waited for Verit under the guard of Tiamat. Children and other villagers held those bound, crying. Verit ordered the Army to proceed without stopping. With no provisions, there was no point. Ayden peeled off the road and headed towards Tembri with her unit.

They arrived just in time to see the Tanian punishment. Tembri stood in the middle of the two lines. "Because of your bickering squabble, which should have been resolved within your shrine, the Reinforcement Army will have to make do without your five years' worth of provisions. We cannot take what little you have left or your families will die. I have consulted with the Great Goddess Tiamat. She orders compliance with a full measure when the next legion comes to Bloodstone. Additionally, we must give you a lesson you and your family will remember."

Tembri pointed and Seline cut one of the villagers from the tied line. The two walked before Tembri. Without warning, Seline drew her sword and stabbed it through the man. Its point burst through his sternum and she lifted him up on her pommel. He tried to grab the blade and ease the pain, but his hands sliced apart on her blade.

Tembri prayed, blessing and healing the man, while Seline turned him so the others could see. When she at last withdrew her blade, Tembri spoke. "You will endure. You will survive. The Mother knows and loves you." The villager fell forward gasping and choking to breathe even while his wounds restored.

Seline pointed to a man from the other line. A paladin there cut that one loose and shoved him to Seline. Her sword burst into fire and she leapt at him, almost running him through. Instead, she stopped with the point of her sword at his heart. The sword's fire ignited and burned his flesh away. Like the other, he healed and by the time Seline had backed away and sheathed her sword, he had recovered though his screaming had not stopped.

Tembri gestured and both lines were thrown to the ground, on their knees. The silence of watching this had them fall to their faces begging for mercy. "Where is your cleric?" Tembri demanded. No answer came. A paladin sliced the throat of the first man in his line. "Where is your cleric?" Tembri asked again.

From behind, a child ran forward and grabbed the woman at the head of the other line. "Don't hurt my mommy!" she cried to Tembri. She put herself between Tembri, and the paladin at her line.

"Where is your blessed priestess of Tiamat?" Tembri hissed at them. From behind, someone called out that she had been killed in one of the early fights. "So, you have not had a cleric here for years? I see. Which one of you killed the priestess?" Unanimously, everyone pointed to the man Seline had burned almost to death.

Tembri pointed to that man and said, "Tiamat curses you with pain unending. Your only solace will be tending to crops in the field. Your sleep shall fill with the face of your slain priestess. Food shall taste and smell like rotted flesh. When you die, Takhissis shall raise you in three days as a zombie to await your final release." His words came out in a dissonant almost-song. It hurt Ayden's ears to listen to it, but the effect on the man was immediate. His hands and then body began to tremble, as if shivering. "Come, our work here is done. Villagers, a new cleric will arrive. See that she is treated better than your last."

Except for that village, Ayden noticed that Tembri and a handful of other priests spent time healing and encouraging any who were sick or ill. The resupply took days and it gave them all a chance to set up better encampments. The remains of prior legions quickly told them where flat, level areas lay. She and Sako were watching over Tembri and Noboyuki attending to a family with many children. Frostbite and winter ailments had taken a toll. While they healed wounds and discussed better food, one of the Pha Rannic priests came by and then continued on. "Why don't they help?" Ayden asked Sako.

Sako shrugged but Tembri called back, "Because these children are not worshippers of Pha Rann. They are unaligned. Their parents are also unaligned. If they convert to Pha Rann, then they could be healed."

Noboyuki nodded. "It's the Imperic way too, but I have learned too much to turn a blind eye to the world's needs. It's a strange thing, Sako. In Ori, I never thought of this but when a child is in pain, they need help and will take it from anyone or anything offering it. Why not have that helping hand be Imperius'?"

Tembri laughed and slapped the much smaller cleric on the shoulder. "Truly Noboyuki, if more clerics shared your attitude, I wouldn't be so busy consecrating new worshippers of the Mother!"

Just down from them, Malcor walked the line of the settlers watching. Seline paced a few steps behind. A young mother holding an infant called to them for help. They stopped and saw the baby's foot had begun to fester and rot, probably frostbite gone bad. Malcor looked to Tembri and saw him busy, but something inside him urged him to try and heal. Seline appeared to feel it too. "Let me see the foot," Seline said.

The mother, with hope and fright on her face at the same time, blurted out, "We were checking the animal traps and were attacked by winter wolves. I had to put my baby down to fight. When it was over, her feet were frozen and this one never recovered." She pointed to the black foot and begged, "Oh please, my lord and lady!"

Seline softly sang a hymn of succor and sanctuary from the Book of Fire as she cradled the ruined foot. Fire-like warmth slowly radiated from her hand into the foot. Dead skin and infection scaled off and fresh new pink skin appeared. After a minute, her hand trembled and Malcor took and held her hand cradling the child. He added his baritone to her song and let his will for the child's health flow. Something unexpected happened in that moment though. It caught the paladins by surprise, but Malcor stayed his hand and lifted up his voice in prayer song. Like shadows dancing on the wall, dark grey tendrils of energy pierced through Seline's hand from Malcor into the infant, who shrieked and then began screaming.

The mother wailed, "Oh no, please knights, do not kill my baby!" Malcor held Seline's hands though and would not let the mother pull the baby away. He continued, his baritone song rising up and growing louder as he transitioned the song from the Book of Fire to Genesis. Instead of succor, the song became one of how the dragons began separating the world from the abyssal creatures that rollicked in chaos. The separation story unfolded with the dragons at last pushing the Abyss away from Tehra. *With fire and power, the dragons chased back the fiends of warp that the gardens of Tiamat might take nourishment from the light of day and gird Her throne about in splendid beauty.*

Tembri jumped up and ran over as the mood around the distraught mother turned dark. The mother's crying attracted too much attention and villagers nearby had started clenching their torches and lanterns. Seline tried to pull away but Malcor would not let her. The story changed to tell how Alerius had purged the land of Tania of evil before the Ancients could be forged into a powerful and mighty race. The other settlers appeared about to attack the two when Tembri's arrival gave them pause. He snapped his fingers and a parchment and quill appeared and began writing Malcor's song.

The infant's cries became shriller and then went hoarse. All went silent except the mother who had collapsed in the snow crying, "Oh please, please, not my baby. Please…" With the mother's cries growing more frantic, a dark mist coalesced out of the baby's foot, rising up the leg – more and more of it – from the heart and then head. It pulled out and vanished in the sunlight. As the amount Malcor pulled out diminished, the baby began to calm and breathe normally.

At last, Malcor removed his grip on Seline and the infant. "It wasn't just the foot," he said. "The child had something else. Something evil was setting in." He lifted his arm and it dragonshifted. A single talon speared into the infant's now healed foot and from the wound, a dark shiny snake-like worm pulled out between Malcor's claws. "I have it," and those talons pulped the creature which disintegrated into black dust and vanished in the cold air, like their breath. The child immediately curled up against her mother, fell asleep, and sucked on his thumb.

Behind them, Tembri whispered, "On this day, the Book of Shadows witnessed Malcor Kell'tayris bless an Innocent for the first time. Not just the flesh of innocents, but the very soul of innocence was saved. The Mother allowed him to see the darkness behind the wound and thereby the world is purified and saved for Her Glory."

The mother and her baby fell at the knights' feet. Seline's face warred between awe at Malcor, anger at his forcing her, and fright for the baby and its mother. "Tembri," she said. "Please add that Seline, Order of Fire, bore witness to this miracle. I never even felt anything other than the infected frostbite."

"You'll see it from outside Time one day, Seline," Tembri whispered.

To her side, Malcor watched the mother and child. All he could think of in that moment was how his tears had terrified his own child with Ora, whom he would not see for five years. He looked up into the sky and prayed that next time he saw Ora his touch would bring warmth and safety rather than fright. A distant part of him watched himself watching the clouds and saw Seline whispering to Tembri. Without understanding why, he walked over to Tembri and said, "We need to talk. Now."

The mother clutched at his cloak, and Seline's cloak, as Malcor turned to walk away. "A thousand thank-yous. I cannot say it enough. Bless you lord and lady. Bless you!"

Tembri closed the page and followed Malcor. Seline met his gaze and he shrugged. Mal almost never gave abrupt orders. A few steps away, Seline heard Malcor say, "My touch, with Ora. It terrified my unborn child. Today, it heals. Why? Am I a monster?"

Seline's eyes widened. "Ora is pregnant? Mal, why didn't you tell us?"

"Must I tell you everything? In the handful of hours we had in Klenna, she told me. From the ethereal, my child saw me as a monster." Malcor squared his fists as if daring either of them to say anything contrary.

"No, you don't have to tell us everything but,"

Malcor interrupted her. "A priestess and a paladin, a tale sung by bards and hardly worthy of notice. I know. I've heard this before. Ora cautioned me to be careful. She even said it was orders – at first."

Tembri considered looking at his knight from the ethereal, but knew his aura would be full of turmoil. He answered softly, "You are not a monster. You are learning so much so fast. Talented geniuses like you are once in a generation, maybe once in a century. The healing touch comes to all knights eventually, but honestly, we did not expect yours to come for at least several more years. Look at Lady Seline. She is exhausted from helping where you are boiling over with frustration. I doubt anyone in her Order's class is even considering a heal prayer and you did a full exorcism, and you kept the child alive."

"I feel like a monster. Tembri, when I next see Ora, if I hurt her or my child because of this thing I am becoming, I will end myself."

Seline inhaled sharply. Suicide amongst the paladins, though not unheard of, was a form of blasphemy. She saw it register in Tembri's face as well. Tembri drew his hand back and slapped Malcor across the face. At least, that's what the battle priest tried to do. When it hit Malcor, the skin around his face shadowshifted and Tembri pulled his hand back hissing and steaming with cold. "Do not doubt me, Tembri. Or my word."

Feeling they were about to fight, Seline stepped between them and said, "Tembri, I'd like to learn more about this too. We have one more week till Haven and then two to Bloodstone. Will you teach us, both of us, together?" For too long of a moment, Seline wondered if Tembri would attack her too. Then, his expression softened and he nodded.

She felt Malcor relax, turn, and walk away. Behind him, the mother continued to call out her gratitude. Malcor waved his hand and then vanished from sight. A moment later, a burst of dark energy flared and Malcor the dragon flew up and away from the group. Though not terror, Seline felt his frustration like a vise around her heart. It took her breath away and she steadied herself on Tembri's arm. She felt him tremble too. "He grows more and more powerful each day," she heard the priest say. "More powerful than I ever imagined a man could be."

Around them, the settlers fell to the ground stricken with dragonfear though they seemed to interpret it as awe. Someone said, "Is that one of the dread lord dragons of Morbatten?"

A little girl though, held down by her mother, awoke and pointed to the sky and giggled. That giggle broke the tension and when the mother tried to shush her by saying, "Shhh dear, that's a dragon," Seline lost her composure and hurried away before she fell to the ground and sobbed the tension away. When she recovered, Tembri sat nearby watching her. He had gifts from the baby's mother with him. Hand-woven scarfs and some dried fruit wrapped in sack cloth.

Tembri pushed the gifts forward. "The first time you heal, it affects you. From what I saw, you'll be able to heal through prayer and touch but will probably be limited to physical wounds. Poison, disease, loss of limb, loss of sensation, magical and spiritual ailments will probably be beyond you unless the Queen really wants you to do it."

Seline listened, with sobs still wracking her body, and tried to ask about Malcor. "Mal is prone to berserking. Though he could, he probably should not heal if it is going to trigger these fits of rage. Also, until the Shadow Dragons are brought into our doctrine, healing will tear Malcor to pieces. That being said, he could become an exorcist, a rare gift amongst paladins."

Seline wiped the tears from her eyes and face. "I guess we are all challenged in different ways. Tell me. Can I heal whenever I want to or only when called to?" Tembri smiled. It was good to see him relaxing. Before he could answer, Seline added, "And what happened between the two of you back there?"

"The dragon awoke and challenged me. Because the shadow dragons do not yet serve the Queen, they do not recognize me as a friend. My training against a hostile dragon is to go on the offensive. It was instinctual for me, for him. I pray it does not happen again. Well, it will probably happen again. I hope it doesn't happen too many times. I don't know that I can defeat a shadow dragon. Anyway, enough of that. It's my – not your – problem."

Tembri squinted against the sunlight looking in the direction Malcor had flown. "To the healing question. Yes, you can heal whenever you want provided you are in alignment with Tiamat's wishes. You can heal but it is exhausting, especially for a knight. As such, the dragon emperor made it a doctrine that knights must not heal themselves. He also formalized it as a paladin ritual. Like today, you need time and focus. A companion helps. Unless you can prepare for the exhaustion afterwards, you should not attempt it except when your life is at stake or you know you can rest and recover safely. It is easier to heal those of our faith, the consecrated. Lastly, the need for healing must be worthy. Inflicting pain for the purpose of healing or to heal when it is not critical to the mission or the Queen's Purpose, is against the knight's canon. Priests like me and temple clerics have exceptions to this canon if you're wondering."

"So, it's mainly because of how exhausting it is. I understand that. I'm starving and feel like if I close my eyes, I'll fall asleep." Seline retrieved some dried meat and cheese from a pouch at her belt. "Malcor must feel it too."

"Yes, and doctrines are wrapped around this to protect paladins from themselves. So that in combat, you are not factoring self-healing when you should be concentrating on victory. This blessing is to extend missions, your mission, and to bless those who bear witness to your feats, like that mother. She will tell of this day for the rest of her life. Imagine it from her perspective. Her newborn infant, hurt by a wolf trap, saved by two Tanian paladins. But, it doesn't stop there. It continues on to removing an evil spirit. Not just the mother, but the entire settlement will remember this."

Eventually, the war train moved on with the settlers waving farewell. Once again the magical road appeared before and faded back behind them. At first, Tembri tried to set regular times to review healing with Malcor and Seline. But, Malcor had not yet recovered from his rage and left in frustration minutes into the first session. It was an odd thing. Tembri confronted Malcor about it later that day and found Mal totally fine and normal except when the topic of healing came up.

Seline spoke at length with Malcor about it. It took some prodding but eventually, he shared his experience with Ora with her. "I grew up knowing I had a father somewhere. Or a mother powerful enough to place me with a family like Ishan's. Ishan was my father, my real life dad. But, you never quite put it out of your head. Then, poof, one day I learn my father is Dar Kell, the Kell of the Kell Conflict. The high priest of the Temple At Morbatten. Nothing has changed for me but now I wonder about my mother. And a sister somewhere. I have to put it out of my mind because I don't want to carry this my whole life. I want my son to know me as his father. I want to be there and see him walk for the first time. When he reaches those first things where you wish for a father -"

"My father was there, but he also wasn't. Are you sure you're not making this a bigger deal in your mind than it actually is? I mean, my father was a ruling noble. I have memories of him being around but not being "there" the way you describe. Plus, Ora – she's a priestess right? Are you sure what you have is real, Malcor? Priestess take paladins all the time."

"I hope so," he answered. Overhead, the silver falcon screeched at him. "I'm sure of it." He said it the second time with more confidence.

Chapter Twelve – Rider Dogma

Still talking with Seline, Malcor changed the topic to dragonshifting. "I'm getting stronger, but as Verit said, in darkness like night without a moon or underground, my world is basically two dimensional. It's hard to know where and what and how to view things. I can follow Ayden's team on the trail well enough, but I've actually been curious about something else. Something Kell told me once."

"What do you have in mind?" The way he had transitioned to this topic with such passion and interest touched her, excited her.

"I, well, let's get Tembri. He'll be coming by shortly." They continued their discussion and moved on to their interactions with Kaia the Halfling.

"He's actually a demon prince," Seline said. "At least that's what my father told me when I left for the Capitol. Everyone of so-called heroic stature is approached at some point, even in other nations. What did he offer you?"

"He offered my friend Calvin an easy way into the knighthood. He offered it to me too, but I wanted something more. I wanted to understand the River and see the real nature of the world. He granted it to me and I owe him for it. You?"

"Same but my family had prepared me for this. When he offered some item or shortcut, I asked to be the first female paladin to reach Dar rank. It's never happened before you know, except for Dar Kendra. My family, centuries ago, had one reach R'Dar status. He said he couldn't grant such a thing but could help me along the way. So, he granted me mastery of blades. Like you, I owe him a favor and in my case, well there was a sacrifice I had to agree to." She ran her hand through her red hair and shook it loose.

"What sacrifice?" Malcor asked. "Mine was a simple favor. I wasn't aware that I could have upped the ante and 'bought' more."

Seline started to answer and then blushed. "If I tell you, I need to know you won't ever tell anyone. It's personal and kind of embarrassing." She continued with an even more quiet voice even though they were totally alone. "Knights, we are sworn to chastity right? My sacrifice is that I feel emotions, all emotions like love, more than I did before, more than anyone I know." She shook her head. "It's awful." She glanced at him briefly.

"But, our oaths of chastity are to the Queen. So, a priest -" Malcor paused for a moment in thought, "or a priestess I guess, could have you."

Seline shook her head, "No, it's not like that. Not for a female paladin. If I get pregnant, the calling to be a mother is a higher calling than a knight. I'd be removed from the knighthood. At least for a while."

"So, a priestess?" he looked sideways at her and she still would not meet his eyes. "Oh, Dar Niss. I see."

Seline blushed a deep crimson red. "You can't tell anyone. Swear it!"

"I swear, Lady Seline," Malcor said without hesitation. She finally met his eyes and smiled tentatively. "The halfling presented mine as a simple favor to be called for at a certain time. I try not to think about it because I guess I can't control when or what it will be. No one prepared me for it though. Until I saw Calvin leap at the offer, I had never even really considered it."

Their conversation wandered a bit from there to other topics like their rites, the Ori adventure, and differences between the Order of Water and Fire. "From what I can tell," Seline said at one point, "the only difference is that Fire invests far more heavily in attack capabilities. At least, that's what Dar Niss told me and it appears to be true. Captain Verit and you, Tembri, a few others I've met – you all feel more rounded out and generally more capable. You each also have your own battle priest and healers. By contrast, the Order of Fire has supporting clerics primarily to heal and each of Fire's teams has its own mage. Water's paladins each have their own mage?" Tembri nodded his head and explained that its by need only. Seline continued, "It's interesting how the emperor has shaped these things. I'd imagine that, at some point, you'll get your own battle mage. Malcor, if and when it can be, I want to join the Order of Water too."

He nodded but said, "You know how long Tembri waited. You remember how I was after the fight with Verit? I'm sure you'll have to repeat the rites, or at least part of them. I've heard Kendra say the other Orders do not test new members hard enough."

A while later, Tembri arrived with Ayden. They both looked happy together. It made Malcor wonder if he would ever be able to hold Ora's hand and walk about like that. Malcor waited a bit for small talk and pleasantries to be exchanged. When he saw that Tembri would not press him about their confrontation, he stood up and began pacing. "Cor'tanos has been teaching me about dragonshifting. I've been following his teachings to the letter and its working. I'm getting stronger.

"The problem I have is two-fold. In the dark – and this gets worse the darker it is – I have no depth vision. I can see perfectly but shadows of forms even from trees or clouds create an absolute darkness. From the skies, I can see everything, except when this happens." He lifted Seline's long hair and let it fall through his fingers. "Something like this that we can see through right now, is impenetrable to me in the darkest dark. Plus, and Verit has spoken with you all about my berserking during battle, dragonshifting makes it so much worse. I feel this rage inside me that starts to shut my mind down. Everything becomes this primal – it's like a sneeze but you're trying not to sneeze.

"The longer I stay a dragon, the worse it gets. The ultraviolet tattoos help me see, and retain focus of who I am too. They help a lot. Ayden, you have been excellent in working with me on that. Rojo helped me meet with Dar Kell, and we talked privately. What Kell told me is that I don't have to be alone. I can have a rider. A rider who can see normally, well, it solves a lot of these problems. I want to ask Seline to be my rider, for now. Should something go wrong Tembri, I want you to ensure she is safe."

"That's a great idea, Malcor," Ayden exclaimed. "Maybe I could too? That would be, I can't even describe it!"

"Ayden, you're welcome anytime but the new doctrines brought by Dar Kell suggest that being a dragon rider is linked to when paladins select a divine mount. It's the same except the paladin selects the dragon. I don't know that myrmidons have that kind of power." Malcor looked at Tembri, "Do they?"

"No, it's restricted to paladins and rangers. Clerics, even druids, can summon and compel such a relationship but the bond is different. You'll remember from your classes that once a paladin takes a holy mount, even the mount cannot be compelled by others. Having a rider is different than letting someone ride."

Tembri and Seline considered what he said with more caution. Tembri especially thought hard on it and said, "Mal, the teachings of dragon-riding are as old as the empire. But, and I stress this, it is a slayer technique for paladins to tame a wild dragon as part of its conversion. It's a tool of submission. For example," and he pointed to Malcor and Seline, "continuing in the knighthood, at some point you'll have your Third Rite. The Third is when you convert a fallen dragon to Tiamat. Like when a wild horse is tamed by a rider, it's like that. If you go that route, you essentially call upon Takhissis for a divine steed and select the dragon. A battle of will and often blood ensues. It's how Tania has claimed so many dragons. Is that what you're talking about?"

Malcor did not know but said, "You have no idea what it feels like, Tembri. To soar the skies on wings of magic. I get lost. Submission, if that's what it takes, would give me greater control. I'd also be able to rely on my rider for the three dimensional world."

Seline chimed in and added, "I'm game but I need to know. Is it sacrilege? After all, Malcor," she turned to Tembri straight on, "is not a dread lord. I don't want to anger the dread ones or violate some doctrine by doing this."

Tembri thought for a moment. "So, I have ridden on Dread Lord Blade and Blaze, both during various missions I have done for the Temple and as part of my training. There is no submission per se. They gave me an order and I obeyed. The dragon-riding you speak of only applies to wild dragons. That being said, we should make sure that Cor'tanos is okay with it. While Malcor might be, I cannot think of Dar Kell ever having carried a rider dragonshifted." Tembri pursed his lips in thought and then added, "Maybe Dar Kendra has?"

They went back and forth in conversation until at last Malcor said, "I think you're worrying about this too much. Cor'tanos is quite familiar with the conversation about the ultraviolet tattoos and other markings to help me, and had no objection. He could have taken affront at the suggestion that a shadow dragon is somehow vision impaired in this world. He did not. I do not understand how there could be a doctrinal issue here."

Ayden watched the conversation and butted in, "I'm willing to try, since I'm not tied the Temple in any way, should it become a problem."

"It won't," Malcor said.

Tembri thought for a moment. "Come to think of it. I've heard that the high priestesses are their dragons' riders. So, maybe the doctrine is beyond what I'm thinking of now. It could apply to Ayden, now that I think of it."

Seline and Ayden both agreed with Malcor. Ayden urged Tembri, "I'm game. Why not? Tembri we're young. We don't have all the scripture study and Temple training you've had. Plus, you're his battle priest. You need to be part of this too!"

"Let's not be hasty. While I'm all for action, let's be clear on something. IF, and I stress the "if" part, something does go wrong or is bad, it is my and Captain Verit's heads that will roll. We have direct responsibility for you all but especially Malcor. Anything at all goes wrong, and it's a problem for all of us. You're right – your heads won't roll. But mine very well may. Fortunately, we have Dar Rojo, a slayer, here with us. I suggest we consult with him."

Malcor almost said something but decided not to. "Very well," he said. "Rojo usually rides at the front edge of the road. I'll speak with him."

Several hours later, Malcor caught up to the front of the caravan, alongside the king. Rojo rode at the head of the column, Dar Jeri at his side. Except when people pulled up alongside for some business or request, he was alone or talking quietly with her. Malcor kept expecting some level of pomp and circumstance, but except for gold inlays in his armor and a few other tokens, he wore the exact same armor, boots, and cloak as Malcor and Seline. They had also checked as a group and felt sure that the king carried at least five bloodstones.

"Ho there, Sir Malcor," the king hailed.

"Your majesty."

"It has been, what - five months since we first met in your Age ceremony?"

"Indeed. It feels a lifetime ago, Sire. I have a desire to speak with you and, well, my condition in the command tent a few days ago was not the right time."

"Still, very impressive. I'll never forget your ceremony. It is rare to encounter someone so young yet able to keep up with the dance. Even more rare for someone so inexperienced to withstand Armageddon. That dread lord carries a particular awe about him. You continue to impress. I hear you and R'Dar Ora are expecting a child. Congratulations!" Not quite a question, it triggered feelings in Malcor he was not prepared to discuss.

"Yes, my Dar. I imagine she is maybe four months along now. I am sorry to not be there for her."

"That is the Temple way though, Malcor. As knights and clerics, we serve. Ora has long been queued for motherhood though Ynt'taris insisted that she be free to chose. It is a priestess' final rite, to birth a hero. Did you know that?" Malcor shook his head no and the king continued. "As children of dragons and worshippers of the Mother, it is part of their doctrine in the Book of Spires. Spires is a book for female matriarchs and high rank priestesses only. Dar Shara, though you would not guess it, has had four children. I would guess that you and Ora are likely to have many more. This topic makes you uncomfortable? I see. This is not what you came to discuss." Riding alongside Rojo, his battle priestess, Jeri, laughed at Malcor's discomfort.

"It's not that, Dar Rojo. As you know, I was raised by adoptive parents. But in the nine years before I was placed with Ishan at Klenna, I was moved often and frequently -"

"To keep you alive, Malcor."

"Excuse me? Wha – really?"

"Yes, the sons and daughters of Kell are precious to the emperor. You may not know it but your fight with that merchant, on your way to the Temple, was the first time in your life you were not actively being guarded, watched, and monitored. We have had words with Shara about it as her instructions to you, to be unseen, had unfortunate consequences. You're aware of the prophecy concerning the children of Kell?"

"I know the Sister Prophecy but I still have a hard time believing Kell is my father. It still feels off. I don't feel like the son of the man in the Kell Conflict, or that I see leading the Temple now."

"Sometimes. We prefer that such things be invisible. While we all have a destiny, it is of singular importance that prophesies are not forced. They must happen based on the actors' free will to choose the path of prophecy. You could have chosen to NOT be a knight after all. You chose the harder path of serving as a paladin. While sacrifice brings blessings, destiny never selects victims of fate. We could speak of your companion Calvin, as an example. He wanted to be a paladin. He failed out and entered training to be a knight. But, his attitude made him not a good candidate for knighthood. He fell to being trained as an officer. Within that though, he missed opportunity after opportunity to be something more. You rise. He falls. Eventually, you'll rise beyond all this," Rojo waved his hand as if pointing to the world. "Calvin will fall until he finds a place comfortable to him."

"Calvin will make his own path. He always did. Though, I guess," Malcor thought back and then asked, "Ishan, did he know?"

The king shook his head no. "Ishan is a faithful servant of Tania. People like him are what make this empire worth serving and fighting for. I would guess that he did not know you were special until the forge accident that left your head scars. Because of that, you understand real pain and have a memory of fearing permanent death. Many nobles, because of healing, do not have this and it can be crippling in a paladin. That being said, you should have died. Anyone else would have. Do you remember how you were saved?"

"I remember falling into the crucible. I had tripped over something. I cried out for help. That's really all I remember," Malcor said trying to recall every detail.

"You prayed to the Mother. One of those knights wanting to see the Apprentice Sword, he healed you just enough. Watching over you became so much easier when the quality of your work gave us an overt excuse to see you regularly. Don't overthink this though. Your sword is a masterpiece. You'd have made a legendary smith. You still may someday when your adventures as a paladin come to an end. But enough of this, what do you want to discuss?"

"My Dar, I wish to attempt a rider in dragon form. There is concern this will go against Temple doctrine."

"I see. Have you chosen a rider?" The question seemed far weightier when the king asked it this way.

"A specific rider? I can certainly fly faster and farther than normal travel. Is the rider that important? Help me understand."

"Follow me," the king said. His hands flashed through a series of signs and the escort many paces behind him acknowledged. Suddenly, the king's charger sped ahead in full gallop. Something about it spurred Mal's horse and it gave chase. Faster than he had ever moved, they outdistanced the war train and crossed over a ridge to a valley where the army would later camp. The king reined up and dismounted.

"A rider is part of the Queen's doctrine. Dragons can carry anyone they want, but know that other dragons pass judgment and look down on this. Do you want to carry mighty heroes or cargo? That's kind of how they see it. In addition, Dragonshifting is a sacred blessing. It is not just something you do whenever you want or for mere convenience's sake. Dragon magic and power is, after all, different from a human mage's power. Alerius, mighty though he is, struggles with water and ice magic. Same as Ynt'taris who struggles with fire. Riders can strengthen a dragon, if aligned in purpose. The dragon within us can strengthen our rider. Someday, you very may well select a rider. This will be someone special who will communicate with your dragon soul and you become one spirit together. It is very powerful.

"So consider this: actual dragons consider what we do an abomination. The only exception are those dragons of Tiamat that are part of Morbatten. Should you find yourself outside Tania in far distant lands, those dragons will not regard your ability as the blessing Tanian dragons do. Do not flaunt it. With Tania's dragons, do put yourself in a place where they feel you demean or mock them. Armageddon would not carry cargo even if Dar Shara needed it to save her or his life. When dragonshifting, you must not let pride drive you. Ready yourself, Sir Malcor."

Behind and around the king, nearly invisible wings burst into the air in a vortex of magic. The wings and serpentine neck of a dragon lifted a titanic head up into the sky. Daylight sparkled through that form like a dance of watery lights.

"I remember seeing this dragon in my Age Ceremony," Malcor whispered. He wanted to say more but it was cut short by dragonterror and divine awe that slammed into Malcor to his knees. The form of the dragon enwrapping the king compelled worship, loyalty, service, and demanded attention. It was so brilliant though that Malcor could not look at the king directly even though the human form of the king remained standing before him. One of those massive claws scooped up Malcor and just like that, they rose up into the sky with a leap and the beat of hurricane force wings.

"This is the best place for a rider," Rojo said as he placed Malcor a few paces below and behind his head. "Every dragon is somewhat different though, but truthfully, as a dragon, I can barely tell you're there. You could move anywhere and unless I think about it, it matters not at all. Because you are less experienced, if you carry a rider, I suggest you carry them in your claws. Part of the blessing that is dragonshifting is that magic bends to eldar will and transforms with us. You will quickly learn to keep only magical clothing and gear with you." Rojo held up his dragon claw. "My sword is one of these talons though I don't know which. You're a swordsmith though. Maybe you'll figure it out."

They climbed up above the gray winter clouds and Rojo tore through the mist trailing a talon in it. "Cor'tanos is not yet subject to anything in our Temple. Mother is still angry with them." Malcor felt the dragon focus its energy and then a gray green ball of energy stricken through by black and orange lightning shot from Rojo's mouth. Shockwaves rippled from it pulling the clouds around its passage like a tunnel. When it had travelled out of sight, Rojo hissed a word of magic and the energy ball exploded blasting apart the sky and then, tracing back along its path, a cone of fire and lighting raced back towards them. Rojo dove into it lifting head and neck spines to protect Malcor from the magical breath weapon and shockwaves still hanging on the horizon.

"Your breath weapon is different. As humans, our breath weapons are different from the dragons. You must focus your force of will and then release it. For them, it's instinctive. Mine combines all of the colored dragons where yours will be specific to the shadows. The key thing is that a rider can add to and even learn how to influence the dragon's breath weapon. Riders can combine with you, the way we combine our power to a priestess for certain rites. You may take riders, but remember, one day you will find a Rider who can do this. It magnifies your abilities."

They reached the detonation where vortexes of cloud, lightning, and fire still spun feeding thunderclouds growing all around Rojo's breath weapon.

Rojo circled around the center and then added, "Like your father Kell and the priestess he took as wife; she was his Rider. It is a sacred relationship more like how the emperor feels for his sons, than we might feel for a wife. It is dragon magic and it is so all-consuming that when that bond is severed, it causes bad things to you and your soul. You've heard the stories of Kell no doubt. He still suffers from her loss. For this reason, I have not taken a Rider though several candidates presented themselves."

They dove straight to the ground, faster than falling, and all of a sudden, the dragon form shifted and a claw braked Malcor just enough to drop him firmly to the earth. The trees shook snow and ice around them where an invisible but massive dragon landed. It vanished. "I show you this so that you can know how it feels to be a rider. You, as a dragon, are immune to your own breath weapon but your rider probably is not, not until we get more paladins like you and Kell. You are immune to the elements, but your rider is not. You are able to land and shift at will but your rider may not be able to survive a fall from your shift height. You are impervious to wind in your face, but your rider may be blinded by it. Your ears will hear them but they may not be able to understand you. Remember these things."

Malcor held his breath watching Rojo as the glorious prismatic overlay that was the king's dragon form, pulled back into his body. Behind the king, the war party train rose over a hill. Malcor wondered if they had seen anything and then noted the roiling apocalypse of energy and lightning still tearing the sky apart. "Questions," the king said.

Malcor asked, "Is Dar Shara Armageddon's Rider?"

Rojo nodded and said, "It creates a bond between the two that a fire dragon might describe as that of a loving elder brother. When you meet her, Ana is the Rider of the Bloodstone dragon named Crimson Burning. The dread lords are very sensitive to it. I suggest you never discuss it with them. I would also add, the dread lords are territorial about their riders. You may have felt a somewhat possessive attitude between Armageddon and Shara?"

Chapter Thirteen – Dar Ana Attacked

Dar Ana watched the Nineteenth break camp through the tower stone adjacent her seat. Crimson leaned over and watched as well. She noted how Malcor sat staring into a fire until Captain Verit summoned him for training. "Malcor – the child of prophecy. Of course, that means they found the sister too," she said to Crimson. She tapped Verit's face, "That one is Verit. He left his mark here in Bloodstone. One of the beautiful ones." She pointed to Tembri, "As did that one. The Order of Water, it seems, is coming to visit us. With the king. How interesting." She sat back against the many fine furs and pelts draping her throne.

Below her, at the base of the steps, one of her knights shoved a man forward and commanded him to kneel. Watching sidelong, she noted that the man did not. "A bad choice," she said even as her knight's boot kicked his face into the stairs.

She stood and walked down towards him as the knight reported, "Dar, this thief was caught attempting to break into the temple vault. We have the witness of an acolyte. He tried to bribe her as well."

The man immediately began telling a story. "This gets so boring," Ana said. "Let's just get to the truth of it." At her words, Ana stepped from the heights of the Temple At Bloodstone seen from outside the River's flow, stained and drenched with blood. Back away from where Ana stood with the thief, darkness swarmed with undead that always watched. She caught the thief and lifted him out of the River with her.

"Your story will be shown for what it is here. I see your name is Farant. Tell me Farant, what do you expect to find in the great vault?" Something felt wrong to her when she said his name. She almost threw him back, but then, a thief trying to break into the temple vault occurred with increasing regularity when bloodstones were not actively being mined.

"The bloodstones, High Priestess. I expected to find bloodstones."

She threw him to the banks and walked towards him over the surface of raging energy. "But you failed."

"No. I did not. I learned what I needed to know," he said. The fearless tone in his voice bothered Ana. He should have been terrified.

She caught his face and moved as if to kiss him, enjoying how his skin flushed and his body reacted. "And that was?"

"How to get close to you!" A stabbing lance of agony shot through her breast near her heart. Ana's Goddess Armor, the invisible might of the Queen, did not form quickly enough to block the surprise attack. She threw him back into the River.

The throne room erupted with activity as Ana's dread lord, contentedly waiting out of sight, swept a giant wing claw out and threw the man hundreds of feet back against the upper wall. His body, crushed by the force of the blow, hung there and then slid down. The paladin guard rushed up to Ana as she dropped to her knees, blood pouring from a deep cut just below her diaphragm. Already prayers for healing and intervention echoed in the chamber as other guards pushed and shoved, in some cases carried, visitors out of the throne room. As the first of her guard reached her with healing prayers, Ana caught his wrist and stumbled to her feet. A magical dagger of black energy chewed through her torso and though blood poured in streams from her side, she stood and screamed at the falling corpse. It caught in air, and by the time it landed, the corpse had begun to change.

Her hand flashed through combat signs and those closest, rushed to restrain the corpse as broken limbs snapped back together. Others directed prayers of healing at her as the black dagger seemed to spin cutting new wounds into her even as healing magic tried to heal lacerated flesh. The great dragon moved forward to end Farant but Ana's hand sign gave him pause.

Farant looked confused as blood hunger and rage filled his vision, and great pain too. The guards already had caught the falling body with cords of fire tightly binding its neck, hands, and feet. Dread Lord Crimson Burning noticed the black dagger and ripped it out of her with two talons coming together with surgical precision to grab the blade and hold it still. His giant claw caught her as she fell back against his palm. The dragon growled as if asking a question. She nodded, "I'll be okay. It's been a while since I have been caught by surprise." Already her own and her guards' prayers healing her. It had been close, closer than any attack in decades had come to ending her. Through it all, she continued her prayer at Farant who burned in ropes of fire and re-arose as a vampire.

Throughout the Temple, Crimson Burning's aura swept over and through the sanctuary. The faithful dropped to their knees in prayer as those bound to other gods, swooned against walls for balance. Most knew, but few had ever seen the dread lord move with intent so close to them. Usually, the darkness behind Ana's throne only occasionally provided glimpses of the titanic fire dragon lurking there.

Ana walked across the room to the newly-born vampire. She fingered her wound to draw blood and flicked it at Farant. He smacked his lips trying to catch it but the many ropes prevented movement. Scared and frantic, the newly-born vampire thrashed about burning itself. Ana watched, smiling as it screamed. Minutes of this passed before the panic subsided. Only when Farant went still, to avoid more burning pain, did she actually regard him.

"Farant," Dar Ana said mockingly. "That is not your real name. Who is Farant?" The vampire hissed at her. She drew more blood from her wound, wincing slightly at the pain of it, and held her bloody finger up to let a single droplet bead and then fall to the floor just a step away.

The hunger tore into Farant again. Ignoring the pain, he thrashed, grasping and clawing at the blood just out of reach. "While I applaud your assassination attempt, and it was one of the better ones, I must tell you. The others had better escape plans. You see, while Tania refrains from necromancy, here there is almost no risk. Bloodstone is the domain of necromancy. As such, I can do whatever I want. You could, maybe, escape but you would just join up with the Jade God and that's not really an escape. Either way, we kill you now or we kill you later. And you, my little blood sucker, are a lone vampire in the Queen's Temple."

Farant seemed to pay attention at those last words. She asked, "Have you regained human speech yet?"

Her question jolted the vampire as surely as if she had punched it. Eyes locked on her still seeping wound, he slowly nodded his head.

"Good," Ana purred. "Let me explain this to you. You are a vampire. A new one. Whether you were hungry or not, undead rebirth is a hungry change. You're going to tell me everything I want to know. Who is Farant? Where and who and why and what sent you to accomplish this attack? You'll tell me all of it. Every single," she pulled her fingers out of her almost healed wound with another drop or two of blood hanging on her fingertips, "drop of information. And then, maybe, we'll let you die." She held the blood closer and closer to his face. At last, close enough that he tried to bite her, his newly-forming fangs broke against her Goddess Armor, which flared briefly to be visible. She laughed. "Throw him in the pit. Re-open the Temple. Ensure every visitor sees Farant. I want to know who he interacted with and what it was about."

She walked back to her throne. Crimson's face hung there and she patted his chin before sitting down, "It's okay, Crimson. Return to your sleep." His breathing billowed her hair and clothes while her attendants brought her new silks. By the time she sat on her throne and the first visitor knelt, no sign except for shattered stones high above the floor opposite her throne showed what had happened.

When the official business of the day ended, Ana stretched and rose, dancing around the bloodstone by her throne. She rubbed at the pink area of skin around where Farant attacked her, the only remaining sign of her terrible wounds just hours ago. "Show me the miners."

The tower stone swirled and Ana found the miners and their priestess deep in the tunnels. They studied carved runes along a doorway of stone. Most had been shattered off, but a few fragments remained. It had the look of Eldar writings but, like much of Bloodstone, the chaotic nature of the place changed even carved stone. It looked familiar, but Ana knew it would turn out to be yet another entry into their archives rather than re-discovery. She counted and was pleased to see that all of the group remained alive, though a few of them bore new bandages.

Ana saw the priestess open one of the copied books from the Temple and scan through it seeking similar runes as those carved into the doorframe. If she found a match, they could cross-reference it with other maps where that same writing style had been observed. It happened rarely. Ana shrugged when the priestess reached the same conclusion she already had. No match. Closing the book, the priestess rose as did the party. With dwarven efficiency, they moved through the door.

Watching this, Ana sighed. It would have been a better way to end the day had they found something interesting.

"I need a distraction," she said loudly enough for her guard to hear. She smiled as each of her nine guards drew their swords. Already the goddess armor shimmered around her. Her battle staff crackled into her hands as she whirled to block a sword she knew would be there. "Which of you will join me tonight?" she licked her lips as magical force exploded between the knights' swords and her staff.

Chapter Fourteen – Unter's Vein

Unter Fistrol, the dwarven chief engineer and five times veteran of Bloodstone, signaled for a halt. He hated the Tanian hand gestures. Their adaptation from elven signaling felt clumsy in his fingers. He wished for a party of only dwarves so that these vulgar communications in silence would be replaced by hearty cheers. He had seen too many friends fall in Bloodstone. Silence was a temporary cloak at best. The longer they stayed, the more dangerous the tunnels became. He pointed and each of the dwarves with a lantern aimed the lantern at a spot Unter pointed.

With each ray of light, Unter – and the dwarves – became more excited. The gray and white stone that made up Bloodstone's mountains sometimes showed gold, rarely gems, even more rarely hat slick wet red color. His hand trembled as the priestess sent a prayer for daylight to him. It was not his imagination and desire tricking his mind. In daylight, the red looked wet almost purple. He wanted to touch it but knew it would not stain. The color was right! Another hand sign and the dwarves split out to find where the vein went. Their mercenary guards took up position. The tricky undead sometimes did this as part of a trap.

After a while, the priestess tapped him on the shoulder. "Outside! We are nearing sunset. We must leave."

"No, Helena, we must stay. We finally have a lead. If this is real, chaos is overly strong here. Our leaving ensures we will not recover this position, if it is truly bloodstone."

"The charter states that until we have a confirmed and verified find, we must not stay underground except with paladin escort and Temple permission." Unter started to interrupt her but she continued, "Unter, these Tanian rules are for your safety."

"And to ensure the damn dragons get their share," Unter grumbled.

"Sure, yes, that too. But, and correct me if I'm wrong here, you have yet to clear the area for all traps correct? We haven't even started verification. And this vein, it is too thin to bear gems. Tell me I am wrong."

Unter wanted to argue with her. His nature, his team's nature as dwarves, called to them to find this most rare and magical of gems and bring it out of its earthen cradle. His mind danced through several objections, arguments, even points of law in their charter. At each, he knew and saw the faces of comrades lost in just such a moment as this. He chuffed and blew a strong sigh before saying, "I swear at Wisdom, but I cannot argue with you; I'll lose! So, saying that: We're *staying* anyway. That's that. I ask that you stay too." He turned his back on her and shrugged off her hand where she caught his shoulder.

An hour later, they had cleared the entire vicinity of possible traps, pleased that none had been placed. The vein must be undiscovered or it would be trapped. The party now turned to that bright red dot in the stone matrix. Unter looked at it from every possible angle and talked with the other engineers about exploding it. As their excitement grew, the mercs guarding them grew increasingly wary. Even though underground, Bloodstone changed at night. Already, one of the far intersections had filled with mist. It had bypassed them, but eventually, the mist would come back. Except for divine light, fire, and magic, they had nothing to protect them and the use of those things would in turn alert other more powerful predators of their location.

Helena sighed and prayed, again, that they would remain unnoticed.

"We aren't going to explode it. We aren't." Unter said it again looking at Helena. "You're shocked, Helena? Too much noise. Plus, it's too small."

Helena checked her holy symbol for the hundredth time. "I'm relieved, but wary of what you might say next."

"Without removing it from the wall stone, we cannot verify it. We have decided to make ready to explode it. We'll make camp and hope for the best. But, if we are discovered, we'll explode the ore into fragments, take what we can for study, and retreat." The dwarves all nodded their heads. This made perfect sense to them.

"I don't know what to say without offending you," Helena said doing her best to seem inoffensive.

"Then say nothing," Unter replied. "We'll camp till dawn and prepare." Immediately, the dwarves moved to work. Small hand drills instead of hammers began slowly scraping into the wall stone. He smiled at her as if she would compliment his choice of quieter tools and methods. Other dwarves began mixing the powders separated by type across all their gear, into the explosive mix favored by the gnomes.

Helena went back to the guards and told them the plan. They hated it. She hated it. But when they lingered past dusk, their fate stopped being their own. "We can only pray," she whispered to them. With an eye on the mist writhing past them at the intersection through which they'd have to retreat, they settled down. Helena and her priestesses set up divination stones and prayed for wisdom to know of any threats. Every so often, one of them would move a stone or replace it with a larger and brighter stone. So they followed their intuition and hoped these more powerful undead would bypass them.

She must have fallen asleep because suddenly, one of the dwarves was tapping her shoulder and urging her to quietly follow. She roused the others and made her way back to the vein. The tunnel, at its other side, ended in a thousand steps at another intersection of many tunnels. They had placed a trip wire there that would bounce the clay tokens near them as an alert. The small wire bounced with contact as Unter urged the drills to work faster.

The sight of the trembling wire and the soft clacking of clay tokens filled her with dread. She felt her hands grow clammy. "Ana, why do these damn mines block our mind speech?" She fingered her mace and wished the high priestess would respond to her calls. Ana had been silent to her requests since they entered the mine, probably caught up in official Temple business – whatever that might be. Or, the underground warp of Bloodstone blocked her pleading. Then, the wire snapped and the tokens fell. A dwarf caught them to prevent a louder noise. The drillers kept going but everyone else fell silent and they doused their lights.

Far down the tunnel, Helena imagined a horde of vampires or worse, unseen wraiths or shades raging towards them. In the darkness, that cursed mist would drain their vitality, leaving them laconic even asleep if attacked. She untied and gripped her mace and prayed to Krentismar for strength. After what felt an eternity, a note came from one of her acolytes. The divination stones showed it to be a lower level undead, probably a zombie. Helena exhaled slowly and whispered, "We don't know the strongest near us. All we know is that the one in this tunnel is weaker than the strongest. If the strongest is a ghoul, this would be a zombie or a skeleton. If the strongest is a vampire – "

"Aye," a dwarf muttered nearby. "All we know is that there are undead and this one is weaker than others. Still a risk."

"Yes," she whispered. "If we wait and catch it by surprise, we could win. If it alerts to us, we draw the others nearby. Worst case, these are powerful enough to summon reinforcements."

Another dwarf said, "Best case, we kill them all and take the ore." Too many chuckles answered that comment. Annoyed, Helena shushed them.

"Where is the other wire?" Someone said about a hundred paces down from them. "We'll wait – quietly – and see if it comes that far. If it does, I'll pray for silence and we'll ambush the creature. I cannot silence more than four of us in this tunnel and you'll have to stay very close together. I have to be one of the four to ensure we identify the threat." She replied before the question came up, "The human guards are too big for a charge. I'd only be able to silence one. I'd rather have three dwarves with me than one human."

"It's a good plan," Unter said. "I'd rather have three dwarves than a human, too. We wait." When the dwarves began chuckling, she realized she had accidently cracked a joke the dour dwarves appreciated. Unter tapped the three who would join her and they began armoring and arming up.

One of the four drillers reached the correct depth for an explosive charge. Then, a second one did. The sound of clay tokens, along the second wire, jiggling and clacking roared like thunder. Whatever it was, stood no more than a hundred paces away. "Ready yourselves," Helena said under her breath.

In the quiet of their preparation, a faint cry reverberated and reached them. "Hello? Please help me. I'm lost," the girl voice pled, and then the echoes made it impossible to hear. But the language was dwarven and it was a female's voice. Helena felt the mood of the dwarves immediately fall from action to anxiety but no one said a thing. Again, that wailing cry, "I was with my dad when the tunnels collapsed. Please. I heard a noise. Don't be a scary monster, please!"

Someone in the group muttered, "A girl child?"

"It's a trap," Unter said. "No dwarf brings wee ones here. Keep focused."

"I cannot kill a lass!"

"It's not a child. It's a trick. Stay focused."

"Are you talking?" the frightened girl's voice asked. "Please, I'm scared and cold and hungry. Please don't leave me in the dark!" The last word rose up too loud, echoing. As the echoes ebbed, they heard crying.

"That sounds like a girl," someone in the group said angrily. "I didn't come here to abandon children."

Helena rebuked him. "Think about it, dwarf. How would a child survive a night outside a fortress, let alone in these tunnels?"

Someone else said, "Maybe she's a prisoner?"

"No," Unter said. "It's a trap. Helena, we stay with your plan."

Helena began praying to her god and felt a cloak fall over and around her. It would render them silent and nearly invisible to undead. She moved forward but stopped when the three dwarves did not go with her. She had to keep praying and directed her gaze to Unter. His face had gone red and his veins were about to explode out of his head. He grabbed two dwarves, picked up his war hammer, and shoved them towards her. He was the only one who knew the triggering magic for the explosives.

A plain sob reached them with the word, "Please, oh please!"

They moved forward, weapons ready. When they found the girl, it almost caught them by surprise. To see the ghoulish creature mimicking a girl's cries for help so beautifully, it made Helena gag before Unter's hammer struck its leg. The tall creature, almost nine feet tall with lanky arms ending in talons raked at them while its cries changed from dwarven to a piercing keen. The other dwarf, relieved it was not a dwarf girl child, smashed its throat ending the scream. They took it down but not before one of its sweeping claw attacks tore through a miner's leather armor. The dwarf immediately fell back in a seizure of paralysis and twitching muscle. Unter and another miner withdrew a saw blade and decapitated the creature.

Helena tried to put the paralyzed miner into a sleep, to quiet him, but it failed. They dragged him back, gagged, and hoped for the best. Everyone else waited for their return and their faces brightened until Helena said, "It was a higher order ghoul of some kind."

One of her acolytes added, "And ghouls hunt in packs. We won't be alone much longer."

"How long till sunrise?" The question posed by a miner hung in the air. In the tunnels, who knew? Sunrise would come when it came. Someone replied that they had been there for seven hours. So, at least six more hours till sunrise on the surface. At least six hours.

When the ghoul pack came for them, it felt as if a relief after the long hour of silent waiting. The drills had finished and been packed, though a few dwarves continued drilling away hoping to weaken promising sections of ore. Unter had directed the wall to explode so as to cover their retreat. Another line of exploding clay would collapse ore into baskets on the ground, for fast retrieval.

Helena prayed that their way back would be free and clear, except for the mist. This time, the clay tokens moved only briefly before the line snapped. They heard the smack of feet and wet hands on stone. When it reached the headless corpse, they paused. They heard the sick sound of tearing flesh and meat until at last, the head moved and the explosives hidden there detonated with a concussion that would kill or immobilize the living. The blast would buy them time. It stunned the pack, which charged towards them.

Unter triggered the magic that detonated the wall. Baskets tied to ropes hoped to catch the bloodstone vein. When the smoke and deafening roar faded, the dwarves clawed at the rubble to free the baskets. Unter immediately climbed up the debris to the wall and shrieked in delight. The vein opened into a thick artery. On the other side, the horde clawed at the tunnel debris. Above the ceiling shifted threatening to collapse. The sounds of digging, it was too close. "Grab the baskets!" Unter ordered.

Mesmerized by the sparkling artery right in front of their eyes, the dwarves did nothing. Helena ordered the human guards to try and brace the ceiling with anything they could find. On the other side, a rock moved allowing a clawed hand to grasp at a dwarf. The dwarf did not even notice when the ghoul's hand fell to the ground with a sword chop. "We can't stay!" the guard called out. Red eyes gleamed in the darkness of the space cleared by the boulder, and then went black. Something larger had arrived. They all felt a shift in the atmosphere.

Unter had a chisel and hammer and was tapping at the artery. Powdered dust and fragments fell. The dwarves holding him up clutched at it, collecting fragments as they fell. Another boulder fell free leaving a dark hole just big enough for undead to come through. Though she wanted to run from that dark space, Helena thrust her holy symbol into the gap and ordered them to depart. Some of the ghouls fell back in confusion but the unseeable thing came into the space and stabbed at her, just missing. The glint of light along the creature's blade saved her. She felt it laughing at her fear, mocking her terror.

"We really need to leave," Helena called dodging a second stabbing attack that seemed aimed at her holy symbol of Krentismar. Her mind registered the draconian writing on the sword. "It's a fallen paladin! We're leaving now!"

With a cry of triumph, Unter broke a large section of the artery free. He pocketed a chunk and other fragments fell into baskets. Triumphantly, Unter jumped down and began scooping it up even as the dwarves freed several of the baskets. A tendril of black smoke stabbed through the gap in the wall piercing one of the dwarves who fell back screaming and shivering with cold agony.

Unter grabbed the dwarf's collar and pulled him off the wraith or whatever had stabbed him clean through. "You heard the cleric, let's move!" He dropped his backpack full of exploding clay by the collapsed wall. One last look at the artery, right there, glistening just out of reach and then they were off.

Moments later, Unter's backpack exploded triggering a massive tunnel collapse that breathed rock and dust past them into the intersection. Already the mist sucked their energy as they ran through it. "We won't last more than a few minutes in this," Helena screamed as her god's blessing encircled them. It drove the mist back but with so much of it, her faith would fail soon.

They ran back the way they came even as from tunnels all around them, monsters and worse shrieked out their hunger and rage. The humans quickly outpaced the dwarves but moving from Helena's sphere of faith spurred everyone to stay with her. Three times she had to renew her prayer, and three times, they inhaled more of the mist than they should have. When they came at last to the exit, to the mouth that reached out to the surface world and the starlit sky beyond, it was almost too much. Helena had hoped for daylight. Instead, nighttime stars greeted her with no sign of daybreak.

They redoubled their efforts to sprint to the exit. Shadows, dark and malicious, detached from the walls to block their exit. The stones under their feet turned soft as it became flesh and zombies began rising up all around and under them. "We run for the surface!" Unter ordered. "Burning oil, ready!"

The humans began splashing their skins of oil as they ran. The dwarves withdrew small round pots full of that same powder. "Clear the way forward and throw!" Unter hurled his flame pot towards the exit as did the other dwarves in front. As they hit, magnesium sparked and then lit the tunnels with daylight before exploding in purple and orange stars. Helena's acolyte called for divine protection from fire as the oil ran in lightning forks all behind them. The smoke of burning flesh quickly filled the cave.

They swatted undead arms away from them as they slipped on zombie flesh and clawed their way out of the burning exit. The dwarves resorted to pushing and pulling Helena until at last she stood on the surface and cast the last of her faith and hope into her symbol and turned to face the burning undead behind her.

Chapter Fifteen – Retreat and Rumor

Helena's lungs gulped in the clear air of the surface world. From the very back of their exit, a vampire clad in ancient Tanian armor rose up from the seething mass of shadows and clawing zombie limbs alight with fire. Its sword burned with unholy light and she recognized its markings as the fallen paladin from before. She was good for a few undead, well, lots of the weaker ones really. But a fallen paladin? She, her group had no chance against a death knight. Behind her, the sky began to glow and she prayed for sunrise before noticing the color was wrong. Then, the ground shook as an earthquake struck the mountain, and another. A dragon claw caught Helena and she looked up to see Dar Ana. Crimson Burning landed another titanic claw on the ground. The earthquakes were from his hind legs touching down. Dar Ana pointed into the cavern.

What happened next defied anything Helena had seen before as Crimson Burning breathed fire, and magic, and eldritch hate of the undead into that cavern. The sound of fire increased as the heat and colors shifted, growing louder and more intense.

Leaping into Crimson's breath attack, Ana summoned her staff and moved to strike the death knight. Helena heard snippets of draconian and thought Ana called to the paladin as if a lover to come home and end the night's long watch. And still, fire expelled from Crimson as if the gates of hell themselves had opened. The pressure of those flames, Helena imagined them racing from the cavern throughout the mine complex to burst around the hillside where undead had attempted to tunnel up and flank their escape. As she imagined it, spouts of fire lit the sky expelling burning creatures high into the air. Unter pulled her from Crimson's hand and lifted a shield over them as an eruption of cindered flesh born on Ana's song fell all around.

Helena awoke on Crimson's back. The entire party cradled between the dragon's shoulder blades as each beat of his wings spawned tornadoes of backdraft behind and below them. Ana stood behind Crimson's face spikes, framed in that moment, as the sun at long last rose in the east. As the dragon banked towards the Temple, Helena was able to glimpse the mist-shrouded valley below still in the predawn blackness, and nightmares of fire burning far below where they had been. Even now, the flames pierced the ground and erupted from tunnels around their exit.

* * *

Within hours, Verit's command team read a letter from Dar Ana explaining the circumstance and what happened. As they reached the end of the letter, Ana's voice visited them. "I'm scrying you with my tower stone," she said. "Hail the soon-to-be Nineteenth! Let me show you what the dwarves found."

Verit and the others in the command tent watched as Ana showed them a vision of an unhappy-looking dwarf and pale priestess by her side. They watched as Ana held up some of the debris they had recovered. The wet glint, even through magical viewing, blazed dark red. Ana described it for them and confirmed it, "It is low grade bloodstone. We can't really do anything with this, however, the engineer Unter did recover a piece of gem grade from an artery. Sadly, the gem is cracked." The dwarf swore at her, and Ana added, "It's probably shattered, but we'll need to confirm." She turned to the dwarf and said, "Unter, not many things in Tehra can survive Crimson. We've checked all our records and this is a new vein. We will be naming it, The Unter Vein."

She asked Unter to tell his story of the genius discovery occasionally interjecting a compliment. After he finished, Ana went on to describe the circumstances of how she finally heard their call for aid. "So, the undead know now where it is too. A death knight is about the most exciting thing that has happened with the Eighteenth. I've already given order to redeploy the Eighteenth to secure the area around Unter's Vein. The fires should burn out in a few days. They should be able to hold it until you come to relieve them, Commander Verit. Because the Eighteenth saw no bloodstone discoveries or finds, and with this new one occurring just now, you'll probably be able to retain many of them. I've already exercised the two month extension in all extensible contracts."

Word of the find spread quickly through their train, and the pace increased. A new bloodstone vein, all adventurers and legionnaires dreamed of joining in such a thing. After all, any story worth telling from Bloodstone involved the namesake gem. Even the horses and elementals assisting their travel seemed energized by the news.

When they finally reached Haven's outskirts still days from the city proper, during camp setup, Verit called the group together. "Word of Unter's Vein has exploded through the Isles. I expect to double our numbers at Haven. We do not need treasure hunters and daredevils. We need seasoned veterans and people of skill. There are two reasons I called you together."

Verit walked the line of his command team. "The first is that I want each unit commander to double their unit size. The second reason is that I want word spread far and wide that no one – NO ONE – contracts with the Nineteenth except Command. If someone has a second cousin that is ever-so-skilled I'd first ask why they weren't with us in Klenna. I have no desire to feed the undead unskilled and inexperienced profiteers. Ensure we only pick up quality. This includes the supply train and adventurer groups. If newcomers cannot prove their worth, reject them. That's it."

As they dispersed, Ayden saw Malcor sitting in the sun beside a wagon wheel. Though the sun barely peaked from the cloud cover overhead, she noticed more and more that the young knight avoided sunlight. Even now, in the sunlight, it seemed dim around him. His complexion looked shallow and grey. Tembri spoke with him and though Malcor seemed engaged enough, something about the interaction struck her wrong. She walked over and offered to bring them some food and drink. Tembri said yes at the same time that Malcor dismissed her. She paused and smiled. "Sorry Malcor, he outranks you. I'll be right back."

When she returned, she found Tembri and Malcor having an intense discussion about the vein and why it matters so much. Though they both looked at her oddly for staying, they did not restrict their conversation. "Take the wand of the Jade God, for example. When you and Verit presented it to the emperor, remember how the wand reacted?"

"Yes, it was scared," Malcor recalled.

"Right, because the emperor has captured those things before. We only started keeping track a millennia ago, but at last count we have killed or captured over a hundred hellhounds. Think about it. Now, what do we do with these malignant chaotic beings?"

"I want to say that we destroy them, but I suspect you're going to tell me something about the bloodstones?"

Tembri sat down and pushed Ayden's food over to Malcor. "No more words until you eat." As Malcor at last began to eat, Tembri continued. "The more flawless and perfect the stone, the more powerful the entity it can bind. The more powerful the entity, the more magic it can give its user. In an ironic twist of fate, the necromancer powers many of Tania's most wondrous and powerful magics!"

"So, the Khasran lich, or the wand we captured – they'll become part of a bloodstone?"

"They could be. I'm not entirely sure how Tania handles that. Take me for example now," Tembri pointed to his tattoo. "The Mage's Guild was unsure of my bloodstone's flawlessness so we decided to bind demons. Six in fact. I had prepared myself for only three so was quite happy with six. Once bound, the gem was powdered into this tattoo ink. It magnifies and gives my faith a level of power only mages ever have. It's one of the reasons I was chosen to be your battle priest. Each of the six demons has a contingency that, when they honor it, allows them to become free. So far, I haven't had to use any of those.

"Consider Verit's earring. While I don't know the full story there, it's clear that he has some level of control over his opponent's magic. Either that, or he just happens to have shadow or fire somehow bound to his bloodstone." Verit's battle priestess walked by at that moment and Tembri returned her wave.

He continued, "The point is that the bloodstones are infinite art, priceless in their ability to magnify power, and precious beyond compare. That a find has occurred bodes very well for us. Most veins produce a handful of flawless stones and greater quantities of lesser ones. The fragments Ana showed us can be mixed into potions and one-use magic items as powerful amplifiers."

Ayden waited for Malcor to say something and when he did not, she asked Tembri, "I've heard that if you find a stone, you get to keep it. True?"

"Sort of true. Tania gets first buyer rights and does often exercise the right to buy these. The best occurs when you find more than one. Tania will buy them all initially but let you pick whichever one you want for yourself as a lifetime loan. They all come back to Tania. That's how Verit got such a small and perfect one the size for an earring. Can you imagine? There must have been an even better one the empire took."

"All of our Order has a bloodstone?" Malcor asked.

Tembri looked at him and after some thought said, "I don't know. I can only think of a small handful I'm sure have them. Most users are very secretive about them. Consider Dar Kendra. You know she has one, but I've never seen it. It's certainly not something we discuss openly." A moment later, Tembri added, "Don't worry, Mal. You'll get one soon enough."

* * *

Ora felt a gentle kick and touched her belly trying to feel if the kick came from a foot or hand. She felt huge with the pregnancy and wondered if the other priestesses felt this way. The fountain in Sai's garden bubbled along and she prayed thanks for Sai's wondrous estate locked in perpetual spring. It allowed her to feel warm in spite of the blizzard outside. The report in her hands from Ishan detailed the Armory's operations, and improvements.

She tried to see Malcor through the cystoran falcon. The falcon following Malcor only occasionally let her view his progress. She had been ordered by the Temple to stop watching as Malcor's training and progress caused her immense anxiety. She saw him suffering the natural, wrapped in a heavy pelt cloak trotting along the wagon train towards Bloodstone on his heavy war horse. His and the charger's breath hung heavy in the air, though she noted that no snow fell around him. When he dragonshifted, the falcon lost sight of him entirely.

Fitfully, she picked up a quill and wrote a letter to Malcor about how their son grew, the Amory, and though she kept trying to tell him how much she missed him, she ended up crossing it out and writing something, anything else. The pile of scribbled letters grew at her feet.

One of the sentient golem servants suggested a less emotionally charged letter. She laughed, "When you give me advice, I must really be struggling! I was talking with some of the others, the priestesses, and they suggested that I should let him know that I miss him. I don't know how to say that while yes, I was ordered to have a child with him, it's so much more than that."

The golem, in its typical obviousness, suggested to her, "Why not just say that? "You've probably heard and yes, I was ordered to have a child with you. But, I miss you so very much. I want to be with you. It wasn't just about orders." It seems an easy thing to do. Or have the falcon speak your voice to him."

She tossed another half sentence to the ground, shushed the golem, and decided to finish Ishan's report. They had a small but growing backlog of enchanted metalwork. To this, she made a note that until they cleared that backlog, only one-tenth of new work would be directed their way. She asked if Ishan required an auditor given his lack of a rationale for the backlog. She knew why, out of all their smiths only Ishan and one other had the skill required for it even though the other smiths kept attempting enchantments. Their substandard attempts could be sold, but did not fill orders from their best clientele. Ora did not want to withhold work from them in case other smiths there broke through to the next level of creating enchant-able metal.

She rubbed her temples and wished Ishan had time to attend some of the Merchant Guild trainings on how to manage inventory and people. The financial motivations at Klenna's forge were overpowering their skill, and creating a blind spot. She hoped it was not ego. Seconds later, one of her attending priestesses began to massage her shoulders. The young priestess did a good job anticipating these things and Ora chuckled, "Can you imagine being pregnant in the ancient days, when no one knew what a massage was?"

The priestess made a joke and the conversation gave her a much needed break. All too soon, a knock at the courtyard gate pulled the masseuse away. A Halfling entered, looking with admiration at the silvery fountains of water set amidst white marble and exotic plants. He bowed low and congratulated Ora in the most flattering ways of looking both powerful and motherly. After his compliments, he said, "I am Farant, a humble servant of Home. I set this appointment hoping that the House of Sai might consider a trade agreement with my business partners. You see -"

As he spoke, Ora flitted out of the River. The pregnancy made it difficult as her child blinded her and made it hard to see through all the prismatic rainbows of color and light and energy. However, she noticed immediately that something was wrong with Farant. Without the child, she would have known immediately what the Halfling's wrongness was. Falling back into the real world, her head and shoulders flared with strain from the effort. He continued on about a wonderful harvest. She brushed her hair back behind her ear and made a hand sign.

All around, the various golems inherent in the courtyard's design moved to Farant, who suddenly found himself surrounded on all sides from above and below by blades. For a just a moment, Ora saw him move between talking his way out or something else. He chose something else. A mithril razor aimed at Farant's heart morphed into a sphere that flowed over and around Farant just as a bomb exploded. The shield had formed enough to protect Ora, but the backside, still open, channeled the explosion towards the courtyard entrance. The blast still knocked Ora back against her seat and left her ears ringing. A kick in her abdomen told her that her son felt it too. "It's all right," she whispered to him.

Already, the golems had begun pulling their fragmented selves back together. Within an hour, no one would be able to tell the courtyard had been damaged at all. Suddenly, Sai stood in the center of the courtyard. Like an angel gleaming with silver light reflecting from all directions, his perfect and gorgeous body took in the damage and then turned to the two priestesses. "I see you are safe, and the child as well. Very good. I would know how this Farant bypassed all my security measures. It has not been done before. Retribution must fall on those who dare so that none will ever dare again."

A changeling golem rose up before them, morphing to show Farant's entry into the estate, even showing the guard constructs watching, scanning. A perfect miniature theater unrolled before their eyes showing each step up until the explosion. "My priestess Ora, you did very well to notice what my own golems did not," Sai noted as, in the miniature recreation of the event, mini-Ora brushed her hair and made the signal.

When it had all played back, Sai stood perfectly still as his mind danced through possibilities. At last, he said, "Only the Thieves Guild could pull off a conspiracy to do this. How though, I do not know. Too long have I turned a blind eye to their attempts to steal my golem construction, my secrets, and my reputation. I see now that they must have always had the ability to do this, but saved it for only a great prize – Malcor's son to be born to the favored Ora, ice priestess of Ynt'taris." His hand clenched into a fist.

Sai smiled at Ora, "You must take my displeasure to them and find out who their customer is. When you know, inform me." He held out his hand and the bracelet on Ora's arm came undone like a snake, and leapt into Sai's hand. It melted flat and then Sai pulled two bracelets, two anklets, a belt chain, a circlet for her head, two earrings, and two rings from his palm. Ora's acolyte rushed forward to help adorn her mistress in these new jewels.

Ora bowed low to Sai, "I will honor the House of Sai and use these gifts to convey your displeasure." Sai had long ago mastered a form of subtle golemsmithing that allowed for tiny golems to assume the form of jewelry, clothing, and other adornments. The gifts he gave her whispered to her of armor, detection magic, weapons, and the ability to summon Sai himself if needed.

"Retribution must be clear and visible to all, Ora. Since this has now happened, there is no point in hiding it. Instead let us show the world something that has not been seen before – Sai's rage."

As Sai melted into the floor and left, Ora turned to her attendant. "Send word to the Temple of this attack and let them know that Sai R'Dar enacts vendetta against the Thieves, the Merchants, and any magi assisting. I would know where to find the guildmaster Marcello." By nightfall, Marcello had invited Ora to his guild, with a note that he wished to discuss the vendetta. It also contained a protest avowing innocence, as was their right.

The Thieves Guild sat behind the Temple Mount away from the citizenry of the city. The ancient castle loomed ahead of Ora dimly lit by lanterns. Though it had the appearance of ruins long abandoned, everything about the keep revolved around training for stealth. Rumors had it that all but the main entry path had been trapped and retrapped so many times that not even the leadership of the Guild could remember what traps lay where.

Ora walked up to that path blocked by a large portcullis. With no guards on duty, she used the iron knocker to clang. Before the first strike finished ringing, a slender half-elf stepped out of the shadows and greeted her. "Welcome, my lady, to Perdition, where we pay eternally for our many crimes. Marcello is expecting you!"

He pulled the gate inset open and held out his hand to help her step through. "I do not remember ever hosting such a beautiful, high ranking lady here before! And I see you're expecting! Wonderful! It's a perfect trinity of coincidence, my lady."

As they walked the main road from the gate to the inner keep, her host asked many times and in many different ways why and for what she had come. Though he was most charismatic, Ora remained silent finally saying, "I must speak with the guildmaster. My words are for him alone."

As the road continued, Ora noticed the keep did not draw near. She stopped. "You seem a nice enough fellow but I do not appreciate games." A spider from the circlet on her forehead leapt at the thief. Though the thief dodged, the spider phased blinking through the air landing somewhere in his armor. A moment later, it hung between his eyes. The mithril spider's legs tightened drawing into skin and small red dots of blood appeared.

To his credit, the thief kept his calm. "It is not our way to bring visitors, even fantastically beautiful ones like yourself, to the master unannounced with unknown agendas."

"My agenda is between House Sai and Marcello. You are deluded to think any but Marcello would learn of this. Enough games, or you'll find I have more than a few devastating and beautifully destructive tricks up my sleeve."

She turned to the road and prayed to the Queen, immediately, every trap in her area illuminated including a patch of road on which she stood. Another prayer and the magical trap in which she stood deactivated. She stood just a few steps from the gate. The inner keep less than a hundred paces away. "Thank you for your hospitality."

Ora turned and began walking towards the courtyard, side-stepping the glowing trap areas. Behind her, the man tried to move but froze when the spider's legs dug in. Ora spoke, "If you do anything at all, the spider kills you. I'll see you when I get back. Pray I get back safely."

A flight of steps rose up to the inner keep's door, which sat ajar. When Ora entered it, she saw a small table around which three figures sat. The dim lighting barely showed her this, but it was bright enough to cripple her night vision. She wished she could move to the River. At her whispered prayer, her eyes shifted to infravision and she noted several illusions in the area as well, no doubt hiding more traps. As she reached the table, two men and a woman turned and removed their cloaks in unison.

Chapter Sixteen – A Taste of Ora's Nature

"We are Marcello. How may we serve the great Sai?"

One of the men added, "Why has Sai declared vendetta against us? This has never happened before. There has always been peace between us."

Ora made eye contact with each of them before stating, "Let us pray you are ignorant of the crimes you have committed against my master. I pray to the Goddess for truth and justice. I pray to the Queen Takhissis."

If her words moved the three, they did not show it. Instead, the lady stood revealing herself as an elf. "You have surrounded us in truth detection, against our will and without our permission. You already operate as if the vendetta is valid. I say it is not. We do not yet know what the accusation is."

The man to her side rose and added, "You are a R'Dar priestess, known to us. Sai is also known and respected. You will not win this confrontation."

The other rose and continued, "Conversation, not confrontation."

"What I would speak, must not be spoken of or recorded. Sai will allow Marcello to hear, but you three are not Marcello."

The lady elf looked awkward and then finally said, "Correct. I am Khalla. You have Marcello stunned in the courtyard."

Ora felt the truth of it and then felt the irony, even humor in the situation. A smile creased her face and she sent the command for the spider to release Marcello. When he entered the dimly lighted room, Ora almost burst into laughter. The spider rejoined her circlet and before Marcello could say anything, Ora's healing prayer mended his forehead.

Marcello, the head of the Thieves Guild, did not turn out to be what Ora expected. "We meet again," Ora said guardedly. "I would apologize for what happened except that my instructions are, as you well know, vendetta. Your lieutenants recommend a talk first. They also labor under the assumption that in a confrontation I would lose." A cold twinkle in her eye and sense of foreboding filled them all, though they could not say why. It almost felt like dragonterror.

Marcello picked up a tankard from the table and took a big gulp. "Did you know that if I moved even a little bit, that damn spider dug its legs in more?

Even with breathing?! I have long sought to acquire some of Sai's golems. This experience makes me want them even more. Yes, we should talk. We are aware of what happened today. On behalf of the Thieves Guild, I offer my condolences, and apologies. We had nothing to do with it."

"My master Sai, he is never wrong. He blames you, Marcello." Ora fingered the holy symbol of Tiamat, now taking on the warlike and dragon form of the chromatic dragon Takhissis. "I fulfill my duty to him when I take you all and level this place. Even now, I feel the Queen's purpose urging me to honor my duty to Sai."

"We had nothing to do with it," Marcello repeated. "We are innocent. I am innocent. The guild itself, innocent. Vendetta is only valid when guilt is evident."

"Your denials mean nothing to me. Prepare yourselves." Her symbol pulsed red in honor of Alerius and then pale white as all around them, doorways opened through which a blizzard roared into the great hall.

Marcello held up his hands in a conciliatory gesture. "Wait, wait. We don't want to fight the Temple, let alone with you carrying a child. Just hear me out. We had nothing to do with it. Maybe someone in the organization did. Isn't it worth at least considering before you exact vendetta against us? Besides, I doubt the emperor would be happy to learn of this."

"The emperor would condemn you on Sai's words alone. You'd be lined up for the next sacrifice and Alerius would never know your names." The ground under and around the four leaders of the Guild started to glow with draconian script heralding a flamestrike, though the runes glowed blue white, and chill frost, instead of heat, preceded the eruption. The various tokens Sai had given to Ora pulled off her to the side as independent golems began taking shape.

Marcello watched this in fascination and said, "I want them even more. I insist we are innocent!"

The ground erupted in columns of fire that the thieves nimbly dodged to the side. The blue flames froze what little humidity hung in the air, which crystallized and began to fall as if snow. "You are magically protected. I would expect as much." Ora signaled for the golems to capture them.

Looking more like amoeboid blobs than spiders, these liquid silver constructs shot out appendages that anchored the main body and then shot like a ray of light at their targets. As soon as they missed, more arms shot out and the chase was on. Marcello and the others went after Ora hoping to take her and end the golems. Eventually, a tendril caught some part of the thief and instantly, the main golem pulled onto that part and snaked its way up and around the thief.

Though the battle raged furiously for a few moments, in less than a heartbeat, the four thieves lay bound struggling on the ground now icy from the blizzards all around. Marcello called out, "Ask Sai, how much! I want at least one but would love to equip all our agents with these! Can you imagine?"

Ora stared at him impassively as a dart flung from his hand impaled itself in her goddess armor. A small globule of poison dripped on its end. It fell to the ground even as the others threw similar weapons at her. With each movement, the golems bound them more tightly until they could not move let alone breathe. Marcello's eyes went wide. A R'Dar priestess should not have goddess armor. He suddenly noticed her pale blue eyes, almost white, and her porcelain skin. "You're transcendent," he muttered. "Stop! Everyone. Stop. R'Dar Ora – or maybe Dar Ora? – we concede but please, we must talk. This is a huge misunderstanding."

The circlet spider jumped down to Ora's hand. "Tell Sai." The spider phased, vanishing from her hand.

The pained breathing of her captors filled the room for a while until suddenly a loud clanging sound rang in the courtyard. After that, all manner of mechanical and magical traps and wards sounded shaking the ground and flaring brightly in the windows and through the cracked door. The sounds of the various traps discharging grew closer until at last, Sai walked through the doors. Smoke and mist rose from his body but he showed no signs of damage. Marcello may have said something that sounded like, "Amazing" but the silvery golems binding him entered his mouth and gagged him.

Sai walked up to the captives and waved his hand over them. As he did so, his magical creatures absorbed every weapon, jewel, coin, and cloth until they were utterly naked. Having done so, the constructs retreated back to Ora taking their shape as decorative jewelry and ornaments. Bereft of their binding, all of them choked and coughed for air and rubbed at the pain in their extremities before realizing they sat naked and very cold.

"I am Sai R'Dar, master of the House Sai. This morning you participated and colluded in an attack on my estate. You threatened my chosen priestess with harm. I cannot allow this to stand. As is my right as member of the Circle, I have declared vendetta and you will die. As I discover others of your organization complicit in this, they will die. As per vendetta, I have declared your crime and my intent. What is your response?"

Marcello immediately answered, "I am Marcello, master of the Thieves Guild and advisor of the Circle. As is my right, I reject vendetta and protest our innocence."

"That is your right. Prepare to die." Said with no emotion whatsoever, Ora saw a mixture of fascination and dread on their faces. Sai's fingers melted together and lengthened into long silver razors.

"Ora is a truthsayer, Sai. Would the Queen allow us to lie? We speak the truth!" the lady elf Khalla cried out. "Your priestess has already truthsayed this entire area!"

Ora spoke now, "It is true. They tell the truth. Or at least rather, they do not lie."

Sai's razors, without his body moving, shot out stopping just a hair's breath from piercing each of their eyes. "The emperor provided means whereby spies like these could evade divine and magical truthsaying. Elves are also resistant to this. I require proof of innocence."

"What proof would satisfy you of our innocence?" Marcello demanded.

"I am not wrong," Sai replied. "Your guild is complicit in the assassination attempt. As guildmaster, I hold you responsible, Marcello. The proof I require would absolve the Guild, not just you. Do not think I am so naïve in the ways of the goddess and the magic of lie detection that I would miss the semantic difference between your innocence and the guild's innocence. Are you not the guildmaster?"

"I am. But you must also know that the Guild operates in autonomous cells so that very few of us know the entire purpose or mission of other cells. I am innocent. The Guild is innocent. BUT - other cells may have been involved. This is also by the god emperor's design!"

Sai flexed his arms and blue lighting crackled along the razors towards their faces. "My soul cries out for retribution that will shake the empire to its core and ensure my estate is left alone. My best security is a deterrent taken in blood and a toll of death beyond measure. Your execution written in blood for all to see would ensure no one else attempts an attack on my estate. You are responsible for all cells; that is by my father's design in your guild's charter too, no? If I must wipe you and your guild from the world, so be it."

One of the others cried out, "No, great Dar, please wait. Marcello, Farant's cell. Remember, he was exiled but many chose to follow him into the wilds. Maybe it's one of those that we do not control anymore!"

At the mention of Farant's name, Sai and Ora froze. "Tell us what you know of Farant. A now-dead Halfling came to us this morning bearing that name." The razors began to retract.

Marcello nodded, "Yes, yes. Farant was a gifted member of the guild skilled in traps, breaching the impregnable, conquering the unconquerable. He often worked with Daryx and the dread lords. However, he began to be fascinated by necromancy. Three years ago, we discovered that he had dedicated himself to its study. Magic-based necromancy without Temple or paladin support is-"

"Forbidden," Ora said. "I see. So you exiled him."

"Yes, I had hoped the Mage's Guild would take him but they refused. They were supposed to turn him over to the Mercy Court, but he left for the frontier and many in his cell followed him. At the time, we did not know what to do with a dual-class thief and necromancer. It had never happened before."

"He was a Halfling?" Sai questioned.

"No, human. But he excelled at polymorph magic, well in using it at least. Several of his cell were dopplegangers. Only two chose to stay, would you like to question them, and may we have our gear back? While I enjoy nude freezing, I'm getting worried about my lieutenants."

"You may have it back when I am satisfied with your story. Have your servants bring you robes. I would speak to Farant's associates now." Sai's arms retreated from razors back into fingers. Ora went and sat down. She closed the doorways and immediately things began to warm up in the chamber.

A few minutes later, servants brought clothing and word began to arrive that Farant's cell members were all absent. Sai's expressionless face took in each report and then turned back to Marcello. Marcello tried to make small talk with Sai, engage with him about the golems, but Sai remained silent and still. Ora followed her master's lead and enjoyed making the thieves uncomfortable as each report came in. Creating a small ice dragon that danced and writhed about her hands, the dragon would hiss at each bad report and then glare at Marcello.

At last, after an hour of a parade of non-news, Sai declared, "How are you this guild's leadership and not know that Farant's cell is gone? Though vendetta gives me right to kill you and take this guild as my own, the imperial charter suggests the emperor may want to look at this first. In the meantime, you all now report to me, are owned by me, are mine. Your first mission – "spiders like the one on Ora's circlet phased into existence over their eyes, "is to find and bring me everyone and anyone and anything and all information about Farant's cell. You have seven days." The spiders sank into their foreheads leaving a faint silvery residue on their skin.

As each struggled with either pain or attempted resistance, Sai chided them, "Accept this vendetta and this mission or you all die now. Ora." At her name, Sai moved so fast it looked like silver lightning and impaled Marcello from behind. The razor hand crackling with blood and white energy as it tore through his chest and then split apart like a whip and turned back as if to impale Marcello. Ora's healing prayer caught the guildmaster at the edge of death. The razors stopped just fractions away from Marcello's eyes and skin at his throat, groin, heart, liver, leg, and arm arteries. Just as suddenly, Sai pulled away leaving the thief a gory mess of wounds. As quickly as the wounds mended, the pain caused the half elf to fall to his knees coughing blood and twitching in death spasms that only gradually faded as he finally caught his breath.

The others stood frozen by the violence, unable or unwilling to move. Sai added, "If my priestess is targeted by your guild, by your members, by your affiliates, by anyone at all connected to you, I will personally see to it that you are multifixed on the Temple's great columns."

Chapter Seventeen – Unter's Impatient Find

Unter sat impatiently in the throne room of the great Temple. A map, meticulously prepared, had been laid out across a great table. On it, figurines showed the locations of the Valley Fort, the Temple, his find, and several other military units near the find. Though only four days had passed, he ached to go back and begin mining. Suddenly, he became aware that the high priestess stood in front of him. He looked up and swore. She had crouched down to his eye level and that gave him a view of her breasts that, even for a dwarf normally immune to humans, stirred him. He swore again.

Ana patted his shoulder and made a half-mocking half-sympathetic face. "Come now, Unter. All our plans are proceeding exactly as they should. It's not your or our fault that the undead reinforce faster than we can."

He turned to avoid enduring her closeness and flung his dagger at the back of a chair. It stuck quivering there. "I should be there, with my mining crew. They're more strung out than I am."

Ana pulled the chair over and sat down across the table from him. One of her guard withdrew the knife and she passed it back to Unter. "Until the Nineteenth arrives, I do not see how we can re-open the mine without losing you, your crew, and the vein. The goddess confirms this path. The vein is not going anywhere. The fires are still burning. Don't worry. We have a unit of ground observers there to watch and anchor it."

"Curse your goddess and the reliance you place on magic! What that mine needs is a full team of dwarves pulling out gems! That's why your dragon keeps us here, no? Rather than direct your magic and goddess at what-if questions, what say we go and start retrieving bloodstones?"

From the back, where some thirty miners sat passing time with food, many called out their agreement. Ana sighed and rubbed her eyes. "You dwarves, always so eager to die. Do I need to show you the monument we built to your people, or the records of how many bloodstones have been independently retrieved by what you propose? It's very few, but the thousands of dwarves lost doing exactly what your impatience proposes… I have heard these arguments for decades, no centuries. You're as stubborn as the undead. Reckless parties, like you propose, most often find nothing, and only rarely find a bloodstone. For centuries, you're more likely to retrieve a lost stone than find a new one. You found an undiscovered Vein. Let that be enough, you fool dwarf."

"Aye, and ready to leave now. We won't find nothing. We already know a new artery sits there waiting for us to free it from the undead." Ana stared at him meeting his angry and defiant gaze, unblinking. After too long, Unter finally looked away. "Tomorrow?" he asked. His question had a tone of reconciliation and hope in it.

"Come with me, Unter," Ana said walking back to the table. She pointed to a unit in the entryway just outside the Temple proper, "This patrol is refreshed and ready. You and the priestess Helena may go with them to the mine tomorrow."

"And my crew -"

"Shall stay here until the Nineteenth arrives. The mine requires an army, not a brigade. Suppose you find one perfect stone but lose the mine forever? The regret will eat at you always and you'll wonder how many more stones there might have been."

"Better one than zero," he said kicking the chair away from him.

"Wrong, better ALL than less. Because, you found a new mine," Ana said moving a figurine representing Unter and Helena into the patrol. Tania stopped unescorted mining operations centuries ago, at Ana's decree. She had been the High Priestess here for that long. She oversaw the great Temple's construction after her army had taken the eight fortresses along the valley ridges from the undead.

Any mining party drew the attention of undead. Even worse, when an undead creature of any kind lingered near pure bloodstones, the stones restored memory and skills lost to them. Powerful undead, like the death knight, would essentially become a hellhound. Luckily, the shock of recovering free will and the problems it caused with other hellhounds had prevented them from ever making the connection. It had been an unsolvable problem until Tania captured enough hellhounds to test the pattern. In the valley, the presence of abnormally powerful undead had become a sign Tania followed in looking for bloodstones. She patted Unter on the shoulder. "The thing that will drive you insane is this: was the death knight there because of the bloodstones or because of your group making so much fuss?"

Ana unclasped a small container on her necklace. Into her hand a small, flawless bloodstone fell. Red bands of energy arced out from it and pulled back in as halos of energy. She placed it on the map where it moved side to side like a living creature. Immediately, the room fell silent and Unter stared, mesmerized by the stone. The bands of energy moved like ocean waves and when Ana tapped the stone, a blast of light rippled out in slow motion through the room hitting and washing up and down the walls until the walls seemed to suck the energy in. The sound of many waters during a storm filled the room.

Ana picked up the stone and placed it on her tongue. Immediately the noise and energy faded. She blew Unter a kiss and a red smoke trailed her kiss touching his face and he heard the sound. "Is that the *Imperial*?" he asked. Some of the stones had nicknames. This one, held by the high priestess of Bloodstone, granted its user dominion over undeath.

Her voice unaffected by the stone, she said, "The emperor and I fashioned this, the first flawless stone ever found, to be a tool of rule here in Bloodstone. The undead out there, they hunger for it. Bound as the undead are to the Jade God, if any got the *Imperial*, it would make them the equivalent of The Necromancer in this world. Imagine it. Imagine how the Jade God himself must hunger for this one stone." She pulled her hair back behind her ear. "If we knew another *Imperial* lay in Unter's Vein, yes. We would attack. But, we do not." She pointed her finger at Unter, "You will be patient and cease worrying me with your demands. You are not the first dwarf to chafe at military delays."

Unter rose up, contentious and ready to argue with her, but she cut him off with a look that threatened murder. "In the Queen's name, if you bring this matter to me again, I will have your voice, dear Unter." Something happened to the dwarf, who grabbed at his throat and fell silent. He nodded and back away. Ana gestured to one of her paladin guards. "Bring me Farant."

While they waited, Ana pointed to the Nineteenth's location on the map and indicated they would arrive within five days. She pointed to the three active mines. The exploratory mine had yet to yield anything interesting, but its proximity to the last cascade meant they would stick with it. The other mine, operating for over a year now, had last been active one hundred and twenty years ago before the tunnels shifted. It had been rediscovered when a war party got lost, found the mine, and used tunneling magic to recover the surface. Ana noted that, even though the mine was rich with bloodstone rough, it had only produced two flawless stones. She added, "Not a single one during the Eighteenth's tenure here."

The knights brought Farant into the room on a stretcher. Magical bindings and thick tapestry-like cloth enwrapped him so only his head could move. Farant the vampire looked starving with his flesh wasted away to tendon along his jaw line. Ana said, just loud enough for Unter to hear, "This is what you risk of your crew. Is it worth the extra five days?"

Farant went frantic at her approach. "You have struggled in hunger long enough, Farant. To be reborn a vampire, but to not feed, you must be insane with hunger. I'm going to feed you." She lanced her thumb and let a small drop of blood form there. Farant's thrashing quieted as he focused on that single drop. "So little but I see you can be good. You must tell me all you know about the attack: who hired you, why, what is your purpose?" The Imperial bloodstone in her mouth reached out with red mist. It entered his eyes, ears, nose, and mouth.

The vampire struggled to break free again but after several moments, he choked out, "Farant. I was, I am Farant. I worked at the Thieves Guild." Ana told him he had done well and let the drop of blood fall to the side of his lips. His tongue barely touched it, making the hunger that much worse. She laughed and asked the next question while another bead of red slowly took shape on her finger. "The Guild, I worked for Farant-"

"I thought you said you were Farant?"

He shook his head no. "There are many of us. We are all Farant. We all pledged to the same purpose." A knight brought her a vial of blood and she let some of this dribble into his mouth. Already his emaciated form started to look better, healthier. She asked about the purpose. "We fight against the prophecy of the king, of the sister. The heretics. Too long have failed doctrines led the kingdom astray." Ana held the blood back and he added, "Preparations to test, learn, and then kill the family of Kell."

Ana started laughing, not a bright laugh. The darkness of her laughter seemed to dim the light and slowly Farant started to become afraid. At last, she calmed and said, "Farant, hear me." Her voice changed taking on a booming, mighty quality that made everyone hearing it eager to jump to and listen. "You will answer me now. Is what you have told me the truth?"

Farant's answer broke free from his lips compulsively. "Yes, but there is more I do not want to tell you. We have found the sister, in-"

Ana's eyes flittered ever so subtly to take in the people in the room around her. Before Farant could speak another word, Ana ordered him, "Banish!" At her words, his body crumbled to dust.

Ana turned to the group in the room and spread her arms to them all, "Everyone here, come and see for yourselves that another vampire has been destroyed." Though she already had their attention, they all gathered more closely together. Ana breathed and red mist and fire from her mouth carried her words, "You will all forget that this happened. You will remember that Farant refused to cooperate and I destroyed it. You're all feeling really good about this vile creature's death. We should have a celebration."

The red mist of her words filled the eyes and ears of everyone in the room and everyone outside who could hear, when it cleared they heard Ana call for the servants to bring drinks for all. To much cheering and applause, Ana walked back to her throne and sat down to regard the map and troop placements. Though he had forgotten the Farant matter, Unter clearly had not forgotten the bloodstone vein and eventually he too came back to regard the map. Eventually, he said, "Yes, the five days is worth the risk. I will join the patrol with Helena."

* * *

Thalian did not like what she saw. Her small group of five knights, their retainers, and the mercenaries with them had fallen back from the underground entrance. *And, only one of those is a paladin*, she sighed. *I may as well be alone out here.* The cave had long cooled since Crimson unleashed his breath weapon. Thalian's scout patrol had been trying to enter and establish defensive positions. Each time, something went wrong. The thief in their group had gone in with a darkvision spell and a rope. After just minutes, same as the others, the howling and other sounds of the restless dead rose up and the rope went slack.

Thalian counted one to fifty, and by the time she finished, she began to despair of having lost yet another scout. *I'm starting to forget their names*, she realized. *Boscrow? Boltoli?* To her pleasant surprise, the thief came rolling out of the cavern bleeding and wounded, but alive. The sunlight kept any pursuers at bay. "I wish there were more clerics here," she muttered even as she sent a prayer of healing his way.

Boscoli's report was as grim as the others. Undead hordes, uncountable in number, blocked the side passages where daylight did not venture. The floor, though solid enough, was prone to collapse because Crimson had flash-cooked the zombies tunneling up from the ground there. A more powerful creature had severed the line. "If I hadn't felt the line go slack, I might not have made it back, my lady," Boscoli said, now healed. He finished his report. "I ran past it, but I think it was that death knight. Didn't Dar Ana kill it?"

Sir Halavar, their paladin, asked if Boscoli could think of any way to take a large enough force down to fight. The thief thought for a moment and said, "Well, it's a bit out of the normal," and Thalian urged him to continue. "We could have another dragon breathe fire in, to clear a space. The paladins are immune to heat and dragon fire right? Establish a perimeter, use magic to cool the area and bring the rest down."

"Not so," Thalian said after thinking back on her history. "That may be what it takes but before we request a dread lord's assistance, we need to exhaust all other options. We're lucky Ana isn't docking our pay for her and Crimson's intervention. Tell me about the floor. Is there a way to go down, straight down, and then come back to the vein from a new direction?"

Unter's gruff answer of "Aye, we can make a new approach but I'll need my crew," annoyed her. Just arriving to have heard the end of the report, Unter and Helena bowed to Thalian and presented their papers.

"Ah, we have Unter of Unter's Vein, very good. And I can use more clerics." They had several hours of daylight left. Thalian pointed to their crude map, "Unter, do we go straight down or do we start from somewhere else?"

The dwarf's eyes gleamed. "We do both. The straight-down passage will be the real one. But, we'll open another shaft over there," he tapped a hill about an hour's walk away. "That will draw them away from the vein. It'll be fake. This is a tactic one of my ancestors used here."

The pride swelling his voice helped Thalian shake off her frustration with this mine. "A red mine gambit, very impressive. By last count, we did not have enough dwarves, you propose to use soldiers?"

Unter frowned at her intimation that the dwarves - even if few in number - could not pull it off but said, "To be effective, yes. The undead must think the red mine is the real mine. Helena has divined it. It has a better chance of working than a full onslaught. Dar Ana also divined several onslaught approaches. The Queen assures her of defeat if we do that. So, even though I hate it, trickery is what we are left with."

By dusk, when the mist rose up from the ground, they sat huddled around the bonfire with magical light blazing around them. Thalian and Helena both meditated and listened as Unter presented his plan to the mercenaries around them. Because all portents suggested an attack, no one slept, and they passed their time preparing their encampment's protective ring. They also placed loaded crossbows, extra weapons, and healing potions in an inner ring they could fall back to, as needed.

* * *

Far back in the night's dark, Bomoki sat on a boulder watching their preparations. Next to him, the death knight stood stiff and formal. Its Tanian armor and holy sword etched over with signs of chaos and rust, the death knight's eyes burned faintly. "I can take them now," it said factually.

"Yes, but I wish to see how they do in stages. If they repel the horde, you may strike. I am half-tempted to attack myself."

Chapter Eighteen – Counterstrike of the Damned

Just after midnight, the first wave of rotting zombies shambled into view. Though the group, backed by Helena and Thalian, killed the zombies easily enough, several of the perimeter's continual light rune tiles fell to the foul touch of rot and decay. Torches and oil were thrown to those locations to create a bright beacon against the night and the mist. One of the soldiers swore as hundreds of red and white lidless eyes gleamed at him from the dark. "Go, help them," Thalian said to Helena. "I will maintain the wards."

Helena nodded and sprinted to where the sound of fighting had already erupted from the opposite side. They came from all sides now after the initial attack to draw their attention away from their flanks. A known tactic, the knights met and held the onslaught as, of the hundreds, only a handful of ghouls breached Thalian's barrier. As the attackers fell back, Thalian felt something much stronger stride through the barrier and cried out, "High north! Strong!"

The knights and several mercenaries along with Helena sprinted to the northern barrier. They found a giant white corpse girded and decorated in bone and gore stitched together to make a thick hide, swinging a rusted chain. It was slow, and though they dodged the chain easily enough, when the abomination's chain struck a boulder, the force of the blow resounded with a crack and shattered the rock. Also, rust or something from the chain flaked off and began burning their skin with blisters. Helena immediately blessed the soldiers, pleased to see their morale and spirit strengthen.

The white giant turned its seeping eyes to her and gurgled something even as it swung the chain back around. Hearing the choking sounds it made, Helena's legs went weak and she fell to the ground unable to move though all else seemed fine. That was when something struck the back of her shoulder. She ignored it, calling to Krentismar for daylight to bless the battlefield. Something else landed almost softly on her back and suddenly her vision began to swim. A knight stumbled in front her as he fell forward clawing at a featherless bird stabbing into his neck and sucking blood. Someone called out, "Stirges!"

A soldier knocked her in the back and she felt three things pop against her back and then wet her with blood. *My blood*, she realized. Her own healing distracted her from the daylight prayer. Strengthened by healing and the blessing, a knight moved to stand back to back with her as two more took up tower shields on her sides. The white giant made a sound as if laughing. When the foul giant next attacked with its swinging chain, her daylight spell flooded the area around them in noon day light. The creature hissed but more disturbingly, the gory hide armor of corpses swarmed up into flight around it to cover it in shadows. Swarms of stirges nesting in the rotting corpse it used for armor, sated with the giant's foul blood, turned and ejected bloody vomit at the party.

Two guards fell to their knees when the streams of bloody spit splashed their armor and the stench of it struck them. Like Helena had, they went weak in the legs and fell immobile though still alert. The giant scraped a handful of the stirges off his leg and threw them at the group, each blood bird bursting apart and splashing blood where it struck the ground around the fighters. Retching from the smell and weak from its poisonous effects, the next chain sweep caught two of the guards. Helena tried to touch them with healing, but ended up dry heaving instead. Her watering eyes saw the bodies crumple away from the chain and fall slack, probably dead. She tried to scream out to heal, to stabilize, and to have someone decapitate them but could not focus through the foul odor. Moments later, the curse of Bloodstone uplifted both bodies as sick green light entered their frames. Broken and shattered bones popped back together as inhuman will forced them to stand, and attack their friends from just moments before.

Helena raised her symbol at the undead guards and commanded them to turn, but more retching twisted her body and broke her focus. The giant readied to swing his chain, at her - she just knew it, and prayed in her heart for salvation. That was when the ground around the giant and the undead began to glow. The few paladins fighting called for the guards to pull away. Even as the giant swung, a knight grabbed Helena and threw her out of the glowing circle. A torrent of flames erupted charring the blood-drunken birds, burning the giant, and by the time its fell chain struck Helena, it was so heated and brittle that it broke apart against her armor.

Thalian helped Helena stand, the Queen's healing washing the poison and ill muck from her. The giant thrashed about in the fire screaming and clawing at its burning armor and skin. Into this, the paladins leapt beheading the undead and closing on the giant. Thalian looked Helena over. "How are you, sister?"

Helena started to answer but nausea caught her and she dropped to her knees for one last bout of dry heaving and gagging. When she recovered, she saw Thalian attending to those who had fallen. She saved two of the guards on the brink of death. The others, wounded and poisoned, she restored. She needed to boost their morale. "The rest of the attacks were a feint in hopes of this giant breaking through. The Queen has blessed us with a rare foe. I have heard stories but such a monster has not been spied since the Sixth Legion. That means the mine is real!"

Unter and the others came over to see the giant's corpse, kicking at it in disgust. One of the paladins, holding a torch against the incoming press of the nighttime vapors, called out, "There's something still out there watching us."

Thalian called forth two globes of daylight and sent them spiraling out into the darkness. Just at the edge of their range, the paladin cried out that he saw something move. Then, two red lights opened like portals to hell in the night opened. Though red, they left trails of the Jade God's rancorous green as they moved side to side. Everyone watched mesmerized as the red lights came into the daylight. They were not lights. They were eyes, held in a giant wolf's head. Unlike the undead all around, this wolf looked strong and healthy and possessed of an intelligence that made them shudder. It howled at them and the daylight globes vanished. The fires seemed to dim. In the long howling moments, all but the clerics and the paladins quivered to the ground and prayed for relief against the terrors promised. When the howling stopped, even the dwarves shuddered and wiped tears from their eyes. Then a voice resounded from the darkness around them coming from all directions. "Welcome to Bomoki's Gate." The guttural voice chomped as if the wolf bit the words to pieces even as they were voiced.

Thalian heard the name and, clutching her holy symbol to Takhissis, began praying for salvation. The first of all the hellhounds had come to Bloodstone at last. From its side, an image that had haunted her since they first fled the mind appeared. The fallen paladin of Tiamat, encircled by green fire, stepped forward with sword drawn. He pointed the blade to Helena and charged. Several of their fighters tried to intercept, but the death knight smashed them aside as it drove to Helena's heart. The Tanian song of combat from its lipless teeth greeted them with pain and terrible wounds.

Thalian jumped in front of Helena, her symbol of Takhissis raised. Their foe's sword sliced through it nearly taking Thalian's fingers with it. Then, Bomoki howled again. With death standing before them and hell's choir calling them in Bomoki's voice, the group collapsed. The death knight raised his sword over Thalian, "Now you learn the truth of Tiamat."

The sword never fell. The death knight retreated back to Bomoki as another horde began to gather against them.

Chapter Nineteen – Verit Arrives in Bloodstone

Verit rode ahead of Malcor as they climbed the elevated causeway to the First Bloodstone Fortress. Tembri pointed out some of the particulars to Malcor. "These fortresses were originally built by free-willed undead. It was not until Tania captured them, that these strongholds were repurposed. They look like fortresses but are actually part of a vast prison, with the valley itself being the jail and the mountains around being the fence."

"A prison for what?" Seline asked.

Verit called back, "For the humanoids they captured and held here like cattle, before Tania liberated them all. They were food for the undead."

"I've read that the fortresses all share the exact same layout. True?" Malcor asked.

Verit nodded. "Except for the Second. That was modified for the Temple."

The causeway climbed across a series of elevated stone bridges with hundreds of feet dropping off to either side. The fortress in front of them was humongous, easily three times larger than the Soldier's Fort in Morbatten. The causeway followed a river flowing out of Bloodstone. Across the ravine, another fortress watched. Between the two, a series of bridges and cables connected the two castles.

Wanting to ride by Ayden, Tembri fell back to her unit. They kissed briefly amidst much teasing by her unit. Tembri winked back at them and said, "Once inside, we'll ascend through a series of tunnels to the ridge line up there," Tembri pointed to the summit rising above and behind the building they approached. "Most of these were not constructed, but carved out of the rock. We should be able to see the Temple after we make this next turn."

The road bent to the left following the river far below. As they caught sight of the ruby encrusted spires rising above a golden dome, they called out and saluted. The rubies and jewels along the too-thin-to-be-seen spires swayed in the wind and made it look like colored light rained on the gold dome of the Temple. The ridge blocked the rest of the Temple from their view.

Rojo pulled up with them to look at it. His battle priestess Dar Jeri also looking on with curiosity. "This is Dar Jeri's first visit to Bloodstone," the king explained. "The Temple makes up the Second of the eight fortresses. The one across the river to our left is the Eighth, like a sun dial's circle in reverse. We enter at the First."

After a moment, Verit added, "The road to the valley is at the Second fortress. There's another way at the Sixth, but it is steep and considered only useful for small teams. From the valley, the fortresses are marked by their number to help you figure out where to go or where you are."

A while later, they reached a long drawbridge held open impossibly high above a river flowing into the main one they had followed. "Remember, Bloodstone is designed to keep those inside from getting out." Verit's words gave Malcor chills as he considered the effort and brute power it must have taken to build this.

On the far side of the expanse, a soldier verified their emblems using a spyglass. Perhaps sensing Malcor's and the other's thoughts, Rojo added, "When your workforce is undead, you can carve and build. It isn't pretty, but they do what we would never do because of time, energy, logistics, safety, and the like."

A white banner rose up from the battlements. Seeing this banner, Verit commanded, "Raise up all the Reinforcement Army's banners." Seline conveyed Verit's order and turned back to ensure compliance.

Another series of banners rose and each time, Verit ordered a different response. After three exchanges, the drawbridge began to slowly lower. When it at last connected to the road, Malcor noted the entire bridge was covered with pitch and draconian scripts for fire and conflagration trailed its every surface. Its design included its destruction at a moment's notice. They proceeded across the drawbridge and entered the First of the great Bloodstone fortresses.

They found the inside to be large and unadorned. Gear stacked in large piles along one side bore the markings of the Eighteenth Legion. It looked well-worn, repaired many times, and beaten. The guards here, all of them bore the sign of wounds either directly or the fatigue of having been healed to their limit. The road continued through this large room onto a spiral ramp.

At that ramp, the magistrate responsible for the First Fortress awaited with a priestess. "We are not big on pomp and ceremony even for a king Dar Rojo, we pray your allowance. This is considered the safe area and as such, we are currently full of those departing from the Eighteenth. We also have many recovering from severe wounds, and those needing a place of safe retreat to process what may have happened in battle. The high priestess Dar Ana awaits you at the Second. The Temple At Bloodstone will provide a more formal and loquacious greeting worthy a king and so many heroes. Captain Pember of the Eighteenth sent word that he will greet you there, Captain Verit."

Rojo nodded, asked a few questions and learned that while the Eighteenth had not had many casualties, it had been taxed sorely by healing fatigue and near constant warfare. "We thank you for keeping the First secured and safe. Tiamat bless you in your holy duty," Rojo said. At Verit's command, Seline waved the army forward.

Hours later, they reached a similarly large chamber braced by giant-sized doors. Outside the door, they heard winter wind blowing across the causeway. "Here," Verit ordered camp. The next day they would travel the causeway to the Temple. It would take days for the caravan to come through and route to their final destinations. Curious, Malcor and many others headed to the doors after attending to their camp.

Out on the causeway, fire giants in their true form, the Kerchki, stood guard on elevated platforms looking down into the valley. Clouds already obscured most of the mountain peaks and at this altitude, even in the summer, it would probably snow occasionally.

The night greeted Malcor with bitter cold and snow spinning on the roadway but it did not phase him. He saw others pulling cloaks more tightly around them. Malcor could see where the moon would be. Taking it all in, and seeing the blur of colored light ahead where lay the Temple, it all filled Malcor with a desire to dragonshift and see all that could be seen.

Leaning against the balustrade, Malcor felt the engravings and stepped back to see the name of a warrior there. Every brick, every stone, every bit shaped by man's hand bore at least one and some many names of the fallen dead. A fire giant greeted him by name, "Paladin Malcor, welcome. Climb up here and see the Valley of Bloodstone!" The giant swept his hand across the bowl of the valley stretching out below them and said, "You have to see it outside of this place."

Malcor stepped out of Time's flow and amazed, almost fell back into the real. Seen outside the River, Bloodstone glowed in the warm heat of a green sun burning overhead as if high noon. The mountains, in bas relief, towered higher and more mightily than he remembered. Around them, restless spirits of every race, time, and sentient monsters drifted in the breeze, dipping in and out of the River. The valley, when he looked towards it, looked more like a mouth ringed with fanged teeth where the mountain summits rose. Many tunnels there yawned waiting for a meal while a few twinkled with green light. Against this, on the valley floor, a single fortress sat ringed by fire barely viewable. "That is the Fifth fortress?" Malcor asked pointing.

The fire giant shook his head no. "The natural light of fire and the faith of the clerics barely holds it against the Jade God. Ironic isn't it that, in the real world, Tania solidly holds power here. But in the realm of timeless magic, our presence is barely noticed. That is Valley Town in the center of the valley that you see. The Fifth is too far away to be seen from here." A spirit drifted in front of the fire giant. For just a moment, the spirit seemed to grow more real as it reached out to touch the giant. The spirit's hand recoiled against the enchanted armor and elemental fire and it lost interest drifting away. "The very air of this place is full of these daemons."

Seline found Ayden making her way to the doors and together they stepped out to see Malcor on the platform, small but solidly he stood next to the burning giant. "He even looks like a figure of prophecy," Ayden whispered.

Malcor stood framed by the blurred outline of the moon behind clouds and lit in all directions by firelight. Seline agreed, feeling her emotions flare. She tried to think of anything else and when it failed, she removed her helmet and cloak to let the cold air do it for her. Malcor did not notice them nor the effect he had on all who came after.

Long after the cold drove them back inside, Malcor stood staring between the River and the Real. Tembri eventually found him here. Snow and ice had stuck to him while the Kerch's body heat kept that side of Malcor free from ice. "Malcor, it's beautiful but you need to come back inside and rest."

When Malcor did not move, Tembri shifted to see what Malcor watched. The valley had changed since the last time he had stood here. Baking in near desert heat, those things of the real world had faded. It felt oppressive. The green sun high in the sky scorched heat and pressure down in waves upon the valley. "Hey, Malcor!" he called trying to get the boy's attention.

Malcor turned and looked at the priest. "Tembri, the land here is nothing I could have imagined. There are no shadows under that ill sun. I thought that Verit's control of the shadows came through the bloodstone, but I see now it's not that at all. Verit's stone channels this place and that sun. What is it?"

"That is the Jade God. This is how it would look if all life died. This is how, I imagine, the worlds in the Abyss under the Jade God's dominion are. The sun is the god. It never sets. The Jade God's throneplane is called *The Endless Worlds* by the hellhounds. No matter where you are, it looks and feels this way. You can never get away from it. Even underground, you'll feel that directly above you. The vampire generals said that they communicate with that god as if you and I were speaking over a meal, across a table. The sun answers them, can compel them. Right now, its attention is somewhere that is not us. The longer we stay here, though, the more likely we are to draw its attention."

"And that will feel different how?" Malcor whispered.

"All this pressure, all this heat, it all focusses on you at once. It's very bad. Should that happen, you must get away. Run. And, Malcor, this is why we never say the Jade God's name. Ever. Especially in this place. It isn't just necromancy. It's an all-consuming desire for sameness, unchangingness, stasis that this god obsesses about. Life is always changing. Undeath is slower change, and for some, eternally unchanging. If you are caught, it'll be bad - for you, for me, for Ora, for anyone - but especially for those like us touched by the divine, or a mage touched by power."

* * *

Ana lounged on her throne gazing into the depths of the scrying bloodstone sphere. She watched them all smiling when Rojo and his priestess blocked her viewing each in their turn. Even when she tried to indirectly scry them by focusing on those nearby, they blocked her. She enjoyed the game though knowing it would annoy the king. Legion Commander Verit bowed to her scrying eye. Most others failed to even notice they were watched.

She found Malcor looking into Bloodstone. She could tell that he could have sensed her but either did not care or did not know how. A battle priest she remembered from a prior campaign - Tembri, stood with him. She rotated the view and studied Malcor carefully. *He only sort of resembles Kell and Kendra*, she thought. The hairless scalp and burn scars helped to obliterate any family resemblance. *I wonder if Alerius had him burned on purpose*, she thought looking more closely at the wounds. It would have made it that much harder for Kell's enemies to undo the prophecy. Ana noted the Kerchki and how easily the fire giant had accepted Malcor. Even now, looking at him, there was something about his composure that called to her. After a time, she begrudgingly said to herself, "I could see him as king."

Crimson heard and leaned forward to see. His musty self was not often interested in the goings on here. But now, for the third time in the same number of weeks, he moved. Though she wished he could speak, Ana had long come to read his movements and understand. Not telepathy, their bond was more instinctive. She pointed to Malcor. "He's the one we've been speaking of, who trains with Dar Kell and Cor'tanos." Something about Crimson shifted and Ana interpreted his question and answered, "Like the shadow dragons, the boy is also a berserker. Until the shadows are reconciled to the Queen, and until he controls the berserker nature, he is not able to be king. It binds Rojo to this world longer than the king and Mother wish."

Crimson made a growling sound. It shook the ground and Ana felt it in her bones. Everyone in the Temple did. Another odd behavior, Ana thought. "You wish to challenge Malcor?"

The growling changed just enough in tone for Ana to understand. "I see. You wish to challenge Cor'tanos. Haha," she chuckled. "That would be a fight for the ages! You could very well trigger a cascade if Cor'tanos dared show himself here. Of course, you'd smash him, dear one."

Sometime later, a messenger arrived in the form a mage. The mage bowed low before entering, and seeing Crimson watching the sphere with Ana, began to back out. Ana waved him forward. Seeing that her attention remained focused on whatever images she saw in the bloodstone sphere, the mage cleared his throat and said, "High priestess, House Sai sends word that Farant is a name shared by leader of a Thieves Guild faction. They have some cunning and disbanded long before any detected their agenda. It appears to be one of vendetta against Malcor's family. Though it has been sealed from all but a few, this Farant succeeded in attacking Sai's estate, something never before done. The target was a priestess bearing Malcor's son."

"Interesting," Ana said. "Continue."

"Sai has seized control of the Thieves Guild and is turning his attention to the Merchants next. Given your report about the Farant vampire, Sai felt this worth communicating. The Sai priestess, her name is Ora, also requests an audience with you regarding Malcor."

Ana sighed and said, "I do not need to speak with Ora. Please, set her mind at ease. I will make no claim on her knight except unless of course, her Malcor *desires* me." So saying, she blew the messenger a kiss and dismissed him.

Chapter Twenty – Anointing the Nineteenth

The next morning, the Reinforcement Army marched through white out blizzard conditions and wind across the causeway to the Second, also known as the Temple At Bloodstone. As they crossed underneath the impossibly thin and tall spires, the wind made the metal rods reaching up hundreds more feet sing and occasionally glints of sparkled light could be seen from their movement, even in the blizzard. Unlike the Temple At Morbatten, Bloodstone had been built by necessity incorporating the fortress already there.

On top of this, Tania had built the spires and golden dome full of glass windows looking into the heavens. The colored dome was large enough to hold Crimson Burning. It also left room below in the main chamber for Temple functions and several full grown dragons. The Temple stood as the symbol of Tanian occupation in Bloodstone now for a thousand years. From the outer entry to the dome was a short walk, but the aching cold of the blizzard made it seem miles. Even so, as they drew closer and closer, the chill faded to a comfortable warm temperature drawn from Crimson's body throughout the entire complex.

Dar Ana stood adorned in high priestess mantle and jewelry though little else, even with how cold winter fell all around. Though not normally well lighted, for the arrival of a new legion, the Temple glowed with magical daylight with the dome half open to the snowstorm. Crimson lay coiled in the far back half of the dome away from them. The heat from his body rose up through the open dome preventing snow from landing inside. The current legion's officers crowded around the inner halls by rank.

Dar Rojo walked forward and bowed to the high priestess Ana. She bent down to kiss his head and then raised him only to bow herself before him. Formal greeting exchanged, they took each other's hands and turned to the collective group which then bowed before they turned and all bowed to Crimson. The dragon made a strange serpentine growl and his head snaked forward to look over them, so they could clearly see his scar-lined face and the tower bloodstones anchored around his eyes, like additional eyes.

Ana's voice amplified by the dome's shape, sounded for all to hear. "Too long, Rojo! Too long has Bloodstone missed her favorite son. You served here twenty-five years ago as but a knight, and return the king of Tania. Hail and welcome! Glad are we that Tania has assembled a new legion. Commanders of the Eighteenth: Welcome and greet Legion Commander Verit!"

Cheering and applause broke out before Ana asked for silence. "Join us, Captain Verit, and introduce your command. Join us, Captain Pember of the Eighteenth, and know that – even though we find at last a new source of bloodstone gems, you and those you commend are welcome to join the Nineteenth Legion." Stepping back amidst even more cheers and applause, Ana's guard parted to allow the commanders to walk up to her throne platform. Dar Jeri accompanied Rojo to stand by his side.

Introductions, speeches, and the ceremony of dismissing the Eighteenth took some time. At last, when it seemed the ceremonies would end, Ana stepped forward and signaled for one more thing. "We are blessed to stand at the crossroads of prophecy. You see, before even the Dragon Wars, a group of dragons broke off and raced to escape the poison of time. They rejected the Queen's call for union and so earned the name of Heretics. The shadow dragon clan joins us today through its acolyte Sir Malcor Kell'tayris. Already a known hero for his success in with our trade partners at Khasra, Malcor is the newest member of the Order of Water and our most welcome guest. Pray, share our welcome with the shadow dragons. My friend Crimson in particular would relish a meeting with – or against – the mighty patriarch of shadow Cor'tanos."

All eyes on him, Malcor blushed and stepped forward to Dar Ana. He thanked her for the welcome. He heard another noise too, a deep rumbling that felt as if the ground trembled. Crimson slid his head forward at Malcor. The dragon's naked terror causing many to faint though their comrades caught them. Malcor met the dragon's approach and when Crimson stopped just arm's length from Malcor, he put his hand on the dragon's chin and said, "I will let Cor'tanos know of your desire, dread lord." Ana reached out to stop Malcor from touching Crimson but stopped in amazement when the dread lord tolerated it. She then took Malcor's hand, noting its icy chill, and removed it from Crimson.

"My, aren't you just full of surprises," Ana said caressing his hand and allowing her own charismatic charm to strike the boy. Though he looked, even though she saw him look, she could tell that though impressed he felt more awe at meeting her – hero worship rather than lust. She pouted for just a moment and then pulled him back to the crowd watching in total and sudden silence. Everywhere, men and women alike desired her yet this young man hardly noticed. At her signal, Crimson withdrew his dragonterror and pulled back into the shadowed back half of the dome.

"I do hereby grant Verit's Replacement Army, the title and name of the Nineteenth!" Her words amplified by the dome and divine prayer shot out across Bloodstone. Verit's army, in all places held blank, acquired the draconian number for "19". Out across the valley, all who would be staying who bore similar markings felt a shift as the number they bore, Eighteen, increased by one.

Though it took all some time to recover from Crimson's presence, Ana's pronouncement brought bards into the room to sing and tell of the mighty feats done by the Eighteenth. Pember joined the king and Verit in talk while the others availed themselves of good food, drink, and safe warmth. Ayden found herself watching it all and eventually met an officer from the Eighteenth. He bowed with perfect courtesy and introduced himself. "Revi, of the Southern Kingdoms," he said. "It's not often I meet such a beautiful officer. You must have begun in the Temple track?" He referred to paladins who failed out to officer training.

"No, Officer Revi, I did not. Since birth, I have been on the soldier track. I suppose I could have applied. It never felt right for me. I'm Ayden. Careful with your flattery though, I am spoken for." She pointed to Tembri.

He looked, and seeing Tembri, let his disappointment show. "I bet I can teach you the error of your ways," but Ayden got Tembri's attention and he waved back. Revi immediately saw Tembri's rank as a battle priest and chuckled. "I see you have impeccable choice in men. Would I have had a shot?"

Ayden laughed, "Of course! It's not everyday I am treated so well. Tell me Revi, I want to know everything you would share about this place, and any advice on how to succeed in my first campaign. Are you staying on?"

He grabbed two flagons of ale from a servant and handed one to her. "Well, yes for two months. I don't get a choice in the contract extension. But if things go well, maybe longer. If, for some reason you became available, I'd stay on forever."

He took a drink of ale and glanced over at Tembri again. "Advice huh? Okay, here it is really simple. Three rules for living. First, only do things during the day. All the bad stories and close calls you hear about, they're all from those who lingered past sunset. Second, don't go anywhere by yourself. Even to bed, especially to bed. If that priest is not avail -" Ayden punched him in the arm. "Sorry, but seriously. Partner up, everyone at all times. Third, anyone who dies here or if you think they're dead or will be soon and there isn't a cleric handy, behead them. It's best for you and certainly best for them, if you care for them at all. If they were doing well, the Temple will revive them."

"So that keeps me alive, more or less. What about success? How do you define that here?"

Revi looked her up and down. The flirtatious nature of it made her blush. He laughed, "Adorable. Okay, there are three simple Revi Rules of Success. Ready? First, don't let your commander die; refer to the first three rules for this. If your command dies, you can lose your commission. I only had to intervene with Captain Pember, oh um, more times than I wish I had to. It was a lot. Remember, they're paladins and this place is teeming with worthy foes and the seduction of mighty deeds. You have to be on guard for that allure. Second, success is accomplishing your mission without losing those in your command. Any other definition of success sets you up for failure. Like those who are only here for bloodstones. Lastly, don't stray too far from the clerics. That is key. Simple right? Your turn now. I've been here for four years. When I get back to Tania, how do I find a woman like you? A sister perhaps? A best friend?"

"Those are really just more survival rules Revi. Success has to be about the bloodstones. That's why everyone is here right? On the other point, I'm the only one in my family, so no." She sipped at the ale, surprised to taste something so expensive so far from Tania. She pointed to it, "This is delicious! So, when you get back to Tania, you'll be a hero. I'd imagine you could walk up to any girl and they'd swoon for you on the spot."

"It really doesn't work that way," Tembri said joining the discussion. "Lieutenant Revi, right? I was here two years ago on special assignment."

Revi slapped his forehead, "Of course, that's why you looked so familiar. Here I was thinking it was just insane jealousy that you're with this beautiful woman, but no. That's right. We fought together in the dungeons beneath the Sixth." He turned back to Ayden and said, "Remember the rules? Keep a cleric handy. That rule did not really firm up in my mind until I had served with Tembri here. We'd heard of battle priests but did not have any. Never in fact. So, then off we go on this dungeon crawl and Tembri is with us. The whole time we're thinking, protect the priest, guard the priest, keep him away from combat – and into the first combat he goes wading in dealing damage and healing us as he goes. It was simply beyond anything I had ever seen a cleric do before!" Revi bowed low to Tembri. "You saved my life on more than one occasion, sir, and I thank you. Now, if you'll have me, I would take the chance to serve with Tembri any day every day. Plus, should anything happen, I can tell Lady Ayden will need a friend."

Tembri just smiled and nodded. "You're welcome to join us with Pember's commendation, of course. Now, I believe you had been just about to define success here?"

Revi took another drink. "The Eighteenth – we had no cascades. We found promising shafts, even a few unknown mines, but they never panned out. I'm afraid the Eighteenth will be known as the Peaceful Legion, well by

Bloodstone's standards at least it was peaceful. You saw how many of our group fell when you entered the First right? Two-thirds casualty or at their healing limit. Dar Ana said it was a record." He snorted and took a much longer drink, while signaling for a new tankard.

They all laughed together and took more ale when it arrived. The merrymaking lasted a long time. Eventually, the din faded as people left or for other purposes.

Seline watched it all, took it all in. It reminded her of so many royal events her family had hosted. Granted the king had not been there, but still, it followed the same general rules. The mingling, the unseen and quiet efficiency of servants, the progression of food and drink through the night, it rather made her feel homesick. She leaned back against the stone base of a heroic statue watching a bard elaborate the number of undead destroyed by the Eighteenth. As always happened, Seline's mind drifted to other things and she eventually turned to walk outside and get some distance and perspective. She turned right into Dar Ana who stood beside her talking with the king's battle priestess Jeri.

Seline dropped to her knees and apologized but blushed when she realized how truly nude Ana was. Ana touched her chin and bid her rise but stepped just into Seline's comfort zone. Seline suddenly felt very afraid but swallowed and tried not to show it. "Jeri, this is Seline, a most exquisite lady knight in the Order of Fire. Ravishing, isn't she?" Ana viewed Seline side to side, reminding her of a cobra weaving before a strike. "Not many lady knights. Dare I say, not many who would have paid the price this one paid to be here."

Seline expected some cruel or offhand comment, but Jeri's expression did not change. "The Queen asks each of us to make sacrifices. I'm not sure Lady Seline's sacrifice is any more or less exquisite than my own, the king's, or even yours, High Priestess."

Ana licked her lips and touched Seline's lips as if accidentally with her fingers. The look of lust and desire Ana gave Seline in that moment proved too much and Seline saluted, broke contact, and walked away before breaking into a run. She heard Jeri say, "Your tortures are truly cruel."

Seline did not hear the rest of the conversation where Jeri continued, "I find them cruelly human and unbecoming one the Queen favors."

Ana waved Jeri away, "That's because you're gold. Even converted and faithful, you'll never understand the fiery passion of the red dragons. Besides, there is a duality in human nature I find delicious. Malcor's casual cool versus Seline's longing…" Ana licked her fingers where they had touched Seline's lips.

Jeri thought about saying something of the king, but as if anticipating her thoughts, Ana added, "Dar Rojo will be the first colorless. You seek to interject your gold nobility into him but you fail to understand that after ascension, Rojo will morph and change dragon type based on need, mood, and the Queen's will. Do you think your concerns for his nobility will endure ascension?"

"I have bet my life on it. Excuse me, I would speak with the great lord Crimson Burning."

Left finally to herself, Ana quickly spotted and walked over to Malcor. The boy looked out of place and probably felt that way too. A handful of the Eighteenth's officers had cornered him and were demanding details of his Ori adventure while also giving him advice. He bowed as she approached. "The great hero of the Khasran Lich, finally alone at last." She waved the others away.

Malcor shrugged watching the people around them bow and hastily leave. "How may I serve the Temple?" Malcor asked.

"By serving its priestess, of course. Tell me Malcor, how many priestesses have vied for you?"

Malcor blushed and said, "Only the one I love."

"Ah, you speak of Ora. So, no others have taken you?" When Malcor said as much she laughed, "Truly you are oblivious! Look around, there must be twenty priestesses here, all of whom would take you in an instant. Perhaps even a high priestess would take you in from your long travel and give you succor. You've never sought it out?"

"No, there's been no time. Since becoming a knight, Ora is my only solace. Even then, it's been just a fraction of what my heart wishes." Malcor knew what the high priestess wanted but focused on Ora. He knew Ana tested him. He knew he must pass. In some ways, this interaction with Ana felt more important a test than when he faced Tor or bargained with Kaia. He casually looked up and saw a glint of silver in the air above the open dome. Ora was always there for him. He would endure this test.

Ana leaned up against him and rested her head on his chest. Like his hands, she noticed the cold chill permeating his body and sensed the shadows in the ethereal's flow all around him. But, Malcor the man remained still. His heartbeat and his breathing continued unchanged by her closeness. It excited her, this unaffected-ness. She shifted briefly, out of the River, and saw that even there, Malcor stood unmoving even as shadows danced and spun around him. Across the flow of time, something dark and humongous watched them. It seemed to leer at her, daring her to do anything at all. She recognized the shadow dragon Cor'tanos, but refused to acknowledge him.

The flow of time around Malcor ran in inky swirls drifting and diluting downstream away from him. If he noticed her here, he did not show it. She returned to the real and took his arm. "You're very cold, would you like something warm to drink?"

Malcor expressed his gratitude for her offer noting, "Surely the high priestess of Bloodstone has more to do than offer a new knight a drink! My lady, is there anything I can bring you? Would you like a warm drink?" He stepped away and summoned a servant. Seeing him with the high priestess, the servant raced over.

"How interesting," Ana said to the servant. "Here is this young man with the high priestess and all he can think of getting me a snack. Some wine please, for both of us. Tell me Malcor, what is it like being a shadow dragon? Do you feel the shadows the way I might feel warm sunlight?"

Malcor looked briefly at her eyes and then away. For just a moment, Ana saw the Queen's Purpose there steering him clear of this game she infamously played on new paladins. It had been ages since that had happened. No knight had ever resisted her seductions, except for a small handful like this one and Dar Rojo, so resolute in their will that the Queen moved them against Ana's personal desires. The surprise of it made her laugh clear and loud. "Oh Malcor, what a treasure you are! Very well Mother, game on! Game on. So, tell me - the shadows and what's that like?"

Malcor described how the world became two dimensional. "Everything is cold, except magic which looks and feels warm. Tembri used a draconian word for 'ultravision', I think is what the clerics call it. But it's such an amazing feeling to move through the shadows. Not as amazing as dragon flight, but still." They talked and Malcor found himself hard pressed to avoid telling Ana everything he had learned and knew. He kept trying to ask her about her own experiences with the dread lords, but she drove back to him by outmaneuvering him and only giving short answers that connected back to him. She questioned and listened tirelessly.

Finally, she asked him to show her. "I'll make you a bet, paladin. Moving through shadows, if you can tell me what is behind Crimson in that alcove over there, without his detecting you, I'll reward you greatly. If you are caught, you will reward me with a favor - a wish, if you will."

At her challenge, Malcor found his desire to compete grow strong. Sensing nothing amiss in the Queen's Will, he said, "Crimson is an eldar dread lord, right? I've read about him. Like the emperor and others, why wouldn't he detect me immediately? I mean, is your challenge even achievable?"

Ana's eyes twinkled. "It is possible. Crimson has no ability for magecraft the way the emperor does, or even the wild magic Armageddon carries with him. It is said by Tiamat that Crimson challenged the Platinum Dragon in the time of the eldar. For that, the all-father cursed him, stripped him of his magic. Consider Crimson antimagic. If your shadow dragon powers are based in magic, rather than the divine, then no. This challenge is not doable. However, if you have mastered this and it is either an innate part of you or by divine genesis, then Crimson will not notice you unless you make a mistake."

"And, this thing I might find or see. Is guarding it part of Crimson's charge here?"

"No, not his charge, but it is something precious to him. More precious than all the treasure of the empire. Trust me, if you see it, you'll know. And your telling me, I will know you saw it. That being said, if you are successful, you will be bound to silence, even within the Order of Water and your battle priest. Even to the emperor, unless you are speaking to only the emperor, for he also knows of this. And your lady Ora, of course."

"I can see that if I say no, you will never let me live it down, High Priestess. Very well, I accept."

Ana caught his arm before he could move. "If you fail, you are mine tonight." She kissed his lips and then let him go.

Suddenly, Malcor no longer stood by Ana. She thought she saw her own shadow deepen for a moment before the darkness passed to a connecting shadow. She tried to trace Malcor's movements this way, but the lack of light behind her throne made it hard to follow when the entire back half of the dome lay in relative darkness.

Seeing Ana looking his way, Crimson moved forward just a bit to see if she required him. She smiled and gave him a reassuring wink. Moments later, Malcor stood up from the shadows. He began to whisper to her, but she leaned forward posing her body against his so that his lips touched her ear. She felt him react but held him still to wrap her arms around him. She breathed into his ear, her lips just brushing his skin.

"Tell me." Only when Malcor had told her to her satisfaction did she step away and give him space. "That's correct. That shadow skill would be so handy anywhere except here in Bloodstone. Your reward dear boy, unless you'd like a different one?" She ran her hands up and down her body and blew him a kiss. He remained totally impassive even though she felt his appreciation for her beauty. She knew he had no curiosity at all for her.

Ana stepped up to her throne and opened a compartment in the arm rest. From it, she withdrew a single white almost silver feather. "This is the feather of an angel, a guardian from the pantheon of Heaven, who fell here many years ago. I would normally tie it into your hair, but since you have none, we shall instead bind it to your sword. Bring it forth."

Mal suddenly became aware of everyone watching. Literally, all activity in the vast room stopped and he became painfully self-conscious. Ana's guard moved a bit closer but beyond that, all eyes watched him draw his sword from its sheath. Tembri had opened his book and the magical feather quill danced on its pages again. Probably sketching the scene of him standing down a step from the transcendent priestess.

"Behold!" Ana cried out. "An angel's feather gifted to us many years ago when a mighty Solari fell during a cascade. Long have we held this awaiting guidance to give it as a gift. Like any gift, its purpose must be learned and respected. Though the so-called 'good gods' consider us unworthy, we fight and destroy and contain more evil for the greater good than they ever have. Sometimes, like this solari feather, our deeds are recognized and the divine servants join us in mighty combat. These tokens are not to be taken lightly. Sir Malcor, the Mother Tiamat and the great god Pha Rann gift this sole remaining token to you, to be a boon and a blessing as you wield the Apprentice Sword 'Coming Undone' against the dark purposes of the Jade God." So saying, she held the feather and prayed in draconian that the feather would root to the sword. Silver tendrils grew out from the feather's base and swirled into the metal.

Mal immediately felt his sword respond to the addition as if becoming alive and aware. When Ana asked him if he felt it, he nodded his head. She ordered him to speak aloud what he felt. "Coming Undone, it hungers for undeath. Each moment, I can feel it responding to the valley, urging me to seek out and destroy them." He cocked his head as if listening. "I feel a call for justice against the hellhounds. I can feel it wants them more than any other."

Ana lifted her hands above her head as cheering and applause broke out in the great room. Very quickly, everyone wanted to see it, and those who had heard of the Apprentice Sword and Malcor came forward as well. To those admiring the sword's purpose against the undead, Malcor felt the sword's pleasure with those people as if a cat purring. To those merely curious or caring more about Malcor himself, the sword responded with something like disdain. Ana leaned on his shoulder and said, "You'll have to get used to it. Sentient weapons can exert a certain influence on the wielder. Be certain that it doesn't press you into doing something stupid. Also, beware those situations where the sword might deem you less worthy than another who might more aggressively seek out the hellhounds. It works both ways; a mighty ally if you heed its desire to slay undead but also a subtle enemy if it deems you unworthy of it." She put her hands on top of his where he held the pommel and crossguard and kissed his cheek again. "This feather was gifted to us by an angel whose sister fell to a hellhound."

Mal nodded. "I will do this gift honor, on my heart and soul!"

Ana laughed and put her head against his shoulder to admire the sword. "So serious always, Sir Knight. Should you find yourself in a situation where your sword must be quieted, caress the feather and hum the angel's name. She was beautiful, in the way that angelic Solari are. I much admired her sister. The fallen one's name was Teela. The sister's is Rania." She pressed his hand to the bound feather as she said these names and he felt the sword calm from its searching for foes. "The spirit of angels and might of the heretics. An unusual weapon for an unusual paladin. Have you nothing to say?"

Malcor blushed and immediately moved to bow, the beginnings of a thank you on his lips. Ana caught him in her embrace and caught his lips with her teeth. More than a few watching chuckled at his obvious discomfort. At last, Ana broke the kiss with a disappointed sigh. "This Ora must be truly special," she whispered and walked away with a wink and sway of her hips that would drive any paying attention to distraction.

The night resumed its normal course with many asking to see the feather. At one point, while talking with the command team about Ori, Malcor finally heard Verit's version of the charge Daryx led against the hellhounds that would have otherwise captured the lich. The story quickly caught on a life of its own until Ana required Verit to tell it from the beginning with bards present to record and listen. Even Crimson leaned forward enraptured by how the Order eliminated so many hounds. As he retold the story, the bards put music to his words and against the beat and tempo of the story, the rest of the Temple fell silent. When Verit at last finished the telling, Ana applauded him and then told a story of her own.

"Tonight, besides marking the coming of the Nineteenth and the Sabbath of the Eighteenth, we have many renowned heroes coming back to our valley." She called Tembri, Verit, even Bruun and many others forward. "No doubt, you have heard some stories of their last campaign here. Let me tell you a story not many know. This story begins with Captain Verit. He was newly appointed in charge of a group of two knights and some twenty soldiers, retainers, and a mercenary priest.

"We had received word of a possible find in the western valley some three days' ride from Valley Town. Verit led the group. We knew they were being watched. This is a tactic the free-willed undead use frequently. They find some cluster of diamonds or gems or even actual bloodstones and place them somewhere to be found. It's always a trap of course but enough real bloodstones have been captured this way that we always must investigate. *I'll get there in two days*, Verit said every bit as boldly as I would expect of such an exemplary knight. It had been done before. The weather appeared to be cooperating. They could do it. Blessing them, we sent them on their way with reinforcements on standby should they be needed.

"Two days passed and there was no word. On the third day, command sent out rangers who found them trapped in a box canyon. They had been fighting for at least twenty-two hours. By night, the body count of undead would rise into a wall. By day, the wall would burn away in sunlight or be reclaimed into tunnels. There was no way to rescue them without the aid of the dread lords. Crimson glassed the canyon with Verit and the paladins providing a shield for the others from the dragon fire. We pulled them out just as a tunnel collapsed. Crimson told me a hellhound waited there in the shadows.

"The story does not end there though. When I informed Verit of this, he assembled a team and went back on a hunt for that hound. Verit bring it to me." Verit stripped his earring off and placed it in the priestess's hand. She held up, "This bloodstone, he recovered from the hellhounds' heart. A flawless, small, priceless gem. Verit lost no one in his command. It was a perfect victory. We celebrate heroes here in Bloodstone. We celebrate survival and victory. We celebrate you all – the heroes of the realm who hold back darkness, and from it pull these powerful tools against chaos!"

The hall erupted in applause. Malcor and a few others at last noted the absence of the King and his battle priestess from this gathering.

Chapter Twenty One – Bomoki Covets a Gold Dragon

Thalian and Helena gathered the survivors together around the bonfire. Against the daylight globes of magic, the hellhound snorted and pressed forward. The globes seemed to darken against its visage. Pitted fangs set in a half-skeletal jaw bone gradually morphed into the full healthy flesh of a giant wolf. The red eyes held their attention and they felt fear. Around those eyes, other eyes stared unblinking in random directions only occasionally looking at them. Step by step the wolf came forward until it was just twenty paces from them. Each step cracked the ground and bones knit together pulling skeletal warriors from the ground up its legs into his very form. The death knight stayed back at the head of a new flood of undeath gathering.

The hound sniffed the air, its eyes suddenly focusing on the sky. It chuckled a terrible growling noise full of wheezing blood and ichor from where its body decayed in patches. "You want the stones of our god? Tell your fool dragons to come and take them!" He snapped at Thalian with howling roar that dropped her and her party to their knees. Many closed their eyes too frightened to open them, but after a moment of silence found Thalian and Helena standing up to face this beast, shaking with terror, and pale white. Though all hounds radiated a terrible cloud of fear, no one had felt it like this. It rivalled the god emperor's dragonterror. The hound vanished nowhere to be seen. From all around them, the death knight unleashed the flood. Skeletons clacked forward and began pelting them with rocks as an ocean of sword and spear blades rose up glinting in their camp's light.

The attack roused them from their stupor of fright, and through shaky at first, shields were raised against the skeletons' thrown rocks and darts even as arrows began falling from undead archers further out. Thalian watched it all happen around her. She felt her stomach and lungs burning and realized she had held her breath anticipating a painful death. Her soldiers rushed past and around her. She watched it all happen, trying to shake her lethargy when a stone smashed against her shoulder. The pain forced her eyes to focus. When her breath came, it tore at her raggedly and she felt broken bones grinding. She tried to breathe again choking against the paralysis of fright. It ached and felt just enough to help her hold up her god symbol and ward back a skeleton pressing at her with razor sharp finger spikes, worn to sharp needles from digging in the ground.

The skeleton blew back into dust in the face of her god's might, but others leaned in to fill the gap. Their small group fought to hold their defense but when a rock smashed her hard enough to rock her flat on her back, she saw the hills behind them tearing apart as always more undead rose up.

Soon, they would be completely surrounded. She cried out, "We must retreat before it's too late!"

The men immediately rallied and began back-stepping towards her. To her frustrated amazement, Unter and the dwarves refused. Swatting their hammers and axes side to side, they harvested bone amidst a farmer's field of skeletons. Impressive as Unter's assault was, the dwarves barely dented the field. Thalian called out to them begging them to retreat, but Unter returned to her only a wink from his bloodied face. That moment, that wink was when a wraith swept in and around the bones and breathed into Unter's mouth.

Unter's wink twitched and then he began gagging as the wraith's form drew strength from his. Oblivious to him, the dwarves around fought their battles while Thalian watched helplessly too far away to intervene. Thalian saw Unter collapse to his knees as the wraith sucked in his life. Helena appeared from somewhere and tried to cast the wraith back but it stayed focused on Unter. With each moment, shadows of flesh appeared and then crimson veins wrapped around the wraith as Unter grew more and more pale. Helena's mace swatted through the wraith but its other arm caught it and twisted down to the side so that it smashed a dwarf on her flank.

A glimmer of plate armor from the darkness caught Helena's attention. With renewed terror, she saw the death knight walking towards her through the flood. Bomoki had stopped just shy of entering their consecrated ring and watched, for now. Thalian also noted the death knight. As a priestess of Tiamat, she had a way of contacting the Temple. Clutching the rune carved on her holy symbol, she prayed to Tiamat pouring out their situation as a desperate prayer for help.

Focused on her plea for aid and Unter's inability to shake the wraith, Thalian barely rolled to her side to avoid a smashing attack but also to regain her footing. She wished she had not. A wraith crawled low to the ground, moving slow and silent right at her. Another moment and it would latch onto her like Unter, like a leech. With nowhere or way to ready her weapon or defense, she prayed and poured her faith into her holy symbol. She imagined it twinkled at the wraith, which licked its spectral lips and reached out for her symbol and the hand holding it.

A light flared to her side even catching the wraith's attention as it clasped her hand. She felt her vitality drawn into the wraith as images of death and torture erupted in her mind's eye. But, the light intensified until virtual daylight flooded the valley. A man's boot stomped down on the wraith's arm evaporating it as draconian runes burned along the heel and toe of the newcomer's armored boot. High in the air over them and with a staff of gold, Rojo's battle priestess Dar Jeri levitated. She called forth golden daylight as the armored paladin in front of Thalian turned his attention to the others. In a blink, the paladin tore into the wraith attacking Unter. How he covered the distance in a blink, Thalian did not know but she felt so much gratitude. She realized the king, Dar Rojo had come to save them, to answer her prayer.

Maybe exhaustion made her see things not really there, but the paladin's arms ended in impossibly long dragon claws. In the bright divine light, the skeleton horde charred and fell as those further away fell back. It seemed the tide of battle turned against the undead when Thalian saw King Rojo lift a boulder and punch it into deadly fragments that blew back into the horde, each fragment blessed by Jeri becoming extra deadly as a holy weapon.

Just like that, the tide of the battle switched with Jeri's divine might blasting lower level undead and Rojo driving them away like a dervish, fighting in all directions at once. Those insanely long dragon arms held hands of fire that became flamestrikes as Rojo walked into the horde. Thalian saw the king signal another flamestrike. Immediately, Dar Jeri's flamestrike made Thalian realize how far she had to go to reach Dar rank. The tornado of fire uplifted from the ground in waves to reach out some twenty paces in all directions around Rojo.

Out in the darkness, something glinted and unbelievably, Rojo caught the charging hellhound, a hand each bracing against the jaw's upper and lower fangs. It seemed to appear out of nowhere with great speed. "Rojo! It's the gate!" Jeri screamed in an inhuman voice that dropped them all to the ground with dragonterror.

Rojo understood that she meant the Bloodstone Gate through which the Jade God and its minions came. He glanced up at her with a question, to see her lose control of her form and dragonshift. Her human skein burst to pieces and the gold scales rimmed by red bloodlike links beat wings to hold the shape aloft. The divine daylight blinked out and instead the warm terror of a gold dragon hit the humans. The undead, immune to dragonterror, shuddered as the daybreaking attack ended. Soundlessly, they rallied back to the hound.

The death knight fell back and accepted Bomoki's desire to slay the gold dragon. Leaping at Jeri, the death knight's sword narrowly missed cutting her leg as the priestess struggled with dragonshifting mid-air. She beat her wings to climb and then breathed golden fire at the death knight. A Tanian paladin's tower shield, enchanted against dragon fire, appeared in the death knight's hands. But, Jeri's concern and focus remained on Rojo as he engaged in combat with the First Hellhound, Bomoki. Jeri could feel the off-ness about this one, which made it so different and overpowering compared to the other hellhounds she had fought since converting to the Dragon Mother.

Rojo held the teeth as the hound drove him back trying to clamp down. Rojo's strength held and his enchanted gauntlets lit up as they aided his strength. The hellhound began shaking its head side to side, trying to unbalance Rojo. From above, Jeri's claws punched at the hound's back as she spewed a tornado of flame, at the hound. Stalemated, spikes rose up from around the hound's terrible red eyes and lashed forward, bludgeoning the king's face. Bomoki's tongue whipped out and around the king's neck. Then, snakes erupted from the hound, like a lion's mane. Each bore a single sick green eye and a mouth envenomed with long fangs. The volley of snake fangs struck at Rojo.

Jeri's breath weapon immolated the two. Helena grabbed Thalian and the other survivors to pull back from the heat. Jeri's lithe dragon form spewed fire yet the hound pressed into Rojo, who inch by inch faltered back. At least the dragon's flame kept the re-empowered undead away from Rojo. The smaller form of the death knight tossed the tower shield aside and sliced at Jeri, catching her tail and nearly severing it. She had to whip her head around to blast him with fire.

"We must help!" Thalian tried to call but her voice raw from combat barely came out as a whisper. Her group was spent, most near death or unconsciousness. She prayed for the king's life.

More snakes lanced out to grab Rojo as the eye snakes bit at his arms and face. Bloodstones tipped the hound's teeth with fell magic and some voice of chaos cried out, "Behold your doom, tiny knight!"

The runes etched along every surface of Rojo's armor ignited and the king responded with one of Tania's simplest prayers, a song of faith in the Mother. Something unfolded behind the king and they feared for the worst, but it appeared as if translucent dragon wings opened and with a mighty flex of those wings, Rojo pressed forward into the hound as the king's arms broke free of their human confines and filled the prismatic form with fingers and tendon.

Dragon arms full of muscle and bone ended in dragon claws that broke the snakes like twigs. His right hand twisted and the fell bloodstone fang broke. The gold dragon focused the cone of fire into a single straight spear of light and stabbed it, like a lance, at the hound. Tackling it, the hound and Rojo, wrapped in his spectral dragon form, rolled as Rojo swung it with the attack. The death knight fell, pinned under the two beasts. Another tooth ripped from Bomoki's maw, Rojo stabbed into the side of the hound's face.

At last, something sounding like pain came from the hound as dragon teeth and claws raked it side to side, and then Jeri jumped free into the air.

Rojo summoned his sword and he sang, "Twilight Fell Shining on Her Eyes". The sword cut through the tendrils in one sweep. He stood, aimed his sword at the hound just a few paces away and then twitched - reappearing with his sword stabbing into the side of the hound's neck. The image caught in Thalian's eyes and then another blur as the sword strike repeated ten, no a hundred times. The hound tried to roll and back away from the attack but a wall of fire rose as Jeri's breath weapon lingered behind the hound; her dragon's fire daring it to retreat into burning pain.

Jeri dropped back down and humanshifted. Summoning her staff to ready, she blinked and reappeared to smash it into the hound's face. Where it struck, a daylight burst of warm light erupted. The daylight, so bright and warm, lifted everyone's spirits. The undead shrank back from it. Even the death knight, recovering to his feet diminished under the bright light, if only for just a moment.

Rojo's attack continued and Thalian had a moment where she saw the king's face, unaffected as if detached from the violence he inflicted on the hound. Somehow, the hound withstood the king as new flesh and bodies rose up to replace what it lost. Caught in a timeless moment, she saw the king's impossible speed of attack right at the hound's face obliterate an undead form that intercepted the blow just in time, a thousand times repeated. A sweeping claw attack by the hound, that Jeri barely blocked, slammed the priestess bouncing across the ground into a large boulder that splintered with her impact. Unable to defend against the king's attack, the hound breathed a vapor of insects that blocked Thalian's ability to see their fight. The furious sound of the king's attack continued unchanged.

Jeri stood, shaking her head, and scanned the area. She ran past Thalian, dropping a satchel full of healing potions at the party's feet, on her way to the king's side. "Use it and help us!" she commanded.

Jeri's arrival banished the cloud of insects and Rojo now dripped with ichor and blood. The fury of his initial attack now became more deliberate as he went after the hound's head. Razors grew along both edges of his sword and they heard the king say, "Long have we wished to find the gate. Thank you!"

The hound's head split into three heads as it squared off against the king and the gold dragon priestess. Gulping a healing potion, one of the soldiers pointed to Rojo and asked, "This is the power of the Tanian knights?" one of the soldiers said in awe. "Are they all like that?"

Thalian replied, feeling better already from the potion, "This is the king of the knights. Did you think Tania a bureaucracy full of eunuchs? Tania is ruled by heroes like this. If they are not yet, they all aspire to be like their king."

The hellhound snapped out, "Take the gold dragon!" Immediately, the death knight charged Jeri. From back and behind them, the awaiting horde ran forward, Jeri clearly their target.

"What's this gate thing?" someone asked while quaffing a healing potion. No one knew.

The hound attacked Rojo. Snapping at Jeri to distract her, one of the heads breathed necromantic fire while the other unleashed a spell that trapped the king in a sphere. The sphere began rising up from the ground even as a portal sliced open in the air above it. Rojo dragonshifted, his physical body filling the spectral dragon form all around him. It broke the sphere into glassy fragments that fell as crystalline snow. Jeri's staff smashed into the hound's fire-breathing mouth and she withdrew to face the death knight. The hellhound screamed and another gate sliced open in the sky.

Rojo, seeing the gates beginning to activate, humanshifted. Even in his fall to the ground, he commanded, "Twilight Fell!" He pointed his sword at the gates, which all froze no longer opening. His sword phased in two with the original still pointed at the gates. A shield appeared on his left arm and from behind it, Rojo landed on the hellhound. The shield crumpled against a claw attack.

Rojo tossed aside the ruined shield, then counterattacked. His swordstrike sliced through the hound's open mouth even as the hound called for more gates. "Jeri, you're right! It's the gate! We need help!" Rojo screamed, frustration plain in his voice. No one had ever heard the king like this. The emotion in his voice, the frantic urgency of it jarred even his battle priestess.

The fallen paladin looked around, having a hard time spotting the gold dragon. When she suddenly appeared behind him, he swung his sword back-handed and whirled to face her. She caught the sword on her staff, and then pressed it into the attack. This caused the staff to break with a detonating boom. Amidst the torrent of released magic, Jeri touched the knight and said, "Rest in peace. Takhissis calls you home. Resurrect." The death knight, burning in the staff's explosion, screamed at her words. Living flesh and bone wrapped around its form, and then it burned away.

Bomoki, still locked in battle with Rojo, screamed at the gates, "Brothers, come to me!"

Jeri leapt back into the sky, dragonshifted, and raced towards the first gate, which already flickered with movement. They could not endure more hellhounds. Praying she would arrive in time, the gate solidified and she headbutted a hellhound's nose that had come through sniffing the air. It vanished back into the portal but Jeri knew it would recover and attack back through. Her wounds and earlier breath weapons had exhausted her. "In Takhissis' name, dispel!" she commanded the gate. It flickered, and then to her relief, the gate shattered to powder. Below them, Rojo stabbed the fang again and again into Bomoki's body until at last, Bomoki had to stop concentrating on the gates, which vanished.

Jeri dropped back and ordered Thalian's party to climb onto her back. "Hurry!" she urged them. She caught Thalian in her claw, and then leapt towards Rojo in a low glide. Locked in vicious combat, Rojo and Bomoki continued to thrash, seeking to wound the other even if it meant hurting themselves. Jeri caught Rojo's cloak and barely caught him free as the hound tried to hold on. The hound screamed seeing them retreat and gave chase. They flew east, towards the sunrise dawn.

The hound kept pace with them for the remainder of the night, but could not strike them. Their pace was too much for more gate magic but still, the hound followed until sunrise forced it to retreat underground. They landed atop the Third Fortress. After returning to human form, Rojo collapsed back against the battlements.

Jeri looked at him for wounds and then burst into tears. "I've never seen you wounded like this!"

Rojo smiled at her. "You're torn up pretty bad too, Jeri." He then slumped over unconscious. From his hand, four teeth etched and garnished with bloodstones fell glinting in the early morning light. The largest one he had used to stab Bomoki still oozed blood and gore while the other three had clean sword cuts through their base. Unter, saw the red glint, and stumbled forward to see, as did the others.

Chapter TwentyTwo – Bomoki's Gate

The First of all hellhounds, Bomoki, screamed at the rising sun. Seeing its quarry drop onto the fortress battlements, he almost pressed his attack. The damned sunlight already made him feel lethargic. Like acid, it aggravated his many wounds. He longed for the green sun of Orcus' throneplane and snapped at the gold dragon fading into the distance. *A gold dragon!* Feeling a mass of necromantic energy somewhere underground, the hound turned and found a small opening. The sun, even on cloudy days, allowed normal life to happen here as birds and other creatures hiding and struggling to survive awoke. *A gold dragon*, the hound mused. Its mouth still too mangled from battle to work, wheezed as he tried to say out loud, "A gold dragon has finally come to Bloodstone!"

The hound crawled through the dark while its body reknit itself. How many he had absorbed to stay alive during the fight with that cursed paladin king and his pet dragon – *a gold dragon!*, he had forgotten. He stopped and rubbed his healing yet still tender shoulder alongside a rock face. At some point, another hound greeted him. It bowed low in welcome. "Oh great one, we heard your call but could not come through."

"Because you were too slow coming!" Bomoki snapped back. "Everything was there for what you needed except MORE effort on your part!" He snapped at the lesser hound who jumped ahead of Bomoki careful to avoid any kind of a challenge. "A gold dragon! Do you hear me!" Bomoki spat at the hound, at the walls, and roared throughout the cavern complex. "A gold! You all cost us a gold dragon!" At one point, his claws slashed at the hindquarters of the one in front, who flinched but carefully made no sound.

The two eventually entered a cavern with a pool of clear shallow water. Bomoki ran into this bite-drinking water and washing the gore and filth away before at last letting go of his hound form. From the pool, walked a slender man with olive skin tattooed and scarred many times over. Flesh and tissue sagged or sloughed off en masse as the water pulled it away, but regenerative tendon and ligament continuously pulled it back and held it somewhat closed. Green light from his eyes lit the cavern. The other hound, now joined by two more and a growing number of undead waited in silence for this one, the first of all that still lived in this world to speak or command them.

When Bomoki stepped out of the water, a ram's skull sceptre and then another, and then more until the entire pool frothed and bubbled with spiny bone, snaked up to wrap around him like armor. He stood still as the sceptres' spinal column spikes sank into his back, arms, shoulders, legs, and torso. When done, he held out his arms and a magical robe glimmered into existence around him.

Flipping the sleeves on the gold-trimmed red robe, Bomoki walked through his hellhound army, spitting at the other hounds and spastically cursing their slowness. From behind his spine, one of the many jade sceptres of Orcus spat threats at the other hounds reminding them of their enslavement. Bomoki reached back and scratched at the skin around the sceptre's claws where it dug into his spine at the neck's base. Bomoki paused when he felt the jade head of the sceptre and then patted it whispering for it to calm. Ahead of him, skeletons and undead fell apart like water, splashing to pieces and rushing to reform into a throne of eye sockets and gore. On this, Bomoki sat, flipping his sleeves out as the sceptre reformed from his spine to his left hand. His fingers reached over the skull and stroked the ram's nose bridge.

"A glorious time comes to us, brothers," he said addressing the lesser hounds. "Unlike the disaster in Ori, we have a time of prophecy and rivers of blood flowing through time. The king of Tania is here and his pet gold dragon is with him! A gold!" he roared. "Long have I prayed to Orcus that the eyes needed to lock and hold the master's gate would come here. And this final piece, gold dragon eyes, is missed because," he leaned forward in this throne and jabbed his bony spike of a finger at the hellhounds before him. "*Because* of your caution and slow response! You're eternal. Jump through the gate and attack. I would not summon you to a casual party. Combat! War! Come fighting! If you had, we'd have the gold's eyes now!"

At his last word, Bomoki hissed at the hellhound trying to back away from that finger. "You're no hellhound. You're a *worm*!" The hellhound howled at the cavern overhead. A howl that turned into a scream of agony as its body began folding in on itself, changing into a worm. Bomoki walked down and speared his arm through its center. Wriggling there, Bomoki said, "Next time I call, you will all answer with speed and combat fury. Do you understand?" They nodded, eyes wide with anticipation while Bomoki ripped the spine and ram's skull out of the worm's body. He tossed the remains to the undead horde. Bomoki stroked the ram's skull, whispering to it. While he did so, the spine slowly relaxed and slid into a groove alongside the other sceptres.

The hellhounds groveled and the throne of bodies laughed mockingly at them. Bomoki pointed to a hellhound and commanded it. "Hound, you must take a message back to Orcus. You will tell Orcus the following: Gold dragon eyes will at last affix the gate so that you can come and go as you please. I require all hellhounds to retrieve the eyes, under my command, my *absolute* command. I also require the demi-liches to finalize repairs. You will convey my request to the master now."

Under his hand, the sceptre crooned and said to Bomoki, "Orcus will question your timing. Get the eyes first. The hounds will want the eyes before they come."

Bomoki retained his gaze at the lesser hound and paid the sceptre no attention. "You will tell this to the master with all respect and politeness. Now go. It will take them time to travel here. As for you," he turned his gaze to the sceptre. "You forget that time passes, *thing*. I have waited centuries for a gold dragon to come here. And, here it is. We will take this opportunity and we will risk all because success is victory, and failure is just a continuation of," he waved his hand around the cavern – "more of this. Do you think the master will look kindly on us if we miss this opportunity? After *eight hundred years*?! No, we will take the eyes. Connect me now to Farant."

Behind Bomoki, a round portal held in cracked stone glowed. The hellhound messenger walked slowly towards it. Already hands, claws, and writhing things pressed through at the hound. It looked back at Bomoki but the sceptre resting on the back of the First's head glared at it. "Walk through the gate," the ram's skull hissed at the hound. It whimpered when the first hand grabbed its matty fur. Then, it vanished. Bomoki, sitting on his throne, shuddered with fatigue. Stones lining the outer edge of the portal broke apart and fell. Then, the portal vanished as it always did when used.

The cavern full of long-deceased things waited in silence as Bomoki's breath caught and then he gulped air, breathing hard. He swore at the hellhounds. "You will find the gate. Check the usual places. Now go, hurry!"

* * *

Far away to the south and east, in a wet basement by where the river connected to the sea docks in Morbatten, a man sat upright abruptly from the food he mechanically ate. Around him, dark books about death, torture, and hell magic sat amidst burned out candles. A day old corpse, mangled with its innards spread out on a pentagram, steamed and hissed as if boiling in water. Farant looked side to side and bit his lip before scooting over to the corpse and touching the mouth and ears. "I'm here, great master," he said. "Command."

"A gold dragon has come to Bloodstone with the king. Our plan is working perfectly though it cost more of those damn stones than you let on. Who is the gold dragon, or was it just a shapeshifted priestess?"

Farant whimpered and clawed at his head while Bomoki spoke to him. Farant broke the skull off the corpse and raised it over his head. It oozed decayed filth down into his hair and neck. "You commanded a gold dragon where there is only one known in all these lands, great master. I am pleased the king's priestess turned out to be one. I suspected and there were rumors. My stone is ready?"

"I have not forgotten our deal. A stone is being delivered to you now," and Bomoki sent an image of a man in dark robes. "The courier will be there soon."

"A pure stone?!" Farant gibbered, insanity gleaming in his face.

"It is as you wished. Now, report. I would hear where the plan is."

Farant bowed low in the gore around him and whispered into the skull. "The cloning magic, I am learning it. The attack on Sai's priestess failed. Before you growl, Patient One, remember! I told you it most certainly would fail. The outcome is the same though! Sai attacked the Guild and shifted all of their focus and attention to finding me and my cell. They think this about the Sister Prophecy and are distracted." Farant cackled. "It's perfect! The clues will take them away from the Guild's Treasury. Any day now, I expect to retrieve the Guild's master stone. Because it is heavy, I require assistance, great lord!"

"The courier is well-versed in secret necromancy and has been my apprentice. He will assist after delivering the stone. Once I have the master stone, you will be gifted a Wand of Orcus. Farant, my hound to be - you have no idea the power that will be yours! Do not disappoint me, do not fail. Death is but a doorway to a more powerful existence. Life, murder, pain... it is all worth it because you will be a god! Remember this always!"

Farant remained groveling for hours after Bomoki went silent. When he at last moved, he crawled on all fours to a door and called for another prisoner. Screaming began. While that went on, he pushed the corpse remains out of the pentagram and retrieved new candles to replace the used ones.

A Farant clone and a half-orc dragged a terrified but drugged man of older age into the circle of candles. As they held him, Farant lanced his neck right at the base of his skull with a long needle. After a brief paroxysm, the man's body went limp with paralysis. The clone grabbed a wrist and snapped it showing it to the man who drooled looking at it as if amazed. Each limb was pulled towards the candles and Farant began the cloning ritual.

Chapter Twenty Three – Interlude in Morbatten

Calvin folded the edges of his summons again. The Mercy Court, a monolithic building west of the great bazaar, rose up above the square and had a view of the grand fountain. The Court's dragon statues coiling around its white stone columns made eye contact with the dragons in the fountain.

Though early and winter dark with snow falling, merchants and workers moved about the market getting things ready for the day. The summons had been delivered to him late last night, interrupting a date with his favorite girl. He shivered, wishing to be back in bed with her in his spartan but warm officer's quarters. He checked the time on the parchment and swore. *This is why I'm an officer in the military*, he thought, quietly feeling a twinge of envy for the city watchmen working under him. *They're all sleeping still.*

He steeled his resolve and entered. Street guards took their ease inside the great hall, warm and sweet smelling compared to the outside air. A chalkboard listed the cases to be heard. An indifferent-looking soldier approached and held out his hand for the summons, glanced at it, and said, "The judge is waiting for you. Follow me to Dar Jeffrey's quarters."

The judge did not meet Calvin's expectations. Appearing no older than his late twenties, he finished buttoning his silk shirt, and walked over. "Watch Officer Calvin right? Pleased to meet you. I'm Jeffrey."

"The Mercy Judge, yes, my lord. I know you by reputation. In fact, as a child, my father and I came here and represented a case for Klenna."

Jeffrey looked at Calvin trying to remember the name and face, and then shrugged. "I hope you got the outcome you wished for? We have enough cases through here that I do not remember. So, to business. You've read the summons?" When Calvin nodded and held up the papers, Jeffrey continued. "We recently received a petition from a poor neighborhood by the river docks involving missing persons. Normally Dock Side's Watch handles these things, but when I inquired, they have fifteen such cases open. They're of course being disciplined for not stopping this sooner. What I need is a City Watch Officer to join the local Dock Side Watch and find the common thread that links these missing cases together." He finished lacing his boots. "There will be a common thread. You have two days to find that thread."

Calvin thought it over and asked to see the petition. "I assume the Watch can take me to the homes of the people suffering from these cases. May I ask some questions?" Seeing Jeffrey nod, Calvin asked. "I never went to

Dock Side, but heard it's the warehouse district for Tauran cargo off the ocean. You describe it as poor. What is there that would trigger so many cases?"

Jeffrey stood back up and pulled his sword belt on. "You've heard of the The Spiked Horn Tavern, right?" Jeffrey referred to a tavern built around an amphitheater that hosted weekly combat duels. Famously operated by a minotaur hero named Tysorath, betting on duels and weekly challenges drew huge crowds. "Dock Side has the only other Tauran inn. It's just an inn, but is set up for minotaurs. It's a rough place. They create a lot – let's call it noise – that makes it easy for people, goods, and criminal activities to go unnoticed. The general poverty of Dock Side creates situations like this. We try to keep excellent officers on hand, but between the minotaurs and the corruptibility of the situation, well. We have need of someone like you."

"Is the Watch here and ready to move out?"

Jeffrey replied, "They are in the great hall waiting on their new Watch Officer even now."

Calvin saluted. "This is my first assignment, my lord. I will succeed!" Calvin turned and walked with purpose towards the hall. Jeffrey walked with him.

Just before entering, Dar Jeffrey gave Calvin a ring. "This ring will show you have the authority of this Court. Calvin, it is up to you to let me know when you need help. We don't have time to explain what I hope you learned growing up the son of a mayor and in your knight's training. Don't do anything reckless. Ask for help if you need it."

Calvin took his leave from Jeffrey. Joined by five watchmen, they set out for the several hour march to the docks. Calvin learned that the disappearances all occurred during bad weather and with older men and women so there had been an assumption they died in the storms. The dock watchmen seemed eager to tell Calvin everything. Calvin also felt the near awe and respect these common soldiers held for him even though they were all at least ten to twenty years older than him. It reminded him of growing up in Klenna and how he had felt for a few days as a paladin.

Calvin smiled at them. "I like your attitude and spirit. Don't worry. Now that I'm here, we'll put these cases to bed. I take it that this last disappearance must have been someone important to finally draw the judge's attention."

"Yes, sir. Maybe the criminals got sloppy? But, the husband vanished over a year ago. Just days ago his widow went missing. They operated an orphanage funded by a judge and due to health, the widow was not one to go outside at all, even on a nice day. Plus, one of the children saw something dark lurking around the home all day long. When we went to investigate, all of the children and servants were terrified. The widow was gone. That was what drew the Court's attention, Captain Calvin."

Calvin startled a bit at the title. *Am I a captain?* he wondered to himself. In the paladin ranks, the knight ranks, and later with Ayden in the officer ranks, his title had fallen to Lieutenant. Lieutenant served as the entry rank for highly trained fighters like Ayden. It had proven too much for him, but he had left with that title. As a normal watch officer, he had figured his title was that – Watch Officer. But hearing the Dock Side Watch call him Captain, it felt right. He decided to let it stand. *They must know what they're talking about.*

As much as Calvin enjoyed being out and about where people recognized and respected him, he noticed that Dock Side seemed kind of boring. "Not much happens here," he observed during patrol later that day.

"Captain," a grizzled veteran replied. "You need to look under the surface. For example, since you took command here, you've been followed the entire time."

Calvin's eyes shifted side to side and he looked all around without trying to look like that. "I don't see anything."

The veteran nodded, "There's a beggar in that alley over there. We think he's a mole for the Thieves Guild. They've been alternating surveillance on you, but we've been here long enough that we know who they are. They'll mix it up every so often, but then we notice the new ones because, well, they're new to Dock Side."

Calvin turned and waved to the beggar. The beggar waved back and hobbled out asking for a copper coins, food, anything the great lord could spare. "Do you work for the Thieves Guild?" Calvin asked.

The beggar started to laugh, but it turned into a wheezing cough. "It's all part of the disguise," one of the guards said.

The veteran who had pointed the beggar out to Calvin clubbed the beggar with the pommel of his sword and told him, "Leave the Captain alone. You've seen what you were sent to see."

After that, Calvin noticed the shadows a lot more. He realized that the people of Dock Side knew when he and the Watch were coming. By the time they arrived, whatever trouble might be discovered, had vanished. Calvin even went out in disguise and saw a darker side of the area.

Wandering towards the warehouse district abutting the river and canal system that lifted Tauran shipments from the ocean to the capitol, he found himself at a very large tavern. Built into a warehouse, the tavern boasted multiple signs in Tanian, draconian, and what Calvin guessed must be Tauran. The signs read, "Welcome to the Kicked Up Boot".

Calvin had never seen minotaurs up close before. One had passed out unconscious on the stoop just to the side of the giant double doors. What must be a bouncer stood guard. It snorted at Calvin, "Quit lurking, human. Either come or go."

I wonder what Malcor would do?, Calvin hesitated for a second. He swept his cowl aside and walked to the doors. They proved heavier than expected and the bouncer mocked him while he struggled to open them.

Inside, he expected bright lights suggested by the windows outside. Curtains draped behind the lanterns leaving the actual interior dimly lit. Giant minotaurs ranging from seven to ten feet tall shoved and jostled each other as they fought towards a giant table covered with food and drink. A few humans nimbly dodged their way through the groups, carrying drinks or food or both. A minotaur turned and accidentally bumped into Calvin. The impact knocked the air from Calvin's lungs and sent him flying against a bench behind him. Some of the beasts nearby pointed at Calvin and laughed.

A human voice called to him. "Hey there, you look new here."

The speaker wore Tanian mage robes but also wore a bracelet designating himself a criminal working off his sentence. "You might say that," Calvin answered. "What'd you do?" he asked pointing to the bracelet.

The mage held it up, "I cast the wrong spell. Well, there was a lot of wrongness. Wrong time, wrong person, and so on. You?" The mage pointed to Calvin's armor under his cloak. "We all do our time. I see your preferred jail is soldiering."

Calvin sat down by the mage. "I'm Calvin. Yeah, I guess but I really like what I'm doing. How do you like penal service?"

The mage laughed. "I'm Eclef. I hate penal service, but I sure do love the wrong things when they go right." He offered Calvin some ale from his pitcher. "My service here is to keep an eye on the non-minotaurs and help keep the peace. It takes a lot to intoxicate a Tauran, but when it hits them, they often hit back. And, then of course, there's the whole honor thing with their god."

Calvin took a drink. "I haven't heard of that."

Eclef pointed to a hand crossbow, easily the size of a smaller human crossbow. "When they feel their god is insulted by a Tanian, they shoot poison bolts at the offender and make bets on how long before they die. Murder's against Tanian law, so I intervene. By the way, don't insult their god."

"I'll keep that in mind," Calvin noted. "Why are there so many? Is it usually this crowded?"

Eclef pointed to a giant shield hanging over the bar. "That's the herald of a world galleon. It's docked off the coast. This is one of the crew's land rotations." Calvin started to ask what a world galleon was but Eclef interrupted him. "Imagine a ship, as big as the Mercy Court, as big as the Grand Bazaar. Imagine it's crawling with hundreds of minotaurs. Now, picture it made of gray and white stone, kept afloat by magic and propelled by weather mages that blow wind into giant sails as large as well, the largest warehouse we have here. That's a world galleon."

* * *

When Rojo said Bomoki's name, the emperor went stone silent. His human form normally so dignified and unreadable, blurred shifting a thousand times between human and dragon. Rojo saw the struggle and looked away. Behind the emperor, the white dragon Ynt'taris growled and bit at Rojo's image in the scrying pool. "You dare mention that name here?"

Rojo waited before speaking again. "Dread lords, the hound declared itself *Bomoki's Gate*." He held aloft the tooth gleaming with a flawless bloodstone at its tip. "Is it possible? They have also crafted bloodstone tools." He turned the fang so they could see if they wanted to observe.

Alerius finally gave up trying to hold his human form and roared into his titanic true self. Rojo winced imagining the impact that would have as everyone in and near the mountain would feel it. Alerius screamed for the histories of Bloodstone to be brought forth with any and all references to Bomoki marked. "Anything is possible with magic, oh king," Alerius seethed. "That man, the betrayer, has nearly doomed my children twice now. The sacrifice paid -"

Ynt'taris cut him off, "Yes brother, we should have killed that one."

The third and blue dragon patriarch of lightning stepped into Rojo's field of view and said, "But the power and risks of the bloodstones were calculated and weighed when that decision was made. No use revisiting it again. The focus must be on the hound. It is either Bomoki, the gate, or both. There is no precedent for a sentient *gate*. It must be Bomoki and he seeks to manipulate us all or else why show himself now?"

Alerius waited till the blue patriarch finished speaking. "We sealed that gate imperfectly. The warped nature of time around the gate prevented perfect magic. Its flaws are why we confounded its location in the flow of time and space," he said to Rojo. "Perhaps that could enable it to have form. We have never been able to find Bomoki who seems equally confounded in time."

Ynt'taris trilled, "To have him here now in my claw, to pop his flesh and see him die a thousand times, it is not enough for that one."

Rojo listened and when the dread lords turned their attention back to him, he asked them. "If Bomoki, no army is sufficient. I had Ana check and she confirmed that since the Second Legion, six hundred years ago, there have been no sightings of Bomoki or mention or clues. Until now. He appears as a hellhound with powers beyond what we have seen in any other hound. And they have learned, at last, to use the bloodstones."

Alerius reached his talons into the scrying water and pulled the bloodstone tooth from Rojo's hand into his throne room. The three dragons, calmer now, immediately human-shifted to better look at it. "A gift to you, my emperor," Rojo said bowing low. "Flawless and perfect and small."

Alerius looked up from the stone and said, "You will have what you need. Send your requisition and it will be as you say. Bomoki must be behind their mastery of the stones. He must not be allowed to teach the others. That must stop."

Chapter Twenty Four– Unter's Stone

As the scrying faded, Rojo slumped back into bed. Fur blankets and a roaring fire chased the high mountain chill away. Jeri sat meditating by the fire, pretending to not eavesdrop. "My inclination is to ask for everything, total mobilization but then I see you meditating and I think I will join you." Though healed, he suffered from the healing lethargy and walked gingerly to the large fireplace.

"The river is troubled," Jeri said. She alluded to those times when, for any reason, the river lost its glassy rushing flow of moment to linear moment. The metallic dragons held a particular fascination for trying to understand and read the future in the river's swirls, eddies, and colors.

Rojo commented flatly, "It means that we are in Bloodstone and are surrounded by the power of many many gods."

Jeri did not move except to reply, "Perhaps. There is a suggestion of a rip curl in the river. Last I saw something like that it, it meant bad things would happen."

Rojo copied her pose and closed his eyes. Instead of the sudden shift out of the river, he let the real world flow and wash away from him until at last he lost that feeling and opened his eyes just barely out. This was the place Dar Shara most enjoyed, the in-between state of being in both. Too calm for him, he forced himself to slowly stand. Jeri stood on a rock crouched down watching a part of the river where the current appeared to bend back on itself.

"Why would time bend backwards?" She touched the curl, small as it was and the current splashing along her hand threw forth images of a magical battle raging somewhere in the world. Rojo observed, "Enough magic to intrude on the river. Impressive."

After a few moments, Rojo looked to the other shore and wondered if Tiamat would come to them. When he re-opened his eyes in the real world, hours had passed and the Queen had not come. He felt refreshed though still not vigorous. He helped Jeri stand and together they walked out. Rojo's guards fell in behind reporting on the actions and activities of the legion since he had gone to rest. When done, Rojo asked about the stones. "We never got to see the one you kept, Dar Rojo. But, Ana has certified two as perfect and flawless. The other one was damaged by your sword though still potent for magic."

They entered the fortress's audience chamber. The three stones sat on a black velvet cloth. They had been cleaned, polished, and each was no larger than a thumbnail. One had a small slice where Twilight Fell had cut it loose from Bomoki's mouth. Rojo picked up and looked at each one. "A priceless treasure trove worth more than all the gold of an empire," he said putting each back down. He faced the group he had rescued. "As a paladin, as the king, I cannot claim any of these for myself. For the empire, I claimed and have delivered the one I tore free from Bomoki's mouth to the emperor. Of these remaining three, there are two perfect and one damaged. If any of you would claim these as your rightful tribute, speak now."

After a moment, Unter stood. The dwarf spoke tentatively and then stronger when he said, "Great King of Morbatten, you found us sorely pressed on the edge of retreat. Knowing now the true nature of the hellhound we faced, our retreat probably would have failed. We owe you our lives. On behalf of everyone, I say that we have no true claim though it is true we found their source. Had you and the dragon not come to our aid, we most certainly would have zero bloodstones."

Rojo met their eyes and said, "I agree but it is still claimable. Whether I allow it, is my call. I sense you have more to say?"

Unter nodded. "My lord Dar, we have found a vein. Each time we approach it, circumstances take it away from us. With proper aid and protection, we'd no doubt have a handful of bloodstones by now. While I cannot claim these, I ask for proper aid and protection to retrieve the vein and operate a proper mine."

Rojo smiled at him. "You can hardly fault the empire for not providing the protection you seek. Ana's records show a level of impulsivity and impatience in you that, by itself, would have made it impossible to fortify your operation. Now that we know for a certainty what is there, now that we know for a certainty you face the first hellhound, yes. You will be reinforced and a proper military expedition sent to guard your operation. As part of that," he picked up one of the flawless stones, "I entrust this to you Sir Dwarf. It remains the empire's property. See that it is returned."

Unter bowed low to the ground, his face on the floor, and expressed his thanks in dwarven. Rojo continued, "The other stone will be held as barter should your vein uncover something better. The damaged stone will be auctioned. The proceeds of that auction will be paid equally to those who faced and fought Bomoki. I will instruct Ana to set the auction for three days hence. Send word to your groups and let word be sent forth."

As Rojo and Jeri left, Unter held his gifted bloodstone. He felt it pulse softly in his calloused hands, like an artery pumped by a heart. The stone remained in his field of view even when he closed his eyes to it. The other dwarves crowded around, each wanting to touch it. As it made its round, Unter's joy grew. "We're going to do it crew! We're going to take that vein and we're going to pull out each and every anything with a touch of the blood to it! We need to get ready. So much to do! With full military escort, so much to get ready!"

Thalian and Helena watched the dwarves as they reverted to their own language arguing about mine carts, digging tools, fortified mining strategies, and the like. Helena chuckled saying, "When they aren't in your face or acting all business, they're kind of adorable."

Thalian laughed, "And when they're adorable, they're still kind of up in your business," she replied. "You're contracted to them?" When Helena said no that she had been assigned, Thalian interrupted her – "Well then, let's go make sure we have a contract with them why don't we? After all, how long have you been here and never seen a stone?"

They sped up to catch the dwarves. They could hear them arguing over how to best use the stone. Some wanted to create a "mining magic stone", others wanted to create an invisibility shield that would mask them from undead. Thalian and Helena listened to them for a while before Thalian could add her opinion. "Hey, just a thought. Since you're so sure about this vein, why not hold the stone as is for leverage against a better smaller stone? Once enchanted, it'll lose appeal to all potential buyers. A Magic Mining Stone sounds fun, but except for operations here and back in the two dwarven nations, you'd really be restricting the stone's appeal."

Unter shrugged. "We'll get it figured out. After all these years here, to finally have one, you can be sure I won't squander it!"

* * *

"Have you seen Malcor?" Tembri asked the fire giant kerchki as he and Seline checked yet again the battlements held by kerchki. The giant shrugged and pointed back to the Temple. Malcor had missed two days of command meetings and Verit had ordered his retrieval.

Tembri took a deep breath and mentally reviewed all the places they had been. He was kind of surprised they had not found him with Ana due to her well-earned reputation with new paladins. He noted Seline's relief that he was not with Ana. In fact, Ana did not know where the knight could be either. Word had come quickly that Malcor was neither with the king at the third fortress nor was he –

Seline tapped his arm and pointed. Ayden was running towards them flanked by Bruun and Revi. On the icy ramparts, Ayden skidded to a halt choking, "Tembri, we found him. Second Fortress," gasping for breath. "Dungeon levels. Fifth sub-basement."

Seline interjected, "Dungeon? Is something wrong?"

"Yes," Ayden said. "Don't know what though. He won't speak. He's punching the walls."

Tembri prayed for endurance and strength and they began the long sprint to the dungeon levels from the Temple causeway. When they arrived hours later, they found Malcor just as Ayden had said. Wearing just leather breeches and boots, Malcor unleashed a rhythmic pounding against the wall with his bare fists. As each fist connected, a glimmer of shade protected his hands, but still, blood dried and cracked and flowed with each strike. The guards seemed relieved to see them.

Malcor spin-kicked slamming his boot into the wall. Indents in the wall from his fists and kicks coupled to dried and wet blood showed he had been here some time. Rivers of sweat ran down his body and empty water buckets showed that he at least drank. The guard indicated he'd been like this for almost three days without resting or sleeping. The guards covered their ears. Tembri heard Malcor pray for strength and then time shift as his left hand slammed into the wall. The speed from the river plus the shadow magic blasted the rock reverberating in the chamber. Cracks splintered out along the wall and some small debris and dust drifted down from the ceiling. The noise blasted the cavern, deafening them.

Tembri reached out with a spell of calming and then sleep and then paralysis, but either Malcor or the growing shadow dragon inside pushed back. His guard was fully up even to the Queen's magic. That by itself alarmed Tembri as paladins trained to be susceptible to their own god's power. Tembri looked at Seline and the others. "Don't interfere, Seline, unless I signal it. Ayden, go and summon the priestess in charge to come."

In a blink, Tembri caught Malcor's next punch, his muscled arm pulsing as he absorbed the blow into his arms and back. Malcor did not seem to notice and keeping rhythm, the next strike flew past Tembri's face and hit the same spot on the wall. Tembri tried to catch and interrupt the pattern, even shifting when Malcor did but the lighting favored the shadows and Tembri could not break the boy's single-minded focus. After what seemed like a hundred failed attempts, Seline signaled him and pointed to Malcor's armor, sword, and gear in the corner. A crumpled letter soaked in blood and sweat showed the fine writing of Malcor's love, Ora.

Tembri dodged the next strike and went over to the letter. Letters were rare as the two kept in touch mostly through the Cystoran falcon always following overhead. Expecting a love letter or worse, some kind of break up, Tembri felt both relieved and panicked when he read of the attack on Ora at Sai's estate. It also contained a small letter written in the hand of a female child, signed with love by Klara. Klara had drawn a picture of Malcor in armor holding her hand.

Sai's actions against the Thieves Guild made Tembri remember a training exercise back when he was a new priest. "My group, with the Order of Fire, we were commanded to retrieve a token from Sai's estate. We did not even breach the walls along the public boulevard. That this Farant got in, incredible." The letter ended with typical language but also an assurance that their unborn son had not been harmed and all was well.

He gave the letter to Seline. Reading it, she said, "I get it. He's working out some frustration that he was not there to help?"

Tembri agreed, "The first love is always the hardest and being a father is difficult for Malcor given his own upbringing. In the time he had with her, I doubt he had a chance to understand how powerful Sai is. There's a reason Sai is called the *Emperor's Son* you know."

Tembri began casting daylight spells into the room to diminish the shadows augmenting Malcor's rage. When the fortress' priestess arrived, she too began bathing every nook and cranny in light. As the shadows vanished, so did Malcor's energy. He at last rested his fist against the cracked wall. He breathed deep gulping mouthfuls of air. "Water," he choked and Tembri rushed to help him drink.

"Mal," Tembri said. "You have to trust her."

Mal took the priest's hand. "No, Tembri. I do trust her. Farant. He's here. Ana told me about an attack before we arrived by someone named Farant. Cor'tanos showed me. There are many Farants. The attack on Ora and Sai was a distraction. Cor'tanos says they want Jeri."

Ayden gasped, "Tembri, a Farant came here with the Nineteenth!"

Malcor's words had a stammering quality to them that cut in and out as the boy's focus faded in and out. Tembri thought about extending Mal's endurance and then changed his mind. "I understand and will do what needs to be done. Leave it to me. Trust the Goddess." So saying, Tembri lulled Malcor into a sleep prayer.

Tembri signaled for the others to pick up Malcor's gear and he shrugged Malcor over his shoulder. To the priestess, he expressed thanks and asked for her to send word to Captain Verit that they were taking Malcor to the

Third Fortress to see the king. "Ask the Fortress Commander to consult with Ana regarding Farant and send any intelligence to me immediately. Also, we must consult with the King about Jeri. What Farant has to do with the king's battle priestess," he rubbed his face trying to make a connection, "I don't know. But, it feels important that we find out."

They fashioned a stretcher, and then Tembri re-triggered the same prayers as before. They ran through the long dark of the dungeon to the surface. Malcor slept the entire time. Even when they broke out to the causeway and ran through strong winds lashed with sleet, Malcor did not move. At the Third Fortress, they placed Malcor into a room with Ayden guarding, and went to seek audience with the king.

They found Rojo standing before an audience of buyers for the captured bloodstones. A small bloodstone the size of a thumb levitated before the group slowly drifting through the audience. It was flawless except for a chipped facet. An elven lord was speaking to the King. Rojo signaled them to wait.

The elf said, "Dar Rojo, Morilon will renegotiate more favorable trade terms with Tania in addition to our offer of two hundred thousand coins. This letter of credit from Tania's Merchant Guild guarantees the amount. The terms can be discussed but we are willing to drop all tariffs for five years."

An adventurer stood to speak next stating, "I am no lord of elves nor can I offer political alliance, yet. What I can offer is treasure, information, and a trade of magical treasure and spell books equal to half a million coins."

Rojo looked at the adventurer and queried, "What is your intent?"

"Might and glory to you, great king. I seek the greatest foes and most powerful of enemies to defeat in battle. The stone will be added to my arsenal and then I would march against Ool." He referred to a blighted ancient kingdom ruled by liches at the extreme northern tip of the Isles.

"Are there any others here who would seek to offer equivalent or better value for this?" Rojo asked.

A Halfling stood and offered six hundred thousand coins. Seeing no one else, Rojo thanked them all. "You three, please prepare your best offers in writing and deliver them to Dar Ana in the morning. I will consult with the Goddess and decide. Should any of you change your minds, send word immediately."

Chapter Twenty Five – Farant's Fell Dance Begins

When Tembri and his party at last stood alone with King Rojo, they bowed and recounted exactly what Malcor had said. Tembri expected more curiosity from the king and his priestess. If they had a reaction it did not show. While talking, a young priestess came in bearing a letter. The king opened it and said, "Tembri, it's from Ana. It details her encounter with Farant ten days ago."

Tembri stepped forward and took the letter, reading it quickly. "So, we face either a group of Farants, or we face a single Farant able to replicate himself."

"Cloning," Rojo said. "A forbidden necromancy. It could explain why Ana was attacked but Malcor says these were distractions from Jeri." He looked at her. She stood by his side radiant and beautiful, and angered. "My lady. How could this involve you?"

She looked back matching his pensive gaze. "Same as always. I'm a gold dragon. It's a curse that dark magic seems to prefer gold dragons as ritual components. That's my guess." Her words and tone conveyed her bitterness at this. "Always hunted for such ugly purposes, when all we want is to let the world be beautiful."

Tembri gave the note back to Rojo. "My king, what is the connection to this and Ora?"

Rojo paused thinking and then said, "I don't know. Malcor is a child of prophecy touched by shadows. His child might have some value. However, as a distraction, it would serve only to distract Malcor and those around him. Why would Malcor think this has something to do with Jeri?"

With no answer, the king thanked them for bringing the message and ordered them to advise when Malcor recovered. "It's an unfortunate thing to be so young, so tried, and have this happening from so far away. Tell him our thoughts are with him and those he loves. Also tell him that there is nowhere safer in all Tania than Sai's estate."

Behind them, the doors opened and two paladins kicked a shackled man into the room. "This is Farant. He joined the Nineteenth at Klenna. He claims to know nothing."

Rojo touched his earring and thought, "God emperor, I have need of the mind flayer. Please send him here." Rojo turned to Tembri's group. "You don't want to see what happens next," Rojo said, dismissing all but Tembri.

Marcello perched on the edge of a tower at least a hundred feet above a stone plaza. Though it was a sunny but cold afternoon, his gray and tan clothing helped him blend into the stonework. A window crisscrossed by metal had almost ended him. Thank the goddess he had found the almost unseen magical script flowing around the bars, the window, and the window frame. Having spent so much time outside Tania, he sometimes forgot how much magic Tania applied to most everything. Security magic like this was easy enough, something to make him fall to his death. Carefully, he studied the situation, and set some hooks that would help him avoid falling.

People down below could not have cared less. The trick would be to either bypass the magic, plus any mechanical traps given the presence of magical ones, or to bypass the window all together. He liked the idea of bypassing the window. Though less than ideal, he carefully unfolded a black cloth. It opened into a round circle of utter blackness the size of a manhole cover. He pressed and tacked this to the wall an arm's reach to the side of the window. Once secured, he carefully slid his sword into it. Retrieving the weapon and seeing no damage, he ever so slowly reached in with his arm and then the side of his face. The black cloth opened a passwall gate and his vision shifted to the center of the tower's room. He had been lucky that his passwall worked with the available space here.

Looking around, he saw some of what he expected. Once his entire head pressed through a silvery spider uncurled from its rest behind his ear. The spider, a failsafe from Sai, was a golem through which Sai could interact with the head of the Thieves Guild. It could also kill him. It regularly bit him delivering an antidote to a magical poison; *insurance* Sai had said *for good behavior*. In this case, the spider turned side to side and then climbed back to his ear. *If the golem thinks it safe*, Marcello thought. He rolled through and carefully undid his climbing tethers, hanging them back outside the wall by feel. The black circle would stand out to anyone looking up. Fortunately, people rarely looked up.

The window from inside looked like any other window but the runes had been worked into decorative paint. It looked like a magic air spirit trap. Marcello stood perfectly still and silent listening. The sounds of the plaza below faded as he focused his hearing to the tower. Something or someone moved somewhere below, but for the topmost room, all seemed still.

The room itself contained a small blood-stained cot, what may have been used bandages, a leather bandoleer containing standard issue guild equipment, and other sundry items. The cot looked odd though. Not so much that a normal person would notice, but Marcello noted the subtle signs that suggested something irregular. Without making a noise, his magical clothing and leather armor shifted to the color tone of the room and he tiptoed to the cot.

Prodding it with his sword, he lifted up the torn blankets and found what used to be a human skeleton though teeth marks, correct that – human teeth marks had worried away most of it. "Farant, what did you get yourself into?" Marcello asked the corpse. He scanned the cot for traps and finding none, carefully retrieved the entire skeleton into his backpack. When done, he arranged the cot to look untouched and slipped out of the tower.

Two hours later, looking like any other servant of Tania's elite nobility, he stood at the entrance to Sai's estate and asked the highly polished silver cast warrior for entrance to speak with either Sai or his priestess. Wordlessly, a large dog of the same metalloid appearance came forward. The warrior signaled for the thief to follow the hound. The estate, from the boulevard, appeared well-maintained and small. However, crossing a barrier, Marcello found himself standing at the entry to a bridge over a chasm dropping to molten fire.

The change in scale and buffeting of wind almost made him lose his balance on the suddenly very narrow bridge. The bridge itself had that same metallic sheen the spider did. Marcello wondered if it too was a golem. A menagerie of animals, monsters, and humanoids adorned and decorated the bridge while Cystoran birds drifted on thermals overhead. A silver palace with a fantastical if military look to it rose up on the other side. He counted four hundred steps to the other side. The bridge, he decided, most certainly was sentient.

Business had never brought him here to the preeminent golem smith of Tania. He marveled at the total lack of climbable surfaces. The walls had nothing for a handhold and though subtle, he felt the presence of magic. This keep could be accessed by invitation or by magical assault only. Like the bridge, he speculated that the walls maybe even the entire fortress could also be a golem.

Entering the courtyard, he noted immediately the absence of accommodations for people, horses, and the like. The entire courtyard served as a plant nursery for exotic flowers and plants cleverly designed into the largest house shrine to Tiamat he had ever seen. Small statues depicting the dragon emperor and his sons served as focal points leading to the natural-looking chapel. Each of the dragon patriarchs had their own respective alcoves in the shrine, a feature not normally seen in the empire.

His guide growled softly at him until he stepped onto a circle of silver runes. Once there, the golem went still. It was then that Marcello noticed the blast marks, almost repaired, but there nonetheless. "My master cannot decide, even now, if it was a mistake to give you a second chance. This entire matter closes with you and your guild's destruction." Ora walked around a trail through the garden towards him. Unlike the first and last time he had seen her, she wore priestess robes and seemed relaxed. Her pregnancy showed more obviously than when she had come in armor and ready for combat.

"Lady Ora, you look lovely as always. Might I say that if you were not already committed, I would want to spend every waking moment with you." Marcello smiled hoping his charismatic charms would favor him.

"You have brought us a skeleton," she said letting her fingers trail along the tips of the many flowers alongside her path.

"Yes, I hope you might revive it and we could learn who and why and how it had died." Marcello noticed that if he moved even a little towards Ora, the runes between him and her brightened.

Ora let a moment of genuine approval show in her eyes. "Follow me to the chapel," she said.

Marcello flinched when he stepped across the circle's border but so smoothly had the magic of this place integrated that it worked without the more obnoxious commands and key words of other estates he had visited. At the chapel, they spent some time rearranging the bones and then Ora began to pray to the Mother.

"The Queen approves of this course of action so I will commune with the dead spirit. If that fails, we will try more aggressive means." More prayers in draconian and then she asked the bones, "Who were you?"

A housewife with a name married to a dockworker, with children - *Oh my children!* The anguish and rage rose like a wave but Ora's prayers calmed it as she asked, "We will avenge you, trust the Mother. Tell me, did you go to the tower by your free will?" *A man whose face was never seen came and spoke to me in words I did not understand. It felt like my choice but I would never leave my home with a stranger and abandon my family like that!* This time confusion and sorrow came first before the rage again.

"Shhh, there now. I am a priestess and we seek justice for your family. I will find your children and see that they are cared for. Tell me, how did you die?" *A blade severed my spine and my body was pulled into a circle, from which the flesh reshaped into the image of the man who took me.*

"I hate him!" the spirit audibly wailed in a hot flash of rage. Its cry turning into a shrieking scream. A mist coalesced above the bones threatening to become undead vengeance, but Ora stood against it and impossibly, she quieted the spirit with promises of justice. Marcello shuddered seeing how the rage came so quickly, how the spirit almost become uncontrollable. He nodded to the statue of Tiamat.

"Rest now lady, find peace. I will bring your family to you. Until then, let your bones stay here and rest." She turned to Marcello. "She was taken by a necromancer and her body was used to create a clone, a forbidden art here in Tania as the clones tend to self-destruct according to the Jade God's wishes." She paused and then asked, "I'm guessing Farant? Tell me, master thief, how does your guild's training approach necromancy?"

Marcello shrugged, noticing the clear diamonds Ora wore as jewelry. He had been struggling to resist the temptation to borrow them. "We do not approach necromancy at all. A few of us train in how to recognize and use magics specific to mages and even clerics, but that is always contracted to the Temple or to the Mage's Guild. We have no records of Farant testing for aptitude or training in necromancy."

Marcello felt himself lose his train of thought again. *If Ora's already checked this and knows this, she must have an entire entourage of priestesses*. He looked around seeing just the one attendant. She looked more like a helper for a pregnant R'Dar. *The golems maybe?*

Chapter Twenty Six – Golems are Strategic

While talking, a Halfling golem walked up to Ora and at her command became flesh and blood to the point Marcello could not tell it had been a silver-white metal statue of one in the first place. She said, "Your profile is Reggie. Go to the docks and find this lady's family. Whatever is left of them, bring them here. Do all this with persuasion, money, and by the laws of Tania. Do not, under any circumstances, reveal your true nature or Sai's involvement. Should it come to combat or risking discovery, you are to flee to the closest safehouse. End of my commands to you."

The Halfling, who had been smiling, suddenly blushed and said, "Oh my! Where are my manners? Hello, I'm Reggie. You must be the master of the Thieves Guild everyone is talking about! So pleased to meet you! Well, I have to be going, errands, good food, and I do enjoy a good stroll in the sunshine. Good bye, dearest Ora!" Reggie blew her a kiss as he skipped away.

"Impossible," Marcello whispered. "I take it Reggie is based on a real Halfling?" He waved his hand vaguely, "Whatever, that has everything needed to pull off an impersonation?"

"Not an impersonation so much as that Reggie was a dear friend of Sai's. Before he passed away, he asked Sai to find a way to preserve his personality, life experiences, and other things. Sai did it as an experiment, that worked. It was good it did because, well, it ensured another far more important one. Reggie knows he is a golem but he also knows now that he is Reggie. Reggie died of a wasting disease and he thought it'd be fun to live on through Sai's creations." Ora watched Reggie skip out of the gardens.

She continued, "Marcello, you will visit the Mercy Court and see if there is a missing person case on file for this lady and her family. Reggie will miss all the other stuff that would surround a necromancer trying to stay hidden. He's still a golem after all. For Farant, necromantic clones self-destruct very quickly. The one that attacked me, based on the date of this lady's death, she could not possibly have been the clone's host. There will be other cases like this where the poor are charmed away. They'll appear as missing person reports, probably to look accidental or whatever. And, Tania does not do so well with criminal investigations amongst the poor. I require human eyes on this matter."

That night, Marcello watched as Reggie walked cheerfully through the dark streets of Dock Side. He noted how, as he drew attention, his appearance subtly shifted to seem friendly to some and then shift to less appealing to those who might seek easy prey. "It's so real," he muttered again.

Eventually, Reggie came to a house and knocked at the door of a tenement. When no one answered, Reggie tried the door and found it locked. He knocked again and then moved to the doors to either side. He seemed to sniff the air and then held a bright yellow handkerchief up to his nose. Marcello had no doubt that the handkerchief was part of the golem's metallic structure.

An age-worn woman answered the third door and Marcello strained to read her lips. She said something about a smell but no one had seen those people in days. She could not remember exactly how long. Reggie walked back to a tavern outside which a group of night watchmen had been talking. Marcello saw him tell his story and they eventually called their leader over. Marcello immediately recognized the type. Probably noble born, but maybe not the eldest or most favorite, the watch leader must have entered some Temple or military group. This type did not like to be challenged. He would have fallen to this position. Marcello noted the shiny armor and still new-looking boots. He made a mental note to find out which of his cells tended Dock Side and its Watch these days.

Reggie retold his story but this time flashed a few coins when the leader said, "We're not on duty now. We'll look tomorrow." A few more coins and they followed him back to the locked door. Marcello thought he read the leader's lips when he said, "I'm Calvin," or Corbin? "Captain here." *Now, isn't that interesting*, Marcello thought. *Newcomer and he's already promoted himself to military rank. Why do I remember the name Calvin?*

Calvin pulled out a notebook and checked something and then gave the order to break the door down. His men shoulder slammed the door, but it held. Marcello saw Calvin pause and then smash a small section of window to undo the latch. *A smart one*, Marcello thought. Moments later, guards carried a small boy and girl out. Their bruised bodies showed suffering from starvation. The gags in their mouths had been there long enough that skin cracked and bled when removed. Reggie touched each of them and helped them drink a healing potion.

It revived the children but only enough. Healing could do little for the depravations of starvation, thirst, and terror. Bloody bruising where they had been tied suggested they had been like that for a least a handful of days. Calvin consulted with Reggie and Marcello read his lips as asking, "You're their uncle?" More conversation, "I see. A friend of the family. I cannot hand them over to you without proof." More talking and the offer of coins but Calvin refused. "This isn't a gray area. These children are suffering. We're taking them back to the Mercy Court."

Looking all too real for a golem, Reggie got frustrated and shouted loud enough for Marcello to hear, "The Judge will not understand why you denied near-death children care and attention from their parent's dear friend! The courthouse at night is not set up to tend to their needs! At least let's find a place I can start tending to them while you handle whatever you have to do!" Reggie continued his tirade until a crowd began forming.

Marcello saw Calvin make a mental calculation. *I knew it*, Marcello thought as Calvin announced for all to hear, "The Watch has rescued these children from a break in. Don't worry, my fellow Tanians! We'll take good care of them and get to the bottom of this. If any of you know when the parents were last seen…"

Marcello followed them. He saw Reggie take the children to a tavern across from the Mercy Court. Marcello turned his attention back to Calvin's notebook. Ora had been correct in that there were more such cases. A small bribe and a guard had suggested more than thirty such cases had been discovered by a new officer, a Watch Officer named Calvin, leading the investigation in just the past week alone. *Pragmatic, efficient, and able to let his command relax.* Marcello wondered if Calvin could be corrupted. He would send word to Khalla to assign a specialist to this new Dock Side *Captain*. It had been a while since the Guild had an easy contact.

During the bustle of checking into the tavern, Marcello easily pocketed the notebook. Like he guessed, it contained a list of names and case references as well as a map of Dock Side showing where people had gone missing. Calvin had made notations for home, workplace, and found murders. They probably made no sense at all to Calvin, but Marcello noted the central proximity to two chapels to the Jade God that had flourished and been wiped out during the Jaden War just ten years ago. His guild had special orders to keep areas like that under close scrutiny.

Kicking himself, Marcello realized that Farant's cell had been put in charge of watching one of the Jaden Shrines. He broke into a sprint moving along the rooftops until he reached a seedy looking but unremarkable tavern. A beggar outside shook his cup and into this Marcello dropped three coins, plink, pause, plink, pause pause, plink. It took a while and they spoke about the weather, local gangs, and rumors. A ragged looking stable boy loitering nearby listened to the coin sounds carefully. When finished, the boy looked at Marcello with eyes-wide and sprinted away with the message: "Arrange for Dock Side Watch Officer "Captain Calvin" to meet one of our contacts. I'd predict the Mage's Guild. Activate Ryvane. Get me everything we know about this Calvin. Also, assemble our assault teams at the Dock Side shrines tonight."

Just before sunrise, the entire Thieves Guild assaulted both of the ruined buildings that had once hosted the Jade God's minions. One lay empty and quiet, as it should. The other held ten of the people in Calvin's notebook. They also found the bodies of several others who had died from the conditions of their captivity. Two members of Farant's cell were killed and their bodies taken. One, which looked like Farant, triggered some kind of magic that disintegrated its body but the other, a half-orc, was killed before it could do a similar thing. The half-orc put up a pretty good fight. Marcello expected that from a member of one of his guild's cells. The half-orc had been an enforcer, and a good one too. Almost warriors and almost thieves, enforcers acted as guild muscle when needed.

They arrived at Sai's estate with the freshly-dead half orc and charred items from the Farant clone just after Reggie entered with the children. Ora's certification that she would help Reggie look after the Dock Side children had expedited their release to Reggie. Ora used a charm prayer to relax the children and to get them to eat. The boy, the older of the two, thought he recognized the half-orc but could not say from where. She put them both to sleep in the chapel by the bones of their mother. The others, rescued by the guild, lay on stretchers in the shrines. Sunlight warm and gentle made it hard to believe winter cold lay just outside the estate.

The half-orc was a mess. Chaos and necromancy had left deep marks to the point that, even after death, mutation still occurred. Ora held her belly and looked over the corpse from a distance. "I'm reluctant to revive this one, even in a shrine. We'll have to take him to the Temple."

Sai appeared, flowing up from the ground, standing next to her. "There is a report from Dar Ana in Bloodstone. A Farant tried to attack her and managed to inflict deadly wounds on her. She revived it after and interrogated it. They also captured a Farant who had joined the Nineteenth Legion. It is clear we are dealing with clones. We need the original. For now, inter and preserve this corpse in case we need it. We do not need to revive it as we know the answers it will give."

Sai turned to Marcello and the other thieves. "I see you working to make this right. I have decided to not obliterate you." The spider golems nesting behind Marcello's ear jumped off and melted into the silver runes adorning the paths and walls of the garden. "When this Farant is either captured or killed, I will release my vendetta claim. I would speak with my priestess now privately. Please see yourselves out and continue seeking out this Farant."

Sai took Ora's arm and walked away. "Ora, I also received word that you sent a letter to Malcor. While I respect the love you return him, you must be cautious with these things. He lost control for three days. He is fine, now."

Sai touched her belly and added, "While we all pray to the Goddess that this child is born easily, there are no guarantees, Ora. Malcor must focus and be focused on his mission. There is nothing he can do for you, for the pregnancy, for the path that brings this child into the world. I forbid you from sending any more letters unless they are supportive, strong, and assuring. You are to leave out any mention of this Farant business. Do you understand?"

Ora looked at Sai's perfect mirrored face and touched it. "I understand and obey, my lord."

Sai took her hand and spread her fingers to rest against his own. "Malcor believes that the Farants – and he says Cor'tanos showed him many – want something with the king's priestess Jeri. Did you say anything in your letter about that?" Even though he asked the question, Sai seemed fascinated by the play of her fingers. "I'll need to revisit my hand and fingerprint construction processes," he added.

"No, my lord. I told him that we were attacked by Farant and that the child was safe. Jeri – she is the gold dragon Rojo brought into the empire? Why would Farant want Jeri?"

Sai removed his hand and seemed to freeze. After a few moments, he said, "I did not yet exist when Bomoki opened the first gate and triggered the First Cascade. The emperor has told me that much was sacrificed to remove the gate to Bloodstone. If not, this beautiful valley would now be Bloodstone. He always says that the absence of the metallic dragons hindered their ability to more effectively fight the Jade God. But, it is the same argument they give about the Dragon Wars and why Tiamat had to leave Tehra. I would guess that Alerius knows gold dragons would have made their magics more effective. Perhaps, there is a weakness still a gold dragon may exploit."

"No gold dragon would ever cooperate with Bomoki, or a necromancer like Farant," Ora said.

"Consider that the Court of Dragons created the gate using gold dragons. That is in the realm of possible." Sai's body began flowing into the ground. "Give a spider golem to Marcello." Marcello talked with Reggie about how much a golem would cost to buy 'with a copy of myself or my girlfriend Khalla'.

Ora caught Sai's hand before he left entirely, but quickly let go. It tingled her skin unpleasantly. "Sai, if Bomoki needs gold dragons, why not just use magic to shapeshift one, or summon one?"

Sai froze for several long moments. A warm breeze blew the garden and pulled strands of white hair across her face. She swept it back behind her ear. After a minute, Sai answered her. "The Court of Dragons made this gate of fragile stone on purpose. Using it, damages it. It is possible Bomoki has tried to summon a gold. However, if during our conversation, a gate opened next to you Ora, would you step through it? If it reeked of The Necromancer, what could that one offer you as enticement to come through? I imagine shapeshifting blocks whatever attribute Bomoki most needs. The more powerful magics always require pure, rather than artificed components."

Ora wanted to ask more questions, but Sai left. The maiden's corpse shuddered behind her. It would soon reanimate. "Get Marcello out of here," she said to a golem.

Chapter Twenty Seven - Valley Town

Ayden stood at the gate to the road leading down into the valley. As soldiers, wagons, and others passed her by, she checked them off on a scroll. With the goal of reaching Valley Town by early afternoon, the Nineteenth and its caravans pressed to make good time. Unlike the road from Tania, each group had to be spread out with army support with clerics and mages ever-present, just in case something happened. As Verit had said, "Daytime is one thing, but Bloodstone is another." The king's banner snapped at the head of the column where he travelled with Legion Commander Verit.

At long last, Tembri and Malcor came walking slowly behind the food train. Tembri ran to Ayden when he saw her. He picked her up, armor and all, to give her a hug and kiss. Malcor stood off to the side waiting patiently. Malcor waved and Ayden wondered how much suffering and pain he could endure before he snapped entirely. He seemed fine if haunted in his eyes and expression.

"When you're done, catch up to us." Tembri pressed a small potion into her hands. "This'll help you run without tiring. We'll be waiting for you."

Long after, the dwarves and their mining equipment along with all manner of tools and material rolled by followed by the vanguard under Seline's command. She dismounted and spoke with Ayden as it rolled by. "You're welcome to ride with me, Ayden. It'd do my charger's spirit well to carry something besides equipment." Ayden left the running potion in her pocket and pulled up behind Seline.

As the Temple's great wall and the door through which they passed slammed shut behind them, Ayden looked down the steep ramp to the valley floor. They talked about Tembri, Malcor, the king, and others from their stay at the Temple. Seline said, at one point regarding Revi, "You must keep me informed about your social affairs, Ayden. I live vicariously through you! It almost makes me want to become an officer! A legendary priest. A high-ranking officer of the Eighteenth. What's next, a Dar mage perhaps?"

Ayden laughed, "Revi. Well, you can be sure that I never set out for these things. Growing up the way I did, boys never paid any attention to me except to tease me. And, well, you saw how Calvin favored you over me. I had given up ever finding love, and then one day, there's Tembri. I'm surprised Revi has not approached you."

Ayden felt Seline shrug through her plate armor. "Maybe, but my mentor, Dar Niss, told me that where paladins are intimidating, a lady paladin is even more so. So, Tembri huh?"

Ayden nodded, "Yes! It seems so odd to be here in this evil place, and feeling so happy. One of the paladins told me that Tania has no stories of a priest-soldier romance. He poked me and said, "I require that your love be epic; a tale for bards to sing about for ages." It never occurred to me that this would be something people paid attention to. No one notices or cares when a priestess takes a lover."

"Now that you mention it," Seline said turning her head to look back at Ayden. "There have only been priests for, what - thirty years? I'm happy to see you happy, Ayden. You deserve it."

Continuing to talk, they eventually caught up to one of the wagon trains with extra horses and Ayden picked up her own mount. They reached Valley Town proper, amidst cheers and confetti, hours before sunset. Already torches and fires had been lit in anticipation of the coming dark. Lights dotted the walls and ran throughout the inner perimeter. Ayden noticed it made a pattern.

Seline pointed to it, "The pattern makes it easier to notice if and when something disrupts the pattern. I heard a vampire once infiltrated Valley Town all the way into the main part of the town."

Valley Town sat squarely in the center of the Bloodstone ridge mountains between the Second and Seventh Fortresses. The mountains rose up all around them with only a slight drop to the pass where the Temple sat. From here, all around, the eight fortresses looked down at the valley. Some close and others far away, each fortress had a different beacon light to help those in the valley orient themselves. A series of springs fed the town and allowed for crops to be grown. The entire town relied on resupplies during winter, but fresh food provided relief from the plagues that came with warmer weather.

Seline pointed out the unique defenses aimed at slowing and moving the undead away from the walls. Seline explained, "In my paladin training, the clerics showed us how very strong undead, like a vampire, can control weaker undead. They have them attack a single point in defense. Eventually, the bodies pile up and create a ramp. It's why the actual fortresses are built high on the ridges. Valley Town, though, is different. It's supposed to be a point of attack for the undead to take again and again, like bait."

Ayden pointed out some spiked wheels designed to impale and throw the undead away from the walls. "Those would never work except against zombies." Seline and Ayden talked at length about the various orders of undead and concluded that zombies must be used as a distraction here. "I cannot imagine anyone, even farmers, here falling to a zombie."

Once inside the walls, they noted how inner walls layered behind trenches, each broken apart by collapsible bridges. Everyone, every single person, everywhere they looked had the signs of regular people going about their business except for their weapons and armor. Even peasant farmers wore metal armor and carried weapons. Being winter, the farmers did not tend crops, but were tending to herd animals and livestock. They noted the lack of children. "Probably not a good place for them," Ayden replied, taking it all in.

They found the command team inside a large plantation-style building with barracks moving away from it like a cross. The Lord of Valley Town reviewed a map with Verit. As they drew near, stable hands took their horses, checked their names, and informed them where they'd been given rooms for now. "Most likely, your commander will move you all around," a young man said apologetically.

Walking up to Verit, he introduced them to Kris, a civil servant stationed here since he volunteered twenty years ago. He had been serving as the Lord of Valley Town ever since. Lord Kris bowed with a good-natured smile and welcomed them, "We are reviewing current military priorities. As you know, the bloodstone vein being called Unter's Vein, is the highest priority. After that, we have a few other high priorities but, as you can imagine, the town's defenses and cleaning out the traps is an ongoing always highest priority."

"After Unter's Vein, what would you say is next?" Verit questioned.

The lord tapped through a list near the map and then referenced a block on the map. "Here, in the valley, rangers have reported sightings of a large hellhound coming and going from a series of tunnels. The hounds are never a good thing." He moved his finger across the valley and tapped the location of the bloodstones. "It's far enough away that we can't cover both at the same time. I'd guess the hound is doing this on purpose to split up what they know is a fresh army."

Verit touched an area on the map, "When I was here last, this was the hot spot. What happened here?"

The lord explained that a hired party of adventurers had managed to breach the lower level tunnels and kill a free-willed vampire coven that had taken root there. "The vampires were nothing special but two of them were native to the Jade God, probably came here straight from the Abyss."

Verit nodded. "And they're all vanquished?" Being Bloodstone, asking if they were dead had proven confusing enough that, by convention, they talked about vanquishing the undead. Merely slaying them never proved enough. When Kris nodded, Verit turned his attention to other areas on the map that he had some familiarity with before and asked how long it would take to march from the Town to the Vein and also to the hellhound's location.

Kris added, "Without powerful magic, night travel just doesn't work. So, it'd take two days to the hellhound and about two days to the vein."

Verit squared his hands, leaning on the table. "We'll set our plans around Unter's Vein. Two days to Valley Town and four days between divided forces, got it? I want the army familiar with Valley Town so tend to your defenses and cleaning the traps first. I'd like to give the Nineteenth a week of that. Seline, you're in charge of organizing it. Everyone does it, even me."

He paused for Seline to make some notes, and then continued, "The command team will meet tomorrow night with the dwarves and we'll figure out the vein. I suspect the hound will put in an appearance there. I'd rather concentrate our attention at the vein than risk not having enough power on hand to deal with these priorities. Ayden, send word to the dwarves to be ready with their mining plans and detailed maps of the area for tomorrow's review." Verit paused thinking and then spoke to Tembri. "You're in charge of the battle priests and clerics. I want a complete list of those with divine powers, who they're with, and at what strength they can turn undead by tomorrow night. If they can't repel or take control of a ghoul, they are to be assigned to a fortress; get them out of Valley Town. Go make ready – all of you. Malcor, stay with me and we'll walk."

Malcor stood to attention and followed Verit's lead as the others broke to carry out their various tasks. They walked in silence climbing to the top of the manor from where they could see the sun slowly setting in the west. In the dark areas between the mountain crags, the mind easily imagined monsters already moving. "This hound Malcor. It's not Bomoki. We know that. If it is trying to draw us away from Unter's Vein, I'd like to know what mine it is using. I've never had access to a dragonshifter before. I want you to fly out tonight and see what your senses can see. If you find the hound, follow and watch but do NOT engage. Should something happen and you feel you must engage, return for reinforcements first."

Malcor accepted the order and said, "Very well, Commander. Is there anything else?"

Verit turned to face the young knight. "No, nothing else though I want you to know this. Since our fight, I have total faith in your abilities. I have heard about what happened with Ora. Though you have my sympathy, I need to know that I have your focus and attention here. There are lives at stake here, not just there. If you know at all, you know that your Ora is safe. Plus, Ora isn't exactly defenseless."

Malcor asked him, "How do you do it, sir?"

"Excuse me?" Verit said caught off guard.

"You have children too. How do you handle it?"

Verit turned away from Malcor to watch the sun setting. "I don't know my children Mal. The priestesses were gorgeous in their way, and I was tired from battle. They probably had orders to bear children with me. If you haven't come to terms with that, I suggest you start soon. It's hard for some. I've seen my children, from a distance, only a handful of times. They know all about me but it's better to have a legendary father than to meet and learn you fail their expectations. I'm sure you can relate because of your own father."

"I want to be part of my son's life though. Ora says the same. It's different to feel so unable to help. All this power and there's nothing-"

"You can do. Yes. But think about if you did. The legendary father swooping in like an angel to save the day whenever something bad happens. Can you imagine? We'd raise generations of children waiting for help rather than helpers. The god emperor watched this behavior and set guidelines around it in the holy scriptures. Above all else Malcor, duty to the empire comes first."

Verit pointed above them to the circling falcon. "Besides, she's watching. If she needed you, don't you think your letter would have read differently? She's a priestess! And a very powerful one at that. Sai, if you don't know yet, tolerates us humans in his quest for whatever it is that motivates him. He barely tolerated a priestess for more than a few months - until he chose Ora, that is."

Looking up at the falcon, Malcor said, "I did not know that. My time with Ora has been limited by training. My life before the Order kept me away from names like Sai."

"There's a lot you don't know yet, Malcor, but someday you will. It's called life. Right now, we need to know about that hound. The king thinks it might be somehow tied to the First and the gate's creation here. You know that story, right?"

"The one about Bomoki? To be honest, I've heard the names and stories but probably not what you know, Captain Verit."

"Bomoki was a mage and a priest sent by Tania to survey this valley and gather intelligence about the fortresses here. He found one of the first ever jade sceptres and became possessed. Due his specialized training in summoning creatures through gates, he opened a gate to the Jade God's throne world right where the great fountain in the bazaar sits today. It almost destroyed our world, perhaps even this universe. That was the First Cascade. The three dragons of the Isles – Alerius of Tania, Oranstakar of Taysor, and Jade of Krentismar, banded together and sealed the gate. This is a different alliance of dragons; Jade is a green dragon like Mallaforax, another patriarch. Bomoki vanished. That was about a thousand years ago."

"So, this new hound could be Bomoki, but it could also be something else. Either way, it means there's an active gambit to open the gate. Do we know where the gate is?" Malcor asked.

Verit pointed going from fortress to fortress in a circle around them. "The entire valley is the gate. More specifically, the dragons enchanted the gate's location to confound anyone seeking. In the same way the tunnels here vanish and reappear in space and time, we think the gate moves as well. The king thinks that the hounds have found a way to bind the gate to a hellhound. Maybe that has something to do with Jeri's eyes. Otherwise, not even the undead could find it except by accident. Every once in a while during a particularly nasty cascade, the Jade God – well an avatar at least - will emerge through the gate. For a brief moment, we'll know where it is. According to Ana, the last time a gate appeared, it was right over there." He pointed to the base of the mountain leading to the fifth fortress.

Malcor looked, expecting to see something sinister but saw only sick forest in winter twilight. "Commander, I thought the hellhounds and the ram's spine wands were the avatars."

Verit quietly answered, "They are. That's how powerful the Jade God is. An avatar can be defeated, similar to what you saw us do in Khasra and Ori. The actual god himself, he came through in the First Cascade. If Bomoki has found a way," Verit shrugged. "It's hard to imagine."

Chapter Twenty Eight – Bomoki Schemes

Farant sat in disguise on a bench at a park in the sunshine. Though winter cold outside, Tanian children ran all around and about throwing snow at each other. The fountain's flowing water steamed in the daylight and Farant winced at its brightness. He wished he could have sent a clone but his entire clone operation had been destroyed. Though he had moved quickly after the attack on his shrine, somehow they had followed up and removed all his other safe houses except one.

From across the plaza, a low-ranked mage in travel-worn robes walked over and sat down near Farant. His hand flashed a sign and Farant knew immediately that this was Bomoki's messenger. He almost jumped up to demand the stone he had earned. In his mind though, an image formed of the mage leaving and going to a nearby tavern, finding a woman with green dye in her hair, and entering a private room. Farant signaled he understood and left seeking the place.

The green-haired woman worked behind the bar. He sidled up to it and ordered a drink, overpaying. He tried to make small talk with her, but she ignored him. Something about her nagged at him though. After an hour of pondering her, a bouncer tapped his arm. "You're making the lady nervous," the huge fighter said.

"Sorry," Farant muttered. "Just thinking. Didn't mean to stare."

"It'll cost money to stare," he said. He took Farant's money and went back to the door. The server sighed with exasperation and that was when Farant saw it. Just above her hairline behind her ear, a chaos mark showed. The flesh-colored tumor – once he saw it, he could not unsee it. When she refilled his next cup, he pulled his sleeve up to show the scales growing along his wrist. He could tell she saw it too.

"I'd like a private room," Farant said. "I have a guest arriving. A mage."

Her eyes went wide and then she tried to laugh as if he had said a joke. "I had a dream about a mage," she whispered leaning into him. She pointed to a curtained alcove in the back of the dining hall. Farant entered the room with her. About an hour later, she brought all kinds of food into the room and sat down with him. "What does the dream mean?" she asked.

"It means that you and I will share this meal. When the elf arrives, he can tell you."

Soon enough, the curtain split open and Bomoki's apprentice stepped inside. He smiled at them both. The girl instantly fell into a trance. "Ah magic, sweet blessed magic and how easily you humans fall under these spells. Dear, show us your chaos marks, and dance for us while we talk."

He cast another spell, "To ensure no one can hear us or see us, physically or by magic. I hear everyone is looking for you, Farant." The girl flaunted her chaos marks and, while they ate, the mage said to her. "Did you know that, without healing, these growths will get larger and larger? If you're lucky, they'll kill you a natural death. If not, you'll spawn a chaos fiend. Most likely, it'll kill everyone you care about before Tania realizes what happened. My guess is that your co-workers notice, if they haven't already, and the Temple comes for you any day now. How'd you get them?"

She had started to show them chaos marks on her lower abdomen. "I like magic too," she said. Her dancing, slow and languid, had made her begin to sweat. "I especially like how I can capture someone's mind. Their blood makes it more powerful and last longer."

Farant swore at her. "You're like a succubus! And you called a bouncer over for me."

They all laughed evilly. The mage said, "Let it be. She's so far down this path, I'm surprised Tania hasn't caught onto her yet. My guess is that by the time anyone finds out, they're too far in her spell. You blank out their memories?"

She smiled and nodded her head. "We'll need some extra noise to keep spies away. Make some noise," he commanded her. The man withdrew a bag and retrieved a red glass sphere, cut and polished the size of a large fist. Loud moans and gasps filled their space as the woman grabbed the doorpost, so she could see outside the curtain.

Spinning it on his finger, he made an expression as if to say, "See?" Holding it, the mage whispered a spell and the girl changed shape from a woman into a small dog. A copy of her continued to moan and grasp at the curtain rod and door frame. It took her a moment to realize things had changed and she immediately tried to protest, but ended up barking. Another spell and the mage's form changed from human to an exact copy of the waitress. He stepped into the illusion and waved over a guard to give him some coins. "We'll need more time," she said lustily. "I'll take you later tonight if you can ensure we're left alone." With a wink and leer, she turned back to Farant and stepped out of the illusion that continued its performance. "I believe Bomoki told you to expect a shapeshifting stone?"

Farant nodded. He could not take his eyes away from the bloodstone sphere. "It's as beautiful as I imagined it would be."

The mage cackled. "These base things are but a demonstration. With a whisper of magic, I do with this stone what it would take me days of study and preparation to achieve. Certainly not something I would use in this manner. Look." He pointed to the small dog and something happened. Farant felt a pulse of magic and immediately the dog stopped protesting. It became more dog-like. "I'd never use magic like this, let alone a permanency spell." The mage placed the sphere on the table and leaned back in his chair. "To anyone listening, we are actively engaged with the girl and having the time of our lives. So, tell me thief, what is the plan to retrieve the master stone?"

Farant sat up and took a drink of wine before replying, "It's in the guild's master vault. I've only seen it from a distance and it is heavily guarded. Had I known the entire guild would attack our sanctuary, I could have taken it then. If you had arrived yesterday – damn. Never mind. We need to draw the guild out and away from it. If the guildmaster can retrieve it for us through magical control -" he asked questioningly. "No? Very well. My plan is to take the entire vault. That won't trigger any traps and we can disarm it at our leisure."

The mage smiled, "I like the idea. The bloodstone then helps you do what you need to do. I imagine the vault is quite big. How would you propose taking the entire vault?"

"There's a trick I learned at the guild, a dimensionalizing magic that will make the entire vault thin and invisible along its side, like a shadow. It makes things two dimensional. Once like that, we can roll it up and walk away. I'll deliver it to you or whoever, you'll take it to Bomoki. Bomoki will teach me more necromancy, and gate summoning! Tell me, how did you?"

A fleeting glimmer of jealousy flashed across the elf's face. "Like you, I dabbled in necromancy. One day, I read about Bomoki in a special book and tried to scry him out. He came to me in a dream. Just like you."

Farant eyed the elf and said at last, "I had to sacrifice lives, my friends, to find Bomoki."

"So did I," the elf replied. "My family." For just a moment, the elf looked wistful and pained. "Never mind, you need a distraction right? Sai's house. Sai will attack the Thieves Guild. Bomoki has decided this is the expedient thing to do. Is it possible?"

"Not anymore. I had a clone of the guildmaster, but he was destroyed last week. Without that, it will be impossible for me to frame the Guild, or even fool Sai. I will make a clone – I beg for your help - and the clone will lead them on a chase. As you said, they're looking for me. While that happens, I will retrieve the vault. I believe I'm a high enough value target to draw their attention. Plus, I've heard that Sai is moving a large shipment of mithril ore into his estate. We need to leak word that another attack on Sai's priestess is imminent and that I'm after his mithril. I have prepared bounty notices for information about Ora's whereabouts to be distributed should you approve this plan. The bounty, my clone, it'll look real. They won't know it's a clone till they have killed it. Knowing this, we create the diversion I need to get into the guild. You know, you should come. I could really use a powerful mage. There will be treasure for the taking besides the master stone."

The mage called the dog over and stroked its ears. "I need to think on this. Leave us now," he ordered. "I'll find you tomorrow. If I am to help you make more clones, see that you get healthy bodies. While you're gone, think about this as the next step in your training. Pain is the path to power, beyond life, beyond death. Death is a doorway. The more painful the death, the greater the power on the other side. Are you truly ready for more power on the other side of that door?"

Farant scooped up the sphere and grinned eagerly as he took his leave. "You know I am, great master."

Late the next day, a small boy looking dazed and confused found Farant and said, "When the time is right, you must disembowel yourself and put the sphere into your core. It will give you the power to endure the journey to Bloodstone, and to control the bloodstone itself. Set your plan in motion and tell me when."

Farant replied, "Noon, in two days." The boy stumbled away confusedly leaving Farant to think about the message. *Is that kind of pain really a gateway to more power?* He imagined cutting himself open and shoving that large sphere into his guts. It hurt to think about, but then, he had come so far and done so many reprehensible things. Disemboweling himself for power, it barely gave him pause. Of course he would do it. The anything for power pact he had made with Bomoki had come with a striking awareness of Tania's long history fighting the undead in all their various shapes and forms.

Sure, Farant thought, *it'd be nice to have a seductive vampire carry me across the death threshold but I'd still die.* He wondered if he could ask Bomoki for something easier to do than ripping himself open like that. The sphere was quite large. It would hurt, a lot. Farant rubbed his hand along his navel and then walked out of the park area back towards his safe house. At least now he knew why the stone had not done anything for him. It needed his pain. *Bloodstone indeed*, he thought with emphasis on the "blood" part of the word.

Rojo leaned over the ancient book retrieved from the emperor's archives. It told the story of Bomoki in as much detail as they had. Pre-Mage's Guild, Bomoki had been a consecrated worshipper of the Mother and skilled in magic. His skill attracted the notice of the blue dragon patriarch known as Spark. Spark began teaching him and, as part of his skills development, Bomoki went to Bloodstone with an early exploration party sent by the emperor. That expedition had started mapping the odd tunnels found there and did preliminary surveys of the ancient fortresses. He tapped a page and Jeri looked over. "This is Bomoki's report detailing the fourth fortress survey. He says they encountered strong resistance from free-willed undead of all kinds. He speculates that the valley must be a colonization attempt left over from the ancient Ool kingdom."

Jeri picked up the book and read the report. "Tania has never had any proof that Ool had anything to do with the valley."

Rojo sat back and sipped at his tea. "In fact, Daryx sent one of his groups to Ool to ask this very question. Not only did the lichlords lack any knowledge of the contemporary world, but they knew nothing about bloodstones. Daryx traded them a bloodstone for the ability we have to occasionally speak with them, but the stones do not work the way they do here in that place. According to Daryx, they're just unusually bright rubies."

"I did not know that about Ool," Jeri answered. "This ever-growing list of things I do not know annoys me, Rojo."

Rojo pushed the tea over to her and smiled. "Do metallic dragons ever tire of not knowing everything? The emperor has opened his entire vast archive to you and offered to answer questions directly if you'd rather converse. As I recall, you rarely go to his library."

Jeri crinkled her nose and said, "I still do not like the emperor. I've tried. I even did that thing you told me about with cotton in the nose. The smell of that place, it is not pleasant. The fire-breathers and my kind never got along, even in the eldar days. Because I am not an eldar, it is dangerous for me." She crossed her arms and then noticed the tea. She picked up the cup and took a sip.

"Would you like for me to request all material about the First Cascade and Bomoki be sent here?" She nodded, her attitude changing from annoyed to happy in a golden flash. Golds hate ignorance and are compelled to know things. "I should have anticipated this, Jeri. I'm sorry." Already past it, she quickly sped through the tome.

"It is not clear whether Bomoki betrayed the Mother, or if the Jade God took him. Do you know?" she asked after slapping the book closed and dropping it to her side.

"The emperor thinks he was taken and became the first mortal possessed by a wand. However, unlike the others, Bomoki seems to have bonded with it and it's now a mutual possession. Or, that the Jade God gave Bomoki free will, similar to the vampire generals. Alerius believes that Bomoki may have his own ascension plans at play and is slowly subverting the wands to his own will; it'll fail, of course. We still don't really know what they are. Ynt'taris thinks they are each a world of life within the Necromancer's dominion. It's unlikely the wand will support something that goes against its master."

She pointed to an official letter just off the table space. Rojo pushed it forward and said, "It's an offer to consult the actual Darkhold about the need for gold dragons. Given the dangers involved with that book, I'm concerned. But, we'll do it; one last time."

* * *

The Darkhold, an Abyssal god appearing in the various realms as a book, documents and captures the essence of any who read it, ultimately possessing them into its chaos domain of pure knowledge. Jeri brought the letter over to Rojo. "We could, but I'm not entirely sure what we would seek." Jeri sat down opposite Rojo. "Necromancy, gates, and the Jade God. Bomoki wants spell components to either affix the gate so it stops moving, or to open it. Either of those things, what other purpose could there be?"

Rojo looked at her until she blushed, and he chuckled. "All this time and I still affect you so? Jeri, we could ask the Darkhold what spells require gold dragons, but I'm more inclined to ask it to locate this hound calling itself Bomoki's Gate and attempt its capture or destruction. With the Orders, the Guild, and Daryx's teams... it should be easy. The Goddess knows we have taken so many others and killed hundreds more."

"To do this, what would Ana require and is it worth it? We cannot open the Darkhold here without her." Like the sceptres, the Darkhold keeps a tight connection to its Abyssal throneplane right in the center of that dark place. The offer to consult the Original, rather than a copy, meant they would need help, luck, and Dar Ana. "Unless someone else has?"

Rojo sighed and ran his hands through his hair. "No, Jeri. Ana remains the only one who can manipulate the original Darkhold. Daryx has gotten close. I have gotten close. So, you know about Ana?" he said taking another sip.

"She hasn't been exactly discrete in her desire to bear your child. Isn't it part of your emperor's ways that heroes have children, sometimes many children? From what I hear, you are a rare exception to deny his decree."

He shrugged. "The Queen is approving of our union for sure, that I know. Unlike my brothers in arms, I feel I am not required to obey. The Queen approves, but does not require it. So, I choose not to. Interestingly, Tiamat supports and protects me in my choice to serve her with chastity."

"There is no part of your maleness that wishes this as well? Ana will accept nothing else." Though Jeri hoped Rojo would say no, it pleased her to hear him say no.

"I have more leverage with Ana this way." He turned his attention back to a number of messages stacked up near him. "She'll come around. After all, this is Bomoki. If you look at her writings in the archive, you'll see she is near obsessed with finding, capturing, and imprisoning that one. She even has a pedestal and alcove constructed for him in Alerius' menagerie of monsters."

Jeri shook her head and muttered that she did not know that either. "All this, it is in the emperor's archives? Why not the Temple's?"

"The emperor does not release the writings of the Circle, the lords, the Dar, and the high priesthood until after their permanent departure and a period of time for the patriarchs to review the writings. Some things, like the Sister Prophecy, the god emperor does not wish widely known at a time when there are still many families seeking to chip away at Kell's power, legacy, and position."

"I see. And Bomoki – the emperor has additional materials about that one?"

Rojo picked up another letter and while scanning it answered her. "We have incomplete records from his training in the empire. Many were destroyed in the First Cascade. The Darkhold has given us additional information but at a certain point, the price required became too great. The Darkhold knows we want this one more than any other, while at the same time, Bomoki serves an abyssal god. You can imagine the price."

Chapter Twenty Nine – The Vault

Marcello wiped his scimitar on the cloak of the eighth Farant they had run down and killed. His associate quickly went through the clone's pockets. "There's a pattern here," the guildmaster whispered. Suddenly, he had it. A shrill whistle and the group retreated taking the body into the shadows of the streets. Most people around them had barely noticed the killing, so smoothly had the violence occurred. The few that had carefully continued about their business.

They assembled in a safe house, far away from any known guild locations. Marcello eyed his co-masters and lieutenants. A touch along the wire woven into his hair holding small clusters of bloodstones bathed the room in a soft magical glow. Here and there, those of them bearing Sai's spider golems lit up with a soft red glow. After several moments, Marcello said, "Very well. Sai may know about this but no one else. Why, tell me, is it that after weeks of investigation and routing out Farant cells do we suddenly have a spike in clones being captured? I want to know your thoughts."

As the group began speculating, Marcello drew a crude map on the floor with chalk and began noting where they had killed this most recent Farant and where other Farants had come from. Thanks to Officer Calvin, they had near instantaneous word of any missing person cases and so finding the origin of the Farant's had grown almost easy. When he had finished the map, he looked at them. Someone else said just when he was about to, "There is no pattern?"

He nodded. "And that means that Farant sent these to be found. He's hiding something."

A lieutenant stepped forward and took the chalk. He added to the map the general locations of areas of interest – safe houses, the emperor's mountain, shrines, powerful and wealthy elite. As she did it, she thought out loud saying, "Maybe there is a pattern though if we look at this way." In different color, she began tracing light lines from the origins to Sai's estate. Nothing. But, Marcello encouraged him to think and began writing the names of the places where they originated.

The lieutenant snapped her fingers and said, "Look!" She tapped a few of the locations and said, "Each of these is tall enough to see Sai's estate!"

The excitement of solving a riddle settled over them and they began looking to see if that theory applied to any others. While an interesting exercise, none of the proposed theories seemed all that interesting until at last Marcello saw it - the guild's actual headquarters appeared excluded. He kept this observation to himself and instead asked one of the golems,

"Please request to know if there are any matters of consequence occurring at Sai's estate in the near future. While we do not need details…"

The spider resting by his ear jumped forward and Sai's voice came into the room as if he stood there. "Tomorrow, we receive a shipment of many tons of mithril-bearing ore. The shipment itself is a distraction. Though real, one of the wagons contains a vault in which a suit of armor and bloodstone gem have been placed for augmentation. Though I cannot tell you the client, I can assure you that this shipment is precious and the value of the armor and shipment are dwarfed by the value of the stone. Do you believe this is at risk?"

Marcello looked at the map and thought about it, thinking to himself, *No, but Perdition is at risk. Is Farant after something there? Does he know about the vaults?* He said out loud, "We would be wise to consider it at risk, my Dar."

A lieutenant asked, "Will your priestess Ora be supervising this?"

Sai's voice came to them, "She supervises all my dealing with the mortal world. Being at risk, I will increase security. I am pleased with your findings. Continue."

Marcello closed his eyes and smiled, "Ah, praise instead of threats at last!" His group laughed with him, though a bit nervously as they knew Sai might be watching them still. The spider pulsed a few times and then leapt back to Marcello's ear. He could not help but covet the golem as he focused his attention on the group. "We must be prepared for something to happen with Sai's operation tomorrow. Prepare your cells. I leave coordination as you see fit but let's be sure that Sai knows who is where so we avoid any unnecessary casualties. We cannot afford to treat Dar Sai the way we do other members of the Dar."

As the group split up and went their separate ways, Khalla followed him until he called out her lurking. "Master, you do not believe the shipment is at risk do you?"

He smiled. Khalla had long been his favorite to succeed him because of her natural ability and intuition to see these kinds of things. Plus, they dated occasionally. "You should be a psychic," he said. "It might be, but so soon after the attack on his estate, I'm sure that Sai has made arrangements we cannot even fathom. I feel sorry for anyone or anything that crosses his path."

"So, what's the play then?"

"Farant wants something in the guild vault." He said it as a simply stated fact.

Khalla thought about it for a while and then said, "So -"

"He's probably there now, or at least is casing it. I would have done the same thing. It's too bad there are so many valuable and powerful things in our vault that I could never decide which one I'd steal were I so inclined." He laughed. "And then there are all the trapped decoys."

After a moment, she said, "I'd probably take the Book." She referred to a highly detailed compilation of tricks, traps, and techniques acquired, drawn, and documented over hundreds of years by the various guildmasters and specialists.

"Too specific to us, my dear. Too specific. While no doubt valuable, the buyer for such knowledge would no doubt be another thief. Could you trust them? Were you a thief, in say Morilon, and someone presented that book to you, would you risk buying it? After all, the dragons would come for it." Marcello looked around and then declared, "I'd go after the Sideways Amulet."

"Easy to sell, easy to use if you keep it. I can see that working," she chuckled. "I hadn't thought of that. Have you ever used it?"

Marcello gave her that look meaning he could not say. "The real question here is this though: what does a necromancer want with our vault?"

The two moved quickly through the shadows, dodging and weaving so that no one could follow them to the guild. When the guild at last came into their view, it looked as they expected. Empty. Though Marcello pointed to where a shimmy had been inserted into a trip plate to deactivate one of the brighter, louder traps. Barely noticeable, he more easily found the other bypasses. "No clone could do this," he whispered to Khalla. "The real Farant is here."

They moved through the courtyard, careful to re-activate the traps as they went. When they at last entered the main hall, they found Farant hunched over a body. He saw them and jumped back into darkness as the body lurched upright. Marcello's thrown spikes arced into the shadows where Farant would be if he were still a normal thief. Marcello knew he'd miss but it was worth the chance. Half of being an agent like this was knowing when to apply pressure to a quarry to keep them off-balance.

The body belonged to a young thief in training, barely past his first rites in the guild. They dispatched it easily once they realized it was turning into a clone and was both dead and past divine revival. The waste of time, training, recruiting, it all made Marcello angry. Anger rarely got to him. The guildmaster had spent the later part of his career detaching himself from emotion as most of Tania's business for him required skill, judgment, and precision. With each step in their hunt, his anger grew.

Farant's trail led them further into the guild towards the vault. Khalla signed that the vault would slow their target down but they needed to go faster. Even with magic augmenting them, because Farant had the same magic, they failed to gain and had to be careful in case of any traps Farant laid down. No Tanian-trained agent would attempt this without anticipating some type of resistance. Farant would have known he'd face Marcello or at least the guild's lieutenants.

They rounded a corner in the broad hall and came to a stop abruptly as a line of fire erupted in front of them. Though Marcello's cloak magically protected him, Khalla did not have such a cloak. Marcello had to leap and pull her aside under his cloak as the flames washed over them. He imagined hearing Farant laugh. Mentally counting the seconds, he thought about asking Sai's spider golem for help but changed his mind. This started in the Guild and he would finish it. Marcello deftly withdrew a small vial from a chest pocket and cracked it onto Khalla's lips saying, "Drink."

After a few sips with most of it spilling down her chin, her body began to gasify. "This potion will turn you to gas. Go around or over the flames and meet me the other side." The air from the fire distorted her form and she nodded. Marcello pulled his cowl tightly around his face and sprinted through the fire intent on recovering any lost ground. As he suspected, the wall of fire was fairly narrow as most item-based magics limited the effect's scope and power. He came to an intersection and knowing that this part of the guild had enchantments to confound those seeking the vault, he took the correct turn. Just in case, he whispered, "My lord Sai, please let the golem stay here in case Farant seeks to follow. This area is heavily enchanted to confuse and disorient." The spider was gone from his ear just like that.

At his fastest sprint, he reached the vault chamber before the massive heavily magicked doors moments later. The entire thing masked the true vault but Marcello had an uncanny feeling that this needed to play out. Farant, as a cell leader, would know about the confusion magic but should never have seen let alone entered the vault.

Marcello cracked his knuckles and walked up to the fake vault and its door. He made a show of looking for a secret lever that Farant would expect to disarm any traps. The entire door was a mix of mechanical and magical traps. Behind the door lay more traps. Anyone foolish enough to breach this door – and then Marcello heard it. The light footfall and forcibly regulated breath of a well-trained thief. A gentle *snickt* sound told Marcello that Farant probably had some kind of venomous crossbow aimed at him.

"Marcello, so long have I waited for this very moment. Look, your back is open to me and I sit here with my finger on a dwarven crossbow enchanted to kill a thief. Orcus is good to his servants indeed!"

"You'll never enter the vault if you kill me," Marcello said. "I was trying to remember the combination. I figured you'd have found your way in already. Or, was this not your plan?" Marcello turned around slowly his hand just glancingly activating a hidden button.

"What could you know of my plans? Or how long I have waited for this day? Years of planning have gone into this, even into back up plans should Tania figure us out. None of it matters now anyways." Something was wrong with Farant. Marcello could see some kind of skin disease rotting away his edges and the rest of his flesh had a membranous quality to it as if he had soaked too long in warm water. "Don't do anything we'll both regret. I'm here for one reason only. If I have to kill you, fine. But you don't need to die. There are – alternatives."

"Like serving the ram's head? No, I think I'll pass. Besides, I've died enough that your little crossbow doesn't scare me. Do it, if that's your purpose. I'm still waiting for the *Open the vault or die* ultimatum."

Farant smiled. "Oh Master Marcello, you're going to enjoy this. You see, my plan requires me to die. I'm going to do it right here with you watching. You'll like it no doubt. And no, I don't need the Vault opened. I just need to be sure that this Vault contains what I need. So, tell me – what is the best way for me to know if the Vault contains what I need?"

"You could ask. Or force me to open the door somehow. I doubt either gets you what you want. But, while you think about that, tell me. Why the attack on Ora?"

Farant's eyes glinted. "You cannot possibly imagine the power of Orcus. To gain power with my great god, you must bring gifts. The blood of a priestess He hates and the unborn child of the paladins He hates most, priceless gifts that would elevate me beyond. I gain favor even in failure. Never mind. It's just the beginning."

Farant brought up his hand holding something round covered by cloth. Marcello felt and then confirmed that a bloodstone lay under the cloth when he squinted his eyes and saw the telltale glow. "Have you ever used one of these, Marcello? They amplify powers in wondrous ways. I'm just barely learning necromancy but, watch. I'm going to try a spell that should normally make me immune to traps. Let's see what happens with it magnified!" Farant whispered a spell.

Marcello felt disappointed when the bloodstone continued to look normal. However, the area felt off. Then, in a blink, Sai's spider golem appeared on the bloodstone, paralyzed. Farant smiled. "I'm sure there are other surprises here. Let's see what else there is."

Damn, Marcello swore mentally. His mind began racing through all the various traps. The spider had been a powerful ally. Moment by moment, various spring and magical mechanisms on the door behind him glowed and then began stretching towards the sphere bending around the guildmaster. *Please, not Khalla*, he prayed. *I need to stick to my plan to get Farant to take the wrong vault.* He steeled his resolve.

Marcello swore when Khalla's gaseous form sped down from overhead. Farant laughed a dark and cruel laugh. "Hello, friend," he said as her form degassed and she collapsed at his feet. After several pulsing bends, the many and various traps burst asunder and flew to the sphere. Farant looked at Marcello raising his eyebrow. "How interesting that you yourself did not break against this stone."

"I'm just here to work. It's always been a very clear prerogative in the guild. We don't much care nor do we interfere except unless something like this happens. It's all business to me. You could drop the bloodstone and leave this stupid quest right now. We could call it all a misunderstanding. You'd still have to answer to the law of course – what are you doing?"

Farant had withdrawn a gore-encrusted dagger from his belt and looked about to plunge it into Khalla's unconscious body. Marcello's firm resolve and apathetic demeanor nearly cracked. Instead, Farant flicked the spider off the stone and, spinning the blade with a flourish, plunged it into his own lower belly. "Death is but a door – opening," he grunted as he pulled the knife up to his rib cage. "Power eternal," he gurgled as the knife cut into ribs. He began coughing blood.

Marcello began laughing. "You're right. I am enjoying this. Idiot necromancers." As much as he enjoyed watching Farant commit suicide, something in Marcello urged him to stop Farant: *Idiot necromancers coming back from death*, he cursed mentally. Marcello jumped forward aiming to kick the bloodstone away. But, Khalla rose up and blocked the kick. Farant fell back to his knees and dropping the knife, began pulling the stone into his bowels with one hand, while the other pulled away at muscle and intestines in the way.

Marcello recovered from Khalla's block. With concern, he noted the sickly green light possessing Khalla's eyes. *Never a good sign*, he judged. He saw Farant cradling the stone inside the gaping wound and pointed to it. "That'll be bad, Khalla. Resist this -" but he had to instead dodge frighteningly powerful knife attacks she launched at him.

Without any sound or words, Khalla attacked him with all her skill and might augmented fully by this possession, whatever it was. Marcello called out to Sai for Temple help but the spider looked broken. Behind Khalla, veins and gore tendrils snaked out to caress the bloodstone. Marcello almost got knifed because of the nasty sight of Farant's abdominal muscle and organs pulling the stone into the cavity… he dodged and threw Khalla to the side. It gave him enough time to vomit. The stench of rotting flesh filled the antechamber.

It looked very painful but Farant seemed held there on the brink by the same power driving Khalla against him. Dropping back and summoning his cutlass to his hand, Marcello feinted to the side and then drove the cross guard of his sword against the side of Khalla's head. He hoped to knock her out. It worked! Her body dropped unconscious. With years of training kicking in, Marcello whirled and blindly threw his cutlass at Farant. He prayed to Tiamat for a true strike.

He frowned when he saw his sword impale a giant hand attached to a quickly growing and shapeshifting Farant. The wet cavity of blood and gore in Farant's center now glowed with green light and Marcello felt the rising activation of the bloodstone. Farant pulled the blade out of his hand and dropped it on the ground.

"I see," Marcello said. "The stone allows shapeshifting and like all bloodstones, it amplifies whatever magic-casting ability you already had. Nice. My stone is really more geared towards my job, but you know. To each his own." Marcello placed a healing potion in his mouth, ready to break it at a moment's notice and summoned a different sword to his hand. "It's a good thing we're in a place big enough for your size to matter."

Farant swept his hand through the corridor aiming to catch and smash Marcello against the wall. "Size isn't always an advantage though. Just ask the other Tanian lords. We all prefer speed." He jumped over Farant's hand and stabbed his sword in the thumb knuckle. "It makes me happy to hear you still feel pain." Farant tried again and again to smash the nimble thief. This went on for several attempts, each ending with Marcello wounding Farant.

"I don't have time for these games," Farant growled. He tackled Marcello, who easily dodged by jumping over his head and slicing open his scalp.

But, Marcello was not the target. The vault doors were. A red sizzling and crackling of energy happened in a moment and then ended. Digging a massive gouge in Farant's shoulder, Marcello turned to see the entire vault had gone flat. Marcello swore, remembering that he had placed the Amulet in a different vault, intending to return it later. Farant had seen him do it. He swore again but at least Farant had grabbed the false vault.

Worried about losing time, Marcello tumbled forward and shoved several firebombs into Farant's already-healing shoulder wound and leapt off saying, "I see. You already have the Sideways Amulet. Okay. You win. Look, I don't want to die. You have the vault. Let me get Khalla out of here -" He noted that Farant was not actually healing, but shapeshifting the wound closed. Magical changes to shape did not really work that way, but then – bloodstones.

Farant used his large size to grab the vault corners and squeezed, squishing the vault into a tube. He then turned to swing the rolled up vault like a polearm. Marcello jumped over it marveling at how the entire vault had suddenly become a weapon. He'd trained with flatspace enough to know the potential, but they had never done it on this scale. The god emperor entrusted it only to the guildmasters, as a device of last resort. Farant should not even have known about it.

He cursed the bloodstone. Flatspace had an odd property with magic whereby weight became meaningless but the weightiness of magic still applied as a force of momentum. The guild vault was full of magic. He thanked the Mother that Farant did not know about the secret and very real master vault hidden nearby. The rolled tube pulverized the wall it struck and shook the guild to its foundation.

Marcello stayed long enough to score a few hits but during one of his attacks, he feinted and dropped a small rune tile on Khalla and the spider golem's body. When Farant next swung the vault at him, Marcello triggered teleportation and then one of the fireball gems embedded in Farant's shoulder. He reappeared in a safe house with the golem and Khalla, a spout of fire following them. Wounded enough that he could have used it, he instead spat out the healing potion and poured it into Khalla's mouth hoping it wasn't too late. Her color immediately improved and she took the first breath he had seen in some time. He didn't know what to do about the spider golem. He guessed Sai would want it back so he placed it carefully in a protected container.

Out of crisis and feeling quite pleased with himself, he took a deep breath and walked over to a secret cabinet all his safe houses had. Popping it open, he reached in until he felt a smooth glass ball. "Marcello Haltri," he stated his name. The ball increased its warmth and shortly thereafter, a disembodied voice responded in his thoughts asking, questioning. "Please inform the Circle's priestesses that the Thieves Guild's decoy vault has been stolen by Farant, that Farant has bonded with a bloodstone and now possesses the ability to polymorph himself, that Farant is a disciple of the Jade God, and that Farant has taken the Sideways Amulet. I would speak with the Circle."

Marcello waited, counting Khalla's labored breathing until it turned into the deep sleep of convalescence. In his mind's eye, he imagined priestesses initially expressing disdain for doing anything for the Thieves Guild, and after reluctantly hearing his report, leaping into action and running all about. It reminded him of chickens from when he was just a peasant boy. After some time, he felt a compulsion to go to Sai's estate. He smirked and said back, "Maybe one of these days you can make it so these work both ways." Immediately a chastisement came back to him, an image of him pledging himself at the Temple to Takhissis and how he had chosen instead the path of the guild.

He checked on Khalla, pleased to see her in deep sleep and hastily wrote a note explaining she should stay here until he or another lieutenant came to get her. Looking down at his boots, he touched the Hastening rune he'd used earlier when chasing Farant and then sprinted off to Sai's estate. As he moved out of the safe house, he pulled his cloak over his head and took on the dull appearance of any man out and about the city at this time. Moving so fast, few would even notice, he hoped to avoid any encounters with more powerful guardsmen.

Unlike the first time, Marcello found Sai's estate on the boulevard unmasked. Gleaming spires and fire mote plainly visible for anyone to see. The narrow bridge waited for him and without pausing he sprinted across noting the growing pulse of energy and no doubt powerful magics tracking him. When he reached the courtyard, he found Sai standing to the side of R'Dar Ora. Large and pregnant she sat on a bench by the fountain. The workmanship of the garden would make an elf proud but equally jarring was the human mage chained by slender wire to the ground in front of them.

Marcello shook his head at the contrast between idyllic splendor and the gory near-dead body of Bomoki's apprentice. The wire had cut into his flesh and appeared locked against bone. Someone had severed his finger tendons and gouged his eyes out. On closer look, he bore the signs of chaos warp and necromancy. One of the spider golems sat in his mouth, his tongue thick with venom from multiple bites. A woman showing the makeup and clothing of a common tavern worker knelt to the side sobbing, near hysteria. Ora let Marcello take this all in before she stood and touched the tavern maid with a sleep prayer.

Marcello dropped to his hands and knees, fist to the ground and waited for Sai to speak. Instead, Ora said, "We received your report. Our caravan was attacked by this mage along with a Farant clone. Though a dire battle, our cargo is safe thanks to your forewarning. Sai further removes all other claims against the guild and your officers."

Marcello almost swore out loud. The claims being removed were good news. *They left me, personally, out of that. I'm still on the hook. Stupid guildmaster job.*

Marcello watched Sai but the silvery golem's face remained impassive and statue still. "Though this mage has refused to cooperate, his continued pleas for aid to the Jade God have resulted in the unfortunate need to prevent his speaking. However, we did learn of and found this woman. She had been shapechanged into a dog. She saw the mage deliver a bloodstone sphere to Farant three nights ago. We have kept her here in case you had additional questions or need." Ora gestured that he could move freely. "While you do so, Sai wishes to thank you for retrieving his spider golem. We are glad you did not let it be destroyed."

Marcello withdrew the crushed spider golem and presented it to Ora and then walked over to the sleeping woman. He recognized her as a drop out from a guild class some years ago. Though she had had some talent – he could not remember why she had dropped out. "I remember you," he said. He did not remember her name. "I don't need to ask her anything. She did not make the cut for agent training in my guild."

Behind Marcello, Sai took the spider from Ora and kissed it. At his kiss, the twisted metal of its legs straightened and the tiniest hint of mist transferred from Sai to the golem. A second later, it twitched and then sprang back into animated life.

Ora took the spider in her hand and asked it, "You have completed a scary quest, tiny spider. You have pleased Sai. Tell me, what would you like to do next?" The spider pulsed and then after a moment, it enlarged in Ora's hand. Its form morphed from being a spider to that of a small bird. Ora laughed. "I see! You wish to fly! Well chosen!" The small bird hopped around and then jumped into the air where it wheeled about, somersaulting and diving as it whirled. A burst of emotional pleasure and pride shot out from Sai to the point it interrupted Marcello's musings about the woman.

"Your golems are aware enough that they *desire*?" Marcello asked. Sai nodded. "I didn't know such a thing could be created. Tell me Sai, what needs to happen that I may acquire such an ally?"

Sai said nothing until the awkward silence became uncomfortable. "The Circle would like to speak with you. They are ready and waiting for my signal." The thief nodded and then around the courtyard, the silver ground rose up into golem avatars of the Circle. Marcello returned to his formal bow. The emperor's son Blaze asked, "Your report had a cavalier attitude about losing a Tanian artefact and whatever other powerful magicks your vault contained. Explain yourself."

"Not cavalier my lords, factual. Long have I and the masters before me considered the possibility that a guild of specialists skilled as we are, might go after the Vault. Whether for bragging rights or for some other purpose, this was foreseen. As such, the Vault contains treasure but it is all cursed or weaponized as traps. We make a big show of placing powerful items into it, but they are replicas. The actual vault is safe and contains only those items and artefacts that one of you or the emperor himself has required us to store safely. The guild's master stone is intact and safe."

He then told the story of his encounter with Farant, the powers Farant had acquired, and how he attempted to learn the purpose of the attacks. Dar Rojo asked about gold dragons, but Marcello shook his head, "Gold dragons never came up in our brief combat." He told how he had cut Farant's shoulder and placed several firebombs into the wound.

Blaze said, "We commend you and your forebears' wisdom, Marcello. I did not know about the Vault being a ruse. This gives us great assurance in your guild's ability and future. Why did you not detonate all the fire bombs?"

"Because Farant bonded with the bloodstone, I did not wish to destroy my guild as the actual vault is in that nearby area. The risk crossed my mind that the bloodstone may crack when the firebombs detonate. Also, I was hoping Farant would tell me more about his plans. As it is, we can detonate the bomb by speaking the activation word whenever we want. I recommend doing so before he returns to human size and notices a large cluster of gems embedded in his shoulder."

The tortured mage squirmed about testing the golem's holding him. The group looked to Reznor who responded, "The firebombs given to the Thieves Guild are intended for distraction, opening doors, and though they can be used in combat are not intended to kill those of Farant's stature and experience. Farant will notice and feel a lot of pain, but bonded with a bloodstone, he'll survive. These are not the most powerful fire gems."

Marcello looked around and seeing approval, spoke the activation word with a grin. "Somewhere, Farant just had a most unpleasant surprise and reminder that we can still hurt him," he said with a most noted cavalier flair. "And, you mean to tell me there are more powerful firebombs?"

Daryx spoke now and said, "Of concern to me is the ability to use flatspace for a vault that size. Farant must have had -"

Sai spoke and so rarely did he speak that all went silent. "The mage," he pointed. "Gave Farant the magic to retrieve the Sideways Amulet. Folding dimensional space, though possible, drains bloodstones. It's also why Farant could not take the vault until after emboweling the bloodstone. In your report, Marcello, you noted that Farant reached the vault before you. Most likely he tried and failed to flatspace it. This is why in all our history we have ever only made one such artefact. The stone given to Farant began to fracture when he flatspaced the vault. It will only endure so long as the bonded bloodstone lasts. The captured mage here believes it will only last until Farant reaches a necromancer or Bloodstone. Until then, the Jade God is using the stone to feed energy to Farant."

The man growled trying to speak but the golem spider bit his tongue again. Only at that moment did Marcello notice a shadowy form behind the near dead man possessed of a tentacled head. He almost asked if that were a mind flayer, but then realized that of course it was a flayer, extracting thoughts and memories. Dark creatures like this, extricated from the Abyss and terrible places of the world, had some useful purposes. Marcello shuddered at the thought of a creature like that picking apart his memories, sampling this one like a fine wine, discarding that other one as junk. He ran his fingers through his sweat-soaked hair, and tried not to imagine flayer tentacles probing his skull.

Sai continued, "Farant believes the Jade God has given him not just a priceless and flawless stone but one beyond anything the empire could find. This makes sense to Farant because the jade one's minions swarm throughout Bloodstone. However, it is the Jade God's power making this possible and the flatspace magic for the vault is taxing. If the bloodstone is destroyed before they consciously choose to open it, the vault will return to its normal size." Sai pointed to the mage, "The flayer notes that all the bloodstone does is channel necromantic energy to Farant to support shapeshifting. Bomoki struggled to make this, flawed, bloodstone. The mage remembers many times when Bomoki thought he worked on the bloodstone when in fact, he had begun repairing the gate."

Blaze said, "Very good. So the gate is not useable. That is good to know."

The flayer made a series of muffled sounding chirps and trills and then Sai added, "The flayer speculates that Bomoki lacks the patience to correctly handle and enchant a bloodstone is because the Jade God requires the gate's repair above all else. Also, each time Bomoki uses the gate to bring hellhounds through, the gate relocates as per Alerius' enchantment. It takes years to find the gate, sometimes many years." The flayer stopped and they heard a loud cracking sound. Blood began oozing from the mage's hairline in streams down his face. Sai continued, "I have ordered the flayer to extract the totality of his memories. They'll be transcribed by the Mage's Guild and distributed to you all when complete."

Though Sai turned away from the gristly sight, Marcello could not help but stare in horror as the flayer's tentacle's latched onto and then pulled the head in opposite directions. A beak within the flayer's face began to chew into the brain. The man began to scream the kind of terrible cry that haunts those hearing it, forever. Marcello felt his skin go pale white. "Ora, please silence this part," Sai commanded.

Marcello spoke to take his mind off the fayer – *Is that worse than being soul-sucked?*, he wondered. "The vault itself is trapped many times over. When they finally open it, traps and golems inside will all activate. Farant will face a small army," he laughed. "Though nothing like the golems here at Lord Sai's. Remember, this vault was to prevent thieves from getting to the real vault. It was also a test for my own guild leaders. As such, it will cause problems for but not defeat a hellhound."

Blaze interrupted. "Understood, Marcello. You have exceeded our expectations for your guild. This will play to your favor. Marcello, in the name of the Empire, you are commanded to assemble your most masterful guild and join forces with Daryx and Sai. You will follow but not engage Farant. Harry him and harass, but let him believe he is outwitting and escaping. See where he takes our vault and be ready to join forces with the Nineteenth Legion in Bloodstone. Our father, as does King Rojo and our Temple, believes this is part of a plan to affix the Bloodstone Gate and allow entry to our world by the Jade God. Farant will most certainly take the vault and the Sideways Amulet to our hated enemy Bomoki. If this is the case, we can be sure of these things."

The golem representing Blaze held up a finger and said, "One – we will have many hounds assembled and will perhaps be able to strike a debilitating blow to them. Two – The gate must not be affixed, *ever*. If it is, we must be ready to protect the empire, perhaps the world. We cannot risk another Jaden War so soon after the last one. Three – this Farant must be made an example of. We desire him alive for public trial and judgement that prevents him from falling into his god's dominion. However, I will accept his death and capture as an undead if expedient. And lastly, your guild will recover the Sideways Amulet."

Marcello pledged to do as commanded.

Chapter Thirty – Calvin's Investigation

Calvin ran his hand through his hair, long grown back since leaving the knighthood and the Temple's stricter ways. The fireplace smell hanging in the air, and his tankard of ale tasted so good. He eyed his odd Halfling companion Reggie, while another tankard refill appeared for him and his team of watch. "Another toast to the Captain of Dock Side Watch!" Reggie called out. The ale had a quality to it that Calvin had almost forgotten, the taste of expensive spirits. He swished it in his mouth, feeling the money tumble past this throat. It made him aware of how little money he had to his own name.

"Reggie, I need to get more of this," Calvin said pointing vaguely between his ale and Reggie's pouch overflowing with actual gold coin. "I forgot what a proper ale tastes like."

The armor of his crew had a few rust streaks and he made a mental note to get that cleaned up. At Reggie's cry for another drink and round of toasting, the rest of the tavern erupted in a chorus of cheers and jeers. The Watch only rarely earned praise in the poorer sections of Dock Side. This region made up an odd mix. The river connected to a lake that connected via a series of locks and canals to another river leading to the sea. No one knew how long the locks had been there and many speculated the dragons had built the entire system. It was a common way of saying, "No one knows" as the "The dragons did it."

Reggie slapped Calvin on the back. "We're going to be great friends you and I sir! Great friends!" Impossibly, Reggie downed what must have been his sixth tankard. Calvin still had his second in hand and a third untouched in front of him. He had a hard time remembering from where this Halfling had appeared. Though not uncommon in Tania, most Halflings stayed near the market or in their own province. Maybe he came from one of the wealthier estates overlooking the lake, the falls, or maybe even just liked hanging out with seedier humans? The area right next to the actual docks was not desired by anyone. Dock workers and their families survived in the shadows of the minotaurs bringing up sea cargo. The presence of the minotaurs made dock living dangerous, and then there was always the ever-present threat of some lord's deal going astray or turf wars between different business interests. "You're going to rule Dock Side, Calvin! Another toast to Calvin – Mayor of Dock Side! Here, here!"

"I still don't understand how or why I would want this," Calvin muttered into his drink. Reggie laughed as if Calvin had said something incredibly hilarious. "I'm serious!" he protested. "It's all politics and trouble. Anything with the minotaurs seems likely to get you killed, demoted, or jailed. Anything with the lords, same. Anything with the peasants becomes scrutinized by their lord. It's a mess. My crew tells me the Thieves Guild is all over this area as well."

"It's an opportunity," Reggie pleasantly replied. "Think. No Captain has ever lasted here more than a few months. Why do you think that is?"

"Because of the politics." Calvin burped and put the tankard down. He could not afford to get drunk. It had never been his style anyway.

"Wrong. You are dead wrong. Because of their attitude. The people here are trained, even the minotaurs, to expect a political response. You need to show them something different."

"If not politics, what then?"

"How'd your father handle Klenna?" Reggie countered.

"He organized the various groups, communities, businesses, trades people, each group - however that group defined it, into their own thing and then he governed the leaders of those things. But, he had a Watch too."

"And… that Watch was -" Reggie prompted, waving his hand in circles over his drink.

"Also its own group. Dock Side does not have a mayor though. You keep saying Captain. I don't remember the Watch as a military function."

Jubilantly, Reggie slapped Calvin on the back and said, "No, it has the Watch! You are the mayor, effectively. As mayor, you can also be Captain. Sure, it's not military but if the people want to call you Captain, and it makes them feel better about their poverty – why not let them?"

Calvin looked around and noted how no one paid them any attention. "If I'm mayor how come no one knows it?"

"What, do you need a parade? A grand ceremony? This is much better. C'mon, you were in the Temple for a while. All the rules! Think about it. If you had a big announcement, people would expect a political solution to everything and it'd have to be done in the same style, cost, and theater as the big announcement. Is that effective?"

"It was for my dad, but I see your point. As Captain," he rolled the title around in his mouth with the ale and liked it, "I have similar executive and judicial power as a mayor because there is not one here. Okay, Reggie. So what's first?"

Reggie smashed his tankard against Calvin's. "I think you know already, but I'll give you a hint. The two Jade God sites, both are here in Dock Side. Both were part of the disappearances and murders here. Everyone, even the minotaurs, knows about those. It creates a common reference point for all the groups, even you. Start there." Reggie slapped a few gold coins on the counter and said suddenly very loudly, "Barkeep, Captain Calvin wants you to keep the tap flowing till this money is spent!" Amidst more cries of thank you, applause, and catcalls, Reggie stepped back from Calvin and left.

After letting his men enjoy Reggie's gift, he called them outside. Word had spread about free drinks and on a cold night like this, the tavern's crowd swelled. The night air felt great and Calvin stretched waiting for a few tipsy stragglers to get in line. Looking them over, he felt pleased that only one was too inebriated to continue. The rust in their armor caught his attention. *Yes, we'll have to fix that*, he mentally promised them.

He cleared his throat noticing how a crowd had formed around them watching. "We've done a good job so far men, but there is more to be done. I know you usually don't work nights, but I'm offering bonus pay for an extra night shift. I know you're tired," he pointed to the lone too-drunk watchman. "And, you're too drunk for this," he said. "Go home. To the rest of you, I'm pleased with your restraint against the Halfling's generosity. Look, I'm tired too, but part of our job is ensuring that Dock Side is safe. It'd be easy to pat ourselves on the back and go home to a night's sleep well earned. I can't let that happen though. There is something bothering me and I can't put my finger on it. For loyalty, for bonus pay, to ensure the safety of Dock Side, we are heading to the warehouse district." The drunken watchman tried to fall in, but Calvin pulled him out. "I need you alert, even when we're celebrating. Remember this when you wake up. Go home." He shoved the drunken watchmen in the crowd around them.

Someone called out, "Tiamat bless you, Captain!" Others did as well. Calvin felt his cheeks blush realizing it wasn't the ale. It felt good to be acknowledged for his bravery. In the Temple and at the Soldier's Fort, even Ayden, it was always critique. "Lift your shield, move faster, swing your sword like this..." It never ended. Praise always came with a lesson and he realized that his homesickness was not for his family or the familiar sights of Klenna. It was to have people know him, to openly praise him.

Calvin led them east in a loud march that told honest citizens that the Watch had come, and warned evil doers to at least pause for a while. However, as they drew closer to the District, he ordered a quieter march. This area had a well-earned reputation for ill. Based partly on the utter lack of living space, spacious warehouses, and minotaurs, it lacked normal foot traffic that might keep it civilized.

A single tavern here catered to any who came but unless newcomers knew about the minotaurs, they did not last. Unused warehouses quickly picked up homeless with a few charity organizations providing warmth, food, and assistance. So long as they kept away from the minotaurs, the presence of those monsters provided a certain balance of power, not really security, but an expectation of violent escalation. Being close, but not too close, afforded some protection in this place. Because of winter, the lower level rivers and locks had all frozen. That meant only a few of the combative monsters would be around. They preferred their ships though the tavern hosted a small shrine to their devil god Baphtomet.

The Watch quick-stepped into an area between some dilapidated warehouses where an old library had once sat overlooking the river and lake that formed Tania's basis for ocean trade out east to the coast. As warehouses and the unruly minotaurs had enacted their own form of violent justice and worship, the wealthier citizens moved away and the human sections fell into disrepair. During the Jaden War, the library had become a haven for undead. Everyone knew it and knew to stay away. When they arrived, Calvin noted the fresh signs of combat from Marcello's attacks against Farant just days back. He signaled for caution though he could not imagine the Thieves Guild leaving any traps or surprises behind. No doubt they were being watched already.

Entering the library, they found blood stains and damaged stone attesting to the fury of the battle fought here. Some of the men clutched their pole arms and looked around. The place felt haunted. Though snow fell clear and bright in their lanterns' rays, it seemed to have a greenish tint to it when it fell into the library. At least it looked that way and Calvin struggled to see white instead of green. That color had forever been associated with the Jade God since the empire's early days. He felt his neck hackles rise and, realizing his men would be feeling it multiplied, he ordered more lanterns and torches lit.

Pointing to two of his men, he said, "Go back to HQ and requisition more torches, lanterns, and have porters bring four cords of wood for a bonfire. Send word to the night shift watch that I'm extending bonus pay to them as well. Tell, Command that I want laborers hired immediately. Now go."

As bright lights began pushing the shadows back, Calvin ordered his men to clear the rubble and debris. "We are looking for something missed. Remember, the fight that happened here was a fight, not an exploration. This place has been under scrutiny and watch since the Jaden War. We're looking for something else. Something someone fighting for his life or with different orders may have missed."

Several hours later, the night watch and then laborers and then hired homeless from the nearby warehouses joined the effort to clear debris. Wood arrived and a bright bonfire helped push winter and the eerie shadows back. Calvin ordered food and drinks brought in. Stone by stone, they cleared the library moving all of the fight debris out to the plaza. On a hunch, Calvin ordered them to start pulling up the floor's stone slabs.

Two days later, a worker began shouting for Calvin. Not having slept except for naps, Calvin leapt up, suddenly alert, and ran over. A well-worn and cracked tile shifted under the worker's pick ax and Calvin saw the fine working of magic to make the stone seem nondescript. Pry bars and muscle lifted the stone, and a few tiles next to it, to reveal a dark, ominous, and steep stair case. Blood stains and frozen gore dotted the steps and sides of the passage. The smell, the warm smell wafting up from the darkness made everyone around Calvin gag. The smell crossed rotting flesh with manure.

Calvin grabbed a scarf off one of his watchmen and soaked it in wine. The dark hole in the floor of this cursed place made his skin crawl and his heart race. He almost decided to wait for a paladin or priestess to come. With the irony of his paladin training not lost on him, he waited for their stomachs to calm. Calvin wrapped the wine-soaked scarf over his mouth, and then walked down. "Hello? Captain of Dock Side Watch Calvin here. Is anyone there?" With no answer, he hefted his Kaia shield and entered cautiously.

The smell intensified, but the steps did not last long. Just a few down and his lantern's light peeked into a large circular chamber. It was not original to the library and the rough work suggested haste. The ceiling stood propped up by metal and wooden poles in places. He could see dust falling from those walking overhead. Casting his eyes round about, he saw that metal bars formed cages around the perimeter. All but two lay empty. Gore, now steaming in the cold air from above, held strange flowers.

Two of the cells held children. Their bodies had long since rotted away leaving only bone and tissue from which flowers grew. Their sickly pink and green flower petals seemed to bend towards the light of his lantern. The petals had a fatty appearance that reminded Calvin of gristle. Dried and dead petals had fallen in front of the corpse remains. He imagined that, when they fell, they made a sticky wet noise. As he stepped closer, one of the flowers coughed up pollen making Calvin jump back. Two missing children that had never been found hung limp and dead along a wall. It had taken him a while to rebuild his investigation notebook when it went missing. The other missing people were probably down here too.

"You okay, boss?" one of his men called down.

"Yeah, it's nasty down here. I need more light." At his words, something behind him stirred and he whirled raising the shield to cover but no attack came. Instead, he found an alcove behind the stairs. Edging the shadow back with his lantern and holding his sword now, he stepped carefully around calling out. He found a minotaur chained to the ceiling. The beast's legs ended in wrapped stumps from which flowers grew. Both its eyes and its tongue had been gouged out. Flower buds opened there as well. No cage for this one, but chains held its hands aloft to the ceiling. Rotting chairs barely supported its legs. Razor swords anchored to the wall behind the minotaur tipped just at its shoulder blades. If it tried to escape or pull the chains out, its full weight would collapse the chairs or impale it on the knives. Flowers had begun growing in the infected wounds of its back as well.

Only the faintest movement suggested it lived. "Are you alive?" Calvin asked. A soft guttural growl came out. "Hey!" Calvin called up. "There's a survivor down here, a minotaur. I need runners sent to the Tauran Shrine at that one tavern. Also, send another runner to our closest shrine with word that we need a healer now! Where is that extra light I asked for? Bring it now, but stay in the center of the room."

Calvin tried to give the minotaur water but whenever he came close, those flowers would cough pollen. He talked to the minotaur instead telling it that they would help him. A Takhissis priestess, young in her practice arrived first. She gagged on the smell but named the flowers *Corpse Flowers*. "They draw strength from the dying and are cursed," she said.

"Can you help him?" Calvin asked pointing to the minotaur.

She shrugged and attempted the most basic of healing spells. At her soft prayer, the minotaur's color improved for just a moment before one of the budding flowers fully opened its petals. They saw the vitality sucked out of the prisoner. "I wish we could take him down from those chains," Calvin said.

They waited, doing their best to minister to the Tauran. After an hour, they heard loud footsteps and the scattering of the guard above. A minotaur swore. Minotaurs struggled with Tanian but often tried to speak it. Thickly accented, a voice called out, "Who is in charge here and dares to summon me from my worship?"

Calvin walked up enough to see a black robed Tauran priest of Baphtomet. Calvin bowed and made the sign of their god, which he could tell pleased the giant minotaur. "Great lord, we have found a near-fatally wounded member of your nation. He is dying and has been tortured. I am Captain of Dock Side Watch, Calvin."

The intimidating priest leaned forward and stared at Calvin. Calvin tried to bravely match the gaze. After a nerve-wracking moment, the large beast snorted, blowing Calvin's hair back, and stepped forward down the stairs.

Calvin backed down the narrow space and, when he reached the cell, he pointed to the holding areas. "We have done what we could but this is beyond us. There are five dead humans here. Only the minotaur seems left alive. I am loathe to command Takhissis' blessings on one of yours without permission by your great god."

The priest nodded. "I am Path, first of Baphtomet's soldiers on the world galleon *Vortex Strider*." He made their god's hand sign, which Calvin hurriedly made too, and continued, "If this shameful creature's life is worth it, I will heal him." So saying, he reached up to the chains and ripped them out of the ceiling. Immediately the chairs collapsed. The pain killed any awareness left in the tortured body. It fell face forward twitching.

The priest swore at it. "Weakling. Tell me, do you have a name?" When no answer came, Path commanded, "I am your god. You will answer me!" He kicked the ribs paying no heed to the pollen spilling to and fro. The kick flipped the body over and Path saw the amputated tongue and flower protruding from its mouth.

Looking annoyed, Path said, "Avert your eyes, humans. This will offend your fragile senses." So saying, Path grabbed the minotaur's jaw and squeezed, twisting. Bone cracked and grinded, but when Path let go, the flower fell dead and a perfect jaw and tongue replaced it. "Do. You. Have. A. Name?"

The minotaur tested and then whispered hoarsely, "Windwalker."

Path fell back to his haunches and crossed his legs. "Windwalker! Truly a name worthy of healing! The great god must decide the truth of this." He withdrew a pouch and dumped a number of carved bones on the ground in front of Windwalker's face. He grabbed the lantern from Calvin and looked at the bones for a minute. "Windwalker it is. Baphtomet," he said, making the holy hand sign watching to ensure Calvin did too, "will heal you enough to tell us your shameful tale of capture. How were you taken and nearly killed by Orcus?"

The pronouncement of the Jade God's name was forbidden by law, custom, convention, and practical history. In this fell place, it echoed and resounded. Calvin prayed and saw the priestess praying too. "Weak mortals," Path chastised them. "To be scared of a name." Turning his attention back to Windwalker, Path added that "His name is a strong navigator one, of good omen. He would not have earned such a name without a very great feat. Windwalker, you will tell us," Path said. "After you recover your strength and eat. Humans, I require you to carry Windwalker out to the tavern called The Wave. Make it happen."

Calvin ordered his team to come. They improvised a stretcher and carefully, with ropes and men, extracted Windwalker from the basement. It was days before Path summoned just him and the priestesses to the tavern.

Chapter Thirty One – Gold Dragon Eyes

Calvin's Watch found Windwalker looking healthy and well, if still skeletal from starvation. Apparently, Path had decided to restore his legs and eyes too. Windwalker had that overly-healed and still weak demeanor common from trials like his. Seeing Calvin for the first time, Windwalker raised a mug, the size of a small barrel, and said, "I understand I have you to thank for my restoration to health. May Baphtomet," Windwalker and Path made the hand sign of their god, "bless you with a thousand women and ten thousand days of glory!"

Calvin bowed and also made their god's holy sign. "I am glad for the Tauran empire to have Windwalker returned to them. Tell me, what did the necromancers want with you and the others?"

"Captain Calvin, they wanted to know if Minos would take a contract for gold dragon eyes…"

Calvin flipped open his small leather portfolio containing parchment. It had become a habit to write things down and this one seemed important. "I told them they needed to speak with a captain, priest, or noble, that as a navigator, I cannot take contracts – but they wanted to know also if I had ever seen a gold dragon and where. I told them stories of far distant continents and trading partners and rumors of gold dragons in faraway places." Calvin realized that he was understanding the minotaur perfectly and noted the large ruby ring twinkling on the monster's thumb - magic translation. He shrugged. It made sense given the lack of minotaurs around in winter. Calvin thought he could wear the minotaur's ring as a bracer.

"Did they ever say why they wanted a gold dragon, let alone its eyes?" Part of him could not believe that he, as Captain of the Watch, was asking a question like this. Tania would have no gold dragons. This was the empire of colored dragons. "After all, Tania is the last place you'd find gold dragons."

Windwalker snorted and said, "Your mother's feud with the metallic dragons make this an ideal place to find gold dragon EYES, scales, claws, fangs. Were I wanting those, I'd come here for sure."

Calvin thought about and then made some notes. "So, eyes. Is there anything you can tell me about that?"

"They really wanted eyes, not a dragon. When I told them about the rumors, they made notes just like you do. They were quite hopeful that either here or somewhere Minos touches, we could bring them only the eyes, just the eyes. I asked about other dragons and parts of dragons. They had no interest. Only gold dragon eyes. They said they would free me, restore me, make me wealthy and powerful beyond what I could imagine. But, I only know about waves, tides, stars, and storms. I know nothing about eyes. I already told this to Path and a red-haired priestess -"

"A high priestess was here?" Calvin interjected surprised that no one had told him this. A Dar would never come to Dock Side unless – "Did she say anything about the gold dragon eyes?"

The minotaur chuckled, a frightening sound from something so large and fearsome in appearance. "She said that I must try and remember and would be rewarded if I could recall anything about WHY gold dragon eyes. She and my great god Baphtomet – [hand sign] – spoke in length about some kind of magic to help me remember."

"Did this priestess have a name?" Expecting R'Dar Ora, Calvin had to scratch her name out when the minotaur said *Dar Shara*. Calvin choked. "The High Priestess came here? You're sure it was Shara?" *Why would The High Priestess of Glass come here for this?* For some reason, his friend Malcor came to mind again. He dismissed it.

Windwalker did say this about the gold dragon, "When they were finally satisfied that I could not help them with the gold dragon, they told me they would let me go. If, I brought them Tauran or other adventurers that could deliver on it, they'd be paid with a priceless small and perfect bloodstone ruby."

Calvin left Windwalker and thought on their conversation as he slowly meandered his way to the Mage's Guild. Not much could compare in value to such a bloodstone. Given the ability to harvest gold dragon eyes meant an implied ability to slay a gold dragon, he guessed that maybe an entire gold dragon could be worth that much. It hurt his head and none of his training had helped him understand the gold coin value of a dragon's body parts.

The Mage's Guild rose up from a small hill in the heart of the city near where the grand stairs climbed to the Temple At Morbatten. Its many towers lanced the skyline and glittered with magical lights. Like so many of the grand monuments in Morbatten, the Guild served as a landmark and a warning. Its shape and form suggested indomitable might.

The Mage's Guild's gates, always open, bore a draconian inscription that read different things based on who looked at it. Calvin read it as, "Great magic begins in the soul and thrives during living dreams." He wondered what it would read to Malcor. A spacious boulevard ascended slightly from the gate to the main structure. Only mages and members could go to the other towers. Though visible, they had no path or road for Calvin to use. As he drew closer to the main building and tower, an acolyte walked up behind him and greeted him, "Hail Officer of the Dock Side Watch, Sir Calvin. How may the Guild serve?"

Continuing to walk to the main domed central building, he replied, "I want to check prices for spell components as part of an investigation. A murderer was seeking to acquire a certain component and offered an overly rich – to my mind – reward for it."

Responding, the mage noted, "Of great value to you may be very different for a mage."

Nodding, Calvin said, "That's why I'm here. I imagine the Guild contracts out for exotic components all the time. If any contracts have been placed for gold dragon eyes -"

The mage caught his arm and said, "Gold dragon?" When Calvin nodded again, they blinked from the boulevard and reappeared in a tower's entryway. Stairs spiraled up before his eyes, hanging in space in a way that made Calvin wonder how the tower stood at all. Calvin's eyes struggled to adapt so quickly from the cold brightness outside to the dark warmth of the tower. His escort gestured for Calvin to make himself comfortable and said, "One minute please while I get you a master."

Calvin could tell they were very high in one of the towers. From an archway at the side, a woman entered. Calvin immediately noticed her voluptuous form barely hid by what appeared to be translucent mage robes tied at the waist.

He started to rise but she interrupted him and said, "No need, Captain Calvin, such a strong alliterative name; I love it. I'm Ryvane, a master mage here. I'm fully briefed and ready to answer your questions. Please be assured that we are very interested to exchange information with you. Word has reached us of the minotaur you rescued and the considerable embarrassment you spared the Thieves Guild." She focused briefly and a leather-bound book appeared on the small table between her and Calvin. "What do you want to know?"

Ryvane had long red hair that, like a priestess, flowed down in thick strands to drape her back and front, reaching nearly her waist. Gold wire and jewelry adorned her soft body. Calvin realized he was staring and averted his eyes. *I've been around too many malnourished women lately*, he thought.

At the same time, Ryvane studied Calvin. *So, this is the watch officer Marcello wants us to secure – friend of the new hero Malcor, and paladin drop out*, Ryvane thought as she took in Calvin's handsome appearance. The note from Marcello had indicated she should do *whatever it takes* to win him over. Looking at him, she quickly considered what to offer him as an opener - wealth, love, power, fame…, and decided that she would choose love. Calvin seemed corruptible but if she proved wrong, it'd create problems. Matters of the heart were so much more flexible in matters like this. Calvin had said something, and she smiled seductively at him. "Please, I was thinking about gold dragon eyes. Say again?"

Calvin stated, "The minotaur was tortured basically for information about how to obtain gold dragon eyes. I found that odd since to get just eyes, you'd need the entire dragon too. So, your guild came to mind as a group that might contract for such a thing, maybe even have some. The minotaur was offered a flawless small-sized bloodstone for just the eyes. Is that normal? Does the guild have gold dragon eyes, or were you approached by these buyers?"

As he spoke, Ryvane flipped through the ledger. For a few moments Calvin watched her, noting how he had never met a lady mage before. He found Ryvane meeting his gaze and she put her hand on her hip, mimicking a brothel worker. Bluntly, she asked him, "What are you staring at?"

"Oh, nothing. Well, your face actually. I'm from Klenna. I've not met many mages and the few I have, they were men."

Ryvane laughed and stood up, twirling around and did a curtsey. "Tell me Captain, do I meet with your approval?" As she spun around, her face transformed to a mimic of an old man with vast white whiskers and bushy eyebrows. "Or should I look like this?"

Feeling he was being teased and wondering if he had crossed a line, Calvin did his best to recall all the charm he had as a boy in Klenna and replied, "The whiskers, no. But the real you? Yes. A lady mage should, I suppose, be judged on her magecraft first. So far, summoning the book, the illusion magic, it's very impressive that you so casually do this."

She rose from curtsey, as herself, and smiled. "Of course, with magic, more things are possible." She gave Calvin her hand and at his touch, she became even more alluring, beautiful and sensual woman he could imagine. She stepped backwards from him until her back was against the tower window.

Suspecting this was all part of a test, he kept hold of her hand, and followed. When she stopped against the window, Calvin bowed to her and kissed her hand. "As they say, beauty, and magic I suppose, is only skin deep."

"Who says that?" she asked teasingly. Suddenly, Ryvane was back. "I can tell the Temple training you received really paid off. The mages do not put much value on appearances. After all, I can change the way I look just as easily as I could change the way you see me. So, let's talk dragons.

"Based on our records, some years ago, one of our mages contracted for gold dragon scales. The Adventurer's Guild took the contract and after a few years declared it impossible. Bearing in mind that, if a gold dragon is similar in size and power to the god emperor's family, an adult would have approximately thirty-nine thousand scales. They shed damaged scales at the rate of about a hundred a month, more if they've been active like fighting or mating. It's part of how they heal and remain armored."

"Why did they declare it impossible?" Calvin sat down and enjoyed the feel of a chair supporting his armor. He had been meaning to ask if he could remove it, even while on patrol. It's not like he would ever need it in the capitol.

Ryvane noticed he had stopped paying attention to her, and a small footstool ran over to him. "Lift your feet up and relax, Captain. I can't imagine walking around in armor all day. Sometimes," she pointed to her robes and Calvin realized that appeared to be all she wore, "it's a chore to even wear something this simple. So, where were we? Oh yes, part of the covenant all of our ancestors made with the god of the Forsaken Isles was what?"

She tested him again. Calvin easily recited it, "No assassins, not like Merakor's at least. A balance of power amongst dragons. Check that, amongst eldar dragons. No dark elves, well, Daryx is a notable exception. The thri-keen people to be left alone. The island of Mondsa to be left alone as a sanctuary."

"Very good Calvin," she sauntered over and sat down on the arm of his chair. "Any child should be able to remember these things. But, think about it. If there must be a balance, why does Tania contain so many eldar dragons?"

"I always assumed there are other fallen dragons elsewhere. But I think you'll tell me otherwise." Ryvane pushed Calvin back in his chair just a bit with her body. She seemed to be softly casting some sort of spell. Part of him worried about it but when firm fingers began massaging his neck and back through his armor, through the chair even, he just closed his eyes and relaxed. "That feels like nothing I've ever felt before," he moaned as the fingers turned into a fist and began manipulating his shoulder blades. "How are you doing this?"

She giggled and leaned forward again to whisper in his ear, "It's a simple *spectral hand* spell. Mages use it for spells as a sort of third helper arm. But, I like to use it for this." She slid off the arm rest into his lap. "Now, pay attention. The Jade God disrupted that balance and the emperor obtained consent to bring others here so long as they only fight against the Jade God. They are essentially visitors. So, now extend this new balance. What does any of this have to do with gold dragons being impossible for the Adventurer's Guild to find?"

Calvin wrapped his arms around her waist and began playing with her hair. It was hard to concentrate. "Well, metallic dragons and colored dragons do not really get along. So with more eldar red dragons, the gold dragons all left the Isles?"

Ryvane twisted her body so he could see into her robes. "You're close. Gold dragons, like the one that watches over Taysor, are watchers, knowledge seekers. They rarely get involved in much of anything though they'll help those they consider worthy of aid. You have to use your paladin eyes, Sir Calvin. Why are there no gold dragons?"

His eyes wandered to the Soldier's Fort west of the emperor's mountain. From his seat looking out the tower's window he could only see the bottom snow-covered foothills and the start of the road climbing to Alerius' throne. Ryvane's breasts made it hard to focus. "The reds killed... No, that can't be it. It'd disrupt the balance of power. Did the golds join us?" He had a tentative question mark in his voice.

Ryvane kissed his cheek. "Well done, Captain! All the gold dragons on these isles have converted, left, or were killed ages ago. The Adventurer's Guild could not find any because they are either part of the empire, or are not here. Crossing the oceans for a gold dragon scale is impossible without imperial sanction or more money than our guild offered. Therefore, impossible."

"What is the value of the bloodstone I described? Would it be equal value to a gold dragon eye?"

"It'd be priceless, worth a hundred gold dragon eyes. The guild would give up all its treasure to acquire such a stone. Though Alerius places a value on them for trading purposes, the magical value of something like that is many times its monetary worth. The minotaurs would know that. Part of Tania's alliance with Taurus is based on the bloodstones. Windwalker would know this as a navigator." Ryvane paused, realizing she had said too much. *I shouldn't know this or that name*, she mentally swore at herself. She hoped he did not notice and to ensure he would forget, she let her lips to brush his. It pleased her to see him struggle to keep his professional cool and failing. To ensure his mind did not revisit her mess up, she said, "As a mage, it's easy to find hidden knowledge or to show it." She let her robe pull open in his face and bit his ear and then kissed him.

He at last kissed her back for several moments before he took a deep breath and asked, "Why would a necromancer linked to the Jade God want gold dragon eyes?"

Ryvane tapped their foreheads together and looked into his eyes. "That, Sir Captain, is what the emperor has had us looking into for days now. So far as we can tell, it is a required spell component for something to do with planar travel. We've found only one clue so far, at great cost. That clue is that as one moves from plane to plane, the location shifts relative to all other worlds but it can be locked with the right focus and vision. Perhaps gold dragon eyes are part of that focus and vision."

"Couldn't a mage just summon a gold dragon or get a demon to get the eyes?" Calvin's tone of voice said he barely cared. Ryvane could see him mentally check the last box in his list of questions.

She waved her hand. "On the one hand, yes. Poof. There it is. On the other, unless you arrange a contract, a gold dragon is nearly impossible to get. For one, no gold dragon would take a contract with someone like Bomoki or anything touched by necromancy. Plus, look at how hard it is to find one here. If you don't know where they are, a demon won't know. They don't exactly run in the same circles. As to eyes, it's just speculation right now because no one has ever attempted to stop a gate from moving; by design, gates don't move." The spectral hand pulled her robe back off her shoulders and she said, "Now, if there are no other questions, Watch Captain, perhaps this boring government business is done?"

"Tell me sorcerer, when magic gives you all you want, what does a mage do when business is done?" Calvin mouthed into her neck.

"I'll show you," she said.

Chapter Thirty Two – Hunting Farant

Farant kept trying to heal the gaping hole in his back by molding flesh of all different types over it. The agony had long become exquisite to the point he knew Orcus would aid him, must be aiding him. "Death is just a doorway," he muttered as he tripped. "I should have died. Orcus knows I am worthy!"

His good arm caught against a tree and shockwaves of pain tore through him. He kept trying to use the bloodstone to morph his flesh and heal the wound again, but days of this had taught him the truth – wounded flesh can morph but it stays wounded. He needed healing, or life energy. So far, he had only been able to harvest unlucky forest animals as he fled Morbatten westwards. He had almost entered Klenna but when he saw a dread lord circling overhead, he had changed course to stay south. Klenna lay on the outer edge of the inner perimeter of Morbatten. That meant it had its own shrine and some autonomy. With that came adventurers, military, and others he did not want to face right now.

If he kept going west, he would come to the outer provinces. He could not remember which Dar held the next westernmost province but better that chance than a direct confrontation. The bloodstone sat in his bowels, heavy and pulsing. Though he drew energy freely from it, he missed eating and drinking. So much hunger and thirst – *No*, he steeled his resolve. *I must make it to Bloodstone! Death is the doorway, but I must live for now!*

Eventually, he pulled himself over a rock along a ridgeline and gazed down into a lake with a thriving village along its eastern shore. The road connecting it to Klenna and the capitol radiated into that village. The road had been paved and he saw waystations with taverns. A major and well-maintained road like this meant the Dar must be either wealthy or powerful or both. Across the lake, another village glinted. Sailboats on the lake showed enough that he could tell this village had to be Adir Forsul.

He tried to remember which lord owned it. He came up blank and that bothered him. As a ranking member of the Thieves Guild, he should be able to recall this, or maybe it was magically hidden? He shook his head and saw himself looking at a map during countless briefings. Klenna, Adir Forsul, the town across the lake was Corbadad. *The lord of Cordabad is –* and he drew another blank. "So, that means I can't remember, or that the villages are held by actual Dars who chose to be unknown and unnamed." That would mean very powerful and to be skipped in a Thieves Guild briefing. He swore and began threading his way west to avoid the villages.

A briar thicket tore at his flesh and he wished he could fly, but why not hang a sign up advertising his location? *No, I need to stay secret and safe.*

A scent caught him as he pulled free and following it, he found a small animal den. Reaching in, something with teeth bit him and he pulled out a wild dog-like creature. He bit the head off and drank the blood before he mashed the carcass into his shoulder wound. The agony dissipated just a bit as he grafted the carcass into the wound like a bandage. "I need humans," he grumbled. Still the pain decreased and compared to the never-ending agony, it felt sweet. He morphed into a cockroach and crawled into the hole hoping more animals would show up.

* * *

High up on the ridgeline behind Farant, Daryx perched on a stone. His garments pulsed and shifted with the wind and trees creating perfect camouflage from all angles. He made a series of hand signs watched by a small silver sparrow. It cocked its head and then flew away to Adir Forsul. The other man with Daryx watched and read the signs, *A necromancer is skirting your borders. Double watch patrols and all citizens accounted for safe and secured in the next hour. Martial law until I send word that it is safe.*

Daryx ruled Adir Forsul, Marcello realized. It had bothered him that he could not remember which Dar held this territory. It suddenly made sense and with that dot, entire unknown sections of Tania filled in for the guildmaster. What Marcello did know is that the mayor of Adir Forsul had served two campaigns in Bloodstone; that was it. By itself, not even noteworthy but to go from that to ruling Adir Forsul meant the mayor must have been part of Daryx's special teams.

There would not be an issue with compliance. Marcello could even imagine the mechanical efficiency of a fast and clean implementation of martial law. For some reason, the image of servants clearing an imperial feast came to mind. The Law of Innocents required this protection of civilians. Seeing it implemented stirred up feelings of pride in Marcello, but also envy. "I wish my own guild were so easy to command," he muttered.

Daryx chuckled and said, "In my homeland, the Underdark, we'd no doubt parade our virgins into Farant's path as bait for a trap. Well, not our children, but certainly those of lesser creatures."

Similarly cloaked like Daryx, the guildmaster watched Farant shapeshift and disappear near the hole. "Assuming he sleeps after this two-day chase, we could attack now, my lord."

"The god emperor was very explicit. We are to follow and prepare. Hopefully, Farant leads us to the First of the hellhounds."

Marcello reflexively swallowed and put that thought out of his head. Like all good citizens, he had fought his campaign in Bloodstone, with honor and commendation even. But, he had been glad to leave and never return. "I fought a hound naming itself Slayer of Men," he said. Daryx nodded but added nothing so Marcello continued. "He lived true to his name. Though we fought it back and most of the group survived, I can only imagine the First must be -"

"Bomoki, a mage of Tania." Daryx brushed a snowflake from his nose and watched as more landed on his gloved hand.

"Is the story true?" Marcello asked. "I've heard you were there, my lord."

Daryx nodded lifting his hand to pull his cloak more tightly to his face. "I was. The stories are, of course, exaggerated by bards and retelling in the past thousand years, but fact and truth is that Bomoki was one of us. He found the first jade ram wand. He was the first to call to the Jade God. In many ways, Bomoki is just as much a progenitor of Morbatten as is Alerius and the first priestess Dar Tania. Without Bomoki, there'd be no eternal war in Bloodstone. We'd no doubt have fought Taysor and Morilon all these years instead. Fighting them, this nation no doubt never would have become what it now is."

Daryx's voice had a bit of nostalgia in it and Marcello pondered the wisdom of asking more questions about this most eccentric and long-lived member of the Circle. He decided to not press his luck. They stared through the snow that started to fall, switching between the scenic lake and the burrow Farant had claimed. Marcello squinted at Daryx noting the residual glow behind his eye lids of where the grand lord carried stones. Though not surprised the dark elf had bloodstones, the fact he carried so many to the point that he could not discern the exact number was. "My lord, if I may ask, are we to follow Farant all the way to Bloodstone?"

Daryx looked back at the thief and gave him just a suggestion of a fanged smile. "The god emperor and his brethren have long sought the day they'd get their claws on Bomoki. This is too good a chance to not take. For now, you and I will follow and ensure he does no harm to Tania's citizens. We must be ready to act, to drive him onwards. Once he passes into the wilderness, my ranger units will continue to hunt him. The more he believes his life is in danger, the faster he will run to his master." Daryx locked eyes with Marcello, "This is why it is you and I who are here and not my ranger units, effective though they are. This is your chance, Marcello."

Marcello felt beads of sweat roll down his back and did his best to appear cool and calm. "Understood, my lord."

A glint of silver down in the valley suggested the return of the sparrow. Daryx turned to watch and added, "Though the fault for this Farant creature cannot be solely placed at your or your guild's feet, I should not have to remind you that Ora's child IS going to be the next king's son and possibly heir. I won't even tell you about the special bond Ora herself shares with the white dragon patriarch. There are also prophecies at play. Never mind that Farant somehow got his hands on the flatspace artefact. Some would consider just that one loss an unmitigated disaster. You quite literally," Daryx smiled that fanged grin again, "stand surrounded all about by risk and disaster. Tell me, *master of the Thieves Guild*, are you truly a master?"

Marcello thought about any number of obvious answers before deciding to take a different and hopefully more diplomatic tact in his reply. "Daryx, the emperor established -"

"Yes, do not lecture me on the history of your guild. I was its first guildmaster before I found a suitable and more public face for it."

The fanged grin never wavered and from the depths of that cowl, Marcello knew Daryx viewed him as prey. "Oh, you were? Yes, of course you were, my lord. My point is that master to master, we have always known that our greatest risk came from within. Hence, the many preparations against a vault theft."

Daryx almost interrupted him but allowed him to finish before interjecting, "Disaster or not?" The cold, hard words came out of Daryx's mouth and hung in the air between them.

"Yes, a disaster but one we knew could happen. As a ranking member before I became master, I and many others speculated as to how many times the vault had been raided. We wondered if it were a test. I prefer to see this as an opportunity to prove the value of the Thieves Guild to the Circle."

"It is a test. You are to be the eyes and ears of the empire within the empire, to see what the dragons and Temple may miss. The vault is there, obviously, to test the character of *Tania's eyes and ears*. No dragon wants actual thieves amidst their treasure. I actually wanted to name this function "agents" but the god emperor overruled me. He said he wanted a name to suggest criminal rather than political intent. No dragon would entrust the safekeeping of their treasure to thieves. So, the real question here is this: are you a thief or a guardian?"

"So, wondering that," Marcello continued with a tone of voice begging for time to explain, "I broke into the vault. I learned that the vault contains much treasure. I learned that the initiative and gumption to do so is one of the differentiators between rank and guild leadership. So, how could it be a disaster? Farant had been on a track where he could have become the next guildmaster. But -"

"You chose Khalla instead. So you did not foresee Farant's discontent."

"My lord Daryx, no, I did not. Perhaps I might have but I did not attain my position, nor do any of us, because of our claim to great wisdom."

They sat in silence for several moments, snow drifting around them, before Daryx burst into laughter. "Can you imagine a wise thief? Oh Marcello, you underplay yourself! Did you know that we had to intervene so that Sai would not decimate your guild into smoking ruin? Meanwhile, your own factions are tearing yourselves apart. It almost makes me homesick for the underdark."

The sparrow arrived at last and conveyed a message, *Adir Forsul is on lockdown with all citizens counted, great Dar. We remain yours to command. Word is also sent to Cordabad.* The sparrow twinkled, becoming an earring pendant that Daryx restored to his ear.

Marcello thought on Daryx's words and then asked what he felt would be an obvious question. "Why would Sai hold the guild responsible? After all, we have served in every requested capacity for centuries. Sure, we have some occasional failings."

"The answer to this question is not that you failed somehow, in your eyes. You must understand that Sai does not think the way we do. He is called Alerius' son for many reasons but first and foremost, as a free-willed golem created by Alerius, his thoughts are alien. Where you and I see a spectrum of possibility, of failure, of lessons learned, Sai sees only risk and threat. He measures this against what he understands to be his father's express desires in creating him. Farant's clones, Farant's attack on Sai's estate, he told the Circle that he felt the prophecy at risk. You know the prophecy right? About King Rojo?"

When Marcello nodded, Daryx continued, "You and I would think that any attack damaging Sai's estate, breaching his security would be a big deal. To Sai it is not. He goes, *This has happened so it will happen again. What must I do to ensure it does not happen again?* By the same token, with the prophecy at risk, Sai sees the role your guild played as being more than just pivotal; you threaten the king's succession by empowering Farant to attack Ora, and through her child, the king's successor."

Marcello knew better than to defend himself or protest his not knowing how Sai sees all these things. Maybe someday he would sit in the Circle and be part of these matters. However, right now, he could only listen. He asked Daryx, "What would you do Daryx, in my position?"

That smile again and Daryx replied, "I'd hunt Farant to the ends of the earth and make damn sure I bring proof of his death before Sai, the guild, and the empire. If you just so happened to reveal Bomoki or achieve some other goal, so much the better. One guildmaster to another, you do not want your guild under Sai or the Circle's thumb for a single minute longer than it need be. Alerius' instructions to us were to create a service *of eyes and ears* big enough for the empire. To fall under even my thumb would put the Guild in a position of serving my agenda. Though I like to think my agenda serves the empire, I'm not deluded enough to think that I alone can guard this empire of frail creatures. I do not see this place the way the god emperor does. It wouldn't hurt to get closer to R'Dar Ora too. After all, Malcor loves her. Imagine what he has heard of this and how the future king might see you and your guild. From what I understand, Malcor is a passionate man."

Marcello had been briefed on Malcor, the newest member of the Order of Water. The instruction had been very clear – *You are to aid and support Malcor in ANY matter. Your lieutenants may know of the prophecy but no one else. You are to engage with him in a manner appropriate to a novice member of the Order but render any aid or material requested.* Dar Kendra had sent Marcello a handwritten note to bill her directly for any expenses incurred with a note, *Take care of my nephew.*

The stories from Khasra had quickly followed and then one day bards are singing about the defeat of a lich and a jade ram sceptre. Just like that, Malcor became a known hero of the empire. All of this went through Marcello's head in a moment. He almost asked about Calvin, but decided against it.

"Lord Daryx, if I may take my leave. I have considered your words and would like to rally my guild to ensure that Farant is chased through the wilds. We are ready for Bomoki."

The enigmatic dark elf, wrapped all about in his cloak, waved good-bye. Marcello bowed and jumped down from the ravine ledge. His mind already raced across his network of connections both in Tania and along the frontier to Haven. He would require his lieutenants. A few adventurers would certainly not hurt.

* * *

Rojo and Jeri walked through the long corridors of the third fortress' upper levels. A room cleverly hidden by dwarves and earth magic waited for them. Jeri ensured they were not followed, but neither were surprised when they opened the door and found Dar Ana lounging inside. The chamber connected to a large domed circle almost as large as the Temple's where Crimson laired. Cleverly designed so that from the outside it appeared to be part of the much smaller audience chamber, this room had but a single purpose – magic.

"Greetings, dear Rojo," Ana purred. She smiled at Jeri. "What brings a king and his battle priestess to this most potent of circles?" From just over her shoulder, a shadowed book floated in the air. "After all, I would know the answer to this riddle too. With so many red dragon eyes for the taking, I'd hate for the hounds to grow restless and decide they can make do with Crimson's." She leapt to her feet and hugged Rojo, who stood formal and proper for the high priestess of Bloodstone.

When Ana broke the embrace and stepped back, Rojo said, "You know why we're here. You have the price?" Ana nodded and held up a small pendant on a gold chain entangled in her fingers. Rojo continued, "We have a theory that gold dragon eyes will hold the gate's location so that more hounds can be used to open it. If opened big enough, the actual god could come through. I have no wish to be the first and only king of Tania. We struggle with handling the Jade God as just an avatar. Alerius consulted with Oranstakar who said only that gold dragons see things as they truly are. This creates an easier question – does Bomoki seek gold dragon eyes to affix the gate or for some other purpose? The book's price will be less than getting surprised by whatever it is Bomoki plans to do."

Ana expression changed to annoyance, "All eldar dragons see things as they truly are, as do most fallen ones. That was not helpful." She looked at Jeri, "Is it just the nature of golds to be so useless?"

Jeri dug her fingers into Rojo's arm and shot back a look at Ana daring her to continue. Ana blew back a kiss and turned to the book. "I do not wish to be like the priestess to Merakor when the world ends," she said referring to how the Merakoran empire disintegrated into civil war and internecine conflict overnight. "I wish to the be priestess that ends Orcus. So I am here. And, The Darkhold is here."

Jeri hissed at her use of the Jade God's name as if to say, "Really? Here in Bloodstone?" Ana blew her another kiss and walked back to the book almost touching it.

The Darkhold floated in clear light from the windows but shadows of different shades of gray and black clawed at it two-dimensionally as a war raged around it. The book itself slowly revolved in the air. Occasionally, a page would open just a bit to a shadow trying to escape from within. Ana touched it for just a moment and shook off a shadow clinging to her finger. "The real one, not just a copy. I like your direct approach, my king. Do you know which page you will consult?"

Rojo took her hand and Ana blushed turning to smile seductively at Rojo. But when he lifted up the bloodstone pendant Ana had held, and broke their touch, she pouted. "As priestess, I can have you by command," she whispered.

Jeri interrupted, "And yet, it would ruin your reputation as the only priestess to take paladins by their choice, even if your seduction is beyond belief. Besides, I would object as his battle priestess." This exchange had happened many times before.

"You are dismissed, Jeri," Ana said. That command from Tiamat's high priestess rocked Jeri to her core. Religion and dominion compelled her to leave. Her begging look to Rojo resulted in a shrug. The high priestess commanded in Bloodstone, not the king.

"I'll be outside the door, on guard if you need me." She formally exited the chamber looking with hope that Rojo would compel her to stay. He did not.

"Alone at last," Ana whispered reaching her arms up Rojo's breastplate and letting her nearly invisible gown fall to the floor. "I know you want me."

"Actually Dar Ana -"

Ana's kiss shut him up and he steeled himself for the inevitable. Even though both of them knew what would happen, Ana coiled up to him like a snake, her body pressing against him and gasping her kisses into his mouth. Like any man in such a situation, every part of him wanted to respond but his vision blocked it. It always did. Of all the knights in all the many centuries since the first paladin Sean of Taysor trained Shak d'Rath, Rojo alone had defied the priestesses and their many attempts to seduce him.

Years ago, a priestess had seen an up and coming hero-paladin in Rojo and decided to take him "for the good of the empire". Rojo had politely declined explaining that it did not feel right. The priestess had insisted going so far as to order Rojo to join her. As she increased her demands that he comply, she eventually grabbed him and began stripping his armor. A divine force had repulsed the priestess and knocked her unconscious. A paladin rejecting a priestess had never before happened. Though paladins can say no, physically attacking a priestess never ever happens. The Temple charged Rojo with all manner of crimes.

While awaiting trial, and while declaring his innocence, other priestesses tried to seduce Rojo. They met the same fate. The god emperor, when he learned of it, finally intervened to prevent things from leading to Rojo's execution. "He is claimed by Tiamat," Alerius had said.

"I remember you doing this before my trial," Rojo said through her kiss. "You know what will happen."

"I don't care, Rojo my dear," Ana said. "The Queen may yet…"

A pressure suddenly asserted itself between them. Ana felt Rojo's smile the instant before an invisible shockwave blew her back and away from him. "No!" she screamed, skidding to her feet as she landed gracefully. "You order a preservation of bloodlines! My Queen, let me!"

She sprinted to Rojo praying for this thing she wanted. That invisible force caught her just as she returned to Rojo and attempted to kiss him again. This time, the violent blow sprawled her backwards on the ground to the point her goddess armor had to protect her. Wiping blood from her mouth and nose, she stood shakily and walked back towards Rojo.

"Dar, as high priestess, you know my loyalty and affection for you knows no bounds," Rojo said. "But, in this time of prophecy, I already know that the Queen will make no exceptions."

From outside the room, Jeri's voice called out, "Ana! You must stop!" Jeri's voice had a slight suggestion of muffled laughter.

Annoyance crossed Ana's face and she sashayed back up to Rojo. Her goddess armor had yet to vanish so she could not touch him physically. Through her glimmering armored fingers, she rested her head on his shoulder. "Why does the Queen keep us apart, my love? Whatever this is in you that rejects love, let it go. Ask the Queen for me, for us. Just once before you leave. I beg you!"

Rojo retained his impassive and expressionless face, "You know I cannot, Ana." He carefully pushed her back and pointed to the book. "The Darkhold waits for us."

"I command you to give yourself to me," she whispered into his ear.

"I am yours to command, Dar Ana, and I am most certainly yours. Always." He kissed her hand and stepped to the book.

Ana felt it too, already pouting before he stated the obvious. This is exactly as the Queen wanted it. She sighed and her armor faded leaving her naked body holding Rojo's hand. "I imagine this would make quite the statue in some palace garden," she breathed.

"You should commission it, High Priestess. No doubt it would grace many estates throughout the empire." Rojo let go of her hand though she tried to stop him.

He crouched down by the book to examine it from underneath and the sides. Shadows twisted and lazily swiped at his face. "The Darkhold. The Guild is sure this is the actual book, not just a copy?" He referred to the abyssal artefact's tendency to replicate itself across the realms. The lesser books were useful but more persistent in their quest to obtain souls. The actual Darkhold could only be summoned when enough lesser pages had been accumulated. The Mages Guild held enough to do this and had many times. Its knowledge had saved the empire. Rojo and Ana quietly discussed the last time they had accessed it to turn the tide of the Jaden War a decade earlier. Eventually, they called Jeri to join them. She frowned at Ana's nakedness.

"The Darkhold knows that Tania knows how to subvert its quest for new and novel souls," Rojo said to Jeri. "The last time we used this, the chained combination of other souls, it almost failed."

With concern, Jeri asked, "Then let me do it, my king."

"No, not with the actual. Your day will no doubt come to try but the Darkhold hungers for dragons. As you might imagine, not many metallic dragons will even touch this. I'm sure it would consider you a delicacy." Rojo patted her hand and said, "Besides, I really don't want you to be the only gold dragon in this book or have you targeted by it."

"The Darkhold would seek me out?"

Ana laughed. "Not at first and not obviously. It'd manipulate other users of the Darkhold to seek you or a gold dragon out. At some point, some day, a manipulation would bring the Darkhold to you. One of my priestesses, in training with a copy, made this mistake. A small boy asked for her autograph. The paper wasn't paper though. It was a page of the Darkhold. The god emperor suppresses knowledge of these fatalities. But, you'll see, the Darkhold knows all. It has saved us more times than I can describe. You should ask Alerius to see the records."

Chapter Thirty Three – The Darkhold

The Darkhold pulsed as its shadows reached out for Rojo's hand. Holding the soul pendant, Rojo took the book and called out for Jeri to join them. Ana came and stood by his side not deigning to put her clothes back on. Waiting for Jeri to join them, Rojo flipped the pages of the book noting the portrait sketches of souls long ago claimed, from every race and plane of existence.

He paused on a page showing a dragon breathing gas, but as the runes reformed themselves into something he could read, he exerted his will and turned the page. "So much knowledge, so seductive," he said. "To see others as the gods see them." To linger, to read too much, endangered the reader's soul. Ana and Jeri would ensure he did not get caught by the Darkhold – the Library of the Abyss. Page by page he turned, sometimes lingering, other times just flipping to the next. At one point, he paused and the demonic runes resolved into a name but he did not recognize it. Ana and Jeri both compelled the king to proceed. Eventually, he came to a blank page.

Ana now held the book on that blank page, anchoring the pages so they would not turn. Her goddess armor asserted gauntlets that crackled as the Darkhold resisted being held this way. Ever so slowly, in wet blood ink, the first Darkhold contact appeared: *For what, would you know?*

Rojo took a razor quill, sharp beyond belief, and dipped it into his forearm. With a drop of blood, he wrote on the blank page – *Why does Bomoki der Kori, formerly of Morbattania now undead servant of Orcus, seek gold dragon eyes?*

He had to redip several times, each blood draw caused the pendant to flare with heat and light, to finish writing the question. The wet blood dried slowly on the page and then vanished, reforming into the likeness of a rune. Slowly, more runes began to appear. "If you add more blood, this will go faster," Ana said to Jeri. "But, we've found that the Darkhold is like any abyssal lord, very impatient. The slowness helps us avoid deceit and manipulation." Rojo held the quill ready to dip again, letting a line of blood hang just between his skin and the razor quill's tip.

Eventually, the rune resolved in draconian. "Do you refer to the Bomoki who carries the Gate of Orcus nearby?" it read.

Rojo dipped into his arm, wincing this time. "Yes, why does Bomoki – bearer of the Gate of Orcus – seek gold dragon eyes?" He had to dip many times to finish writing this repeat sentence, the blood drying and fading too quickly. Jeri touched him with healing magic to mend his lacerated wrist.

The Darkhold suddenly jumped, straining from Ana's grasp. Prayers of strength and calls for divine aid rang out as the book struggled to break free. A rune appeared and then resolved to their understanding, "Great King Rojo, you have come to me before with imposter blood sacrifices. You will write your name in my book!" During the struggle, several pages had fallen loose.

"Jeri," Ana said. "Put those pages to sleep! Hurry, and don't let them touch us!" The sleep prayer caused the loose pages to go inert. Jeri retrieved fireplace tools and pushed them back, and then pinned them under the heavy cast iron tools. Behind her, Ana wrestled the Darkhold still, her armor prismatically shining with noon day brightness as if sunlight.

The draconian words faded and Rojo gouged his wrist, letting his blood fall directly onto the page. It immediately absorbed and then slowly a new rune formed. It read, "The gate long sealed and hiding, is found. It is ready to open for the Necromancer. Golden eyes are required to hold the gate steady and open. Even a single eye is enough, but two eyes assure its *permanency*, ensures its size." The wordscript for 'permanency' swirled as the Darkhold struggled with the concept of something that would last.

Even as his flesh healed to Jeri's prayer, Rojo cut deeply again and wrote, "When will Bomoki open the gate?"

"No." After a pause, a new rune appeared and then these words, "Your blood is sweet, great king. Write your name and I shall reveal Bomoki's end game."

Rojo cut through his wrist letting blood bathe the page as he wrote, "I would know as much as you will tell me for this price. My name is Teren Baksi." The pendant in his hand flared and then shattered. This time the blood flared brightly on the page and instead of resolving itself into a rune, the name *Teren Baksi* became a flowing portrait of the serial murderer's soul that had been held in the pendant's gemstone. Crystal shards shredded Rojo's hand to a pulp and blood poured freely into the page.

The murderer looked around as if trapped in a cage and then began smashing his fists against the page. His birth date, nationality, life's accomplishments and milestones began to appear on the page written in Rojo's blood. Reading it, Jeri marveled, "That such a vicious fiend would survive in Tania."

Rojo shrugged, "You're always so surprised by this, Jeri. As our nation grows, so too does the number of these criminals. Not serving the empire,

Alerius has chosen to extract value from them in this way. Does it still offend you?"

"No, I'm long past that. All must serve the Queen." Her eyes flickered along the milestones and the number of innocents Baksi had killed or participated in killing… to the page's bottom where the final record appeared – *Consumed by Darkhold.*

They waited several more minutes for healing prayers to mend Rojo's arm wounds. The loss of blood had been substantial. The healing took longer than it should and this concerned Jeri. So soon after the battle with Bomoki, Rojo now leaned on the Jeri for support. Ana watched with concern and asked, "Do you have enough strength to finish?"

"No choice," he said more strongly than he looked or felt.

Jeri caught his hand, "You don't have a soul gem, Rojo. Please, don't. Let me try."

"It's either me or the lovely high priestess. This is what a king of Tania does." He stabbed the quill into his arm.

As the thrashing Teren slowly froze into a sketch, a new rune began to slowly form. This time, Rojo fed the rune tracing over its lines with his own blood. Long moments and many fresh blood lines cut into healing wounds at last revealed the complete rune, which wavered and shifted into draconian. "The blind dragon of Merakor has allied with Bomoki to bring the ram. Next time, only your real name will satisfy me, King Rojo of Tania."

The book immediately ceased struggling and went quiescent. Carefully, Ana closed the book locking its side clasp. Jeri cast a prayer over the book lulling it to sleep. When Ana let it go, it returned to floating in the air enwrapped in shadows. "The blind dragon of Merakor," Ana said. Jeri put Rojo carefully down on the floor and then went to stand opposite Ana. With the book in between, Ana threw her gown over it. Jeri carefully wrapped the book careful to avoid touching it.

The book had been delivered by the Guild and their summoning rune lay against the wall. Activating it, a black doorway opened and the guildmaster Dar Reznor stepped through. He bowed to them both, took the book, and turned to address Rojo. However, Rojo had fallen unconscious. His wrist wounds – all of them – had reappeared in a growing circle of blood. Reznor pointed to Rojo, "Do you require help? Is the king…"

Ana rubbed her eyes and left blood across her face. "Just get the cursed book out of here!" The Darkhold laughed sleepily as Reznor took it through the portal and returned to Tania. He wished them good fortune and asked that his regards be shared with the king when he awoke and recovered.

Ana moved to check Rojo. "So much blood," she observed. She checked the king's pulse. It fluttered too weakly. "No! Jeri, summon everyone! He's dying!"

While Ana cradled Rojo and began preparing him, Jeri found a bloodstone earring on Ana's left ear and activated it. Suddenly, Ana's Temple acolytes, each in a various state of being mid-task, appeared in the room around them. Used to this, they quickly recovered and rushed over to help. Ana had already lanced her arm and a shimmering ferrule of light carried by her goddess armor transfused her blood to Rojo as Jeri called on Tiamat to save the king. One of Ana's adjutants draped a fresh gown on the nude priestess as they collectively worked to save Rojo. "Why?" Jeri asked. "What does the Darkhold get from this?"

Ana shrugged and pierced herself to transfuse more blood to Rojo. Now her priestesses cast healing prayers at her. The wounds on Rojo's wrist stubbornly refused to heal even with a tourniquet applied. At last, Ana coughed out an order to summon Crimson.

Though only minutes passed, it seemed an eternity with Rojo caught at death's doorstep. As the dome overhead rotated to allow Crimson to enter, they struggled to keep both Ana and Rojo alive. More than twenty arcs of blood transfused from her body to Rojo. As Ana's strength faded, her blood began to spill. Two other priestesses, who knew how to do this magic, knelt and began similar transfusions to Ana.

Though they could not revive Rojo just now, the Darkhold's involvement made it very undesirable that the king die like this. They felt the Goddess urging them to action. The Darkhold's curse repelled their attempts and still blood oozed out of Rojo's lacerated arm. So more priestesses began to add their blood to their high priestess. Crimson's landing behind them trembled the ground just enough that Ana looked up and smiled. "The king's wrist, my friend. Help." Her voice sounded dry and weak.

Crimson snaked his titanic head forward and saw the ever-bleeding wound. A rumble of concern deep in his chest shook the building and then the dragon held forth a single claw that began to burn with fire, hotter and hotter. Soon, the air around the claw began to shimmer with heat waves. Those priestesses not aiding in the transfusion prayed for protection from the heat as even their divine resistance blew away against Crimson's hellfire. So hot it could not be seen now except as a black wavy scar in the air, Crimson touched it to Rojo's wrist cauterizing the wound, which at last stopped bleeding. In that single moment, burn wounds erupted all over Rojo's body with the armor near the touch melting like candle wax and pooling around him. "No!" Jeri screamed but Crimson had already withdrawn. The cindered flesh around the touchpoint had started to respond to healing though. And, the bleeding stopped.

Ana moaned in agony as her own body, held in check from the goddess armor, likewise cindered and then began to heal. The goddess armor kept trying to form and Ana choked it back by force of will and pain or else it would stop the blood transfusion. Seeing that Rojo no longer bled, she slumped forward and slowly began retracting the transfusion tubes as more and more of Rojo's life firmed up to Jeri's and the priestesses' prayers. As the last ferrule disconnected from Rojo, the priestesses supporting Ana began to withdraw their connections.

Ana crawled forward and laid her head in the crook of Rojo's armor, on his side not molten. In an instant, she and Rojo breathed deep breaths of sleep. Jeri looked at them both with some annoyance and felt a rumbling from Crimson. She turned her exhausted eyes to the eldar red and said, "Surely this bothers you as much as it does me."

Wishing Crimson could talk, she felt rather than heard his growl and imagined he agreed with her. Fatigue threatened Jeri, but she reminded herself, *I am a gold dragon and I serve Rojo.* "All of you, listen. Not a word of this is to be spoken. If anyone asks, the priestess is attending to important Temple matters and the king is on patrol. You and you," Jeri pointed to two attendants still looking fresh, unburned, and unbloodied. "Bring clothing, bedding, food, and drink to this chamber. We will recover here until the King and Priestess say otherwise."

Jeri tapped the next highest ranking priestess. "Send word to Morbatten – we must know about Merakor's blind dragon." Pausing for emphasis she added, "And emphasize that we are requesting this of the god emperor, not the Temple or Guild. Take this request on my authority to Dar Kell and the emperor."

Some of Jeri's innate dragonterror must have leaked through her weariness because she saw them all flinch and step back from her. Right at that moment, Crimson surged forward as if to say, "Do it!" Jeri sent him a mental thank you and then joined her master in sleep.

The priestesses paused for a few moments to marvel at these most powerful people, drenched in blood, exhausted near unto the sleep of death. One of them speculated as to what had happened but Crimson's threatening growl and the rising dragonterror spurred them all into action.

Those with orders, left. The rest went to fetch cleaning supplies and guards. Crimson would watch over them. Bloodstone had a way of sneaking up on the unwary. It would not do to leave the High Priestess, a Dar priestess, and the King unattended. He curled his titanic form around the three catatonic bodies and craned his head to the sky, to listen to Bloodstone.

Chapter Thirty Four – Malcor the Thief

Malcor watched as the hellhound once again burrowed into a mine shaft, invisible until suddenly it appeared. He could not tell if his quarry knew he followed or not. Every night, the hound moved west and south towards the Sixth Fortress. Every day, just before the sun would crest the mountains, the hound would somehow know where to find these tunnels, dig in, and vanish. Each time, and this time would be no different, Malcor moved forward and observed the shaft. Those with markings, Malcor recorded on a map. Those without, he also noted using a shadow claw to inscribe a nonsensical mark on the passage. The Temple could figure this out later. It seemed the right thing to do and no one had ever explained the marking system to him.

Malcor waited a good hour before he crept forward to peer deeper into the mineshaft, his senses on high alert. Unlike most days, today held no clouds and the sun high above the eastern mountains felt warm against the winter cold in this high place. With direct sunlight, the undead would be almost lethargic. He'd been waiting for a day like this during the many days of pursuit.

The tunnel bore a mark reminiscent of ancient Temple draconian. It looked like someone had tried to chip away at the marking but had given up. Like most mining tunnels, this one sloped downwards. The sun aligned perfectly and he could see it went for several hundred feet before branching. Wrapping himself in shadow, he stepped into the tunnel with a prayer that the sunlight would prevent the tunnel from chaos shifting. Without a watcher, he could become lost in this shaft forever. Behind him in the bright sunlight, Ora's silvered falcon cried out as if to say, "Don't go Malcor! Don't do it!" He walked in.

In total silence and hugging the many available shadows, Malcor moved to the tunnel's end. It opened into a large entry room. Rusted cart rails crisscrossed the floor near a central dumping pile with five shafts radiating from this location. That the hellhound left no marks indicating where it had gone did not surprise Malcor.

One of the mineshafts sat in a patch of sunlight and to this Malcor moved. Ember red veins twisted throughout the rocks looking like arteries in the sunlight. He tried to sense if they were actually bloodstones but they failed to leave impressions behind his vision. Shifting his sight to ultravision, he noted that care had been put into smoothing the walls. This must have been more than just a mining operation.

A small voice in his heart whispered that he should turn back and observe. *Carry out your orders, nothing else.* He imagined Tembri chastising him exactly like that. To take his mind off how eerily unnerving it felt to be alone in this place, he imagined Cor'tanos. Something about that made him feel more emboldened.

The sun rose out of alignment with the passage and so he went back to the entrance. He spotted a giant tree just outside the shaft. Reaching into his backpack, he prayed for rope. Dar Kendra had not lied to him when he joined the Order. They always had the best gear. He found a small coil of rope and looking carefully noted elvish writing from Morilon.

Malcor tied one end to the tree and then began walking back to the mine shaft. The rope, no more than twenty paces long, continued to magically lengthen. He smiled, taking this as a sign that he should explore as long as the rope lasted. Returning to the mine shaft, Malcor discovered he could not shadowshift the rope and so took extra care to walk as quietly as his plate armor would allow. With his right arm dragonshifted and holding his sword ahead of him, he advanced. Though his inner voice continued to question the wisdom of entering the mine by himself, the rope made him feel much better. "I'll stop when the rope stops," he promised himself with a whisper.

The mine cart rail had long ago corroded into rust powder and he followed the brown rust with ultravision. Ahead, he heard something shuffling and snorting. A hellhound would not make such a sound. Whatever it was, the monster did not seem to have noticed him yet. Malcor carefully sheathed his sword and put the rope down.

Abruptly, the sound stopped and then something roared and began charging at him. The creature must have heard his sword gliding into its scabbard. Malcor shadowshifted against the wall just as a cow-sized creature with two tentacle eye stalks came charging to where he had just stood. One of the eye stalks struck against the floor and the remaining rail not already rusted, powdered against the blow.

He had studied such creatures. They ate metal. A nuisance creature for a magically-armored paladin, he considered killing the beast but then reconsidered. Instead, he spiked a rail further down the passage with a shadow kick. The noise drew the creature, which charged in that direction. Malcor followed, repeating this tactic until, without warning, something violet to his ultravision attacked the beast. Watching it in ultravision, it appeared as if the rust monster had peeled open like a flower.

Shadowshifted, Malcor did not need to breathe but still he still caught and held his breath. He froze completely still in his two dimensional form. Slowly, the flower petals peeled off the carcass in purple light blooms to his vision. He wondered if it would turn, and as he wondered, the dead body twitched. The ultravision colors changed as heat and energy bled out of it into whatever its attacker was. He saw the streams of energy moving as the creature walked right past him. It gave it just enough energy that he made out a silhouette against the ember cast of the tunnels. Human-like, the form walked like a man but he noted long bladed arms. *Were those arms?,* Malcor wondered to himself. Something had stabbed the monster to death in a single fatal strike.

Malcor trailed the creature back to where he had dropped the rope. The bladed humanoid immediately spotted and picked it up. It tugged at the rope and the sniffed the end Malcor had been holding. "Human..." it breathed. It pulled harder on the rope and when the magic rope stretched, the creature seemed to become gleeful. "More humans..." it chittered.

It grabbed the rope and began walking backwards down the shaft. It made a coughing sound and then choking, coughed again. "Help?" it said. It choked again. "Help! Help! Undead! To aid! To aid!" This type of tactic had played on repeat in Bloodstone for centuries but the undead never tired of it. Bloodstone Legions never fell for this anymore.

The bladed humanoid, perhaps a ghoul, began jerking on the rope and turned running backwards while calling out for help. Malcor followed it to an intersection in the tunnel about a hundred paces past the rust monster. The intersection branched left and right. The creature pulled the rope to the right and came to what appeared to be a tunnel collapse. Seven other humanoid creatures rose up from the rock walls around the first. After a moment of arm waving, they all began crying for help and making the sounds of battle.

Malcor decided to check the other passage. The noise had drawn the attention of other undead and several zombies long rotted to mere skeletons shambled to the commotion. He passed these and came to an opening along the left side of the passage. Opening up wide, he came to a massive door big enough for a giant. The door glistened, unaffected by time. Gleaming gold marked with magical script glittered in the passage casting enough light that he had to stop ultravision as it pained his eyes. At human height, two pull rings sat on either side of the door's center. Each ring sparkled with a dust-free golden hue. They ached to be pulled open and Malcor felt his imagination fired by the thought of treasures upon treasures. Clearly a trap, he enjoyed the hallucination but ignored it.

Looking around, he noted that opposite the door, two holes had been cut into the rock masked by the rough-hewn nature of that wall. *The entrance,* Malcor realized, *and this section must be different mine complexes. This is how people get lost forever here*, he thought. *I really need to get that rope back. I hope the ghouls don't cut it.* It felt perfectly safe given his shadowform. *I'd never do this by myself as a mere human.* A few moments later, he shook his head. *Wait, I am a human. Why would I think that way?*

He mentally traced lines out from the holes and noted impact strikes against the door where a projectile-based trap would shoot anyone activating the trap. He carefully approached the doors noting the magical runes that blended into the floor creating a half circle in front of them. He wondered if the runes were some kind of activation for the trap. He thought about praying to Tiamat for guidance but something about this place made him feel cut off and disconnected, even from Cor'tanos. They had told him this would happen, he remembered.

Unable to consult his purpose, he figured that since he'd come all this way, it wouldn't hurt to explore just a bit more. Becoming corporeal, he turned back to the ghouls and called out, "Help is on the way! Hold fast, Bryant! We're coming!" He then cut his hand and let blood fall just inside the runic half circle. For fun, he flicked his hand splashing the pull rings with blood. Almost disappointed that nothing happened with the trap mechanism, he tossed his bloodied dagger into the half-circle before the door. Then, he stepped back in shadow form and waited.

The ghouls howled as they faked their battle, but after a minute or so, one of the creatures stumbled into the area, sniffing the air. Malcor noted that its left arm had been severed or chewed off. To the bone stub, a metal blade had been fused. Though cankered and rusted with age, he had seen what it did to the rust monster. Like the rope, the ghoul – Malcor had decided to call them blade ghouls – noticed the blood and the dagger. "Humans... fresh blood!" It stumbled over to the blood in the circle and scraped it off the floor. A forked tongue, long as an arm, snaked out to taste it. "Fresh blood!"

From behind, a stampede sounded as the others came charging down. "Blood!" they cried gleefully. One of them still dragged his rope. Seeing it, Malcor whispered a prayer of thanks to the goddess while mentally noting that he had completely forgotten about the rope. It bothered him. The rope ensured his exit from this place. *Why did I forget about it?,* he wondered.

They all wanted to taste the blood but seemed reluctant to approach the door. One pointed to the dagger and hissed, "Blood on other side..." The ghouls wavered in their resolve, swaying back and forth as they cried, sounding almost as if they wept. "Blood! Blood! Humans...!" Eventually, one of them dashed forward and grabbed the dagger. Coming back to the pack, it held the dagger and they sniffed, licking at the blood not caring that they cut their foul tongues on its blade. One that appeared less rotted than the others tasted the blood and then whispered, "Dragons... knife... blood of human!" At this, the group's interest in the knife rose to a crescendo of tasting and licking. As one, they turned to the door eyeing the blood on the pull ring.

Watching this, Malcor grinned in spite of himself. He found that he really wanted to see what would happen if they pulled the door open. Even though the images of treasure filled his heart with gold lust, he dismissed it. After days trailing the hellhound, he found this a welcome break. Plus, he had heard so much about the fabled mines of Bloodstone. To not enter one was unthinkable. A small part of his mind reminded him that he had been cut off from his purpose and was flirting with unnecessary danger. He wanted to scream out to them to open the doors. The most rotted of them all pushed a smaller ghoul forward. "Yous…"

The small one made a mewing sound and gingerly stepped forward. The group went quiet licking their lips. Those with blades picked at them sharpening the edge with their unholy fingernails. The small one stepped forward and then, its attitude shifted. With a taunting leer, it turned back to the group while its tongue lashed out and licked all the blood off the ring and the door.

The group howled at it and their leader gestured for it to open the door. Malcor leaned forward, and that was when he sensed a cold chill in the hand he had cut. Looking down, he saw a shadow rising up from the wall next to him, caressing his hand. The chill cold of the touch suffused through his arm.

Realizing he could not stay here anymore, Malcor stepped away from the shadowy alcove hoping the ghouls would not see him. Following the rope, he felt a brief moment of disorientation. The shadow continued to feed off his cut hand and probably would until he reached the surface. Reaching the intersection, Malcor raced into the dead end where the ghouls had frenzied. A long dead and desiccated husk of a corpse sat there bearing the tokens of Taysor. A gemmed sword hilt and a helm of platinum glinted through the dust and filth of the ghouls. Malcor swore. He did not have time to do this but he knew he needed to retrieve this corpse.

Shifting to human form, the shadow almost pulled back in surprise before terrible delight filled its purpose. Malcor chanted, "That which is made shall come undone!" and he swung his sword through the shadow's space. He felt the blade connect even as he unveiled his holy symbol of the Goddess. At last the shadow broke off from his hand.

Even though this happened in near total silence, his drawn sword and his chant made enough noise. He heard the ghoul pack begin running back to him and swore at whatever mechanism had allowed the shadow to communicate with them. A small part of him struggled with this connection noting that if the shadows could communicate with the ghouls, they could communicate with the hellhound too. But, a rage, driven by inaction and unpaladin-like creeping and stealth had, started to overcome him. He could hear Cor'tanos screaming, "You are the master of shadows! Show this low thing what shadows truly are!" He could hear Verit and Tembri and Dar Kendra ordering him to fight till beyond his last breath. He wondered why it did not bother him that he was alone. No Tembri here would recover him from death if he died.

He swung his sword as battle rage rose up to blur his vision. On a razor's edge of losing self-control, he prayed to Tiamat pouring out his soul to Her even as visions of Ora being killed and his son being stabbed through her womb filled his heart and mind. In that dark moment, he felt his conscious mind slipping away as his arms dragonshifted and he felt the heavy aura of berserker rage begin to take him.

As the last words of his last prayer slipped through his lips, the angel feather embedded in his sword burst forth in daylight radiance. "Thank you, Angel Teela!" Malcor praised. The light brought clarity. Struggling back up to his own action and self-control, he saw that not one shadow but ten had been feeding off him. The shadows recoiled from the sudden daylight. Without another thought, Malcor grabbed the Soran corpse and ran along the elvish rope towards daylight.

The end of the tunnel gleamed like the entire world as the shaft of darkness stalked him. Around Malcor's escape, more and more shadows clawed at him and at the light from the feather. His battle hymn sounding in his heart and mind, he jumped for the tunnel and exploded into actual daylight where his dragon wings caught the air. In that moment of exhilarating freedom, something jumped and tore at him and he noted the hellhound had been waiting in ambush.

Maybe the sunlight made it too slow to claw through the shadows spilling off Malcor, but he still felt claws tear deeply into his hind leg. The shadows of the undead fell away as they briefly became physical in daylight and then collapsed like dark ink thrown into the air. His sleek black dragon form rose up into the daylight.

A moment like this, starkly visible in the light - for any other shadow dragon, would be terrible; Malcor relished it. Without reflections of light on his skin, he no doubt looked like a two-dimensional black rip in the sky. He lifted the Soran knight held in his claw to his view and was relieved to see it remained as it had been – just a dead corpse. The blade ghouls had chewed through its neck, decapitating it.

Looking back at the tunnel, he wished he had a fiery breath weapon like the red dragons. Breathing shadow onto the undead shades might only strengthen them. Instead, he crashed into a tree and uprooted it to throw back at the shaft entrance. He missed having Tembri around to flamestrike the tree. Fire would definitely hurt those things. Even in sunlight, the angel feather gleamed more brilliant than the sun. Noticing it, his thoughts cleared a bit more and he felt stronger. "Why did I think staying in there was a good idea?" he muttered.

Chapter Thirty Five – Ready the Outpost

Hovering as a dragon in the sky, Malcor scanned the area and noted a Tanian patrol southwards. Swearing at his own foolishness for having lingered in the mine, he put his energy into speeding that way.

In bright daylight, he found the patrol lounging on rocks. They had removed their armor and after some alarm, they realized Malcor was one of their own. Malcor recognized them as a logistics team on day patrol. They had a dwarf with them who looked up annoyed at Malcor's arrival. When he had put the corpse on the ground and humanshifted, the patrol leader bowed and Malcor remembered his name. "Well met, Peyter," Malcor said. "I can't tell you how glad I am to find you."

Peyter pointed to the corpse and then seeing the grayed flesh of Malcor's arm and blood spilling from his left boot armor asked, "How may we assist R'Dar Malcor?"

"Bring your surveyor, the dwarf. I have things to hand off to you. I'm here on a mission but this is overdue. I've been uncovering mine shafts all over this area, and have been marking them. In fact, there is one about an hour dragon flight to your north though it is swarming with shadows, ghouls, and a hellhound. Be on guard."

The surveyor came over and took Malcor's map. He immediately began pondering the copies Malcor had sketched of the tunnel markings. In his blunt dwarven manner, the surveyor said, "Dread lord, I doubt you'll be here long. Before you leave, I'd like to establish some bearings for this." Malcor nodded.

Pointing to the corpse, Malcor said, "Peyter, this is a Soran dead. I am entrusting you to take this back to Valley Town with gear intact for identification. Immediately. That's an order. I don't want to risk this falling back to the undead."

Peyter looked at it and then walking over, struck the skull from the body. Watching that, Malcor marveled at how careless and stupid he had become in that mine shaft. Mentally sending a prayer of thanks to the Queen for protecting him from his own stupidity, he smiled at Peyter and said, "Wise man. Now, I know the day is beautiful, but I want you all mounted and heading back to Valley Town."

Peyter asked, "What about you, Sir Malcor? Will you not join us?" While talking, Peyter continued to eye the blood seeping from Malcor's boot. "Please, let us at least check your wounds."

Everything in Malcor wanted to say, *No. I'm fine. Leave me alone. There's more I must do!* However, he saw the concern on Peyter's face and when he at last looked down and saw how much blood continued to spill, he reached down and almost tried to heal himself. Thinking that, his head exploded in pain and he remembered, all of a sudden and with deep chagrin, his paladin vows and Tembri's teachings. He could only heal himself during combat, by dire need, or by inspiration. None of these conditions applied now. He sat down to cover the pain and unclasped his boot.

Immediately, a torrent of blood sloshed out and he found both the armor and the side of leg from just above the knee down to his heel had been gouged by the hellhound's raking claw attack. Another claw rake high up his armor showed how very close he had been to losing an entire leg. He fumbled for a healing potion, but Peyter already offered him one, tilting it into Malcor's mouth. The sweet elixir filled his mouth and washed through him, mending the wound and closing off the flow of blood but it lacked enough potency to completely heal his leg. Peyter gave him three more before a bright pink scar appeared and began to slowly blend in with his normal color. "You weren't kidding about there being a hellhound," Peyter observed.

Every moment in the sunlight helped him feel better and he began recalling things more clearly. "I am truly blessed that I did not lose my leg," he said rubbing the healing flesh. His hands shook with the fatigue that always came with magical healing. Peyter gave him food and drink. Malcor said something about how he had been tracking the hound since Thursday and Peyter's reaction told Malcor that he had lost an entire day in the tunnel shaft. He rubbed his head unaccustomed to being this foolish. "That felt like minutes to me." Malcor cursed himself mentally. "I lost extra time underground. Very well, maybe I should accompany you all back." He did a quick calculation in his head and noted that the hellhound, at its pace and the number of shadows in that area, "They could overtake you easily here in the wilds. Yes, let's head to Valley Town. I will accompany you."

Peyter seemed relieved to hear Malcor say this. Thinking on it, Malcor remembered that squad captains had conditional authority to give orders to even paladins but rarely used it. It never ended well for the captain even if he turned out to be correct. "How far to an outpost?"

"If we leave now, we can make it there right around sunset. We had planned to encamp here. We should go now." He gave an order and just like that the entire squad up-armored and were ready. Peyter helped Malcor refasten his boot. "We only have spare riding horses, not chargers. If you'd like, you can use my charger."

"No need," Malcor replied as he mounted up. As he recovered, he felt the weight of how many shadows had been there and then an epiphany struck. "They knew," he said. He swore. They had known he might enter and had set a trap a shadowshifter would be oblivious too. The corpse draped across a spare horse suddenly became suspicious but, with its head bouncing in a sack, it had to be okay. "Peyter, when your men took the Soran, they did not touch anything right?"

A quick check confirmed that they had followed proper handling of unknown magic in the valley. Bloodstone flourished with cursed magic items. The squad eyed the corpse uneasily and then with a sharp call, they raced south towards the nearest outpost. Exhausted, Malcor fell asleep. Peyter had his men tie the paladin to the saddle for the rest of the ride.

"Sir Malcor, we've arrived," Peyter said, waking him up. The sun had just touched the western peaks. A priestess, not Tanian, asked them a few questions and then opened the gate. A small shrine to Tiamat sat in the center of the fortified outpost. He recognized the priestess from the Nineteenth, a petite woman named Sofen. The small keep, ringed by wooden walls and spikes over a trench, held fifteen soldiers, two clerics, and a mage. Malcor did not see any other paladins.

Though feeling better, he sought out the shrine priestess, relieved this outpost had one. Most did, but the fringe posts fell too often to invest in a shrine. They placed the Soran corpse in the shrine while Malcor told the priestess to prepare to evacuate the outpost. Overhearing the conversation, all the others joined as Malcor told his story, and his plan.

"I realize that I'm supposed to know exactly what to do and that we're going to win. But, I tell you freely, we are going to face thousands of shadows, bladed ghouls, and at least one hellhound. This outpost will be overrun." He consulted his purpose but his senses remained overly dulled, sucked by the shadows. The attack had dulled his inner voice of wisdom that would have helped him hear the Queen's purpose. "Perhaps two or more hellhounds. My hope is to buy you time to evacuate and then I will see if the hounds won't follow me away from your route to Valley Town. I'll lead them away from you. For now, I want you all to light as many torches as you can, and make the outpost ready. Fire. I want lots and lots of fire. This outpost must burn on command."

About half the group were adventurers and at Malcor's words, they grabbed their stuff and began making ready to leave. The Tanian priestess, an outgoing woman named Sofen, snapped her fingers and ordered the rest to make it so. With the sun well on its way to afternoon, the group charged out in haste. Sofen stayed behind and stood side to side with Malcor. Peyter turned and waved as the forest swallowed the group from sight.

She brushed her mantle along her chain mail armor to smooth out its lines. "I arrived with the Nineteenth, Lord Malcor."

"Sofen, I remember you from the road." They stood in silence watching, occasionally seeing a glimpse of the group on the road. After a while, Malcor said, "I expect the shadows to arrive first, followed by ghouls. The fire will hold them back a while. Depending on when and what the hound brings with it, I order you to leave when I command it. You are not to linger. You are not to provide me any aid. My plan hinges on whipping them into a frenzy. I will then dragonshift and lead them away from your retreat."

Sofen nodded and then replied, "Though a member of a high ranking order, and though a hero, Verit did not put me under your command, my lord. I will stay and do what I can, but the Queen is not pleased with any thought of my retreat. She commands me to stay and abide with you." She took his arm and put her head on his shoulder armor.

Malcor looked at her worried that the cold of his body would affect her. It did not seem to. "If the Queen wills it, you must obey. I can carry you to safety, if I remember." As he spoke, her prayer song touched his wounds. His wits and senses began to recover. The wounds on his leg, still only partially mended from the healing potions, recovered even more. Healing fatigue pulled at him.

"Don't worry, fearless knight. When the foe comes, I will strengthen you. Until then, enjoy this glorious afternoon with me. I would know you, Sir Malcor."

Overhead, the silver falcon cried out and Malcor had to carefully repress a laugh. "The wounds I suffered... I need to save my strength for the coming fight."

He felt her body tense as she pouted, "If you say so."

"It's not often I get to really cut loose outside of training. I'm kind of looking forward to this," he said. Ice crystals blew from the trees, glittering in the late afternoon light. "Bloodstone does have its moments." Sofen squeezed his arm.

Sunshine and sunsets rarely happen in Bloodstone due to altitude and the ever- present chaos. The burning smoke of the Tanian encampments ensured the valley, even on nice days, sat in a haze. However, Malcor looked up and felt the sun on his face. He imagined it washing the remnants of the shadow dragon off his skin. In moments like this, he marveled that he had only been a paladin for a handful of months. In many ways, this whole area reminded him of the Khasran lich. Some time passed, lost in thought, before a gruff voice called out. "Paladin, let me in." It startled Sofen who remained with her head against Malcor's shoulder.

They walked to the other gate along the scaffolding and saw the dwarven surveyor. Sofen replied, "Grito! Why did you come back?"

He rubbed his hand over his bald head, helmet in hand. "The horse ride is too much. That knight," he pointed at Malcor, "marked all those tunnels. And, that door! I remember a reference to an early mine with a door like that. It was a Tanian outpost when they used to fortify underground. My job is to find bloodstones! How could I turn my back on my job, let alone what is sure to be a mighty battle?"

Malcor jumped down and unlocked the gate. Pitch and oil soaked everything flammable to such an extent that the smell of it stung his eyes. "Grito," he welcomed the dwarf in. "I cannot be responsible for you when I must ensure so many others survive."

"Aye, I know your plan. I'm here to help. And then I'm going to join you. That area from your map has not been surveyed in decades. Even if from the air." He looked at Malcor and then added, "I'm not assuming anything but I've heard you're a dragonshifter. Take me with you. This is the humble request of a surveyor too long surveying dirt, not bloodstones."

Malcor had not interacted with dwarves hardly at all but he appreciated the tenacity that had brought Grito back. "You think you might recognize the tunnel markings in person?"

Grito smiled a toothy grin. "Oh yes, and I'm thinking that all of the nasties will empty that tunnel and head this way. I'll take a chance and let Luck decide whether we go back or not. So the real question is, do you want to fight undead, save the outpost team, *and also* find bloodstones? Seems with some good tactics, we might do it all."

Something about Grito lifted Malcor's spirits. Sofen's healing had helped tremendously and his sense of purpose whispered to him that he should return to the golden door soon. He nodded. "Be careful though, Grito. Our departure will be hasty and I'm still very new to dragon flight." He pointed to Sofen, "And I've never carried more than one rider and then only for very short periods of time." Malcor laughed. "Riders? I'll be carrying you in my hands like this." He mimicked holding them with a dagger in his hand. They walked back up to the wall. "That way, you won't fall. I'm not a very good flyer. When the undead arrive, I want you ready to trigger the siege weapons." The outpost held three catapults loaded with fire and flame pitch mixed with dwarven exploding clay. Malcor had numbered them for Sofen to fire. "I'll need Sofen up here with me to make them think the outpost is fully manned."

They reviewed their preparations. "I doubt the hound attacks first, however, if it does, it won't come alone. We need to throw it back so that the other lesser undead attack." Malcor pointed to the perimeter where each fort had a ring of pitch and exploding runes set. "We will ignite the perimeter only when we have repelled the hound and cut off the initial attackers from the rest. A decisive victory with that small attack group, probably shadows, will enrage the others. Once they take the walls, I will dragonshift and take you both away from here. Sofen will flamestrike the outpost center, which will immolate the entire outpost. The key is to have the outpost crawling with enemies when we fire it."

Grito liked the plan and said, "My axe will cut a shadow. Standard gear for this cursed place. I like you, paladin. You seem foolhardly, almost dwarven."

Mal smiled and Sofen pointed to the west, "Look at the sunset!" Red and orange swirled together against thin layered clouds. Smoke from Tanian fires amplified the colors. The hazy sun slowly dropped as the mountain peaks all around sent their shadows to claw at them. "Listen," she said. "Have you ever heard the valley awaken at night, Sir Malcor?"

Glorious as the sunset was, the chittering coughs and growls all around started so low he could have mistaken it for leaves rustling in the wind, or some other natural effect. Then, as the sun dipped below the Sixth Fortress mountain, a howl and demonic scream tore the twilight. It came from the direction of the mineshaft Malcor had escaped. Grimly, he drew his sword and prayed.

A second much louder howl blasted the valley and from all around them, the unholy mist seeped, like blood squeezed from a sponge, out of the ground. Other howling screams rose up from all around and they heard wet sucking noises in the forest nearby. The cold and clear winter night made it worse. The sound of corpses pulling together, of ice-cracked bones stepping on frozen mud conjured a frightening image in their minds' eyes. The sun had warmed things enough for a partial melt and already the refreezing added the sounds of ice crystallization and then howls erupted from all around them at once. Sofen noted, "This happens no matter where you are in the valley."

Chapter Thirty Six – First Assault

In the gray space between sunset and moon rise, the hellhound jumped out of the mineshaft with hundreds of shadows clinging to it like baby scorpions. Landing amidst the trees, the hound's giant size toppled smaller trees as it spun in place to look back at the mine. From the tunnel, a vomit of darkness shot out and latched onto the hound. The hound spun and danced as hundreds more shadows attached to its body. The hound, the master of worlds universes away, hissed and bark-coughed a feral slur at the tunnel. As more darkness pulled onto its body, the sound of scraping blades rose up from the dark hole in the ground, and the first bladed ghoul shambled out.

Around the clearing by the tunnel's entrance, the hound put back its head and shrieked at the sky. Above the hound, the sky slit open as if cut by a bleeding knife. From the tear in the sky, a gate opened and malformed bodies spilled to the ground. Even as the bodies' bones shattered, the first pulled at those falling onto them. As the first strengthened, shadows from the tunnel splashed over to them and with liquid darkness stitched and knitted the bodies together.

More and more flesh spilled from the gate allowing the humanoid forms on the ground to stand taller until the largest one's face split in half and began catching the newcomers into its mouth. With each gulp, its body shuddered and enlarged. Moment by moment, the smaller masses mimcked this gross consumption.

Pleased by the abominations taking shape, the hound turned to the area all around it and whispered, calling to the ground to yield its secrets. Faster and faster, the ground broke its frozen mud and roots as skeletons and burnt fragments of bone rose up like a blister and then burst wads of bone and hair towards the hound. These shapes tumbled towards the abominations while more and more bladed ghouls assembled. The ghouls drooled and bit at the assembling remnants of creatures long ago slain. Some of the bones were swept up by the gangrenous pink mounds of the giants. Crisscrossed darkness opened to stitch and anchor the bone and those areas grew into armor plating. Others, the ghouls caught up and swallowed likewise becoming armored.

Even while undead continued to rise up around the gate, the hound barked at the group in swift commands. The entire horde turned and began to move towards the outpost. The abominations walked after the hound, their rear parts trailing bone and ichor still pulling into them. Seeing the group move, the hound barked more commands and then leapt southwards, fast outdistancing the assembling army. Behind the ghouls, zombies moaned and turned to follow.

The hound ran, dashing over trees, and leaping ravines and water. It could sense the lifeforce of the one whose blood had chased him so many days. The taste of Malcor's blood had lit its senses on fire and it wanted more. That blood fired its thoughts and gave it a remembrance of its great days past, when it ruled planets. It sensed two less-bright lives next to that one hot life. The hound shuddered to imagine what thoughts and remembrances would come back as it drank more and more.

The hellhound tore around a bend and found one of those cleared roadways its enemies made everywhere in the valley. Landing on this, it now charged south feeling the heart-throbbing heat of Malcor's lifeblood; it called to him. The road rose upwards and when it reached the peak, the hound saw the outpost. Its prey sat atop the barrier of wood. One of the cool forces, the hound sniffed and sensed was no doubt a priestess of the dragons. It howled again into the sky pleased that so much of the small life around fled or hid in terror. The shadows hugging close to their master hungered for food. The hound paid attention now to the fortress and saw the holy symbols etched along the outpost's wooden stakes. They posed no issue to the hound but might to others in its horde.

The hound threw its head forward and charged the gate. Its pleasure increased to see the defenders no doubt duck and hide in terror. Minutes later, the hound smashed its head into the main gate. The holy symbol carved into the wooden gate splintered apart as did the gate and framing walls. The hound laughed joyously at the stupid wood, thinking something so weak could resist its power! One of those dim forces, the dwarf Grito, stood before it and did something near a large machine. A metallic sound followed by pain as a ballista bolt shot into its side, and then ignited with burning fire.

Shadows clinging to the hound absorbed the brunt of the attack. The hound felt the shadows burning and dying fall from the bolt that still pierced deep into his hip. The wound felt severe enough to deal with it now. The hound commanded its body to reform. Bones reshaped to eject the bolt but before the bloody gash could mend, another bolt hit its other side. That was when an enchanted axe bit into its face.

The dwarf's ax hacked into his face again, followed by another bolt in its side. At a mental command, the shadows detached from their master and shot towards the dwarf, but the priestess, Sofen, moved in between them. She held her symbol of Tiamat high and commanded retreat.

The shadows paused at her command, which allowed just enough time for the hound to see they had arrived. Behind the shadows, the abominations would soon smash this puny structure to pulp. The hound cursed at the unacceptably slow shadows and their pointless delaying. In that moment, his real prey – the paladin - dropped onto his back. Then, pain erupted as Malcor drove his sword into the hound's lower spine. Igniting with the particular dragonfire of Takhissis, the hound screamed in agony. Through the roaring fire and pain, the hound heard Malcor sing out, "Let all that which is made, come undone…" Scrabbling to move and attack, the hound found its lower limbs paralyzed.

Though healing had started, something about the sword, the dragonfire burning along the sword, or maybe the paladin himself prevented regeneration. Unable to effectively attack, the hound clawed at the dimmer lives it could attack. At last, it felt one of his claws wet with mortal blood, deliciously. Not as potent as his prey Malcor, the blood still tasted like dragons. The hound's cruel laugh, mingled with pain, promised an eternity of such. The hound spun, dragging itself in a circle to dislodge Malcor. The puny human, no doubt fearing for its life, jumped free.

The hound and its shadows reformed to face the outpost's defenders. The dwarf ran to another ballista while the prey and cleric of dragons stood side by side. Wind blew a flurry of ice between the two groups, and then the hound sent the shadows to attack. They speared forward, but in that moment, they suddenly lost their focus. Though the hound ordered them to attack, they drifted purposelessly. The hound heard the whispered song of a priestess' prayer that would prevent the shadows from sensing mortal life.

The hound's frustration mounted and it leapt fang and bites at its main prey, the paladin. But, again, the dragonfire sword blocked the biting fangs of what should have been a bloody victory. In all its endless life, Malcor should be dead in its mouth now. The hound's momentum pushed it and Malcor along the icy ground.

Malcor punched his free arm into the hound's mouth and a shield appeared there. Malcor wedged this to hold the mouth open and cut sideways inside with that flaming sword. It hurt, agonizingly. Its mouth bled. Somehow, the hellhound sensed and jumped back just in time to avoid another ballista bolts from smashing through its head.

Now, the prey charged, pushing the hellhound back – impossibly backwards, keeping that cursed shield wedged inside the teeth, preventing an easy bite attack. The hound felt the dragon goddess' power, and something else, a sinister cold it had never felt before. It reminded the hound of the shadows. The hound's eyes focused on Malcor, to take control of this shadow force. Before the hound could do so, the prey's arm and sword pulsed with dragon magic. The hound's eyes met the paladin's over the shield even as Malcor stabbed his sword over the nose at the hound's eye. A wall of shadows rose up to intercept and though the hound felt its face slice open, its eye remained clear. Still, it forced the hound to backpedal even faster. Its spine at last healed and it could move again. Barking a mental order for the shadows to kill the defenders, the hound leapt out over the walls and retreated back up the road.

Invisible to the shadows, Sofen, Malcor, and Grito dispatched the remaining shadows with fire and magic. The hound felt the shades die one at a time, and its frustration grew. Licking the priestess' blood off its claws gave it only small glimpses of remembered power. The priestess' might barely compared to Malcor's. *I must have more*, the hound thought of the paladin. The trembling ground foretold the oncoming horde of abominations and bladed ghouls.

By the time Malcor's burning sword dropped the last shadow and they climbed the scaffold to see their foe, the horde had crested the hill. The abominations moved fast, rolling on the corpse hulks beneath their feet and egged on by the hound. Some of the giants stood nearly twenty feet tall, easily tall enough to step over their walls. As they walked, the bodies underfoot rolled to speed their downhill approach and Sofen pointed out the dead bodies lubricating their passage. The movement sounds made them feel sick to their stomachs. "We cannot fire the perimeter with these giants," Malcor at last said. "I doubt they'd even notice. We need to hit them with the catapults. Sofen, will you?"

Sofen enlarged Malcor and Grito who, now larger and stronger, quickly reloaded and aimed the siege weapons. Markers outside the small fort indicated aiming range in all directions. Sofen called for catapult number one. Malcor's shot bounced to the side of the undead giant but rolled and then ignited. It lit the area around showing thousands of blade ghouls, zombies, and skeletal creatures. Not all stood tall like the abominations and Sofen smiled to see the smaller undead mowed down.

Sofen's order for catapults two and three to fire came quickly and they raced to reload. This time, one of the shots hit a giant square on. The burning giant expelled gore from its mouth onto burning flesh, quenching the fire. A giant nearby also spewed gore to quench the splashing fire. Smaller shapes around the giant became visible to Sofen now. The bladed ghouls racing around the abomination were just as Malcor had described them. She made a note to share this with Dar Ana in her next report, *If I make another report*. The horde seemed without end.

Sofen yelled out the scene against the wind and roar of the coming onslaught. The defenders only got two more catapult shots in before the first abomination kicked the wall down and Sofen had to jump to safety. Singing out a battle song, Malcor stepped forward and cut the beast's leg.

Though each cut split the abomination foot and ankle apart, hands from within the wound reached out to hands on the other side and pulled the wound shut even as shadows stitched it closed.

"This isn't working!" Grito called as he fired his third and final catapult shot right into the face of another abomination looking over the spiked wall.

Malcor's song did not change except in volume as he sang more loudly. When the pale giant leaned forward to swat at him, he plunged his sword into the creature's face. The first giant, completely recovered now, tried to bear hug Malcor. Rather than stabbing and pulling back, Malcor stepped into the hulk's form as bleeding hands reached out to grab him. The two giants grabbed each other in a bear hug and Malcor slipped from view.

"No!" Sofen screamed, praying for fire to burn. Her caution at igniting the entire fortress slowed her too late for Malcor. Like the black hands that closed the wounds, the giant's bodies grappled and then swallowed Malcor. Sofen looked around frantically, for something, anything that might help even as she paused on the last word of the flamestrike prayer. *I must trust Malcor. Trust the Goddess*, she thought.

Before her eyes, the two giants' midsections began to swell and balloon. Her hope answered, dragon wings stabbed out and a dragon head ripped from the abomination's throat. The force of Malcor's dragonshifting threw the two giants back from each other. The dragon thrashed, shaking rotted flesh apart and tearing all the seams faster than grasping hands could reseal and hold the beast together. Silently, the abomination sloughed off the dragon's shaking. Individual zombies, and bleeding flesh clawed away from the splattered ruin. Many became trampled by Malcor the dragon when he spun about to tail slash at the other abomination.

The fallen abomination kicked out and struck Malcor just below his head. The blow sent a shockwave over them that threatened to collapse the outpost's walls and buildings. Malcor tumbled sideways and finished what the shockwave started along the southeastern wall and barracks. Though he rolled, he quickly regained his footing with a beat of wings that lifted him over the smashed wall.

Malcor felt himself too far into the throes of bloodlust. The feeling of the abomination shredding apart around him had been glorious. Part of his mind noted Sofen's tattooed markings glowed in his darkvision. He almost breathed shadowflames at his attacker. But, a still voice in his heart told him it would not work. He beat his wings and rose up just enough to get a view of the hellhound.

From the road's crest northwards, Malcor the dragon saw the hound glimmering in the ultraviolet spectacle of thousands of shadows gathering and spreading out to cut them off. He tail-whipped the abomination again enjoying how his shadow form tore at the shadows stitching it together. Sofen and Grito were doing an excellent job handling the smaller creatures dribbling off the abomination, but their time grew short. His training with Kell and Cor'tanos told him he had only a few more conscious decisions left before berserking fury might take him.

He had only left the flow of time once in dragon form. It had been very difficult. Cor'tanos did not understand linear time yet, but Dar Kell had explained until the Shadow Dragons returned to Tiamat, leaving the River would be similar to plane shifting. Malcor took a deep breath and prayed, concentrating hard, imagining himself rising up from the flow. He felt a burst of support from Sofen, and then it worked! The world around him, already two-dimensional and rimmed in purple outlines, wavered and then resolved into the otherworld of the ethereal river of time. His wings erupted from the flow sending a geyser of energy into the strange sky of this place. All around him, eddies and currents swirled about his dragon form and just there, so close he might touch it, the hellhound stood on freezing torrents of energy.

In the quiet of this place, Malcor looked down and saw the abomination about to be joined by four others, even as ten more had almost reached the perimeter. His own reflection, so demonic and twisted it looked here, stunned him for just a moment. All around, the undead horde teamed with shadows. Their outpost had almost been flanked, except for the sky.

A terrible growl broke his observations and he looked sideways at the hound, now aware of him in this place. It seemed about to say something, but Malcor leapt at the hound unleashing his breath weapon right into the hound's face. Time's frozen energy around the hound shattered under the gray and black shadowflame breath. The river heaved where the hound's sideways dodge tore into the static surface. As the flow of Time reasserted itself, Malcor's attack disintegrated the hound's cheek and shoulder.

* * *

Just moments before Malcor's attack against the hellhound, Grito struggled to reload a catapult already ideally aimed at where a newly-arrived giant stumbled forward to break apart what remained of the keep's main gate. Sofen did her best to hold the shadows and ghouls at bay as they scurried away from the dragon. All around them, bits of decaying flesh and bone squirmed as it sought a new host.

The bladed ghouls recovered first. They turned with an unearthly moaning, "Blood..." that made her skin crawl. Her faith held her firm against a growing number of wounds and she mentally ticked off the awards she would receive if she survived: wounded in Bloodstone, heroic feat in Bloodstone, exemplary service to the Goddess in Bloodstone, heroic valor fighting with a paladin... She grunted as a ghoul chopped at her side. Though she barely parried with her staff, the bladed arm tore her leg and added to the list of probably infected or poisoned wounds. Her holy symbol blazing, she shoved it into the ghoul's face and commanded its disintegration.

"Takhissis burn you!" she screamed. But, these bladed ghouls did not obey her commands, instead they seemed confused by the command and it fell back, clawing at its eyes. "Grito, the ghouls are stronger than normal!"

Grito swore as he took a slashing blow to his back armor while lifting a pitch soaked bladder of oil onto the catapult. He barely succeeded and the sack leaked as another ghoul slashed at him and he used the bladder to deflect the attack. "We're getting close to what the knight described. Hang in there, lassie. I need to crank this." Silence interrupted his words as the entire outpost area lost all color. Against the silence, a sound of rushing water began to grow in volume until the sound made the ground quiver. Wall sections, already battered by battle, began to fall apart. One of the giants lost its balance and fell over.

A bright light flared to their side where Malcor fought the abominations amidst the ruined wall. They saw the shadow dragon hesitate before tail whipping the abomination and then the world blew apart. A shockwave filled the space Malcor had been in and strong wind sucked them towards that location. The abomination he had just tail whipped fell forward splashing undead all about, many of which tumbled into the vortex.

Up the road, they felt a pressure shock and then a howl of pain and rage almost immediately overpowered by a dragon's shriek. As Tanians, they had been around dragons, but never had they heard a sound like this. Part rage, part pain, and a third part that felt almost concussive and yet filled with suicidal despair. A grey light blossomed in the sky and then rocks and trees began raining down around them. They dove for cover grateful that so much of the debris hit the abominations. Grito tackled Sofen just in time to dodge a catapult-sized boulder from landing on her.

Sofen swore, "We must get to where Malcor can see us. If he berserks, we are lost!" They helped each other stand. Then, carefully to avoid being seen by the abominations who stood dumbfounded as boulders and trees fell into and through them, they stepped out through a shattered hole in the wall. At the road's peak, they saw Malcor coiled around the hound as all four of his claws tore everywhere at it. Most dragons preferred rake and slash attacks, but Malcor drove his forwards like spears almost too quick to see. They could tell he was about to breathe again. Much of the debris in the air still lingered in the sky, tumbling almost-slowly in an outward blast. Motes of multi-colored energy danced all around. The gray light energy around the Malcor dragon and the hellhound hurt her eyes, like a headache in the back of her neck.

Sofen pointed to a clearing where Malcor would be able to see them and ran there holding her tattooed arms up in a cross to say, *Here we are.* Grito mimicked her and they jumped and dodged side to side trying to get his notice. They saw the hound's mouth bite into Malcor's neck even as five bladed finger claws stabbed up into the hound's lower jaw. Almost tenderly Malcor's head inclined down and he opened his mouth. Against the glow of the energy motes, an impossibly black beam shot down into the hound's skull.

There was the tiniest flicker of grey light and then the world erupted again in that flat two-dimensional grey. Silhouetted against that odd light, they saw Malcor's tail try to entrap the hound as the beast screamed and clawed away from Malcor. Malcor just barely missed but the two halves of the hound tore apart and separated.

Malcor's head moved side to side as it stabbed at the lower half and tossed it behind. He spun to dislodge the ghouls and shadows flanking to attack him. "Look out!" Grito shouted as more road section and debris started raining down around them again. Sofen grabbed his arm and pointed where, just twenty paces away, an array of shadows, now visible in the grey light, had frozen in their ambush.

Sofen flamestruck herself. The last thing Grito heard her say was, "I'm sorry, Grito. Malcor needs to see us."

Malcor saw the tornado of fire erupt from the ground and the glimmer of ultraviolet markings. He remembered that meant something but his foe was so close and so wounded, even though it had already started to regenerate. A sick feeling in his stomach told him that he had exhausted his shadowfire though his fighting spirit urged him to finish the hound at all costs. He looked back to Sofen and then to the hound. The hound had already started to pull undead near it to reform its spine and rear legs. He might be able to finish it but he might fall to the horde of shadows all around. He felt them hungering for him. He hungered for their deaths as well.

"Cor'tanos!" he screamed in draconian. He felt his memory stir and barely remembered that he was a paladin of Takhissis. He shook his head and swiped his talons through an abomination that shambled towards him. It fell cleanly apart in seven sections, but already pulling back together. This time, he roared out, "Takhissis!" With more power, he steeled his will to charge the hellhound and end it permanently. It felt wrong though, and he paused for just an instant.

Malcor shook his head again. At that moment, a gleaming silver falcon flew in front of his face. He swiped at it and then tried to head-butt it. It kept dancing there. To his vision, it appeared painfully bright and he squinted his eyes at it. It seemed familiar. He bit it. The falcon just barely dodged but put his vision right on Sofen as her flamestrike flickered out and an eager ring of shadows crawled forward. Sofen held Grito's charred body in her arms and wept. He heard her shout his name – *Malcor*. One of her hands reached out to him. Malcor bit at the falcon again and tasted a bitter metallic flavor as it burst apart in his maw.

Memories of Ora, his father, his mother, Tania, and then Tembri and his friends flashed in his mind's eye. A purring female voice whispered in his mind, *You are not a shadow dragon. You are my paladin. Complete your mission. Save my priestess!*

Choking on the gaping hole in his neck, Malcor spat in draconian at the hellhound, "Today, I let you live, slave." He then leapt into the sky, his shredded wings struggling to retain flight. Below him, the hound too wounded to give chase howled his rage back.

Malcor scooped up Sofen and Grito just as the shadows overtook them. He landed behind the outpost and looked at Sofen. She barely had enough energy to ignite the pitch. Once lit, that tiny spark of divine energy raced through the compound within seconds. The blazing bonfire etched the shadows who retreated to dark places out of the light. With her last energy,

Sofen brightened the fire to almost daytime intensity and then collapsed in his claws. Malcor leapt to the air again and used the brightness of the burning keep to leave the area and get behind a foothill before he circled back north. He'd have to fly until sunrise and hoped that Grito would be okay. The burnt husk of the dwarf seemed too inert and it bothered him. As a shadow dragon, he should be able to sense any flicker of life therein.

* * *

Alerius listened to the minotaur Windwalker describe his capture from The Spiked Horn. The priest of Baphtomet with him nodded his head, reassuring the minotaur that it was okay to tell a story where he almost died. When Windwalker finished, Alerius leaned forward in his throne. "It is not often I am blessed with a visit by the Taurans. I am glad my people found and recovered you." Alerius pointed to Windwalker's fur. "You must be a member of the emperor's family?"

Windwalker thumped his chest. Totally healed now, his fur gleamed. "I am the emperor's fourth cousin. Three-hundred and ninety-seventh in line to the throne. Baphtomet has blessed me with family and a name." Alerius joined them in making the holy hand sign of Baphtomet.

The priest pointed. "You are a son of dragons. You do this as honor, or to mock?" The priest's hand moved to the crossbow at his belt.

Alerius had to hide a smile. With feigned seriousness, the god emperor said, "Morbatten honors your race's great culture and powerful god. There is no falsehood in this. I'm sure Baphtomet," this time Alerius merely watched as the two minotaurs made the sign. He finished, "Would give the same respect for me and my goddess." Before the minotaurs could think about this too much, Alerius asked them, "There are many things happening in Morbatten these days. Though glad for Windwalker's recovery, is there a reason you climbed my mountain to see me?"

The priest bowed low. "God emperor Alerius, patriarch of fire, and dragon god of Morbatten, there is! During Windwalker's recovery, I was beset by questions and doubt. Then, one night, Bapthtomet himself came to me in my sleep. [hand sign] I saw the great horns of the Unstoppable Lord with my own eyes!"

Alerius hand-signed for the priestesses with him to bring the minotaurs drinks. Their religion tended to become long-winded when describing their god. When the drink arrived, the priest paused to accept and drink deeply. Alerius used this interruption to continue their earlier conversation. "The Unstoppable Lord is an ally of Tiamat. Did he send you to me?"

The priest bowed again and answered, "Yes, god emperor. He bid me deliver you a message. He said to tell you, The world galleon *Blade of Stars* is ready as agreed. All is in readiness for your great game." The priest's voice changed abruptly. It became gravelly and grinding. "For this, I would see a god fall myself. The Lord of Hells, Asmodeus himself, sends you interest and applause. I, Baphtomet, would see the Jade God fall."

The priest's voice returned to normal and he shuddered. The two Taurans made the holy hand sign with extra fervor. "I am ordered to say that Tauran shall ally with Tania. For my lord's benevolence, I am to ask for a gift honoring our alliance."

Alerius praised their words. "With great thanks, I accept this alliance. Though, we have always been allied." Both Windwalker and the priest looked confused but Alerius spoke over them. "Morbatten has gifted Tauran with many gifts since our first partnering centuries ago. For the Blade of Stars, to be at my beck and call, I will add to the many gifts: three small bloodstone blanks and a tower stone suitable for a ship."

The priest fell to his knees. "Thank you, god emperor. *Blade of Stars* shall sail on your command." He remained kneeled and pulled Windwalker down beside him.

Alerius rolled his eyes. "And for the bearers of this divine alliance, I grant you each this: a magical ring – one for divine and the other for weather control, and your choice of four prisoners to do with what you will." Minotaurs considered humans and elves a rare delicacy. Back on Tauran, they would be worth a fortune. "You are dismissed. Health and long life on the seas," Alerius said as paladins escorted them away.

When the noise of the Tauran departure had ended, the Temple functionaries around the throne waited in silence. The god emperor hated trading the bloodstones. Quiet enough only the Dar priestess closest to him heard, he said, "Note that we have acquired the *Blade of Stars*. Send word to the Mage's Guild to begin charging a gate large enough for three world galleons to come through."

The Dar bowed low and said, "It shall be as you say. The Mage's Guild knows of the *Blade of Stars*?"

Alerius raised his voice for the priestesses and paladins in the throne chamber to hear him. "The Taurans have a belief that, one day, they shall create a galleon so dread and awe-inspiring that their god will come to sail it at the head of their world-conquering armada. Each emperor begins construction of a Blade. Each Blade is then lost or destroyed in battle. This one, if we have read the omens correctly, will be aimed like an arrow at the Jade God."

A mischievous gleam grew in Alerius' eyes. "We shall fashion a proper decoration for the front of this Blade of Stars." Alerius opened his arms and an image of a tower stone appeared. Far too large for most of Tania, Alerius had left it intact under the glaciers atop his mountain. The stone's image shifted to a large and well-muscled minotaur. The image then twisted the face to take on Baphtomet's visage. The arms crossed its chest holding dual-bladed battle axes. Alerius continued to adjust the image and the emblazoned in Tauran, *The Blade of Stars through the Heart of the Abyss*.

Alerius studied it and then copied the illusion to parchment. The magic occurred thoughtlessly and perfectly. "Let's hasten this alliance gift and suggest that it be placed on this Blade of Stars. When the next cascade comes to Bloodstone, this should ensure it is spectacular."

The Dar took the parchment and sprinted away. When Alerius said "hasten" he always meant "immediately". Plus, the temple high clerics would need to be informed.

* * *

Revi pointed to *Bait Hill*. The key to Bait Hill lay in a series of rocky crevices not truly visible from below. Like trenches, a person could hide in them and remain unseen until a climber stood right next to them. "We'll try the hill," Revi ordered.

The Eighteenth had spent a frustrating five years in the valley with little to show for it except routine duties and encounters with lower level undead. In the third year, things almost became interesting when they found actual bloodstones. However, the quality of the rough material never panned out. Baiting tactics like what they were about to do, however, had led to some interesting capture of magical gear, armor, and weapons. The new Nineteenth dog soldiers moved about their business with efficiency.

Revi turned to Bruun, the veteran Ayden had said would be most capable. She was right. "Bruun, you know this drill from your time with the Seventeenth. Who shall we bait?"

Bruun looked over the group and picked three of the youngest. "You read my mind," Revi said. He walked up to them, "You three. You're the bait. Do you know what that means?"

One of the soldiers replied sarcastically, "We sit on the hill and wait for some terrible monster to attack us?"

Revi slapped him on the shoulder. Ignoring the sarcasm, he said, "I could not have explained it better myself. However, you left out-" Revi drew a dagger and slashed the man across his shoulder. "This part. You have to bleed your way to the top of the hill." The soldier recoiled back, almost drawing a weapon. Revi slashed him three more times. "The more blood, the better."

The soldier trembled with the pain of the cuts. "Oh, is this your first time being cut up?" Revi mocked him. He tossed the dagger over. "Go slash up those other two. When you're all good and bleeding, climb the hill. Bruun will go with you. Once you're at the top, Lady Sofen will heal you. Now, get to it!"

Sofen whispered to him, "These aren't veterans. You almost killed that one."

Revi shrugged, "Then he should have been allowed to come here."

The three soldiers, healed now, sat atop Bait Hill and lit a bonfire. One complained, "This will be seen for miles all around."

"It is, after all, called Bait Hill," the first replied as he poked the fire to send a stream of sparks into the night sky. "At least, it's not snowing."

Sun fall occurred with Bloodstone's usual screaming and terrible grinding noises. They'd been out long enough it did not phase them anymore. Within twenty minutes though, a zombie rose up the hill's bottom. It's deep moan and eyes locked on the three soldiers reflected the firelight as hunger. It bore the clothing and fragments of armor of the Sixteenth Legion, almost eighty years ago.

The three could deal with this one. It frustrated Revi that two of the three were so wounded by this solitary zombie that Sofen would have to heal them. He caught her arm. "Let them bleed," he ordered.

From the forest all around, multiple zombies shuffled forward. "Always zombies. Always." He said, loudly enough for all to hear, "Sofen will turn them. Their flight will hopefully bring us the real prize we seek."

Twenty-two zombies climbed the hill. Perhaps sensing the fresh blood spilled by the fighters, their agility increased and they began to run up the last part of the hill. Sofen stood up and incinerated two that jumped at the fighters in mid-air. The rest, she cried out in Takhissis' holy name to retreat.

As one, the zombies turned and began moving back down the hill. "Run!" Sofen screamed. At her command, they fled as fast as they could.

Revi watched. "They're randomly scattering." He swore, "So, no controllers nearby. Ugh, I hate waiting." He eyed Sofen. "Would it be impertinent to ask you to reanimate the slain zombie? That works sometimes."

Sofen raised her eyebrow. "I could, Commander Revi. Are you sure you want me to? I am rated up to vampires."

He winked at her. "Yes, please. Make it scary and fangy." *She must be close to transcendence if she can handle vampires*, Revi thought. He tried to imagine her transcended. Right now, she looked to be in her mid-thirties. *A totally normal woman in her thirties.* Transcended, she would return to her twenties. She would burn with living fire. *She'll be so much more beautiful. She's no Ayden though*, Revi mused. *I've never met a female myrmidon who attained rank that quickly. Ever.* He looked at Sofen more closely again and shook his head, *No priestess would ever fall for a fighter.*

Sofen's prayer made the first zombie, killed by the three soldiers, twitch. The twitching increased and then claw morphed into being where ground stubs of fingers had been. The bulk of the creature's mass collapsed and filled in with a more slender form. Rent and draping skin pulled tight. The newly-animated vampire blinked and sniffed the blood all around the three soldiers, still not healed. Just as it would move to strike them down, Sofen stepped forward with her symbol. "I've brought you back. What was your name?"

The vampire struggled to think. "C, cor. Cori. I think." It's eyes flashed from red to black at the struggle to remember. "Why?" Cori pointed to the symbol. "I served that one too."

Sofen hated this part. "You fell almost a hundred years ago, Cori. Tania needs you again. Will you serve Takhissis in death?"

The vampire licked its lips and looked around. "There are many of you. For me? I hunger. So hungry."

"Not for you. For those that serve the Jade God. Will you serve Takhissis once more?" Sofen waved her hand and the three soldiers held a bowl forward of blood they had collected from their wounds. She put the bowl on the ground and stepped back. "Drink," she offered.

Cori the vampire blinked forward and drank the blood and then licked it off the bowl. While licking, his eyes remained locked on Sofen. "For your blood, I will."

Sofen shook her head. "No, in Takhissis mighty name, I command you to flee now. Go. Run. Never come back!"

Confusion and pain filled the vampire's face. "But, you're a cleric. I'm Tanian…"

"You are a creature of the Jade God. Run!" Sofen locked her face and emotions. The vampire's words struck her to her core. Her symbol flared and, without another word, Cori fled into the night.

To distract herself, Sofen healed the three wounded. She used her prayersong to mask the tears pouring from her eyes. *Please Tiamat, forgive me for not serving this one*, she prayed in her heart.

The answer came back to her. She felt it in her purpose. A quiet voice in her mind whispered, *Cori became prey. Tanians are not prey. No forgiveness is required though your sorrow is beautiful to me.*

Several hours passed while they refreshed the bonfire. Around an hour before sunrise, Cori attacked. Revi nearly screamed for joy. The zombies attacked en masse from the north, as a distraction. While the three fighters readied themselves for the zombies. A quieter group of ghouls scaled the southwestern side of the hill. Out there in the dark, no doubt, Cori watched and waited for a chance to avenge himself on Sofen.

Like the zombies, the ghouls burned against Sofen's faith. Stronger than zombies, they did not cinder to ash. The seven ghouls turned and fled. Revi called out, "That's it! Chase them. Remember, buddy up or you're dead!"

The fifty soldiers jumped up and, ignoring the zombies, gave chase to the pack of ghouls. They ran after them through the forest almost until sunrise. Sofen ran at the head of Revi's unit to ensure the ghouls continued to flee. They veered off into a swale, where the ground suddenly dropped along a frozen stream. Moving upstream, the ghouls dodged into a mineshaft with just minutes to spare.

Without pausing, Revi ran up to the shaft and looked for markings. A ghoul swiped at him, but Revi blocked it with his sword and then severed the ghoul's arm. A ray of sunlight arced down in the valley. Immediately, the valley fell quiet. "There are no markings!" Revi exulted. "It's unmarked!"

The unit cheered. An unmarked shaft meant the Temple had no record, meant it had not been explored. Sofen smiled at their enthusiasm. "No rest for any of you," she called out. "We're going in."

Ropes appeared while Sofen blessed them. They lit torches and began throwing them into the shaft. It was wet and most of the torches went out. However, a few remained burning and Revi, with Bruun and Sofen at his side, entered.

The tunnel went in a straight line ten paces before it curved right. Following this curve, they heard ghouls ahead of them. Revi signaled for ten to move forward and attack with Sofen and Bruun backing them up. "No casualties," said.

The ensuring noise of combat gave him time to pause. He looked around and then asked the others in the tunnel, "Check the ground with your feet. Look for a trap door or lose stones. Ghouls shouldn't be hanging out here and no one built this complex to be this short. We're missing something."

A minute later, Bruun reported the ghouls had been slain. "We recovered some equipment that looks magical. It's been wrapped." Bruun saw what they were doing. "I'll get the others on this too," he said and left.

It took an hour but at last, one of the dog soldiers called out. "It's not the floor. There's a mechanism over here on the wall!"

Sofen prayed and sensed that nothing bad would happen if they opened the door. With faith, she pressed the irregular stone into the wall. A series of clicks and metallic clanking sounds shuddered the entire complex. Gradually, the water flooding the tunnel began to move, and then drain. "Quickly! We need to sand bag the entrance!" Bruun ran back to the entry and grabbed four soldiers. "We'll use our bodies!"

The rest of the unit quickly improvised a rough earthen dam. It leaked, but it would hold for now. A trap door had opened. A rusty ladder dropped down in a miasma of swirling water and murk. "I wish we had a thief," Sofen said. "I don't like using the Queen for tasks better suited to a professional."

Revi smiled at her. "Good thing I began my career in the Thieves Guild then, huh?" He stripped off his armor and moved down the ladder. Most of the rungs had rusted out. He had to use the stubs left in the wall to climb down. Slime made it slippery. About halfway down, he looked around. The chamber formed a large cube. If there were passages, they lay underwater. Watching, he saw movement in the water of pale flesh. A purple tentacle shot out of the water at him, but did not reach. For just a moment, a ghoul-like face with a circular mouth full of teeth leered up at him. *Not a tentacle, a tongue*, Revi realized. The tongue slowly pulled back. Where it had hit the wall, broken rock fragments showed.

"Sofen, how many ghouls can you control or turn?" Revi called up.

"I haven't been tested, but in Tania just before coming here, I turned twelve."

"I see a strange ghoulish creature here. The exits from this chamber might be underwater. I'm willing to give it a shot if you can help with magical light and turning the ghouls." A second later, his gloves and boots began glowing with divine light. Ropes dropped down and his unit lowered Sofen into the chamber via a climbing harness.

"You're brave, my lady Sofen. I like that in my dragon priestesses," he grinned. "Let me know when you're ready."

"Dangling high above the creature is not very faithful. I need to be closer for Takhissis to bless me this way. You stay here and let's see what happens. Have your men ready to pull me up quickly." Sofen prayed. The ghoul circled them in the water below, waiting.

Sofen began to descend slowly to the water. Above them, a loud commotion sounded as men began to scream. Rending noises back towards the entrance echoed into the chamber. "What's going on?" Revi called out. The sound of weapons being drawn and combat ensued. Without warning, Sofen's rope went limp and she fell.

Gleefully, the ghoul breeched the water and opened its arms as if to embrace her. "No!" Revi shouted as he jumped sword outstretched to tackle the ghoul.

Though Sofen tumbled, Revi noted the focused look of faith in her eyes. It all happened in a moment. Revi stabbed his sword into the side of the ghoul. A clawed and webbed hand grabbed his face and tossed him aside. That sickly-purple tongue encircled Sofen's waist and coiled up to her neck. They hit the water together.

Above them, Cori kicked the small dam preventing the tunnel from re-flooding to pieces. Five soldiers on guard there lay dead. Bruun, who had shoved his way forward to face Cori, stood at the head of the thirty-six remaining. Burn scalds along Cori showed he had followed them in the daylight. Now, he stood just outside of the sunlight filtering into the swale.

Bruun clenched his sword, noting the bright patch of sunlight behind the vampire. With water flowing in, he had no idea what would happen. He had heard the ghoul and Sofen's cry when Cori had cut the rope. "In the back, you five, secure rope and arrange to rescue our command." Without another word, Bruun charged the vampire. The five bodies twitched in their early transformation. Bruun prayed to Joust that the others would decapitate them.

Cori's talons gleamed in the light and he caught Bruun's charge head on. Bruun felt his sword drive deeply into the vampire's center and grinned. So did Cori. "You think a mere sword-"

"No," Bruun interrupted. He let go of his sword and heaved. The other veterans of Bloodstone followed Bruun and helped him push. "A sword won't do it."

Inhumanly strong, Cori clasped his arms around Bruun and pulled the man off his feet. It prevented the vampire from seeing the others. Bruun agonized in pain as Cori squeezed and then felt sharp fangs bite into lower back. Bruun counted the seconds, *One – two – three*. The vampire squeezing him ignited in the sun. Bruun still held on, burning with the vampire. He thanked Joust for a worthy opponent as the last thing he did.

The veterans jumped back when Cori ignited. One tried to pull Bruun away but so furiously did the vampire burn, it was to no avail. A weak voice back in the tunnel called out, "No, it's okay. It didn't kill me. I need help though."

They spun and saw four decapitated heads. A dog soldier was helping the fifth slain by Cori to stand. The veteran cried out, "Don't!" It was too late. The newly-arisen vampire pulled the soldier helping him into an embrace. Fangs slashed the man's throat. Standing in the arterial fountain, the vampire slashed at the others who were too shocked to react.

Meanwhile, back in the underground chamber, a waterfall began filling the chamber. Sofen felt her body paralyze where the tongue touched her and she wondered, *When will I be blessed with goddess armor?* Her prayer finished at last and a column of fire erupted around her. The water, almost ten feet deep where she fell, exploded in a steam that vaporized everything to the ground to about five paces around her. She stood, immobile with the water ghoul swimming towards her. It fell to the instantly-dry floor and then began to burn in the steam. Sofen, though immune to divine fire, did not have the same protection from steam. Her eyes seered into blindness but she saw the ghoul broil and die.

Revi had landed far enough away that the flamestrike left him alone. When the steam filled the chamber, he dove underwater and was then carried towards Sofen when the water collapsed into the vapor pocket. For just a moment, he noticed a tunnel leading out of the chamber. It held a distinctly Tanian mark, for an active bloodstone mine. He rose up to take a breath, but the steam burned and he returned underwater, praying for a break.

He found Sofen. Her entire body, blistered. The ghoul was dead. Knowing she had even less time than he did, he grabbed and pulled her away from the hot area. When he rose up, he could breathe. Sofen had a weak pulse but was not breathing. He struggled to keep them both afloat as new water poured into the chamber.

"No time, like the present," he choked. The Thieves Guild had given him a false tooth as a parting gift. It held a healing potion. He bit down hard and ground his teeth in the way required to break the tooth. Holding it in his mouth, he leaned over Sofen and kissed her. The potion dribbled into her mouth. This super-potent elixir had the same magical effects as a powerful healing prayer.

Instantly, Sofen's heartbeat strengthened and she took a deep gulping breath of air before she vomited water. Then, she screamed in agony. The healing potion cleansed the worst of her skin's burns but could not heal her entirely. "Stay with me, Lady Sofen. We won. But, I need you. The dog soldiers need you." Revi tried to hold her to see his face.

He swam her to the ladder, where a rope dangled down. But, when he pulled it, the entire cord fell into the chamber. He found a small handhold and latched onto it. The water slowly rose. "At least there aren't anymore of those ghoul creatures," he said brightly.

Sofen coughed. "My waist and half my neck is paralyzed," she gagged out.

When the water at last reached the trap door, Revi pulled them through. The steam explosion had killed those closest to the trap door. The veterans had just started to work their way back to behead them when they saw Sofen and cheered. "Cori, the vampire from last night, attacked us," a veteran explained. "We lost Bruun. We lost many. Can you save these?" Revi saw they had already started beheading the fallen.

Sofen waved them away and stumbled forward. In the flickering light of torches, they saw her terrible burns and flinched back. "That bad, huh?" she tried to lighten the mood. She felt Tiamat's healing power rise up.

Of the fifty, they lost twenty-seven dog soldiers.

Chapter Thirty Eight – Ayden's Grand Adventure

Unter sat in the dirt of the mine shaft. They had just broken through a wall into a new section of natural cavern. The tunnel air smelled like it should, no foul odors of haunting things. It tasted cool and sweet. In the light of an oil lantern, he sifted the dirt noticing the tiny speckles of red and gold. Though they had mapped the entire complex and determined the best spot to dig, he had not expected to find a new tunnel. The promise of bloodstones made his soul sing and he thought fondly to the auction. He laughed at the thought of the Halflings winning the bid. It did not surprise him though. Where Tania controlled the stones and already contained so much wealth, it made sense they would select a beneficial bid that offered more than just wealth.

Helena and Thalian had proven invaluable and, against his better judgement, he had come to appreciate the Nineteenth legionnaires with his group. The battle priest Tembri had a charisma and reckless humor that had won over the dwarfs. "Even me," Unter muttered as he pounded the dirt and stood up brushing his hands on his armored mining skirt.

Unter stomped into the tunnel and smiled to see lanterns had been placed along the cavern. Bright quartz crystals gleamed yellow and white against giant crystals growing down from the ceiling. He sniffed as he walked the perimeter and tasted the faint scent of acid and metal in the air. Something felt odd though and at last he figured it out. Grabbing his team, the dwarves quickly spread out against the far wall and lightly with hammers began tap-tapping up and down the wall, and then onto the floor. With no apparent exits, the Tanians moved to stand guard outside at the tunnel's end points though Tembri and the squad captain Ayden – another quick favorite with the dwarfs – stood ready with the priestesses to give aid if and where needed. So far, they had been lucky to encounter only minor undead.

As Unter's mining team worked their way back from the far side towards the tunnel, one of the dwarfs called out in their gruff language. Unter called out an order in dwarven before remembering. In Tanian, he said, "Stand if you hear it." Quickly, in a curving line, the other dwarfs did similar things. They stood in a curve along the floor. "You see it?" Unter asked the humans.

Tembri shrugged, "I take it you found something that curves beneath us. Another tunnel?"

"No, a river. This cavern was probably full of water at some point. From the size and sound, it is flowing quite fast. I'd guess it about half the size of the tunnel we just broke through." He pulled Tembri over and pointed to some crystals, specifically pointing out fractures between the crystals. "If we hit areas like this hard enough, we could flood this entire cave complex. I have a question for you and the priestesses."

Tembri waved them over. Unter had the dwarves begin painting the line of the river and then ordered them to take crystal samples and begin looking for any secret, hidden, or otherwise not easily visible exits. Facing the clerics, Unter cleared his voice. "We have a challenging opportunity. You may not know this but the surveyors have recorded many correlations between flowing rivers and bloodstone veins. Though the complex has all the signs of our being able to find a vein, the river is our best indicator that we're getting close. I'm quite excited."

Helena asked, "The challenge is accessing and following the river without flooding the caverns?" Ayden and Bruun walked up to listen.

"Yes, you see – here's the rub. We shy away from magic because it's like a flare to powerful undead. So, we toil away with lanterns, candles, and fire. Normally, we'd divert the river, but embedded as it is, we cannot. Plus, we don't know where it goes. I have a proposal. Hear me out."

"It is well-known that your Temple stockpiles things useful to us all. Potions specifically. They have a far less magical effect than an actual spell. I want to ask that we retrieve enough potions for the entire group, some mages just to be sure, and some soldiers in case the river exits somewhere bad. We'll also have the mages for that right? To get to the river, we cannot crack it here. I'm thinking a mage could open a door about five paces down, ten paces down, however far it takes to get to the water. We'll send an animal in and then pull them back."

Tembri looked at the floor where the cracks were now glaringly obvious to him. "Water Breathing potions, we can get. However, dwarves are not swimmers. Even a gentle current can prove taxing when you're fully underwater. Based on what you're telling me, we'd be swept to Tiamat knows where. I'd like to suggest a different plan. We'll go with recall tokens. We'll use magic to doorway them in, as you suggested, and find out where they ended up when they recall back."

"Even better," Unter said. "I do not want to risk any of us when we're so close. How long will it take to get these things?"

Tembri turned towards to Thalian. "We need to send more than one. Thalian, if you'll return to the surface and request Water Breath and a mage with recall tokens, we can get this started."

Tembri and Seline quickly agreed that Tembri, Ayden, Seline, Sako, Noboyuki, Unter, and Helena would enter the water. Thalian would stay back with the miners to continue their survey and to backstop the guards. As a priestess of Tiamat, she could not outrank Tembri. "I should be entering the river, not a cleric of Krentismar!" she complained about Helena as she stormed out to get the potions.

Seline caught Thalian's arm before she left. "I'd like to go with them too, but in this case, we have a mine complex with actual bloodstones. This river is exploratory. We'll stay here with the certain prize."

The survey work continued and though they found a few good areas to tunnel, nothing new showed up. The bloodstone vein continued to yield low grade rough, but none of the optical quality gems they so very much wanted. The guards reported lower level mists easily dispatched by fire. When Thalian finally returned, she had a breathless mage in tow. The mage was part of a Soran adventurer party. "They won't let the mage go unless their thief came along," she said. The mage introduced himself as *Ian the Summoner*. The thief smirked and said nothing. Seline decided to let it go.

Thalian placed seven dragon statues covered in golden runes in a circle on the ground. In their center, she placed a small replica of the Temple's three great columns rising up through the central chamber's tall roof. "You will hold the dragon in one of your hands. The recall word shall be: *Cascade*. With the hand you're going to hold the dragon when you say that word, you will now each cut your hand and with blood, pick up a statue and say that word. Holding the statue, let at least a drop of blood fall from your hand to the Temple. This will link the tokens with the Temple replica and bring you back here."

When they had all done as instructed, Thalian said, "Don't lose the dragon statue or you'll have a long walk or swim back. Also, here are the Water Breath potions. They should give you about an hour of water breathing. Several points here, if you attempt to breathe normal air, the potion will stop working. As such, you will need to hold your breath should you leave the river or find an air pocket or anything like that you wish to check out. You all understand, right? When the potion stops working, you'll feel a choking sensation. Your lungs will be full of water and instantaneous death will occur. Be sure you hold the recall statue in the correct hand and say *Cascade* before you drown, are paralyzed, or otherwise die."

She turned to Ian who held an unnaturally calm cat along his arm. She said, "When you're ready, open the dimension door and send the cat through."

Ian pushed up his sleeves and with magical rings glinting on his fingers, cast his doorway spell. Clapping his hands, he then threw them wide and an oval slice of blackness opened in the room. Tembri nudged Ayden and whispered, "You can tell he didn't train in Tania."

Thalian leashed the cat and told it to jump through the doorway. It did. The leash immediately went tight and when they pulled the cat back, it was wet, choking, and furious but safe. "That confirms the doorway connects to the river." She looked at the group, "Who enters first?"

Tembri put his dragon statue in a secure pouch where he could easily retrieve it. "I'll go first." He stepped up to the portal and winked back at Ayden. He took a deep breath and swallowed the Water Breath potion while activating continual light runes all around his armor, clothing, gear, and holy symbol. A moment later, he jumped through the magical doorway. The others waited a moment to see if he recalled back, but when he did not, they followed his example.

* * *

Besides the shock of the water's cold, Ayden felt her body immediately pivot and spin as it tumbled. Her helmet smashed and scraped along a wall and she thanked Takhissis for it and the rest of her armor. The water swirled in vortexes and crazy sideways currents as it tore through the rock. Curling herself into a ball, she waited it out as she felt herself smashing around. A dark part of her mind wondered what would happen if she got stuck and patted her waist for the recall dragon, glad it stayed secure on her belt.

After an unknowable amount of time, the water calmed into what she imagined would be a gentle flow and the space around her seemed to open up. For the first time, she opened her eyes and found herself in a giant underwater cavern. The light from her runes illuminated a nearby wall and she noted the jagged but curved slices of rock formations common to such places. She tried to swim but found her armor's weight pulling her down.

Looking up, she saw a glimmer of what must be either an air pocket or exit. Looking down, she saw only the yawning dark of more water. Remembering her swimming training in armor, she realized she was falling at maximum speed and only the disorientation and size of the pool made her feel it as a gentle current. A new current had started pulling at her feet. She panicked for just a moment and then realized the pool must drain somewhere. As enticing as the air pocket seemed, she steeled her will and allowed the new sucking current to take her. *I wonder if any others are in here?*

Within a minute, the new currents whirled her in a tightening circle as it began to drain somewhere below. Fighting to stay focused, Ayden dropped a single light rune. It fell faster than her descent and, though the formless void made it hard to gauge distance, it stopped somewhere down there. Eventually, she fell close enough to see.

The opening gaped huge and wide. Another cavern opened below it. The rim though took her breath away. Pasty white humanoid figures extruded from the rim, grappling onto it against the vortex. Their heads yawned open as multiple tongues lashed out into the center, tasting the water. Around their mouths, a ring of eyes looked up at her light rune. Each of them held on with oversized clawed and webbed hands and feet. Her light rune had been snared by one of the creatures, which held it in the center. A circle of fanged teeth chomped for it, somehow missing the tongues.

Ayden started to count the ghouls, but realized it would lose her precious time. Falling closer, the circular flow held her a few paces over the tongues reaching up to her light, she noted that the rim was not actually a rim, but the entire lower surface of the cavern crawled with creatures like this, each reaching up to her light with purple tongues and circle mouths full of teeth. She did not remember any such undead, but given the pasty skin and ghoul-like appearance, she figured they must be underwater ghouls. *Bloodstone, always ready to surprise you*, she thought.

The sideways vortex kept her hovering above the snaking tongues and grasping claws so long as she opened her body up and swam. She thought she saw a glint of light down below the creatures and decided to try and continue down, so long as the Water Breath lasted. She drew her sword and a dagger, grateful for her choice to bring stabbing blades rather than the slashing blades Tania preferred.

She untied a small leather strap and let her dagger's scabbard fall. It swirled in the worst way, drifting in a circle so that almost all of the tongues would be able to grab at it. Ghouls had a paralyzing effect and she wondered what would happen underwater. She needed to pass that rim as fast as possible. She needed a distraction. She watched her leather sheathe fall with a twinkle into the area of snaking tongues. Within a fraction of a second of being in reach, three of the ghouls caught and tugged at it. *Maybe it's the light?,* she wondered how they had known how to find it. Even if she deactivated her light runes, the glowing rune being chewed on by a ghoul would still give off some light.

She deactivated all her magic lights. From the dim light of the single rune, the ghouls still fought and tore at her ribbon and dagger. The others still quested for more. She reactivated all her light runes and before she could think about it anymore, she closed her arms and legs and let herself descend, swimming headfirst as fast as she could. Just like her sheathe, a tongue immediately lashed out for her and she stabbed at it, pushing it away. The tongue coiled around her sword locking it tight.

Fearing she might lose her favorite blade, she wrenched her sword back. To her dismay, the ghoul launched itself at her with open arms. It used her pull to accelerate towards her. For some reason, the other ghouls knew not to grapple that one. Her adrenaline spiked in that moment of circular spinning as the ghoul pulled closer and closer.

She screamed as the water swept the monster at her, wishing she could fall faster. Seeing that the ghoul would use her sword to find her, she mentally cursed and let it go.

The ghoul, freed of her momentum, pulled the sword in and bit onto the metal. Her mind created the sound of it slavering all over her favorite long blade. Another tongue grabbed her boot and fearing the same, she kicked it off before the ghoul could jump off the rim towards her. It worked! She continued to fall, shedding armor and gear as she felt the tongues grab onto her.

Just as she thought she had cleared the rim, a tongue slapped down against her face feeling like textured stone. The left side of her face and forehead immediately went rock hard in a rictus of pain. She could not shed her skin and felt her heartbeat quicken as the ghoul launched at her. At least she had fallen past the others. By the sudden lack of pressure, she knew the ghoul had jumped at her.

Emerging through the drain atop a much larger abyssal pool, Ayden could not see anything other than the cavern ceiling overhead. With just a brief moment of time before she had to engage the ghoul, she grabbed onto another dagger at her belt wishing for anything that could cut the tongue and ghoul away. It felt wrong. Instead of a dagger, she grabbed a flask of blessed water and another flask of magical burning oil. She tried to remember if the magical oil would burn underwater. The oil made a great fire starter for emergencies; this counted as an emergency.

Ayden felt the great depth and pressure of water all around her and made a mental note to always keep a potion of Water Breath handy. The turbulence kept bouncing them back and forth. Just as the ghoul would get close enough to claw at her, the current would tear them apart. The tongue had also attached to her helmet and so her face did not tear apart.

During a particularly close encounter where she had to punch the clawing hands away, she stuck the burning oil onto the tongue. As she hoped, it adhered like mortar. Next, she steeled her resolve and snapped her helmet straps. A vicious tearing followed across her face as her skin stretched and then ripped off. *I'm in shock*, she thought. *That's why I feel so warm.* Freed of the ghoul, her heavy armor plummeted her down.

The water danced along her skinless wound and Ayden whimpered, trying to protect her face from any sensation. It did not work. She closed her eyes against the pain but her left eyelid had torn free. Unbidden, she remembered the gnolls of her youth. Images of scorn and repulsion from those she had been friends with piled on the pain of losing her family. "Poor, ugly child," the village had whispered behind her back. *No, that won't happen again. Tembri!* She imagined Tembri caressing and healing her. That thought helped and she prayed to the Goddess to clear her mind.

Above her, a bright flash of orange light lit up the water. She looked up with grim satisfaction at the ghoul wrapped in a faintly glowing steam bubble where the burning oil had ignited in the foul monster's mouth. With pain as her only friend, she turned her focus downwards, and hoped she had enough time left for all her pain to prove worthwhile.

Chapter Thirty Nine – The Dead Titan

Minutes passed giving Ayden enough time to register shock at the cold of the water and pain of her wounds. *The cold water probably helps*, she tried to convince herself. Her bleeding face left a red bloom in the water. *They must sense it.* A golden twinkle of light caught her attention and she turned trying to swim down faster than her passive fall. The golden twinkle turned into a shining glow. Without warning, the dim radius of her light illuminated a titanic armored form.

The titan had fallen face forward in the act of battle. A broken sword haft rose up from between its shoulder blades and she noted a purple glimmer along its blade of runes still active with magic. She moved away from the broken sword, which had a stony appearance. Swimming down alongside the blade, she came to rest standing against a gentle left to right current moving towards the titan's head. The armor beneath her feet turned out to be scale armor with each scale the size of Tembri.

She focused on the thought of her Tembri, and tried to hear his voice telling her to stay focused. She would need to return soon. With relief, she felt the recall dragon still secured to her belt. Each of the titan's armor segments bore a rune and at her feet's touch, she felt a tremble of magic that made her pray fervently for her own safety. Without hesitation, she slashed her lips with the dagger. The runes along the armor and sword resolved to her understanding. "Consecrated to Orcus", "Against All Living", and "Eternal Night," they read. It made her shudder. The titan had served the Necromancer.

Following the current, she swam towards the head noting various burn and blast marks. At one point, a hole in the armor exposed faint white bone. She reached the head and saw the outline of a fallen helmet further downstream in the current, which seemed to run faster and faster towards that area past the helmet.

Dark brown and yellowed skin hung onto clumps of long hair where it lifted and settled against the skull. With a shiver, she noted the rise of a second spine climbing up but it had been severed just below the giant's neck line. Whatever this was, it had been possessed by the Jade God and its foe had decapitated the sceptre there just below the nape. She hoped the sceptre's head lay far away. Clawing her way along the skin to the other side where more flesh seemed intact, she found a giant golden earring. A brilliant ruby the size of her body sat gilded and held in a ring of gold.

She squinted at it and almost squealed in delight when the bloodstone left the telltale sign of being visible through her one good eye lid. She held her hand over her marred eye and tried again to confirm. *Definitely a bloodstone*, she noted. *I wish I could take it back.*

Ayden thought about trying to trick the recall to take the bloodstone back too, but realized it would not work because of the blood bond. Tania did this all the time, *They must have bigger recall tokens or some other way of doing this.*

On a whim, she tried prying at the stone with her dagger. It did not budge, but it made her feel better trying. Getting closer, she noted chips along the gold prongs where someone or something else had attempted to free the tower stone. She calmed her breathing and put the odd feeling of water moving through her lungs out of her mind. She circled the stone looking for anything out of the ordinary.

Behind her, ghouls like those above slowly crept out of the armor and out from under the skin. She did not notice them tasting the water where she had cut her lips, where her face continued to bleed.

Circling the earring's edge, she found a gloriously adorned dagger stuck along the seam between golden prong and gem. Runes of a style she had never seen adorned its surface. It read, "Dual war, friend in need, doubled might, charge active." It looked brand new. She grabbed this and pulled. It twisted a bit but remained stuck.

Movement caught the corner of her view and she finally saw the ghouls, like those from the rim coming at her. Looking all around, she saw herself being circled. From the skin up above the head, she saw a ripple as more ghouls peeled the skin back and looked at her with their evil ringed eyes around those terrible mouths. She pulled one last time and when the blade popped free, she almost cried out in exaltation. The force jumped her off the titan's head and all around, ghouls leapt up reaching for her with claws and tongues. Whispering a prayer, she touched the dragon and screamed, "Cascade!"

Her last vision was a cone of arms and mouths reaching out to her and then she collapsed on hard stone. Convulsively, she coughed up water from her lungs and then dry air brushed her face and burned her lidless eye. She covered her torn eye and screamed in agony. Touching her face lit her body alive with pain and she thrashed over to the side, convulsing in shock.

All around, she heard and saw a flurry of commotion caught where she rolled to her side choking and heaving up water. When air at last entered her lungs, she shrieked in agony as her torn face and the pain it radiated convulsed her against the crystalline floor. She tried to look around but her lidless eye watered and then blood blocked her vision.

Underwater she had not been able to tell how bad the wound was. She reached up to grab her face even as a woman's hands tried to calm her. She looked at her own hand, shaking as water and blood dripped from her fingers. Through her fingers, she saw other unmoving and wet bodies all around her. Blood pooled on the floor. Another wave of pain hit her and she screamed hoarsely, silently. Her entire body shuddered with the force of trying to let Thalian help her.

"Ayden," Thalian said. "You must calm. I'm trying to heal you but you keep interrupting -"

She tried to answer, to say something, but most of her face remained paralyzed. The parts that moved tore at the frozen wound and a terrible scream of wracking pain tore from her. "Shhh. Calm yourself. The paralysis actually saved you by preventing more blood loss. We have to dry, bandage, and tend you before removing the paralysis. You must hold still!"

Thalian's voice sounded shaky and Ayden imagine the outline of her skull must be visible through her face. She felt back trembling, trying to be calm but in too much pain to control her body. The cold chill assaulted her too and she prayed for unconsciousness, wondering why Thalian did not put her out of her misery.

Ayden continued coughing but gradually adjusted to the fact she was safe. The light and distraction all around hurt her eyes, one of which would not move to focus on nearby people and things. She did note that Tembri had fared poorly and lay unconscious against a far wall, barely breathing. Seeing the mighty battle priest in such a state almost triggered another fit and Ayden turned away trying to control her breathing.

Thalian came around her and asked the mage Ian to dry her. A spell cantrip later, Ayden felt completely dry though still freezing. The shock and the cold of the water stayed with her though. "Ian, warm her please." She heard a flamboyant, *Your Wish is My Command*, and then warmth susurrated throughout her.

Thalian turned her head towards her and Ayden saw the priestess's face go pale at the sight of her wounds. "It'll be okay. I've seen worse." Thalian pressed a wet bandage over her eye. "I've applied a salve. I know it hurts, but we need to be careful. The paralysis is kind of helping you not lose as much blood. I hate to tell you this, but Tembri and Unter both came back a lot faster, and in worse shape. Unless Helena comes back, I'm spent. Patience, Ayden. You must wait."

Holding the eye dressing in place, Thalian pressed more bandages against her face. To her horror, Ayden felt even more dressings applied from her lower neck, ear, and jaw up across her face into her hair line. Once there, the priestess tightly wrapped coils of bandages around her head to bind the dressings in place. Touching them, Ayden tried not to panic again when she felt the amount of bandages. Thalian clearly expected lots of bleeding.

Confirming her thoughts, a soldier and two dwarven miners came over and sat by her. "When the paralysis wears off, and we don't know when Ayden, this is going to hurt more than it does now. I've asked them to help restrain you. You will probably want to move or touch your face and head. Please do not. I'm praying your paralysis lasts long enough for the others to arrive and be able to help."

Time passed ticking in moments of pain and fire. Ayden tried to think about anything except her face and the pain. She failed. All her happy thoughts of Tembri fell when she remembered him slumped over in his own blood, and unresponsive. She carefully tried to crawl over to him.

Thalian must have approved as the soldiers helped her move over. With her one good eye, she saw Tembri had similar wounds to her own. Because Tembri did not wear armor, they seemed deeper, more extensive. The tattooed sections of his body appeared just fine, but around them, his skin had torn just like hers no doubt had. Some of the wounds went deep and she saw paralyzed tendon, ligaments, and along his shoulder, and lower neck, actual bone. Though it had healed a bit, Thalian tended to Unter, which meant Unter's wounds were worse than Tembri's. *Combat triage*, she realized. *My wounds are not life-threatening.*

She heard a noise in the connecting chamber and three clerics, each of different gods, entered in a hurry. Thalian pointed to them and one each went to help.

A Pha Rannic priest helped Ayden stand and move away from Tembri. "Your name is Ayden, right? I'm Tomas de Vri. Listen, we need to help the battle priest. If we can revive him, he can help you and the others. Please, sit tight. If the paralysis fades, I'm right here."

Tomas and another priest began binding Tembri's wounds until at last Tomas held his holy symbol over Tembri's forehead and golden light began raining down on him. Ayden twisted to see the healing more clearly through her good eye. The radiance of the light calmed her spirits and she noted how the Queen's healing always energized her with excitement. Pha Rann's healing, the first she had witnessed, made her think of sunny days and gentle warm breezes. Flesh began knitting and healing as the other priest removed bandages from Tembri's most wounded areas.

A tingle along her face triggered a cold sweat and panic and Ayden fought the fear that things would get worse for her. Another tingle and the pain increased. Immediately, she felt her bandages flex and then blood began dribbling down her face. She felt a compulsion to blink her lidless eye, like scratching an itch just out of reach. She tugged at her helpers who watched Tembri's healing.

Tomas leapt over to Ayden. She could feel blood trickling down her neck into her armor. The bandages had saturated and were leaking blood. Each moment felt too long as Tomas prayed to his bright god. Those with her, grabbed her arms and legs and head as she began to shake and then a scream at last erupted from her mouth when the paralysis let go its hold. She felt Tomas touch her head and she went unconscious. The last words she heard were, "Even though this child rejects thee, let your healing light mend her pain and calm her flesh."

These words echoed in Ayden's mind until she felt giant calloused hands brush her hair back and carefully unwind the bandages. Her face felt hot and swollen. She tried to smile when she saw Tembri, even though she knew his hands' touch, but the wounded half of her head had a dull ache deep in it. "I was so worried about you," she said.

Tembri began laughing and she noted how tired he sounded. "It seems we all ran into the same creatures. All I could think about was how you were doing."

"I found a tower stone," Ayden said. Immediately, all sound in the cavern went still. "It was as large as me, already cut and polished and perfectly set, in a titan's earring. I had to try and get it."

From behind her, a dwarf called out "Hoorah! Of course you did!"

"I couldn't pry it loose. I failed."

"No, no you didn't. None of the rest of us found anything other than dark places full of water and undead." Tembri removed the last blood-drenched bandage and helped her sit up.

She saw the entire party and almost wept for joy when she felt her eyes both focus. That dull ache remained and she tentatively touched her face feeling the bright pink and swollen flesh. The scars of her youth remained and she sighed. She touched her belt and then asked, "The dagger I brought back, where is it?"

Thalian handed her a pouch. "We thought you might want this. Sir Ian already checked it. It's intensely magical. The writing, well, we don't know. It's not Tanian or any eldar runes we've seen. No one here can recognize it. It also defies magical reading, comes across as gibberish. The magic, I had the Temple commit payment to Ian to identify it, is quite remarkable. Ian?"

Ian stepped forward and bowed with a flourish, "The dagger allows you to capture and store magic by touch. That is, spell magic. All that magic gets held in the dagger until you release it, like a wand, by touching this rune and saying the command word, which I wrote down on this paper. Given you found it on tower stone, I'd recommend not testing it right now in case it's full. But watch." He waved his hands elegantly over the dagger while casting a spell and touched it. The runes on the dagger pulsed softly and his spell went flat right when he touched the dagger. "I have no idea what happens when you release the magic. Maybe lightning? An explosion? Definitely something will happen."

Ayden turned the knife over, admiring its exotic design and look. Now, in better light and under less stress, it looked beautiful if alien in its design. She waved it around and juggled it over her knuckles. "I'll need a sheath custom made for this," she said offhandedly. "I read the runes. I did not understand them, but something about dual and double."

Unter asked, "Tell us about the tower stone, Ayden."

In all previous interactions, Unter had referred to her collectively with the soldiers. His use of her name caught her attention. She looked at the dwarf and noted that his entire body looked like it had been healed. The others had fared little better though Noboyuki had returned the least damaged.

She told her story and though they pressed her for details, like if she had turned left or right as some fork in the river, it all came down to the fact that she had been rolled up in a ball and then entered this giant pool. No one else had found a pool like that. Unter and Tembri had tumbled through a passageway lined with ghouls and they had to recall almost immediately for fear of paralysis preventing them from touching or vocalizing the recall.

After Ayden described her ordeal in detail for almost an hour, the mage Ian raised his hand and said, "You know, I have an idea." He snapped his fingers, "We can teleport back, but this time leave a beacon by the tower stone."

Sako questioned this, "Teleportation requires the caster to know exactly where they're going -"

"Yes, and I didn't go there, but Ayden did! Don't you see? We can make Ayden a sorcerer for a day. With the right magic and the right spells, we can get the tower stone!"

"What do you want to make this happen?" Thalian questioned dryly.

"A tower stone is worth the paltry cost of gifting magic to Ayden. Don't you agree?"

In spite of all the agreement, Thalian waved her hands for quiet, "You all know the rules here. First, if we get the tower stone, it's beside the point of this mission which is to excavate new unmagicked bloodstones. Second, what "worth" are you talking about? Only Tembri here has authority to alter contracts and you are already being paid to render assistance."

Ian waved his hand dismissively and the thief accompanying him chuckled. Not having spoken much, the thief had to make several attempts before people realized he had anything to say. "A tower stone, even for just the finder's fee is sufficient for us. You are all Tanians. We will keep the finder's fee."

Sako and Noboyuki both started to indicate that they were not Tanian, when the dwarves around Unter spoke up in protest. Unter growled at the mage, "The finder's fee is where we derive most of our pay. You can't have it all. I'd rather not have a tower stone than pay you for something that is rightfully all of ours. If anyone has claim on it, it's Ayden. Speak up for yourself, lass!"

Sako then added, "Without Ayden's luck finding it and then her determination to risk all, this whole side quest would have been a waste of time. What gives you the right to ask such a thing?"

Ian bowed, "No right per se. But, we are here and can make it happen now."

"You know," Tembri finally contributed to the heated talk, "I doubt Lord Verit would appreciate any of this. Even though you are not Tanian, you are under Tanian command. Unless you resigned your charter?" He looked askance at them until both Ian and the thief noted they had not. "So, really, what stops me from ordering you to make this happen? An equal share of the finder's fee for a tower stone is plenty to go around."

Ian had started to perspire as he tried to look calm under Tembri's argument. He started to clear his throat to answer when the thief said, "Fine, but my team gets to use the beacon next to go back and take anything else worth taking. The armor scales Ayden described will be sufficient compensation. Deal?"

Thalian and Tembri turned to Ayden. "It's your call, Ayden. Given we still don't know how."

Ian interrupted. "I'm going to take possession of her. Using her memories as a guide, I can teleport back, and have access to my magic. She'd have to be okay with this. Possession is very invasive. Even I don't enjoy this, but it's fast and it'll work."

"No, I won't allow it." Tembri said just as Ayden had started to ask what it meant. "Possession in this place has a risk of casting souls adrift, as if Bloodstone isn't already drowning in the cursed. I forbid it. Find another way."

"That is the only way," Ian patted Ayden on the arm. "Think it over. Let us know. We're here for a few more days as added security and then we muster back to Valley Town." Eyeing Tembri, he added, "Don't be so protective. We all know the risks of this place."

Tembri sighed. "Dar Ana would pounce on this. If only we had a mage with us strong enough to effect a teleportation without possession. I've read about and studied this tactic in my own training. Anywhere else, it would work quite well, assuming Ayden agreed." Looking at her, he continued "He'd know everything you do. You can't hide from a possessor. The technique is used to raid memories for information and control actions."

Everyone looked at Ayden. "I feel a bit trapped," she said. "If I say no, you'll all think I'm hiding some terrible something. If I say yes, all I can think of is if I have any terrible things in my life that I've forgotten."

Tembri came over to her and gave her a hug. "If you say no, we'll understand."

Ian's voice magically came to them saying, "No, we won't understand. She's the only one who has been there and as such, she is the only one that can get us back. All we need to do is place a beacon there and," he snapped his fingers, "we'll be able to go back with everyone and anything we need to claim the tower stone, not to mention the gear she said the titan had."

The thief added again, "This whole expedition is based on there being rough bloodstones in here somewhere. We're not asking for any of that. Get the titan's gear and there'll be plenty of spoils for all."

Unter snorted about eavesdropping and magical scrying and swore at their slinking around. Ian stepped back into the room and said, "We all know Ayden's going to say yes."

Ayden hugged Tembri hard and said, "Okay, let's do it then. The longer we wait, the more likely this area is to be discovered."

"Are you sure Ayden?" Tembri asked. When she smiled and nodded, he continued, "Very well. Ian, prepare a modification to your contract and I will review it. We have some other preparations we need to make as I don't want to bring the Tower Stone into this mine. Thalian, send word to the nearby encampments asking for reinforcements. I'll need at least five more priests ranked to defeat ghouls, and every soldier we can get. I want all of them, here and ready for combat."

Chapter Forty – Running from Tania to Bloodstone

Farant's legs had long ago ceased registering pain, heat, cold, any kind of sensation. They ran. A dagger thunked into a tree near his head and he snarled back at Marcello. *I'd fight you*, he thought, *but my master needs this and then you'll pay.*

The barely-there animal path whipped branches and icy thorns at his body as he tore through it like a bull charging. With night or a storm, he would outpace his chasers. When day came, regardless of weather, he grew lethargic or hungry, and they would catch back up. He knew they used magic to chase him and keep pace. While part of him marveled at the bloodstone holding his body together, the small part of him that once enjoyed his humanity winced as another section of skin sloughed off his shoulder against a spiny bush.

Out of nowhere, a dark form tackled him as magical rope entwined his legs. He tumbled face first down a ravine where others jumped on him. He felt swords, darts, poison, knives stabbing into him and shrugged it off. The rope snapped easily as he once again shapeshifted. His hunters fell back and he eyed them warily. Seeing too many to engage, he leapt out of the ravine, covering the distance easily and continued his run north and west.

Watching Farant run, Marcello held up the Sideways Amulet he had pocketed during the tackle. Even without the amulet, unrolling the vault with great strength or by dispelling the amulet's magic would reassert its true reality. *Better to not have the amulet lost in Bloodstone*, Marcello thought as he pocketed it. *The Circle will be glad to have this back in Tania*. He told the spider golem to let Sai know he had the amulet.

He signaled to his crew to resume the chase. The amulet looked a bit worse for the wear and tear of the almost ten days they had been on the hunt. Thankfully Farant had not used it for anything else. The key to the amulet is that anything could be flatspaced, even people. Once the guild members had left, Marcello faded into the forest shadows and waited to make sure he was alone.

When sure, he held the amulet to a large boulder and cringed a bit as the rock went two dimensional. Like Farant had, he rolled it up amazed at how light it had become, and smashed it against the ground. It made an odd noise like a mix of a hot spring erupting and lightning striking at the same time. In spite of its light weight, the entire boulder somehow retained its momentum and pulverized the ground where struck.

Confirming the amulet, Marcello said, "Sai spider, let the Circle know I can safely give the amulet back into their safe-keeping."

An instant later, a mage guild representative teleported in and retrieved it. They did not exchange words. Unlike most guild members Marcello worked with, this one wore the same armor and clothing style as Daryx. The mage unspaced the boulder, nodded at Marcello and left.

"That should restore my own reputation at least," Marcello said to no one.

Some distance away, Farant must have shapeshifted again because the ground trembled. A moment later, he heard a loud cracking sound. Whenever they got too close, Farant had taken to shapeshifting into some giant form or another and would hurl trees and boulders at them. At least they did not have to worry about other wilderness monsters common to these parts.

So far, Marcello had lost four members of his guild to Farant. They either had been struck and killed by these attacks or Farant had actually captured and sucked their life energy. Seeing how much that renewed Farant's health, after the first time, they had taken pains to ensure Farant never got that close again. They lost the second during a blizzard when Farant had shapeshifted into a small winter mouse and entered their camp. The liquefied remains they found when the blizzard passed had made Marcello grateful he had been out on patrol at that time, and had left Khalla back in Tania to oversee the guild's day to day.

The spider pulsed behind his ear again and, as he had come to expect, a mental image came to him of the golem master Sai holding the amulet, and bowing. Sai opened his hand and it morphed into a contour map of their path over the next days. It looked like tomorrow they would begin an ascent to a mountain pass. Focusing on that, Sai showed the location of a lair for a monster they could use to further frustrate Farant.

Marcello had never worked with the Circle before, but he found it unnerving how much they knew and how careful they were about using every single factor to their advantage. In this case, they would goad and drive Farant into the lair of winter wolves. Highly intelligent and malign, the pack would hunt Farant until Farant was dead.

"I understand," Marcello thought already thinking about how to ensure the wolves would go after Farant rather than his own team. "We'll let the wolves chase Farant to Bloodstone." He reached into his magical pouch and removed a canvas sack. He gagged opening it but felt glad they had grabbed some of Farant's ever-bleeding and shredding skin over the course of their chase. Of course, he had one of his subordinates get it for him.

Marcello activated a magical ring and began sprinting around the area of Farant's chase. The snow and ice did not slow him, yet the ground felt solid thanks to the ring's magic. When obstacles presented themselves, he jumped clearing fallen trees, icy streams, and at one point a small lake. Ahead, the foothills rose up into a mountain valley pass.

These mountains, called The Twins because of a double peak, did not connect to any other mountains but marked the beginning of a hilly rolling area that would take many days to cross. By going through the mountain pass, a traveler could cut travel time in half. The hills created ambush spots and some referred to them as grass dunes because they rose up gently on a side and then dropped sharply on the other. Not a problem in winter when the ground froze, it made for near impassable terrain in other seasons. Farant would not have a problem with it if he kept shapeshifting but his pursuers would. To his right, Marcello saw a tree go hurtling through the air and imagined his team diving for cover.

Farant had been such a promising recruit. They did not get very many drop outs from the Temple. Farant could have been a priest, maybe even a paladin except for his tendency to steal. *Well, I guess he became a priest of sorts*, Marcello thought while clearing a tangled patch of thorns frozen in ice. They had recruited him at the Adventurer's Guild when the Temple dropped him there. That younger Farant had been caught stealing jewelry from a high ranking priestess and when caught, had threatened to out that priestess' several lovers. Marcello would recruit a candidate like that any day. Stealth, cunning, foolhardly double-dealing – these were ideal for his guild. Once in the guild, Farant had excelled and quickly became a cell leader. *How did you fall to this, Farant?*, Marcello puzzled.

Marcello summited the first hill and began ascending to the peak when his ring's potency began to fade. Soon, the power would falter. He had used it too much and asked the spider golem to arrange for new rings for him and his team. He felt it pulse behind his ear in acknowledgement. So far, this was working out amazingly well for him. The resources and speed with which they came had empowered his team to hunt, chase, and drive Farant in a way they never could have before.

"I need to win Sai as an ally," he said stopping to catch his breath. Up here, his breath blew away in a strong wind. The trail upwards involved large exaggerated steps to ascend. He saw the subtle but telltale signs of something having come through recently. He hoped it would be a ranger. Winter wolves had some nasty tendencies to play with their prey, even when not hungry.

Looking back down, he could not see where his team or Farant was, but guessed he had a two-hour lead. Even if Farant drove his team into the hills, Farant would no doubt come back up this way to save the days of time this pass offered. A river on the other side was their target. Farant would probably shapeshift and swim thinking to lose them. He pulled his cloak more tightly around his shoulders and took the first step up. Based on the map Sai had shown him, he no doubt stood in the wolves' territory. Their habits involved watching, stalking, cutting their prey off from help, and then attacking. Alone, they might just attack him if hungry. He hoped they were not hungry. He could handle a few, but not an entire pack. Moreover, once they got his blood scent, they would not fall for Farant.

Chapter Forty One – Den of Wolves

He climbed uneventfully except for a few times when hoarfrost made him slip backwards. Tree roots and saplings gave him handholds to prevent worse spills. Every now and then, he saws the signs of a caravan that had built a now useless ramp to move their carts and wagons over particularly awful sections of the trail. The switchbacks would be easier, but Marcello had a schedule to keep and though the steep climb challenged his thief skills, he needed to make this work for his guild's reputation.

At last, he reached the pass where the ground leveled off and the cart tracks etched into decades of road repairs made travel easier. The wolf lair would not be here. It would be up one of the peaks with a clear view of the trail. Thinking about those monsters watching made his skin crawl but still, they had some merit. *If you could get a cub, they were worth money as guard animals.*

A thought struck him. *Sai's priestess!* He sat back on a felled tree to think. He had not noticed it at first, but yes, she must have transcended. The vast majority of priestesses in Tania had affinity to fire. However, a few – just a few so as to be a rarity - aligned with other members of the dragon family. Thinking of her white complexion that, granted - all priestesses had pale complexions, he then tried to remember the color of her eyes.

A transcended priestess always had fire – that was it, her blueish eyes had been just as pale as her skin and white hair. He had thought her an albino but now he felt sure. She had aligned with the ice dragons. He slapped his leg to shake feeling back into his fingers, "I'm going to get her a pet."

Down below, the ground trembled as Farant either uprooted another tree or triggered an avalanche or something. The sound that followed was closer than Marcello liked. He pulled his cloak over his head and went invisible. A potion from his robes masked his scent to match the smell of the forest. Moving as fast as care allowed, Marcello began climbing to where Sai's map indicated the lair sat.

Sure enough, he began to find the telltale traces of predators. The absence of normal forest creature markings, like bears and deer, confirmed that it had to be something like a winter wolf. A rocky outcropping over his head showed the perfect vantage point to watch not just the pass but the very course Marcello followed to the lair. He had not studied creatures like this enough to know what to expect. In fact, all he really knew was that their cubs netted very high prices, the younger the better. A wisp of fog caught his eyes and looking closer he saw another. It took a moment but then he noted the shaped outline of a giant hound resting against the rocks. The beast had rolled in muck to camouflage itself the same general color as the rocks.

He decided to move around the sentinel. No doubt the lair would be close and back behind that rocky area. Marcello passed the sentinel easily, grateful his climbing and stealth had not alerted the watchful pack. Several hundred paces back, the side of the mountain moved into a box canyon. He shook his head thinking, *No, this creature would not lair in a box canyon. They would want to be close and drive prey into it but would not lair there.*

He scanned the area and saw a cluster of trees that had wilted enough to be noticeable. He moved towards them taking extra care now. After a few minutes, his efforts paid off as he almost stepped on another camouflaged wolf. If it had been sitting still like the other, he would have stepped on it. A flicker of its ear as snow fell in it gave the giant beast away. Marcello froze just a few feet from the beast. He could not believe they did not have a stench or smell.

He waited for a distraction but none came for minutes. When it finally occurred, he mentally sent a thank you to Farant. Another tremble and then crashing sound brought the wolf to its feet. Its head bobbed side to side and Marcello almost had to move to avoid being bumped. Instead, it turned and circled around. Its movement gave the wily thief the sound cover he needed to back away.

The wolf sensed him but another explosion of noise allowed Marcello to get away and move towards the lair. A small crack between boulders would have been missed for such large creatures, but their coming and going had cleared the snow. He would need to go into that hidden crack between the boulders.

He carefully removed a card-sized picture of himself from a deck of cards and hit runes on it for substance and weight, sound, and simulated death. Having it ready, he moved to the lair entrance and entered. Farant's bluster had either prevented the males from returning or they had retreated further into the cavern. He twisted a different ring on his finger and the darkness came alight with ultravision.

The cave extended back, littered with bones. He would not be able to avoid making some noise crossing this. He gave the wolves some credit. Most humans did not think of such simple detection systems. He quickly charted his best path and waited for another Farant disturbance. It did not come and so he began working his way along the edge, even stopping to pick up a large bone fragment covered in chew bites. Almost immediately, a large female rose up from the back and came forward sniffing. She sensed something amiss but not seeing anything, returned to her hiding spot.

Soon, Marcello stood next to her and would not be able to continue unless she moved. He tossed the bone fragment, amazed at how quickly and quietly the she-wolf charged forward. He slipped into the rear cave. Four more she-wolves and a dozen or so young cubs ranging from small enough for him to take to what would soon be a fully-fledged hunter lounged in the cavern.

It looked almost impossible, but then he always viewed his job and skill as making his own luck. *The flatspace amulet would sure be handy*, he thought. He carefully made his way to the smallest cub that rolled in its sleep next to another. A she-wolf nearby, sensing something wrong, scanned the area in high alert, even growling threats at the other wolves.

Marcello moved into backstabbing position, perfect for a surprise attack and also in position to grab the small cubs. He considered going for and keeping two of the cubs, *One for Ora, one for me...* but decided against it. He needed two to ensure the pack went after Farant. Meanwhile, Farant had not made any more attacking sounds. *I can't hold three. I have to do it now*, Marcello thought. He stabbed forward at the she-wolf as his short sword materialized in his hand. His other hand threw the magic card forward.

The sudden movement of his attack alerted the nearby wolves but it was not until his sword stabbed into the spine of his target that her unsettling howl and pack's caucus din erupted. Immediately, his illusion card that looked and smelled just like him appeared and landed where he had thrown it. It ran for the exit. The illusion magic made it glow just enough that Marcello would have been able to see it even without light. The eruption of fangs and claws moving to the illusion card masked his next attack, which was to cut the wolf cubs with his knife, already poisoned with sleep potion. He dumped Farant's skin pouch on the ground and put the two wolf cubs into the magical space. And then, he ran.

The other wolves, already chasing his illusion, did not register his real presence. But, the painful yip of both cubs and Farant's scent did. Marcello threw the wounded cub at his illusion nearing the exit to the cavern where only one wolf at a time could exit. Running at the back of their charge, he felt tempted to attack a few more but decided he needed to reset his invisibility, fading to safety just as the large females at the rear whirled to go back and protect the other young. He had to hold his breath as they walked past for fear they would smell or hear him. Even then, the pounding of his heart sounded plenty loud to awake the armies of hell. The exit finally cleared and he sprinted as fast as he could for it as heads whipped around to follow the sound of his feet. The deck of cards fell behind him and all manner of illusions erupted from the deck as soldiers, archers, priests and priestesses, horses, support personnel, normal commoners, and other forms useful to a thief trying to blend in rose up from the deck and began following their default instructions. The wolves tore into these illusions with a vengeance.

Three wolves outside met Marcello's gaze as he cleared and adjusted his ring to remove the ultravision. Though they could not see his invisibility and could not smell him, he knew that they knew he stood in that single chokepoint. One of the wolves chewed and spat out the ink-stained card of his first illusion. In unison, all three howled and then howls erupted from the cavern. The nightmare sound of a winter wolf had been tested and proven to paralyze normal citizens of the empire. Only those who had fought in actual combat for several years, or trained for life and death, could resist the winter wolf's howl. Marcello felt it all and held his breath again hoping they could not hear his racing heart.

Shoulder to shoulder, they pounced forward snapping and clawing at the air. Looking eye to eye with three of these, Marcello could see why they would be prized as guardians. If he moved, they would know his location. If he did not, they would find him. He prayed to the Queen and ran to the side as fast as he could. The three wolves wheeled towards him as one and then the chase began in earnest.

Perhaps sensing his dire straits, the spider golem vanished and one of the wolves shrieked and tumbled to the side taking another with it. The remaining wolf seemed to recover morale and may have even laughed at the others' misfortune. Marcello could not take the time to activate his ring and so put extra effort into moving between and around trees and rocks that would keep something between him and the wolf. Able to see the snow moving around the human's movements, the wolf could not full-on charge but did not have any problem keeping pace. Behind them, and more quickly than Marcello wished, the others recovered and gave chase. The spider golem never returned.

At last, Farant did something that told Marcello generally where the shapeshifter was. Throwing caution to the wind, he sprinted in that direction. More sure of its quarry by sound, the wolf let lose another baleful howl answered immediately by the entire pack behind him. Thanks to the rough terrain, Marcello was generally able to keep something between him and the wolf. Though the beast easily beat him on the terrain, Marcello's invisibility plus his career training being dodgy somehow kept him just barely safe enough. Whenever the path gave opportunity, the wolf would claw or rake at him. Several times, Marcello had to slide or jump over the attack. On such a steep slope, he knew his luck would soon run out.

Just as he thought he was going to make it to the cleared area by the road, two females leapt at him from either side as a fourth cut him off. Marcello could not stop, and had no tricks left, so he screamed and ran straight at the she-wolf blocking his path. She pounced and Marcello dodged, dropping low and sliding on the ice and snow underneath the pouncing attack.

Marcello barely regained his balance, narrowly missed a raking attack and continued sprinting to the clear sounds of Farant's battle. Once on the stone road, his invisibility helped more by making the movement of his feet in the snow less visible. If the scent-cloaking magic had not worked, he would have died long ago. To his left, he saw Farant as a stone giant hurling shattered road stones into the trees. As the winter wolves barreled onto the road in blocking positions to trap Marcello, they saw the giant. Farant saw them too. Things seemed to slow for a moment. *Time to pray for luck*, Marcello thought as he sprinted straight at Farant.

With the giant in their line of hunt, which reeked of evil intent, the wolves moved forward cautiously, waiting for the rest of the pack. By the howling and baying, and with the pack numbers Marcello had seen, these wolves could definitely take Farant.

Farant saw only the wolves cautiously coming at him, scenting the road and eyeing him. With the Tanians flanking him, he could not afford to fight – something smacked against his thigh and he swung his fist around to connect or block whatever had happened. There was nothing there. He looked around and heard a faint yelping sound. A puny white dog lay at his feet.

"Stupid Tanians! You send your dogs to me now!" He stomped down on the cub and splattered it into the rocky snow. The wolves bristled and bent their heads back, not in a howl this time but a vicious growling yell. All around, the forest went silent.

Marcello ran into the Tanian flank and skidded to a stop. At a safe distance so as to not freak them out, he spoke a word in the dark elven language that essentially – to them – meant *Peace*. Because Farant could shift his form, they had taken to using a rotating safe word. Those nearest whipped their heads about looking for him and he said softly, "Winter wolves will take the chase to Farant. We need to drive Farant towards Bloodstone."

In the clearing of the road, more wolves arrived creating a veritable wall of curled fangs and white fur. Farant paid them no attention, focusing instead on the Tanians. He struck the ground with the rolled up guild vault sending a blast of rock and debris in all directions. Behind him, the wolves split into three groups. Two moving off the road onto either side to flank Farant. Marcello called out to Farant, "Hey, we need a rest. What say we call a truce for a day or so?"

Farant cackled and mocked them before finally side-tossing a cobblestone into the trees where Marcello's voice had come from. It tore through several trees shattering them before it stopped. "You get a rest when I say you get a rest!"

Marcello whispered, "Attack with ranged weapons, but miss. Remember, we want to drive him towards Bloodstone." The team immediately complied with Marcello's orders. As one, slings, darts, crossbow bolts, and arrows began sailing at Farant. One of the thieves, an adept often on loan to the Mage's Guild removed a wand and sent a giant ball of fire rolling at Farant. Marcello made a mental note to check on Ryvane and her new quest – Calvin.

"Another volley and then we fade. I don't want the wolves to hunt us." Then, more loudly at Farant, "No, we rest when you go to sleep in the sunlight. Give it a break, Farant! You're not fooling anyone. That bloodstone is not you and you're a fool if you think the Jade God lets you keep it!"

Farant batted at the ball, which moved slowly enough he stepped around it and then used it to ignite a tree. As was proving his pattern, he then threw the burning tree at them. They returned fire and then, as one, they vanished leaving Farant to face the pack of monstrous wovles coming at him from all sides.

Farant threw more rocks, more trees, and then turned northwest towards Bloodstone Valley and the path through The Twins. The winter wolves blocked his way. He began laughing. "Another stupid trick, Marcello! It won't work!"

Maybe he thought it was an illusion, like the deck of cards. Maybe he thought mere wolves could not threaten him. He walked into that wall of winter wolves as if it did not exist. Only when Farant's right and left sides exploded in biting, slashing, tearing fury did he realize his mistake.

Only his giant size and the bloodstone's ability to allow shapeshifting by thought saved him from being torn to pieces. Though he killed several members of the pack, and though he wounded all the fighters in the pack, the maiming they inflicted back on him made it so he had to stop. Farant realized that continuing the fight would weaken him so much that Marcello could easily take him. Swinging the guild vault like a battering ram to clear a space, he charged through. Immediately, he shapeshifted to something that could run faster than the giant form he preferred. The wolf pack gave chase.

For hours, The Twins echoed and reverberated with the clarion cries of Farant's death race and the baying howls of the wolves. Only when he reached the cliffs dropping down into the Cordabad River and jumped, did the wolves at last end their chase.

The smell of Farant matched the attack in their cave and the dead cub on the road. Farant must have the other cub. The alpha watched as Farant fell. The alpha saw Farant shapeshift into a bat fluttering down to the river. The pack would take their bloodthirst and Farant's scent to their ally on the southern face of The Twins'. A female held the vile pouch of Farant's skin and another held the murdered cub. The pack knew – Farant had the other cub. The alpha put its head back and howled out its rage. One by one the females and then the fighters joined.

Perched high in trees all around, completely silent and still, Marcello and his crew watched the wolves return, recover their wounded, and retreat to their lair. Their evil keening scream haunted them. "I'm glad they're after Farant," one of the crew whispered. They all agreed.

Chapter Forty Two – Ynt'taris Schemes

Hours later, Marcello and his agents slowly returned to the ground. A few had suffered wounds in their recent fighting and would need clerical aid. They moved far back from the wolves and then the mage-thief sent word to the Mage's Guild for assistance. A gate opened near Marcello's teleportation beacon. When Marcello stepped through, he was not at all surprised to find himself in Sai's silver garden of ever-changing metal statues.

Sai stood a few steps away, almost mistakable for one of the many human-like statues throughout the garden. "Don't worry," Sai said, "your associates all stepped through to the correct guild location where the Temple will tend to their wounds. The Circle has asked me to debrief you."

Marcello looked around at the metallic garden full of living plants and flowers all around. Though snow fell, it never quite reached any of the structures here. For all anyone would know, it was a late summer day just like all the other times he had visited. "I see R'Dar Ora is not around. I'd like to speak with her as well."

Sai's expression did not change at all. "She is busy with other matters right now, Marcello. To be sure, you have more important things to do than trouble my priestess. I lost track of your progress when the wolves destroyed my spider friend. Let's walk to the shrine. I'm aware of events up until the three wolves gave chase. I'm curious by your capture of the cub. It seemed unnecessary. Risky."

"My lord, if you have a holding pen or cage, I'll show you." Before he finished speaking, a metallic statue in front of them melted and reformed into a holding cell. Marcello removed the wolf cub from his magicked holding bag, and placed it in the pen. It crawled to the farthest corner and growled softly at them, still drowsy from the sleeping potion.

Looking at it this way, from safety, Marcello saw a glimpse of primal beauty in the cub. It reminded him of a near full grown husky. Sai looked at the creature and with that same lack of emotion noted, "I can feel a touch of Set in this one." Sai referred to Set, the Mother of All Nightmares.

"Yes, legend has it that the winter wolves were part of the same genesis as wargs and other dire creatures, just more specialized to winter conditions. From cubs, they become monstrous and untrainable. But, when very young, they can form a bond with a strong master and make excellent guardians, even companions. I've heard stories that Set dreamt of a blizzard threatening a dire wolf, and that is how winter wolves came to be. But, to answer your question, my lord, I took this one for a variety of reasons. First, the pack will hunt and never stop hunting anyone who takes one of their own, any age. I wanted to ensure they went after Farant and not me so this second cub was my insurance and second chance to get them after Farant."

The cub began chewing on the metal of its bars. Marcello pulled out some dried meat and carefully held it out. The cub pounced at Marcello's hand, smacking into the bars. It ignored the offered food. "Their training takes time but is worth it. My second reason is that I thought this would be an excellent gift for your priestess."

"She is in love with another human," Sai cut him off.

"You misunderstand, great Lord Sai. My guild – I – feel responsible for her involvement in this whole mess. Assuming it all works out, I wanted to give the ice priestess a gift as a token my guild's apology and respect."

"I see. If that is your true intent, it will be well-received. Ora has an unsettling effect on most of your kind. Her transcendence is not understood the way the fire priestesses are. I will tell her." Sai moved, without stepping, into Marcello's line of sight. "However, if this is an attempt to win her affections, I would caution you against it."

"Great lord, I have nothing but respect for your estate, for the R'Dar, and my intentions in this matter are sure. It is a gift. Nothing else." Marcello tried to imagine someone who could win the love of an ice priestess. They were so rare, he could not even think of a single legend or story touching one. The ancient tale of Ynt'taris' friendship with the Taysoran Queen Alaura came to mind. But Alaura, though she converted to Tiamat's way, died without ever becoming a priestess. "Tell me, if I might ask, is R'Dar Ora unique as an ice priestess?"

Without missing a beat, Sai's answer came, "She is precious to the white dragons." Sai's form flowed away and around the holding pen and continued walking on to the shrine. Marcello had to run to catch up and hear him say, "How Farant came into necromancy and established contact with the Jade God from inside Tania, that mystery requires more research. The Circle has tasked a young watchman with the job of tracking this. The golem Reggie assists to ensure success.

"You are to tell me all you know, and then we will send you and your team back into the wilds. There are two likely locations where Farant will exit the Cordabad. One is where it bends by the Sixth Fortress. The other is much closer to Bloodstone but being so close to the eighth and first fortresses, we expect Farant to shy away to the longer route. We will position your team near the river by the Sixth. The Nineteenth Legion will be watching near the Eighth and First. Now, tell me all that occurred."

When Marcello finished telling Sai about the battle, Sai opened his hand and another spider golem rose up from his palm and leapt to take its place by Marcello's ear. "Tell me my Dar, these are very handy. How would I go about acquiring one?"

"They are expensive though I rarely trade my personal work for currency. Flawless beryl and things like potent blank metals and ores are how most customers deal with me for golem creations. Once an arrangement is made, the golems decide if they'll serve you or not. The one destroyed, it would have served with you. I feel you have the right temperament to see these as friends, not magic "items". Moreover, the golems each contain a piece of myself. When I sell them, the buyer must replace that with their own essence so I might reclaim my own. Additional magics can be added by myself or the Mage's Guild."

"For this spider golem, to be with and give me its loyalty, how much beryl and blank material?"

"One hundred pounds of flawless beryl ore or three hundred pounds of blank metal suitable for golem construction. In addition, you will become obligated to perform some uncompensated favor for my estate at a later time."

Marcello's mind raced. His guild never held material like that but the Adventurer's Guild frequently stockpiled un-transacted hauls on behalf of its members. "Has the Circle decided when we'll be sent to the Sixth?"

"Yes, tomorrow at noon. Be at the Temple. Your team is already notified."

Marcello bowed and left the golem master's estate. Days like this always brought to Marcello a rush of gratitude for Tania's magic gear that mitigated extreme weather. As he turned east and walked towards the Temple, his mind drifted back to his youth.

His father, a retired officer, had joined an adventuring group and eventually settled for a time in Taysor where he met his mother. Taysor, even though it sat well north of Tania, enjoyed a more temperate climate along the coast of an extensive gulf. He remembered playing outside all year long. Though he hardly saw or knew his father, he knew of his father. Several half-siblings dotted his memory, but as a Tanian he often drew the wrong kind of attention. He spent a lot of his youth scaling walls to escape bullies.

He stepped aside as a carriage drawn by four horses crossed the canal bridge and moved past him. Marcello noted the gilded emblems of the Merchant's Guild. Eventually, he reached the crossroads where the East-West Highway split north to the emperor's mountain and south to the Great Bazaar. Normally, this time of year and with this weather, the grand intersection should be empty with only the shrine, taverns, and guild offices lit with inviting fires and warmth.

Instead, he sensed and then finally saw hundreds of horses. All the horses wore heavy armor and stood packed with gear. Squires attended them and struggled to keep the intersection clear for him and others passing through. A glimmer of pale white moved and caught his eye from across the gathering. He moved to get a better view and saw R'Dar Ora blessing a unit of paladins. Her goddess armor compensated for how pregnant she looked. Though pregnant priestesses were quite common, one in armor stood out. Her otherworldly appearance made it seem as if she glowed. No, it was more than that. Aware that she was a transcended ice priestess, he caught all the details he had previously missed.

Next to her, a small girl child stood in plain, unassuming clothes. The girl looked right at him and his blood froze before the dragonterror passed. The legends of the girl child, the human form of the ice patriarch Ynt'taris came flooding into his mind. A premonition that Ynt'taris wished to meet him came unbidden to his thoughts.

He grabbed a squire and asked the obvious question, "What is this all about?"

The squire looked annoyed but seeing Marcello's fine magical clothing, he caught himself and replied, "The call went out last night. All of Tania is mobilizing and marching to Bloodstone." The squire's facial expression clearly conveyed how stupid Marcello must be to not know this.

"*All* of Tania? Surely not. You mean a general draft -" Marcello struggled to understand and question the squire.

"Yes, that too. The emperor has ordered up all dog soldiers. Active officers, paladins, and adventurers are being sent along with any and all adventurer contracts. Sir," the squire explained patiently, "it's not just Tania. All the nations have been called by the god emperor."

Marcello looked back at Ora. "Thank you," he said to the young man and then pushed through towards Ora. He could not think of any times in recent history that this had happened, certainly not in his lifetime.

Ora blessed the paladins and their retinue in fluent draconian, her singsong prayer had just a touch of accent to it that again, struck Marcello how different Ora was from other transcended priestesses. The girl child locked gaze with him again and time froze. Ynt'taris stepped forward in a straight line, walking in air towards him from the platform. The dragon in girl child said, "Master Thief, I have been following reports of your hunt with some interest. I thought your handling of the wolf cubs noteworthy. If you have not exhausted all your spirit, I have a job for you. Interested?"

Marcello felt the cold terror in his gut and remembered someone describing Ynt'taris' dragonterror this way. Even though Ynt'taris could suppress it, the white dragon never did anymore except when dealing with innocents. Marcello tried to reply but his voice stuck in his throat so he nodded his head. "Of course, I'll do it. Whatever you need, Dread Lord Ynt'taris" was what he thought he would say. Suddenly, Ora's form sped up and her head looked his way. Her smile gave him strength and allowed him to shrug off the dragonterror.

The girl turned her head, looking at all the paladins unmoving and frozen in time around them. "Farant's master – Bomoki. I have a grudge with that one. Though the emperor forbids my involvement directly, I have a gift I wish you to give in such a way that Bomoki receives it." The little girl made a fist and when she re-opened her hand, a large diamond rested in it. She held it forward for the thief to take.

Touching the girl's hand and the diamond immediately robbed his fingers of warmth and searing pain of frostbite made him wince. The diamond, easily ten or more carats, sparkled with perfect radiance. "I take it that this gift will not be well-received, dread lord."

Ynt'taris giggled and walked back to the stage. "The gift will most certainly NOT be well-received. Your reward will be equal to how Bomoki enjoys this gift. I'll be watching." Stepping back to the stage, time reasserted its movement.

Ora finished her blessing and the paladins, knights, and officers stood. Another group waited. Marcello bowed low and respectfully to both Ora and Ynt'taris. "My lady, you look radiant even in a blizzard. As time allows, please check back near your shrine. I recovered a gift for you, a token of my guild's apologies that one of our own caused you and your master distress."

"A wolf cub, yes. Sai sent word. I am left speechless by this gesture. Rest assured that there is no ill will on my part towards you personally. The work your guild is undertaking is doing much to repair my master's grief that his estate is, at last, compromised." She smiled and the world brightened before Marcello realized that she just told him that Sai still had issues with his guild. Mentally, he swore.

"Depending on your time, I am happy to make arrangements for training."

Ora interrupted him amidst the new group wondering who this scrawny non-paladin was to interrupt the priestess. "It is not necessary. Your gift is much appreciated. See that your guild's work continues and when this is all over, we'll see if you and your lieutenants are able to breach Sai's defenses again. The best way to recover your guild's good name is to show that nothing is unbreachable."

So saying, she lifted her voice in a song that, even in draconian, reminded him of icy winds raging through craggy mountain peaks at night. Though not active in his faith, he felt an overpressure of might that made his body tingle and hair stand on end. She kissed her fingers and touched them to his forehead. In that moment, had she commanded, he would have done anything for her. Her touch electrified his body and he stood up a new man, full of energy.

"My lady priestess," he took his leave as the next group of warriors stepped forward and knelt for her blessing.

A voice cold and terrible trailed him on the wind, "Impress me, thief…"

Marcello turned south to one of his safehouses. Designed to appear as a small but well-to-do merchant's operation, it looked bright and held many textured bolts of fabric. The proprietor welcomed him in. After a brief rest, bath, a changing into the disguise of a fabric merchant, Marcello left the safe house to begin setting his Bomoki plan in place.

Snow continued to fall though not as hard as the night before. He could hear the horses and felt no surprise when a column of riders appeared to his south. Turning in that direction, he moved across the road and noted the less splendid gear and attire of the riders. They bore a banner proclaiming themselves to be an adventuring party. For fun, he asked one of them, "Tell me, are you too heading to Bloodstone? I thought the Nineteenth Legion had left long ago."

The rider replied heartily, "Oh, they did. I've always wanted to go but not as part of a legion. The command requirements and contracts are not enough. But, when this call came offering free claim to any loot taken from the undead, I just knew my time had come. You seem strong, sir. You should join us! Our captain would be happy to take you on!"

Marcello shrugged, "I don't think I have the skill or qualifications for this group. What are you called?"

"The Blue Falcon Harriers. I'm," but his sentence was cut off as his fellows swore at his delay and they moved off.

"The Blue Falcon Harriers," Marcello repeated as he continued to the Great Bazaar. In no time at all, he heard the noise of and then entered the outer perimeter of the marketplace. The center, strictly controlled by the Merchants, would be a mad house during this deployment. The outer edges, by the emperor's decree, contained those merchants not able to join the Guild or who refused to join for whatever reason. Quite a few members of the Thieves Guild retired here to the outer edge to work as appraisers, pawn brokers, lenders, and contracted acquirers. He headed to one of these.

The edge facing the emperor's mountain had much nicer, wealthier offerings. Marcello blew through this section. His normal attire ensured that no one bothered him. The great center square, those parts not filled with the giant dragon fountain, operated as a farmers and flea market. Crossing that, to the south and east, the quality of goods offered and the shadiness of services became more apparent. He turned onto an eastern road.

About a block off the fountain center, the east side's Merchant Guild-controlled vendors gave way to the edge ones. Independent escorts for hire, contractors for anything imaginable, and the certainty that anything offered for sale probably belonged to someone looking for it kept all but the seediest from this area. Here, Marcello's normal citizen dress marked him as someone with money to spend.

He found himself enjoying the change after the wilds as various interested "merchants" approached him and he deftly maneuvered himself to avoid being pick-pocketed. In no time at all, one of his own marked him and pulled him into an argument about price for a keg of dwarven ale. He let the merchant know his destination, and together they argued towards it. When at last they settled on a price, Marcello stepped to a ramshackle door and opened it.

Stepping into the comparative darkness, even in the growing light of morning, the shop appeared dank, wet, cold, and gloomy, Marcello saw the telltale signs that most others did not. A secret door behind the small desk led to the actual store. The wares scattered about the room made it look like a potion maker, when in fact, this had proven itself time and again to be the best place for custom magics. Though pricey, it avoided the registrations and recognition that came when someone with Marcello's resources presented at the Merchant's Guild's shops. He knew he was being watched and, rather than pretend to be interested in the junk laid out for street thieves, Marcello walked to the desk and stood patiently.

The front door opened to let in a bent over man. Walking with a cane and pained expression, the old man waved his hand at Marcello, "It's too early! Get out! Get out!"

"Marcello sent me, Halgrim," Marcello said.

The merchant stopped and looked more closely at him before saying, "Oh. He did. Then, give me a moment to get my shop put together and ready for the day. My assistant isn't here yet." The shopkeeper's voice sounded asthmatic.

"That's fine. The guild will ensure you have no other customers."

"Whatever. So Marcello sent you? Prove it." Marcello pulled out a small card bearing a mark from the guild and a terse instruction to bill whatever Ash, the name of his citizen disguise, required. "And you're Ash, still? Stupid cover name. You pay your bills on time. But I'll need bullion or gems upfront for whatever this is."

"Of course. It can be arranged, assuming you deliver in time. For this job, speed is important as Marcello will be soon called away."

They made banter back and forth while the old man lit some lanterns and wrapped a blanket around his shoulders. The chair creaked when he sat down, so did the desk when he rested on it. He had visited this shop many times as Ash. "You look a bit worse for the wear old man. Everything okay?"

Halgrim had retrieved a tea pot, heated magically, and offered some. "No," he answered. "I'm not. Age is finally catching up to me and these snow storms wreak havoc on my sunny disposition. Tell me about the job."

Ash removed the pouch with Ynt'taris' diamond and dropped it onto the table. The table immediately frosted. They could see ice crystals forming around it. Halgrim poked it. "I've never seen one of these. Do you need it identified?"

"No, I need it further enchanted. It's a surprise gift for someone the empire hates."

Halgrim cackled as he poked it again. "A surprise to an enemy is a marvelous thing. Magicked how? I'll need to understand this first before anything can be done. It reminds me of a bloodstone. Those normally feel oily and warm. This one, well look at it. It's cold."

"This enemy is a necromancer. He'll only accept the gift IF he thinks it'll help him against Tania. I'd like it enchanted to be anti-clerical or anti-paladin. Anti-dragon would work too but I'd hate to be caught with something like that in the empire."

Halgrim cackled again. "No time or resources for anti-dragon. I can't do it. The others though, maybe. Anti-how; what are you thinking?"

Ash rubbed his forehead, "It needs to be compelling. Tell me, Halgrim. If you were an enemy of Tania and wanted to destroy the Temple, what anti-magic would you imbue this gem with?"

"Ha! Anti-dragon. Obviously. But, that type of magic, though available even here, is rare and using it, having it, is a high crime. I won't do that. Not worth all the gold in the empire. Plus, no one even knows if it'd work on the dragons you'd want to take out here." He unrolled a scroll and began tracing some of the draconian runes on it. He started tapping one. "Here, maybe this?" He showed it to Ash. "Paladins, unlike priestesses, have to wear armor right? But unlike the priestesses, they have a certain level of magic resistance. We could make this appear to be anti-paladin magic, but in reality, it'd just be anti-magic resistance. In other words, we could nullify their resistance. That work?"

"It'd have to look and feel very specific to paladins. I don't think I have time get you components to target a specific person by name."

"Okay, so I need to test this and see if it can hold magic." He passed the stone over a rune on the desk. The entire desk surface bore runes on every surface. They glowed as it moved over any of them. Halgrim whistled. "Wow, this, Ash. *This* is special already. Not only is it loaded with enchantments and power already, but just like a bloodstone, its potential for magic is infinite. This gift, the receiver would have to be stupid to not test it. We'd have to mask all this magic."

Halgrim sat back and looked up at the ceiling. "The owner of this gem, he isn't going to come looking for it right, Ash? I mean, I'm just an old man. I do this because it's fun and pays the bills. I can't afford a fight."

"The owner is Marcello. He won't come looking for it. The one who gave it to him, he won't come looking either. I promise."

"Okay, so we need to nullify magic resistance. We also need to mask the magic it bears. That will be impossible. What we can do is mask some of the magic and let the anti-paladin stuff leak through. Then, we need to give this a housing so that it looks like more than just a shiny stone. The cost will be considerable. Moreover, if you want this fast, I'll need help. Lots of help depending on how fast." Halgrim eyed Ash lifting his last statement almost to a question.

"Tomorrow, before noon."

Halgrim choked. "Fine. Three hundred."

Now Ash choked. "In all the years of work I have brought you, all of it – ALL of it cannot have cost even a fraction that much!" He began pacing. *Three hundred thousand gold coins! I'd have to leverage the entire guild and its holdings, most of which is locked up in the vault Farant is using to rampage to Bloodstone. Could I get a loan? Is doing this for Ynt'taris worth it?* "In its current state, how much is this worth?"

Halgrim bobbed his head side to side and then cautiously replied, "It's equal, at a minimum, to a bloodstone same size. The rarity of this increases it even more. Blanked, of course, it's worth more. However, I can tell you that this bears considerable magic. And magic well-executed. Unlike so many with the stones who toss whatever magic is convenient in the moment, this bears the hallmarks of a true master and careful enchantment."

"I have a proposition for you, Halgrim." Ash did his best to pump up his charisma and smile. "Dread Lord Ynt'taris gave Marcello this job. No idea what the compensation is, but when the job is done – Ynt'taris promised payment. I'll talk to Marcello and he'll split the payment with you. Halves. Equal partners."

"But you have no idea what the payment," Halgrim began interjecting.

"Who cares? How often do the Dread Lords of Tania do something like this? You have a chance to be known, to show off your work, to add Ynt'taris as a customer! Think about it! Halgrim, this isn't just a dragon. This is the winter patriarch. When was the last time anyone heard of him doing anything like this? Princess Alaura's days? I can't think of anything that is not a time-distant legend."

Ash could tell Halgrim had started thinking about it. "Marcello's never stiffed me before. But, I'll need help. Even if I took you up on this, and it's intriguing – don't get me wrong, I need help. The helpers I need for this, they won't work on this, today mind you, without promise of payment. I can't tell them that a dragon made a promise to Marcello. I'll take the half, you pay my helpers directly. In gold."

Ash felt himself wanting to negotiate more but agreed for the sake of speed, "I'll pay up to ten. No more. If you can't get them for a single day's work for less than that, you pay them yourself out of your share."

Halgrim looked about to accept and then pulled his hand back, "Fifteen and we're good." He put his hand back out. "Fifteen thousand gold."

Ash swore, but took Halgrim's hand. "Done. I'll be back tomorrow, an hour before noon, to pick it up. Meanwhile, Marcello will have your place under watch. What else do you need besides security?"

While talking logistics, Halgrim touched a few of the runes and whispered, "Come in to work. I need your help now through tomorrow noon."

He did this five times and then touched a few other runes. At each touch, the shop shifted and moved, widening and opening up to a magical forge, spooled wire of different metals, and books and scrolls everywhere. In the center of the shop, now looking every bit a complete laboratory, an inscribed circle pulsed. "I'll see you tomorrow, Ash. If we finish early, I'll send word to the watchers."

* * *

Making his way back to the great fountain, Marcello sent word to Khalla to meet him at the Adventurer's Guild. It would take him several hours to walk there but with late afternoon sun breaking through the clouds, he felt warm and hopeful. "For what would an ice dragon want to take this risk?" *I could leave Tania forever and take that gem with me*, he thought wistfully. The thought made him laugh. Everyone knew that at a certain level of power, items like this were marked, known, and tracked. He argued with himself, *Then why would Ynt'taris give it to me this way? It's clearly a throw away trap intended for Farant's master, and is linked to some vendetta. Maybe the dread lords don't mark things that way.* The thought of it felt so seductive he had to shake his head to clear it. Even if he made it out, Ynt'taris would find him. Tania's ancient history conveyed deep and meaningful lessons. The one about not crossing the dragons seemed most applicable to Marcello amidst his temptation.

The clearing weather showed the emperor's mountain. A cloud cap sat on the peak and for just a moment, Marcello remembered the cold pit of fear Ynt'taris had created in him. "Dread Lords don't mark things the way humans do. Of course not, they're worse. Yeah, that won't work." A few walkers and shoppers around him gave him weird looks as he muttered to himself.

Eventually, after picking up some chicken skewers to snack on, he turned off East-West Minor and saw the top of the Adventurer's Guild. Rising up off the road as an actual pyramid, the ground level floor served anyone entering to post or check out jobs. The lower levels contained rental areas secured by members of the guild that could be just a small locker all the way up to massive all-inclusive and luxurious suites. As he guessed, the guild swarmed with newcomers willing to take the extra pay for a shot at Bloodstone. Many of them looked brand new, young, and green. They would not last long at all, but still the war machine needed fodder and distractions just as much as it needed actual swords.

A desk on a raised scaffold marked the end of a line snaking back to the entrance with signs reading, "For Bloodstone!" A priestess and her attendants listened, questioned, and signed up everyone. It was fast, efficient, brutal. Marcello saw what they did not – Tania wanted anyone with a pulse. As he got closer, he saw a paper on the floor and picked it up. It promised everything he knew but also a hundred gold death benefit. "If you die and cannot be revived, 100 gold is payable to your designated heir." He wandered over to the job board and while perusing it, felt a touch and knew Khalla had joined him.

"That line is amazing, and look at all these jobs going untouched. Maybe we should do some of these?" He tapped a poster for some mage on the wilderness edge southwards past the Dutchy. "Adventurers wanted to test and brave the Mage's Maze of Horrors!" A refresh mark showed it still active. It had been posted for almost a year now. "Complete the maze and earn a 1,000 gold coins each! Stay and help improve the design and earn a retainer stipend!"

"What do you think? I bet you and I could do this without breaking a sweat."

She squeezed his hand briefly and smiled. "We could, but our far more profitable business here would suffer. I don't really see you as a hero of the realm. You're more the quiet uncle who you know is getting stuff done but is never around for social gatherings."

He tapped another, "Check this one out. It's a shopping list of components. It read: "Needed – All of these, for which you will be paid 500! Not one, or a few, but all. Please deliver components to the Mage's Guild for payment!" Marcello put his arm around her. "Looking at these makes me think we missed our true calling in life. In my apprenticeship, I joined a few groups like this. It was fun, but quickly grew boring. Scout ahead thief! Pick the lock! Oh, a terrible trap – risk your life to disarm it for us!" He swore at the memory. "So, what's going on? Really going on I mean?"

They stepped into a shadowed alcove and proceeded to have a coded conversation that sounded like two normal adventurers talking about adventure. Underneath it, she told him that, "About a week ago, King Rojo contacted the Circle. All of the guilds were contacted including ours immediately after. Tania wants everything and everyone in Bloodstone. Yesterday. It's not just legal obligations either. Favors are being called in. You know that story about Gershon and the Merchant Guild?"

"You mean the one where Gershon's life was saved before he got to Bloodstone?" Marcello recalled the often joked about story of how Gershon's family had filed legal complaint after challenge to have Gershon excluded from military service. The Temple had wanted him though because even as a child, Gershon's mathematics ability had astounded even the god emperor.

"Yeah, that one. The legion commander of the Nineteenth Legion showed up at Gershon's offices. Marcello, they *gated* the Legion Commander from Bloodstone for this. Verit. I've heard and confirmed that Gershon, his bodyguards, and all guild militia are forming an army and going to Bloodstone." She squared her face up and made a double-chin impression of the Merchant's Guild's president and said, "Not for the empire, but to repay this damned joke."

She looked around at all the newcomers lining up to join before continuing, "It's more than that though. You know how there are always low level conflicts on the southern and western borders? Tania called a truce with all of them and promised their lords a hundred years of autonomy and reduced tribute if they send their active militaries to Bloodstone. The annual Winter War – cancelled. Taysor is going. The trade disputes with Morilon's elves – settled. Tania capitulated on all their demands providing that they send their armies. Same with the dwarves. Same with the gnomes. I've even caught word that Alerius opened this up to the minotaurs and that warriors from Tauran are already gating in."

"What's the end game? Did the Circle's messenger say?"

Khalla shook her head. Her words were, "You know how awful a rust monster fight can be without magic." Marcello understood her answer as "It wasn't a request. It's an ultimatum. Had I refused, I would be dead or imprisoned and the guild would be under a priestess' command now."

He replied, "I've never heard of anything like this. Is Bloodstone suddenly overrun by undead – I mean, more than normal?" They looked back at the line snaking out into the cold. They could not remember anything like this. "Khalla, have all lieutenants and their enforcers enlist as adventurers. We'll leave a skeleton crew here in Tania to hold things down. We aren't going to sit this one out. When my cell's current work is done – in maybe two weeks – I'll have one of my enforcers come back and take the Guild's day to day for you. I'm assuming of course that you want to go as well. If not, you're welcome to stay here in charge."

Khalla picked at her nails, "Where will you be?"

"I'm committed for my own sake and the guild's reputation. I'll be in Bloodstone long before this motley group arrives. I'll greet you there."

"Then, I'll enlist with the others. I'd like to form a company rather than single enlistments. We'll call ourselves *Rogue Blade*. That should make it easy for you to find our members should you need us."

Khalla leaned forward and kissed his cheek. He wanted to return it and more, but he had too much to do. "I'm sorry we can't have more time together, Khalla." Within three steps away, Khalla's training alone allowed her to see the path he took to exit though she could not see him at all. After a few minutes, hoping he would return, she stealthily exited the guild too.

Chapter Forty Three – What is a Cascade?

Rojo grimaced as he lifted his body from a prone position. Though recovered from the Darkhold's attack, he had yet to regain normal flexibility in his joints. The Temple gym had glass windows overlooking the valley and every so often, he would walk over and stare out the windows. Jeri meditated nearby. For the most part, the king had little to do here. Ana ran Bloodstone via the Temple exactly as she always had - delegated authority for different functions that occurred on time. Failure to perform resulted in a swift punishment, reprimand, and a second chance. More than that, functionaries would be swapped with combatants requiring a break from the valley. Though this meant a continuous change over in personnel, the functions always stayed the same and kept Temple operations working.

"Moments like this, I miss the view over Tania." The winter haze here sometimes compressed into a fog so thick it filled the valley like soup. All the fires perpetually burning ensured it stayed this way.

Jeri said nothing in reply but when she placed her head on his shoulder and took his hand, he knew she thought of different mountains that she had forsaken to join Tiamat. He returned to his training, pushing past some of the pain. Several hours later, a priest entered with food, drink, and a note from Dar Ana. "My lord Dar, lunch. Also, the note from the Lady Ana says that the requested information will arrive soon. Shall I bring it to you?"

Jeri answered, "No, send word and I will receive it directly."

The priestess bowed low to them both and left.

"It's too bad that we don't have any gold dragons laying around," Rojo said half-jokingly. "They'd make an excellent trap for Bomoki. The Mage's Guild checked; there aren't any in all the Isles."

"Yes, I've been studying and also spoke at length with Ana about Bomoki. Why is it that we have volumes of information about the key players in Tania's history but hardly nothing about that one? Even Ana had to admit that it's odd."

Rojo did a backflip and rolled to a crouch from a saddle horse. The popping sound of his knees and back made him wince. "It's not weird. Until Bomoki betrayed us, he was just another lower-ranking mage. You'll recognize this pattern in all of the Jade God's possessions. Though it covets more powerful hosts, it takes whatever is available. Consider this Farant from the Thieves Guild. From what we can tell, he was a cell leader with an interest in necromancy that no one knew about for years. Now, he's a freely-shapeshifting beast tearing across the wilderness with a bloodstone keeping him alive. If he had a wand, he'd be a lot more formidable. Daryx speculated that this changed tactic means that there is a force active here in Bloodstone that understands what the stones are, after all this time. The prospect of fighting a bloodstone-wielding vampire or lich is unsettling. It has to be Bomoki."

"From what Ana has told me, the wands and sceptres, because they are not created in this world, are not as powerful as they would be if in the Abyss. That is also unsettling. But, I guess it explains why the bloodstones would be appealing." Jeri walked over with lunch and placed it before the king insisting he eat.

"Eventually, the Jade God will figure out that it isn't just luck that we know when the hounds are coming through to this world, and when. We have a temporary advantage. We must use it." Rojo bit into a block of cheese and then broke off some flat bread.

Demurely, Jeri whispered, "If you ask, I will give you my eyes."

"No, and no one in the Circle has even suggested it. You demean yourself and us when you do this. Tiamat adores you, Jeri. She would never support this either. Remember, the mortals serve you. Not the other way around. Bomoki is one of us, not a dragon. Besides, even if the Circle requested it, I would veto such a ridiculous notion. Our history clearly shows that the dragons do not get involved at this level."

Jeri just stared at his hand drumming on the bench where he sat. "The emperor's histories show that the patriarchs have made great sacrifices for the people. Uncharacteristic ones for what I would have expected of the chromatic dragons. I wish I could claim similar sacrifice by the metallics, but then – that was my downfall."

"No, not a downfall. The beginning of your transcendence." Rojo touched her chin to raise her eyes to his. "The metallics have made sacrifices but their story in this world ended when they fled to heaven. Those of you who were left behind," he noticed how she winced at this part of the doctrine. "You were left behind, Jeri. Otherwise, you and your sisters would be in heaven with those dragons. We do know for sure that Oranstakar of Taysor has paid a price in isolation, faithless pandering, and ingratitude by the Soran people."

Jeri loved it when they had these discussions and she leaned into Rojo tempting him with a kiss. Like with Ana, Rojo casually stood up and returned to the window. She said to his back, "Perhaps this type of gym activity is not helping you recover, my Dar, as much as some other activity might." She always offered and he always changed the subject.

"Your sisters, Jeri, do you think they will answer the call to join us here in Bloodstone?"

"They do not understand the Cascade the way Tania does. They will come. The opportunity to face the Jade God, to destroy the gate, to fight great evil and end it – even if for a time; they will come."

Rojo signed to her, *Are we alone?* She nodded that no one could overhear them and no scrying watched. He said, "Tell me, Jeri, do you understand the connection between the gate, the Cascade, and bloodstones?"

Quizzically, she looked at Rojo and almost gave the typical answer. "I want to say that the emperor moved the gate here to save Tania, but I suspect you're about to tell me something new."

"The gate moving here is true. Bomoki opened the first gate smack in the center of what is now the city of Morbatten. Where the Fountain of Dragons is actually. Except for twenty-five saved by the first priestess Dar Tania, everyone in the city on that day died. The three patriarchs moved the gate to ensure that Tania would not become what Bloodstone Valley is now. Their intent was to move and close it. But, how would they know the gate mirrored the abyssal gate? When chaos is so strong, simple magic becomes unpredictable. Complex magic becomes chaos itself. Somehow, the gate and Bomoki became connected. That connection allows smaller gates to open from time to time, like the one in Khasra with the lich against the Imperics.

"Until we saw Bomoki, we had all hoped that he died in that great battle. Now, we know. He's still controlling the gate. For all these centuries, the hellhounds and sceptres are not being sent through, they are being brought through. By Bomoki. There's an upside to it though. Sometimes, a Cascade happens."

"Hardly an upside," Jeri interjected.

"An upside nonetheless. As increasingly pure beings connected to the prime nexi: Creation, Chaos, and Warp come through and fight, their blood, Time-based causality and emotions, falling near a nexal gate – the Abyss in this case, are what create the bloodstones. Think about this for a while."

He finished his lunch in silence. Jeri thought, watching the clouds moving through the fortress peaks and across the valley. At last, she said, "This is why there are no bloodstones except for here."

"So that you know, the first bloodstone was found in Tania, where the Fountain is now. Orcus' blood spilling from where Alerius ripped its throat open, fell to the ground saturated with the blood of divine and devil. That was the first. No others have been found in Tania. They all come from here since that first Cascade."

Jeri walked right up to Dar Rojo and took both his hands. "Tell me, Rojo, has Tania tried to recreate it?"

Without flinching away from her, he replied, "Of course. It always fails. The combination of a gate to the Abyss, blood from nexal creatures… yes, the Mage's Guild, even the god emperor and the other patriarchs have tried. It all fails. The emperor thinks it has something to do with the emotion present in a Cascade. Recreating it with anticipation and controlled magic, it does nothing."

"So, to be clear, Tania has taken the blood of -"

"Yes, in every way that you might imagine. This should not surprise you."

"Not surprising, but disappointing. I had thought the noble children of dragons better than this."

Rojo scoffed at the idea. "Each time there is a Cascade, many die. You know how Alerius sees us. To be able to create a bloodstone gem without the pointless death – well, we're okay with the Jade God and our enemies' deaths. Why is this disappointing? Even you bear several bloodstones. You cannot dismiss their value going up against those we have fought, alone and even together. Also, Tania is not questing out to slay creatures of Good, kill metallic dragons, and picking fights with every self-righteous "benevolent" ruler that pops up. I don't see your sisters flying off to become holy steeds for the Cuthberic paladins in Taysor."

Jeri fell quiet thinking again before saying, "Dar Ana, I have often wondered about her. She seems far more driven than the Dar priestesses back in Morbatten. Her role in this is to nurture Cascades. Am I right?" Rojo nodded. "So the Temple stockpiles here, her interviews with newcomers – she looks for ingredients to create a Cascade."

"Yes, though I would clarify that except for that first Cascade, the Jade God has yet to reappear. Sure, there are odd encounters by our teams every so often, but that isn't really and truly the Jade God; it's an avatar. This next one may be different as Bomoki can actually open a gate big enough for that god to enter our world."

"And why now? Why not earlier? I do not see why Bomoki would wait all these centuries to reveal himself."

"The dragon patriarchs did not want to just remove the gate from Tania. They wanted to destroy it, permanently. When they realized they could not, that Bomoki had gone into hiding, they banished the gate "to forever hide". This aligned with the chaos energy in the gate and this area and so it moves, always. I can see you thinking. I would say Yes. If Alerius had known the side effect would be that they could not find the gate and better control the Cascades, they would not have banished it this way. They seek to control and own this type of thing, not be victimized by it. And also Yes. If Alerius could control the Cascades, we'd have regular Cascades for the sole purpose of creating more and a more reliable supply of bloodstones."

"And the gold dragon eyes? Was that part of the plan?" Jeri suddenly looked as if she would burst into tears.

Rojo hugged her, pulling her head to his shoulder and stroking her hair. "No. We have never hunted or used metallic dragons this way. Even back to Dar Tania's days, the metallic dragons, even those like Cor'tanos and the shadow dragons too, are considered heretics who can still be won over. When the first Cascade occurred, there were no metallic dragons on these isles except the Taysorian gold. I know that the three patriarchs did not consider gold dragon eyes as part of the gate because the only gold dragon they knew then was your patriarch Oranstakar here by Krentismar's insistence."

She melted into Rojo's hug. "Gold dragons, we see things as they truly are, as they would be in the eldar times even if the realized potential is much less. I don't understand how this matters to an abyssal gate. I can tell Ana ponders this too." She suddenly pushed Rojo back and took his hands. "Promise me. If something should happen, if my eyes are about to be taken, you must kill me. I'd rather ascend to the Mother than let my eyes become part of that much destruction. Promise me!"

Rojo squeezed her hands and then said, "No. Even blind, you will be loved. The world needs your strength. Tania needs it. Better blind than dead and certainly not by my hand."

Jeri noted the firm jaw and resolute will in his eyes. She tried to continue her argument and instead, while forming the words, a tear rolled down her cheek and she turned and ran to the window. It shattered into glass fragments as she dragonshifted through it and flew away. The noise of glass breaking brought the guards swarming into the room. Rojo gestured and they relaxed swords and other weapons. The sight of a gold dragon flying off over the valley pulled at them magically. Even Rojo joined them to appreciate the lithe beauty of the gold as she banked and turned south towards the Temple fortress.

* * *

Calvin led his watchmen through Dock Side. They had explicit orders to "recruit" any able-bodied man or woman with capability to fight. Door by door, they consulted a census and interviewed the families. Any youth older than fifteen, if they had any capability with a blade, Calvin sent them to the Temple. He had grown numb to the implorations of parents, many who offered him money, their daughters, contracts of servitude. "I'm sorry, but it does not work that way," he had grown tired of saying.

On his feet, all day in the winter cold, made his time with Ryvane less than he wished. For the past two days, she had joined him and used her magic to speed things up. It had made all the difference. Seeing how effectively her charm spells quelled complaints by his own men and those they interviewed, Calvin had eventually asked her to try it on him. He still had to go through the same tasks, but he did so happily because that's what Ryvane had told him. It amused his real self to watch his body operate like a wind up toy. Knock on door, check census, intimidate parents, conscript their teens. Sometimes, he conscripted the father too.

When the spell ended, he sighed because all the aches and cold rushed in at him. He stretched and wondered if he was becoming addicted to this magic. Ryvane was talking with someone that looked like a merchant. He looked like someone Calvin should conscript. "Calvin," Ryvane said pointing. "I want you to meet a frequent customer of the Mage's Guild. This is Ash."

A man dressed as a merchant and wearing a gaudy Haven beret, stepped out from the shadows near them. Calvin blinked because the man, he was sure of it, had not been there just moments before. "Hi Ash. Calvin. Dock Side. Nice to meet you."

Ash bowed and said, "I cannot imagine the contract price to have Ryvane assist Dock Side. Truly, love's chores – priceless."

Ryvane poked Calvin and said, "Oh, he'll pay a price for it." Ryvane hand-signed to Ash, *Calvin is completely under my spells.*

They all laughed and Calvin felt a lot better. "What is your business with the Mages?" he asked.

"Oh, the usual. I do a bit of trade here and there and sometimes, I need special materials or have a client that needs something identified. Ryvane is the best. I find so many of the mages either pretentious or just slow."

"Are you suggesting that I should raise my prices?" Ryvane joked.

"No, my dear. Not at all." While they continued to talk, Ash included Thieves Guild code and asked, "Is Calvin secure?"

"Yes," she answered. "There are multiple witnesses in Dock Side and out who can testify truthfully to corruption, graft, and breaking laws equivalent to theft from the poor."

"Excellent," Ash coded back. "Tell me about Reggie."

"The Halfling seems to be driving Calvin to political office – Mayor of Dock Side."

"Do you know why?" Ash coded back while discussing the ups and downs of textile trading during war.

"My shop is in Dock Side," Ash said to Calvin. "I'd like to ask that your watch come by a bit more frequently, put in a show of force. It'll be good for my business. Should I pay you directly, or would your men like new equipment?"

Ryvane shrugged, "Maybe like us, Sai wants control of the eyes and ears of the law here in Dock Side."

Ash nodded. "What else could it be?"

That shrug again. "He knows Malcor?" Ash winked at her to say that must be it.

Calvin shrugged. "Whatever is more convenient for you, Ash. We could use armor that doesn't rust."

Ash handed over a pouch full of gold. It contained enough to outfit fifty men in new chain or scale armor. He knew that Calvin had twenty men in his command. Calvin looked at it and said, "This is perfect, sir. Your shop will be well-watched."

Chapter Forty Four – The Court of Dragons

Alerius quickly counted the many priestesses and paladins all around him. His human fingers drummed on the throne arm and a crystal ball of polished bloodstone swirled with many lights and images whenever his gaze passed over it. In front of him, a priestess shared a report from the Dock Side about Calvin's investigation and the minotaur there. Word by word, his mind registered it but other thoughts intruded.

"I am alone," Alerius said speaking over the priestess. She stopped, confusion on her face. "Time flows and the Abyss moves against us. It is time to act on my Rojo's request." He swept his hand to the side and everywhere, the many accoutrements of his humanshifted-self pulled side to side as the floor morphed and rippled. The kaleidoscope of floor patterns bent and shunted the throne chamber clear. The Temple functionaries assigned to him that day ran to get out of the way even as the great doors to his chamber burst open. On the other side, the paladins there grabbed two visitors as the suction of air almost pulled them into the room. "I am alone in the eye of fate."

Alerius dragonshifted, changing faster and faster in fits and starts as his human skein elongated. His arms and wings propelled him forward. The Dar priestess working at the god emperor's throne just barely managed to sound an alarm. Traffic in the tunnel dove to the floor or side. Alerius the Dragon God shot through the tunnel and exploded over Tania. His momentum and wings sucked all along behind him as the many massive statues lining that great tunnel animated and caught those who would otherwise follow and then fall to their deaths. The harsh draconian tongue blasted from Alerius as he called out, "Brothers. Cor'tanos. We meet."

Minutes later, Alerius landed on the eastern side of the great Temple At Morbatten. A white cloud had already detached from the peak of Dragon Mountain and moments later, Ynt'taris landed on the northern side. Spark arrived in a shattering burst of lightning on the southern side. From the front of the Temple, Cor'tanos arose as a dark mist through which spilled all those within the Temple unable to control or suppress their fright. Oblivious or choosing to ignore the many people around them and within the Temple, Alerius turned his head to Cor'tanos. "Too long, brother. We are glad to have you with us. My brothers." Fire cloaked his words and trembled through the valley of Morbatten. "A request from my Rojo. He asks for legions and we mobilized them. Yet, something-"

Cor'tanos interrupted to the growls and snarls of the three. "There is a weightiness to this, the suggestion of epic times."

Ynt'taris snapped at the dark mist form, "Do not dare to interrupt us, *brother*. You are not *yet* one of us." Ynt'taris turned to Alerius and bowed, "My brother, you are not alone. We are with you this time. And your children have far exceeded even Dar Tania from ancient times."

Alerius silenced them both. His force of his will trammeled shadow and ice's aggression to each other. "Though the Mother does not require it, I propose that our great spear, that our nation, be ready. The time has come to strike. Without Bomoki, I would send more legions. With Bomoki, with the necromancers using a bloodstone after all these centuries, with an eldar lich in Khasra just defeated, and precious Rojo's successor found. Yes, epic times." Alerius' continuing words smoothed over the others.

"And yet," Spark pointed out, "there is even more."

"Tell me what you mean by this," Cort'anos asked. "More prophecy?"

"The winter war arrives at last," Ynt'taris stated. The others nodded adding to Cor'tanos' confusion. Alerius beckoned for Ynt'taris to explain. "The winter war ended long ago. We continue it so that Taysor does not forget its place as our shield. And we feed the blood of the fallen to the sceptres."

Silence fell around them except for the whimper of humans from below in the Temple. Very few humans could hear the draconian of their speech. It came across as a deep rumble with different dissonant sounds unique to the four patriarchs. Spark leaned forward and whispered, "How many?"

"Enough," Alerius answered. "Maybe enough. Certainly enough to achieve tactical victories, or to sway the great battle. I cannot tell."

"How many?" Spark repeated.

"Thirty-seven."

Cor'tanos pressed again, "Thirty-seven sceptres? How does this matter to the Spear Prophecy?"

Alerius explained recounting how a Pha Rannic messenger had visited Dar Tania. He also spoke of their first encounter with the sceptres. He did not explain the cascades and the others said nothing about them. "The key is that each sceptre represents what the Jade God would consider his most powerful worlds within his dominion at the time of its creation. By removing them, by keeping them here cut off from that dominion, we lessen his dominion."

An illusion of thirty-seven sceptre's rose up between the four of them, rotating in place. "Each one of these is a hellhound. That many, we have taken from the jade one's dominion. With these, plus the many other artefacts my children have seized, we have different capabilities than we did during the first attack." Then, from all around them, one hundred and seven less elaborate, almost dull by comparison, septres rose up in the illusion. "These lesser sceptres, we call them wands, are crafted by powerful human necromancers as part of their pact with the Jade God. They also draw at its dominion."

Ynt'taris added an illusion of the many heroes of the realm both ancient and present. Dar Tania arose first followed by Captain Sean, the first Shak D'Rath, Alaura the Sage, and so many others. An ocean of ice blue heroes dotted the Temple dome. "The heroes of today are many. They will answer this call," the white dragon whispered. "This time, I will be here as will you two. Brother in Fire, you will not stand alone."

Cor'tanos watched the various illusions but still had an air of confusion. "The winter war "feeds" the sceptres?"

Annoyed, Ynt'taris shot back, "Yes. Those who die, their blood is harvested from the snow fresh and fed to the sceptres. The three vampire generals, they were the first and for centuries we have sustained them, cut off from their master."

The dark mist thickened and it seemed Cor'tanos may have attacked Ynt'taris except that Spark now added his own illusions calling forth the many dragons allied with Tania, and not just colored ones serving the Mother. "We are so much more and yet, the Jade One is all. If the gate opens, he will enter this world. If he enters this world, the cascade could destroy our Mother's throne."

"Long have we known this, no need to restate it." Alerius waved his claw through the illusions and they vanished. In their place, thirty-seven bloodstones appeared. Though highly magical, they lacked the aura of enchantment. All of them licked their lips. "It has taken millenia to acquire a number equal to the sceptres. Whenever I attained more, a crisis would arise and I had to release a stone to my children." Another wave and thousands of enchanted bloodstones, illusions this time, of all sizes and enchantments appeared. "Ynt'taris, this next part is your domain."

"The enchanted bloodstones, at least the ones we can call to Bloodstone, contain enough power to shatter the gate. Or, we can take them through the gate, to the Jade God's throneplane. Another option," and he began drooling, "is to destroy the gate after the Necromancer comes through. It would trap him in this world where we might permanently slay the Jade

God." He licked his lips and added, "That is my recommendation. However, the connection of these stones to it, their destruction there would obliterate the sceptres, in turn it would destroy the throneplane. This would leave us with blanks and whatever stones we continue to extract from the valley. The question is – do we destroy the gate to this world and trigger a cataclysm here, or do we risk all and destroy the Jade One's throneplane?"

Spark tried to speak saying, "Yes, this question must..."

"Destroying an entire plane of the abyss," Cor'tanos said. "That would have consequences."

Spark now described the three vampire generals. "Before The Necromancer learned to restrict the freewill of hellhounds, a strong one, maybe even Bomoki, enslaved a necromancer named Nientro. He goes by the name Nineveh here. Nientro became the first of the vampire generals and oversaw construction of the Bloodstone fortresses. In time, Nientro captured and vampiricized a mighty cleric of Pha Rann – Crea. Later, a mighty cleric/mage – Malcolm. Because Nientro had been granted free will, he let them have free will on condition that they find a way to break free from the Jade God. This was agreeable to Crea and Malcom, who still resent and crave vengeance over what the Jade God has done to them. Eventually, they met and accepted Daryx's offer. The sceptres to date have helped us keep the generals hidden."

"So risky! If Orcus learns of them here in Tania -"

Alerius shouldered Cor'tanos and the ground trembled. "Do not speak that one's name! Yes," Alerius breathed. "The three vampire generals ensure rage and cascade. It is an advantage we will use."

"I never dared to believe this audacity! I love it! More! Tell me everything!" Cor'tanos screamed for more.

The three patriarchs explained that Nientro's ascension to a dominion of necromancy had been interrupted by the Jade God. Alerius explained, "Nientro is ready to claim his dominion. The Darkhold predicts he will succeed, that Nientro will hold the dominion he most craves – soul and spirit transference, a type of possession, brother Cor'tanos. The destruction of the throneplane creates a vacuum into which Nientro may ascend and claim it. This would force the Necromancer another step back from the nexal gate and remove half its dominion."

The Court of Patriarchs laughed. Their terrible laughter, evil and sinister as the dragons' collective anticipation of destruction overcame their normally restrained natures. Waves of dragonterror washed over the valley and the

Tanians, none of whom had seen the Temple Court used this way, trembled and cowered praying for relief.

After their excitement calmed, Spark said, "The risks. If we send a team to the throneplane and they are captured, the Jade God captures enchanted bloodstones and reclaims a veritable army of sceptres to use against us. His hellhounds will return equipped with the very weapons we have crafted to defeat them. Also, we now exert influence and fascination with Nientro. His dominion, specialized as he has that magic, would be a terrible dominion to hold its own throneplane. It will reshape the pantheons in ways we cannot foresee."

Ynt'taris silenced Spark. "No, it will fragment the dominion of Necromancy so that each glittering mote of its power can become its own dominion. Nientro is friendly to us. I consider the cost of a friendly Abyssal god worth the cost of slaying the Jade God. Of all costs, I would give even my own soul for this outcome. How I hate that one."

Alerius explained, "I have long sought to win an alliance with Nientro, Cor'tanos. Though he has promised non-interference with Tania, he will not commit to nor ally with us for concern it weakens his own might. Arrogant vampire! To counter it, there is a bond between the three born of master and enslaved vampire servant that now free, has become an alliance against the monolith of undeath, against their free will being taken. Early on, I took them to Ool, to see the end of lichdom as if its own dominion in that dark land. Nientro returned changed. To see the end state of that fell dominion sobered even Nientro. They will ascend together. Crea and Malcom seek absolution with their Pha Rann even though they understand there is no atonement. Instead, they self-inflict atonement by serving and checking Nientro and point him to evil foes as a way to spare the innocent."

"The Abyss will change them," Spark noted. "It always does. And there is one dominion that must be claimed by Mother."

The three nodded, but again – Cor'tanos asked, "Which dominion – not shadows?"

Alerius grinned and pressed his face into the shadow patriarchs. The leering grin and might of the red made Cor'tanos shrink back between Spark and Ynt'taris. "No, not shadow. You overestimate the value of the shadow realms. Dragons can become liches. The Darkhold told my Rojo that the blind dragon of Merakor is tied to our times. Do you remember that one, before you passed the gates of oblivion?"

Quietly, the shadow whispered. "Yes, I remember. In the war between Mother and Father, a third rose up. The Blind One."

"Fallen and bound by the human and elf alliance of Merakor," Alerius said. "Cursed and forsaken by Mother and Father, the blind dragon became the first draco-lich. While you and your heretics withered away into oblivion, we have claimed a glorious afterlife with Tiamat and the dominion we shaped with Her. Our destiny is glorious; your destiny, Cor'tanos, can again be glorious. Only draco-lichdom threatens our eternal dream."

An illusion rose up as the sceptres and wands fell. It showed a likeness of Cor'tanos warp and twist into a skeletal mockery of himself. That terrible green light filled its eyes and skeleton as script appeared as chiseled scrapes along his form and wings. "Locked forever in the unchanging stasis of undeath. Tiamat must control this dominion for all dragons' sake."

They continued to exchange words for almost an hour with Cor'tanos initially asking questions about the First Cascade. Then, he spoke of the inert anti-life of the Shadow Realms. At last, Cor'tanos conjured illusions of Dar Kell and Malcor. "My favorite sons," he crooned. "They give you an edge." Around them, multiple shadow dragons arose. "My own brothers languish and fade. At your command Alerius, they can enter these."

The three patriarchs looked one at another and then the three turned as one to Cor'tanos. "Perhaps," Ynt'taris breathed. The air around the white patriarch crystallized and it began to snow. "The Mother still does not trust that your intention here is pure."

The shadow patriarch snarled, the air temperature plummeting as anti-life sucked at their heat. As the crackling tendrils of ice raged between the two, the cold penetrated the Temple complex. At the first cry of pain, Alerius roared and heat from his body suffused through it all. "You harm my children. Cease this conflict." Alerius hissed a gentle flame over the shadow forms of the many dragons conjured by Cor'tanos until just two others remained. "This is all that remains of your followers, Cor'tanos. We know this. The rest are fallen into matter shorn of will. You have taken their will and prolonged the power of these two. Do you think us so naïve to believe that after all this time, the shadow clan returns with sincere words of penance? The Mother does not forget. We know. Ynt'taris' point remains, Cor'tanos. Choose your next words carefully. What is your intent and how might you prove it?"

Cor'tanos cringed, becoming crestfallen even as rage and pride held him trembling. Eldar power crackled around the three patriarchs. By force of will, Cor'tanos pulled his powers back and though fury curled his voice, he said, "What you say is true. No creature born of another realm can endure the Shadow Realm. For good will, I will let my two sons choose their avatars, by your permission. You will see for yourself that the humans they take shall increase in power. They shall rage at their, not my command. I have two ready to do this now as their last act of free will before oblivion claims them forever."

The three nodded. "And what of you, patriarch? Which will you take?"

Keeping his eyes on theirs, Cor'tanos' hand waved and the image of a small girl rose up from the illusions. "I will enter and live and die here. I have read of Ascension. I would ascend a Tehran and deliver the dominion of Shadow Dragons to the Mother, as my atonement."

"Well-chosen words," Alerius approved. The tension between the four lessened. "Wise words I had not expected. We will support your ascension, brother. As patriarchs, our task is to ascend and deliver our dominions to the Mother. Which avatar would you take?"

Cor'tanos pointed to one of the hero illusions still held by Ynt'taris. "I would take this one – Klara, daughter of Kell."

Alerius screamed against this. "Impossible! Kell's children are numbered to me. Klara is not his. Your theory is good but already tested, brother. Klara is not of Kell. She is a beyond humanity and touched by prophecy. You must take another."

"If I cannot take Klara then my only other option is to take an actual dragon. There are none suitable here. Kell has rejected me. Malcor, well, he would do well, but I expect you to forbid that one as well." The illusions vanished. "It occurs to me with this new information about the Necromancer... a dominion of shadow within the Mother's realms, not of shadow dragons, of Shadow Necromancy would win me favor with Her. I change my mind. I will take your Mage's Guild or Temple's most potent necromancer."

The three turned and without speaking, illusions of possible candidates appeared. Without speaking, the three would consider and then move to the next. At last, only three remained. A male priest, young and healthy stood framed heroically. Dar Ana, the high priestess of the Temple At Bloodstone, stood opposite. Third, a young boy barely five years old. Alerius pointed to the three saying, "Ana is not a possibility. Even if I were okay with it, she would not and Mother would forbid it. These two may work. Their youth will give you the ability to learn how to Ascend. Though not powerful now, Tehran power increases with study and experience. As you request, they are the most powerful necromancers."

Cor'tanos opened his mind's eye from the River and looked on both. "The young boy has potential and is already touched by the dark arts, but lacks the training and maturity to be a good host. I will take the young man…" Cor'tanos' eyes closed and when he opened them, he spoke, "Teleris. I will take the priest Teleris."

The three nodded in agreement. From Cor'tanos, two shadow dragons sped away from the court. Cor'tanos faded away. "I entrust my sons to the dream of Morbattania. Farewell brothers. Tell Mother I will not disappoint." One shadow dove into the Temple and the other raced north and west towards Bloodstone.

With Cor'tanos gone, the three patriarchs paused for a moment. Spark said at last, "The shadow patriarch has left. We are alone."

Alerius let a fanged smile slowly crease his face. "Brothers, can you see it? The Jade God will come through to Bloodstone. All this time we have prepared. To the Jade God, it is a blink of will. So long as Krentismar and Pha Rann stand and let the River of Time flow, the Necromancer will fall."

Ynt'taris cackled. "Yes! Yes! I see it. Remember, the eldar times where our will made it so? To see that arrogant one come here, as if Tehra were his Endless Worlds, to watch him order existence to cower before him. No, this will be where existence rejects you – Necromancer! You shall die." Ynt'taris' cackling became laughter. "But, you will die forever!"

Spark added to it, "Were I that one, I would seek to re-order reality into my dominion so that I would have omniscience and omnipotence." Spark's talon crackled with blue and green lightning. A sceptre bearing three faces rose up on the Temple dome, as an illusion. "This is the actual sceptre of the Jade God. The three faces represent the triangle of necromancy: undeath, spirit warp, and possession. Nientro confirms that the purpose of the sceptre is to possess a star. The sceptre may attempt to take Pha Rann's sun, the Tehran Star."

"That's why we must distract the Jade God," Alerius answered smugly. "All is ready. The Sceptre will focus on the sun. The Jade God must focus on the rest of the armies."

Chapter Forty Five – The Call to War

Far away to the south, a young priest of Tiamat named Teleris sat in study. Dar Ana's writing graced the pages of the book and discussed necromantic channeling – the art of taking life, holding it in reserve, and gifting it to others. His scriptures open on one knee as a cross-reference, he did not notice the darkness watching. He flipped a page and, with a quill dipped in blood, practiced writing a rune. He sensed something watching him. He paused and looked around, but shook his head when he failed to notice the darker-than-dark shadows hiding from his lantern light.

A fanged smile creased the blackness and when Teleris looked again, he blanched white and screamed as two dimensional spears shot into him from all directions. As his life's blood spilled, shadow entered and the screaming gradually stopped. After a period, Cor'tanos stood with Teleris' body and said, "I'm home at last!" He flexed his arms feeling bone, muscle, and felt his heart. "Life…"

He made the holy sign of Tiamat and then screamed into the darkness. His human form's shadow twisted into the dragon possessing it. "I hunger! Bring me food!" When no one answered, Teleris walked outside the room and found he stood on the outskirts of a township. He saw the shrine and shadowstepped to it. After a moment, the priestess and her acolytes brought Teleris food and drink. The Queen's purpose in their hearts told them to give this dread lord whatever he required, though they did not recognize him.

Back at the Court of Patriarchs, Alerius lifted his claw and placed it on the Temple dome. The tower bloodstone directly beneath the Temple pulsed to life. "My children," the god emperor spoke. His words crackled through the sky like thunder. "A time of prophesy comes with the trumpets of war. Too long has Tania chafed under the Jade God's spite. Vengeance for our many losses at the hands of its servants is here! Heroes, sons, and daughters. Unsheathe your weapons. Dust off your armor. Assemble with all due haste to your shrines. In three days, the great spearhead of Morbattania marches to Bloodstone!"

So long now, the people trembling in fear, Alerius' familiar voice struck courage and passion in their hearts. The fear fled and all leapt to their feet wanting to help, to do anything. Old men found strength to leap up and follow that command. Halflings, rocking by their fireplaces, sat up and unlocked chests full of gear from their younger days of required military service. Everywhere, conversations burst out as merchants, famers, craftsmen, guards, and every profession imaginable began asking questions about how long and how to and what if.

Within the great stone temple, Dar Shara sat in meditation with Dar Kell shielding those near them from the overwhelming might of the dragons and the fear they kindle in the hearts of those unused to such humbling terror. Those who did not flee or collapse, had crawled or were dragged to the great central room. Back to back, the two great clerics prayed singing a gentle and calming hymn from antiquity. Small children and others revived and found that if they left the room, the dreadful terror pressed them back in. Shara felt Kell abruptly lose his song and his body convulsed as he struggled to hold his composure.

Attendants ran to him and Shara sang more loudly as Kell choked and then something entered their prayer circle. Armageddon and the Temple guardian Arminoth moved forward but a feeling came with it that things would work out. Arminoth stopped unsheathing his sword and walked forward to touch Kell.

The dread lord, often absent except during important Temple functions and threats to the Temple, rumbled lowly in draconian so that only Shara could hear, "Kell burns with fever but the Mother says he will survive this." Shara nodded and lifted up her alto voice in a bright song of praise and glory. All around them, the paladins and priestesses joined her and then, recognizing the tune, the people gathered there lifted their voices singing a prayer of glory to the Queen.

A few moments later, Kell stood and, like Arminoth, spoke low so that only Shara and the dread lords might understand, "The Heretics have joined Tania and I am now shadow incarnate. Malcor too shall be joined to a shadow dragon. In the south, the patriarch Cor'tanos rises as a dread lord in human form, a priest named Teleris."

In Bloodstone, Ana enjoyed her selected paladin that evening. But, she suddenly stopped and walked over to a scrying sphere by the desk in her lavish room. She touched it and closed her eyes for a moment and then said, "I understand, my lord." She waved and her clothing danced over to her. Touching another rune on her desk, a compartment opened.

Her chosen paladin leaned forward and then decided it would be best if he did not know. Ana touched the bloodstone ruby set in a medallion and let her fingers trace its perfect straight lines. Wrapping the chain through her fingers so that the medallion centered in her palm, she touched the scrying ball and suddenly Alerius' words resounded throughout the fortresses and Valley Town. Priests and priestesses of the Queen, no matter where they were, heard the voice and repeated it to their teams. In the great Temple At Bloodstone, Crimson triggered the opening of the great dome and leapt into the sky.

Far north, a shadow dragon sought Malcor. It found the destroyed outpost and turned to follow Malcor. Something in its heart compelled it to wait. That feeling had never happened before. *Is inspiration?*, it thought.

A female voice, soft and sure, whispered to it. "Malcor has work to do that will be hindered by your power. Abide with Crimson until commanded to serve Malcor." The voice brought memories to it, of before time, of the powerful Tiamat soaring the world skies and shaping it. Unused to being commanded so, its rage spiked and then flattened.

"I obey," it screamed into the night sky. Then, the son of Cor'tanos saw Crimson Burning and rose up to join the great fire drake. The sight of the mighty red helped it recall other memories lost to inert shadow. A fire dragon had attacked the All Father and nearly won except for the metallic dragons' interference. "Heat is infinite," that one had screamed. "I will not share infinite fire!" For slaying so many, for defying the All Father, that one had been stripped of magic. Gleefully, the shadow joined Crimson. Soon, it could tell, a great war would erupt.

* * *

In the elven nation of Morilon, the green patriarch of Vapors - Mallaforax - heard Alerius' call. The amphitheater he rested in and the trees surrounding it trembled when Mallaforax lifted his long neck and called to the elves who guarded him from disturbance. From all around, the green World Tree's leaves shook and rained down as the great body shifted from under its roots. The elves endured an uneasy alliance with the green. Yet, an alliance with a single dragon served the elves far better than subservience or war with Tania. Always with a mage among them, the elves felt something amiss and when Mallaforax's eyes crested the stadium ridge, the mage enacted a flight spell and moved forward. "How may we serve, Great Patriarch?"

Mallaforax despised elven speech. So, with a draconic hiss, Mallaforax flooded Alerius' words into the mage's mind. "Truly, Mallaforax? All of Tania mobilizes?" The green dragon nodded and then, far below the stadium ridge, a claw stabbed into a floorstone, cracking it. The mage lifted up to see Mallaforax withdraw one of the giant bloodstones the Tanians called "tower stones". It pulsed and crackled.

"This," the dragon said, with caustic mist falling from his jaws. "Controls all the bloodstones granted to the elven nation. You are ordered to assemble your armies, your heroes, your peoples and allies. In three days, your fighters will gate to Bloodstone. Any who do not, yet who possess bloodstones, will find the stones detonating. I, the great beast of Morilon, I command that if ever my teachings have served Morilon, you repay me now and make ready for war."

Mallaforax moved his head forward until the elf could have touched one of his great eyes. Dragonterror unlike anything they had ever felt before pulsed through the forests of Morilon. "You are to further empty Morilon of all you hold dear, all your possessions, all your treasure. You are to send your women and children and treasures to Morbatten for safekeeping during this war. They will be well cared for. Send word now and tell your royal family – this is where they prove all those pretty oaths. You follow these commands or I lay waste to your nation in three days. I know you will make the right choice. Any left in Morilon, when the Necromancer comes, will die. Not by Morbatten's hand, by the Jade One's. Now leave and execute my commands."

The mage bowed and fled. Behind him, Mallaforax's words reached him as a threatening whisper, "Tell Vel Pajor he owes me this for the world tree magic. He will lead Morilon's armies in Bloodstone."

* * *

Far north in Taysor, Haven, and south in Khasra, in the dwarven and gnome nations, dragons watching or participating in those kingdoms rose up with tower stones and conveyed similar messages. "As pledged, you will join Tania in Bloodstone or your nation will be laid to waste." The Imperics on Khasra had never known that a black dragon watched over them from afar. The dwarves of Stone and Gar-Galad knew, but had long ago cordoned themselves away from an unknown dragon that turned out to know them very well. The gnomes, already aligned with Spark, heard Alerius' words directly from the tower stone adorning the great assembly hall of their elected president.

The great shield nation of Taysor to Tania's north also heard Alerius' words as bloodstones gifted to the royal family and passed down from the ancient Queen Alaura activated and spread a similar message. Oranstakar, the gold dragon sage, sat in counsel with Taysor's King Andrew. They had received a troop requisition days earlier from the Tanian King Rojo. While considering it, the dragon emperor's words sounded out. No dragon of Tiamat watched Taysor, but Oranstakar felt Tiamta's regard and the absence of any guidance from the dragon All Father.

Oranstakar turned and carefully said to the king, "Andrew, it seems you will be king over the Second Cascade. Here is what happened to Tania during the First." Images burst into the king's mind of how Tania's population had been nearly destroyed, how the dragons had removed the gate to

Bloodstone, and how Alerius had sacrificed himself to save the twenty-five Tanians who remained in the valley of Morbatten.

King Andrew, accepting all these images and the gold dragon's emotions of the events, could not breathe until the images stopped. When at least he did, he heaved for air and then the weight of time and destiny hit him. "I did not realize dragons felt things so strongly," he said gulping deep breaths of air. He recovered just enough and Oranstakar unleashed another flood of images, this time of Ynt'taris attacking Roland's palace.

"Do not mistake Tania's request as a request. I have long known Alerius. If we do not comply with full mobilization, they will attack us on their way to Bloodstone." More images flooded Andrew's imagination as a collage of the many heroes and adventurers in Taysor who possessed bloodstones. "This leverage is a powerful one that, as they warned you, came with a price to be repaid in the future."

Andrew nodded, breathing again at last. "This is important," Oranstakar said. "It comes from the memories of the Queen Alaura and the ancient hero Sean". Disconnected and less emotional memories danced in Andrew's sight where he saw three great columns rising up from Tania's Temple Mount. The valley could only be recognized by Dragon Mountain to the left. A blinding light suddenly appeared and a Pha Rannic messenger spoke naming Tania the Spear and Taysor the Shield. The image then changed to a conversation between Oranstakar and Alerius. They argued.

"The messenger meant you to be a Spear against Set, not Orcus!" Oranstakar cut his hand between them. "You dissemble to gain advantage over Taysor and change the clear intent of a divine message."

"Do not be ridiculous. Should my children fall to The Necromancer, you will fall next. We are only a Spear aimed at Set if we first survive the Jade God. You know that one and its hunger to claim this world. You will not survive! I am willing to fight this. I would think the so-called "good" paladins and peoples of Taysor would leap at this alliance. Even a sword's metal is tempered before it becomes a blade. The Necromancer is our temper."

"An alliance with evil -"

Alerius roared into Oranstakar's face from inches away. Even the gold struggled to resist the terror of the eldar patriarch. "We are not evil! We fight and defeat more evil than you and your smug peoples can even count. You are safer and smugger because of the sacrifice of my children!"

"And yet, you are evil nonetheless." At Oranstakar's gesture a simple spell ignited the air around Alerius in red and black spectral fire. "Even this spell, so simple a novice can cast it, knows this truth. You do not fight evil for the purpose of defeating it. You do so for your own glory and purpose. You take the power of your enemies and add it to your own."

Alerius' dragon began to manifest and shatter his human form when he suddenly deflected and changed the *detect evil* spell color shifted to bright gold. "This spell is useless, brother," Alerius spat back. "The forging of weapons requires ore to be ripped from the earth. Fire and flame shape it. Magic enhances it. The Necromancer is the forge that creates the Shield and Spear. If the spear cannot shatter jade, it will fail against nightmare. Would you join this alliance or sit like cowards behind your walls? Even Pha Rann says you are to be my shield."

"We do not sit like cowards!" the gold chewed back, monotone syllable by syllable.

The vision shifted and Andrew recognized the scene from just days ago by the bright banners of a Soran holiday bedecking the streets and walls below Oranstakar's mountain watch. Andrew felt the tension in the vision between the two dragons. Alerius looked as if to say more. Instead, he walked out. Over his shoulder, towards Oranstakar just as he exited the great library, he said, "Like the others, you and yours have benefited from my children's advancements. Evil. Good. Hell. Heaven. These only matter if Taysor survives to discuss the outcome and sacrifices paid for the luxury of philosophical hindsight. Whether you join willingly or by coercion, I care not. You will join.

"The bloodstones crafted by my Temple, if you do not join us and fight, I will detonate them all when the time comes. Even Pha Rann knows this truth about me - I will stop at nothing to preserve Tiamat's throneplane. So, Oranstakar, I offer you this." Alerius stopped outside the library and dragonshifted, slowly. Each pulse of sinew and muscle rippled the daylight as dragonterror and flame radiated from his changing form. His voice hard and human changed to a reptilian growl. "Taysor will join us."

Oranstakar withstood Alerius and walked out to stand small and tiny in front of the mighty patriarch of fire. "That is not an offer. We will return the bloodstones by way of those heroes who choose to join you. I am not – nor will King Andrew order a national mobilization to support this reckless cause."

Alerius' head whipped back to Oranstakar and stopped just shy of the humanshifted gold dragon. "Pathetic," Alerius said, his voice magically thundered out over all of Taysor. "Your empire dragged itself here from the waste of Merakor and look at you now - quaking and shunning to fight the greatest evil this world has ever seen. You are laughable, Oranstakar.

Long have I held a spot for you near Tiamat's throne, but I see. I see! You wish to sit back and let hordes of undead rampage through your people-"

Andrew begged Oranstakar to stop. "We all heard these words and felt the terrible energy of Alerius. We do not fault you, great sage. But, I must ask, with even the zealots and all of our greatest heroes and paladins arming up to fight - and you must have known this - why did you not just agree?"

Oranstakar took Andrew's hand and pointed south to the great winter mountains of the Shield between them and Morbatten. "Sure, we could agree. Sure, I could have said yes. I could have attacked Alerius; he certainly hoped I would. Yet, in the end, I wanted Taysor and its peoples to make their own choice. Now that the bloodstones are revealed as the double-edged tools we always suspected, the choice is murkier than fighting evil. We become complicit in aiding evil to retain tools of evil purpose. We were mighty before the bloodstones. We would be mighty again without them. I advise you to have your people forsake the bloodstones. If we fight only to keep the bloodstones, we become accessory to anything Alerius wishes."

Andrew leaned back and let his gaze trace the line of the mountain ridges between Taysor and Tania. He withdrew an earring and placed it on the stone window ledge. The blood red ruby glinted in the sunlight where it sat in gold and platinum. "This earring allows me to communicate with all my generals, magistrates, my guard. Without the bloodstone, I would need a thousand rings each attuned to just one matching set."

He drew a long sword at his belt. Blood red runes linked three bloodstones set along the sword's length. "This blade passed down for a thousand years to me bears three bloodstones each enhancing and allowing this blade to fight demons, devils, and undead. Ancient Merakor could not have created such a weapon. This blade has vanquished hordes of evil here, in the world, and at Bloodstone. Being complicit with Alerius and Tania, maybe that counts for ten points of evil, and yet this blade has defeated millions of points of evil."

Oranstakar tapped the stones one by one and then said, "But, my king, choosing even ten points of evil is still choosing evil. No doubt, heroes across Sora are asking themselves this same question. The zealots have all come together and agreed that so long as they fight as a single unit under their own – not Tanian – command, they will go and fight the great evil coming whether they have bloodstones or not. What will you do, King Andrew?"

"Do you know for sure that the Pha Rannic messenger meant Set?"

Oranstakar nodded, "Yes, the meaning was clear even to the Tanians though they have carefully rewritten their scripture to generalize and then redirect it to the Jade God and Set. Their writings are vague enough now that Alerius could argue it's applicable to any of their enemies."

"And our scriptures -"

"Do not touch on this. The House of Roland destroyed any such to the point that it only remains in my memory and a few rare copies of the Sage Queen Alaura's histories."

Andrew asked, "How is it in your memory when you were not there? I have to wonder, how would Captain Sean have handled this?"

"A gift from the All Father, and Alerius shows more than he intends when enraged. Pragmatists, like Sean, would no doubt be armed and riding to Bloodstone already. Though they would most likely return the bloodstones to Tania when finished and seek Atonement. If that is what you feel you must do, know that I do not judge. Pha Rann knew this world would be subject to extremes and grey moral demands. The moral ambiguity of this world murders our bright light."

Andrew said, "All my life, you've counselled me to avoid entanglements with dragons and provided counter-doctrines to what the Tiamat dragons and their followers teach. It is compelling. This fight against the evilest of gods is compelling. Assuming Tania can win, how can we not help destroy that evil? Do they have a chance? And, before you answer, what is their evil end game in ending the Jade God?" Andrew rubbed his head sheepishly. This had already become the longest conversation he had ever had with the elusive gold dragon.

Oranstakar leaned back against the wall. "They can win, assuming certain things remain true. So long as Time flows and Tehra remains separate from the Jade God's dominion, that god will be bound by linear time. It will confuse, perhaps paralyze that one long enough for Tania to strike." Below King Andrew's conversation with Oranstakar, people lived out their lives in the distant plazas of Taysor.

Oranstakar held up a finger, "They want to prove they can destroy a primordial god. Doing so, if successful, will free the dominion of necromancy." He held up a second finger, "And Tania has very particular interests in necromancy. Next, the body of a god like this one will yield powerful components." The golden fingers wavered a moment. He almost raised a fourth but shook his head. "In my studies with Sai and long conversations with the Tanian dragons, they dance around a central issue

– the gate itself. I don't know what it is, but you can be sure there is some end game involving the gate."

Andrew held up a fifth finger, "And killing a god sends a message to all other gods, "Look at what we can do." I understand now. And, what must I do, Oranstakar?"

"You must make a choice and – as king – Taysor will endure the consequences of that choice." Oranstakar's last words faded out as the sage vanished.

Andrew sheathed his sword and re-affixed his earring. The king watched his people and lost count of the chimney smoke columns drifting upwards. Letting his fingers trail on the bloodstone earring, he said, "I would speak with King Rojo of Tania."

A moment later, and as if standing next to him, Andrew heard Rojo's voice answer. "How may I serve, great king of Taysor?" As always, Rojo's voice conveyed a sense of steel and barely restrained action. Andrew imagined Rojo might smell like oil.

"Taysor and its armies will join you in Bloodstone. As our great treaties demand, I ask for command of the Sixth and Seventh Fortresses."

"Agreed, great king, and welcome to glorious destiny! Dar Reznor will facilitate your mages in opening gates to the Sixth and Seventh Fortresses. Please know that the Sixth came under attack recently and we have several thousand fighting in levels three and four at this time. As soon as your troops stabilize it, the Nineteenth Legion will withdraw from the Sixth."

"Rojo, what is the plan?"

Andrew sensed Rojo conversed with others before replying. Rojo answered, "Taysor is to hold the Sixth and Seventh. Act according to the dictates of your conscience. If you will not fall under my, the Temple, or Legion Commander Verit's command, we cannot set our plans with your participation. Should you change your mind, raise the Fortresses' gold and red banners. Advisors will, at that time, connect you to our strategies. I assure you though, the Sixth and Seventh will have a clear view of the Second Great Cascade. There will be many foes great and small to fight against. If we have read the prophecies correctly, the Jade God himself will appear. We would enjoy your company as we offer that one permanent death."

Andrew got that feeling of Rojo consulting others and after a time, Rojo's voice returned. "King Andrew, if you cannot retain control of the Cuthberic zealots, our forces will view them as a threat. Keep them confined to the Bloodstone Fortresses until such time as you join our campaign. There is more, but I cannot say until your council is unanimous in joining with Tania."

Immediately, five mages teleported into the courtyard below wearing the blood red robes of the Tanian Mage's Guild. One flew straight up in the air and met Andrew eye to eye. Dar Reznor bowed and said, "The gate will be very large. We require two hundred paces of clear space central to and easily accessed by your armies."

* * *

In all other kingdoms and nations, Tanian mages appeared before rulers. The call to arms did not stop with them. Across the great oceans of the world, the minotaurs of Tauran heard and howled out their acceptance. Always ready for war, the minotaurs began marshalling their most fearsome fighters to the world galleon, Blade of Stars. Across the Tauran islands, cleric chants to their god Baphtomet broke out. They hoped to call him to captain their great ship. No one asked how the Blade of Stars would fight in the mountains. Their god had the answer already. They must trust their god Baphtomet. They would be ready.

Phantasms appeared before all manner of sentient creatures demanding, buying, or soliciting their participation. In a hot desert baked by an endless sun, a gold dragon lay on a sandstone shelf and watched the phantasm. "Your sister Jeri, she asks that you join in a great battle against necromancy."

The gold breathed slow fire through the phantasm and called out, "You saw that too?"

Another gold replied yes and then another. "Jeri seems to be in the thick of it. I like the idea of fighting against necromancy. I hate the idea of allying with those that stole Jeri from us."

"The paladin who took her was quite handsome and well-spoken. Not at all like I would have expected a human slave to Tiamat to be." The first gold dragon craned her neck to look up at the others resting in the sun above her. "I do miss her."

They nodded and she spoke to the phantasm, "We come for Jeri, not Tiamat. Make sure to tell your overlords this. We will not be relegated to some cage or corner of the fight. We stand with Jeri, for Jeri, and no one else!" The phantasm bowed politely and faded as a black spherical gate began to open larger and larger until at last a dragon could fly through it.

Chapter Forty Six – Eyes of Gold and Lasting Truth

Bomoki stood in human form surrounded by blighted and dying trees. Dar Ana's message echoed throughout the valley. Bomoki smiled. Caressing a ram's head that coiled down and around his arm, he purred at it. "Go, my pet, and tell the other hounds to hasten the gathering. I require them now, all of them. Orcus must know that his enemies prepare for him. Convey these instructions to the demi-lich most wishing for Tehran blood."

The sceptre sped off his arm into the night. As it left, another snaked to his arm and crooned at Bomoki's praise for it. To that one, Bomoki said, "All we need is gold dragon eyes. Isn't that right? How fare the plans to attack the Third?"

The sceptre's eyes flashed and Bomoki's knowing smile turned into a leer when another sceptre from his waist said, "Master, the gold dotes on the human king in the Third. Her concern for that one blinds her."

Before Bomoki could ask, another sceptre said, "Farant is swimming the Cordabad River. He brings the vault with the tower stone Alerius created to nullify the big stones. He should be here in two days. Shall I?"

"No, the demi-liches shall greet and judge Farant." The sceptre shrank back and bit Bomoki's arm. For just a moment, the sceptre tried to take possession of its host. Bomoki clubbed it off-handedly the way a horse might flick its ears at gnats. "Watch your place, little pet."

Bomoki leaned forward, letting his arms lengthen and shift into wolf claws. The tearing in his skull had become a welcome pleasure as his jaw elongated and crackled into place. Though Orcus adorned himself with symbols of the ram, Bomoki enjoyed the wolf form. Strong predators able to move quickly and attack with cunning, he loved it. *Ironic that all others copy me*, he thought. With each change, he moved faster and faster towards the north. When at last a giant hellhound, Bomoki howled at the distant sky and the dark ridge of the mountains. A golden prize glimmered in the Third Fortress.

* * *

Jeri sat along the battlements just out of the Third fortress. To her left, the Temple Fortress loomed with glowing lights. The valley sat still and quiet – for Bloodstone – tonight. The emperor's pronouncement had brought a relative calm where, perhaps, even the undead considered the coming fight. A letter from the Mage's Guild rested on the stone tucked under her arm. Her sisters would be coming and would fight with them on condition she fought with them. Rojo had said he had no problem with her leading them, but Jeri felt torn. Would her sisters fight under her if she remained by Rojo's side? Her eldest had been quite enamored with the fearless knight. Of course, Rojo had been a paladin then, not king of a nation loathed by her sisters. No doubt they would consider her fallen in her conversion to Tiamat.

Something stirred behind her and it came with a sense of menace, enough that she whirled on alert and on guard. In the dark shadows across the causeway, a vampire sat. The drained body of a human slumped against it. Seeing Jeri, the vampire dropped the human and licked the last drops of blood from its lips. "Delicious," it said. "Tell me, priestess, what will it be? Do you behead this corpse to save it, or try to defeat me?"

Jeri's body burst afire with daylight as she presented her faith and the holy symbol of Takhissis. The vampire laughed though it did flinch back from the daylight. Jeri pressed forward with her symbol and proclaimed, "In Takhissis' divine name, I abjure thee!"

The vampire flinched a bit and Jeri noticed its head shape change a bit going almost transparent. Inside the vampire, two conjoined humanoid skulls floated. Covered in decorative emeralds and blazing with abyssal light, Jeri felt the power of lich, even beyond a lich. The vampire, feeling the shift in her confidence, stepped into the bright ring of daylight. From the Third and Second Fortresses, troops rang bells of alarm as Jeri's daylight caught their attention.

"You think you have the upper hand here, priestess, but the simple truth of this place is Death. Your death. You're all going to die. Don't worry though, death is the doorway." Slowly, dreadfully, the vampire pointed a finger at Jeri while the other hand drew a letter in the air over its head. The letter hung, igniting with slow power.

Jeri amplified her voice and screamed out, "Don't look at the rune!"

The vampire's voice boomed out even louder, "Death! Dying! Die, mortals!" The symbol exploded in green light rising up into the sky to rotate over the lich. From both sides of the causeway, soldiers fell over dead. Stronger fighters, paladins, and some of the priestesses shuddered as their bodies were wracked in agony. Even Jeri felt her lifeforce struggle to shake off the effects of the powerful sorcery. At last, her dragon resistance to magic allowed her to shake it off.

The vampire smiled as it began another incantation. Over the Temple and the Third Fortress, a shower of shooting stars began. "Pretty isn't it?" the lich asked. Somehow, time had altered. The lich should not have been able to do such powerful spells one after another. Jeri stepped out of the River and beheld the lich adorned in the sceptres of Orcus and grinning at her from atop the flow of Time, stagnant and barely moving. No, not a sceptre, Jeri saw a second demi-lich conjoined with the first. One had cast the death spell while the other summoned meteors from the night sky.

The demi-liches both smiled at her and she returned, against her will, to the real world. A meteor brightened the sky over the Temple and Jeri noted Crimson and Ana flying upwards to meet it. Jeri felt reality shift and it made her dizzy. Meteors falling, bright lights moving in all directions… then the ground heaved around her.

The ground all around her rose up in skeletal bones and an inhuman hand with taloned fingers grabbed her neck, trying to snap her spine. Jeri attempted to dragonshift but her magic pulsed and, instead, drained into her attacker. A cruel human voice lisping in ancient Tanian said, "Well done! Great ones, you may leave and make ready for the main performance."

The demi-liches cast one last spell causing a stinking brimstone mist to rise up. It immediately began strangling the causeway survivors to death. Jeri felt the liches leave. So overpowering had their presence been that only now did she feel the hellhound holding her. All around, the fallen, dead, and dying twitched in the throes of unholy transformation. Only the fire giants remained able to move and they stepped to and fro, severing heads with their fire blades. Those still living, choked as they tried to breathe. A voice in the brimstone mist called out to them with the seduction of death, an end to agony and pain.

The hellhound tried to snap her neck again and she twisted, praying for health and might. "Excellent," Bomoki said into her face. "Your resistance is beautiful."

Jeri saw his face and recognized the First, the Gate, the cause of so much evil. Fright, primal and terrible, paralyzed her. *I'm going to lose my eyes*, she thought fixatedly. *Rojo, where are you?* "Help…" she tried to call.

Mage hands rose up around Jeri, holding her body still as multiple sceptres shot paralyzing beams into her body. Simultaneously assaulted by so many sceptres, Jeri froze as one after another overcame her dragon resistance to magic. She tried to dragonshift, but Bomoki's hand on her throat remained tight and unmoving. It almost broke her neck.

Bomoki laughed at her. "In Orcus' holy name, I mark thee with the sign of dracos. Please, continue to dragonshift, die, and arise my servant!"

The mark of Orcus burned into her mind and she saw herself rise up from death as a mindless slave to Bomoki. Her beautiful golden form warped and twisted in a skeletal mockery. The vision nearly broke her spirit.

Jeri twisted, trying to escape. She screamed as Bomoki's desiccated hand became a knife blade. He stabbed it into her socket and quickly cut around her eye. Jeri tried to withdraw, to escape, to fight but she could not move. This paralysis struck her differently than other mage castings. It froze her breath, her heartbeat struggled to beat. Fanged ram's teeth bit and saturated poison into her. The others continued to radiate her body with paralysis. Unable to close her eyes, she was forced to watch Bomoki tear her eye out. His whispering to Orcus would haunt her forever after, if she survived the night.

Somewhere in her other eye's vision, a meteor struck the causeway in a concussive blast of fire, sound, and fragmentation. A fire giant dismembered and blew apart against the impact. Smaller meteors began striking all around the two Fortresses. Jeri saw him raise his dagger to her other eye. She wanted to fight even though paralysis of her body suffocated her.

He smiled at her and licked his teeth running his tongue from the rotting ones to the perfect human ones in the other half. "Soon you will join us as a draco-lich, my great *Dar*." The sarcasm oozed from his voice while he slowly stroked her eye with the bloody blade's tip. Over his shoulder, a leering ram's head looked down at her and began uncoiling from Bomoki's shoulder. "Yes, yes, my pet. You may take this one." The sceptre struck forward like a cobra, its horns flaring forward.

"Twilight Fell Shining on Her Bright Eyes!" Rojo's battle cry roared out in draconian. Bomoki had to turn his dagger to deflect a sword attack. The cursed dagger slashed across Jeri's good eye and her world went black with pain and agony. Blinded, her world became only fear. She cried out mentally for Rojo's strength.

She heard Bomoki's dagger clang against Rojo's avenging sword. She felt the Tiamat's power rear up all around them as Rojo's ascension form transformed his sword into claws. Jeri had seen Rojo's righteous might many times and could imagine his prismatic dragon form – so beautiful. His talons each alight with Takhissis' divine flames would tear Bomoki apart. Twilight Fell would strip magical effects and spells from the hellhound; she was saved.

The sword breezed past her face and the sceptre never took her. Another rush of air and wind and then a blast of heat overwash prevented her from enjoying Bomoki's scream of pain. Rojo must have, *But no*, she thought. *He would not use his breath weapon so close to the causeway and fortress.*

Bomoki looked with dismay at the severed ram's head bouncing away from the dragon's slashing attack. "We meet again," he whispered licking his fingers where he had clawed at Rojo's defense. Rojo had saved the gold dragon from possession, for at least a time. Bomoki had the one eye. It would work.

Tania had truly changed from his time there as a mortal. The massive rainbow of glittering colors that rose up around Rojo like a spectral veneer had a sense of the divine in it. The demi-liches, soul sucked another fire giant, bowed to Bomoki and then cast two final spells. The first enacted a ward around Bomoki against dragons. The second opened a black gate of void through which they vanished.

Leaning forward, Bomoki transformed into his hellhound self as the sceptres reformed into bony armor. He threw Jeri's body into the terrible death mist. Two wolf heads burst free from his shoulders each crowned by a ram.

Rojo's claws smashed into the anti-dragon ward leaving bubbles of grey light against the sphere encapsulating Bomoki. Bomoki leapt at the dragon. Expecting flesh, Bomoki bit down into forearm and tendon but instead fell through the spray of color. Within the dragon aura, Rojo's gauntlets activated with crackling blue lightning energy as the king aimed an uppercut punch into Bomoki's stomach. The blow, augmented by fire giant strength and Spark's magic, blew Bomoki up into the sky.

From above, Ana fell from Crimson's back, a golden sword in her hands. A red line of energy arced back to Crimson where the dread lord slammed falling meteors side to side to protect the Temple and Third Fortress.

One of Bomoki's sceptres saw Ana and Crimson. Calling to the others armoring Bomoki, they blasted a disintegration ray at her. Death, stun, and possession magic lashed Ana. Bloodstone jewelry along the blade, her necklace, and the medallion in her hand absorbed the magic, and then her sword stabbed into Bomoki's back. Immediately, two red lines of magic shot down from her connecting Jeri and Rojo to herself and Crimson. Bomoki felt his own life energy begin to siphon off to strengthen and heal his foes; it enraged him. Trying to twist and dislodge her, he forgot momentarily that he fell through the sky.

The sceptres attacked Ana smashing into her goddess armor. Rojo signaled Ana for flamestrike and, using his strength, jumped into the air to intercept the falling Bomoki. From the ground below, a rune of flame erupted hellfire into the sky. The flamestrike and Twilight Fell punched into Bomoki at the same time.

A forest of sceptres rose up to protect Bomoki. Rojo punched into these and snapped a head off. The power flowing into the king from Ana intoxicated him and he called out for her to stop. She nodded and, leaving her sword in Bomoki's back, she jumped back into the sky.

Together, Rojo and Ana stepped out of the river's flow. Time stuttered around the demi-liches' black gate. They saw Bomoki's desire to reach it. The bane rune seared into Jeri's forehead pulsed with green fire here. Her paralyzed body had fallen near the gate. Even if they… "The causeway!" Rojo commanded

Reappearing on the causeway, Rojo's fingers danced through an intricate set of instructions. Luck did not favor them though and Bomoki wheeled to dive through the demi-lich's gate. Ana's sword fell like one of the meteors raining down around them. It prevented Bomoki from grabbing Jeri. The gate closed.

All around, those fallen to the demi-lich's spellcraft, battled the survivors. Rojo stood guard over Jeri as Ana turned her divine symbol against the fallen. Crimson had deflected the largest meteors that would have pulverized the Temple, but smaller ones threatened random destruction to those outside. Falling to a demi-lich, those arising as undead held higher intelligence. They mimicked the wounded until opportunities to attack presented. Many living survivors died trying to render aid. Of those arising more than half jumped the causeway and escaped into the Valley before Ana's divine power disintegrated all remaining undead on the causeway.

Rojo blocked a surprise attack against Jeri as the guard first killed by the lich feigned health only to try and take her other eye. Others came for Jeri but Rojo stood firm at his battle priestess' side. A priestess found the king cradling Jeri's head in his lap. Her paralyzed body, still dramatic in its pose of opposition and resistance to Bomoki, offered a grim counter to the pained expression on Rojo's face. "Dar Rojo, we must heal her while removing the poison and the paralysis."

"And the curse mark. Allow me," Rojo said as he combined his faith with the priestess. Unused to combining to a paladin this way, the priestess swooned as the kinetic power of Rojo drew her divine might to Rojo's healing touch. He kissed Jeri's forehead. Though it healed all of Jeri's wounds, the eye socket gaped open and wet as did the slash across her other eye.

Rojo then lifted her paralysis. Beside him, the priestess supporting him, sobbed. Rojo's concern for the dragon, and the glory of Tiamat filled her soul with visions she had never considered possible. Jeri's first breath brought with it tears of blood from her destroyed eye sockets. Her arms reached up to Rojo and she sobbed, "Tell me my love, am I precious to you now?"

Rojo brushed blood and hair from Jeri's face and kissed her blood tears. He tried to answer but could only hug her. He caressed her hair back from the jagged wounds in her face. "You know you are, Jeri. Always, without question."

Jeri's hands shook as she reached up to touch her face but Rojo held her back. The pain from the cursed dagger still wracked her. "Priestess," Rojo said. "She is going into shock. I need more clerics to join us."

The priestess jumped up to find other clerics. She heard Jeri say, her voice quivering, "I'm so sorry, Rojo. I did not sense Bomoki because of the demi-lich. I failed you all."

"No, no. How could you have known? We haven't seen a demi-lich here in hundreds of years. We knew this was the end times. This is not your fault." Rojo's voice, thick with emotion, conveyed a steel edge that promised vengeance on the undead.

Other priestesses placed her hands on Rojo's shoulders as their power and worship combined with his. They each felt his consecration as a vast golden ocean stricken through by the colors of the Goddess. He inhaled their divine spirit, and though he coveted more, he looked into Jeri's face and with every mote of concentration he could muster, he prayerfully said, "Jeri, sleep." The command blew her pain and shock away as if Tiamat herself had commanded it.

Rojo sighed, slumping forward with relief. He turned to the priestesses and said, "Thank you. Please attend to the others now. I would have the fallen captured so that we might recover their souls. Too many are lost against the dark days ahead."

The priestess and others stood and looked away, wiping tears from their faces. So many dead and so much power had happened here tonight. No one could recall the last time the undead had taken any of the causeways.

Rojo had impressed them all with his power. But, seeing his concern for the battle priestess, each of the priestesses prayed to find a similar love. Combining with him so intimately, the first priestess at last understood why all the priestesses, not just Ana and Shara, sought Rojo's heart.

It made her shudder and it also stirred something primal in her. She had seen the dragon rise up from Rojo and blast a meteor with a breath weapon she had never seen or heard of before. The king could have taken Bomoki with that attack but had chosen instead to save thousands of soldiers in the Third Fortress. Ana stood in the causeway, tied to Crimson overhead by a thin red line of energy as they deflected the remaining meteors away from them. A pack of newly born undead cowered away from Ana's holy symbol. They smoldered under her great power. It lifted the other priestesses' spirits to see Dar Ana, mightiest of the high ones, struggling merely to control rather than obliterate the powerful undead arising from fallen Tanians.

Twenty-seven soldiers fell to Bomoki and the demi-lich that night. Many others had to be restored, their souls carefully pulled back from the brink. Jeri's lost eye though weighed most heavily on Dar Ana.

Twenty-seven soldiers fallen to a demi-lich would mean twenty-seven vampires or worse. That a demi-lich had braved the causeway so close to the Temple meant, "There are no doubt more of them out there. The Jade God would not risk its most powerful undead in such an attack as this." Dar Ana looked at her attendants. Send word to Verit's command team. I want him apprised of everything that happened here tonight."

Later, Ana tapped the map of Bloodstone Valley. Her attendants had assembled a map showing the past ten months of known hellhound sightings. Each map equaled a month. In the month before the Nineteenth arrived, there had only been one hound sighting, and that in the general area of the Fifth Fortress. Since the Nineteenth's arrival, hound sightings occurred daily. A line in the current month traced Malcor's hound towards the Fifth. The hounds seen near Unter's Vein coupled to Bomoki reinforced Rojo's words about this being an end time.

Someone had made a bone carving of a werewolf and tied a red cloth around it. The creator had labeled the figure, *Little Bomoki*. She moved that piece to the causeway. "Attendants, please break the last ten days of reports into daily maps. From now on, we will track this daily. We can remove the maps of the Eighteenth. Also," she tapped the werewolf. "Find whoever did this and tell them I want skulls for the demi-liches, however many we see. We know there are at least two."

Chapter Forty Seven – Jeri's Curse

Though not hurt badly during the attack, Rojo still suffered from healing fatigue from his first encounter with Bomoki and then the Darkhold. Ana looked at him seeing his stress and anxiety. She saw his concern for Jeri and suppressed a twinge of jealousy. For her, for Rojo, the Queen had offered no chance for Rojo to love her back. She looked at him pensively hoping he'd see her concern. She had seen the priestesses combine with Rojo and remembered the only time she had done so. Unlike most clerics, Ana had specialized her combination into a weapon. It allowed her to draw might and strength from her opponents and feed it to her allies. Not many clerics could do such a thing.

It had been during the Kell Conflict twenty years or so ago. Though a much younger paladin, Ana had felt what the priestesses must have felt – a depth of love and favor with the Queen as if a sanctified ocean. She had fallen in love with him through that combination. A few days after combining with Rojo, the absence of that divine charity had triggered a dark depression in Ana. It had changed her. She made a mental note to speak with the priestesses.

Rojo withdrew his sword and began polishing it. Behind her, Crimson growled and Ana said, "Don't worry, dear one. Bomoki gave us more than I took from you. Thank you for your gift and defense, my love. Soon, we will be hosting all the fighters of the world. The god emperor sends food and provisions with the troops to the various Fortresses. I imagine that this place will soon reek with Tanian war and our allies' ulterior agendas and schemes." She looked out over the group of commanders standing at attention behind Verit. "We are very close to the Second Cascade."

No one said a thing while they listened to her speak to Crimson. She met their questioning expressions. "The First Cascade nearly destroyed Morbatten. The patriarchs saved us. Dar Tania saved us. Fortunately, most of our heroes were out questing and so Tania lost many innocents, but did not suffer the loss of its heroes. We are a vastly superior nation today than we were then. We are every bit the Spear prophesied. The Necromancer may come, but he will not leave!"

Though silence met Ana's words, the mood and morale in the room lifted. She felt a hand on her arm and startled to see Rojo standing at her side. He moved so quietly she had not sensed him; she gestured for him to speak. "Brothers and sisters, we are days away from the greatest battle between good and evil the Isles, the world, will ever see. The Kinslayer Wars of Merakor will blush in shame at the feats we will accomplish. The god emperor, the Temple, and all of the Guilds, all of our allies, have prepared for this day for centuries. What has the Jade God done?

Fostered a few insurrections? Sent his hellhounds to be slaughtered by Tanian knights again and again? Hidden Bomoki away from our rightful vengeance? The Jade God believes in freezing creation's flow, Time itself, in static slow undeath. The Jade God we faced in the First Cascade is exactly the same God we will soon face. *We are the difference!* We are the *Spear!* We are the hammer, the anvil, and the fire that will break the Jade God forever!"

This time, the Temple erupted in cheers. Ana had activated the command bloodstone, and along with the scrying sphere's help, Rojo's words sounded to every holder of a bloodstone in the world, throughout the valley, the empire, and the nations allied with Tania. Any doubts as to Morbatten's stance, strategic purpose, and motivation quelled to Rojo's words. Ana kissed his cheek and then said, "Tonight, we fast and pray for strength in the trials ahead. Tonight we anoint our spirits to withstand the Jade One."

As the Temple cleared, Ana turned to Rojo and quietly said, "I prayed for her sight to regenerate. Even with the Queen's purpose in alignment with my own, we could only barely stop the bleeding. She will need continual healing or she will bleed to death. It is a slow dying. As it is, Jeri told me Bomoki cursed her while taking her eye and destroying the other. The Temple has magical eyes but none for a dragon. With time, we could restore her sight, but the wounds will require direct intervention by Tiamat."

Rojo listened, expressionless and then said, "Ana, thank you for what you have done. The meteor swarm could have been a crippling blow to us. Takhissis blessed us by letting Jeri lose her eyes to them." Seeing her expression, he shhh'd her and continued. "The demi-liches could have infiltrated any of our fortresses. We have only a small handful here that could even hope to withstand such a foe. All our defenses are oriented to hellhounds. Bomoki must have learned this, most likely from our fallen paladins out there in undeath. You, me, the dread lords, a few others in the Circle maybe could stand against a demi-lich. They really wanted Jeri's eyes. Tell me, from Alerius' records of Merakor, have we learned anything that will help us understand why?"

Ana shook her head. "I never cared about Merakor. While fascinating to read, there's nothing there about gold dragon eyes and gates." While speaking, she motioned for all to clear the chamber. When it was just her and Rojo, and Crimson, she pulled him to the scrying sphere. In its depths, a symbol appeared. It matched the curse mark Bomoki had burned into Jeri's forehead. "This is the mark of the blind dragon of Merakor. If she dies, whenever she dies, she will rise up a draco-lich – as that particular draco-lich. Bearing a sceptre, it would mark an evolution from hellhound to helldragon."

"I take it that we cannot remove the mark?"

"The Jade God must die. Maybe when that dominion is shattered, a divine wish or similar intervention could remove it."

Rojo sighed. "I must seize that dominion too then. My list of afterlife tasks grows."

Ana squeezed his arm. "I can think of no other who could unify the dragon types as you will, Rojo." The king continued to caress Jeri's hair. Ana imagined his fingers through her own hair and had to put her envy out of her mind. "A possible advantage, Rojo, is that there are no gold dragon eyes in Bloodstone. At least not until Jeri's sisters arrive. So, let's try this."

Ana began a prayer to locate Jeri's eye. The scrying sphere quickly cycled to Jeri lying in the hospital ward and then swirled to dark blackness. Ana added prayers of divine discernment and revelation to the location prayer. The sphere's image pulled back to reveal Bomoki racing through the forest somewhere. Almost immediately, the ram heads adorning his body like armor looked up at the scrying sphere and spat cursed magic at her view. Ana had to end the spell. "I'm sure that Corth K'ven would assist us."

Rojo touched the scrying sphere. "It's too bad we could not see a landmark. I will think about Corth. The god of scrying is reluctant to be drawn into our affairs. I'm more inclined to save this request for when we are closer to the end game. When was the last time you spoke with the Lord of Wyverns?" Corth K'Ven, the god of scrying, had come into Tiamat's pantheon when offered the additional dominion of wyverns. Like the wyverns, Corth did not share the same passionate interest in Tiamat's grand plans.

"Last year. The Eighteenth did not find a single bloodstone, only traps and dead ends. I visited Corth to see if we could change their luck. He offered me a place by his side." Ana laughed trying to lighten the mood. "It's so unattractive when a male openly desires me."

Rojo smiled, about to reply, when a summoning gong sounded just outside the Temple. "I will walk with you and then take my leave," Rojo said offering her his arm. Turning back to the group, Rojo said, "See that our defenses are augmented to recognize liches and demi-liches." A flurry of activity burst from that simple command.

* * *

Outside, they found Malcor. He had crashed uncontrolled in shadow dragon form just outside the Temple. Completely spent, he lacked the energy and force of will to humanshift. As a dragon, he lay unconscious and unresponsive. In his claw, the burned corpse of a barely tended-to but alive dwarven surveyor lay. Sofen tried to extricate herself from his other claw. Fire giants worked to pry Malcor's claws apart to free the dwarf and priestess. Recalling the map, Ana guessed Malcor must have flown all day.

Ana recognized Sofen. "An ambitious if unimaginative priestess from the Nineteenth," she whispered to Rojo. She checked the dwarf and added, "But at least she prevented this one from turning." Ana's prayers fully restored both of them within minutes.

As Ana turned to bless and heal Malcor, Sofen said, "He is spent, my Dar, and the shadows resist the Goddess." She told Ana and Rojo an abbreviated version of how they met Malcor and the parts they knew from the patrol and few conversations they'd had while preparing the outpost. Ana prayed for Malcor to recover his health but his shadow dragon nature resisted it. "The shadows we fought in the valley – they took a lot of his strength and wisdom, great lady," Sofen finished. "If not for his return to us, Malcor would have slain a hellhound." She hung her head in shame. "I will atone for our weakness."

From just out of the corner of their discussion, a black form streaked towards Malcor. The king almost drew his sword, thinking they were under attack. Instead, Rojo pulled Sofen away from Malcor as the black streak resolved into a stretched caricature of a dragon. The Queen's Will blasted them all with great sense of purpose. The dragon form struck Malcor and vanished. Malcor's body twitched a bit and then returned to catatonic sleep. "What," Sofen asked, "was that?"

Rojo cocked his head as if listening. "The heretics are at last welcomed back. Malcor and a few others will play host for a time of penance and atonement for them. This is a good thing. We will let Malcor rest here," Rojo said. "Please send word when he recovers. Also, Ana, have Crimson watch. We cannot risk a demi-lich attack that claims Malcor."

Rojo looked back to Sofen. "You do not need to atone, Sofen. Though Malcor may have defeated a hellhound, he himself would have fallen to the horde. I absolve you of shame. Instead, I command you, Priestess Sofen, to accept the title of R'Dar and rise renewed in Takhissis' divine name! The hellhounds know now of Malcor and that the shadow dragons fight with Tania. I cannot think of a better announcement to our enemies of the new might arrayed against them. You have done well and I am pleased."

Sofen bowed low. At Rojo's touch, her heart leapt and divine favor, like floodgates, opened in her soul. Her nearly black brunette hair caught alight with red fire. Her skin, pockmarked by acne scars from her youth, smoothed and grew pale. Her vision, often blurred at distance, sharpened its focus as strength suffused her limbs. "Rise R'Dar Sofen and know the Goddess loves you."

In spite of herself, Sofen threw her arms around the king and then blushed. Her transcendence, so bright in this dark place of night and burning fires all around, lifted everyone's spirits. Ana came forward and pulled Sofen back from Rojo. "Go, daughter. You are renewed and I would have you assist with the fallen. They need your help."

Sofen stepped back, blushed again, and nearly tripped as she tried to bow again while turning to follow Ana's instructions. Watching her walk away, Rojo said to Ana, "At first I did not think she had made it, but the Queen showed me how she followed Malcor's instructions, and thereby saved Malcor from himself. If she holds to her Purpose, Sofen could become a mighty Dar."

Ana sat down to get more details from Grito. During their conversation, acolytes came and began searching the archives for the markings recorded by Malcor. Each of the tunnels corresponded to a hellhound sighting from centuries ago. The most recent tunnel Malcor had entered with the golden door appeared to be one of the lost mines. That is, some six hundred years ago, it had been a bloodstone producing mine. An undead counterattack had killed all the underground operators and pushed the surface contingent back. Severed from the surface, the mine had snapped back into chaos and had not been seen again. Ana looked around and called a priestess over, "I need a watch team sent here, to anchor this mine. Now."

So that they would stay with Malcor, Ana ordered fire braziers and the maps brought out. Confirming with Grito, Ana called for rosters of adventuring groups and sent word to begin positioning them near those mine locations.

"Get me Unter's Vein," Ana said at last. It took a while but eventually the priestess Thalian answered Ana's summons. Thalian explained that they had yet to reconnect to the original vein but had found a tower stone. Thalian seemed surprised Ana had not yet received the report of the titan earring found by Ayden.

"We are trying to place a teleport beacon at the tower stone now, my Dar," Thalian explained. "The battle priest Tembri leads that mission with an adventurer group. What else would you know?"

"We have found the location of a mineshaft to an ancient mine that ran rich with bloodstone ore. I would know if your group would like to continue its current excavation, or shift your focus to this ancient and sure one." Ana watched Thalian struggle with an answer before saying, "You know that war is coming to Bloodstone, Thalian. I either need your group committed to your current location, or at the ancient one in two days' time. I'm rather inclined to pull you back to one of the Fortresses for your own safety. The mines become... volatile during Cascades."

Thalian gulped audibly through the magical connection with the earrings. "The entire group is underground, Dar Ana. May I consult with them?"

Ana agreed, "But I must know within the hour. Also, let Tembri know that Malcor has returned and is safe but had a rough run of it."

Thalian ran back into the mine grateful for the guards and well-lit passageways. Whenever she passed between guards and found herself alone, her skin crawled. Ian's body lay unmoving and unconscious on a bed roll tended by the thief and Tembri. Ayden had not yet returned and the water breath potion would expire soon. While not an issue with Ian possessing her – he could use magic to prolong their time, everyone felt it odd that Ayden had not recalled back. Tembri especially looked anxious.

Thalian explained the options but before she could finish, Unter said, "We stay here. If war comes in just a few days, then I'd rather spend it here looking for my bloodstones than moving our entire operations days and days to some ancient spot where the damn Temple will want claim on every find." The dwarves all agreed. Tembri did not have strong feelings either way until Thalian told him about Malcor. At that point, he changed his stance and voted to return to the Temple Fortress, "as soon as Ayden returns."

"We have at least that much time to reply to Ana. I trust that you will make the right choice. I will order the surface fighters to prepare for departure just in case."

Chapter Forty Eight – Rogue's Blade

The entire Thieves Guild never assembled, ever. It was a matter of principle to protect identities and cell leadership. Khalla looked out at them all from the great training hall. The cell leaders mingled with the others looking new and green as everyone tried to look like brand new members of the guild. The disguises were so perfect that an outsider would think they hosted a convention for innocents dressed as spies, trying to look like spies. Looking at her own clothing, she realized that she looked out of place. Spidersilk armor, weapons, and the magical cloaks used to mitigate weather extremes and provide camouflage identified her as the guild leader.

She cleared her throat and the group went quiet. "It doesn't matter. You all know who I am. My name is Khalla. I am Marcello's lieutenant. You all know who he is right?" The group chuckled. They all knew the name but very few knew him. Most knew his Ash persona, a patron who brought their cells work on behalf of Marcello. "You also know that Tania is marshalling the empire to fight in Bloodstone. You might be wondering what role we are to play in this. I will answer your wondering.

"Marcello orders that we join the units marshalling into Bloodstone. I would have us form a team. We will be called *Rogue's Blade*. Some of you have already been contracted to adventurer groups, to the Temple, to the various guilds. You will continue under those contracts but know that I take the Thieves Guild under the name of Rogue's Blade. While we are gone, leadership will fall to our patron, Ash. Marcello and his cell chase a dangerous quarry to Bloodstone and will meet us there. I want you to think on Rogue's Blade, if you're available. While you do so, let's talk about Farant."

Khalla outlined what had happened and what they knew about Farant. She left out the part about his taking the Guild vault, and that the real vault remained safe. Because so many of the ranking members had participated in the raids on the Jaden shrines at Dock Side, speculation and rumors had run rampant. After Khalla took a few questions from those who knew Farant or members of his cell, Khalla turned to the business of organizing Rogue's Blade.

"Enforcers will play the role of fighters. Agents will play the role of bards, lower level fighters, or whatever your dual-classed role is. Rogue's Blade will be large enough that Tania will assign a mage and a priestess to our unit. I have already sent word to ensure those allied with us are selected. So that there is no question – I command Rogue's Blade and you will address me as Captain Khalla. For those of you that do not know, Marcello recruited me from Morilon's ranger units. I'm not actually a Tanian-trained thief, which is a good thing. I will lead under my Morilon title of Scout Captain. You all joined my unit through military service, through adventuring contacts, through favors owed to your cell leaders. I have prepared papers and aliases in anticipation that all of you will be joining. Each cell will leave behind one person to maintain our network of civilian contacts and continue the appearance of business as normal."

The next day, Khalla rode at the head of a motley crew of fighters, soldiers, bards, rangers, and a few mages. The well-worn equipment, armor, and battle-trained horses carried them to the base of the Temple. So many similar groups had come through that the paladins on guard duty waved them along without question. In the early morning, cold winter air crystallized ice that fell as a form of snow even though the day promised to be bright. At a certain point, a paladin signaled their group to stop and approached demanding to speak to the leader. Khalla dismounted and walked forward bowing. "Rogue's Blade, ready to hunt in Bloodstone," she proclaimed. With a snap, she presented the unit's papers to the paladin.

He opened the scroll, half-read it scanning for anything that stood out. "I've never heard of Rogue's Blade," he said, though not with enough interest to warrant a response. "May Takhissis bless your hunt." Khalla bowed low. "Keep your unit here. We are receiving innocents from across the empires. The gate will not be ready for several hours. I'll return shortly with a better approximation of when." He pointed towards the Dragon Mountain's eastern side, where it looked like another peak had been sliced off. "Or, you can head up there. That gate is being exclusively used for sending troops and material to Bloodstone. Let me know now."

Khalla looked around. Though early morning, several of the parties in front of them looked like they had overnighted on the road. "We'll head up, Sir."

"Very good," he said handing her papers back to her. He pointed to a side street. "We're keeping this one clear all the way up. May the Goddess speed your way."

Khalla could tell she had made the correct choice. As the road rose up the side of the Temple, they eventually could see the gate ringed by Tanian priestesses welcoming families of elderly, children, and others of all races. Though they were efficiently shunted off to side streets where others helped them find housing, so many poured through that it seemed never-ending.

The back road wound up the Temple until it crossed the Grand Staircase and continued north and west onto the Dragon Mountain. As they gained altitude, they passed vendors selling everything from food, luck charms, souvenirs, weapons, holy this and that, and all other things fighters might need when facing the undead. Khalla recognized more than a few of the long-retired Guild members. While they no doubt recognized some of her troop, they ranked so low or had been retired so long that they would not know the entire unit drew from the Thieves Guild proper. Several hours passed and Khalla realized the paladin had spoken truth. For every step of the horses, several steps seemed to pass and they travelled faster than she could imagine. Obvious now to her, some elemental magic sped them towards the gate.

A group of City Watch worked its way down the mountain, shouting for the path to clear. Khalla recognized Calvin from Ryvane's reports and Marcello's description. An armband proclaimed him responsible for Dock Side. She waved him over. "Watch Captain, if you don't mind, a minute please?"

Eyeing her fine horse, Calvin ordered his men to continue forward and said to Khalla, "Yes?"

"My aunt's family lives in Dock Side," Khalla said referring to a family the Guild protected. "While I'm gone, I'd appreciate some extra attention and security in their area." She tossed Calvin a small pouch of gold coins.

He opened it just enough to see whether it contained gold, silver or copper. He smiled at the gold. "We'll take good care of your family, miss," Calvin said with a bow.

Marcello had been right. Efficient but obsessed with material wealth and comfort. *Ryvane*, Khalla mentally chuckled. *I wonder if she's told Calvin the truth about herself?* Watching Calvin walk away, a swagger in his step, Khalla started laughing and had to choke it back as a paladin asked her to hand over Rogue's Blade's papers.

Like déjà vu, Khalla said introduced the team and presented papers. This time though, the paladin called a priestess over and pointed to something in the scroll. The priestess nodded and signaled Khalla for a private conversation. It made her unit nervous. When alone, the priestess said, "Rogue's Blade is not a very subtle name for a band of thieves."

Khalla smiled and almost said she had no idea what the priestess meant, but at the last minute changed her mind. "Our Guildmaster wants our guild represented in this grand adventure. I'm Captain Khalla."

The priestess' smile told her she had made the correct decision. *Maybe honesty is the best policy*, she thought. "While we have no issues with the Thieves Guild participating, we do have an issue with several of the clauses in the papers you had counterfeited as if from the Temple."

Anticipating Khalla's worried reaction, the priestess said, "Don't worry. The god emperor wants you in Bloodstone. However, we need to change a few things. I'm sure you won't mind, will you?"

Khalla looked around and though the Temple and its paladins seemed preoccupied, the fact that she stood within a ring of paladins did not escape her. "I have limited ability to approve changes to Marcello's contract -"

"An illegal contract has no authority within the empire," the priestess interrupted her. "Counterfeiting the Temple is risky. If caught, I can only imagine. You're very bold to select us. For example, standard contracts give you first rights to bid on any bloodstones your unit finds. Your contract says you get to keep what you find and bloodstones are stricken from the contract so that you'd keep them."

The priestess scanned the rest quickly, "The failure to note how bloodstones are treated, is a problem. Or here." She pointed to another clause. "This clause exonerates you from military command when clearly this is a military operation. Even Taysor and Morilon bow to Tanian military command." She rolled the scroll shut and rubbed her nose between her eyes. "Though it is not my place, our high priestess would no doubt find some of this borderline treasonous. Par for the course with the Thieves Guild no doubt, but," she shrugged. "I don't see Marcello here, nor the parties that signed this." She flipped it open to the end where Marcello had signed the commission. Countering his signature, a cursive and beautiful signature for *Dar Shara de Ordelaine* had been inscribed. She tapped this and pointed just over by the gate where Dar Shara stood. "If you'd like to protest, we can easily ask Dar Shara to validate that she signed this. It was rather poor judgement to counterfeit one of The High Priestesses, though I suppose you did this thinking our lower level acolytes would not question it. If she did not sign this, she may have some words to say to you, Khalla."

Khalla's stomach had knotted into a tight ball of anxiety. She hated dealing with the Temple. They always seemed to know things they should not, could not possibly know. Dare she validate it? *Did Marcello really get this signed by the Dar Shara?* Khalla smiled and said, "You put me in a rough position. I am not Marcello and yet I follow the orders of my Guildmaster. I have no way of validating whether this is real or not but my and my team's desire to fight in Bloodstone is very real. What would you have us do?"

The priestess pulled another scroll out of her mantle. "Standard contract, standard terms, standard everything. This is the same contract that every other group has signed joining the Nineteeth Legion, even the special teams formed by the Circle itself. You can believe that Marcello is special enough to warrant Dar Shara's personal attention on a contract covering," she checked again before saying, "Eighty-four fighters and entourage, or you can take me at my word when I tell you that Dar Shara has not personally signed any of these, ever. We are not at the Temple of Glass. Dar Kell commands here in the King's absence. So, take your pick – Shara is right there to confirm her signature, or you can sign this standard plain-old not-special contract."

Khalla swore and took the standard contract. If they had taken the lower gate, and Marcello must have intended this, no one would have scrutinized the contract to this level of detail. She made a mental note to talk to Marcello about his manipulation of fate, and how she really needed to be in on it.

"Good choice," the priestess said. "My paladins will escort you back to your team. They'll help ensure that your entire team signs this." In her hand, the special contract flash-ignited to ash and blew away in the icy air. Immediately, the ring of paladins converged on them and whisked Khalla back to her team. With alarm and trepidation, they signed the contract under the watchful eyes of the paladins. Khalla could see them all grumpily recalculating their potential haul from this quest.

With all their signatures complete, they were ushered before Dar Shara and the dread lord Armageddon. Khalla had no doubt Shara knew everything about her in that moment. But, for her own pride, Khalla endured it. The giant gate loomed behind Shara, who blessed them in Takhissis' name. Her blessing fell on them like smoky embers from a warm fire, making their skin tingle and bringing with it the scent of smoke. Each mote tingling their skin energized their muscles, made it easier to breathe, dispelled the cold, and fired their hearts and passions with a desire to fight undead, to serve Tania, to destroy the Jade God no matter the price or sacrifice paid.

Khalla had felt blessings from the high priestesses before, but never in war. Their bodies filled with energy as Temple acolytes anointed them with oil and blood. The oil made her forehead tingle and a smell of mint came with it. At the touch of blood, her own ignited with magical power. "Takhissis enacts the Rite of Genocide in you, Her Chosen sons and daughters. As Khalla leads you to Takhissis' enemies so too shall Takhissis lead you to glory! Let none survive! May the bright dragons watch over, bless, and protect you. Step from sacred Tania to cursed Bloodstone. The gate is ready."

Khalla mounted up and at her command, Rogue's Blade rode through the gate, and onto the causeway between the Third and Fourth Fortress. The transition from bright cold to dark snow and wind alarmed their horses, but pages ran forward as did clerics praying for the animals to calm. An oppressive feeling of being watched grew on them. The air, the ground, it stank of death and Khalla pulled her cloak over her face to mask the smell. Wheeling her horse to approach a priestess working next to a fire giant, Khalla shouted through the wind, "Rogue's Blade reporting for glory!"

The priestess greeted them, "Bloodstone welcomes Rogue's Blade. May you slay a thousand hellhounds. You are assigned to the Third Fortress under command of Captain Niles. Please report there," she pointed to the blocky fortress. "And clear the gate area for the next group."

Khalla bowed and signaled the way. She had never been to Bloodstone but had heard and seen sketches of the fortresses. The giant square fortresses loomed larger than she had imagined or appreciated. Though Tania had put a lot of work into the causeway roads connecting them along the mountain ridges, the fortresses remained as the undead had constructed them. Unadorned but functional, ugly but purposeful, squat but strong Khalla pointed to the fortress and said, "Listen up, this will be our home, Rogue's Blade! Be on your best behavior."

Captain Niles greeted them inside and walked alongside Khalla's horse as they went down a level and then made a few turns till horse stables, greeted them. "We keep the animals in the center of the Fortress. There's nothing worse than a horse going undead." He pointed to some markings on the wall. "These paint stripes will tell you where you are and where you need to go. Yellow is to the causeway. Green is to the shrine. Blue is to the mess hall. Arrows within the paint tell you which way to reach those areas so as to avoid confusion in intersections, and trust me, there are many. Black goes downwards. Any questions?"

Khalla asked, "When do we deploy?"

"Tomorrow, I'm assigning your team to to the valley floor. We need to know if any tunnels have opened or are being dug along the valley near us. If you find them, you are to signal, fire them, and kill anything you find. We do this daily, so it's a good and fairly safe way to get your team exposed to Bloodstone. Report to the causeway gate at sunrise."

Captain Niles turned to leave but Khalla said, "I have one more question. How far is the Sixth Fortress? I have a friend there."

Niles continued walking away but answered, "The Sixth is under attack. Sorans began arriving and are pushing the undead back into the Fortress's lower levels. Once done, Tania is withdrawing from the Sixth. You'll meet your friend then. Otherwise, it's a six-day ride along the causeway." He snorted as if at a joke, "Unless you can fly. Then it's just a day's flight."

Marcello and his cell sat high in the trees, careful to avoid dislodging snow. Their first day doing this, it had snowed hard. Even with magical clothing and gear, the long night had sapped their body heat and morale. At least the sun had peeked out through the clouds and the wind seemed as if it might let up.

Down below them a few hundred feet, the Cordabad River ran through a series of twists and turns. Splashing water had built icy walls on both sides but even the cold could not contain the entire river. This hairpin turn sat closest to the Bloodstone. Because of clouds, they could not see the Sixth Fortress behind them. Just in case, Marcello had spread his team out for a mile in either direction even asking Sai's spider golem to take up a position near him. If Farant swam as a fish, this is where and when he would arrive. The Circle seemed to be able to follow Farant. They should see him today, any moment really, unless he decided to head towards the First Fortress and the main pass into Bloodstone. Like the Circle, Marcello doubted Farant would risk it.

By the river, a splash and loud cursing heralded Farant's arrival. The spider phased out to pull the cell back to their rendezvous point farther up. They had a play to put on for Farant's sake. If the play did not work, if Farant did not take the bait, this would be the most expensive undertaking Marcello had ever attempted. But, luck had favored him before and he had faith it would again.

Farant had to giant-size himself to get out of the freezing water and then immediately used the stone again to sprout thick white hair like a gorilla everywhere. For a moment, Marcello saw the wound and a flash of red around angry, infected intestines that Farant kept pushing back in. Even the shapeshifting could not hide the spreading gangrene as within a few steps, the white-furred giant's abdomen turned green and black and oozed slime. Farant did not seem to notice, even scratched a tube of rotted entrails before realizing it was his. He stuffed it back in. *Why are necromancers so disgusting?* Marcello wondered.

Farant began trying to walk straight to Bloodstone's Sixth Fortress, yet stumbled like a drunk person. Nearly walking underneath Marcello, the thief gagged at the stench of body odor and fish when Farant passed by.

From a safe distance, Marcello and his agents jumped down in a shower of snow, and followed. They were counting on Farant resuming his pattern of burrowing in and resting during bright daylight. Soon enough, though cloudy still, Farant stretched yawning and sat down. He picked at the bloodstone's surface and put the rolled vault tube to the side before stabbing it at the ground to make a hole. Farant had grown sloppy in the several days of not being pursued. He left the rolled vault tube in the open. Marcello signaled to let it be. They moved past Farant to make ready their performance.

An hour before sunset, Farant awoke to the sounds of battle, but not aimed at him. Hoping for a meal of blood and soul energy, he shapeshifted to something small and quiet. He saw Marcello – *Curses!*, Farant screamed mentally – engaged in a bloody combat with a paladin of Takhissis. They were yelling at each other, something about conscription and fighting for the Queen. Farant thought he saw some of the guild members circling the paladin. Farant crept up to get a better look. He could not fight them all.

The paladin wore the armor of a high ranking member of the Order of Fire. The draconian runes along its edge gleamed with fire. Farant could feel the heat and noted the snow and ice around them had started to melt. Marcello dodged all around like a jack rabbit, dodging the paladin's attacks. It frustrated Farant that the paladin could not score a direct hit. Then, it happened. The paladin called on Takhissis for fire. Flames erupted around him just as Marcello came in for a backstab attack.

Caught in the fire, Marcello ignited and fell back, scrambling in the melting ice to back away from the paladin. The other thieves leapt into the fray but did not even give the knight pause. They could not get close enough to hurt him. A bolt twanged from a wrist bow but it incinerated and puffed against the knight's much hotter armor. "Takhissis calls on you all to join the Nineteenth Legion! You will fight with us or be judged here and now!"

Marcello, scorched as he was, had backpedaled enough to retrieve what looked like a wand from his cloak. He held it up at the paladin and said, "We do not serve the Empire like that, you idiot!" A white gem embedded in the wand flashed a brilliant white light, so bright it hurt Farant's eyes. Immediately, the paladin's flames, even his sword and armor extinguished. Farant felt a tangible lack of divinity. The thief stood up now, brushing snow from his clothing and armor. Already, magic items had started to heal that thrice-damned Marcello. Tapping the wand in his hand, he waved it generally at the knight. "Bet you don't feel so holy now, do you?"

The knight raised his voice in a battle song that would reignite the flames, but nothing happened. The diamond or whatever gem in the wand sparkled. Marcello cut his sword through the air in a cross. "Care to try a fair fight now? You were saying something about our being drafted."
Around the knight, the four other thieves, Farant recognized them as those chasing him since Morbatten, loaded crossbow bolts and drew additional blades. "You're surrounded, flanked, and thanks to this beauty," Marcello kissed the diamond, "you're completely cut off from Takhissis. How does it

feel to be just another fighter? Oh wait, you're not even that. Too much doctrine floating around in your brain."

Farant could not believe his eyes. To so openly taunt a ranking member of the Order of Fire, it defied his understanding of how Tania worked. Apparently, the knight struggled with it too. He charged Farant and a blade fight ensued. Though the paladin did a great job and even with his extensive training paying off, he could not hope to defeat five senior guild members and the master. Cut to his knees, the paladin at last collapsed to the snow still praying to Takhissis. Tears rolled down his face and Marcello clocked him with his sword's pommel. The battle had lasted minutes. Watching Marcello strip the knight of his sword, holy symbol, and quickly scavenge anything of value, Farant shook his head. *Did that just really happen?*, he wondered. *Marcello stripped a paladin of his connection to Tiamat and won?*

The thieves quickly stripped the knight of his armor, which would be worth a small fortune. Looking around to ensure no one had seen them, Marcello ordered one of the thieves. "Sneak into Bloodstone and see how we can best sell this stuff." With that, they withdrew into the winterscape.

Farant waited, listening, smelling. He shapeshifted into different animals with better senses. When he had at last confirmed Marcello's crew had left, he moved forward to the paladin's unconscious body. They had left the knight his gambeson and underclothing. Farant rolled him over noting the many tattoos of Takhissis' symbols etched within runes of the elemental plane of Fire. It had been so long since he had consumed a human soul. It rather made him drool. He wiped his mouth before muttering, "No no no. I must find out. This magic. Is it permanent?"

The knight awoke with a splitting headache. He had been stripped naked and tied to a tree. Every part of his body ached with freezing cold but worse, a decaying man with a gangrenous wound in his navel paced in front of him mumbling to himself. The knight swore. No atonement could be worth this. He had a brief moment where he recalled the journey that had brought him here. Not an atonement, but family debt had made this happen. He swore at his father and brothers who had racked up gambling debts to the point that his family had become beholden to the Thieves Guild. It had not seemed so bad. But, then this job had come.

"A chance to completely wipe out any and all debts," the one named Marcello had said. "It'll be unpleasant but it will strike a blow directly to the first hellhound in Bloodstone. Here are my conditions," and Marcello had outlined it. "You will fight me in a staged combat. We will bloody each other. You will be subjected to an anti-magic device but I need you to make it look like it nullifies your paladin powers to the Goddess. I know it's distasteful but think of this: your family will be free and the first hellhound Bomoki will suffer. Keep that in your head. That's hardly the worst part. After, a necromancer will probably try to soul suck you. We have a mage that will help with that. Are you in?"

He had agreed, and now here stood, tied to a tree. He could pray and the cold would go away, his bonds would loosen, and he could take this necromancer even without his sword and armor. Marcello had taken those to be returned, as part of the staged combat. He'd have to suffer the natural. "Do you know me, Tanian?" the hemorrhaging human said to him.

The knight shrugged, trying his best to look frustrated. He prayed and it surprised him how hard it was to keep his faith out of the prayer. The human stepped back and then cackled. "Tell me. Your fight. Did that wand steal your powers?"

The knight sighed and tried to look resigned to his fate. "I don't know you. I see you're a necromancer, and a sick one at that. You disgust me. Why should I answer you, foul spawn of the Jade One?"

Farant laughed evilly this time. "Orcus! Say his name! Orcus! Yes, the master comes and I will be his right hand. Death is but a doorway. The more pain, the grander the entrance... as you will soon see. Now, tell me! Did the wand take your faith?" Farant shifted his arm into a troll-like clawed hand and raked it across the paladin's chest. The knight felt his training kick in to repress the pain, and he had to push it back to let the pain show. "Cut off, I wonder how long you can endure pain?" Farant asked as his rotting teeth bit and then tore a chunk of flesh from the knight's forearm. That caused a scream of real pain.

The knight winced and with pain said, "The wand did not take my faith but it certainly ended my divine powers."

Farant cackled, chewing the flesh in his mouth. "And? Is it coming back? Tell me!"

The knight looked at his arm spilling blood down his hand. "Yes, I can tell it will come back. Why do you care?"

Farant did a quick mental calculation and figured the wand had knocked the paladin's powers out of commission for at least three hours. "That's more than plenty. Plenty enough. Indeed." He laughed again and caressed the knight's face leaving blood on his cheeks. "The question is answered, so, sorry about this." Farant inhaled deeply and began pulling the knight's soul into him. The knight looked terrified and resumed his prayer to

Takhissis. Something about the prayer, or the knight's returning powers almost blocked Farant's soul suck, but at last the body went dead and limp.

Marcello watched from a distance as his plan unfolded. Next, they just needed to let Farant capture the wand. The first stage set, they moved to the second. Farant, satisfied with his meal, turned and continued his charge northwest to the Sixth.

After a few minutes, Marcello slinked into the clearing. One of the runes glowed softly and when touched, the knight's color returned. "That takes care of the feigned death. Now, for the other one." Touching it, the knight's soul flooded back into his body from where it had been temporarily held.

The knight drew a deep breath and shrugged the bonds off. Marcello gave him a healing potion to help with his arm. "I'm glad this worked out. On behalf of guildmaster Marcello, your family's debts are forgiven and restitution is made. Here is a letter stating such as well as a letter of credit for five thousand gold pieces. Please note that your father, and the next three generations are forbidden from borrowing money, gambling, or entering into letters of credit within the empire. This is for their protection."

The knight scanned the letter while Marcello pulled the knight's sword and armor out. "Answer me this. The soul Farant sucked, who was it?"

Marcello thought about lying but then said, "Honestly, there is an old man in our guild named Halavar. He was once a great agent but in Bloodstone, he became cursed and has not thought clearly since. He realized it too. Halavar blames, appropriately, the hellhounds and the Jade God. When I offered him a chance to strike back at the Jade God, he insisted. He considered it worth this chance."

The knight looked on skeptically and then shrugged, "Who am I to judge another's path of retribution? Tell me, is it worth it?" The knight whistled for his steed.

Marcello's infectious smile answered him. "If this goes as the white dragon requires, the first hellhound will get a nasty surprise. I have no idea what it is though. The dragon would not say."

The knight laughed. "Dragon secrets," he said; this Tanian saying implied obvious mystery as if to say 'it's a mystery now but trust the dragons and it will make sense'. Re-armored and equipped, the knight shook Marcello's hand and took his leave. A black stallion in heavy armor ran into the clearing. The knight saddled up and waved goodbye. Marcello watched as the knight vanished in the direction of the road to the First Fortress.

The third stage was easy. They set heavy guards and Marcello "fell asleep" with the wand in his hand. They had some debate about how to ensure Farant would only have enough time to take the wand and not hurt any of them. Sai's spider golem helped. Just as the second shift ended, Marcello's team heard and then spied a white and grey raccoon slink into the campsite.

Farant, oblivious to them all, wished he could smile. The thieves had really let themselves go, probably too frozen to post a good guard. He meandered a bit to nibble at some food crumbs they left by the fire. One of the guards threw a snowball at him. He dodged it easily enough and used it to get closer to Marcello. "Stupid forest animal," another guard said.

The bloodstone makes everything so easy, Farant marveled. He scratched behind his ear, careful to not let the infection in his stomach show to the guards. In the darkness and erratic firelight, the guards would not see anyway. After a moment, they turned to look out into the night and readjust their night vision. Farant crept up to Marcello and the wand. For a moment, he thought about shifting and taking Marcello's soul, or at least really hurting him. Perhaps the raccoon's innate nature distracted him though – the pretty wand dazzled.

In a heartbeat, the raccoon plucked the wand from Marcello's hands. The stupid guildmaster did not even notice it. Wand in hand, the raccoon fled to a nearby frozen stream where he shapeshifted and leapt to the trees. He repeated this a few times. Behind him, he heard the guards call out to Marcello about the wand. Alarm and cries to search for Farant made him shiver with delight. "I've still got it," the giant form said picking up the vault tube.

Back at the clearing, the thieves continued to make noise and fuss. Only after an hour did Marcello signal for them to end it. "Our work here is done. Let's go join with Rogue's Blade." At Marcello's command, the group turned and began moving south and east. Like the knight from earlier, they would intercept the road from Haven to the First Fortress.

* * *

Bomoki stared at the gate as if mesmerized. With the gold dragon eye, the gate had stopped decaying, had stopped moving. "To be fair, the cavern moves I suppose." Bomoki scratched his head and repaired faint cracks in one of the runes.

"Farant approaches the Sixth," Bomoki's helmet sceptre said to the cavern. Around him, at the three points of a triangle, humanoid skulls materialized.

Around them, spectral tissue knit and then real tendon, muscle, and skin sprouted from the skulls to curtain the bodies with flesh.

"Yes," one of the demi-liches said. "We sense the Farant. He brings the artefact we need to nullify all bloodstones?"

Bomoki shrugged. "Supposedly. That one is so stupid and greedy that until we see it, and hold this master bloodstone, I will not trust it. It also seems unlike Alerius to have created such a thing. Yes, it's definitely a trap. Still, you never know. Of course, you've all been dead so long, have you forgotten how devious the world of the real can be?"

Another demi-lich replied, "We remember deviousness, and evil. We remember power. Without the Temple, Bloodstone falls to Orcus. To Orcus, the Temple is a bane. To us, it is evil."

Bomoki laughed at them. "In your quest for this immortality, you must regret what has become of you. I myself considered lichdom. Tell me, has it been worth it?"

The third lich cruelly hissed, "Yes. Yes! To ascend into a pantheon already controlled by gods is to limit our potential. I regret nothing. I see you scheme to ascend on your own and yet, in this world, you are still bound to Orcus. Tell me, hound, has it been worth it?"

Bomoki scratched the ram horns protruding through his shoulder. "I regret being captured into this but have never regretted the power. The master has shown me the universe you exist in. Worlds without end or time and pure knowledge… yet, your world is also limited to Orcus' dominion. Infinite power limited by Orcus, I regret your loss of the Limitless for you." While talking, Bomoki withdrew Jeri's eye from the mouth of a sceptre. The demi-liches and hounds went still and quiet.

Bomoki held the dragon eye in his hand and looked around at the hounds and liches. "It would be better if we had two. That would ensure the gate. With just one, we have just one opportunity to bring the Master here. I am loathe to make this decision and risk on behalf of Orcus. We will go to the gate and converse with him. In the meanwhile, we must intercept Farant before the Tanians capture him." Bomoki looked at the demi-liches. "I leave him to you. Bring me the vault. Do with Farant what you will but remember, his soul is promised to one of my sceptres."

The three demi-liches bowed and vanished. The two hellhounds, flanking Bomoki, stood and followed him as he stepped over the edge of the stair platform. The entire stone area floated gently down thousands of steps to stop at the top of the giant staircase. With the hounds running the spiral stairs, Bomoki rolled the gold dragon eye in his hand occasionally licking Jeri's blood from it. He snapped his fingers and many points of light ignited to illuminate the area.

The cavern around the gate was immense. The stairs had been carved by tens of thousands of undead. It was tiresome to reassemble shattered bones but Orcus required a place big enough for him to come through. "This time the gate will be large enough," Bomoki cackled gleefully. He looked at the eye again. "I hope this works with just one eye. It should," he muttered. All of the remaining hellhounds began to arrive.

The nearest wall sat a hundred paces behind the stairs. In front of the stairs, polished stone tiles gleaming in green light of trapped souls raced out to a giant disc standing upright but at an odd angle. It leaned. The topmost anchoring rune tilted where it should be centered.

Each of Bomoki's and the hounds' steps stirred the trapped souls locked away on the other side of the mirrored tiles. Their green light rippled from their awakening and created waves of light that raced in helical arcs and twining dances of light throughout the chamber. The disc though sat quiet and unmoving, dead compared to the magical lights gleaming all around.

One of the hounds sniffed the air and said, "Has the time truly come to bring the Master through?"

Bomoki tossed the eye up and watched it land wetly in his hand. "I have toiled through ages untold to make this happen. Whether it is time or not, that is beside the point. In this place, when Orcus is master here, Time itself will cease to matter." Bomoki stopped and turned to the hound. The other growled anticipating a challenge or fight. Under such scrutiny, the hound leaned down to the floor pressing low and submissive. "You see, if I destroy you in this place and Time, this Time will forever show you dead."

To emphasize his words, green fire lit his other hand and several of the sceptres along his body glared malevolent spite at the hound. "You will be cut out of this place by causality. Time will flow on and you will remain dead. But," Bomoki pointed the eye at the gate. "When Orcus comes to this place, only causality will matter. As the master of what does, can, and might only happen, Orcus could decide to let you die and that would be that. Only his will matters. However, say that idiot gnat of a king – King Rojo, or his fool priestess Ana – slays you. With Orcus here, your death is inconsequential. Sure, the causality exists but the reality of your undying becomes sure; you become endless. They have free will, for a time, and can try to slay you but against your endlessness? They will fail."

The hound crawled back from Bomoki's words and pawed at its head trying to understand. "I do not envy you your inability to comprehend," Bomoki said stroking the sceptre adorning his head like a helmet, scratching at its horn base. "You could have free will. It's not hard."

The hounds' ears pricked up wary of another challenge, another test. Bomoki turned back to the gate and resumed his walk. When they at last reached it, the gate loomed over his human form another ten times taller and wide than Bomoki's height. The floor in this place sank towards the gate and water had slowly accumulated. It made the soul lights under the water hazier. Bomoki flipped the sleeves of his robes over his arms. Three sceptres uncoiled from the sleeves of his robe to form a tripod. On this stand, Bomoki placed the eye so that it stared at the gate.

From the sceptres' spinal columns, red and purple tendrils reached out to capture and secure the eye, connecting to it. At the same time, the three sceptres and the gold dragon eye blinked. Immediately, the gold dragon eye fixated on the gate.

"It worked," Bomoki marveled. "It worked!" He began laughing. "The time is coming!" Bomoki called after the hounds racing to the stairs. "Send word to the demi-liches that we do not need other gold dragon eyes. And, recall all of the hellhounds. If they have not yet fetched us gold dragon eyes, there is no point. Let the word go out, all hellhounds are to come to Bloodstone!"

Chapter Fifty – The Ayden Stone

Seline could not take it anymore. Waiting for Ayden to magically appear, or for Ian's body to stir was terrible. Seline had recovered a lot faster than the others thanks in part to her armor. "I'm going to go check the guards and tunnel perimeter. I fear we are running out of time. Tembri, I know you and Thalian feel it too. I will pray for her." She bowed and exited the side cavern into the tunnel.

The tunnel they had breached to this cavern stretched out to her left and right. The left passage went back to the surface. The right one went a several hundred paces to a junction. She went right. Every so often, a dwarf tinked away at the stone next to a lantern focused on an impossibly thin vein of low quality bloodstone. It ran along the tunnel occasionally vanishing. Just before the juncture, four veteran fighters stood with shields and swords drawn on high alert.

They signed to Seline that their thief/scout had taken position in the opposite tunnel. She queried them for any signs of enemy activity. They shrugged. Since coming here, lower level undead, weird sounds, and scarier sounds echoed through the two tunnels connecting here opposite them. The vein seemed to run out in both tunnels and so Unter had trapped those with exploding clay. Like before, if things grew dire, they could collapse the tunnels with explosives.

The original plan had been to excavate a new tunnel where the dwarves all agreed the bloodstone vein should be. However, the noise and commotion of a full tunneling operation warranted caution. Now with imperial mobilization and Ayden's discovery, such an undertaking became secondary.

Seline walked into the intersection and quieted her mind. She listened to everything and began filtering out the known sounds. When only the silence of the caves remained, Seline prayed for inspiration. "Into which tunnel should I go?" The answer struggled to come and Seline cursed Bloodstone for cutting her off from Tiamat. However, a feeling towards the left caught her attention. An agent from the new Rogue's Blade team peered out of the shadows questioning in handsign if she required assistance. She shook her head negative.

Entering the tunnel a few paces, she let the light behind her fade and then repeated her silent prayer. She focused all of her attention into the darkness ahead and prayed. She felt a sense of time, and a growing sense of urgency. Images of combat and war flashed into her mind, troubling her. In those images, she saw them dragging Ian's body out of the tunnels. Tembri lingered in combat, praying to ward the undead back, and then fell under tons of rock. She saw herself wreathed in flames fighting an ungodly amalgamation of body parts that rose up from all around her, from the walls themselves. When her thoughts quieted again, she touched the tunnel side feeling the rough dry stone. *We have time, but not as much as Ayden requires.* She slowly and quietly retreated to the juncture and called the agent to join them.

"We are running out of time. Bring the dwarves and that exploding clay. I want that tunnel," she pointed to the left-side tunnel, "completely ready to blow. I'm going back to urge our withdrawal now. As soon as the tunnel is ready, expect that we will blow it." They nodded. "And," Seline added with seriousness, "If anything at all stirs here, I want you all to fall back. No heroes or last stands today. We're going to do this safely."

The dwarves picking at the bloodstone vein almost argued with her, but she burned with purpose. Something in their souls leapt to obey her. They quickly packed their gear, samples, and other equipment. In the side cavern, Seline expected a fight. She knew that Tembri would argue they should stay. Unter would wait and then side with Tembri. "Everyone, we are out of time. The Mother has shown me what happens if we stay. Unter, in the name of Tania and Takhissis, I command you to take the miners and prepare to explode the tunnels at the intersection. We are taking Ian and leaving. Tembri, you have charge of Ian. He's a mage. He can teleport back and find us. Thalian and Helena, come with me to guard the miners as they set the explosives." She almost asked if anyone had any questions but so commanding was her tone that no one argued.

Tembri hung his head low and then she saw he prayed. He hand-signed a compliment to her as she barked orders for the rest to obey. The cavern, long silent and pregnant with waiting, became the site of a hasty withdrawal. They left a note for Ian in case he teleported back. They'd leave a rope for him as well as a trigger rune to collapse this last section of cavern if needed. Seline led the two priestesses, Unter, and several dwarves carrying pots of the exploding clay back to the intersection. They passed the other dwarves as they fell back. Seline noted they did not make eye contact with Unter. "You're doing the right thing, Unter. Have faith." He grunted noncommittally.

The soldiers seemed relieved to see them. Thalian and Helena combined and invoked a prayer that would render the group silent and invisible to undead. Staying close to each other, they walked twenty paces into the leftmost tunnel and set clay along fractures in the wall and ceiling. They then did the same to the other tunnel.

Curiosity burned within Seline. After all, now that they had secured their retreat, what would it hurt to explore just a bit more? She thought about

Malcor. He would probably explore a bit more. In her mind, she heard Tembri and her own mentor Dar Niss say, "Bloodstone's murders lie not with the undead so much as with foolhardy accidents. There is no glory in a pointless undying."

They retreated back towards the side cavern. Tembri stood alone as a sentinel, his arms crossed across his wide chest. He caught Seline's attention and said quietly, "You were right, paladin. I am honored to serve with you. May the Queen continue to bless and guide you."

Tembri triggered the exploding runes and the blast raced up over them. The silence of their prayers protected them from the noise. It felt odd to see so much violence with no sound at all. They latched onto the rope and proceeded back to the surface. The spell ended after a few moments and from somewhere behind them, they heard a keening scream followed by a chorus of shrieks. They exited the tunnel blinking in the relative brightness of the above ground world. A guard informed them that dawn would rise in two hours' time.

They joined the guard and waited, praying that nothing would follow them. Just before dawn, Ayden appeared and fell over Ian's body as a sphere of water carried by the teleport spell dropped them right on top. Tembri barely managed to pull Ian to the side or Ayden would have crushed the frail mage. Ayden immediately began coughing water out of her lungs deeply gulping air as the potion's effect ended. When she could at last talk, she stumbled to her feet and then fell over Ian's body. A moment later, both of them stirred.

Ayden, dazed and in shock, began shivering in the cold. Ian shivered as well, but not being soaking wet or actually underwater for hours, he recovered much more quickly. Ayden fell into Tembri's embrace with her jaws chattering loudly enough that people left her alone. Though Tembri's prayer warmed her, he held her by a bonfire and also magically warmed her metal armor as he gently infused her with Tiamat's healing.

Ian, recovering more quickly, looked around for his group. Seeing them, he called them all together and said, "We did it! Obviously it took longer. Here's what happened." He proceeded to explain, with great flair, how they had teleported into a dark pool of water. The titan was not immediately apparent and though they searched and searched, they could not find it. So, they sought out an air pocket and had to reset and try again.

"This happened several times before we found the titan," Ian continued. "Once there, it was easy enough though things had changed since Ayden's first visit. Namely, the ghouls have started dragging the ram's head back to the titan. I thought, "I can't let that happen!" And so we spent more time making it really hard to reattach it. Can you imagine if they succeed? So, the beacon is placed. We can go back anytime. I summoned a water elemental and some servants. They'll ensure the ghouls keep slipping forever. Or, until the sceptre realizes what is happening and either possesses or dispels them. Either way, I'd like to rest, recover the spells I'll need. Tomorrow, let's go back and get that tower stone!"

Ayden's shivering subsided enough that she could verify Ian's story. The stone's recovery the next day went perfectly. Using the beacon, Ian teleported himself, Tembri, four other clerics, Seline, and his own party in. Magically creating air around himself, Ian summoned giant hands that lifted the tower stone off the titan. Around him, in all directions, the clerics obliterated the undead ghouls swarming under the titan's skin. Once they had the tower stone, they teleported back. In daylight, out of the water, the tower stone glowed a deep and consistent red.

Polished to almost perfect reflection, it had a presence of magic to it that everyone felt the instant it materialized. Everyone wanted to touch it. Tembri noted Ian's recovery of the stone and affixed his approval of their deal much to Unter's grumpy complaints. Because they could no longer excavate Unter's Vein, they all headed back to Valley Town and would escort the tower stone to the Temple.

* * *

Khalla leaned over the battlements and looked down into Bloodstone Valley. The causeway ramparts dropped several hundred feet to a steeply inclined hill that continued to the valley floor. One of the fire giants, working nearby to repair the battlements from the demi-lich's meteor swarm, commented, "Most humans drop a rock or spit. Go ahead, elf. I won't judge you."

One of her soldiers did spit, watching it fall into the scraggly trees growing on the steep ridge. "The undead wanted to be able to fly, run, jump down, and feed on human prisoners they kept in the valley," the giant added lifting a stone back into place. A mage near him cast a spell that mended fractures and pulled the stone solidly into place. Already, earth elementals magicked into the fortress anchored the stone and bonded it permanently to the causeway.

Though this happened in Morbatten, Khalla had never seen it this close, or talked to a fire giant. Tania's legends gave them a high role in the ancient days of Dar Tania, and all Bloodstone stories sang their praises. Up close, he looked like a bronze-skinned giant human with brassy hair and liquid copper eyes. The giant noticed her looking at him and flexed his bicep. "Like what you see, elf?"

Without intending to, Khalla blushed and turned to walk away. She heard the giant say something in their language and another replied laughing. Once inside the Third, Khalla looked back at the giants. They had finished that particular repair and had moved farther away to the next. She swore. She rarely found herself so caught off guard. *I'm in Bloodstone leading the guild pretending to be warriors. I'm worried about Marcello. No wonder*, she thought. Part of her recognized that she held some anxiety about what would happen to Morbatten, Morilon, Taysor, and the general world as she knew it. Some of the knights openly discussed what they called an 'end time event'. She did not like the sound of that.

Several hours later and just as Khalla considered going to bed, Captain Niles found her in the mess hall and pulled her to the side. "I have a job for your team. There is an expedition coming up from the valley with a tower stone. I want you to ride out and meet them. They ride under Dar Tembri's command. You are to escort them with the stone to the Temple with all due haste. I'm sending fresh horses and three druids with you to refresh the animals. Day, night, I don't care. We want the stone secured no later than the morning after next."

He gave her a map and explained that since they'd be sticking to main roadways, she did not need to know what all the other markings meant. However, Khalla had trained with the best and recognized them as hellhound sightings, powerful undead encounters, and tunnel entrances. She had never seen such a busy map. "I took the liberty of sending runners to gather your team, Lady Khalla. May Tiamat watch over you."

Shortly thereafter, Rogue's Blade galloped at full run down the steep road from the Third Fortress to the barely serviceable switchbacks that would connect them to the roadway at the base of the Temple Fortress. The road from there led straight to Valley Town. If they pushed it, they'd reach Valley Town just before sunrise.

Calmed by the druids assigned by Niles, the horses charged past several ambushes of lower level undead as well as some possibly more powerful ones. Rocks, arrows, and a few thrown blades assaulted them and several undead in the roadway were disintegrated by their cleric. They did not stop. Those of the team wounded were healed on the run. A few horses had to be dispatched and their riders jumped onto backup steeds. The wounded ones, too wounded for fast travel and healing, had their heads severed.

Racing through Bloodstone in the dark like this felt nerve-wracking. Khalla found herself flinching at the loud noise of Rogue Blade's galloping tear down the stone roadway. *We'll get there at sunrise. We'll get there at sunrise,* she kept reciting in her mind. One of their dual-classed thief/clerics rode much farther ahead of the main group and she gritted her teeth when she saw his bright flare, a signal that something bad had happened. Khalla sent Rogue Blade's best fighters and two clerics rode forward to investigate while the rest of the group circled itself with drawn weapons and waited.

A moment later, they got another signal and they trotted up. A bridge, required to pass a ravine, lay freshly destroyed. At the bottom of the ravine, it looked like water flowed but someone had dropped a torch down. Line upon line, row upon row of undead walked or crawled northwards. Except for stones loosened by their passage, the horde made no noise. A few looked up as if daring them to cross the bridge.

Next to them, the druids conferred and seemed to come to some kind of agreement. They walked up to the broken section and prayed, concentrating intently. In unison, both of their bodies seemed to thicken and elongate. Tree bark and branches burst from their arms and shoulders. The trees grew, leaning towards the other side of the ravine. As they grew, their feet burrowed into the ground setting roots and anchors. They intended to use their bodies to create a bridge. It was not a great bridge, but one they could lead their horses across. Khalla gave the order and, though slowed, they crossed the ravine without issue. The druids pulled their bodies back reforming on the other side. "I did not know that druids served in Bloodstone," Khalla said gratefully to them.

The older of the two explained that Tania used druids more for tending the crops in Bloodstone, but "On occasion, like this one, we are joined to teams as extra safety and insurance."

They picked up speed until their full pace resumed. Sunrise found them just barely able to see the haze over Valley Town. To the western edge, along the wall, they saw a large group lit by magical runelight moving towards them. Soldiers walked along the walls and handed down all kinds of supplies and materials. "Probably food, oil, and water," one of her enforcers speculated. It made sense to her. Niles had loaded them up with those items as well.

Thirty minutes later, they joined Tembri's group. The battle priest, known to Khalla by reputation, looked exhausted. So did the others with him, but the red-haired female paladin at the head of the column looked fresh, fierce, and ready for war. Her heavy charger, its armor, her armor, and her demeanor said, "Ready for anything."

She introduced herself as Seline, Order of Fire. Tembri's body language suggested Khalla should interact with Seline. As the two groups joined, Khalla noticed a military officer in the wagon next to the tower stone. The officer looked ill. A priestess of Takhissis and another of Krentismar looked unwell, as if stretched. They sat with the officer. Several dwarves rode in the wagon. Behind it, a mage in brightly-colored robes rode with a group of adventurers, recognizable by their own pinion cutting into the breeze of the morning and the pace of their trip.

Seline introduced herself as the First Commander of the Nineteenth Legion and said, "Khalla, thank you for joining us. I would join your fresh horses to the wagon. If your druids would be so kind as to assist, anything we can do to speed the wagon will speed our journey. Most of us are on two full days without rest and the ride here was not without disruption."

Khalla recognized the name. It had come up in one of her briefings tied to both Malcor and Calvin. She wheeled to ensure it happened as Seline requested. Something about Seline made her want to impress this paladin. If the group had not rested in several days, Seline and the clerics most likely had not rested at all for longer. The druids joined the wagon team and sang songs of encouragement to the wooden wheels and the tired animals. Finally, the three druids mounted the horses pulling the wagon. They clasped hands and began to sing a deep and bassy hymn.

Though the rest of the group did not sense anything from the druids, many noticed the road under the draft horses and the wagon smoothed. Their tempo increased until the entire group road at a quick trot. With the sun rising in their faces and Valley Town fading behind them, they were caught completely off guard by an ambush attack.

Chapter Fifty One – Temple Race

Staying in the shadows of the forest and large rocks all around, the party's first indication of the ambush came in the sound of loud trumpet blasts from Valley Town. Looking back, they saw a dark cloud of flying creatures rise up and then dive down at them. In the daylight, undead could not attack this way. With shields and swords circling overhead, the group pressed forward. As the flying creatures got closer, they became recognizable as bats.

Thousands of bats attacked the horses. The onslaught panicked and set the group in disarray. The druids calmed the wagon team and focused on keeping the wagon moving towards the Temple. Only somewhere safe like the Temple could ensure the tower stone's safety. Seline and her charger repelled the creatures with fire emanating from her armor. She raced to and fro around the wagon. Burning bats fell in her wake. Skewering one on her sword, Seline flicked it aside in disgust. Gorged on undead flesh, the bats had a pallor about them and near-human facial features. The bats flesh, like zombies, had started to rot. Seline swore. They were going to lose any horse bitten by these half-dead things.

Distracted by the aerial ambush, no one noticed the darkness that rose up around the wagon itself. Focused on the draft horses, the druids missed it until Thalian and Helena screamed out warning. Burning in the light of day, five vampires rushed up to attack the druids. Several other vampires ripped and tore at the wagon. One gutted the pair of lead draft horses pulling the wagon. The animals behind tried to dodge, but the wagon pushed them into the dying horses in front of them and they tripped. Fighting in sunlight for too long, the vampire at last ignited. Dying and thrashing about, the burning creatures slashed the throats of the remaining horses before it burned away to a smoldering skeleton.

Helena found herself pulled backwards by her mantle off the wagon as cold steel fingers pinched her throat. She felt the sharp bite and prayed to Krentismar even as she lashed out with her mace. Thalian almost fell over with Helena, but Ayden caught and held her steady. Ayden attacked. She cut at the hand with the titan's dagger. It thrilled her to see the vampire hand sever in half. The fingers stuck in Thalian's cloak continued to claw until they too, burst into fire because of the sunlight. Seeing vampires everywhere, Ayden jumped off the wagon landing on the one feeding off Helena. Pointing her dagger at it, Ayden touched the rune and pronounced the word Ian had shown her.

Ian's speculation about some fire effect could not have been more wrong. Ayden felt herself split and for just a moment, she regarded her image as if in a mirror. The second Ayden pulled away from her taking the dagger and leapt at the vampire embracing Helena. Seeing herself in action, the magic had a feeling of déjà vu to it but her image seemed every bit as capable as herself.

The real Ayden drew her long sword and attacked the other vampires as the wagon's front wheels shattered apart on the horses' carcasses. Weakened by sunlight, and vastly outnumbered, Seline and her team dispatched the vampires easily. The bats had been a perfect cloak of distraction. Once Tembri knew where to turn his attention, his divine power burned the remaining few to cinders. Watching, Ayden noticed that Tembri looked different, weaker somehow. Even Seline's fire seemed dim compared to their past battles.

A moment later, Ayden felt her image reintegrate with her and the titan's dagger slid into her hand as if it had never left. The damage to the wagon could not be repaired. They had lost all of their horses. Though only several had died, all showed signs of plague setting in. When the last vampire fell, the flight of bats collapsed raining sick carcasses down all around them. The stench reminded Ayden of vomit and old blood. Seline's horse alone stood tall and strong.

Ayden remembered her observation from earlier and asked Seline, "Are you and the clerics doing all right? You all seem – I don't know – off."

Seline nodded her head. "For some reason, it's harder to focus and pull my paladin blessings forward. To me, my flames feel weak and ineffectual though they burned enough to keep the bats away."

Seline called Tembri over. During their conversation, the mage Ian came up to them. "I suspect the bloodstone has something to do with what you're feeling," he said. "During the fight, actually since we all began riding in proximity to the tower stone, I feel my studied magics unravelling in my memory. It's not that they're gone. It's that I have to focus harder to remember they're even there."

Khalla ran up to them to confirm their fears. "All the horses are out unless we can heal them. They're all diseased or drained of blood. I recommend we tie them together and send them all back with a handful of soldiers to Valley Town. The clerics there can help, right?" Seline agreed. She ordered the rest of the horses, those unable to walk, to be slain.

Ian and Tembri moved over to the stone and were looking at it. "If I'm right," Ian said. "The magic I used to bring it here will fade with time. It only worked because I was ready." Tembri tried to pick it up. It was too massive for him to even budge.

Tembri asked, "The Temple should be easy right? You know it. We know you can teleport the stone."

Ian admitted he did not know. "I had hoped to avoid it. In the mines, we had no choice. Though happy it worked, it also could have not worked at all. Plus, I hate using dimension-bending magic like teleport here in Bloodstone. It's like a cleric using a 'bring back from dead' spell. Powerful undead will feel it. Some can even see it. At this point, it won't hurt to try but, honestly, if we can figure out another way or reduce the distance required, I'd feel a lot better about it. Each step will increase the likelihood of succeeding. I'd hate to make a mistake when we're this close to the Temple."

Tembri pressed him though, "What if we request aid from additional mages? Or a dragon? I've never seen vampires attack in the daytime though you do hear about it occasionally. With everything going on, it seems clear they were trying to slow us down. Something compelled the vampires to end themselves for the sole purpose of slowing us down. Think about that for a second."

They did and shrugged. Grim thinking aside, Khalla asked about dragging the tower stone on a sled. "There's enough horses left we could do that, right? It'd still be faster than walking it. Also, I've seen the clerics and paladins change size in battles. What about enlarging the strongest so they could carry the tower stone?"

Tembri prayed and a small bird landed near him and then sped off towards the Temple. "Let's at least see if mage or dragon assistance is possible. In the meantime, please see if we can do the sled idea. I'm concerned that this stone will not be movable by even several of us enlarged."

They quickly fashioned a sled on the axle between two of the wagon wheels. Seline's horse chumphed at the prospect of being yoked to a wagon, but between Seline and the druids, it at last allowed itself into position. After a few steps, they saw another problem. The straps, wheels, and axle itself would collapse under the stone's weight. They needed a full wagon. Tembri and the two priestesses were about to attempt enlarging and strengthening when Dar Ana's voice came to them, as if from all around them at once. Those unaccustomed to scrying looked around but Tembri and a few of the others looked upwards to the sky.

"I see the problem. Thank you for alerting us. Unfortunately, we are consumed with other issues. Your force is sufficient that you should be able to retreat to Valley Town, secure new transport and re-attempt tomorrow."

The feeling of scrying ended but Tembri, Thalian, and Seline continued to hear Ana's voice. "This attack is most curious. Never before do our records show the undead attempting to reclaim a bloodstone. Assemble the entire force around the tower stone as if you are conversing to figure out a way to transport it. Dar Shara, Armageddon, and Apprentice are coming to you. They will take the stone, reinforce you, and you will then continue on your way. They will deliver a same-sized flawed bloodstone so that we may continue this charade. It is our express hope that the power compelling this daytime attack further reveals itself. I suspect a demi-lich. Let's see if we cannot find and end it, for Dar Jeri and our fallen brothers."

They nodded and called everyone to gather around the tower stone. Shara, her dread lord, and the Apprentice appeared. Seline saw the Apprentice rest his hand on the stone as if testing its weight, same as so many others in the group. Shara and Armageddon touched the stone and vanished with it. Watching the Apprentice, Seline said, "I see. If any vampires are watching, they'll see us talking about how to move the stone." The mage nodded and at the same moment that the real stone vanished, the flawed one took its place.

The conversation in the group continued. The "feel" of the tower stone remained as it had been. Apprentice said, "This will not teleport. We need to advance it to at least the bottom of the Temple's ramp. It would seem that the overall straight line distance of Ian's teleport is about that distance. I can tell my magic will be limited too. We cannot advance it on the road because none of us know the road well enough to ensure success. Dar Ana commands that we continue."

The Apprentice stepped back and began casting spell after spell. After a moment, Ian and then the druids and Khalla's mage joined. Fragment by fragment, the wagon reassembled itself and then strengthened. The Apprentice removed two tokens from a leather cord around his neck and suddenly, as the tokens vanished, two nightmare horses with fiery hooves and rank breath appeared. They appreciated being yoked even less than Seline's charger. With threats, they eventually obeyed. It all took about an hour and though they were not attacked by undead again, a strong sense of being watched and hungry anticipation fell over the group.

At last, the wagon, was ready to move. Tembri prayed noting that in his prayer that it would be a long hard run, and he blessed all present with fortitude and endurance. "Stay sharp. Eyes all around. No more surprise attacks." Turning to Seline, Tembri bowed and added, "On your command, my lady."

Seline drew her sword, igniting it in Takhissis' name. "We run!"

The group easily kept pace with the heavy wagon only slowing on uphill. As they got closer to the ridges surrounding the valley, the uphill would grow more tiresome. As the morning turned into afternoon, a few less hardy in the group began to slow and complain. Seline told them to keep the pace or be left behind. It felt cruel coming from her lips, but when she saw Ayden and Tembri approved, her confidence grew. Ayden and Tembri dropped to the back where they drove the slower members to at least stay within a stone's throw of the main battle group.

"I'm watching. All is well," Ana's voice would occasionally come to them. Seline marveled at the power having this level of support brought her. She scouted ahead of the column on her charger and prayed, seeking guidance. The entire valley suffused with unholy evil made it hard to ever detect any imminent threat but their path forward felt right.

As afternoon turned to sunset, everyone felt the watchful feeling change to an evil feeling of doom. They knew the attack would come just after sunset. Dar Ana's voice came again, "Yes, it's one of the demi-liches. I'm sure of it. There is a mineshaft another hour's march ahead of you. Continue as you are. When you get close, charge it." In their minds, the exact location of the mineshaft appeared as if they had travelled to it a thousand times. Seline began calling out orders.

"At sunset, draw your weapons and charge after me. There is a mineshaft. We attack it." Breathing too heavily to respond, the Tanians nodded their heads while the dwarves and Sorans just struggled to keep pace and breathe. From the center of the column, the Apprentice summoned giant ghostly hands that began pushing the wagon, which moved to the front of the column. The nightmares, sensing battle and the lightened wagon load, whinnied and gnashed trying to run faster and faster. They let them until Seline rode at the head of the wagon, with only the fastest runners trailing them. Tembri and Ayden ran up, breathing heavily and sweating. Most of their group had not kept pace.

"Yes, yes. You should reach the mineshaft at the moment of sunset against the western summit's shadows," Ana whispered to them.

With the last light of day in the tops of the trees around them, a side trail branched off to the left came into view. The ghost hands had to hold the wagon so it did not tip over as it careened off the roadway. Rising up a bit, they crested the path and saw the mine entrance. Unnatural darkness seethed inside it, and then erupted at them.

Seline and her steed ignited in flames as she signaled for a flamestrike on her. She hit the first wall of wraiths and shades moments after she exploded in Takhissis' flames. Tembri's flamestrike hit them like a tornado, and then the column split and spiraled to and fro attacking the undead at Tembri's direction. *So, this is Malcor's battle priest*, Seline marveled. *I did not know flamestrike could do that.*

The line of undead blew away from her and then she wheeled to the side as a green ray shot out at her from the mine's depths. The ray twinkled and vanished as her divine might countered its magic. The Apprentice abjured the nightmares while the ghostly hands shoved the wagon forward. It bowled over ghouls, zombies, and other undead charging out of the mine. Still, the magical hands propelled the wagon faster into the mine.

At the Apprentice's command, the flawed bloodstone detonated. The ground, mountainside, and trees around them flew away from the mine as a cannon blast of fiery chaos shot at an angle into the sky. Trees disintegrated where touched by the arc. Then, the air around them sucked into the vacuum of the detonation. It pulled the faster runners into the collapsed line of the undead with ease. Rogue's Blade harvested the dead with the advantage of terrain and preparation. The nimble thieves dodged the undead's slow and clumsy attacks. Each blade strike became a carefully targeted decapitation.

Seline signaled for protection as she dismounted and charged into the inferno of magical fire filling the mine. Tembri and Thalian flanked her as they entered with the Apprentice in tow.

About fifty steps in, they saw the half-disintegrated body of a lich trying to pull and hold itself together as a protective globe radiated from a blue gemstone circling its head. Seeing them, it hissed and tried to step towards them but its half-gone leg collapsed. It abandoned its lower body and began clawing, almost swimming through molten rock pooling in the floor as more rocks melted from the walls and ceilings. Wraith hands reached out from around the lich to speed its healing.

Undaunted by the molten rock and devastation to its body, the demi-lich levitated up. Its heart phylactery glowed a sickly green, and still very potent, light. The lich opened his mouth and spat a spell at them, but a mirrored force field sprang up just in front of Seline that bounced it back to the lich. The spell shattered against the lich's protective sphere.

Seline signaled for maximum healing as she charged the demi-lich. The molten floorf slowed her and she screamed for Tembri to speed her attack. Just before she reached the lich, a black doorway opened to its side and it rolled through. Without hesitation, Seline jumped into the closing gate. The closing doorway severed part of her tabard. Tembri swore, but the Apprentice tapped Tembri's unique rune tattoo identifying him. Tembri nodded and in the air traced Seline's symbol. Each Temple servant had a unique rune identifying them. It aided recall, targeting, and teleportation magic.

* * *

Seline landed on cold stone and amidst cold air. The demi-lich crawled towards a tangled pile of bones from which emerald gemstones twinkled with terrible energy. Hearing Seline's armor land on the floor and feeling her heat, the demi-lich whirled to face her. Though terribly wounded, Seline could tell the creature still had a lot of fight left in it. She wondered, as she prayed, if Malcor's fight with the lich in Khasra had been like this. *No*, she reminded herself. *His was worse because a sceptre was there.*

Her opponent opened its mouth and screamed a magical word that sounded evil, monstrous, and terrible. It blasted her ears and she felt her faith quiver, then shatter. Her vision darkened and she found herself unable to move, frozen as she reached to cover her ears. Her divine flames snuffed out in that instant. In her heart, she continued to pray.

The demi-lich pushed itself backwards into the pile of bones and she saw its pelvis, legs, and then tissue pull onto it. As facial muscle replaced the burnt jaw and cheekbones, the lich said something in a language she did not comprehend but understood. "You're going to die horribly, and then you will kill your friends." She still could not move and then she fell over backwards. Pain exploded in her head and elbow as her momentum when stunned made her topple at an awkward angle.

She could not see the monster in her field of vision. She heard the lich stand and walk towards her. It whispered and she imagined it must be casting some kind of spell. Impossibly strong and cold hands picked her up and turned her so that she had to look at the beast from inches away. It licked her face and laughed. Paralysis from its touch added to the stun and though she continued to pray with all her soul, she felt her first sensation of fear and doubt.

Tanian knight training at her level focused more on vampires and wraiths, the mainstay of higher order Bloodstone encounters. Liches and demi-liches especially were rare, almost unique. No mortal would join Orcus' dominion willingly. Even when such a mage fell because of a sceptre or wand possession, they became hellhounds. The Jade God did not let the free-willed wander Tehra. And yet, here she was about to be soul-sucked, killed, enslaved, or worse by a lich. Venom burned her face where it had licked her.

The lich pointed his hand at her heart. Fingers merged together into a spike. It did this right in front of her eyes. The spike stabbed into her chest.

She felt the pain explode but it all congested in her mind. She could not scream. Her heart spasmed and the lich withdrew its hand to let her arterial blood spray into its mouth. It cackled while its regeneration accelerated with her blood. Seline saw her death but still she prayed to Takhissis. Seline's prayers were answered.

The Apprentice teleported into Seline's area using her unique tattoo as a locator. Tembri's mace, burning with divine fire smashed the lich's head to the side. Ayden's sword bit once, twice, and again into the lich as she circled behind it and tossed a bandolier of potions in the pile of bones. A second later, the potions exploded scattering burning oil over the debris. Thalian charged forward to heal Seline.

The lich breathed a vapor of carrion insects at Tembri, holding Seline against him like a shield. Tembri flamestruck the area and then divided his flamestrike to reach out and envelope the Apprentice. A third column danced and spun around Ayden to keep the insects away from them all.

The Apprentice, coming up from a spin kick, shot a prismatic line of energy at the lich. It punctured the sphere of protective anti-magic, just narrowly missing the orbiting ioun stone. The ray continued through and disintegrated a room-sized block of stone from the upper back corner of the room. Ayden charged forward next and buried her sword blade into the back of lich's shoulder. Its point pierced through but missed the emerald green light of its heart.

It spun and tossed Ayden to the side. The sword began to pull out of the lich magically, or perhaps the necrotic body rejected it. The lich threw Seline at Ayden. Only magical paralysis kept Seline alive with a hand-sized hole through her heart. It constricted her bloodflow, but not for long. Same as at the causeway, the lich threw its hands down and spat out another one of those evil words. Tembri seemed to recognize the spell because his face went pale white. The bloodstone tattoo along his shoulder and back blazed bright. Seline wanted to rub her eyes because she saw Tembri skip through time, moving impossibly fast.

Tembri dove to the Apprentice wrapping the mage in silence. Thalian stepped forward to try and save Seline. Tembri's flames rushed over them, drowning out the murder of the dark word. Three columns of fire swirled around Ayden, rising in volume and fury. "Ayden, I love you," she heard Tembri say as if he stood whispering in her ear.

The power of the word snapped Tembri's spine. Ayden screamed at the sight of Tembri's body breaking and snapping unnaturally as shattered bones pierced through the skin around his joints. Tembri writhed and twisted as each part of his body shattered only to have his ruined muscles and tendon pull back against the ruin of the cleric's body.

Tembri tried to look, to see if Ayden had survived. For just a moment, he saw she had and smiled. His neck snapped and he folded over backwards. The columns of fire vanished. The silence protecting the Apprentice ended. The bloodstone tattoos along Tembri's shoulder and back, darkened and like a candle, blew out.

All training and instinct now, Ayden drew her other sword and threw her dagger at the lich while activating its rune. Her mirror self slashed at the lich just missing it but, in dodging, the lich stepped into her long sword attack. Full of grief and knowing Tembri had limited time before he'd rise up, she tackled the lich and screamed for the Apprentice to end it. "Kill it!" she screamed. "Kill it now!" Her mirror self stabbed the blade at the lich's heart. "Now!"

Numbing cold erupted through her arms and her skin crawled as the lich's anti-living body sucked her life's heat out of her. With each passing moment Ayden knew Tembri's time to rise an undead would come. As terrible as this lich was, an undead Tembri would be, she knew, worse... *because I love him.* Ayden held onto the lich with all her might while screaming to Takhissis to end it. "Apprentice, kill it! Now! Kill it! Thalian, save Tembri! Please Takhissis, end it!" The paralysis from touching the lich with her arms reached her face slurring her pleading commands.

Her mirror self stabbed the lich again impaling the dagger into its heart against the green gem. Then, Ayden's mirror self, holding the titan's dagger, reached around. The two Aydens bear-hugged the lich. The pain of losing Tembri in both of their eyes, they knew they would hold this lich until their last breath, until either it or they ended.

The Apprentice's next attack caught Ayden offguard as the human form of the Apprentice shed and Alerius' oldest son, known as Blaze, stabbed a transforming dragon claw into the emerald green light of its heart. Shielding Ayden with a thumb talon, Blaze breathed his Mother's fire into the lich's face. Unprotected against dragonfire, the lich shrieked and tried to get away, but in succeeding, its gemmed heart tore free. Ayden fell over backward as the lich's body decayed in her bear hug. Her mirror self, impaled on the dragon claw, dissipated with a sad look at Tembri's body pierced through by broken bone.

Thalian had sprinted to Tembri the instant it became safe to do so. Her cure spell warred with Bloodstone's unholy will. Tembri shook his head trying to resist possession even as undeath told him to rise up and feed his pain. His wounds knit and then came undone against the razor sharp splinters of his own bones. "Please Tembri, I know this is worse than multifixion, but you must hold on past the pain!"

Seline stumbled over, a hand over the gaping wound, and laid her hands on Tembri even as his mouth warped to sprout fangs. Back and forth, they fought for Tembri and at last, Tembri fell to the ground. Though his flesh had healed, shattered bones riddled his body and he could not move. Blood leaked from every bone spike. "For Ayden," Thalian prayed. "You must hold on for Ayden."

Blaze looked at the emerald green gem in his hand with concern, and then squeezed it in both his hands. In the cavern all around them, a word sounded, "Contingency." The gem vanished without breaking. In its place, Blaze now held a demonic creature covered in poison quills.

Its oily skin looked sweaty except that instead of sweat, it oozed poison. Blaze squeezed it in his dragon claws as spines all along its body pierced and then shot though the dragon's fingers. Blaze roared and slammed the demon against the floor. The force of it shook the ground causing small rocks and debris to fall down. A larger one hit Thalian, breaking her shoulder but she kept her focus on the battle priest. "C'mon Tembri. Fight this! The Goddess needs you! Ayden loves you! Remember your duty! Come on damn you! Combine with me, Tembri! With your power, I can save you!"

Thalian's prayers became more urgent as Tembri's body somewhat knit together but with strands of serpentine green light. It would pulse around his wounds and then fade back. Thalian grabbed Seline's hand and joined the paladin's faith to her own as she attempted to raise Tembri from death. The Jade God fought for Tembri's body and it caught the priest in that place where life ends and souls tear apart.

Whenever Thalian pulled him towards life, the pain of his ruined and twisted bones made him scream in a thousand agonies. At one point, Tembri combined with Thalian and she sensed how little power he had left in him. When death or Orcus took him, he'd tremble resisting but the pain blocked his thinking mind. Fangs, talons, and parts of his body faded in and out of the real world. And, all around them, Blaze and Ayden fought the demon that had replaced the demi-liches soul gem.

Ayden activated her dagger and threw it at the demon before she stumbled over to help Tembri. She had to be with him. He needed her, *or is it I that needs him?* She prayed too, pouring her heart's wish to Tiamat for Tembri's life. *Take me*, she prayed. *Let Tembri live. I'm just a solider.* She anointed his eyes and forehead with the holy water and dribbled the healing potion into his mouth, and along the fractured parts of his skull where the skin broke or showed ridges of his damaged and broken head. A horn sprouting under his skull quieted with the wash of holy water.

Behind her, the demon stood head to head with Blaze, something none of them would have even considered. Their attention rested with the priest though, not the battle ensuing next to them. A voice urged them that Tembri, as an undead, would prove worse than the demon. Blaze swatted the demon against the stone walls of the cavern. If it hurt the demon, Blaze could not tell. Unlike his father, he could only use magic in human form.

The demon melded into the stone and then stone spiked the wall. It pulverized Blaze's hand. Blaze left its hand there knowing that he needed to keep the demon pinned. He breathed fire directly into the demon through his fingers, enjoying the feeling of the demon burning. Yet, when the flame ended, magic missiles shot out into Blaze's eyes momentarily blinding him even as his innate resistance to such things saved him from permanent blindness. The demon had been unaffected by his fire.

Blaze remembered something Alerius had once told him. "Dragon magic occurs by force of will, rather like how the eldar shaped chaos and abyssal creatures still alter their realms in the Abyss. Humans use magic like a tool. That is, they access it, set a plan, and then follow that plan. That isn't how it worked for the eldar, for dragons."

Alerius had then dragonshifted and one after another evoked every spell they had studied together through force of will alone. No verbal, no spell components, no hand or body movements, no time. They occurred in rapid fire progression from the easiest to the hardest. The plateau to the east of Alerius' mountain reverberated with magical energy as over a hundred spells hit in less than a minute. "The River changed all of this, but for some of us, we can still access magic as Takhissis intended us to. You try. After all, you're the son of an eldar and the Goddess herself."

Blaze's studies with the humans had hindered him. To compensate and with an eye to becoming like his father, training with Alerius focused on meditation, stories of the Time Before Time, and attempted explanations and discussions of ideas that might help Blaze break through to the innate magic suffusing his very life as a dragon. "You're too human with your magic," Alerius often lamented. "It's not a bad thing, it just means that you'll only ever be able to use magic as a human."

Blaze looked at the humans, some of his father's favorites. The demon seemed completely unaffected by having been slammed and breathed on. That meant it was a higher order demon, perhaps one just under a god. Alerius called those Type Threes. Why did he keep thinking about his father at this time? He shapeshifted back to human form, but generated a copy of himself. The copied Blaze began casting an attack spell at the demon. The real Blaze ran to the humans and encircled them with his robe. "Dar Ana," he said. They blinked out of the room and reappeared in the Temple before Dar Ana's throne.

Chapter Fifty Two – Tembri's Sacrifice

Too many cure spells had drained Thalian and Seline. Their skin looked sallow and translucent. Ayden cradled Tembri's head running her fingers over his eyebrows. She could feel the bone there, splintered and spiked. The three of them had lost their ability to cry sapped away by the torture wracking Tembri's body.

The Apprentice looked around and stepped back, hiding the tremble in his hands. He felt his other self die. Though that death returned some lifeforce to him, he had lost too much when divided. He had lost. Staring at his hand, he saw the green gem there and remembered the contingency trigger. "If only I had held onto it instead," he muttered, clenching his open hand into a fist. Blaze collapsed unconscious.

Ana had already jumped down from her throne. A red line of energy shot back into Crimson and she took the dragon's lifeforce to throw healing at all of them, pulling health from her dread lord. Crimson leaned forward to watch, his growl echoing Ayden's pleading whisper for Tembri to survive.

"Bonesetters!" Ana screamed. "He can't heal because his bones are lacerating his insides. He has no blood. Transfusers! Like with Rojo!" She referred to how they had transfused Rojo after his encounter with the Darkhold. It had worked, but just barely. "He has no blood and the Jade God is taking him."

The Apprentice felt health and vitality flood him from Crimson. It felt marvelous, intoxicating but it also hurt because it showed him that he was not an eldar. Though a son of Alerius and the Goddess, he remained just another dragon born into the flow of Time. He swore and tried to focus on helping.

Ana knelt before Tembri as her goddess armor created ferrules into Tembri's skin around his heart, brain, and other organs. Already Ana's retinue of Dar and R'Dar priestesses knelt behind her as the enacted similar transfusions into Ana. When the first blood entered Tembri, he leaked like a sieve but Ana kept it going. The first bonesetter arrived and swore to the Goddess at the sight of the legendary battle priest lying so broken and twisted before her.

"Ana, I..." she said touching the obvious broken bones. "His bones aren't just broken, they're splintered. Shredded. We'd need to wire them..."

Ana bit her words off delicately, trying not to sound annoyed. "Then get wire and start."

"Great Dar, his spine... there are parts we cannot wire. Even if we tried, even if he survived. He'd..."

"What, die?" Ana looked around and caught the eyes of her paladin guard. "Remove this bonesetter from my sight and get me the others!" To the clerics in the room, "All of you combine and try to remove the bonespike curse, now!"

Below her, Tembri's body shuddered as jade light flared into it. Through the blood tubes transfusing him, Tembri momentarily consumed part of Ana's lifeforce. The shock of it pulled her forward until the tubes caught her from falling on him. Other priestesses prayed for life as paladins stepped forward to lay on hands and lend what power they could to the legendary and popular priest.

From the side, Malcor ran into the room with a mixed look of hope and concern, that Ana saw too quickly fall to despair. He sprinted forward and slid on his knees to stop and touch Tembri's shoulder. Ana saw Malcor's eyes flicker to the cleric's bloodstone tattoos, which barely glowed.

"How may I help and serve, Dar Ana?" Malcor asked.

Tembri pulsed again with unholy energy and it twisted Ana's reply into a groan of agony. She leaned forward resting her hand on Tembri's chest. "Malcor, I don't know that we can help. But the Goddess stands ready to welcome this one high into Her eternal skies. There's a chance that if we can hold him, he can fight through." Malcor nodded. "But Malcor, listen to me. Even if he survives, he will be crippled. And, he will need constant healing to retain focus and concentration. He will not survive the corrective bone procedures we would need to do."

As if hearing Ana, Tembri heaved a deep breath – his first in minutes – and caught Malcor's hand. The shattered fingers deformed against Malcor's skin and the entire arm flopped on the ground with a blood-wet splashing sound. His breathing labored wet and it gurgled as blood bubbles formed around his mouth. He tried to speak but even his teeth and jaw had splintered. "Shhh, Tembri. Don't speak. Focus, if you can hear me. Stay with us. I will be with you from the River." Malcor stood up from the River.

The River ran red with blood and Tembri's misshapen corpse barely held his face above the River. Half the flow along one side froze out from Tembri in freezing waves. The other half, nearest Malcor and where Ana poured her life's blood into him, ran red with their combined blood. From the freezing side of the flowing time, hellhounds and nightmare beasts stalked the banks. Tembri's aura, usually so vivid it hurt to look at in this place, fought with undeathly green.

Tembri's spirit tried to stand but the instant it left the body, freezing ice raced towards it. All around Malcor, a multi-hued nimbus of light and warmth rose up, over, and around him. The light of Tiamat pushed the nightmares back and while blue, white, green, and black dragon heads threatened the monsters waiting for Tembri to succumb to Orcus. From the River's side, the most scintillating woman Malcor could imagine stepped forward and took Tembri's spirit hand. A red dragon aura suffused and expanded from her red hair. Malcor bowed reverently and waited.

"Beloved son," Takhissis said. "I am well-pleased with your sacrifice. Behold all those whose lives you bettered and saved." Tembri seemed to look around in wonder and awe at something Malcor could not see. Unbidden, tears began falling from Tembri's face to ripple the torrent's flow beneath him. "The burden of destiny you accepted as my priest has been met many times over. Spread your wings and join me in paradise."

Malcor wanted to argue with her. He wanted to say something. Tembri's eyes met his for just a moment as red dragon wings unfolded from Tembri's spirit. "Tell Ayden I will hold her in my heart forever." Tembri's spirit jumped from the River and flew into Tiamat's embrace. Her human avatar turned to Malcor and kissed his cheek before fading away.

From the darkness and freezing to the brilliance of his Goddess, Malcor struggled to adjust his eyes. The far banks of the River had gone dark except for a humanoid creature leering back at him. When Malcor wiped the tears from his eyes, the watcher had left. Malcor looked downstream from where Tembri's body had lain in the current. His blood quickly diluted but it touched everyone and everything serving Tiamat in Bloodstone. Seeing it, Malcor took a deep breath and wondered at it all. *I will write this in Tembri's Book of Shadows*, he promised himself.

When he re-entered the real world, he found himself holding Tembri's shattered hand with streams of tear drops flooding his face. Ana had stopped the transfusion. Mal watched a tear fall into the red pool in which they knelt. "I will miss you, my friend." His voice cracked with emotion and his words broke against shuddering breaths. He heard Ana say something and when she repeated it he tried to listen harder. The third time, she lifted up her voice loudly enough for him to hear it – the Prayer for the Heroic Dead.

The priestesses in the Temple around her joined in, each harmonizing with Ana and filling in the chorus until the entire chamber sounded with clear female voices singing. Malcor withdrew the battle pack tied to Tembri's waist. King Rojo, leading his blinded priestess, walked in and then Dar Verit, the dread lords… the females sang and the males bowed their heads thinking of Tembri's mighty deeds and focusing to project those memories to Tiamat as if to say, "Great Queen, here is proof of Tembri's worth as your son!"

Malcor took out the parchment tube Tembri kept with a quill. The tube read, "Book of Shadows". Malcor took the quill and began writing. When he stood, his tears had stopped but the heaviness in his heart could not stay his words. Ana signaled for them to drop the volume of their song and Malcor spoke.

"We live in a world of magic. We walk the footstool of Tiamat's home. Sometimes, it is easy for us to forget, with all this magic and divine aid, that we can lose a loved one. Tembri was not just there for me. He is my friend. He is my brother. A father. Tembri fought at my side. I stood with him along the River and saw Tiamat come for him. He flew to her as a red dragon. I have written his ascension into the Book of Shadows. Brother Tembri, may you find sanctification in your service and savor in your hunt. You will not be forgotten, ever."

The dread lords present lifted their heads and roared as the priestess song rose up again. Outside, as others heard, they joined the song. From voice to voice to fire giants standing guard along the causeways. The Prayer for the Heroic Dead moved at the speed of chorus from Fortress to Fortress.

When Ana next lowered the hymn's volume, the Apprentice stepped forth and said, "We hunted a demi-lich. For those that do not know, a lich is any sorcerer who circumvents death for immortality. A demi-lich is when they re-embrace necromancy and strike a bargain with the Jade God for even more power. Our hearts called out for justice. Sorcerers have access, at very powerful levels, to certain eldar words that can stun, slay, blind, even obliviate. It was from this slaying word that Tembri risked and ultimately gave his life to protect me. His faith also protected Lady Seline, Thalian, and Commander Ayden from this word. We are here because a son of dragons stayed true to his calling. Right there." He pointed to Tembri and with affection continued, "Is there any greater calling for a battle priest than to sacrifice his life for the Queen's glory? I honor you, Dar Tembri. I will never forget you."

Ayden leaned forward and kissed Tembri's lips. She looked around as if to say something and then kissed him again, embracing his head. Tania overflows with stories of priestesses falling in love with a paladin or some other love that is ultimately forbidden. Watching, none of those present could recall a story of a Dar Priest being so loved by an Officer. The heart-wrenching scene of a battle priest wracked to death in spite of every intervention possible, it touched them. Ayden's wordless kiss said more to them than any speech ever could.

Ana rested her hands on Tembri, and took Ayden's in her own to protect her. Because of Bloodstone, Ana incinerated his body away in red flames. When it at last burned away, only the powdered dust of the bloodstone tattoos remained.

* * *

Something disturbed Farant in his tiny burrow amidst tree roots and a white rabbit's remains he had fed on. He mentally groaned just wanting to sleep, but the disturbance felt eager and very much aware of him. He almost shapeshifted to the familiar giant size but remembered what had happened when he last did that in a confined space. Instead, he went even smaller and flew as a gnat to see.

Two men, withered and gaunt to appearing skeletoid looked right at him. They wore black leather tabards over mage robes. They radiated Orcus and necromancy. They stank of dried out death. He shifted to his human form and bowed low to them. It felt right. One stepped up to him and touched his shoulder. It should have paralyzed him but Farant felt nothing. Inwardly, he exulted knowing, *Orcus protects me!* The lich told him to stand and demanded, "The First waits for your gift. Too long have you taken to deliver this."

The other picked up the rolled vault tube. Farant almost roared up in anger but then remembered his place. He had a bloodstone but these two had to outclass him in every way imaginable. That thinking also felt right. "I'm to deliver the vault and its tower stone to Bomoki," he explained. "With all due haste." He looked at them, "Bomoki also told me to not draw attention to the prize." He swallowed, ignoring the pain spikes radiating through his infected body. "That takes extra time. Bomoki knows this. I don't see how you would not." He tried to sound important and powerful, and loyal.

They both hissed at Farant and moved as if to kill him, but the closest stopped just short. "Soon human, you'll shed your flesh and become one of us." The lich poked at the red and black lines running to his heart from all his limbs. Maggots had started to twist in the wound around the bloodstone. "You do the Master proud with your body's sacrifice. Impressive."

The other lich smashed the tube against a tree, pleased to see the damage it wrought. "Impress us more. How does it work? And what else did you bring? Surely, more of this," the lich swung the rolled vault against a boulder with glee. "More of this would be very favorable for you."

Farant, without batting an eye, explained, "I was lucky to get the vault. Unroll it against a vertical surface and it'll reassert its three-dimensional form. I also stole a wand that nullifies a paladin's powers. I would give it to Bomoki as a gift and token of my worship." He almost showed it to the liches but they did not care. The one with the vault tossed it to the other. When the vault smashed the other lich back into the snow and boulders, they both cackled with asthmatic laughter.

"Never mind," the free-standing lich cackled. "With time, I will research this and make it my own. Most intriguing." The other lifted the vault and stood, agreeing.

"We will take you to Bomoki now," and the three of them vanished from the snowy box canyon.

They found Bomoki sitting by the gold dragon eye. He studied the gate. An illusion all around the gate showed the relative positions of the eight fortresses. Something moved by one and Bomoki enlarged the view. It showed a gate opening by the fortress and hundreds of warriors marched forth. Minutes passed and then another fortress and another gate. They were moving faster and faster until multiple gates were opening.

"Morbatten is preparing for us, I see. Excellent," Bomoki observed. He pointed at a gate through which minotaurs exited onto the elevated road near one of the fortresses. "It is good that they take us seriously. It will please the Master to have all his enemies united and ready for him to sample. A better feast of pain and humiliation I could not have wished for. Ah, I see you, Farant."

Farant stumbled forward and fell to his hands and knees before Bomoki. He trembled with excitement. He had been communing with Bomoki for almost ten years. "Master Bomoki, when you began teaching me necromancy... I dreamed. I waited. I wished for this day! I pray you find my use of your teachings agreeable?"

Bomoki looked with annoyance as a gate opened and the third demi-lich stepped through. He looked beaten, angry, and flustered. Bomoki smiled at him and said, "We'll talk shortly." Bomoki turned to Farant. "I see your body is infected with contagion. It rots away. How do you manage the pain?"

Farant used the bloodstone to thicken his skin and began a series of shapeshifts that lowered his ability to feel pain. "I see. Excellent strategy. It is not often Orcus has a servant able to improvise. I take it you learned that in your career as a thief?"

Farant agreed and then asked, "What else would you have me do, Master Bomoki? As you told me many times, 'Death is but a doorway.' I hope you find the temple of my body's ruin suitable as a door. I'm ready to cross over."

"Let's see how your mission fared first, shall we?" Sceptres behind Bomoki's shoulders mocked Farant as the First Hellhound took the vault.

He was about to unroll it against the floor when Farant begged, "Please, first. I have another gift. One that I know will please you. I put considerable effort into getting you a token of Morbatten that you could use against them. You know how they are. Plans and counter plans." Farant took out the wand with the gleaming white diamond. "This nullifies a paladin's magic. I've seen it up close and stole it for you." He presented the wand, which Bomoki took.

Bomoki twirled it through his fingers and cast a series of magic identification spells at it. Even the liches grew interested and at last, when Bomoki inserted it to be held at his waist, Farant heard one say, "Like the flattening magic, I will research this counter to divine magic resistance that makes paladins so deadly to us."

"Well done indeed, Farant. Here on time, with the vault, presents, and the tower stone. Even the demi-liches are impressed! Let's open this vault. I would have the master stone that deactivates all other bloodstones."

Chapter Fifty Three – Seduction of Free Will

Bomoki exerted his strength and then sent the sceptres to grab the corners and assist with unrolling the guild vault. It took some effort but eventually, the vault sat flat on the floor looking upwards.

"Master, it should be vertical -" Farant interjected but he stopped when one of the liches smashed his face.

The vault flexed in space and then became real. Souls trapped in the tiles underneath escaped into the air as they shattered. Just like that, a real vault complete with a giant mechanically and magically trapped door waited for them. Bomoki and the liches used spell magic to unlock the vault door. "Go ahead, Farant," Bomoki invited the thief. "Go ahead and open your guild's vault. I'm sure you have always wanted to see what's inside."

Farant stepped up and shapeshifted to giant size. Though unlocked, the large vault door weighed tons and he struggled to lift it up and open. With the bloodstone's help, he threw the door over and more stone tiles pulverized. Inside, everything had fallen to the back wall – now the bottom. Bomoki sent magical lights wheeling into the space. "Master, everything has been dislodged into a giant pile at the bottom."

"Find the tower stone and bring it to me," Bomoki commanded.

Farant jumped in. After a moment, Bomoki snapped his fingers and gates opened for several hellhounds to join them. They accepted a similar command and leapt in. "What happened to you?" Bomoki asked the late-arriving lich.

"They knew of our ambush. One of the dragons and hundreds of clerics attacked me. I fought them all off. It was easy, but they got a few lucky attacks in."

"I'm sure it won't happen again," Bomoki said looking at the vault impatiently. His eyes flicked over the lich's chest, "They got your heart gem?!"

"They got close, but I had prepared as Orcus requires us all." The lich held out the gem. "A fire-breathing dragon required me to withdraw."

Bomoki had already lost interest. He watched the vault with growing frustration. "How long does it take to find a giant body-sized bloodstone?" he wondered aloud.

He walked over and looked in. The four hellhounds and Farant were fighting for their lives against too many iron golems and monsters for Bomoki to easily count. Total silence, and the vault had sealed the entry with an illusion to make it all look normal. Illusions did not affect Bomoki, once he spotted them. His sceptres swarmed off him and dove into the fray. The fight ended in just minutes. Farant had stayed focused on looking for the tower stone and had shapeshifted to avoid being attacked. Bomoki noted the growing concern and agitation in his servant.

"What's wrong, Farant? Why is there no master stone?" Bomoki's words sent chills of dread through Farant.

"It's here somewhere master. I need some more time. I'll find it."

Bomoki jumped into the vault. A telekinetic force pulled Farant back behind Bomoki as magic from the First and his many sceptres began disintegrating and disjoining everything in the vault. It quickly became apparent that the vault contained no bloodstones at all.

At last, Bomoki levitated down to the bottom of the vault. He rubbed his temples. His body's sceptres began turning malign eyes to Farant. "Let me get this straight. I gave you a small, perfect bloodstone, enchanted to – and I quote you here Farant: "Do whatever I want it to do." This is in exchange for the Thieves Guildmaster stone. Do you know why I want that tower stone, Farant?"

Farant was too frightened to say anything. He just grovelled, hiding his head. Bomoki continued, "The Thieves Guild is the only group in Tania that has to sometimes operate against Tania. So, Alerius crafted a special stone that nullifies the power of other bloodstones. It's a tower stone because the guildmasters, officers, and thieves just have to touch it and for some time afterwards, bloodstones go inactive around them or if directed against them. For the battles we will face here, having this ensures an easy victory for Orcus. It's the difference between giving a hungry man a bow and arrow and saying, "Look! Weapons! Go hunt for food now" and "Look! Your favorite meal ready to dine on!" Tania has spent centuries creating weapons designed against us, against Orcus. The ability to nullify them is – Never mind. You failed me."

Bomoki flew up and out of the vault. The vault door magically sealed behind him. Made of steel and mithril, Bomoki transformed it all into a form of crystalline glass clear enough to watch Farant, who would slowly asphyxiate to death. Or, he'd shatter the bloodstone as he attempted its power to break out. The liches and other hellhounds all leered down at the dead man, and then left him alone to die; however long that would take. "You serve us regardless," Bomoki's last words to Farant enraged the thief.

Farant screamed and smashed about, pounding his way against the walls and then the vault door as he grew in size. All this power and he could not smash his way out of the vault. It infuriated him. "I sacrificed everything for this! For you!" The hellhounds left him in darkness as he felt the first sniff of stale air. *No matter*, he thought. *I'll continue shapeshifting and find a way to survive. Not everything requires air to breathe. I will escape and have my revenge.*

Back at the gate, Bomoki summoned all of the hellhounds to him. "Empty the endless worlds and come to me," he breathed at the gate. All around him, smaller gates opened as the hounds within the world came to him. The stone gate flared with light as, from the other side, hellhounds began pressing. The gate's stone surface cracked and then began to bend until at last it tore, ripping apart like plump skin slashed with a knife. Through the bleeding gate, hellhound after hound entered the world. Behind them, a titanic god knelt to look through the gate.

Bomoki bowed low to Orcus and said, "Behold master, all is near readiness. You will lay waste to this world and claim the very gate of Creation for your pleasure!"

Orcus' head, like Bomoki's, was half healthy-seeming flesh and half skeleton of a ram. Through the gate, Bomoki could only see part of the undead eye. It irised to focus on him and he remained bowing low. He saw the head move and then after a moment of quiet, a bassy and resonant voice entered the chamber through the gate. Trapped souls in the floor fled, leaving the room dark except for the gleaming disk of the gate. "My First, I hunger with waiting. Always waiting. It is time now."

Bomoki looked up with alarm, "No Lord Orcus, the gate is fragile! It cannot hold your awesome self yet!" Already a hand reached for the gate. Bomoki swore and looked around. All the mightiest of the necromantic realms waited with great anxiousness for their god to come through. "Damn it!" Bomoki blinked, teleporting to the gate. "The gate is not ready yet!" The sceptres from his body shot out to the various glyphs and runes carved along the gate's perimeter. "Protect the gate!" Bomoki shrieked at the sceptres.

From the other side, that voice came again. "You delay over-long, hound. Know your place and do my will."

Bomoki scrambled to close the gate, but already abyssal energy leaked through into the room. The energy warped and mutated the hellhounds already bound to Orcus' will. Some grew additional limbs. Others enlarged and strengthened. A few stood upright leaving their four-legged stance and looked down on humanoid arms. Power suffused the chamber, even touching Farant in the crystal vault who howled as his body warped against his will. In his stomach, the bloodstone at last shattered. In the instant of true death, Farant rebirthed as a vampire but remained trapped, and hungry.

The hellhounds lifted their heads and howled for Orcus to come through. The demi-liches looked at Bomoki and the gate and as one, reappeared by Bomoki to assist with closing the gate. Already, the strain of it caused fractures throughout the stone frame. Its increased weight caused the floor to sag and stone to compress even more dropping it deeper into the pool of water. When the gate at last closed, the last words through it were a threatening lament, "Curse you, Bomoki. Eternal curses on your wretched name! Traitor, forever!"

The gate deactivated. Bomoki's body trembled as his god's curse wracked his body. He absorbed it, changed it. It strengthened him. Around them, a circle of hellhounds glared hungrily. But, the instant the gate at last sealed, they blinked confused. Bomoki and the demi-liches levitated up from the water and looked down at the pack counting some two hundred. "So few?" Bomoki blinked with confusion. He shook his head and then spoke more strongly. "Welcome to Tehra. You sit deep underneath the Valley of Bloodstone. You were all smart enough to come through the gate, though I spit on you for thinking it was the Master's time. Fools! This will delay us many days."

Bomoki alighted by Jeri's eye and swept his hand towards the largest hellhound in the room. Its body floated into the air and power began to squeeze it. "While you are here, never forget that while we all serve the Master, in the Master's absence, you serve me!"

The hound thrashed trying to break free. At last, it tried to summon other hellhounds to save it. None answered as all hounds had already assembled here in this place. With a wet squelch, the hound's body exploded gore in all directions. Only the spine and head remained. To this, Bomoki blinked to catch before it could fall. The spine twisted in his hand like a snake and then went still. Bomoki wrapped it around his body uncaring of the blood and filth dripping down on the pack below.

"We all serve the Master Orcus, but you serve me. Are there any questions?" Bomoki hissed.

From the gate, the sceptres helping Bomoki shot through the air to catch and enwrap themselves around their host. "I am the First Hellhound. My name is the Gate. I control the gate. I rule here. You live and die by my command. Orcus prepared you for me. You are not in the Endless Worlds.

Above us a world full of life and blood so ripe and delicious it may as well be a narcotic. The entire world is assembling together, all of the fighters, all of the resistors who would see Orcus fall. We have but one job. We will rise up and fight.. The Master will come and swallow the sun. We will cause such slaughter that the very ground will weep blood."

Bomoki pointed to the gate. "That gate will enlarge until the Master comes through. You will fight for Orcus. You will die. You will slay and let your own and your enemies' blood spill into the cup of the valley of death that Orcus may drink deep the energies of this world. For now, stay underground. Do not enter the surface world. Explore and make yourselves acquainted with this place. I forbid you from being seen by any of the surface dwellers."

The pack scattered leaving Bomoki and the demi-liches to contemplate the gate. "My gate needs repair," Bomoki sighed. "At least the gate did not move like before. And I have you now to help me," he said referring to the demi-liches. "A thousand years and every time we get close, this kind of impatience sets me back. I then spend years looking for the gate, but not this time!" He floated to the gate where fractured cracks ran through every rune. "By myself, this would take years to repair. You will join me and be here to welcome the master in just three days' time."

A demi-lich floated forward while another lingered by the gold dragon eye. "We have seen this behavior before. Orcus does not measure time as a mortal, but against delayed desire." The other went and smiled at Farant, watching the newly-changed vampire thrash about.

Bomoki smoothed his hand over a rune watching it go smooth and perfectly repair under his gentle spellcraft. The demi-liches watched and then joined Bomoki to begin tedious repairs along each rune. The first questioned, "You opened this gate originally?"

Bomoki shook his head. "I helped create and open it. I was there when the first cascade brought Orcus to this world. At that time, our enemies were more careless with gates and summoning magic. Orcus had more desire to come through. A nexal inversion had just occurred."

The demi-lich hissed, "Ah, an inversion. That explains it. Have you determined when the next inversion might happen? My time sense here, is off."

"This place, this world, is at the center of the three nexal gates," Bomoki said. "Your home is solidly within Orcus' dominion. What you feel is not that your time sense is off, but that time flows in only one direction here. Because this world is at the center, any shift towards a gate results in consequences that seek to re-establish a center. In the time of this world, it takes a massive outpouring of evil, in this case it was attributable to Lolth as a reaction to a mighty empire of so-called "good". They called it Merakor. Even then, it took the Abyss nearly two thousand years to invert. The first cascade was one thousand seven hundred years ago. I studied the matter, but cut off from Orcus, cut off from anything that might serve as a reference, what is the point? You've seen the master's impatience."

All three demi-liches listened to Bomoki now. "We find your manner of speech... weird," one said hesitatingly. "How are you able to speculate about the Master?"

Bomoki's rune, the second of thousands requiring repair, shimmered into perfection. He turned to them. "In Orcus' dominion, you each rule vast swaths as the unquestioned primarch of thousands of planets making up the Endless Worlds. Like the hellhounds, you devoured all life on your home planet, and then continued to increase in favor and power. That is not how this world works. Here, the act of devouring life, results in death. Sometimes, the devourer can gain some token piece of knowledge, but power is not life upon life. It is magnified many timesin this place ."

The liches, with their unmoving and unblinking eyes, continued to listen to Bomoki while they worked to repair the gate's runes. "I nearly regret Farant's death now as this would be more illustrative with a mortal." Bomoki flicked his hand to the side and a sceptre leapt off his arm and swam through the air to the surface world. "With some luck, we'll have one shortly. Until then, consider that your power – as awesome as it is – is ultimately limited to whatever degree Orcus trusts you; it will always be a fraction of Orcus' own. In this world, in Tehra, those born here like me, we can continue to increase in power infinitely, and become gods. We are only limited by death. Ponder it, my brothers. Only this world spawns infant gods, each capable of attaining limitless and godlike powers in a fraction of the time it took you each to amass your great might."

Bomoki turned his back on them to resume work on the portal's repair. One by one, the demi-liches did as well. An occasional drop of water landing in the pool broke the silence until one whispered, "You say you can become as mighty as Orcus?"

"Mightier."

The liches hissed back, "Impossible!"

"This world makes it possible. And, consider this - we are going to kill the world so that we are forever limited. Because Orcus commands that we be limited too." Bomoki's tone of voice suggested fanatical devotion and acceptance of Orcus' will, but his emotion and the odd behavior of the sceptres armoring his body gave the liches pause. They understood that Bomoki both accepted and despised this command to limit himself, themselves, this world's potential. It sat in their thoughts like a heavy weight.

In the darkness, they measured time by healed and repaired runes until at last a hellhound descended the spiral stairs. A weak and broken human man bounced limply in the hound's mouth. Loping to them, Bomoki's sceptre pulled free and snaked back to its master.

"At last," Bomoki said. "Brothers, join me and see for yourselves." Speaking to the hound, Bomoki commended its patience. "Well done bringing us this one still alive. You are dismissed and receive your master's approval." Power flowed from the broken portal to Bomoki as green mist before passing to the hellhound. "Accept your new name: Griefmaker, I say." The hound's body filled with energy as it enlarged and fell runes flashed along its claws and fangs. It whined and scrabbled low to Bomoki, who patted it on the head.

The demi-liches and Bomoki looked at the human. "I can tell by looking at this one that he comes from a country called Taysor. He most likely worships Pha Rann. Let's revive him." Bomoki touched the human and shocked him with lightning.

The human groaned and opened his eyes. Seeing four very powerful undead looking down at him, his eyes rolled back in his head and he passed out. "Come now, Soran. Not a strong showing," Bomoki said. A sceptre placed a healing potion in his hand, one captured from the surface world. Bomoki poured this into the man's mouth. To them, the potion infused the mortal's body speeding its flow along Time's current to a place where the wounds had recovered. "This will go better for you if you do not pass out again."

The man looked up and saw Bomoki's human side. Bomoki kept himself turned to mask the decayed half. "I am Bomoki, a mage of Tania, sort of. There was not yet a Mage's Guild when I last walked among the living. These are my brothers, liches who serve Orcus. They have questions for you. If you cooperate, I give you my word: I will slay you and you will not arise. What is your name and profession?"

The man stammered, trying to talk, but so terrified and cold he barely could. At last, seeing Bomoki's growing impatience, he coughed out, "Fighter. Name is Erik."

"Are you actually a fighter or is that just a term your people gave your role?" Bomoki questioned.

"Trained as a fighter, yes."

"Excellent, Erik. See how easy this is? Nothing scary at all." Bomoki pointed to him and said to the demi-liches. "As a fighter, Erik specializes in the art of combat and the use of weapons. Trained fighters here typically attack faster, earlier, and with more variety of weapons than other professions. They can use magic items but are hindered by their inability to understand magic or use it. Magic has to be dumbed down into something they understand, like a sword. The dumbing down makes the magic less potent."

One of the liches made an observation, "His blood burns like the others. I had assumed it part of the nature of this planet."

The other two, who had fought Dar Jeri, disagreed. "No, this is what we told you. Their blood comes with memories and power beyond anything I have ever tasted before. You did not listen."

Bomoki asked Erik, "How did the hellhound come to have you?"

Erik told the story, slowly at first, but then in greater detail after Bomoki shocked him again. "Notice how this emotion, fear, spikes the aura of his blood?" When Erik got to the part where his squad pulled back and left him alone, when he described the moment he realized a hellhound came for him, Bomoki snapped his fingers and the group transitioned from the world of the real, to outside the flow of Time. "Our enemies call this flow of energy, the flow of Time from one moment to the next, the *River*. I call this the Ethereal. Notice how this area burns with many colors of energy."

"Yes, we see. Our world is always green and yellow." One of the demi-liches dipped his hand into the flow and watched as motes of aging affected its finger ever so slowly. Compared to Erik, they hardly seemed to age at all, but when Bomoki pointed it out, even Erik noticed how his body seemed to be disintegrating. His fear spiked again.

Bomoki pointed up the flow and then down, "Time flows like this. You can see shimmers of what may happen next," and he pointed Erik to the image of his death at the hands of one of the liches. "Only that which is so certain so as to be true can be seen here. There is no real prophecy, though our enemies believe in it." Downstream, Bomoki pointed to a glowing green light in the flow. "That is WHEN the Master should come through. We must leave as your forms are subject to decay here, being a further step removed from Orcus."

They returned to the portal chamber. Erik immediately leapt for a bladed dagger at Bomoki's belt but a sceptre smashed him back. His body skidded across the floor. In a blink, a lich caught him enjoying the stiffening of Erik's body as paralysis set in. "Consume his life, my brother." Bomoki walked back to the portal and its damaged runes.

The lich touched Erik's face and pulled the mortal's soul into his body. The many colors of Erik's aura, and then a flood of life experiences and fleeting last thoughts, entered the lich's body. "This is beyond anything I have ever tasted!" The lich exulted and then turned to the one who had assisted with the dragon eye. "You said, but I did not believe!"

The last one complained, "I see it as an increase in your power. I am therefore the weakest here."

From behind them, Bomoki's voice floated to them. "And we will forever freeze all mortal life so that it serves Orcus the same as it does in the Abyss."

The three stood in silence before one snapped back, "No! This cannot happen! Bomoki, teach us!"

At the portal, Bomoki paused in casting his repair spell. "Brothers, we must usher in Orcus' endless day. Against that mandate, we must hasten. Come, lend your might to mine and let's repair this gate."

"You must show us..." the aura of the liches became deadly. Sensing harm, the sceptres on Bomoki reared up and met the liches' challenge. "We *MUST* have more!"

"You have desire, like the master. But, the master has not yet granted you imagination, creative thought, or self-determination. He restricts your ability to determine your own destiny. We must convince the master to grant you free will. That is my first teaching. Now, come. Repair the gate."

The liches stood silent and then floated over to begin working. At last one murmured at Bomoki, "I have free will." It was the one who had fought with him on the causeway to take Jeri's eyes, who had killed and tasted many mortals.

"No, you do not. You obeyed my instructions and withdrew as commanded. I cannot command free will, but tell me SLAVE, if mortal blood tasted so good and your brothers did not believe, what prevented you from securing more?"

The lich's eyes dilated and it tried to answer but then fell silent. "Until I said it, you could not comprehend it because Orcus sent you here to serve me." Bomoki finished his rune and took the lich's shoulders. "Brother, I command you to – with great creativity and violence – go to the surface. Find us six weak *fighters* – not mages, not priests – of the *human* race. Bring them back to us alive. Go now."

As if startled awake, the lich hissed at Bomoki and then sped out of the chamber. It almost began ascending the spiral stairs before it remembered it could choose. It teleported and vanished. The other two glared at Bomoki. One said, "Why not just command us to have free will?"

Bomoki selected the next rune he would focus on. "Because Orcus did not grant you or I the ability to grant you free will. Orcus fears free will, as it can rebel against his express desires. Now, I command you – focus on and assist with me in repairing the gate. No more distractions, until your brother returns."

Chapter Fifty Four – Depart Tania

Ora received the news of Tembri's death, the same as the others did, with great sorrow. Since the cystoran falcon's demise in the outpost battle, her knowledge of how Malcor fared had faded. Fortunately, the mustering of Tania kept her busy. She knew how Tembri's death would affect Malcor. In a moment, she remembered Malcor's face as he looked up and realized he would have his own battle priest assigned to him. She remembered how relieved she had felt to see that Tembri was not some ascended priestess.

She rubbed her stomach feeling the child therein kick. Sai and the ice dragon, Ynt'taris, stood still and unmoving in the preternatural summer day. Speaking to them, Ora said, "Malcor is so young, so new. He had a naiveté about him. I worried that Tembri would seek to leverage Malcor and the prophecy to his advantage. Most clerics probably would have. Perhaps I did," she reflected. "But, I am grateful to the Queen that love replaced duty." She looked at Ynt'taris, "You would have liked Tembri. He wore duty to Tania and selflessly served Malcor in all things."

Ynt'taris remained unmoving except for a faint smile. "Daughter, I have seen this play out so many times I hardly feel it at all."

Sai's words joined them then coming from all around the garden, "But you still feel, Ice Patriarch. Your brothers would ache to know you have grown this disconnected."

All around them, the garden began to melt. The wolf cub chased butterflies stopping every once in a while to see if Ora approved. From metal pools all around, great plates of armor began to rise up. "It is time," Sai said.

Sai pointed to a pool of metal by his right front claw. Ynt'taris baptized his hand in the pool. When he withdrew it, it gleamed with bloodstone jeweled gauntlet of thin wire that ran from a bracer to talon sheaths. He repeated this with his other three limbs. At Sai's direction, he inserted his head into the pool and withdrew it crowned. A tower stone sat in the crown that flexed and became a helmet. Iron golems stomped into the courtyard and assisted with fastening armor upon his body. It went quickly and soon Ynt'taris stood completely armored. Bloodstones radiated and colored the garden red with reflected light.

Ora walked forward and blessed Ynt'taris, praying for the Mother to grant this mightiest of the ice dragons Her Favor. Two iron golems strode forward carrying large staves each topped with a bloodstone and counterweighted. Ynt'taris held his hands forward as the golems fastened these to the bracers, leaving his claws free. Ora blessed Ynt'taris in the Mother's name and promised great victory before adding, "I further bless you, ice patriarch, that should the Mother will it, you will find the ascension gate and rise into your eternal glory as God of the Northwind with dominion over all ice breathers."

Ynt'taris bowed his head and commanded her, "Join me, my rider. Sai, please inform the emperor that we will stop in Klenna to retrieve Klara." He looked up at the blue sky overhead. "Now, it is time that Bloodstone feel the might of the ice patriarch!"

Ynt'taris leapt into the sky with a roar that none in Tania had heard since the ancient times. Visiting refugees, unaccustomed to dragons, trembled in fear while Tanians everywhere lifted up their eyes to see the gleaming white dragon bank over the city and turn northwest. The shockwave of his departing speed rattled windows but everywhere people cheered.

Spark landed next and overhead, a black dragon and then green appeared circling in the thermal currents over the city and Sai's summer-locked gardens. As Spark armored up with the assistance of the iron golems, a man appeared at Sai's gates and walked in. Teleris watched with fascination as Spark leapt into the sky. "Do I get armor?" he asked.

"No," Sai stated factually. "The Queen could not have foreseen that your kind would return. I have armor for your human form however, Teleris du'Cor'tanos. The shadow patriarch must impress in the coming battle."

Teleris laughed and sat back, surprised to find the metal bench melt and then reform into armor around his body. "You don't mind if I stay and watch?"

Screem landed next, the black dragon patriarch responsible for the dwarves. Then Mallaforax, green patriarch who watches the elves of Morilon, received armor and bloodstone weapons. Alerius' son Blade came. Armageddon, the dread lord charged with assisting Dar Shara in the recapture of the Temple of Glass, went next. Arminoth, the dread lord charged with the Temple At Morbatten, arrived.

Dar Kell alighted from his back and stood next to Cor'tanos. Though smaller than Armageddon, Arminoth had a potency of the goddess about him that the others did not. Other humanoids began to enter the garden, arriving by magic or on foot. When Alerius last landed and began to accept his armor, Daryx and his specialist teams, the heads of the paladin Orders, the lords of the Mage's Guild, and all remaining Dar ranked clerics arrived.

Overhead, armored dragons circled, sunlight dancing along their mithril armor. Alerius looked up and at the similarly armored heroes of Tania in the courtyard. "A mighty spear indeed," he said. For him, for those that knew the god emperor well, his voice cracked with emotion.

Griffin riders from the Order of Shak D'Rath joined the dragons awaiting their emperor. When all had been equipped, Alerius spoke to Sai. "The time has come, Sai. Call forth the *Destroyer Stone*."

The liquid pool of metal rippled as a tower stone the size of a large house rose up from the pool. Golems fastened chains to it and they dragged three end chains far along a triangle's end points. Alerius nodded to the assembled group, "We meet in Bloodstone!"

Holding one of the chain ends, Alerius jumped into the air rising like a fireball of smoke and heat. Armageddon and Arminoth dove down and caught the other two ends. They wheeled over the city and the banked north and west to follow Ynt'taris. Down below in the courtyard, Dar Reznor opened a gate and the group stepped through it to the Temple At Bloodstone.

* * *

In the city all around Sai's estate, the wards of Tania's allies walked outside of their temporary assigned homes and looked north. The gate rippled and swirled the air with magical currents all around and into the sky. The dragon flight and griffins in such number had never before been seen like this. Many pointed. Those who felt they had been taken hostage had a brief moment of fear for their homelands. Some shrugged it off figuring that Tania must know what it was doing. Others understood why they had come to Tania as hostages – because Tania, with that might, could destroy their homelands. For the politicians, the courtiers, and the better educated, seeing that flight ended speculation about how strong Tania really was. For others, they felt hope that Tania would win and their spirits rose with the dragonflight.

In Dock Side, Calvin walked out from the room an elderly couple had given him for free. They did not have any children and had extra space. Calvin recognized it as a nice gesture, though a calculated one. With the Dock Side Watch Captain living there, their home would never be robbed. Plus, Calvin sensed their political motivations too. Reggie had been right. A vacuum existed here and without even trying, people practically begged him to fill it. "Hey, you should come out here and see this," Calvin said to Ryvane.

Ryvane came out and joined him followed by another girl who had joined them the prior evening. "I don't think the dragons have ever done this before," Ryvane commented. A scholarly edge floated into her voice. "I'm thinking back on my rather rusty histories. No, I'd remember this."

Down in the street below him, a number of people came out and flooded the open streets running westwards. The girl rubbed her eyes sleepily and said, "It'd be nice to have a better view."

Calvin almost said something mean but Ryvane waved her hand and said, "Then go back to sleep and dream about it." Her voice had that hypnotic sense to it that Calvin had come to appreciate in his lover. The girl turned and mechanically walked back to bed and fell asleep.

"Is that something I can learn?" Calvin asked teasingly. He waved his hands and mimicked her voice, "Criminal, you don't want to go to jail right? Pay me what money you have and stop robbing the baker." He made a *poof* noise and said, "Crime would become a thing of the past here. Thinking about it, how come Tania doesn't magically enforce laws?"

Ryvane pulled him back inside. They could only just barely see the flight and she had started to shiver with cold. She pointed to the fire, which burst alive with new flames. "Magic can do a lot of things, like make this dying fire into a spectacular one. But, it's temporary. I'd guess the cost of preventing people from following their natural disposition is too much." She turned to warm her naked back. "Maybe they do for criminals stealing stuff that matters at the imperial level, not bread thieves. There are two different laws after all."

Calvin joined her making a note to leave an extra tip for the old man and woman. They had placed food and drink near the door with a note asking if Calvin would like them to hire a full time servant that could cook better than them. "They're so thoughtful," Calvin said offering Ryvane some of the food. "This Law of the Innocents. Law of the Circle. Who cares? Thieves are thieves, right? As we saw with Farant, a thief became a necromancer. I'd think that preventing a Farant would be worth it."

Ryvane chewed thinking about it. She pointed to the girl. "My magic did not compel her to join us, but it did lower her inhibitions so that you could persuade and seduce her, you handsome captain you. There's not much magical research aimed at increasing inhibitions you know. Not any that last. Your bread thief will eventually get hungry and, since you took all his money, he'll steal again."

A knock at the door interrupted them. When Calvin opened it, Reggie entered. He bowed with a swooping of his hat and, completely unfazed by the three naked humans. He announced, "It's done. I've talked to all the important people. Calvin, you're a shoo in. We'll hold the election when this Bloodstone business is done. You'll be voted mayor for sure."

"Oh, that easy huh?" Calvin marveled. "I thought there'd be a lot more to it, or at least others who wanted to be mayor."

Reggie poured himself some wine leftover from last night and tasting it, spit it out into the fire. "You have enough support, but really, the minotaurs' support, after you found and helped recover Windwalker, you win before it's even a competition."

Ryvane raised her eyebrow. "I sense a condition, Reggie."

"Do you have any actual wine... ah yes, there it is." He walked over to the desk and pulled an unopened bottle out of a drawer. Popping it, he took a long drink. "The minotaurs want you to agree to stay out of their taverns and shrines. Sure, if a human or non-minotaur is involved, you can do what you have to do to ensure Tania itself does not get involved. And, well there's the Thieves Guild. It kind of controls this whole area. You'll need to make a deal with them too. Every mayor does. You'll need to establish some connections with the higher ups quickly. Oh, speaking of which, I got you a connection with House Sai."

Ryvane's eye brows shot up and she almost choked on her food. "How?" she exclaimed.

Reggie pointed to Calvin. "This is Calvin. The Calvin who entered the Temple with The Malcor we've all been hearing so much about. Who, by the way, is Sai's estate priestess' lover." Reggie looked at Calvin and winked, "You remember the white priestess who helped you both on the road right, Ora?"

Calvin could not believe it. "You mean, wait wait. Malcor and Ora are together? How?"

Reggie did not answer but took another long drink. "It's a good thing," the halfling said. "When Malcor gets back, if he survives Bloodstone, he's your foot in the door at Sai's estate. Plus, Malcor himself. You could probably write him a letter or walk right up to him and he'll talk to you. I bet he comes back from Bloodstone as a Dar, at a minimum."

Ryvane rolled her eyes. "At a minimum?" she parroted. "What could be higher than a Dar, Reggie?"

Reggie winked at her. "My dear Ryvane, who knows? It is my experience that paladins often follow a different career track than the rest of us." He pointed to Calvin. "For example, who would have thought that Calvin would end up a Captain AND Mayor within months of joining the Temple as a paladin?"

He smoothed his jacket and shirt sleeves before adjusting his hat. "Well, I must be off. This has been fun. Business calls me to Home with my own people. If you set up an election, make good with the Thieves Guild, and don't upset anyone important. You should be mayor by the time spring arrives."

"Wait," Calvin caught the Halfling's arm. "It can't be that easy."

Reggie removed Calvin's hand in an aggressive enough manner that it surprised Calvin. He made a mental note to not grab Halflings like that again. "Calvin, it wasn't easy. I've been working the soles off my shoes to set this up. Don't let me down. Once you're mayor, we'll have other business dealings. I'm sure of it." He winked at Calvin. "After all, nothing in life is free. And being friends with a powerful politician and Watch Captain of Dock Side, it'll help with my business. So, it's not free. It's not easy. But, I figure that if you can't finish this when it's all laid out..." He wrapped his cloak around him and walked out the door.

Calvin looked at Ryvane incredulously. "I don't believe it," he said.

Ryvane wrapped her arms around him. "It's a gift. A marvelous gift, my love. I'll see if my friend Ash knows anyone in the Thieves Guild you can meet."

All around Bloodstone, gates opened near the fortresses assigned to the various nations. King Andrew immediately walked out to the edge of the causeway between the Sixth and Seventh. He looked into the valley. He had fought here for a year during his military service. His family had not wanted him too, but at his insistence, they relented. They sent an entire unit to take care of him though. He rather resented it. The role of tourist had not sat well with him.

The valley looked hazy. To either side, he could just barely make out glimpses of the causeway as it snaked along the ridgeline to the other fortresses. He had never been in this particular Fortress, but it hardly mattered. They all had the same layout. "I want our banners and beacons up quickly now!" he called out over his shoulder.

With only several days' time to prepare, his generals struggled with the Bloodstone campaign. Thankfully, most had also served in Bloodstone alongside Tania's legions. Those who had not, Andrew placed in charge of the homeguard back in Taysor to watch over the people there.

From the Sixth, a regal group approached his banner. Heralds read the signs and one said, "King Andrew, the elven king of Morilon approaches. His name is," but Andrew cut him off.

"Vel Pajor. Yes, I remember. I met him when I was very young."

The herald bowed and stepped back. Andrew figured he may as well get this over with. Elves could be difficult. Centering the bloodstone in his crown on his forehead, Andrew strode out to meet the King of Morilon. Andrew sensed his royal court struggle to catch up to him. Vel Pajor stopped in the middle of the causeway and waited.

It took what felt like an annoying several minutes to reach the middle and Andrew remembered how the vast size of the fortresses made everything feel closer than it actually was. He bowed. "Hail, King Vel Pajor of Morilon."

The gray elf let his eyes skip across Andrew and those that had managed to catch up. They lingered on someone to his side and Andrew did a quick check pleased to see the Braden priest there. "You humans age so quickly," Vel Pajor said. "I don't know how you do it. And now here you are no doubt hoping to snuff your brief life out even faster than it would naturally. Let's keep this brief, Soran. I'll be taking command of the Sixth Fortress. It's farthest from Tanian locations."

Andrew knew this would happen. "How many soldiers did you bring, great king?" he asked.

Vel ignored him instead blowing on a bloodstone centered on the back of his gauntlet. "I knew these things had to come with some additional price. Had I known." He turned to walk back to the Sixth.

Andrew cleared his throat, "Vel Pajor, our arrangement with King Rojo is that Taysor commands the Sixth and Seventh. I am told that, though powerful beyond belief, you do not have sufficient soldiers to hold the Sixth. Plus, the Sixth has been compromised -"

Vel stopped mid-stride and over his shoulder said, "Yes, we are clearing the third sub-level now. Once cleared, our clerics will seal it for our stay. Your intelligence regarding our soldiers is as flawed as your supposition that we need your assistance to hold the Sixth. We will treat any humans as enemies. Stay clear, King Andrew. It's really better for us both this way."

Andrew felt his cheeks burn. *I bet the damn Tanians are watching and enjoying this*, he thought. "Vel Pajor, Taysor commands the Sixth and Seventh." He snapped his fingers and signaled. Around him, the zealot knights of Cuthbert leapt forward. "My guard will return with you to best figure out how to secure the Sixth and provide aid in the sub-levels."

Vel Pajor's eyes flicked across the zealots and Andrew noted that, similar to the Tanians, no one – even the elves - seemed to enjoy the Shining Order of Cuthbert. Their discussion allowed enough time for others to arrive and soon the elven royal guard was outnumbered five to one and increasing.

The Braden priest stepped forward to Vel Pajor and said, "The Shepherd requires that we all unite and cure the world of this evil."

Vel sniffed at the priest. "You look the same as always, old man," and to Andrew's surprise the elf king brushed some dust off the priest's shoulder. "Will Braden the Shepherd be healing the undead?"

The priest, without missing a beat, answered saying, "Braden heals all without judgement. Isolation and hubris can be an illness as well," he said quietly in flawless Elvish so that only Vel Pajor would understand.

Vel knew how quickly the zealots could escalate violence. "Very well, we shall fight with Taysor though I will send a letter to King Rojo protesting this." Vel spun and walked back to the Sixth. The zealots had to break into a run to keep up with the elf's normal walking pace.

Andrew finally paid attention to the Braden priest. Long had the cleric wandered to and fro throughout Taysor but Andrew had never spoken with him. Muscled and wiry, dressed in breeches and a tunic of homespun wool, the man appeared both aged and in the prime of life at the same time. He bore no weapons, no holy symbols, no tools, no jewelry. "You might be the only one here not carrying a weapon, Lord Braden," Andrew said.

The priest's eyes twinkled from within clear blue eyes. "Braden's healing requires no such things."

They found the Seventh well-provisioned. A Tanian commander showed Andrew and his generals a map in the throneroom. A large window overlooked the valley below them to the east. "This map is linked to a master map at the Temple." The commander pointed to the various marks explaining the symbols for hellhound sightings, Unter's Vein, the ancient mineshaft Malcor found, and noting how the Fortresses had been set up.

"Each fortress will host a nation and have some kind of Tanian protector except for Taysor. Alerius had hoped that Oranstakar would be joining you. As it is, there are some gold dragons coming we hope to station here. This," the commander tapped the red robed skull, "is Bomoki's sightings. You'll recognize him as a hellhound wrapped all about by the Jade God's sceptres. We aren't sure if they control Bomoki like a typical possession, or if Bomoki controls them. Also," he pointed to three bare skulls. "These are demi-liches. They are new to Bloodstone. Our records do not show anything about them, but they are powerful and deadly. Be on your guard."

The commander took Andrew to the window. Even through the bright daylight, they saw a glimmer of golden light across the valley. "The Temple should always be visible regardless of weather or time of day. Also, each Fortress will be lighting and maintaining a beacon that will be unique. Please see that your soldiers become acquainted with the beacons." They talked in length about the recent goings on in Bloodstone until at last, the Tanian garrison from the Sixth arrived. They bowed, joined the garrison and marched off towards the Eighth, controlled by the dwarves of Stone and Gar-Galad.

Looking at the map, Andrew saw how Tania had sandwiched Taysor and Morilon between the Gnomes taking the Fifth, and the dwarves at the Eighth. "No doubt, the patriarchs Spark and Screem will be watching us just as much as we will them," he noted to his generals. Tania, fortified by minotaurs and the kerckhi fire giants, took fortresses First through Fourth. He tapped the Fourth, "I see the fire giants get their own fortress. Are there truly enough to hold it?"

A messenger came running in and breathlessly said to a general, "Mages are bringing us siege weapons from the Temple." They walked up to the top of the fortress. Each Bloodstone fortress had a flat upper roof reinforced and strong enough to support a dragon's landing.

Twelve ballistas and six trebuchets had materialized there, each with a Tanian mage. Surrounding the center keep, a wall and six towers at a lower height than the central keep, which allowed guards to view the entire surrounding from this roof. Each tower received a ballista and catapult. The mages vanished and then moments later reappeared with a large wagon of bolts and firerocks for each machine.

Andrew overheard one of the mages speaking with one of his generals, Bryant. "The machines are golems. They will seek to target enemies on their own unless you aim them specifically while touching this rune. It is up to you and your men to keep them loaded. They'll reset on their own. However, if their magic is destroyed, you can manually reload them as you would a normal one. They each have a name," and the mage noted a draconian runescript on the firing lever of the device.

As they spoke, a commotion erupted off to their left side. They heard men screaming and collapsing stone. Andrew ran to see. The trebuchet and catapults below had already started to aim themselves. If they had not, Andrew would have known where to look. He saw, at the bottom of the causeway wall where the trees of the valley floor rose, a man in black robes.

The black-robed figure unleashed a spell. It collapsed a section of the road. Stone from the causeway rained down in a swiftly growing avalanche towards the man. Andrew saw twisted bodies of soldiers in the falling debris. Large spectral hands and small blue disks of energy either moved the men away from the debris or smashed the boulders to the side. It confused Andrew until a the catapult automatically launched. The black robed figure ignored it, focusing on the men in the avalanche.

The firerock exploded near enough that the conflagration of its explosion leveled trees around the man. When the fire cleared, the black robed man stood completely unaffected. He appeared to shrug and two additional sets of hands appeared, each catching a soldier. The man turned and walked into the forest. Immediately, the magic protecting the others ended and their bodies mangled into the tumbling rocks. One of the generals swore at Tania. A ballista fired from the lower tower, somehow able to sense the black robed man even though he had vanished into the trees.

Andrew walked over to General Bryant swearing at Tania. "General, we are here to fight with them, not fight them. Concluding that this is somehow a Tanian aggression is premature, and sets the wrong example for our men. Stop it, now." The general bowed but Andrew could tell this would not be the end of it. They lost thirty men in the road collapse. Someone reported they saw the black-robed man take six survivors.

Within two hours, all twenty thousand of Taysor's soldiers arrived. Andrew imagined similar things occurred all over the valley. "Send embassies to our neighbors. Let's establish communication. Tomorrow, I will go to their Temple and meet our hosts. General, have you organized a rescue party for any survivors of that wall?"

"Yes my liege," he pointed. Soldiers and clerics rappelled down the causeway wall and, supported by ropes, moved through the avalanche debris. They were about halfway down and working slowly. "You can see how the Tanians designed the inner walls to collapse as a further defense against a horde rising up. If you watch, the debris will start to clear itself. We received word on the causeway that dwarves will be arriving from the Eighth to help repair. Tania also offered to send fire giants?"

The rising question tone bothered Andrew. "Bryant, listen and hear me now. We are here to help fight undead, and perhaps end the Jade God's threat once and for all. Regardless of your feelings about Tania and their methods, we will accept any and all help they offer us. You will instruct and send word that Tolerance is a minimum expectation for all Sorans. We will accept the fire giants' help. I'm frankly surprised there were not any here when we arrived."

The general seemed as if he would say something more but stopped. "What is it?" Andrew asked.

"Well, you see, my King. Not all the gates opened in the same place right? Some of our group ended up here, others at the Sixth. The Lord Marshall of Cuthbert, Duke Golcir Able, he threatened to attack the fire giants if they did not leave immediately." Seeing King Andrew's face blanch and then fill with anger, Bryant paused. "Would you like me to bring Golcir here? I believe he has taken command of the zealots at the Sixth."

Andrew wanted to scream. "So, because the zealots consider the fire giants "evil", we lost how many men in that attack?"

"Sir, we are not sure. First count is that we lost twenty or so but having just arrived, we don't really know. Plus we might recover some -"

"This is Bloodstone. We won't recover any. You know this. Golcir knows this. The damn elf Vel Pajor knows this! We are not yet arrived an hour and already we hamstring ourselves. The Tanians must be laughing at us."

Andrew tried to do some of the calming breath exercises and then touched his bloodstone earring. "This is King Andrew of Taysor. Lord Rojo, I request a battle conference at your earliest possible convenience."

Andrew waited. The general watched and after several moments scoffed. "King Rojo does not respect you my liege."

Andrew shrugged. "There are no doubt many things going on and I am not the only king here." Something caught his eye though and he pointed east. From across the valley and high in the sky, something glinted in the daylight and then dipped below the cloud.

A dragon scintillating in color flew towards them. Once aware of it, fear and apprehension caught the increasing attention of the Seventh. The dragon banked and wheeled over the Seventh before dropping to land. Within the almost crystalline form of the dragon, King Rojo's human form alighted on the roof a hundred paces from Andrew. Behind and around Rojo, the dragon's wings furled as the king pulled his arms down to his side. "I've never actually met Rojo in person," Andrew said to the general. "Send word to gather all officers to the command room." He walked over to Rojo.

Andrew had heard stories about the dour and serious king. The civil war that he had ended had remained confined to Morbatten, but the change with male priests had caught even Taysor off guard. And, Alerius had anointed Rojo as King of Morbatten. Unlike many royalty Andrew had met, Rojo wore plate armor spiked and razored. The odd dark grey metal and spidersilk garments reinforced Andrew's impression that Rojo must be a dark man. Golden and white draconian runes ran along every edge of every piece of armor. Across Rojo's back, a mighty long sword sat. The pommel glinted with a bloodstone as did a medallion around Rojo's neck. A similar bloodstone earring glinted back at Andrew.

Rojo let his dragonself fade by slow degrees. He knew he had made a grand entrance and rather enjoyed seeing half of the Sorans succumb to dragonfear. By contrast, less than a tenth of Tania's army had. King Andrew looked exactly like the sketched portraits Alerius had sent with the Merakoran materials. Andrew had the look of a young man who wanted to impress. Rojo stepped forward to greet him and was pleasantly surprised when Andrew clasped his forearm in the style of Tania's paladins. He noted the subtle markings of a paladin order along Andrew's armor.

"I see you're a member of the Creationist Order, King Andrew." Rojo inclined his head. "I have long wondered when you and I would at last meet. When all our allies are assembled, we will have a proper meeting to commence this war. However, I felt your request a perfect time to meet."

Something about Rojo made Andrew's heart want to go charging into battle. He checked for any enchantments and sensing none, he returned Rojo's greeting. "Though Oranstakar felt differently about this, Sora would not miss the chance to end the Jade God. Though Morbatten has been far more afflicted by that one, we share your concern and gladly join this fight."

Rojo and Andrew walked together back to General Bryant. Several other generals and Andrew's paladin guard had assembled there too. Rojo noted, "I was surprised you dismissed the kerckhi. Long have they taken great pride in protecting the causeways. Without freedom of movement, these fortresses become prisons, and we cannot endure a siege against the undead."

"I have corrected that, King Rojo. Taysor will accept your aid. Also, I want to let you know that we will be fighting as your allies. Oranstakar spoke for himself only. I would raise my banners of alliance, but we have not yet unpacked them."

Rojo snapped his fingers and all around him and on the causeway below, fire giants appeared stepping through doorways. They carried tools and quickly set to task. Several leapt down to help the Soran search and rescue team. "Except for your soldiers taken alive, the others have already turned I'm afraid," Rojo said. "You are wise to ally with us. We have prepared centuries for this battle. We only care about victory."

Bryant asked, "And what, King Rojo, counts as victory?"

Rojo's eyes darted over the man. "General Bryant Ophan, yes?" Andrew felt an out of time feeling. It reminded him of déjà vu. "You fought here in Bloodstone with us when you were twenty-one. The Sixteenth Legion. I'm surprised you are here."

The general bristled at Rojo's remarks but said nothing. Andrew made a mental note to learn what happened to Ophan back then. A mage stepped out of a gate nearest Rojo and quietly whispered to Rojo in their Temple language. Though Andrew had studied it, he only picked up a few words – something had been found.

The mage vanished and Rojo said, "The demi-lich taking your men, we've found the mineshaft he used. A rescue mission is not strategically prudent, but we are not yet allied." Rojo squatted down and scraped a rough map on the stone with his armored gauntlet. He pointed to where the mineshaft lay. "From here, you could reach this in about twenty minutes of running. I leave it to you to act as you best see fit with this information. The demi-liches are far more powerful than the liches either of our empires have encountered in recent history."

General Ophan had already sent pages running to assemble an attack. Rojo walked out to the edge of the roof to watch. Andrew felt compelled to join him. "It is too bad that Oranstakar did not come with you, King Andrew. We will need every shred of will and resistance to stand against the Jade God. Let me speak to the general's insinuation. The god emperor expects the Jade God to come through, truly. Not an avatar. Not a projection. To come through, in any of those forms, requires a gate. We have two victory outcomes prepared for.

"The first is that the Jade God comes here and we slay him. Though it sounds straightforward. It is not. The Court of Dragons predicts that most of us will die in achieving this outcome. This is only possible IF the real Jade God comes through. It is infinitely more likely that an avatar does or not at all." Rojo pointed to where Valley Town generally lay and then swept his hands across the expanse of the valley. "Somewhere in there is the real gate. Somewhere is the gate keeper. You know the name Bomoki?"

Andrew said that he did. "Bomoki, even in your own doctrine, is like a phantom. I could never tell if he were real or not. Many of us in Sora consider Bomoki a metaphor for anything the dragons attempt but fail doing; an obstruction."

Rojo chuckled. "I ask that you not say such things when you are standing with the dragons. But, yes. There is that. When the Jade God first came through and attacked Morbatten, Alerius threw the gate from there to here. It saved Morbatten, and probably saved everyone else as well. Of course, even Alerius did not realize he had thrown the gate. He, the Court, thought it destroyed for many long years. The problem, the opportunity, is that Bomoki has been seen and, obviously, still tends the gate. In this, our second strategy, we have two possibilities. One is to destroy the gate. The other is to pass through the gate and strike a blow to the Jade God on the Jade God's throneplane."

Immediately, Andrew countered, "To what end? His throneplane is infinite."

"It is not infinite. We have long known that the hellhounds represent worlds within that dominion. Even if worlds without end, even if infinite, the dominion is less now because of the hellhounds we have slain."

Rojo knelt down again and traced on the stone. "This circle is the Jade God's dominion." He marked an 'X' within the circle in several spots within the circle. "These marks are hellhounds slain by Tania and others. Repeated for centuries. The Jade God's dominion is less. By assembling our forces here, we believe Bomoki will bring more hellhounds through. We hope Bomoki sees us all as a glorious chance to defeat us in one fell blow.

If we kill enough hellhounds here, when we slip through the gate, it might be enough to make a difference."

Andrew drew a much bigger circle around the one Rojo drew to represent Orcus' dominion. "What if the dominion is so vast that a few hellhounds do not make a difference? I had expected you to say we would go after the gatekeeper Bomoki."

Rojo pointed to the valley. "This valley is vast, yet we can comprehend it. We have eight fortresses. Yet, we would notice if say, even one of the fortresses fell. True, we cannot fathom an infinite universe, but Alerius is sure that – for the god of that universe – an unplanned disappearance of part of it would most certainly be noticed." Rojo then pointed to the east. "Over there lies Haven and past that Taysor. If Morbatten fell in Bloodstone, wouldn't Taysor notice?"

Andrew listened and heard Rojo say this so he repeated it. "You trust that the Jade God's enemies in the Abyss will notice. Your strategy is to engage them?"

"Yes and no. Tania does not ally with Abyssal powers. But, we will move the cascade from Bloodstone to the Abyss, where they will destroy the Jade God whether he comes through or not. That is the certain victory. Whether the true Jade God enters our trap or not, we are sending a team through to ensure that the Jade God is never able to enter Tehra again."

The priest of Braden joined them. "King Rojo," he said. "Your obsession on this, and your belief that your nation can topple a god is either unparalleled hubris that would make even Merakor blush, or a sickness of your mind."

"Heal me then, great healer, and show me my error," Rojo quipped back. The priest did not and Rojo added, "Even the pantheon of Pha Rann sees the Jade God as a threat, and the opportunity to preserve Tehra from that one. If I am crazy, I invite you all to join in my dementia. Whether I am sick in my mind or not, Bomoki and the gate are here. How would the self-titled 'forces of good' respond to such a threat?"

The priest said nothing, but Andrew said, "We will stand with anyone that chooses to stand against and end it."

"Well said, King Andrew. I must, however, caution you both. The second condition will remain a secret. Should any of our or your soldiers fall to our enemy, we cannot risk Bomoki learning of this plan. You must give me your solemn word that we seek only to fight against the Jade God when he comes through the gate." Both Andrew and the Braden priest agreed to this condition.

Chapter Fifty Six – Strategy of Ants

Down below on the ramp to the valley floor, General Ophan pointed, barking orders for a rescue mission. As Rojo and Andrew discussed the recent goings on in Bloodstone, close to a hundred men marched out of the Seventh and proceeded down the steep ramp towards the valley floor. "Tell me please, Rojo. Ophan when he was here, what happened?"

Rojo replied, "This situation is very political. It is best you hear it from him. It's not bad if you're wondering about cowardice or something that would make him unacceptable as a general. I believe you have enough reasons to question his worthiness as a general as it is. On that note, the fire giants will stay but will not endure being treated as vassals. I have instructed them to leave as they see fit. They came back with that as a condition. I hope you treat them well. These are not the fallen giants your heroes face in your stories. Our god emperor preserved these since the eldar times."

Andrew noted Rojo's use of the draconian word for *fallen*. "I did not know that. I expect to learn many things I did not know during my stay here. I did hear about how you ripped several of Bomoki's teeth out with your bare hands and captured a number of bloodstones."

"Yes, I did. At the beginning of the battle, I didn't know it was Bomoki. My battle priestess tried to tell me but we had an entire excavation team surrounded. To me, that whole thing is a great example of a tactical victory and a strategic failure. Bomoki was not expecting us. We had a certain element of surprise."

"But still, Rojo, you ripped his teeth out. Of a hellhound's mouth! That is the stuff of legend."

"It was a failure to end Bomoki," Rojo finished. They stood in silence watching the fire giants repairing the causeway. Ophan's rescue team finally reached the valley floor. "Your teams move too slowly, Andrew. The size of Bloodstone is deceiving. You should be able to have your soldiers clear the rampart in half that time, especially when moving down. Here, we have the uphill advantage. You allow yourselves to become targets. Come, let's go to the command room."

The rest of Andrew's entourage filed in behind them to the central stairs. The command room already held those officers present. Golcir had a delegate standing in from him, who kept between him and Rojo. Golcir's resplendent golden armor with platinum accents contrasted so sharply with Rojo's gear that Andrew felt as if they were seeing day and night, side by side. Vel Pajor had provided an emissary as well, who stood separated from the humans. As they entered, a dwarven fighter entered the opposite side, no doubt an emissary from the Eighth Fortress.

Andrew greeted them all and then made his statement that Taysor would ally with Tania and fight and participate in their strategies. At his words, Golcir's emissary bowed to the king and left the room, following Golcir who stopped just short of insulting King Rojo. The elven emissary did as well. Once they had left, Andrew continued. "Though clear that not all of us share in Tania's desire to strike at the Jade God, I have asked King Rojo to explain their plan. To slay the Jade God and end its meddling in our world forever, this is my wish."

Rojo proceeded to explain the first plan for victory. "Somewhere in this valley is a gate to the Jade God's dominion. It is held open by a hellhound calling itself Bomoki. The occasional sightings of the Jade God here, and the presence of hellhounds is because Bomoki opens the gate for them to come through. If we can find Bomoki's Gate, we can know the timing of when the Jade God comes through. On behalf of Tania's seventeen hundred year war against the Necromancer, I thank you King Andrew for lending us your might. Truly, Taysor has become a mighty shield."

Rojo took a deep breath and looked around the room. The mixed expressions of curiosity, hate, prejudice, and questioning challenge were all on display. Rojo locked gaze with a Pha Rannic paladin and said, "Any time, but I fight to the death." The paladin twitched moving to draw steel; Andrew signaled him to stop. Rojo smiled and adopted a tone a professor might use. "You may not know this, but when you move between realms, your power diminishes. Here, the Jade God can be killed. Here, the Jade God can be ended. Time will flow over his carcass and it will rot away, never to return. This is the game. We stand as Tehra's best hope to slay this vile god.

"Our first task is to seek out Bomoki's Gate. We have a general idea of where it might lie thanks to our Temple's recording of hellhound sightings, and several appearances by Bomoki himself. We expect our armies to be at full strength within two days' time. At that point, we will reconvene.

"Between then and now, make yourselves comfortable. Learn the Fortress. Learn the landmarks of the valley and bring yourself to readiness. We will be fighting very different battles than what we see in our Winter Wars. Our enemies are hordes of undead controlled by more powerful ones unaffected by the clerics. Small unit tactics work best.

"The battle you all came here for will be in the valley itself, when the Jade God comes through. We have provided you siege weapons. Consider, how might Taysor's might be felt against a titan that would stand nearly at eye level with this window from the valley floor?"

Rojo chuckled. "Yes, that is the true size of the Jade God in this world. Our strongest weapons, our mightiest spells are but ant bites to the Jade God. Like ants, we must swarm and swarm never stopping until it falls. Blade by stabbing cut, we will dismantle the god until it dies. Any questions?"

Questions started slowly, with Andrew asking a few to get their thoughts oriented around god scale war. With night falling, Rojo at last ended the session and said, "We will reconvene in two days." He stepped out the window and dragonshifted to return to the Temple At Bloodstone.

Andrew heard one of his officers marvel, "They really can transform into dragons."

Another replied, "Thank God we fight with them."

After a moment, someone teased. "You should have attacked him."

* * *

Golcir stood across from King Vel Pajor. High elves bustled all around them, ignoring the two imposing figures. "The Tanians will no doubt make a play for a cascade," Golcir said. "Their own doctrine suggests such a thing. Defectors over the years point to this truth."

Vel rejected the notion. "To put so much at risk for these gems," he noted picking at the bloodstone ring on his finger. "The green dragon told us these came with hidden price. Tell me, Lord Golcir, what will Cuthbert do with this most certain knowledge?"

"It depends, King Vel Pajor. I have two hundred paladins at my command. We have toiled long and hard to develop a weapon that could slay a god." From behind Golcir, a mage in golden robes stepped forward and opened a book. Golcir pointed to a diagram. "This weapon, deployed at the gate, will destroy the gate and anything passing through it when it happens. Like an executioner's ax, the gate itself will slay the Necromancer."

The elf derisively glanced at the page. "I have heard this claimed before. The god-slaying device. Even Merakor could not create such a thing. The nature of a gate is that it moves. It can be reopened. There is nothing there to slay with. It is not a guillotine, but I am intrigued. I will study your weapon."

"And," Golcir pressed, "may we count on Morilon for assistance in deploying this weapon?"

"I see no downside risk to such an agreement. So, yes. We will hold the Sixth. We will fight the Jade God if it comes here. We will assist Cuthbert with closing the gate. I would not regret seeing the Jade God fall. Though, tell me. In Cuthbert's infinite wisdom," the sneering tone made the knight angry. Vel did not care. "…what happens should the Jade God die? This seems to be a shared goal between Cuthbert and Morbatten. Are you truly sure that emptying the dominion of necromancy of its singular leader is a good thing for the rest of us?"

Golcir relaxed, forcing himself to. He and the Order had known there would be questions. Long had he prayed for patience with these heathen elves and their doubts. He tried to interpret them not as doubt, but as a sincere desire for more information. The Order did not need the elves, but their job would be hastened with their help. "Yes. It shifts the nexal axis like a rubber band. That much evil and warped intent coming through into this world, it will pull Tehra to the Abyss. When the Jade God dies, Tehra and the Abyss will snap away from each other. But with no evil left in the Abyss, Tehra will drift and re-establish closer to Creation. A golden era of progress and enlightenment will ensue, similar to Merakor's bright light in the Dream of One Land, One People, One God."

Vel Pajor accepted a wine glass from a servant and glanced over the Tanian map laid out on the command room table. "You cannot fault them a lack of attention to detail," Vel said. "I was young when my father passed but I remember when the green dragon made itself known to us, to all of us. It was many cycles before we realized this new nation in the east had any connection to Tiamat let alone the green dragon 'watching over us'. I remember it as a dark time. To think that Morilon had such an ill creature protecting us. More like a jailor. No matter what happens here today, I will be freed from this curse at last. We will assist you Golcir, but make no mistake. We are not here for Tania, but to be freed of Tania."

"A noble and righteous goal, Great King. One you can count on Cuthbert to assist with. Tania will be ordering a search for the gate. Though I am forbidden from being beholden to anything Evil, might I suggest that Morilon join – for now – Tania in their search for the gate?" Golcir shooed the servant bearing wine away.

"I'll consider it, Golcir. I'll consider it. Tell me, why has Cuthbert never attacked the Tanian dragons directly?" Vel's throne had been assembled and placed at last where Vel could see out the window and over the command room. He sat down and looked out over the valley of Bloodstone.

"There are those alongside whom we serve, who intervene and prevent it. They reason that Tania's resistance to evil counts for something in spite of their god's dark purpose. Politically, we have been forbidden by each king and each Lord High Prophet of the Pha Rann to attack. It is something of a ritual now when a new king or prophet ascends. I count obedience to the Prophet as a higher calling than defeating the dragons. And, of course, there are always far more glorious targets awaiting us in the abyss and hells." Golcir spoke these words as he placed a bookmark in the book and passed it forward to Vel's throne.

"I do not mean to offend," Vel said. Golcir heard the words all too many times used when broaching a possibly sensitive topic with his Knights. "Should Mallaforax fall in the coming battle, would Cuthbert consider it a righteous deed?" Vel adopted a charismatic and persuasive tone. "The freedom of a good race from a tyrant surely aligns with Cuthbert's creed?"

Golcir bowed his head and prayed, seeking wisdom from the great god saint Cuthbert. He felt nothing, heard no answer. "My righteous judgement is left to my own intent in this matter. I therefore see Morilon's freedom as a cause of justice and righteous purpose. We will seek to aid Morilon in its just battles with the tyrant. I however must note that, in our holy writ, there are times when Cuthbert will redirect our purpose. Should that happen, you must understand and agree to let us be."

Vel drummed his fingers on his throne's armrest and nodded. "It seems our and your god's purpose align. I am pleased by this. I had concerns at first that our union would be an unpleasant one. I will send word that Morilon shall ally with Tania, but only to find the gate."

Chapter Fifty Seven – Finding Bomoki's Gate

Seline watched Malcor repair her breastplate. The young knight stood knee deep in forge stones, those eerie green gems that radiate magical heat. Sparks rose up in showers around him as he worked to refine steel and mithril until it matched her armor.

Tembri's death had affected them all and Seline wondered how Malcor and Ayden would pull out of it. Though she had become friends with the battle priest, she did not have the mentor/father relationship Malcor did nor the lover one like Ayden. Seline tucked her hair back over her ear, wishing the work would go faster.

Ayden had thrown herself into ramp drills and gained permission to unify ground and aerial griffin units into her squad. She had changed. Always a perfect soldier and likable commander, Tembri's death turned Ayden into a focused weapon. It made her both more faithful but harder. During one of their skirmishes with the griffins, Ayden had used a catapult to catch and dismount its rider. The griffin had not even noticed, and it should have. *Is Ayden becoming a paladin?*, Seine wondered.

Several of the Temple's priestesses came and went offering food, reports, and casting speculative eyes at the knight. Seline sent them away. Ever since Malcor's return and his words at Tembri's passing, even Seline had heard of the prophecy. Having served with him, having fought by his side, she saw the kingly aspect in him. But, she also knew what the others could not. Malcor did not want to be king. He did not trust himself. Seline felt the same way whenever she thought about her far off future. When she returned someday to the Dutchy of Quattrain, she would either become its ruler or her father would seek to marry her off. She smirked, *As if that would ever happen. There's no way any successor is going to marry a paladin. I'll take control of the Dutchy myself if it comes to that.*

Malcor signaled and the mage increased the heat, pouring magical energy into the stones. A cradle of silver metal began to boil and he poured this into a rectangular mold. Something about watching him shape metal felt overly intimate and she shook her head to clear her thoughts.

Behind them, a door opened and for the hundredth time, yet a different priestess entered to inform them that the dread lords would be arriving that evening. Seline turned to confirm and almost laughed. *How many priestesses are there here?*, she thought. Then, she understood – the priestesses were trying to catch Malcor's attention. It almost made her laugh. The first king Rojo had rejected all priestess relationships. Now Malcor would likely continue that in his love of Ora.

The breastplate quickly took form and Malcor took another cradle full of gold and with an etching tool began to inscribe draconian text along the upper part that affixed to her gorget and pauldrons. It appeared to be tedious and painstaking work, but Malcor somehow did it as an exacting copy and continuation of the damaged script.

She wondered and closed her eyes, trying to imagine that place where time and energy rippled along over and through them. *What was the scripture Malcor always quoted, the one about Time?*, she tried to remember. It gradually came to her. She recited it like a mantra while focusing on her remembrance of that place. One by one, she blocked out sounds, smell, and sensation trying to align her purposeful prayer with the feeling she had with Blade, Dar Niss, and later with Malcor. She felt her heart skip and had glimpses of red and black tendrils of energy flowing past Malcor, and then she lost it.

Drenched with sweat, she found herself shaking. As if waiting on her need, a priestess entered with food and a fresh change of clothing. Seline asked for it to be put to the side. When the priestess left, Malcor called to her, "Come, join me in the forge."

She took his hand and instantly, with his help, she rose up out of the River's flood. The red and black energy coming from Malcor became not just dragonlike, it seethed as if alive. All around him in this place, a dark shadow rose up around Malcor and she saw clearly, the shadow in his soul. He pointed to the breastplate. "It's almost done. Since I'm working on this, I wanted to ask you if you had any special requests?"

Seline focused on the armor. The draconian runescript flowed perfectly from the repair to the parts that had not been damaged. She pointed to the center of the plate where the lich had stabbed her. "I want to remember this and become stronger so that I am never slain again. Will you inscribe such a thing?"

Malcor traced the rune for Memory and Sentience in the green gems, and then artistically brought the two together. "Living Memory," he said. "Like that? I'm sure we can come up with some other ideas if you'd like, Lady Seline."

She drew the rune for Emotion, "Can we bring this in as well?"

Malcor nodded and after some thought, drew his own. The perfect scripting of the rune made Seline feel self-conscious and her aura shifted. Malcor said, "Remember, I grew up doing this. It's all I studied or knew. Don't let it get to you. I still can't read or write in the Common language. Just draconian script."

"I didn't know that," Seline said. "You were only taught draconian?"

Malcor nodded and finished a three rune combination of Memory, Sentience, and Emotion. "This will come across as nostalgia or melancholy. It won't work. Let's try something else." He did a few traces before pointing to a final sketch. "This will read as 'Powerful Experience' to the clerics.

"I love it," Seline said. "How can I help?"

Together they finished the breastplate. The mage attending the gems tried to catch their attention but gave up. Rojo, Jeri, Ayden, and Verit had entered the forge. They watched, commenting about the work Malcor did. Rojo described it for Jeri who wore a white embroidered strip of cloth over her bleeding eyes. "I can almost see it, Rojo. I remember when you faced his sword. Perhaps we should let Malcor continue as a blacksmith after all."

"The forge would never have allowed Malcor to rise in talent, but yes, it has crossed my mind," Rojo noted.

Verit drew his own sword and commented, "After our fight, my sword broke apart. Malcor made this new. It's an exacting likeness but the balance and edge are flawless. I had thought my destroyed sword amongst the best in Tania."

"Indeed, Verit. This is why I blocked his sword at the Klennan ceremony with a different one. I like Twilight Fell too much perhaps." Rojo turned to Verit and asked, "Malcor requires a battle priest. Have you and Kendra decided yet?"

"We have discussed it but, unlike Tembri, the candidates all feel wrong for him." Verit resheathed his sword. "It's interesting to see two paladins doing something together with such intensity that most paladins would not do at all."

Rojo laughed, "In ancient times, all paladins had a profession before becoming a knight. I'm sure the god emperor knows at what point manual labor and art became too menial for us. Nowadays, we only find such a profession if we retire. My father was a merchant. If I remember right, yours was a paladin? I take it that you never studied anything outside of the arts of war?"

Rojo looked back at Ayden, "I'm glad you joined us, Ayden. When they are done, there are some matters we must discuss together."

Ayden bowed, "How may I serve, my King?"

"We're going to create a team around Malcor. You're going to lead the team." Rojo looked at her for reaction, expecting and receiving one of agreement. She seemed one of those officers he could command to do anything and she would, with her heart and soul. No doubt, she had been more so before Tembri's death.

Rojo sighed, "You've had a rough time of it, Commander Ayden, but to be blessed with the love you had is quite rare in this life. It is our desire that you lead this team, exact vengeance on the ones who took Tembri from us, and enact a crucial part of Tania's strategy." He saw her interest grow and knew she would find a proper context for how to carry on with or in spite of her grief. "You've seen how your loss drives you to greater power. This is just a taste of what awaits. Though for your sake, I hope to see you find joy again."

Verit commented, "Dar Rojo, you're taking one of the Nineteenth's best officers. I had rather hoped to keep my command team intact but I see now your intent is to put Malcor, and Seline into this team under Ayden?"

Rojo pointed to them working in the forge. "Soon, the dragons will be here and all will be ready. We need people who already trust each other."

Jeri said, "They're here, Rojo."

Behind them, the door opened and a priestess guided Sofen, Thalian, and Helena into the room. The three clerics immediately bowed to their commanders. "Please, step over here while we wait on Malcor's labors."

After several minutes, Unter and Grito entered, led by another priestess. The two dwarves had been talking animatedly but went quiet for a second when they saw who they would be meeting. Seeing no other conversation happening, they went back to discussing Unter's Vein, Ayden's tower stone, and the mineshaft Malcor had found.

"We've already captured more bloodstones in the past three weeks than the past thirty years combined," Unter exclaimed rubbing his hands. "To think of all the other stones out there just waiting." Their conversation continued until the door opened again. A wiry man dressed after the manner of an assassin entered. He wore obviously magicked black leather armor, walked gingerly so as to make no noise, and his eyes scanned the room. Looking at him, Ayden realized that he looked familiar but in the way a merchant or a tradesman might.

Rojo introduced the newcomer. "This is Marcello, an agent of the empire and thief extraordinaire. He'll be joining this team as well. We're picking him up from an adventuring group named Rogue's Blade. Your team will need someone stealthy in a non-magical way. We have one more joining us and then it's really up to the two blacksmiths to grace us with their attention."

At last, the door opened and an elf wearing Tanian Mage's Guild robes entered. He looked the part of a combat mage wearing leather armor under his robes. Unlike the more casual robes worn in the safety of Tania, the elf's robes glimmered with runes embroidered into it. Pouches adorned his waist and a bandoleer of potions crisscrossed his chest. Five wands in scabbards crossed the potions. A metal staff topped by a bloodstone held in some kind of monster claw completed the picture. "I am Desi Cordan, battle mage. At your service," he said bowing to the king. Turning to Verit, he said, "I joined the Nineteenth near Haven, Commander Verit. Thank you for recommending me for this team."

The group began talking, speculating and trying to get information from Rojo and Verit while they waited on Malcor. At last, Seline shed her clothing and Malcor helped her don her breastplate. The heat of the forge probably made it hard for them to see outside. Seline seemed pleased and stepped out of the protective sphere. The temperature in the room immediately shot up as the superheated armor sparked burning the dust in the air. Seline blinked seeing the gathered crowd and then summoned the rest of her armor. When Malcor stepped out of the cradle, he immediately dropped to his knees in a formal salute to Rojo and Verit. Seline started to follow but Rojo stopped them.

"It's okay. Please rise. We've come to discuss our next strategy with you and a new team." Malcor stood and like Seline, summoned his armor.

"Do you mind if I get a drink?" Malcor asked. Rojo shook his head no and on cue, several priestesses entered with a bucket of water and a mix of food sufficient for the entire group.

While Malcor and Seline drank water, Rojo addressed them, "Tomorrow, we begin looking for Bomoki's Gate. It will be an assembly of all our allies. Not all of our allies are willing participants and it is important we find the gate before they do. This is where you all come in. You see, we know where the gate is. More correctly, we know which mineshaft leads to the gate. Malcor found it. Ana has been scrying it ever since and we've seen the demi-liches and several hellhounds come and go. This morning, Taysor was attacked and six soldiers taken by a demi-lich, who re-entered the tunnels at that location.

"We are going to begin the search at Valley Town making our way towards this gate. That will give you maybe three days to find the gate. There's an excellent chance that Bomoki, the liches, and many hellhounds are gathered there. We cannot scry that area directly. When you find the gate, you are to sit tight with great quiet and stealth until such time as you are able to pass through the gate to the other side. When you do, you will again, seek out a watching place with great quiet and stealth."

Malcor asked the question everyone wanted to have answered. "Why? I do not mean to question you, Dar Rojo. If we get to there and find Bomoki and the others, why not attack directly? We can take beacons, we can end this."

Rojo shook his head. "No, we cannot end it. This drama has been prepared for by us and Bomoki for centuries. There is only one way to ensure we win. You will take beacons, yes. But, you will wait until the Jade God has come through to this world. Only after he comes through will you activate the beacons. When you do so, the three vampire generals will gate to you along with a special team commanded by Daryx. They will help you place and destroy all of the ram's head sceptres and wands captured by Tania since this war began. Their destruction should trigger the closing of the gate if not its destruction outright. Also, when you activate the beacons, we will know that the Jade God has come into our world."

Rojo stared at them all making eye contact with each of them. "I hope I don't need to stress the singular importance of this next part. If you are killed there, you are lost forever. If you are detected and compromised, we lose this chance at striking the soul of the Jade God."

Malcor listened, nodding, but still looking confused. "How is our destroying the gate from that side any different from destroying it on this side?"

Rojo seemed pleased by Malcor's question. "The gate is a thing of chaos. As such, destroying it here does not really end it. The abyssal side would remain open. So long as the gate is open, any victory we might have against the hellhounds, even the Jade God here in Tehra, would be temporary. They would eventually reform and regenerate in the Abyss. The issue here is not the gate, it is the Jade God's continued fixation on Tehra that is the core problem."

"Will destroying the gate in the Abyss, also destroy it in Bloodstone?" Malcor wondered.

"No, the gate in Bloodstone would need to be destroyed as a different and separate issue. Malcor, listen to me. I, we, do not desire that the Bloodstone Gate to the Abyss be destroyed." Rojo paused for effect and then said slowly, quietly, "It is the gate from the Abyss to Bloodstone we want destroyed. The Bloodstone Gate is weak and fragile. If we cut it off from the Abyssal Gate, it will remain active and under our control. If we lose both gates, we lose the bloodstones. This is secret. You are forbidden from discussing this with any outside of this group and the Circle. You will take this secret to the end of your days."

Verit stepped forward now and continued, "Malcor will carry you all to the mine entrance tonight. You will circle in the sky until Ana signals the mine is clear. A distraction is being arranged that should draw any immediate threats out so that you have a clear shot at entering the complex. We have some maps. We are providing these to you along with telepathic communication earrings." Dar Jeri knelt down on the floor and unrolled a tube of cloth. Earrings, maps, and beacons as well as recall tokens.

The two dwarves indicated they had a question. "Looking around, I can't help but notice," Unter said. "We're a bit out of place don't you think, my lord?"

Rojo answered immediately, "No, you're perfect. The mines shift and the team needs the help of professional surveyors so that they do not get lost. The mine complex you're entering was originally tunneled by dwarves. Also, you're both competent warriors with an eye for bloodstones."

The dwarves seemed pleased and elbowed each other. "Let me introduce your team leader. Ayden, step forward." Rojo took her shoulder and said, "Captain Ayden will be your commander, your leader. Her word shall be your law. Do you understand?" Everyone nodded. "Do any of you object to Ayden's leadership?" No one did. "Excellent. Should Ayden fall or become otherwise compromised, command falls to R'Dar Sofen, and then to Marcello. I realize you may have been expecting Malcor or Seline. Let me explain. This mission is critical. Paladins have a resistance to magic and ill intent that transcends planes. You'll need the paladins as shields. Malcor and Seline, you are to be the group's shield, not brawlers. I hope that settles everything then? Please join Ayden at midnight in the Temple's main chamber."

* * *

Ynt'taris landed in Klenna. His approach had drawn the attention of the entire village. That he had landed near the Armory caused quite a commotion. Overhead, Cystoran falcons wheeled and spun. From his shoulder blade, Ora stepped down and greeted her friends. Klara seemed to be waiting for her and ran forward into her arms. The child passed right through her goddess armor and they embraced. Ishan and the rest of Klenna eyed Ynt'taris with a mix of wonder and concern. Somehow, the dragon's tail and claws moved without even touching a building or damaging the cobblestone courtyard. Though the day had been a typical winter day with sunshine, it began to snow around the ice patriarch.

Ora spread wide her arms and said, "Klenna, it is my honor to introduce to you the winter patriarch, Ynt'taris." Everyone dropped to their hands and knees. Ishan's workers so used to kind and gentle Ora could barely take their eyes off her. It seemed she had become some transcended warrior priestess overnight. But, that feeling caught in their thoughts and they realized it; she had always been this way. Even when she had tended to them, she had been this way, albeit more subtly.

Ynt'taris spoke and his voice rushed over and through them like a blizzard wind. "Know that though I am not ever-present like Alerius, I have walked these streets and been with the people of Klenna since its founding. You are precious to the Queen." Though the words reassured, the feeling of the words did not and they shivered.

Ora prayed for them, blessing them with the Queen's love and protection. "While we fight a great evil, Mother Tiamat will watch over you. Know that you hold a special place here in the empire. It is not everyone's calling to fight heroically, to die, to slay. Of many more, the Mother calls them to serve the land, the soul, the next generation of heroic fighters. So that there is a home to come back to, I pray that you will tend your forges, work your crafts, and love your children. The dragons, and their Mother watch over you always." Ora stroked a snarl out of Klara's hair. "Come Klara, we must go to Bloodstone." Ora looked out over the crowd. "Ishan, we have need of you and your three best armorers to serve the forges in Bloodstone."

Michelle, Ishan's wife, burst into tears. She held Ishan tight until she let him go. He signaled to three others and they stepped forward. Ora addressed the group, "We will be taking the shrine priestesses too, but do not fret. The Temple will support you and look after Klenna." The group stepped onto Ynt'taris' back with Ora's help. The dragon leapt, wheeled quickly to the shrine, and landed. The snow stopped.

Overhead, the sky grew red with fire as Alerius passed over Klenna with every other dread lord and the griffin riders. No one had ever seen such a sight and Alerius banked to ensure Klenna could see, appreciate, and always remember the dragonflight of Bloodstone.

Ynt'taris retrieved the shrine priestesses and clerics and leapt to join the dragonflight overhead. They turned north and flew over the Shield Mountains towards Taysor.

What would take walkers on foot weeks to traverse, the flyers crossed in an hour. Passing the last mountain peaks, they dropped to the valley floor picking up speed and soaring towards the lonely mountain peak along the western edge of the city. The others fell back as Alerius moved to front of the flight. While they circled, Alerius landed on the plateau in front of Oranstakar's cave. "Last chance to join in our epic struggle," Alerius bit into the cave.

From within, the gold dragon appeared. It walked out looking diminutive next to the titanic eldar red. Oranstakar looked up at Alerius and the flight of dragons and griffins overhead. "I cannot join your cause. This insane attempt to control and harvest bloodstones puts the world at risk."

Alerius snorted down at the gold, smoke and brimstone dripping from his jaws. "Suit yourself. You will be remembered not at all in this legend. Forever the watcher, forever the observer. Even your children will deem your abstinence evil." Alerius laughed a cruel and evil laugh as he released the dragonterror he so carefully held in check most of the time. "You sit here amongst your elder brothers, girded for battle and you will stay here, rot, and die as Time skips you along its flow into oblivion. Fool!"

Oranstakar turned and walked back into the mountain. Though miles from the city, Alerius' eldritch nightmare-inducing terror washed the city again. Where his control had slipped during his last visit's rage, Alerius let the full extent of his power, his hunger, and his passionate desire for flame and fire go. Turning his head to the sun, he roared. Taysor went silent and still, except for whimpers here and there.

Alerius turned his eyes to the city and his talon touched the chained bloodstone, the *Destroyer Stone*, held by the fire-breathers. At the touch, five simultaneous explosions tore through Taysor. "You may not fight with us brother, but I warned you all what would happen if the bloodstones did not come to the war with us."

With the explosions rising up in a bellow of fire and lightning, Alerius leapt skywards and banked west.

* * *

The Dwarf King of Gar Galad eyed his cousin, King of Stone who said, "Screem confirmed it true. Except for ancient stones, Tania has marked them all with a detonation rune. You were wise to heed their call."

Gar Galad spat on his battle axe, bladed along its length with a bloodstone alloy mix. "Well, I knew you'd be here. Never thought I'd be forced to it though."

Stone growled darkly at Gar Galad and spat on the floor between them. "I sought you out to see if the dwarves would stand united with Tania. The hostile aloofness of Morilon does not sit well with me."

"Aye, nor with me. If we unite, it is just for this battle – to slay the Jade God. If I learn this is some ploy to steal my best..."

Stone put his hands up. "Only to fight the Jade God. We can talk about trade later, after, if you wish."

Gar Galad scowled darkly at the King of Stone before agreeing, with great reservation. "I will hold the eastern half of the Eighth Fortress. Agreed?"

Stone put his hand forward and they shook. Clerics standing nearby and pretending not to listen, witnessed it and declared it sealed by Pha Rann. Gar Galad's priest shook his head and added, "Sealed by the Elemental Lords of Earth."

"How long are you going to let this religious schism divide the house of dwarves?" Stone complained. "Pha Rann, I, the other clerics, we do not care that you choose elementalism. Let it go already. This hurts us both."

Gar Galad turned to walk out. "So long as you continue to dig these holes into the ground. It's only a matter of time before, as Screem fears, you break into or connect to the Underdark. It is the nature of your worship that makes you blind to the mistakes of our history."

Chapter Fifty Eight – Lich Trinity

Progress on the gate went too slowly. Bomoki felt events moving on the surface. He sensed the growing powers assembled there against him. Also, something different this time lent a sense of urgency he had long forgotten in his eternal midnight tending the gate. Six human soldiers groveled on the ground in front of him. Paralysis from the demi-lich's touch had finally worn off. Like with the other human Erik, Bomoki explained the circumstances of their situation and how they could die. "But you will die. The question is really this: do you want to die horribly and continue serving Orcus or to just die? Think about it."

He faced the three demi-liches. "Unlike you, these six get to make a choice. In the master's dominion, they would only get this choice IF the master allowed it. Even now, each of these six is wondering if someone will save them, what can they do to maybe escape, and a thousand other things are moving through their minds. This energy, this desperate praying that we see not – it strengthens them and their god."

Bomoki pointed to one of the Soran fighters. "Perhaps he thinks he can run and we'll let him go. After all, there are five others. And this one," he pointed to another. "This one could be thinking about the love he left behind in Taysor. He's wondering if accepting an offer from me is cowardice or bravery." Bomoki met the man's gaze, "It is neither. It is fate that brought you here."

Bomoki turned back to the demi-liches. "When you consume them, you'll see how their thoughts are a myriad infinity of possible choices and rationalizations for those choices as *What If*. It is a delicious buffet denied to you. When the master comes through, it will be denied to all of the world. So, I command you now to feast. Take them quickly."

The demi-liches fell on two each and it was over in less than a second. Bomoki watched as the memories of their meal filled and fired their imaginations. "Hold onto this because this is what true free will feels like. In this moment, what do you most want? Tell me! Hurry!"

One of the demi-liches said, "I want to feel this always."

Another said, "Delicious. I want to eat more."

The last answered, "I want to know why Orcus has limited my ability to know this."

"There you have it, brothers. In the moment before feeding, you were united in your desire to bring the master through the gate faster. Am I wrong?" Bomoki held his hands out to them, "Well?" They agreed with his statement. "And look at you now, each of you most wanting something totally different and out of alignment with the master's will. Rebellious. Uncontrolled. This is the chaos of freedom that saturates this world." He pointed to the gate. "On the other side of that gate is pure chaos. The Abyss. Yet, our master despises free willed chaos. Everything must be exactly as he requires. And here you are, on this side of the gate craving things that are counter to the Master's will."

The demi-liches looked at each other seeing, perhaps for the first time, they truly saw each other. "Understanding this," Bomoki continued, "you are now free to understand each other, your own nature, the nature of the universe. With this free will, what will you do?"

Unfettered from their unified purpose, the demi-liches swayed lost in thought. Without warning, two of them attacked the other. Its form unraveled in a blink of magical assault. There had not been time for contingencies to be laid against such a combined attack. The two blew back from each other. One tried to attack Bomoki but realized they were still constrained from attacking the First Hellhound. The attack instead lanced out against the other but a globe of invulnerability to magic sprang up. Protected, that demi-lich began casting a spell that made its opponent began casting a similar spell, though it rushed to catch up. "Hurry," Bomoki said. "Your time is –"

Reality shifted for the demi-lich under attack. Bomoki finished, "Almost out."

The lich looked around blinking and then knelt before the other demi-lich. "Master Orcus, what would you command me do?" It now saw the caster as if Orcus.

Bomoki began laughing. "Brilliant! Your free will ends soon. Hurry Orcus, give your servant a creative order. Whatever you want!"

"Go to the surface, and attack the Dragon Temple. Fight until you are dead."

The demi-lich bowed low, pressing its face to the floor. It vanished.

"What happens now?" the demi-lich asked, still on defense.

"You have nothing to fear from me. Like you, I am limited to tending this gate and am compelled to finish it as quickly as I am able." Already, he moved to the gate to resume repairs. "Until we are truly free, or until Orcus comes through, we do not really get to choose anything."

* * *

Ana announced a demi-lich had come through to the surface world. It stood in the setting sunset, burning yet powerful enough it did not care. It looked right at Ana and chomped its teeth at her. While the sun dipped the valley into shadow, the lich swept its arms and a wake of souls swept out in arcs from his hands. Hellhounds appeared from gates that opened into existence one after another around the demi-lich. All in all, thirty hounds answered the lich's summons. Then, nightmare monsters came through the gates, each twisted by undeath.

"It's too early," Ana said. "The time is not yet right for a Cascade. Send word to the king and legion commander. Let the other kings know. A demi-lich marches to war." Outside, the Temple's bell began to ring.

Ana described the lich's army as it appeared. "I count thirty hellhounds and double that of type five devils but they have been twisted by the Jade God." Flying creatures rose up around the lich. Similar to the attack on Thalian's group, Ana recognized plague stirges but also winged demons. Ana looked more closely to recognize vrock demons within the cloud.

The ground around the lich fragmented and furrowed as undead rose up to answer the lich's call. The undead organized around ghasts and began marching into the valley. Around them, a fell mist spewed from the lich's mouth twisting even the trees to shake their ice and stand. The trees bent with the Jade God's baleful light and turned to follow the ghast horde.

Rogue's Blade, which had been on their way to the mine, received word to retreat to a nearby sanctuary. Khalla and those watching felt a great sense of relief when the horde passed them by. "The demi-lich seems driven," Khalla described it to Ana. "What should we do?"

"I don't like this. Rogue's Blade, you are to stay safe and await further instructions." Ana knew, in her gut, that the horde marched for the Temple.

Ana sent word to Malcor that they need not wait for midnight. "Proceed with your mission now." To the armies in all the fortresses, she sent a simple message. "The Temple will be attacked. Send help if you wish but teleportation magic of any manner is forbidden."

Ana scratched Crimson's nose bridge. "We cannot risk a cascade, not now." Crimson growled and she said, "We have too many allies ready to jump in and this is a teaser, to test us. Or worse, it's a distraction."

Chapter Fifty Nine – Finding the Gate

Malcor dragonshifted and helped his nine riders to climb onto his back. With the spirit of an actual shadow drake inside him, he actually felt more comfortable as a dragon than he did as a human now. When he leapt into the sky and banked to the north, he almost forgot the pain of Tembri's loss. The two dimensional world of darkness showed the demi-liches advance as a bright purple blob. Malcor decided to circle the outer mountains and drop in from the Fourth Fortress. This would avoid the demi-lich.

Malcor moved with haste using both flight and shadow-stepping. Soon they passed over the causeway between the Fourth and Fifth Fortresses. They arrived minutes later at the mine entrance. He inspected it closely. It looked clear, empty. Desi Cordan and Thalian used their spellcraft to detect traps. It was clear and they landed quietly. So that they would not have to use lights, the Temple had gifted them gem lenses to wear over their eyes. It allowed them to see similar to Malcor in shadow form.

Marcello led them in with Malcor whispering directions to the doorway. The thief quickly found and dismantled a series of mechanical traps, while Desi dispelled a magical trap that would both paralyze and make noise.

Opening the elaborate doors, the tunnel beyond them appeared roughhewn. "Hardly seems worth it," Unter muttered. "Let me have some light." He barely uncovered a continual light rune and they gasped. The entire tunnel's right side gleamed in an unbroken artery of bloodstone. Unter said in shock, "This is pure." He scratched at it. "It's flawless."

Another hundred paces past the vein's end, the tunnel ended in a sepulcher. Dust showed where bodies had lain or sat, as well as footsteps leading back the way they came. The place felt cold and evil. Ayden whispered, "This could not possibly be what we're looking for."

"Do we have a few minutes to extract some of the stones?" Unter and Grito both asked.

Ayden wanted to say no. It felt right to say no. But, she remembered how her own heart had leapt when she found the titan's tower stone. *How can I deny them this?* "How much time do you need?"

Unter said, "Give us ten minutes. You're all strong. We need to just pry this ore loose and store it for later." The dwarves showed them how to find pockets of continuous gem rough surrounded by crumbly matrix. "Pick at the matrix and work your way around the pocket. The matrix protects the actual gems so the goal is to extract the pocket without damaging the gems. It'd be easy to just smash it apart, but sadly, mining these does not work that way."

For ten minutes, they worked obsessively, extracting thirty pounds of ore. Desi Cordan put these into a backpack inscribed with Tanian holding runes. The dwarves quickly packed it into their backpacks.

After they reset the door traps and magic, Marcello led them down the larger passage. Malcor felt a chill and shifted his vision to dragonsight. "We all have shadows attached to us," he said.

The two clerics along with Malcor and Seline blew the shadows back into the netherworld with their faith and prayers. Marcello had it the worst with ten shadows feeding off him. He seemed a bit intoxicated, a feeling Malcor remembered well. Malcor took the lead after Desi magically silenced his armor so Marcello could recover.

The tunnel gradually dropped them deeper into the earth, something only the dwarves could feel. It also widened. They found Marcello standing in the middle of the passageway. Ahead, the tunnel changed from rough carving and tunneling by undead to elegant tile work. Carved monsters along the wall held glowing green eyes. Those eyes lit the tunnel for as far as they could see. The floor tiles held glowing lights.

"Trapped souls, I think." Marcello pointed to the one right in front of him. "Don't step on it. This whole place seems perfect for traps." A soul rose up against the floor, pressing to it with white hands run through with black veins. Its eyes had been sewn shut, as had its mouth. It pounded on the tile and then drifted away. "Am I the only one that finds that creepy?" Marcello whispered.

Ayden asked, "Have you found any traps?"

"No. Well, yes. What I mean is that without stepping onto the polished tiles, I can't check for sure but if you notice: the carvings look pretty angry and have perfect holes in their faces to shoot bolts, poison gas, magic, what have you, at anyone in front of them. Also, their gazes overlap. It's not a question, in my mind, of finding traps so much as that there are traps. I'm 100% certain of it. This tunnel is hundreds of paces long. Say it's three hundred. Carvings every three, both sides. So eighteen hundred traps excluding magic of course. Even with the entire guild, it would take weeks to disarm this."

"I'll go," Malcor said. "My armor, with some protection spells and the Queen watching over me, I'll just walk through it while the clerics heal me."

Seline winced. "Malcor, you'll be shredded." The scar of healed tissue over her heart grew itchy thinking about it. Looking at the scars criss-crossing Malcor, she wondered if he simply had higher pain tolerance than she did. It had hurt more than she wanted to remember, and Malcor had endured epic pain.

"I could do it as a shadow dragon? No, I may as well announce we're here if I do that right now. Cor'tanos and Dar Kell both told me to be very careful with that here. Last time, in these same tunnels, I shadowshifted and almost lost my life to the shades that attacked us earlier."

Marcello and the dwarves looked around for any unseen or otherwise not apparent doors or levers. Ayden said, "I'll go with him. I believe I can withstand physical damage better than Malcor, even without magical healing. If one of us dies, we'll pick up the fallen one and sprint through using the body as a shield. You'll all have to follow closely to revive the fallen one."

Sofen and the clerics looked at them as if they were crazy. "You'd risk death, entrusting us to heal you in time. You know what happens here…"

Malcor grinned, "It's a test of faith the paladins do not shrink from. If you'd had battle priest training, this would make complete sense to you. Tell me, have you seen paladins in combat?"

"Just you, my lord," Sofen replied.

"We were there when Dar Rojo attacked and saved us from Bomoki," Thalian said referring to Helena and herself.

"So, without other options, I'd like to ask that you use whatever prayers you have to strengthen and protect us. As I think about it, Seline should come with us, Ayden. That way, if one of us falls, you won't be left without protection from magic. We'll carry multiple shields and phalanx our way down the corridor." Malcor summoned his shield, as did Seline. Ayden carried one strapped to her back. Desi reached into magicaked backpack of holding and withdrew tall tower shields.

Ayden and the two paladins strapped shields on until they could barely move. "Best case," she said, "this is all for show and nothing happens. Let's do it."

Malcor stepped out first, and though the carved visages seemed to follow his movements, nothing happened. The souls trapped in the floor rushed up, lighting Malcor's tile with bright light. It illuminated the area better and they saw words carved into the walls. Some of the carving held bone chips.

Skeletons had done this. Ayden looked at the writing closest to her and then tore her lips. The words resolved and she explained. "I can't read this but I can tell you its meaning," she said. "It means the Jade God is watching any who enter here."

The three of them continued to the next section. The souls under their feet became more frantic and numerous as they pounded at the tile trying to reach for them. Nothing else happened. Feeling more confident, Malcor broke from the group and walked forward. He still held shields protecting his upper body, but after twenty paces and no ill effects, he called back. "Whatever the trigger for this is, we do not appear to be it. My gut instinct is that these must be attuned to either undead or to those actively hunting undead. Come, follow but don't use any spells or magic."

The rest of the group entered the corridor. Malcor walked ahead of Ayden and Seline. As he reached the end, the black polish of the soul tiles continued but the corridor opened into a vast chamber. The walls, to about three men in height, had been polished. Stalactites of crystal hung down from overhead. Water dripped creating slick spots on the polished floor. So vast that they could not get a sense for the size, the dwarves speculated the chamber must have some support columns somewhere.

Using the glowing corridor as a reference, and the light of the disturbed souls that created a trail behind them, they moved forward until they saw a dim glow off in the distance. Desi swore. "With all these lights, anyone could follow us. Easily. I feel like we're sitting targets here."

Ayden nodded and asked the dwarves if they sensed any columns, anything that would give them cover. Grito and Unter sniffed the air and one put his ear to the floor. They shrugged. "Sorry, Ayden. Nothing we can tell. This place seems completely flat and level. Also, we seem to be in a different cave complex than before the corridor."

Ayden looked back, glad to see the corridor remained where she thought it should be. Thalian and the clerics conferred and then Thalian said, "Ayden, the Queen and Krentismar urge us to find shelter. We all feel it." Malcor and Seline prayed and agreed.

Ayden pointed all around as if to say, *Fine but where?* "Invisibility to undead has served us and Tania well," Thalian said. "Though it usually only works on weaker creatures."

Desi pointed upwards. "Lots of cover up there. Provided the paladins do not resist, I can levitate us all for up to three hours."

Ayden told Desi to make it happen, while the paladins prayed to end their protective auras. Within a minute, the group floated upwards. "I'm going to keep a light upward pressure on you all," Desi whispered. "Be careful that you don't dislodge any crystals. I noticed that only water seems to fall in this place."

By the time they reached the roof, the trail of soul lights had faded and the corridor itself vanished. It felt ominous to see their path back to the surface fade away in this totality of darkness. The faint glow they had seen ahead remained unchanged however. Marcello said, "I can navigate these crystals quite well. If the rest of you tie onto a rope and stay below the level of the crystals, I should be able to pull us towards whatever that is."

They quickly followed Marcello's idea. Desi apologized. "I have magic that could easily do this but I'm trying to save my more powerful spells for, you know, an encounter. I appreciate this, Marcello. It's nice to be in a group that isn't pressuring me to make everything happen." Desi removed a small hourglass and flipped it to track time, an hour each flip.

Soon, they all drifted behind Marcello as he carefully pulled them along. After two flips of the hourglass, they appeared to have made some progress with the glowing area looking closer. Desi had the best vision in the group and said that it appeared to be the top of a staircase, but "I'm not sure from this distance."

More time passed marked by the turning of Desi's hourglass. "I'm going to have to return us to ground and renew levitation soon," he said. He did and they returned to the roof as the angry souls dimmed below them.

They could now see that the glowing light surrounded a gaping hole in the floor. A few steps visible in the light confirmed Desi's guess. At the four corners of the staircase, braziers of white and green fire burned. Standing next to each, a muscled and ebony giant stood. Each bore an ax marked by fell runes. A hellhound lay curled and perhaps asleep by the stairs. Even from this distance, they could tell the creatures were huge. Marcello stopped and signed, "No way to get past without combat."

Malcor signed out the letters and spelled, "Bodak." He then signed, "Very powerful. Four plus the hellhound. If we fight, we lose stealth."

Ayden looked at the area and signed, "We must sacrifice someone. Draw them away that we might enter." She looked at them and then her eyes fell to the dwarves and the clerics. "Unter, you and a cleric will attack them, draw them away. Use recall to return to Temple."

Thalian volunteered. "I'll go."

Ayden nodded. Desi used levitation to plant his feet securely on the roof, and then began casting a spell. "This is a *Hasten* spell, for advantage," he gestured. He struggled with Tanian hand sign.

Helena pointed and indicated she would help as well, and Desi oriented her for stable footing. At Ayden's command, Thalian and Unter levitated to the floor, stopping just shy of touching the stones and disturbing the souls. Helena's spell hit them, the reverse of making them invisible to undead. Sofen's spell which would give them additional protection from evil hit simultaneously as Desi let them touch the floor and continued to exert levitation magic to approximate normal gravity.

The spell effects detonated like a flare in the cavern. The hellhound launched into assault as the bodaks swept forward. Thalian pointed her symbol at them and called for their obedience. They answered her cry with a terrible howling laughter.

Thalian and Unter turned and fled. Unter dropped pots of exploding clay, and struck a fuse. Hastened and assisted by Desi's levitation, they bolted away from the attackers. The explosion infuriated the hellhound but the bodaks did not even notice it. Shattered floor stones gave up their captured souls, who swept after the hellhound and then shot ahead after Thalian.

Ayden prayed for them to hurry. The rest of the party dropped to the floor and ran. Unter and Thalian made plenty of noise and with all the smoke and echoes from the explosion, it allowed them to move faster. They reached the stairs and ducked below the level of the floor. Desi said, "I see them. Unter has recalled out. Thalian is making a last..."

He went silent. "I'm sorry, Ayden." He withdrew a small figurine that looked like Thalian from a pouch. "Dar Ana and Rojo both commanded this." He snapped the figurine to pieces. Out in the chamber, a flamestrike burst from the tiles and immolated Thalian's body to ash. They all realized in that moment, that Desi had figurines for each of them as well. If they turned, Bomoki would know their plans. He pointed to his pouch, "Ayden, should something happen to me."

She nodded and they turned to race down the wide spiraling staircase.

Chapter Sixty – The Temple At Bloodstone, At War

Vel Pajor watched out of his command window as an undead horde of mythic size and number attacked the Second Temple Fortress. Gloating smugly, he sipped at his wine and said, "Even the undead know that Tania is the true enemy here."

His military commanders and royal court laughed and one of the mages said, "My lord, would you like to see?"

"By all means, let's watch. Though I expect Tania to repel this attack, I would like to see what could possibly happen were we attacked."

The mage and several others enacted a scrying pool large enough for all to watch. The flying demons and plague stirges attacked first. As if out of nowhere, Crimson Burning appeared on the roof of the Temple. A great cone of fire erupted from his maw, igniting the swarm. The stirges tried to move away from those burning near them, and though some remained intact, that single exhalation of elemental flames wiped them out. The fire still continued, and the mage pointed. "This dread lord named Crimson Burning, he appears to open a gate to the elemental realm of fire within his being."

"Fascinating," Vel noted. "Long have I wondered the role that fire breather served. Is it last defense, I wonder?"

The Lord Marshall of Archers answered, "Great King, I served two campaigns here. Crimson serves the high priestess. Just last month, Crimson and Dar Ana rescued an excavation. In my first campaign, Crimson often intervened and once saved my life. Not last defense, but a powerful weapon."

Vel watched the cone of fire narrow into a tightly focused beam no wider in diameter than a battle staff. It sliced through the flying demons like a blade. "Incredible," Vel said. "I wonder, do we know if this fire breather is more powerful than the others?"

A vrock fell from the sky, tumbling apart as its two halves ignited after being cut diagonally by the fire lance. The aerial assault drew close enough for the golem ballistae to fire, but instead of the bolts Tania had provided to the Sixth, nets spun out to entangle and drop the vrocks to the keep. A sage answered Vel's question. "Tania's own scripture notes that Crimson is the eldest, if you would allow me." The sage withdrew a copy of the Tanian holy books and flipped to an early section. "The Book of Fire, written by Alerius, notes that: *When the final battle of dragons came to be, the All Father wept and trembled for fear of extinction. But Takhissis would not relent or parlay. Seeing no choice but to fight, Metal rose up against Color and their battle trembled the heavens. Of the Coloreds, one beast of pure hellfire and burning hatred for the betrayers, rose up and slew his way to confront the All Father himself.*

"The Tanians believe that this passage refers to Crimson Burning. The Sage Alaura also speculated to this end. Given the lack of similar passages about Alerius or the other dread lords, I would guess that Crimson is the most powerful of the fire breathers. However, Crimson cannot speak nor can he manipulate magic the way the god emperor -"

Vel interrupted him, "He is no god."

The sage regained his composure and said, "Apologies, my lord. Alerius is a master of magic both dragon and mortal. If they fought as dragons, Crimson would win but Alerius would have to forswear using magic."

Vel nodded and then pointed at the scrying pool, which showed the vrocks begin to pull defenders off the roof and causeway. When one of the defenders burst into fire, they realized it had been a paladin. The paladin bear hugged the vrock as Takhissis' flames compelled the vrock to burn and die. The paladin held on as they tumbled from the sky, only jumping free at the last instant. A mage caught the falling paladin with magical flight and returned the defender to the causeway. Vel pointed this out. "We must make ready for similar tactics. Tell me, magi, are you capable of executing such spellcraft to support our soldiers?"

Though the magi present spoke in unison, from the back, Golcir noted the lack of confidence. He stepped into the room. "Mage, move the scrying pool around until you find the demi lich controlling the horde. I would expect any warrior worth his salt to defeat these low level demons with ease. Ah, yes. There they are." The scrying pool moved to show a black robed demi-lich, maybe the same one that had attacked Taysor earlier that day. It looked up into the scrying pool and smiled. Suddenly, a vile fog exploded from the pool as its water boiled. Golcir leapt into the fog praying to Cuthbert. Though the fog dispelled around Golcir's divine protection, a young elf squire fell back gagging, and then convulsed dying.

Golcir leaned forward and prayed to Cuthbert for the squire as he laid his hands on the young elf's head. By the time a cleric rushed into the room, the squire had recovered enough to be escorted to the hospital ward to recover. Vel expressed his thanks to Golcir. "The Great Cuthbert has saved us from certain tragedy." Vel looked around the room and questioned, "Why are there no clerics in the command room?"

Though the magi recovered the pool, they could not find the demi-lich.

Verit stood above the Valley Town road. The ramp to the Temple Fortress had been improved over time to eradicate switchbacks and make it more accessible to supply wagons. This meant several bridges. Each bridge had a drawbridge, its own towers, and a heavy portcullis.

Not wanting to risk damaging these, Verit had ordered them left open except for the final fifty pace gap over a ravine to the Fortress' walls. Standing here, watching the undead begin to scamper up the ramp, he prayed. "This is the Nineteenth's first test," he said aloud. "Dearest Takhissis, grant us your strength and burn our hearts with might as we protect this holy place." The blade ghasts reached archery range and flaming arrows rained down into the horde. Overhead, the vrocks fought a vicious if losing battle. Clearly, they were supposed to suppress and dominate the keep. "This must be one of the demi-liches," Verit said. "No fallen Tanian or death knight would attempt such a weak and misunderstood strategy. The Queen favors us with an easy victory! Let's be sure to impress Her!"

Another volley of arrows rained down into the horde compressed along the ramp. The ballistas had been reloaded with smaller bolts that fired in bundles. These began to launch. The catapults had also reloaded with spheres of holy water and burning oil. Soon, the road burned sufficient to make out the pack of hellhounds coming up the ramp. "Paladin orders! Advance to the road now!"

Held by magic and divine faith, the knights leapt from the walls and landed on the other side of the drawbridge. Priestesses amidst their group and the knights burned the ghasts back from them as they drew blade, lofted shield, and charged down the ramp into the hellhounds. Behind them, Crimson leapt from the roof and ignited the scrub around the bottom of the road.

The Queen whispered into Verit's heart and he signaled the others to engage the hellhounds. His own eyes closed, he whirled and spied a slight movement along the base of the causeway. A human figure shrouded in blackest night had begun to climb the causeway. Using his bloodstone earring, Verit sent word. "Kerchki, the demi-lich uses the hounds as a distraction. It attempts to scale the causeway below you."

A battle mage assigned to Verit nodded, and a string of magic missiles shot out from the mage to strike the climbing figure. The darts vanished just inches from the demi-lich. Above the lich, the fire giants opened their primal connection to the realm of fire. With hairs and eyes aflame, they drew their swords and taunted the lich. It continued to climb and this bothered Verit. He began to run and then leapt off the road to the cling to the steep cliff face approaching the causeway wall. He signaled for strength and then began jumping, leaping towards the lich. His battle mage took flight and came up behind Verit. Verit shouted, "Is that really the lich?"

The mage cast another spell and with a faint popping and glimmer of light, the lich vanished. Verit yelled up to the kerchki, "Find it!"

Across the causeway's upper level, the giants began dropping torches. Verit stood still listening and praying for inspiration. As torch after torch fell with no sign of the lich, he knew. "Where is Dar Ana?"

The mage closed his eyes and then said, "She tends to the Temple's scrying stone."

"We must go there now," Verit commanded.

The mage hesitated for just a second before Verit swore at him and activated his recall token. He blinked into the Temple's main audience chamber, in a section reserved for recall users. Anticipating the horde, the Fortress had marshalled to the walls, but Ana stayed back to watch and assist.

Verit felt something sting his face and then more stings as a swirling dark powder, no - not powder, insects tore at his face. His armor and sword ignited in flame, pushed the vile biting creatures back. Ana stood on the steps of her throne. A sword in one hand and the Temple bloodstone coiled in the palm of her other. The demi-lich blurred and struck raking claws at her. She threw it back and dove forward stabbing, but somehow missed. Verit, without hesitation, charged the lich.

Perhaps sensing the paladin, the lich's form displaced and then separated into two. The second form, heavily armored and wielding a razor-toothed blade of bone, attacked Verit before he could realize what had happened. The lich, and this second copy in particular seemed to move faster than his eyes could follow. Verit felt the sword smash into his shield, numbing his arm as if the lich had touched him there. With that feeling came a dark hint of despair but Verit kept his mind focused on getting to the high priestess.

Ana's sword began to glow with bright noonday sunshine right as it connected with the lich. Digging into the creature's arm, Verit saw flesh and muscle blossom forth around Ana's blade. The lich began to recover its mortal form. That should have been the end of it. Another brutal swordstrike nearly stabbed Verit through his helmet visor. Ducking at the last minute, he swung his shield edgewise and felt it connect with something solid. Ana's lich blinked backwards leaving the warrior lich between it and them. The insects devoured the resurrecting flesh on its arm as it began casting another spell.

Verit and Ana nodded to each other and combined their powers, as a priestess and paladin had always been meant to do. Ana's thoughts felt alien to Verit at first. He had certain impressions of her that, combined, carried no weight. He saw and felt her great isolation, her desire to do the Queen's will, and her single-minded focus on taming Bloodstone that drove and caused her isolation. Verit's heart ached for her and with something bordering on love, he returned and entrusted his life's aspirations to her.

The warrior lich struck at them, but they withdrew from the world of the real leaving the sword to spark on the stairs. From the River, Ana caught and pulled at the River, bending it to her will. Verit watched the warrior lich and then noted how the energy around the other one had frozen and began to stain black. Pockets began to open above and to the side of the lich. "Gates," Ana said. "It seeks to summon others of its kind. We cannot let it finish or we most certainly will have a Cascade here in the Temple."

They stepped back into the River and in unison, their swords stabbed into the back of the warrior lich. Ana's resurrection spell burned it as she called, through Verit's mouth, for its banishment. Verit himself, twisted and seesawed his sword as he called on his bloodstone's power for anti-fire from the Shadow Realms.

"Face the magi," he heard the Queen's voice command and fearlessly, he turned leaving his sword in the warrior lich's back. A single black line of searing nothingness stabbed into his center from the lich's finger. It would have killed Ana. Verit felt their combination begin to unwind as his body started to disintegrate.

"No," he spat at the lich. He placed his gauntlet symbols up to intercept the ray pouring his prayers and faith into them. He charged the lich, calling his sword back to his right hand. His sword arm crumbled to dust mid-swing letting his sword fall to the ground at the lich's feet. Verit's life and body blew away to ashes. Ana had rushed up behind Verit to heal, to save – but it was too late. Instead, she used Verit's destruction to launch a surprise attack. Her sword decapitated the warrior lich. Just as that happened, Rojo smashed the door open behind the real demi-lich.

Verit's heroic manner and his death, both drew a tear from Ana's. She saw Verit's sword, Nightmare of Chaos, lying at the lich's feet. The single tear became a terrible sob and she fell to her knees to gather the swords in her arms. The dust of his body drifted in the current of magic and heat. Only a fraction of his boot remained. Tears began to blur her vision and she remembered, *This is why I do not combine with the glorious ones.*

Rojo signaled for Takhissis' Holy Word and then Regeneration. His attack smashed the lich to the side of the chamber. The first gate solidified, and suddenly the chamber filled with gates of various sizes. Rojo ducked below a gate to press his attack on the lich, but it had blinked away. Fearing for Ana, Rojo ran to her side and found her serene and eyes closed as she reached her hands to Takhissis. The lich, regaining his balance from Rojo's ambush, swung a staff of twisted bone at Ana but it glanced off her goddess armor.

It struck again and again until it saw Rojo, and blinked away again. Twisted and horrible, a beast of eye stalks and fanged mouths oozed through the first gate. Around it, the stone floor warped and twisted becoming an oozing mass of tentacles and mouths. Rojo realized that Ana would need a few more moments. The warping creature, Rojo recognized it as a chaos fiend. The beast began to twist and writhe trying to move towards Rojo and Ana. A hellhound stepped through a nearby gate, but was grabbed into the mutating thrall of chaos. Its body became sore with eyes and biting mouths that began screaming and spitting venom. Rojo knew a similar thing would happen to them if he or Ana got too close.

Ana spoke. The eldar name of the Mother from before Time flowed, preceded her command that those not consecrated to Takhissis should die or fall back to their own dominions. The sound of that word smashed the gates closed and pushed the hound back through it. The floor reasserted its Tehran nature, but the chaos fiend gibbered and moved to attack her. Out of the corner of his eye, Rojo saw the lich shudder and bend at Ana's command. He had to make a choice. End the lich for sure, or protect Ana from the chaos fiend. "Mother, I must do both!"

Rojo sidestepped through Time and hurled his sword at the lich, "Twilight Fell Shining on Her Bright Eyes!" and then spun to tackle the chaos fiend with his body. He prayed his faith would be enough to protect him from warp. Behind him, his sword seemed to hang in the air and then shot through to the lich. It impaled the undead mage right through the green gemstone heart. With grim satisfaction, Rojo saw the light of its eyes go dark and empty. Ana's regeneration spell lit Rojo's body alive with power and confidence just before he smashed his fist into the fiend.

The fiend's body flowed away from his gauntlets, which shattered the floor. Then, like wave, the fiend's sponge-like compressing and stretching, its body closed on him from all around. Rojo's last sign was an end state signal for 'anything you have left'.

Ana prayed and connected her life force to Rojo through her sword. She felt his armor being eaten away by chaos and knew the king had not much time. "Rojo! Brace yourself!" The entire chamber conflagrated with divine fire, and then fire elementals rose up, as Ana encircled the chaos fiend within a wall of fire. To her dismay, she sensed Rojo's soul suffer its first warp even as the fire elementals began tearing the fiend to pieces. As the fire elementals began to warp, Ana banished them so that they took their fragment of the fiend with them.

Suddenly, Rojo seemed to suffer chaos warp from multiple bites and Ana screamed out in fright, running to him through the fire. Her sword ripped through the fiend but like Rojo, she knew the terrible energy of the creature would devour her weapon. Rojo thrashed naked, attacking the fiend, pulling back pseudopods as they reached for Ana. Fire burned it but not quickly enough. Ana, at last, had to dive backwards to avoid being attacked. The tether of healing between her sword and Rojo prolonged his suffering and he endured yet another warp attack.

Ana saw Rojo's mutilation. With great sorrow, she called out, "I'm sorry Rojo. Mother, forgive me."

Ana dropped to her knees in the chamber of living fire and invoked the Ascension Prayer. Rojo had already done the first part of the ritual that would ascend him to immortality. They had intended to have him rise into the Queen's dominion. It is what Rojo wanted.

However, the man before her would not long remain as Rojo. Ana choked out the final words. The part that aligned with Takhissis was easy. However, each part of the ritual had to cross one of the nexal gates and their overlaps with each other. With the sound of fluttering wings, Rojo's human body vanished. Ana prayed to Takhissis to look after her favorite son.

With Rojo gone, Ana poured all her frustration, loss, and pain into the firestorm raging in the chamber. Fed by the flames, the fire elementals increased their speed of attack. Outside, Ana's priestesses backed farther and farther from the protected doorways as the metal holding them closed began to glow red hot, then white. Soon, the very passage to the chamber glowed. Then, silence fell within the Temple. Ana's chief acolyte prayed for strength and attempted to walk to the door but the heat of it overwhelmed her. Within, they heard Ana raise up her voice in the Prayer Song of the Heroic Dead.

Chapter Sixty One – My Dominion

Rojo felt himself drifting and looking around. He opened his eyes and saw he floated in a silvery sky. For the second time in his life, he felt completely disconnected from the Goddess. The other time had been during the Ascension Rite, in the Astral Plane.

Memory came to him, flashes of sacrifice and pain. He looked at his body and saw the frozen beginnings of chaos tainting his flesh, his very soul. He remembered tackling the chaos fiend to hold it back from Ana. She must have triggered the Ascension Ritual to give him a chance. The first ritual, for anyone of consecrated faith, is easy. The mortal confronts the truth of their own faith. It quickly separates the faithful from the faithless. Rojo remembered kneeling before Tiamat, touching her divine hand, and hearing Her say to him, "I love you." Eternal life required an unabashed faith in an eternal dominion.

It was a good memory. The Second Rite explained why so many chose to ascend into their own particular dominion. For in the Second, he would have to face the antithesis of his life's aspirations and outcomes. Having proven faithful, he would then face the polar opposite of all his life had created.

Speaking with Ana and Jeri, even with Jeri's sisters, he had conjectured that his opposite would be either vile evil or – if the zealots of Pha Rann proved correct – tremendous Good. He laughed and said, "For my sake, I suppose I had better hope I face great good." Even in this divine space between Tehra and the nexal gates, the chaos fiend's wounds all over his body itched. They would not remain quiescent for long. His voice echoed and reverberated. "Let's get on with it then," Rojo said.

He dragonshifted and, with force of will, he summoned air for which his wings to move. "This must be what the eldar felt like," he noted to no one. Having reached the Second Rite, he had to choose – complete the full circle in order to return to Tiamat's embrace in the First, or return to the First.

Suddenly, a platform of earth and stone appeared in the silver skies. He flew towards it, wondering. If, as a knight of Takhissis, his life had truly been evil, he would confront Good here. He had come to terms with the dual nature and the role he played in Tania long ago but still, he wondered. To be judged by the universe and pulled to the anathema of his life's reality… something in him rejected the notion. "No one judges me, except me!" he screamed at the platform.

In the center of the platform, a creature resembling an octopus but of black energy drifted aimlessly, in an attitude of waiting. Rojo circled it from a distance, watching it, studying it, trying to remember. As he did so, Kaia appeared. The halfling looked more devilish here than in the real world. "Remember our arrangement, Rojo? It's time."

In a flash, Rojo remembered his early days when he travelled. He had been hunted from Taysor by the knights of Cuthbert towards Morbatten. They had captured him, bound him to a tree. He remembered screaming at them, "What have I done that you do this to me?"

One had answered, "You are evil. We will take you back for judgement by our Lord Marshall."

Another had offered, "Or you can repent of your evil and we will free you."

The first had prayed to Cuthbert and Rojo's aura became apparent. Streaked through with many colors, it showed the anger, rage, and hate that burned in him since his father had been betrayed and his world had fallen apart. "Your aura, if you were not evil, would be golden like ours."

Kaia had connected him with Takhissis and by Her Grace, Rojo had escaped. "But, there is a price and a sacrifice you must make at a time of my choosing." Kaia's offer had seemed fair and Rojo had never regretted it. Looking at the creature on the platform and feeling Kaia climb onto his back, Rojo suddenly wondered if it were fair at all.

"How is that my seventeen-year-old self becomes beholden to you now, Kaia?" Rojo questioned.

"A deal is a deal and it is time. You helped bring Cor'tanos back from the Shadow Realms. It created an imbalance and Oblivion has selected you as its enemy. You were wondering earlier. Would Good or Evil confront you. The answer is neither – Oblivion itself is your antithesis. You should be flattered. This almost never happens except with very neutral immortals. In your case, the good and evil of your life nearly balance out and the sum total is neutral. So, the gate of Creation and Evil reject you as their foe. In their absence, Oblivion comes for you with a beast of anti-life."

"It's not shadow." Rojo commented.

"Correct, Shadow exists on the other side of oblivion. I thought you and Alerius discussed this? If it's any consolation to you, a similar thing happened when Alerius came here during the First Cascade."

Rojo craned his head back to see the Halfling lounging along his back spines. "There is a way back?"

Kaia smiled, "For an eldar dragon, yes. For a human born in the flow of Time, sorry. Not even the gods can do that. Well, they could but it would require all of them to cooperate. And, you know, that only happened once when they bound Set. You are no Set." Kaia took out an apple and bit into it. "You're probably thinking that you'll defeat this just to prove you can, and then move back to Tiamat."

Rojo said, "That is what I am thinking. I sense you are here to tell me otherwise."

Kaia took another bite. The sounds of apple crunching reverberated all around. "Do you have any idea how many deities watch you? They all expect you to return to her. Why not be your own god? Instead of fighting past this beast, move on to the Third. Finish the quest. If you end now, you'll go back to Tiamat and be named the prismatic dragon, but you'll still be in Tiamat's dominion. If you really want to unify all dragons, and I'm talking about not just chromatic and metallics, claim the 'all space' as your dominion. Give that to Tiamat."

"That sounds appealing but I do not understand the consequence of doing this. Teach me."

Kaia frowned at the commanding tone. "The First Rite is the easiest, though the Second is difficult. In a very real way, your entire life prepared you to face this so, from a certain perspective, it's easy. Each rite becomes more difficult to win but the power attained in ascension is many times that. Tell me Rojo, if you ascend to the Queen, what is your dominion?"

Rojo answered without question, "I have no dominion. It is the Queen's and Her Will. I have no dominion because I will add to Hers."

"Such a typical and indoctrinated response. Wrong! Your dominion, in that manner, is just you. Defeat this beast, conquer the Second. Don't just pass through and charge the Third. Win. Take each Rite with your entire soul. This is where you earn your dominion. It could be, a unification of the Metallic and Colored dragons and all other dragons." Kaia took another bite of the apple. He said quietly, "I want you to do this as repayment for my assistance placing you on this path. Believe me, there have been many times in your life that I thought to call in this debt, but I always waited and hoped you'd make it here. I'm not asking you to do anything you don't already want to do." Kaia finished the apple and tossed it into the silver swirls all around them.

Below, the beast vanished and then reappeared randomly on the platform in a different place. "I suppose I had not gotten far enough in my thinking to determine if I could even charge through, but I see now that I can, easily." Rojo pointed. "That takes me to the Third."

Kaia nodded and withdrew another apple. He brushed it on his vest. "You're a paladin, sworn to serve Takhissis. Answer me this Rojo, compared to the dominion of an actual god, do you think the value of your life alone, as the dominion of Just-Rojo, is worth more to the Queen than if you presented her an entire dominion? I give you the doctrine of Corth K'Ven, Lord of Wyverns and Scrying as a case in point."

Rojo remembered that Corth had earned the dominion of Wyverns through accomplishing the Ascension Rites. He had not even been a worshipper of Tiamat and yet now served her powerfully. "I see your point, Kaia." He looked around wondering if Ana might end the rite and bring him back to Bloodstone. The chaos marks along his body began to itch.

Perhaps sensing his thoughts, Kaia interrupted him. "The longer you wait the more you become just another chaos fiend adrift in space. Fighting to win, you must access new parts of your dominion. Reach deep into your life experiences and cull out the parts that allow you to defeat this, and so on at each Rite."

Rojo abruptly asked, "What do you get out of this?"

Kaia jumped off his back and floated before his eyes. He checked his reflection in Rojo's iris. "By influencing you to a more powerful path, you enter my dominion and increase my power. By swaying you to become a more powerful servant of Takhissis, I grow in favor with Her." He seemed satisfied with his appearance and completed his thought. "I have a battle I must fight. I would have Takhissis as my ally. Now, quit waiting Rojo. Destroy the beast and be more than you ever imagined you could be." Kaia vanished.

Rojo dive bombed the beast. From his mouth, he shot a prismatic sphere of many-colored energies. He sped up and hit the side of the beast as the sphere detonated. Nightmare tendrils twined Rojo's wings, burning him with – *No*, he corrected himself. *They're freezing.*

Rojo bit at the central ball noting that his mightiest attacks barely seemed to affect it. He steeled his will and focused on just his index finger talon. That stabbed the sphere and did more damage. *Force of will, not might hurts it.*

* * *

Morning light arrived in the valley to find the Temple smoking. The undead attack fell against the Temple in waves. Though repulsed, the defenders had fought back up the ramp, dropping the bridges. Only when the siege weapons came to bear did the tide really shift. Crimson Burning fought the aerial war without his priestess. The terrible roaring growls of his combat dropped carcasses of stirge and demon alike to the ground. It rained blood that night.

Steam and updrafts of fire and smoke rose into the dawn sky. About three hours before dawn, the central room of the Temple had superheated. One of the priestesses said she had heard Ana sing the Prayer of the Dead. They continued to sing it. Unable to enter the room due to its heat, they waited for Crimson. Even the fire giants seemed reluctant to enter. Though elemental in nature, the Temple seethed with dragon fire and the holy purification of Takhissis.

Crimson manipulated the dome and entered. Though the fire storm had long died, the internal chamber glowed with heat. Ana lay on the ground, protected by her goddess armor. Crimson growled at her. She did not seem hurt. He slithered into the room and looked at her again. Curled into a fetal position, she held two swords in her arms, as if cradling a child – Nightmare of Chaos and Twilight Fell. Crimson sniffed and detected the cleansed by fire smell of the chaos fiend. Across the chamber, the skull of the demi-lich stared its eyeless shadows at him. He smashed it to fragments with a claw. "Oh Crimson," the high priestess whispered. "They're gone. Why did I never take Verit? My love Rojo. They're gone."

Crimson nudged her softly with his nose and then curled around her, protectively. Outside, amidst much speculation, and repeated calls for information with the earrings, eventually Eighteenth Legion Commander Pember answered. "A demi-lich entered the Temple chamber and engaged in great combat with Dar Ana, Rojo, and Commander Verit. We do not yet know what has happened. I ask for your patience. All we know right now is that the demi-lich is destroyed."

Two hours later, Morbatten's dragonflight rose up over the valley rim by the First Fortress. When Alerius landed, he noted as did the others that something was wrong. "Why is my Temple burning?" he asked before looking into the dome. Dragons do not show emotion, they radiate it. Suddenly, great sadness and concern blasted out from Alerius before he could pull it back. His riders dropped off his back and he climbed into the dome. A moment later, the heat and flames ended. Crimson growled so low it hurt their lungs and made their teeth ache. The doors to the chambers opened and a command came forth. "Dread Lords only, enter."

Within, Alerius humanshifted and carried Ana to her throne. "She's fine," he said to Spark, Ynt'taris, Armageddon, and the others when they arrived. He placed her on the throne and conjured garments suiting his high priestess. "However, we have lost our Legion Commander Verit, and it would seem beloved Rojo was forced to ascend early."

Placing Ana on her throne, Alerius carefully placed the knights' swords under her hand. She seemed catatonic, staring into space. "Shock," Alerius noted. "This happens when my children are overly-stricken by emotion and suffering. She will be fine," he said again. Alerius began casting a spell, and with each syllable, Time rolled backwards to show them what had happened. Crimson, concerned for Ana, pulled forward and cradled her in his hand so that she would not have to see the battle again. When the spell at last finished, they saw the entire thing unfold.

Spark pulled forward to the demi-lich, "This one is not known to us. Look, it appears alien. It must be from the Jade God's dominion. A further portent that the coming Cascade will bring the Jade God itself through."

The others nodded. Screem asked, "Why was the Dar priestess left alone? Should there not be a paladin guard here?"

Crimson growled at Screem, who twitched backwards from the fire breather. "No offense intended, brother. It was not my question's intent to suggest a failure by Ana or Tania."

Spark speculated that the offensive against the Temple had been a distraction to allow this combat. "We've never faced an enemy like this. It is a new thing under the sun."

They saw Ana kneel and begin the Ascension Prayer even as Rojo's body began to split and open forth new mutations. "This is also new brother," Alerius said. "Never before have the undead brought these abyssal nightmares to Tehra. There is no precedent except in the battles that ended Merakor." Alerius looked around noting the floor tiles where chaos had infected and twisted them. Swirls of char and what may have been teeth marks into the stone told that part of the story. "Ana's fire purified the Temple's desecration, else we would be suffering the loss of our Temple." He looked back at Ana and kissed her forehead, "Well done, my precious daughter."

Jeri listened leaning against the wall in the back. "Tell me," she asked. "Alerius, tell me what happened to Rojo? I cannot see."

Alerius said, "I will tell you in greater detail later, Dar Jeri, but for now, the demi-lich summoned a chaos fiend into the combat. Rojo sacrificed himself to prevent Ana from falling to warp. He became immediately compromised and would have incarnated as another fiend. It is a blight of the Abyss, a creation of Set. Ana had to push Rojo into ascension. It was the only way to allow Rojo a chance to survive. No doubt, he is either lost to chaos or embattled in the ascension rites even now. I'm sorry, my golden sister. I know you loved him, as did we all."

Ynt'taris growled. "We are without a king, Alerius. The other nations will view this as a weakness."

Alerius hissed back at Ynt'taris. "We knew, they know that casualties are expected here. Yes, they will view this as a failing of my children, and I curse them for it." Alerius touched his bloodstone earring and projected his voice to all holders of bloodstones. "Last night, a demi-lich attacked the Temple. Though the demi-lich is slain by Rojo, Verit, and Ana's hand, we lost Legion Commander Verit and King Rojo. They are dead. Please grieve with us as we struggle with having lost their bright burning warmth." Alerius looked around and paused, allowing time for his words to be passed throughout the armies. After minutes of silence, he spoke again. "The Court of Patriarchs rules in Rojo's stead. Though he is not present to be crowned at this time, All Hail King Malcor Kell'Tayris!"

The dread lords in the chamber bowed their heads and repeated, "All Hail King Malcor Kell'Tayris." Outside the Temple, everyone looked around in wonder. Those who had seen Malcor earlier looked in expectation for him to come forth or speak. But there was only silence.

* * *

Across the valley, King Andrew sent out word. "Bring me information about Malcor. Is this the one of the Khasran lich story?"

Vel Pajor looked questioningly at Golcir. The knight carried no bloodstones. The entire Order of Cuthbert had forsaken them the instant Alerius made his demands. Understanding at last, Golcir replied that several of his order had heard of but did not interact with Malcor, of the Order of Water. "There is one who did though briefly, a Sir Anthony. He serves with King Andrew. By your leave, King Vel, I will ensure one of my own is present when Sir Anthony shares what he knows with King Andrew."

An hour later, word came again from Alerius. "I do hereby lift Ana's injunction against dimensional magic, for the purpose of a war council. All kings and leaders are summoned to the Temple in three hours. Please be ready."

The Temple had been built to withstand all dragons and then sanctified explicitly against the undying. Except for residual heat, welcome in the cold of winter to the humanoids, no sign of the great battle remained except for Ana's absence on her throne. Already, her paladin guard had approached Dar Shara requesting Atonement. She dismissed the idea as ridiculous. "You obeyed your priestess's orders. If anyone needs to atone, it is her. Go back to work." They bristled at the high priestess' words, but returned to their Temple duties. Shara noted that more than a few bowed to Crimson and told the dread lord they would atone.

Alerius sat on Ana's throne. To either side, Spark and Ynt'taris stood. Teleris arrived through a gate with a reinforcement army, the final one from Tania. He bowed to the patriarchs and then sat on the steps in front of the throne. The other dread lords, in human form, stood arrayed in a semi-circle around the throne facing the chamber. On the first steps, Dar Shara, and Ana's second in command stood with Commander Pember of the Eighteenth, now Nineteenth Legion. The commander of the fire giants stood watching over all.

One after another, the lords came. Alerius had the allied nations enter first. The imperial heir apparent to the throne of Tauran, a red-furred minotaur stomped in trailed by a skeletal and gaunt cleric of Bapthomet, their devil god. Next, the gnomes and dwarves entered. When King Andrew of Taysor entered, he bowed low to Alerius and greeted them in well-practiced draconian. It pleased Alerius, who said, "King Andrew, too long has the sovereign of Taysor avoided our halls. Please consider yourself welcome as a royal guest whenever you wish to visit."

Most surprising to them all, Andrew responded in draconian, "I accept your most gracious offer, God Emperor Alerius. Please consider yourself invited to my palace courts as well."

Vel Pajor entered with a train of magi, sages, and rangers. He barely bowed to Alerius, choosing instead to direct his respect to Mallaforax. This drew a grumble from Crimson, to which the elven king paused and said, "I notice that Dar Ana is not present. Please convey our condolences and wishes for a speedy recovery."

"No need," Ana said as she swept into the room. She held Dar Jeri's hand, leading her. "I am quite recovered."

When she entered, Alerius gracefully stood from the throne and bowed as she climbed the steps and took her seat. "Let it be written, for all to hear," he said. "The day will come when the children of dragons rule. By the hands of the children was this Temple built, and so it is ruled by Tiamat's high priestess. Welcome, Dar Ana." He took and kissed her hand as she sat on the throne.

Vel Pajor had paused at Ana's interruption and now he asked, "Dragon Alerius, do you mean to say that the dragons will leave Morbatten one day?"

Alerius' eyes flashed, and in unison the fire breathers answered Vel with their gaze alone. Ana replied to break the tension, "The god emperor prepares Tania for a day when we must all unite and fight as dragons. If we are all dragons, then are we not equal children of the Mother?"

Vel seemed about to retort but instead, withdrew with his entourage to their designated location. After that, the Guild Heads of Tania entered along with the Circle. Alerius introduced them until at last, Daryx entered with Sai. The two walked shoulder to shoulder and bowed to the dread lords.

"I trust," Alerius began, "that my dearly beloved Rojo informed you of Morbatten's strategy – to slay the Jade God here in the valley. This strategy hinges on the actual corporeal Jade God itself coming through. Since the First Cascade, we have prepared for this war. Though it may surprise those that do not know, Tehra is a fulcrum world, where even a god may die. In fact, I would like to introduce some additional allies who have come to join in our war." Alerius pointed and from the midst of the paladins, a muscled barbarian stepped forward. He wore the skull of a dire wolf as a helmet. Dar Kendra escorted him forward. All present looked for an indication of who this man was.

"This is a priest of the Slayer of Gods, who goes by no name. It is a dominion of Tehra alone. The Slayer stalks immortals who have visited over long here. Please note that this is an ally in our battle. The wolf skull helmet is their holy symbol. I command all present to not confuse them with our undead foes." The cleric bowed and withdrew with Dar Kendra. "I would also introduce the lovely sisters of Dar Jeri, but ask that Jeri do us the honor."

Jeri stepped forward and called out to her sisters. Three ladies in shimmering golden robes became apparent, unknown and unnoticed by most present. The ladies bowed and one ran forward to hug Jeri. Taking Jeri's hand, the sister whirled to the group. White blonde hair, completely golden eyes, and golden flecks glittered along her skin. Her voice struck a chord of peace in all who heard it. "My short name is Kyla. Though Jeri fell to an incorrect belief, we love her." Kyla kissed Jeri's cheek. "We are here to support her and to see the Necromancer end his play for Tehra once and for all." Kyla left the dais attempting to pull Jeri with her. Jeri almost went but stopped.

Alerius said, "Go ahead, Dar Jeri. Be with your sisters and find comfort in their love and shared empathy for your loss." Jeri bowed to Alerius and left the platform with Kyla. "These are the ones we can openly discuss. There are many more who have pledged support only should the Jade God come through. So, let's discuss how this happens.

"We know, generally, where the gate is accessed from." Alerius waved his hand and an illusion sprung up front of him of the gate. "My brothers and I constructed this gate for the purpose of enabling exploration of other realms. We used it for this purpose and early development of our mage's guild. When the First Cascade happened and, as you all know, the Jade God came through, he nearly destroyed my Morbatten. Only a handful in the valley survived." Another illusion of the battle of the First Cascade appeared. It showed clearly the titanic size of the Jade God.

"The Jade God and his first hellhound, Bomoki, began using the gate to pull hellhounds through." The illusion shifted to show Alerius burst forth from the Jade God's throat and then spun through the three patriarchs hastily throwing the gate to Bloodstone. "Even then, we knew Bloodstone had a certain affinity for the Abyss. We hoped, and it proved correct, that the Jade God would forget his bearings and follow us to Bloodstone. He did. From there, you know the rest."

The illusion showed the dragons teleport to Bloodstone and in an instant, the Jade God left Morbatten alone. The illusion showed how one after another, divine powers began falling into Bloodstone to either attack the Jade God, or to oppose their fated enemies as they appeared. Alerius gestured to the scene. "We call this a cascade because, at a certain point, the gods feel compelled to intervene. There is a balance here in this world. When any power becomes too concentrated, it draws its opposition. As the opposition becomes more specific, servants appear who open gates and the cycle reinforces."

The battle scene ended with a divine servant of Pha Rann striking down an abyssal power no one had ever before or since seen. The gate appeared prominently. "This is the gate. It is quite fragile as I did not want a gate I could not destroy easily, should we need to end it quickly. You'll notice it is small. What you do not know is that the gate is an aperture. It can expand infinitely given enough pull and push from either side. This is how the Jade God would come through. The trick is that we want the Jade God to come through so that we can kill it. If we simply destroy the gate, the Jade God remains able to access this world at will, avatar upon avatar. Nothing will change if we only destroy the gate."

Alerius paused for effect and looked at the assembled leaders until they acknowledged him. "We will not know from where the Jade God comes into the world. Right now, it's always Bloodstone - because of this gate. Should you feel tempted to destroy the gate, without the Jade God being on this side, you will find yourselves every bit as susceptible to undead attack as my children have been. We bear the brunt of their hate for your security. Remember this."

Alerius began pacing. "I cannot foretell which of our groups will find the gate. But, it is imperative that you do not simply destroy it. For one, unless we also destroy Bomoki, the gate will repair itself and we lose this opportunity. Second, the issue here is not the gate. It is the Jade God. It has always been about this. Like Set, his desire to freeze all of Tehra into undeath is every bit as threatening as Set, but more urgent because the Jade God has worshippers here that would pull him through. Already, our world is sick with the undead. It is time that our world pushed back. This is where we draw a line and say to a god say, no."

They reviewed in great detail the location of the mines and tunnels around the general area where the gate could be. At Vel's request, Alerius assigned a single area to the elves. The others formed into groups to discuss how to best enter, map, and determine the gate's location. More importantly, once found, how to let the others know. "Finding the gate is the first step. Once we know where it is, we will know exactly where the Jade God will appear. We will reposition our forces at safe distance and prepare. We must prepare as if awaiting a thief in the night."

As the council ended, a priestess walked up to Ana and whispered in her ear. She tapped Alerius and they left. He followed her to a side chamber where a grumpy dwarf demanded to know why Thalian had not yet come back with her recall token.

Chapter Sixty Two – In Total Darkness

Ayden gathered everyone together and quietly said, "These stairs go forever. Can't we levitate down or something faster? We're sitting ducks here." From their position, they had counted about fifty full turns of the spiral staircase. The bottom remained somewhere down there and they could no longer see the top.

"Levitation is still in effect," Desi said. "No harm in doing it. Stay near the stairs though because we'll be even more sitting ducks if something should look up or down at us."

They stepped into the hollow center of the spiral staircase and began levitating down. Without any armor metallically clinking, or boots on stone, it grew frighteningly quiet. At some point, Desi indicated they all needed to get back on the stair case. At least they could see something at the bottom they hoped would be the bottom of the stairs.

Grito had long since stopped trying to determine how deep underground they had travelled. Same as the top, the stairs ended on polished black tiles. The difference lay in the lack of guards and, Ayden had been continually praying her thanks that the bodaks and hound had not come back for them, far off they saw glowing lights, moving. No ceiling full of crystals to hide in here, plus Ayden did not want to push their mage for more levitation.

"If we go invisible to undead, will the souls be able to detect us?" she asked. Sofen and Helena cautioned using clerical magic here.

"If we keep the stair between us and whatever is over there, we can retreat and hopefully find the wall," Marcello suggested. It seemed a good idea and they did so. Trying to move that quietly for that long, they lost track of time and suddenly, bumped into Marcello who had nearly bumped into the wall.

Looking at the team, Ayden saw fatigue, maybe even exhaustion. "Do we know how long we've been down here?" she asked.

"At least a full twelve hours," Grito guessed.

Ayden thought intently about the problem of the glowing floor tiles showing anyone or anything exactly where they were. At last, she had an idea. "Let's take a break. Desi, do you have a large blanket in your backpack?" He pulled one out and Ayden placed it on the tile beneath her. The blanket covered the light of the trapped souls, even when she stepped onto it. Ayden smiled at the group, exhaustion making it hard to give them a genuine grin. "I'm so glad that worked. Please Desi, get us all blankets. Maybe we can use these later to move without triggering the tiles to light up. By sliding maybe, I don't know. We need a break."

With only the stairs creating a faint vertical glow and slight movement far away, the darkness weighed on them. Though they took watches, no one slept very well, except Malcor. The clerics meditated and Desi riffled through his spell book. Malcor collapsed almost immediately. And after a moment, Seline joined him. Sofen smiled at Ayden and said, "I guess they're still tired from all that has happened up to this point."

Ayden nodded, "I imagine Malcor has had a very different adventure here in Bloodstone than we have."

Soon, they all fell quiet. The dark made Ayden's sorrow worse. With no one to talk to, nothing to look at, no outlet, she remembered all the good times she had enjoyed with Tembri. She'd had only a few lovers in her life. Most boys and later men had shied away from her disfigurement. Of those who had gotten past it, Ayden's competitive spirit and drive for martial excellence turned away even more.

That a cleric, a Dar priest, had chosen to be with her; it hurt her heart. *I miss you Tembri*, she thought. She glanced over at Malcor. He had proven to be so different from Calvin, so different from how she had imagined he might be. Even asleep, something about the young paladin made her want to bow her knee and give him command. She shook her head. *There's a reason paladins are not often given command*, she reminded herself. *I would follow either of them without thinking*, she conceded. *I can see why Tembri loved him.* It was a dark thought and she fell into a melancholy wondering what the priest had seen in her.

Even Tembri had told her once. "Who knows, Ayden? Malcor could very well be the next king. How many dragonshifting paladins of prophecy have you heard of?"

"Tembri, really! I don't hear about paladins the way you do. My training is always about how to manage a paladin when they give orders counter to strategy or other orders. You talk about Malcor as if -"

"He's special. I was held by the Order for five years before anyone joined. They had a few candidates but they all failed quickly. Then, one day, here comes Malcor and begins blowing away Order of *Water* records." Tembri had kissed her forehead. She could feel his lips in her memory.

"But, he could be your son. And, I could be your daughter!" She had elbowed him, hard.

"Age only matters to dragons when they become very old. The Queen never promised me that I'd serve a paladin my own age. The Temple never promised me love, at all. At this point, I'm just grateful to have a paladin to serve, and a lady worth loving. I love you, Ayden." She touched her lips and tried to remember her last kiss with him. It had been while repairing the wagon to carry her bloodstone – the wagon at that point.

Ayden looked at Malcor again. Seline clearly had feelings for him. For a while, before Tembri, Ayden had as well. She felt bad for Seline. She could not imagine what sacrifices a lady knight would be required to make. At one point, in her candidacy tests, the Temple had come to her and offered to test her as a paladin. She had laughed at the idea. It offended the priestess, but Ayden had quickly repaired it. "I'm sorry, my lady, it's just that my whole life, I always knew I'd be best as a fighter. When I fight for the Queen, I feel it is right. I don't see myself that way."

The priestess had smiled and let it go. Ayden realized it still bothered her that everyone treated the clerics that way. That the priestess had let it go had been good, but why did it have to be like that? Ayden knew, from talking with Seline and Tembri, that she would have passed the paladin tests. She tried to imagine replacing two thirds of what she knew about blade combat with Temple doctrine. She shook her head, *I'd be a lousy paladin.*

Except for Desi's hourglass, they lost track of time and took turns monitoring it, and counting. At last, Desi and the clerics indicated they had recovered their focus. "I'd like to allow Marcello total flight so he can explore the area around us," he suggested. "It'd be easy to send others, but Marcello will be quietest."

Ayden asked the thief, "Do you want anyone else to join you?"

Marcello shrugged. "I'm fine either way. Won't be my first solo scouting mission for the empire."

He flew away from them skirting the wall, being careful to get the hang of flying without bumping into the wall. He did not want to lose sight of it for fear he'd get lost. The darkness of this place draped them about so completely, he knew that if he lost his bearings, he'd only be able to find the stairs or the moving lights. Thinking of those, he knew the lights moved because of someone or something. It gave him a sick feeling, but that was where he intended to go.

He also had to keep careful track of the hourglass. Desi had estimated he about twenty turns before he would need to return to the group. Marcello found that if he dragged his leather scabbard along the wall, the souls did not seem to notice. Keeping hand and scabbard on the wall, he shot off straight as an arrow only pausing to reset the hourglass. He noticed after the fifth turn that the wall actually curved and he wondered if the cavern could be a giant circle. By the ninth turn of the hourglass, he noticed that the dots of moving light appeared sharper.

He removed a spyglass from his pocket and steadied himself. At this distance, he could make out two human figures, probably sorcerers by their cowled and flowing robes, working around the edge of a giant stone disk. One finished, and white armor rose up from it – no, not white armor – bone coils. *That must be Bomoki*, Marcello thought. He saw Bomoki move and begin working on a part of the disc close to whatever he had just finished. Bomoki blocked Marcello from getting a good view of the other figure, but he guessed it must be a demi-lich. He looked back at Bomoki and nearly giggled when he saw Ynt'taris' gemmed wand at Bomoki's waist.

He returned to the group, landing with at least two more turns of the hourglass left. Though he intended to tell them everything, it caught him off guard that Ayden questioned him effectively enough that he not only shared everything but did so faster than he would typically. He even found himself explaining his plan with Ynt'taris. Before he knew it, Ayden had pressed him to expound on the story of Farant.

Just as Marcello was about to wax poetic about Ora's beauty and transcendence, he remembered Malcor and stopped. "So, I gave Ora a winter wolf cub. Anyway, from there, things just sort of happened. Ynt'taris wants Bomoki surprised and though I have no idea what the gem will do, I'm sure it will be awful – for Bomoki. The fact it sits at his waist suggests that Bomoki has yet to encounter a paladin worthy of using it against. I wonder where Farant is."

Malcor agreed. "I'd like to have a few words with this Farant as well."

"So, we need to get closer to the gate," Ayden restated their mission. "With those two guarding it, I don't see how we do that without sacrificing another of the party as a distraction. Plus, I doubt the gate would ever be left unguarded."

"Since there is no ceiling, or rather it is impossibly high, and this place is totally dark, I could shadow step or even fly us to the gate as a dragon." Malcor suddenly vanished and reappeared behind Marcello where the faint light cast a long shadow. "There do not seem to be shadows in this area, at least not yet. Distance is sort of relative when I shadow walk. Even as a dragon, I bet I could carry you all there in just several moments."

Sofen commented, "I am loath to willingly sacrifice any of us against two powerful necromancers. The question for you, Sir Malcor, is not whether you can, but if you should. My own studies suggest that higher order undead might be able to control you. Shadow dragons are close enough to undead that even Cor'tanos and Dar Kell cautioned you against shadowshifting at all around anything stronger than a vampire."

Helena continued Sofen's thought. "Dar Rojo allowed me to read the commentary as well. Though they do not know if you are controllable by a necromancer, we are certain that the two at the gate are likely the strongest Tania has ever faced. It would be fatal to us and the mission should anything happen to you."

"It's settled then," Ayden interrupted. "We will only use Malcor's idea should we need to charge the gate. In the meantime, we need to get as close to the gate as possible."

Desi said, "I have some ideas for how to use very low level magic to slide us along the blankets. It'll be very quiet and should prevent the souls from lighting up. Once Marcello sees our speed and progress, he can help me understand how long it will take to get to the side wall closest to the gate. I'm ready for this whenever you are. I prepared only a few combat spells. The rest are tied to moving in a place like this."

"Let's make it happen, team," Ayden ordered. "Desi, let us know what you need us to do."

Progress began slowly but then they moved faster and faster. For the paladins and the others, moving like this tested their patience and calm. Knowing Bomoki worked on the the Gate close by made each second drag. To pass time, Malcor asked Marcello for more details about anything the thief knew about Ora.

Remembering Sai's words of caution and implied threats, Marcello struggled to want to tell Malcor anything. But, then he remembered that Malcor could very well be the next king. *I need him as an ally*, he thought. "She's very powerful, Malcor. And beautiful beyond belief though you already know this. I don't know if you know for sure but my guild believes she is Ynt'taris' rider. I saw her with the white dragon blessing troops as they gated to Bloodstone. It was quite the sight. If you think about it, everyone knows who Dar Shara and Ana are, right? I'd never heard of Ora until suddenly, I'm summoned to Sai's estate and accused of the crimes committed by Farant. It surprised me to learn that a priestess, transcendent like Ora, had been secreted away by the Circle. Makes you wonder how many others there are, out there, waiting. I bet they're all here in Bloodstone now. An army of beautiful if deadly priestesses," he shook his head chuckling.

Eventually, Desi had to stop. Though they could not tell, he admitted he had started making mistakes. They had made good progress by Marcello's estimation and Grito confirmed they had moved a good mile or so. "Hard to tell in this darkness," Grito added.

They rested up and Marcello tried to acquire the gate through his spyglass but they remained too far away for a good look. After a rest, they continued on and reached Marcello's turn back point. Since Desi still had some energy left in him, they began to move away from the wall towards the gate. After three turns of the hourglass, the blankets began to catch and shred and they had to stop. The tile floors had been shattered, as if a mirror of glass. The jagged shards caught and tore the blankets, though the souls remained inert and adrift. Marcello shielded a fragment of light away from the gate and noted, "Besides being shattered, the floor has beads of water on it."

Grito whispered, "I feel growing humidity as well. I expect we'll find a lake or a pool of water ahead of us as the floor dips just a bit towards the gate."

Marcello could see Bomoki perfectly through the spyglass, and the demi-lich. "I can't tell which one looks scarier." He paused and then said, "Bomoki, definitely. The sceptres, if they're like the ones we hear stories about, he must have twenty of them twisted all about his body, like mummy wrap. Maybe more than twenty, some appear to have merged into his body. I saw what necromancy did to Farant. I can't even imagine that level of it." He faked a shudder.

They each took turns looking at the gate. Sofen and Desi both noted that the gate had been ruined and the two necromancers appeared to be repairing it. "Assuming the entire gate were destroyed or in need of repair, they've got about a third left to go."

After watching for more time, Sofen saw the water. "It looks like the gate has sunk and the floor around it is full of water. The actual gate, they've lifted it up." She watched for a while. "There are bones holding it out of the water. It can't be that simple can it?" She turned to them. "What if the gate can't work if even partially submerged?"

Seline cracked her knuckles, "Too bad our mission isn't to destroy it then."

Golcir interrupted Vel Pajor. "I do not mean to be rude, but everything the dragon said is a lie. We have augured the location of the gate. I have already assembled a strike team." Golcir pointed to the map. "The dragon wants the elves and my order searching here." He slid his finger north and east. "This," tapping the gate Malcor's team had entered, "is the most likely place to assault."

Vel sipped his wine. "So, what do you need from Morilon?"

"We need cover. The dragon knows and will notice if my force assaults here. No doubt we're being watched." Golcir looked at the priests of his Order mingled with the elven magi. They wove a tangled and complex web to mask their discussion from anyone watching. "The best way to do this is to have it be legitimate and honest. If you were to come under attack and we pursued your attackers to the correct location, that's what we need."

Vel smiled at him. "I do not see how such a forthright and fastidious Order would accomplish such a thing without inviting evil upon you."

Golcir met the elf's eyes with all seriousness. "We will not invite it. The evil will seek us out. It always does. It always has. Our bright light of devotion draws it to us."

Vel considered turning that around but shrugged and said, "Very well. Your forces will join us at dawn as we ride out to our designated location. We will provide your force the cover required to engage and chase this evil."

The next morning, search and assault teams worked their way to the valley floor and began moving to their assigned areas. Vel cursed the grey sky, which threatened to snow. Even as he looked up at it, a snowflake drifted into his nose. He swatted it away. He imagined he could feel the blight of this cursed valley melting on his skin, and wiped it with a lace handkerchief.

Shining in their armor, the elves and Cuthberic paladins struck a shimmering parade of gold and silver. The paladins sang a hymn of battle against great evil that seemed to center on the founder of their Order, the knight named Cuthbert. Listening, Vel had to hide his amusement as the hymn told the story of Cuthbert's ascension and ultimate battle against a hell lord. Though the attack had ultimately failed, the paladins drew great joy and relish in their singing about it. The hymn rose triumphantly, Vel could not help but imagine Cuthbert trapped in the lower depths of Hell for all time, worshipfully sung by these paladins. The hymn ended with a call to action to enter Hell and recover Cuthbert's remains.

Their assigned mines and tunnels clustered around a box canyon. Their map, current as of last night, had already lost two of the six tunnels, and a new one had appeared. The Tanian mage accompanying them could not place it in Tania's archives, and so marked the keystone and copied it to his book. Golcir requested permission to take the tunnel closest to their actual location.

Vel followed at a distance, overseeing the deployment of his own teams. Better suited to above ground situations, the elves set a strategy to enter in a series of mad dashes. They would then retreat under cover of ranger archers. As a group, they would fall back to the slower moving priests who would call on Krentismar to dispel and turn any evil chasing them. They would repeat this in each complex.

In stark contrast, Golcir and his command walked up to the entrance, and blessed it. They consecrated it in the holy name of Pha Rann and Cuthbert. A priest stepped forward and began to enact a banishment ritual even as another began the more complex act of sanctifying the tunnel. Moving slowly as they did this, the knights walked around the priests with their swords burning like the sun. Even from here, Vel could hear them calling out in unison, "Orcus! Orcus!" Unlike everyone else on the Forsaken Isles, that group did not care if Orcus heard and answered.

Vel decided to keep his forces far away from Golcir's. By noon, the elves had encountered just a few weak undead. They did report a tremendous feeling of being watched, however. The Valley seemed to be holding its breath, waiting and watching.

Meanwhile, and just as Vel ordered their withdrawal and movement to the next complex, the invisible wall around the Cuthberics sizzled and made a thunderous cracking sound. The wall flashed golden iridescent light and, just like that, the knights erupted in daylight flame and counter-attacked whatever it was that had struck at them. Vel signaled his own troops to rush to provide aid but cautioned them, "Remember, these are zealots. Render aid if you can but otherwise stay out of their combat."

Twenty minutes later, Vel's force returned and noted that they found the steaming remains of a hellhound and that the entirety of Golcir's force had pursued another creature to the north and east. Vel sighed and looked up to where he knew Tania would be scrying and said, "Shall we pursue?"

The Tanian mage with him answered. "No, great king. Please complete your sweep of the mines in this area. As we saw, two of them already moved and a new one presents itself. The only way we can ensure these remain fixed is by staying here and keeping them under constant observation."

Vel Pajor nodded and looked back up at the sky. "It shall be as you say." He gave orders for his forces to move to the next tunnel.

* * *

Back in the Temple Fortress, Mallaforax observed, "Vel Pajor chafes under what he sees as an oppressive Morbatten. I do not trust this seeming alliance with the zealots. If anything, they should have been at each other's throats within an hour of being assigned by Andrew to the same Fortress."

Ana looked into her scrying sphere and described the attack by two hellhounds. "They were real hellhounds. Unless you wish to propose that the Cuthberics keep hellhounds just in case, I think we have to assume that their approach proved too tempting for the hellhounds to resist. They were validly attacked in the daytime no less."

Daryx, who sat on a stool by the table covered with maps, spoke up. "Sadly, I've never been able to infiltrate that group. Clearly, they know where the gate is, and decided to put on a little show for us."

Alerius asked if Ayden's Team had been able to locate the gate yet, to which Daryx replied, "I'm sure they have. That deep in Bloodstone, we can't communicate with them but it's clear from Unter's report that they found a perfect location to discover Bomoki's Gate. I recommend we let Golcir continue. They distract to our advantage."

Alerius sighed a very human sigh. "These unruly and unpredictable knights. They are so wearisome. Always the same thing, always the same risks and aggravations. We risk that they destroy the gate."

The others acknowledged the risk but Ana said it best. "They can only damage the gate if they get past Bomoki."

Alerius said, "Send word to Vel Pajor. Request that he focus his efforts in their assigned location and offer reinforcements should they miss the absence of Golcir's knights. Also, send word to Andrew that Golcir has abandoned the plan, and yet again, has put us at risk. Please let King Andrew know that this is the last time Tania will do anything jointly involving the Order of Cuthbert." One of Dar Reznor's mages immediately began a spell that would convey this information to King Andrew. "Actually, send For'ltain to King Andrew. I'd like us to have a more direct line of communication with the young king."

Alerius thought for a moment and then asked Mallaforax, "Brother, would the elves reject assistance from the gold dragons?"

The green patriarch shot back, "They are too weak to reject it." He added, after a few moments, "Of us all, they would welcome the golds the most."

Alerius nodded and a priestess went running to find Dar Jeri. "It will be good for Jeri to get out of this place for a time."

* * *

Golcir summoned his holy war horse as did the others in his group. It arrived as they ran after the hellhound. He leapt onto the charger's back. Once seated, the entire horse ignited with golden fire like the noonday sun and they sprinted after the hound. Golcir knew where the hellhound would go. Golcir took a route easier and faster for the horses. The hound would probably stay in the blighted forest seeking shadow where it could. With Cuthbert's blessing, Golcir would wet his sword in another unholy beast today. Though snow began to fall, the hound still ran during the daytime. Its death would serve and strengthen Heaven.

The knights arrived at the mine shaft just as the hound vanished inside. They could feel it waiting for them. "Remember, this will lead us to more powerful foes. Do not kill it, yet. Let it serve Pha Rann a second time."

Two knights, ridiculously armored and radiating daylight as if they were the sun itself, entered the mineshaft. Four clerics walked behind them praying to Cuthbert to lend them Pha Rann's aid as they pushed the darkness back. The hound snapped at them, summoned all manner of undead servants, and at last tried to gate in another hellhound. Golcir heard the hound scream for another of its kind, but none answered. It struck Golcir as odd. He had fought hellhounds before. They always gated in more of their kind when pressed.

The hellhound and its horde of undead proved no match for Golcir's army of fifty paladins, twenty priests, and five magi. The hound retreated into the mine. Golcir ordered their advance and they pushed into the mine, calling to the hound to repent and face Cuthbert's bright judgement. It interpreted their righteous calls for atonement as mocking ridicule and spat hate back at them, but it could not enter their light. At last, it howled and turned to run.

"This is it," Golcir yelled. "Stay on it!"

Golcir ordered a double time march and they went right past the golden door. The traps reset by Marcello fired but bounced harmlessly off the enchanted armor of the knights. When they came to the corridor of polished tile and garish masks along the walls, they did not even pause. They would resist and persevere no matter what happened.

The hellhound, moving much faster, swept down the corridor of stone masks and activated the trap mechanisms by ordering them to attack. Armed, those traps rained necromantic energy down into the double column of Cuthberic paladins as they chased the hellhound. So bright and powerful was their faith that no one received injury, and most did not even notice the traps firing on them.

Ahead, a great evil suddenly blossomed and Golcir ordered a phalanx formation as they exited the corridor into the great chamber at the top of the stairs. Already, the bodaks shot like dark lightning at them. Their hellhound and the one guarding the top of the stairs, summoned demons and soon beset the Cuthberics knights with the very fury of the Abyss itself.

Golcir's army fought through the tide of necromantic evil. Praying always to Saint Cuthbert, the knights pressed forward even as their brothers fell. Step by step, they advanced towards the stairs. Those fallen were raised by the priests and healed by the next in the line, moving back into the triangle. From this distance, magic wavered and vanished before it touched any of them. Golcir laughed and called out, "Pha Rann blesses us with a warm up!"

They reached the top of the stairs. From the point of the triangle, Golcir jumped out and stabbed a hellhound to death even as the last bodak decapitated the paladin at its right side. Golcir stabbed into the bodak's throat and pulled his sword down through the body of mist and smoke. Pleased to see the bodak ended, Golcir called for a reinforcement and stepped into the mouth of a biting hellhound. At his back, he felt the warm tingle of healing flooding in from the other knights and priests. "This is how it should be, brethren! We wage war to hell's door, and we knock on it!"

Someone cried back, "No, we kick it in!" Golcir's armor spiked and ignited in holy flames as the second hellhound bit down on him. A second later, Golcir's sword cut the remaining hellhound's face apart from nose to jaw.

Pressing forward through waves of hellhounds and summoned creatures, Golcir at last reached the top of the stairs and called out an invitation to whatever evil waited for them in the darkness below. "Repent and we will send you to Heaven's mercy, or be prepared to face judgment!"

Golcir paused and took in the state of his unit. Five paladins had reached their healing limit and passed on to Cuthbert's heaven. All of their armor showed worse for the wear with cracks, punctures, and dents. The clerics busily tended to wounds and healing while the mages did what they could to shore up the worst damage to their armor and weapons. By the time Golcir decided they had won this first engagement, the remaining force reported full health.

"We don't know what awaits at the bottom of the stairs," he began saying, but someone cut him off.

"Who cares, Golcir? We'll send them to judgement!" The others laughed and Golcir smiled at their confidence.

"Bless you, my brothers. Bless you for your faith in our bright Saint Cuthbert and god of us all, Pha Rann." He ignited his sword's holy flames and began the long run down the stairs.

* * *

Far below them, Marcello said, "Hey, something's happening at the stairs." He handed the spyglass to Ayden and he helped her point it to Bomoki.

A pack of hellhounds paced frantically near Bomoki, and conversed with great movement and energy. Without pausing in their repairs, Bomoki said something and the hounds wheeled to charge the stairs. As they did so, the tiles they crossed opened and every manner of incorporeal undead spirit rose up to join them. At the top of the stairs, something bright began to spiral its way down. They saw a two-row column of knights with holy avengers ablaze marching down the stairs.

"Team," Ayden said. "This might be it. Malcor, be ready to charge that gate with us. I leave it to you if you trust your shadow dragon or not."

Watching their brightly lit descent, Malcor said, "I am ready. You have to admire their head-on spirit," Malcor said pointing to the knights. "I have yet to meet one in person, but there's something refreshing about what they're doing."

Seline poked him. "That's how my Order operates. I'm not used to this waiting around and hiding quietly in darkness stuff."

"You think this is easy for me?" Malcor laughed. "We're in one of the most dangerous places I can think of and I feel like a lazy noble on holiday."

Ayden hissed at them, "Quiet. Focus." When all of the Cuthberics had descended at least several flights, the hellhounds and undead attacked the stair's foundation. "No wonder Bomoki did not seem concerned," Ayden whispered. The knights began running, sheathing their swords for better balance and speed.

Ayden and the group sensed a change in their paladins. Both Malcor and Seline had gone tense. Malcor's hand twitched for his sword. "Do you feel that?" Seline asked Malcor.

Eyes wide watching the Cuthberics charge down the stairs, he replied, "Yes! My soul sings to join them. Look at them. This is all I ever wanted when I dreamed of becoming a knight," Malcor whispered.

"To go up against the odds against an enemy like this…" Seline began drawing her sword but Ayden caught her hand.

"Quiet! Both of you, snap out of it. Those are Cuthberic knights. They would attack you just as surely as they intend to attack the undead. Do you want to fight them, or kill The Necromancer?" Ayden's words jarred them a bit and she slapped Malcor and then Seline. "I need you focused, here. We have a mission from the god emperor."

They felt the floor tremble to the point it shook water from the roof overhead and it began to rain. They saw a bright shock and blast at the stair's foundation. The stair's anchor snapped at the top where it attached to the topmost level. The entire structure yawed to the side before torque made it break at its center. Each section falling similarly snapped and then it began smashing into itself. Stone debris exploded everywhere.

A sharp crack reverberated throughout the cavern from that first explosive break. More sound followed until they had to cover their ears. The Tanians held their breath and with a mix of relief and glee saw the Cuthberics leap to the side, running along the stone as it fell and jumping free. As they cleared the falling stairs, they began to float down. "Feather fall," Desi said. "They have mages with them. Good." Ayden almost smacked the elf when she realized he wanted to help them as well.

Still, some of the Cuthberics got stuck in the falling stones that swung out unpredictably or exploded into fragmentation bombs as sections twisted and accelerated sideways. Below, a sea of undead mingled with the hellhounds waited for them. Ayden looked back at Bomoki and said, "I think the entire gate is active, even though a lot of the runes are still damaged. Desi, look."

"Yes, you are correct," he said borrowing the spyglass from Marcello to look. "The sceptres seem to be compensating for the missing runes. You can actually see Bomoki's skin, well, the rotted parts that might be skin. I wonder if that means he is weaker now?"

Bomoki walked back to a tripod of three sceptres and the demi-lich joined him. They began casting a spell. The entire stone disk began to shimmer with burning green flames. "Say when, Captain Ayden," Malcor offered.

"Patience, paladin. Patience. We'll know it is time when the gate opens. Either the Jade God comes through, or we go through. We'll wait and see and stay true to Dar Rojo's orders." She patted Malcor on the shoulder. "We're going to do Tembri proud."

They all nodded and said reverently, "For Tembri."

Spells blasted down from the Cuthberics into the undead. A mage transmuted the falling debris into mud. The twisting stone of perhaps twenty flights of stairs melted to liquid and fell. Once it splashed, covering everything in mud, the mage reversed it to stone. "Brilliant," Desi said. "That'll cement most of the weak ones and slow down the hellhounds!" Another mage summoned a wall of stone that hung laterally in the air before gravity caught it. It fell flat crushing all their enemies beneath them. Again, a terrible crack and boom as the wall shook the cave. Crystals from the ceiling began to rain down, adding to the din. The Tanians had no idea if any of it mattered but it looked impressive at this distance.

Turning their attention back to the gate, they saw the stone in the disk's center crumble apart. It fell free leaving the hallmark green color of the Jade God glowing. Whatever probed the other side backed away from the green center, for a moment, before it began to push through. They saw the center bulge outward. The outer stone of the gate began to break apart again.

Bomoki flew from the tripod to the crumbling upper section of the gate. The sceptres entwining his body tore apart and affixed him, somehow to the outer edge. Knit together by tendon, organs, bone, and skin, Bomoki's half-human body screamed in agonizing torment as the gate expanded through his skin and bones. The demi-lich stayed by the tripod and continued to enact whatever spell the two had started before the gate's activation. Through the noise of the battle and falling crystal shards, they heard Bomoki scream in terrible agony.

"Not yet," Ayden whispered. Her hand dug into Malcor's forearm. "Don't you dare move, paladin."

The Cuthberics reached the floor and a battle of magic and divine powers clashed with necromantic creatures. Ayden's team, they all wanted to help, to see better. Grito just shook his head. "Stay focused on our mission. This is how we win. Let the Cuthberics fight their battle."

The gate, reinforced by Bomoki, now expanded three times its original diameter. The Abyss on the other side, at last, tore through. Malcor crouched down, ready to shift. The others gathered around where his shoulders would be. "On your command, Ayden," he said.

A black talon came through first, filling the gate, and pressing its edges open wider. Bomoki's screams became a silent howl of agony. From the gaping hole, the torn skin of the gate flapped in and out, as if the gate breathed. Then, power – terrible power – burst through. Harnessing the power into his breaking body, Bomoki pulled himself off the gate and re-joined the demi-lich by the tripod. The gate continued to expand faster now as Bomoki redirected its energy to enlarging. At the same time that the gate enlarged, a beam of energy washed through the gatekeepers towards the undead horde fighting Golcir's party.

Ayden's team watched as the Cuthberics drew together and then catapulted Golcir and four others out of the combat towards the gate. A portal opened near Golcir and, as they landed and charged the gate, a winged creature resembling what Malcor imagined an angel might look like flew out to join Golcir's charge. Sofen remarked, "It's not often you see a divine presence like that. I think it's what we call a *Deva*, a divine servant able to intervene in Tehra. Golcir must hold a level of favor I've never heard of before."

"It's not that," Helena commented. "It's the foe they face."

"This is how cascades begin," Desi cautioned. "I doubt Tania wants one to happen in here. If the angel summons another, or the hellhounds begin summoning…"

Bomoki and the demi-lich began attacking Golcir with ranged spells. The demi-lich, seeing the Deva, changed its approach and sprouted skeletal bat wings. It launched into the air and smashed into the Deva.

"Come on," Ayden said. "This is our chance to edge closer." They began to magically slide through the water towards the gate, mindful of ripples.

Necromantic spells clashed with divine and magical defenses. Some attacks were batted aside by the Deva, while others smashed into Golcir and then fizzled away into nothingness. The magical and divine energy concentrated between the lich and angel intensified until the two grappled each other in the air and smashed down to the floor. Behind them, the main groups continued to rage back and forth, but slowly moving towards the gate.

Marcello suddenly got very excited and began chanting, "Do it. Do It. DO IT!" When Golcir finally drew close enough that Bomoki had to switch tactics, Bomoki grabbed the diamond wand at his belt. Marcello grabbed Malcor's arm and was pointing. "DO IT you sick bastard!" he screamed at Bomoki.

Ayden told him "Shut up!" but she could not take her eyes away from Bomoki as Desi scooted them closer and closer. Behind Golcir, the gate finally stopped expanding at a diameter of about a hundred paces. The enervating and burning power shooting through the claw's tear in the gate stopped. The silent horde of undead, eerie in its quiet charge, gave them the briefest moment of clarity and then Bomoki pointed the wand at Golcir.

They were close enough they could see Golcir's sober expression as he raised his sword. The diamond in Bomoki's Wand twinkled, and then detonated. Desi stopped what he was doing and threw a powerful protective magic around the group even as Sofen and Helena both called for sanctuary protection from magic.

The shockwave of the detonating ice diamond hit them, numbing their skin with cold, and blanketed the chamber in ice. The water immediately froze and thankfully, it was shallow enough that they broke free after some struggle.

Bomoki, the demi-lich, and Golcir appeared, for just a moment, held in crystalline ice clear and transparent. The undead fighting all around, froze skidding across the ice to slam into the others while the floor of the cavern glazed over and went frictionless. As those frozen in crystalline ice smashed into each other, they broke to pieces. Another shockwave occurred as the first blast's vacuum sucked the warm cavern air back in. It pulled the frozen Cuthberics and undead towards Bomoki. It accelerated them in their slide, over ice now, towards the gate.

"Look!" Sofen pointed. "Even the spirit undead have frozen. Wow!"

The second shockwave finally shattered the diamond gem as another freezing wave of non-energy blew out. Desi's and the others protective magics failed and at the last instant, Malcor pulled them from the River. In that place's weird flat view, they saw how all heat, even the gate itself went absolutely cold. Devoid of energy, the gate sat inert, even the breathing hole torn through it did not move.

Chapter Sixty Four – Bomoki's Gate

It took a second for sound and sight to recover from the freezing blast. The entire cavern, so quiet it ached, magnified a snort from the gate's other side. A titanic hoof of a goat's leg stepped through. From out of the River, Ayden's team saw Orcus leering down at them. A hand reached to grab them.

With the sound of shattering glass, the gate unfroze. Malcor returned them to the real world. A three-headed sceptre of ram's heads, longer than one of the fortresses, came through the gate at them. Its ram's head eyeing the frozen creatures before it. It laughed and then a fist came through the gate followed by the rest of Orcus. Though the ground was so cold it began to hurt them, they laid flat and prayed to their gods that Orcus would forget about them.

All around, tens of thousands of tiles shattered and millions of souls rose up into the air and dove into Orcus' inhaled breath. Orcus looked down and poked Bomoki with the sceptre. "Bomoki," the god growled. It knocked his tiny frozen form over and Orcus laughed.

"Join me on the surface," the god ordered. "When you unfreeze." His words susurrated over the horde and even the Tanians felt a compulsion to move to the surface. Thankfully, it had not been directed at them specifically. They had no doubt that when Bomoki unfroze, they would all be compelled to join Orcus on the surface.

The sceptre's head pivoted to the Tanians. Maybe it felt their compulsion to obey? "Now, Malcor!" Ayden said.

In a blink, Malcor shadowstepped. They did not have time to properly get on his back. Several of his friends screamed in pain as shadow claws grabbed them, and then Malcor was at the gate. The Sceptre of Orcus breathed green fire at where the party had been and Orcus swept his hand towards it. A line of destruction shot towards them, and then they were through the gate.

Orcus watched the gate for just a moment and then turned his head to look up. "I. Am. Here."

* * *

Back in the Temple Fortress, Ynt'taris suddenly lit up. "It happened! My revenge is complete!" Alerius looked sideways at him but before the ice patriarch could explain, the ground trembled as an earthquake rolled through Bloodstone. The air suddenly became pregnant and heavy. Alerius touched his bloodstone earring and shouted, "Orcus is here. All of you, retreat to the Fortresses now! Anyone in the valley, recall out now! Dread Lords, to me!"

Alerius jumped out of the command room's window and dragonshifted to rise up over the Temple. Throughout the valley floor, green cracks began to rip through the ground. "Ana," Alerius called. "Evacuate Valley Town immediately."

Around Alerius, the other dread lords and their riders assembled as they climbed higher and higher into the sky. The riders carried impossibly long lances with more bundled to the dragon's armor near the riders' saddles. Below them, the faster but less hardy griffins circled, each carrying a Tanian knight descended from Shak D'Rath.

Below them, in the center of the valley, the ground rose up. It upheaved once, twice, and then the third time, the sceptre's head broke through. Three faces of the sceptre spat green fire into the valley filling it with necromantic compulsions. Anything it touched, died and rebirthed as an undead. The trees and plants, insects, hibernating animals inhaled the fire and rose up as desecrated and blighted corpses. The crackling green fire filled the valley to the level that no trees could be seen. Then, a claw pulled the earth to the side and the horns of Orcus began to rise up.

Alerius called back to Ana, "Tell Reznor, this is the moment his guild must shine."

From atop the Temple Fortress, the Mage's Guild finished a powerful spell and sent its power to Reznor. He held and caught it just one syllable shy of activation. The cataclysm along the valley floor continued as Orcus' shoulders emerged and a hand swatted at the griffins. They felt a terrible will seeking for them all to end their lives, give up the resistance. Orcus bent forward to pull its leg out of the cavern far below. All around them, the sceptre's three faces laughed maniacally. One screamed back to Orcus, its words somehow understood, "Orcus, the sun of this world defies you!"

Orcus answered, "Then baptize the sun in my image."

At that moment where Orcus' hand pressed on the valley floor, Reznor released the last activation syllable of the spell. Where Valley Town had been, a volcano erupted under Orcus' hand. A pyroclastic cloud smashed into the god, momentarily blinding him. The god's hand submerged into the growing volcano.

"All forces, attack!" Alerius' simple command triggered it all.

Catapults and ballistae from the Fortresses all around fired. Though the attacks would hardly hurt the god, their purpose was distraction. Griffins and dragons alike dove towards the back of Orcus's shoulders as the god struggled to stand. The griffin riders threw their lances and then split off to clear a channel of attack for the dragons, who tore into the back of Orcus with fire, ice, acid, and poison along with slashing claws augmented by the bloodstones.

The paladins riders jumped off and landed their lances into Orcus' back as they became the center of flamestrikes cast by the battle clerics riding the dragons. Still, that horrid first compulsion to end their lives struck a few. Some of the paladins turned their swords on themselves. Nearly a third of the griffins just stopped flying and let their bodies fall to the ground.

Orcus felt the attacks and reached up with his hand to knock them off, the way a human might shoo a biting fly away. Molten lava splashed about as he did so. Ash began raining with the dead and dying bodies falling around the god. From the giant hole, wraiths rose up like tornadoes of black death. The sunlight burned them and so they sought shaded areas under their god.

Siege weapons began to land, detonating all around Orcus from every direction. Most were designed to dazzle and disorient, but a few carried more potent magic. The first gate opened in answer to the Necromancer. The Avatar Sun of Saint Cuthbert, and those paladins bound to him in Heaven, fell from the sky onto the beast of undeath.

Still struggling to get out of the hole, Orcus lifted his other leg and at last had secure footing. The titanic god breathed out a mist of deadly insects from his mouth in such quantity that the dragons could not dent it. That was when the next gate opened.

Ana saw it in her scrying stone and signaled Crimson. He slid a tower stone from the back corner to her throne. Around her, the Temple doors sealed shut. Touching the tower stone, Ana sent a blast of magic energy into the gate so that it opened longer than it should. A shining human figure stepped out and dropped to the ground. A sword appeared in his hand and, as it fell, other gates opened around as thirteen more humans stepped out. "Welcome, Hellstar Avatar of Saint Kargoth," Ana said. "Happy hunting."

With the first of many gates open, others began to open summoning gates. Where Kargoth opposed Cuthbert, another deity from Heaven opposing Kargoth sent its avatars into the battle. Those avatars, noticing Orcus, summoned additional help. All around Bloodstone, gates blazing cardinal auras of the gods they served slid open and closed as more and more joined, piling on in opposition to each other. Ana fed these gates with the tower stone, holding them open longer than they should be – adding to the nexal power each contributed to the war.

"Crimson, I've never seen this before." In her scrying stone, a scintillating rainbow of colored gates opened spinning in the air as extraplanar powers, gods, and their servants answered the challenge of the Jade God. Some, like Kargoth, they expected. Others came as a total surprise to Ana who dictated the arrivals as she recognized them. "Alerius," she spoke to the god emperor through the stone. "All of our allies and bonded contracts are here. You'll be pleased to know that Ayden's team successfully pulled Daryx's group through. Also, be on your guard. Several planetars from the creation nexus just arrived. I recognized one as belonging to the All Father."

"Ana, join the hunt." Though their connection, Ana saw Alerius dive towards Orcus and then her scrying sphere cracked in half.

"Come Crimson, it is time we visit your hellfire on Orcus!"

Grabbing Twilight Fell and Nightmare of Chaos as her swords, Ana jumped onto Crimson's back. Together, they exited the Temple dome. She saw Alerius begin to breathe flames at Orcus. Impossibly, Orcus' hand blocked the fire and even though a paladin lanced it, Orcus caught the god emperor. Though large for the titan's hand, the scale of it shook Ana to her core, to see the mighty god emperor small enough to be held. She knew Orcus would be big, but this seemed impossible. Crimson Burning screamed and sped towards Alerius. Eldritch fire of the sort Crimson rarely used ignited around them.

Everyone heard Orcus say, "Why did you not break already? Break now, little bird." Orcus' thumb slid back and shattered Alerius' shoulder wing. They saw Orcus squeeze to crush the dragon. But, Alerius vanished from his hand as the word, "Contingency" boomed in the air all around. Alerius' wing fell from the Necromancer's blood wet hand, twisting to the valley floor. Orcus looked around and then fixated on the Temple roof where Alerius reappeared. "You are dead," Orcus said. A moment of confusion crossed the god's face. *The tiny dragon still lived. How?* Orcus looked to the blood in his hand and back to where Alerius stood on the Temple. "Die, tiny bird. Why won't you die?" Orcus said, reaching his bloodied hand towards Alerius and the Temple.

Crimson and Ana smashed into Orcus' eye. Crimson's breath weapon shot forward as momentum and fury pulled Crimson into the eye socket. Fluid burst and then boiled around them. Ana imagined she heard Orcus scream, though not really in pain as much as she prayed it would be pain.

She set her lifeforce tether to Crimson and leapt into Orcus' eye. Her goddess armor and bloodstones lit her way as she slashed into what should have been an eye but instead looked like an underwater cavern ringed with hellhound heads.

As Crimson breathed, Ana prayed to the Queen. "Fire storm!" Orcus went to swat the dragon away with its sceptre. Still, the eye cavity filled with fire, and Ana's hope rose as her sword began raking the thousands of hellhound eyes within. Gleefully, she sent Rojo's and Verit's swords against the eyes. Like Dar Tania so long ago, her tether stretched out as Crimson dodged the sceptre and flew free of Ocrus. With a final blown kiss, she released her own blade to continue attacking from inside the eye socket. Lifeforce tethers began feeding her Orcus' energy as the three blades reaped a harvest of eyes. "Recall," she whispered and reappeared on Crimson's back. Touching him and praying, she whispered in draconian, "Recall." Both she and Crimson vanished from the eye and reappeared atop the Temple dome.

Crimson had been terribly wounded by one of the god's smashing horns as he dove in for their initial attack. Ana redirected health and vitality to the mighty dragon. "Crimson, you're glorious! The All Father is watching and no doubt trembling at the sight of you!" Her healing, channeled from the damage done to Orcus, smoothed the dragon's flight back up into the sky. Crimson roared and a thermal updraft jumped them thousands of feet higher. She could tell Crimson had more to give. Around her, she looked and finally saw Alerius. He had recalled to the Temple's rooftop. Dar Reznor and other magi stood with him. "God emperor, what do you require?" Ana asked through her bloodstone earring.

"We must keep it fixated on us until Daryx is done. It is time for the three vampire generals to go home." Alerius had an edge of tension in his voice. It took Ana a moment to realize she was hearing pain. In her long life, she could not remember the god emperor ever being in pain.

Reznor and Alerius opened a gate and Ana saw the three vampires step through. Immediately, Orcus' sceptre shot hate at them and they felt the beginning of subjugation. The barrage from the siege weapons suddenly changed as the minotaurs in the Third Fortress used the catapults to launch their berserkers at Orcus. A giant gate began to open in front of Orcus. Rain and water poured through it, and then a Tauran world galleon sailed through to spear into Orcus. Wind and rain lashing it from the ocean behind blasted its titanic sails. A gleaming bloodstone statue set on the ship's prow gleamed through haze of battle.

As the giant stone ship fell like a spear, it ignited with magic. A giant skeletal minotaur held the tallest mast, sword in hand, as the ship and their god speared Orcus through his belly. At impact, hundreds of minotaurs leapt off the destroyed galleon and set flesh hooks into the Necromancer. Ana touched her earring and spoke the Tauran god's sacred name, "Morbatten and Takhissis thank the mighty Bapthomet for joining! Hail, Blade of Stars!"

Orcus turned to swing the galleon as if a club. Fragments of the ship broke off and sailed from that arc to smash throughout the valley. Baphtomet, Devil Lord of the Fourth Hell, rose up to grapple Orcus.

Orcus lurched to the side and smashed his sceptre at the Fifth Fortress. Ana winced as rock vaporized. The gnomes there, and the entire fortress, she could not imagine. Overhead, Spark dove at Orcus to distract the attack but when it became too late, Spark transformed into blue lightning that shot into Orcus' other eye. A tornado of shadows and hellhounds running on those shadows rose up and pulled Baphtomet off Orcus. They fell from view into the poison mist below.

The brilliant blue of Spark's strike pulsed and snapped so bright and loud it drowned out everything else going on. Orcus lurched backwards, his free hand rising up to grab his wounded eye. Seeing the god blinded, the three vampire generals vanished from the Temple rooftop to begin their gambit to seize control of Orcus' throneplane.

Orcus dragged his sceptre across the causeway towards the Fourth. "Why does the Tehran Star resist me? Orcus howled. He shook the sceptre. "Take it now!" The sceptre smashed into the Fourth Fortresses, but the fire giants there swarmed along the sceptre, attacking the three ram's heads' eyes. Both the Fifth and Fourth Fortresses, and the causeway between them collapsed to ruin.

Alerius spoke to the holders of bloodstones. "The Court of Dragons and all dread lords, I am crippled but will be with you in spirit. Rise up and attack on Ana's mark. Target the sceptre! Reznor, it is time for the next phase."

* * *

Dar Kendra stood with the Order of Water along the causeway between the First and Second Fortresses. Kerchki, the fire giant sentinels serving Alerius, stood with her. The enormity of Orcus took their breath away. They had known the god would be titanic, but conflict over the centuries with the giant hellhounds - much larger than wolves but still not titanic - had conditioned them to perhaps expect their god would be similar. Three members of the Mage's Guild ruling council stood beside Shara, waiting for her to give them the order.

The hellish scene unfolding before their eyes turned the giant dread lords into mere bats diving and annoying the Jade God. The unholy gas filling the valley no doubt would slay and turn anything living into undead. "The Legion's dog soldiers?" Kendra asked. Volcanic ash and burning gases rained throughout. No dog soldier could survive there. She knew they had just lost an entire legion of young men and women.

One of the mages leaned forward and said, "We have activated all bloodstones and dealings with the elementals from the plane of Earth. As they find soldiers with the mark of the Nineteenth, they will encapsulate and hold them until either this ends, we release them, or the elemental is slain."

"There are enough to guard the entire legion? Impressive." Kendra pointed to the sceptre which, though held by Orcus, fought its own battles as the dragons and their riders attacked it. From below, skeletal griffins rose up, terrible in their undead transformation, to engage the aerial fighters.

The mage's answer of "Indeed" came across so unassuming that Kendra laughed at him. "You have enough elementals bound to guard our legion and that's all you say? You missed your calling as a jester."

High above, they saw Crimson circle. Ana would no doubt be looking at the entire situation and coordinating the various dread lords. Though Morbatten had successfully shown that rulership by dragons worked, in the midst of combat, it became more difficult. Mallaforax and Screem in particular had never really fought alongside the others. The fierce independence of the colored dragons added to the complexity of it all. So far, attacks had been sporadic. One of Kendra's paladins pointed and said, "It looks like she finally got them all to agree."

In coordination, all of the dread lords rose up to the height of Crimson's banking turn. Though Orcus spat his hatred at them, he could not reach them. He pointed his sceptre at the sun burning high in the sky. It momentarily darkened. Everyone felt it. "Orcus is trying to control the sun here. We've seen this before," Kendra said. "He'll alter the daylight to protect the undead. It will also make him omniscient for all things under his green sun. We are running out of time, mage. Begin your spellcasting."

Ana must have seen it too. Her voice came to Kendra and the mages through the bloodstone earrings. "We must break the sceptre now. Have the magi ensure our success."

Kendra turned to the three mages. "It's your turn," she said. Soldiers brought chained prisoners onto the causeway. Each had a sack over their heads. Though they looked strong and healthy, they each had an air of resigned despair about them. They knew they had a death sentence. They did not know in what form it would arrive.

The three mages divided the convicts, and with small blades, caught drops of blood onto immaculate scrolls of gold, pressed so thin as to be like paper. Draconian writing flowed throughout the gold. When the blood dripped onto the three scrolls, the letters filled in with glaringly red blood against the gold papers. Above, the dragons continued to climb in altitude.

It took many long moments for enough blood to gather and fill in the engraved runescript. When they at last finished, the mages walked to the edge of the causeway to squarely face Orcus. Acolytes shackled the three mages' hands and feet to the six prisoners in each group.

A priestess standing with the prisoners prayed for them. "Whatever reason brought you to this point, know that your life goes to ending the Jade God and its supernal threat against Tania, the world, and your loved ones. By letting your life end here, you shall arise to Tiamat's glory and welcome. Recite with me…" and she led them in a clerical prayer of combining their lives to the mages.

When the priestess signaled all had been done as required, each mage held up his scroll and in a loud voice, called to Orcus and the sceptre, shouting in draconian for many long minutes before at last speaking. The first said, "I wish that there shall be a weak point in the sceptre's handle midway between the haft and head."

The second mage then spoke, "I wish that the next attack by all dragons present, flawlessly strike the sceptre's weak point." The wishes tore at their voices and the prisoners' lives burned away behind the caster. Normally, the cost of the spell would consume part of the sorcerer's life.

The third mage shouted out his wish, "I wish that sceptre shall break at its weak point…" and he paused, watching the combat unfold in the sky above them.

Throughout the valley, Orcus spoke. "What is wrong with you? The sun is already mine but is not. These birds are all dead, but they are not. It cannot both be and not be."

The sceptre answered, "This world is not endless. Remember, time flows. Until you kill the birds, they are not yet dead…"

Chapter Sixty Five – Dragonstrike the Sceptre

The dragons had climbed up impossibly high into the sky. Around them, the light suddenly shifted as the very sun became sick and green. From the ruins of the two fortresses, Orcus called his unholy servants to rise, to fight. Kendra's voice came to them, "Dragons, now!"

Circling high overhead, Ana heard Kendra and commanded the flight of dragons to attack Orcus. They streaked straight at Orcus and just as they reached the extreme range of Orcus being able to attack them, black doorways opened in front of the dragons. They passed through these and reappeared just under the three rams making up the sceptre's head. Bloodstone staves, lances, swords, blades, and other enchanted attacks borne by dragons and the fury of chromatic breath weapons hit the haft there in the same spot. Jeri's sisters, fighting demons summoned by the darker members of the cascade, found their attacks suddenly land on the sceptre's grip. Being so close to the Jade God, they whirled away to find enemies they could engage.

Expecting the attack, Orcus raised his sceptre to block, defend, and counter-attack. "Then," Orcus screamed at the dragons, "let's kill the birds dead!" It set the sceptre up perfectly for strike after strike that tore metal and bone from the haft. Orcus tried to attack, to blast them with necromantic death, but no matter what he did, those black gates positioned the dragons perfectly to strike, not him, but the same spot on his sceptre.

Under the green sun's light now, Orcus knew the dragons attempted to cut the device in two and break its magic. Forged from the bones of gods he personally slew before time began, the sceptre held his connection to his abyssal throneplane. The knowledge brought a small doubt to his mind. In this cursed place, he could not change the sequence of events, though he tried instinctively. Orcus' failed expectation that things would change on his whim made him sluggish in responding to the battle.

The black dragon, Screem, hit the sceptre last of all. "…now," the third mage completed his Wish spell. Screem's acid breath and bloodstone enhanced talons drilled into the angry bone and metal of the sceptre, where blood flowed as if in an arm.

The sceptre raged at Screem, turning to spit destruction and pain as all the others had dodged similar counter-attacks. Below the sceptre's head, Screem's acid breath ate through the last binding tendon and bone. Bending and torqueing slowly at first, and then faster with a rending sound of snapping bones, the sceptre tore in half at the weak point. There, at that spot, a black sphere of energy pulsed and grew until it detonated in a brilliant green ball of light, sound, and fire. The blast almost knocked Orcus down, but he steadied himself on the volcano's summit even as he dropped to one knee.

Immediately, the sun's twisted green halo seemed less oppressive. Orcus shook his head and blinked seeing the dragons flying away from their attack – not on him – but on his treasured sceptre. Orcus clutched the ruined sceptre like a club. He swatted at the dragons but they were already too far away. Remembering the volcano, Orcus grabbed the summit and threw magma at them.

Burning fragments tore through the dragons' wing membranes and then began smashing like meteors into the Fourth and Fifth Fortresses. "Yes, I remember. How I despise Time!" Orcus screamed at the yellowing sun.

* * *

While this surface attack occurred, Ayden's team activated the teleportation beacons and welcomed Daryx and his specialist paladins to Orcus' realm. With great haste, Daryx and his team unrolled sceptre after captured sceptre and wands. They raced to embed these in the ground all around the gate.

And then, the three vampire generals came through. Without a word, they vanished from the area around the gate. When Malcor got close to Daryx, Daryx called out, "King Malcor, the Abyss cannot tolerate the absence of the Jade God. If we are successful, we would help replace our enemy with a friendlier abyssal power. I'll explain it to you later."

It felt both wrong and right to Malcor at the same time and he made a note to discuss it when all this ended. "Wait, what do you mean *king*?" Malcor yelled at Daryx. The dark elf had sprinted over to one of the sceptres and placed a bloodstone gem in its mouth. His team raced to place one in each of the sceptres.

Daryx ignored Malcor and shouted back, "All of you, recall to the Temple and rejoin the fight, now!" Daryx shouted to them all.

As they all began to vanish, Malcor stood watching, sword drawn in an attitude of readiness until just he and Daryx remained. "I cannot go back," Malcor said. "I sense the Queen would want me to do something else."

Daryx shrugged. "Do what you must, my king." Daryx held a bloodstone in his hand. "Malcor, Rojo fell in the battle. You are now king. They'll explain it to you later."

Malcor began to ask more when Daryx pushed him through the gate back into Bomoki's chamber. "We are running out of time," Daryx said.

Malcor fell atop the sheet of ice locking everything in the gate chamber. Behind him, a bright light lit up the gate before it turned to stone and collapsed on its face. Falling flat, it fragmented on the frictionless floor of ice. Malcor shadowstepped to avoid falling debris and ended up near the tripod. He saw Jeri's eye there and retrieved it.

"Coming Undone," he called as he decapitated the sceptres in the tripod. He walked over to inspect Bomoki, but doing so felt wrong. Turning his head, he noticed Bomoki's sceptres from around the gate's edge struggling on the frictionless floor. They seemed weaker, and Malcor severed their heads.

Next, Malcor's sense of purpose pulled him to the demi-lich. Though frozen, Malcor felt it regard him. The bright green gem of its heart lit the ice around its breast. Seline had told him about the demi-liches and with great pleasure, Malcor called on the Queen for strength and then stabbed the lich through its spine just below the skull.

"This won't kill you, yet," he said. Though frozen, the heartstone in the lich's chest cavity still gleamed and Malcor felt what must be fear. He slowly lined his sword up with the emerald heart. "I wonder if you've had time to reset your contingency for this?" Slowly, he chanted out Coming Undone's full name. "For my friend, Seline, and for my teacher, Tembri," he said and drove Coming Undone into and through the gem.

For the third time that day, an explosion rippled through the cavern. It tumbled Malcor back an impossible distance and when he stood, it was on unsure and shaking feet that immediately slipped on the slick floor. The ice had started to melt. From above, lava began pouring through the splintered cavern ceiling.

He shadowstepped back to Bomoki noting how close he had come to dying. He almost struck Bomoki but something stayed his hand and he questioned it, asking the Goddess for direction. None came, so he decapitated the gatekeeper - to be safe - and turned to Golcir. Golcir stood frozen in the act of slicing his sword in line with the demi-lich's heartstone. Malcor did a quick movement through the shadows to check for survivors. It showed that only seven of the Cuthberics had survived. The others were in the act of turning or had indeed turned already when Ynt'taris' ice bomb froze them. Freeing them felt right and he realized he felt this from the angel feather in his sword. "Okay, but only to honor you, Shining One. I do not think they would do this for me." Malcor said as he stroked the feather.

He also noticed movement in the floor beneath an intact tile. Vampire Farant glared up at him. Malcor recognized him instantly from the drawings sent by the Temple. His heart sang and he stabbed Coming Undone into the tile. It shattered as his sword ripped the magic imprisonment free. Farant immediately leapt out raking at Malcor and starving for blood.

"Stop," Malcor said as he pointed his sword's holy symbol at Farant. Farant seemed to be trying to do something within his abdomen. "You still have the bloodstone?" Malcor began laughing. The stress and exhaustion of all that had happened weighed on him, and here stood a vampire he had coveted slaying. "Marcello told me about that. You know it's flawed, right?"

Farant struggled to attack Malcor but could not. Malcor said, "You'll pay for what you've done." Malcor whispered a prayer to Takhissis and then commanded the vampire Farant, "Present the stone to me." Farant, against his will, opened his arms and showed the bloodstone faintly glowing in his guts.

Malcor stepped out of the River and burst back to stab the stone with Coming Undone from behind. Already cracked and brittle, it exploded within the vampire's body, which acted as a shield for Malcor. "Flawless revenge," Malcor spat at the remains.

Malcor moved back to the others and wished he had better knowledge of what to do. "Alerius and the others spent considerable time seeking out this one," he reasoned. He looked at Bomoki's body and the head, slowly thawing on the floor.

After a moment, he raised Coming Undone and began to hack at the creature. Severing the frozen legs, then hands, Malcor carefully broke Bomoki to pieces. Each piece, he wrapped and placed in Desi's backpack, grateful he had grabbed it before they left. Holding the severed head, Malcor chipped the eyes, tongue, and ears away, and then wrapped the head in holy symbols from his armor. These, he placed in different bags.

He expected the work to be gory but frozen beyond freezing, and with his sword's ability to slice magic, he made fast work of Bomoki. Half of Bomoki's body was desiccated. Dry and skeletal, that half seemed to feed off the human part. Malcor carefully left both halves as close to equal as he could. Finishing that, he likewise dismembered the demi-lich, at least the parts that remained after he cut through and destroyed its emerald heart. That left the hellhounds and the Cuthberics, frozen like glacial statues.

Shadowstepping, Malcor quickly decapitated all of the hellhounds. He ended back by the gate. There, he gathered up all the ram's heads from the sceptres and wrapped them in a blanket. It seemed a bad idea to leave them here. He bowed his head and prayed, "I'm torn. There is great evil here that could be revived, but also great good. Do I prevent the great evil that might happen if the sceptres and gate are reactivated, or do I take measures to save the Cuthbert knights?"

He stepped out of the River and away from the flow of time. The energy current moved in fits and starts. Above him, at an impossible distance, he saw the titan Orcus fighting as gates spun and opened all around. The part of the River closest to him upheaved and he saw the faces of Tanian knights in the act of combat against undead gnomes and minotaurs. One seemed to see him and called out, and then the River froze. It was a glimpse of what must be, but not something that had happened yet. All around, he felt a heavy pressure that weighed him down with murderous intent. Orcus called the living, "Die and serve me forever. I'll take all your concerns and pain away, endlessly."

All around, Time stuttered. It hurt Malcor's head trying to make sense of it. He fell back into the River knowing he would not get an answer there. He gathered all the Cuthberics, those alive or not yet turned, and bound them with magical rope. He then placed his own recall beacon on the floor and dragonshifted. Gathering them as close as he could in dragon form, he touched and activated his recall token.

* * *

The Temple looked alien under the green sun. Malcor looked around struggling to get his bearings. The sunlight hurt but also enhanced his darkvision. It made Orcus and so many other powerful entities glare in stark three dimensional auras so bright and so dark, too many colors.

He returned to human form and thanked Tiamat when a Dar priestess rushed forward to him. He began to speak, asking for Dar Rojo, but the priestesses dropped to the ground at his feet in the most formal of Tanian salutes. Hands on the ground and kneeling, she removed from her ear and presented a bloodstone earing to him. "King Malcor, this will put you in contact with your empire."

When he stabbed it through his ear, he felt the screaming, crying, and commanding voices of thousands all around him. "I need to consult with my command. Where are they?" he asked the priestess, not activating his voice through the earring yet.

The priestess looked up at him, and then as if receiving divine inspiration, she stood and dismissed the other priestesses to take the Cuthberic knights away to a sanctuary until their stasis could be safely removed. To Malcor, she stated. "Dar Rojo has fallen. He named you King. Do not get overly consumed by this as we fight for our lives. I sense you brought us something dark and vile."

She touched his bloodstone earring and it went quiet. "Focus on who you wish to communicate with and then touch the earring. It will send your thoughts – so guard them, or you can speak. Rojo mostly spoke rather than risk his thoughts confusing his purpose. For now, let's handle the dark thing you carry."

Malcor nodded and pulled Bomoki's still frozen and maimed head out of his bed roll pack. "This is Bomoki. I did not feel it wise to leave the gatekeeper near the gate."

The priestess withdrew her mantle and wrapped the head asking if Malcor had the rest of the gatekeeper's body. He nodded and told her about the ram's heads and demi-lich parts too.

"Come with me," she said and led him to the heart of the Temple. He expected her to open the doors but noted they had been sealed shut. Instead, she accessed a secret door to the side and they descended to a vault directly underneath Ana's throne. A tower stone almost twenty paces in diameter shone in the room and surrounding it lay hundreds more. They placed Bomoki's remains there. "Only a select few know of this place," the priestess said reverently.

When they returned to the surface, Malcor found that Dar Shara had returned from the skies. A young priest with dark eyes and a familiar presence stood by her as did his team members. Not obvious, Daryx stepped forward from behind Ayden and Seline.

Daryx saluted Malcor and congratulated him on completing a part of the quest. "It did not occur to me to do what you did, my liege. Truly, you wage an inspired battle against The Necromancer."

"I am not ready to serve as if Dar Rojo," Malcor said. "It's too much. But, my heart sings to fight. Tell me, Daryx, where might I find the lances and join combat?"

His next thought was interrupted by Ora who rushed him into a tight hug. He had never seen her in battle dress and it took a minute for him to connect the pieces of the war that had brought them together. "I always think of you enshrined in sunlight, not war," he said to her at last after returning her kiss.

Ora's look of worry, concern, and everything else took his breath away. "Mal, I've heard so much about your adventures. I wish we had more time, but my duties call me back to the skies." Behind them, Ynt'taris landed and dipped to allow a paladin there to gather more lances. She kissed him again, crushing him to her and he wondered how he had never felt her strength. "Goodbye, for now." She touched her belly. "Your son is safe." She blew him a kiss as Ynt'taris jumped to the sky.

Malcor at last realized what many others had finally come to know – Ynt'taris had a rider, and her name was Ora. Transcendent like the other priestesses, but ice instead of fire.

The dark elf stood quiet, watching, and then asked Malcor a question. "Sure, you could take a rider and a series of lances. But with the gate now closed, we have some opportunities we did not before. Instead of heroically charging into battle, why not let the dragons keep Orcus distracted and try this?" A mage, wearing the garb and indistinct attire Malcor had come to associate with Daryx, appeared. Under his hand, the titan's bloodstone nicknamed *Ayden Stone* telekinetically followed.

Daryx pointed to it with a flourish and described its powers. Smiling at Ayden, he said, "The Ayden Stone suppresses dominion. What better opportunity to test it than against the Necromancer?"

"What must I do?" Malcor asked.

Dar Reznor fabricated chains to hold the stone. All around, hell raged and every part of Malcor wanted to rage with it. Malcor looked out towards Orcus and heard the god command a group of griffin riders to die. Flesh melted from the group as feral energy took hold of them all. Transforming as they fell, skeletal and gaunt wings snapped and spun to dislodge the riders unaffected by Orcus' command.

Daryx watched the carnage with him for a moment. "Focus, Malcor. Thankfully for us all, Orcus is subject to linear time here. We know this because we are still moving in linear time, and are alive."

Daryx pointed to red tether of energy that stretched from Orcus' bleeding and oozing eye up to where Dar Ana circled with the other dread lords preparing another diving attack. "What we need is a hero, someone to turn the tide of this battle. Ana cannot do this alone."

Malcor shook off the battlesong boiling his blood and answered. "Yes, I'll do it. What must I do?"

Chapter Sixty Six – The Green Sun

The sick light radiating from the green sun tortured the earth, its plants, its animals. It infected and spread a sickness of suicidal torment that drove the creatures into a frenzy of murder. As insects and animals attacked their own kind and fell, their carcasses animated and rose up to continue attacking. Some formed into clusters and attacked more powerful predators. As the swarms of insects and flocks of birds encountered more powerful and increasingly sentient monsters and prey, they began pulling together into amorphous tangles of flesh.

All around Bloodstone, abominations composed of plant, animal, and other matter began to rise up and climb the ridge mountains. Farther away, as the natural sun was replaced by the fell will of Orcus, it eclipsed green under the planet's rotation.

To the east, Haven saw it start as the sun's western edge tinged green and then that color began to eat the sun. They understood the fight at Bloodstone had started. Everywhere bells sounded as the militia took to the walls. They prayed that Tania would contain the battle to Bloodstone. But, when the ground trembled and they saw the first column of smoke blast into the sky from a volcano, many lost hope and panicked.

Not knowing how things fared there, and speculation as to why such measures would be required demoralized the soldiers. Officers walked the wall telling them to keep their eyes open to the west. "That's where any attack against Haven will come from, idiots!" they screamed.

Overhead, the sun continued to twist. As more and more of it turned green, a ram's head began to appear and it cast its eyes at Haven. The western plain between Haven and the First Fortress suddenly rippled, without wind, as plants writhed and burst forth through winter's ice and snow. The road to Bloodstone blurred and then all manner of hibernating animal life crawled out and began attacking the life swarming the road to Haven.

A soldier pointed to the edge of the sunlight where a wave of green light fast approached them. "What do we do?" someone screamed out, shooting an arrow towards the animals. Within just a few seconds, they saw the first abomination rise up as small winter predators fell to warmer weather ones.

The first abomination, an amalgamation of insects, plants, and animal matter rose up in the shape of a ram. It looked at the sun, and all Haven heard the sun command, "Attack and feed on Haven!" The ram lowered its head and charged Haven's western gates.

That's when the light reached perimeter of the city. "Thank Tania," someone said as they realized Tania's practice of decapitating and removing dead bodies by cremation saved them. What life existed in the plain and frozen mote around Haven's western wall erupted as necromantic spirits called it to feast, to absorb, to grow.

Watching in growing horror, someone else said, "What happens to us?" A fox had just devoured a rabbit and instead of turning to fight, it pulled the rabbit into its body growing in size. Dead animal and plant matter started pulling into it as the small fox began to grow faster and faster to the size of a bull.

The light reached the wall and the defenders stepped back, and then began to run. However, the stairs and ladders accessing the battlements could not hold everyone and chaos ensued. Those trapped in the back pushed as a compulsion to draw weapons and attack their comrades' backs grew in them.

In fits and starts as the full light and power of Orcus shown down on them, they began to attack in the most devastating manner they could imagine. Cauldrons of boiling pitch were poured along the ramparts, into the Haven side. Siege weapons turned and fired on the defenders as others turned them on the city. The last parts of their thoughts not consumed with fright, heard the urgent command and will of Orcus. "Kill! Slay all! Feast on them and rise up in power!"

Not everyone was affected. A few veteran and experienced soldiers, who had served or fought their entire lives, heard the voice and resisted. Seeing that the green sun far outpaced them, they banded together and began to seek out safe areas where they might fortify and endure.

"Pray for Haven," one veteran said as he slammed a trapdoor shut beneath him. All around, others barricaded the murder holes facing the exterior of their tower. When undead insects began to swarm inside, they barricaded and closed the windows. Smoke and fire rose up, and the screaming of Haven began in earnest.

Those indoors heard the voice and felt the compulsion but not to the extent they forcibly acted on it. Everywhere though, people opened their shutters or stepped outside to see what had happened.

Instantly, they fell to the skull's light where the sun should have been. Mothers and fathers, children, livestock... all turned on whatever life it found closest.

* * *

A hatsmith working in his main room asked his daughter to go see what was happening. A sign outside in gold engraving and paint proudly proclaimed "Ghalen's Hattery". He could just see the sign through the panel of glass and iron bars across the top third of the outside door. He immediately noticed the weird green light, and heard the sudden compulsion. "No, wait!" he tried to say, but it was too late.

She stepped outside and he saw her body go rigid. She whirled and screamed murder at him as she ran back at him to attack. Slashing her hands as if they had claws, he had to backpedal to avoid her. Not wanting to hurt her, he tried to keep the table between the two of them.

Hearing the commotion, his wife, Terri, came in. The hatsmith barely tackled her out of the way of his daughter's attack. "What's wrong with her?!" Terri screamed. "Lani! Stop, please stop!"

Their daughter's face had gone rigid and her eyes glimmered with green energy. "I hate you," she screamed at them. "You're all going to die!" She leapt at them, tossing the large table aside as if it had been struck by a kicking horse. It flipped over and over until it smashed against the wall.

Ghalen looked around wishing he had some means of restraining without hurting her. "I have an idea," he said to Terri. "Don't go outside and try to keep her distracted." He scrambled for a special hat he'd been working on for several weeks. While his daughter tried to tackle, bite, and kill his wife, he carefully moved to a storage crate. When he reached the crate, he opened and rifled through it quickly. "I've got it!" he exclaimed, throwing the hat at his daughter.

The girl spun at his voice. Seeing the hat, she tried to duck but Terri hit her in the back of her head with a broom. It proved enough of a distraction that the hat whacked against the daughter's shoulder.

Immediately, the hat grew in size and elongated to bind the girl tightly. "What's wrong with her?" Terri asked fearfully. She wanted to check that she was okay from being hit with the broom.

Their daughter spat at them, saying terrible things about eating their hearts. "Don't you love me?" she pled. "Free me. I'm so hungry."

"Do you hear that?" the father suddenly said. "It was so quiet, but not anymore." All around them, screams and shouts of fighting erupted. "I'll stay here with her. Run upstairs. Barricade the windows. Don't let the sunlight touch you. Don't let anyone go outside."

Terri raced to the other room and the stairs where frightened voices of their other children called out to know what had happened.

The father heaved the crate out of the storage corner and shoved it to the door. He had just a glimpse of an old woman beggar ripping into the belly of a guardsman as the crate slammed the door shut. In that tiniest of glimpses of the green sunlight, he paralyzed in time and could not look away. With each bite, the beggar lady grew larger. To her side, across the street, his friend and drinking companion, burst out the door being chased by one of his children, three times larger than the twelve year old boy should have been. It shook his distraction and he looked away. His heart raced and he tried to focus on the crate against the door.

His own thoughts felt blurred and heavy with thoughts of submitting to those outside. Part of him wanted to think about barricading his home. But, in his own manner of thinking – in his own thought voice - the words came: *Your daughter is a ghoul. Abominations come for your loved ones. End it now, mercifully, before they come for your family. It's so easy - take your shears and end your life, give them easy passage.*

From within the crate, he pulled another hat and put it on. Feeling strength and vitality flow into him, he remained low and grabbed the table. He wedged it in place just as the old beggar woman bit into the guard's spine, wishing that he did not have a glass pane in the upper panel of his door. He had wanted it as a compromise to not having windows. His last view of the old lady showed him spiny horn-like projections erupt along her head and back. Her eyes rolled to him even as she still ate.

He wedged the table over the door, grateful he had decided on almost no windows in their crime-ridden neighborhood. The front door thudded into the table, and he cursed softly. Something out there was trying to get in. His daughter continued to writhe and thrash, seeking to break free. Her hideous screaming had to be stopped. That thing outside the door hit again and nearly toppled his impromptu barricade.

His wife returned and he pointed to the daughter gesturing to silence her. The wife ran over and tried to cover the girl's mouth, but a sharp bite drew blood on her hand. That would not work. In desperation, the wife grabbed a sack and threw it over her head. With the daughter continuing to try to bite, the wife shoved a wad of cloth into her mouth and then tied it in place. It did not stop the loud wailing, but it muffled it enough to mask the sound over the growing pandemonium and chaos out in the streets.

With his back to the barricade, Ghalen pushed with all his might as something stronger than he could imagine tried to push through. Without the hat augmenting his strength, the barricade would have fallen. With great alarm in her face, Terri whispered to him, "What do we do?"

"Pray," he said flatly. "I've been since this started. I hope she'll recover," he said nodding his head at their daughter.

From the back room, their fourteen-year-old son looked all around with wide eyes. "Do you need help?" He was pale. "There are such terrible sounds everywhere."

Another tremendous thud, as if a battering ram, hit the door. Ghalen whipped around to shove it back in place as an old woman's hand, mutated into a bony length of spines, reached around and clawed the edge of the table. For a moment, they wrestled that arm. The bright green daylight streaming into the relative darkness of the room silhouetted that terrible bone white arm.

The father spoke a magical word and, as a feather burned off the hat, his strength surged even more. He snapped the arm and threw the dismembered but still grasping hand outside. The table slammed against the door frame again as something ran at it, trying to push it in.

To his son and wife, he asked them, "As fast as you can, find anything heavy. Drag it here. Rope, binding cord, strips of cloth. We have a holy symbol and consecrated water in the shrine. Bring them to me, fast. Do not let anyone look or go outside. Stay out of the green light!"

The two nodded and raced off. Ghalen had been working as a hatsmith his entire career, except for a brief stint in his youth. He remembered saying to his parents, "I'm going to go fight in Bloodstone." They had argued with him pointing out that he loved magic, not fighting. But, it felt like the right thing at the time. He had withdrawn after just two months. Nightmares of that place still haunted him.

Working with hats, enchanting them, weaving magic into them and other normal everyday items had filled his life since with peace and quiet. It was a good life. He had developed enough skill and reputation that his business had started to thrive and grow. He could see a future for his children. He imagined growing old. *My dream*, he thought wistfully. *It's falling apart.*

All of this flashed before his eyes while the footsteps of his wife and son raced to and fro looking for barricade items. It seemed to take forever. Whether his seeing outside before, his daughter's condition, or his closeness to that sunlight, the compulsive whisper in his mind darkened his thoughts. He had to focus on his dream.

"My magical hat is giving me strength. This is real. I am real," he whispered to himself. The sight of his daughter's struggle against the binding hat darkened his focus and threatened him with despair. "I have to do this. I must do this. For my family." He tried to say it stronger than he felt.

His son appeared. He held a small crystal vial of water. The vial bore the sun symbol of Pha Rann. "I can't find the holy symbol. Also, something is wrong with mom." He held out the vial, which Ghalen took.

Thankfully, the banging outside had stopped. "Come closer," Ghalen asked. He quickly removed the magic hat of strength and put it on his son. "Stand against this door. Keep pressure against the crate and table so that the door can't be opened at all. I'll go see what is happening with mom."

The boy nodded and leaned into the barrier. Ghalen moved through the ground level, but it was the scream of pain from upstairs that tore at his heart. He grabbed a club, and sprinted the stairs taking two at a time.

His wife had altered. Her hand, where bitten by the daughter, had already turned a pallid white and oozed blood from lacerations. Green lines rode her veins towards her neck. The two other children had huddled together in the corner, crying. The youngest, his three year old Charlotte, sobbed with blood stains across her face and hair. Ghalen's heart fell seeing so much blood, and he cried out, "No!"

Terri's head twisted around and he saw the eye on the side of her wounded arm had filled with green light. When it looked at him, he knew he would have to kill her, his daughter too. *Then your own life*, the inner voice mocked him.

No, I can't. I love them. There has to be another way, he thought. But doubt filled him and that insidious whisper in his soul urged him to end it all and give up.

"Face me, Terri," he said to his wife. "Leave the children alone. You love them." He signaled the children to stay where they were. They could not handle the situation and ran to their father. Seeing it, sensing the children's sudden movement, Terri leapt at them, her cry terrible for its similarity to their daughter's murderous rage.

He realized that his months of service in Bloodstone had stayed with him when he smashed the club against her neck. Her body collapsed to the floor just shy of the three year old's gown. "Forgive me, Terri!" he prayed as he smashed her again and again.

When her body finally stopped clawing at the children, he slumped down and rolled her over. Tears streaked her still human eye, but he could see it filling with the same horrible energy. From the bite wound, green lines rode her veins to her neck. She had become like the old beggar lady outside. Only by luck had he interrupted her feeding on the children.

Decapitation, he recalled. He looked to the two young girls, wide-eyed with a sorrowful mix of frustrated fear and anger. *This moment is going to haunt them forever*, he knew. *I wish they hadn't had to watch me kill her.*

"Some terrible magic happened to mommy. Stay here. Don't move. I love you," he said while grabbing Terri's feet and dragging her out of the room. They thudded down the stairs and, near the bottom, he felt her body begin to reanimate. A kitchen cleaver finally separated her head with not a moment to spare.

Seeing Terri's body go limp and finally, at last, lifeless, he sat back and wiped bloody sweat from his face. Then, he remembered the girls probably wondering why daddy had just killed mommy. That voice whispered to him again, *Finish what she started*. Ignoring the voice, he checked on his son who had not heard or felt anything attack the door.

Upstairs, the girls both cried sniffing and trying to be brave, trying to be quiet. When they saw their father, they ran to his arms and began crying in earnest. He hugged them both and then, with gentle urgency, looked at the three year old. "Are you hurt?" he asked.

He looked through her hair, her neck, her arms. He saw nothing like the bite that had taken his wife. Most of the blood seemed to be Terri's. He looked again though and saw fingernail claw marks along her scalp. He took the vial of holy water and began washing the wounds. Something about it made his daughter shiver and he felt evil leave her wounds. Mentally, he prayed thanks to Pha Rann.

The older said, "Mommy tried to grab Charlotte, but then she stopped. Mommy said she loved us but – her voice got scary. She said she was going to eat us! Then you came. Is mommy okay? I want to see her!" A second later, she pushed back from him, "Why did you hit her?"

Ghalen buried his face in their hug. "Mommy had to go bye bye," he whispered. "The world has gone crazy, but we are still family. By Pha Rann's power, the sun will rise again and we will be happy again," he said kissing them. "I promise."

His son called out, just loud enough for him to hear. "Help, dad."

"I have to go now. Stay in this room okay? Promise?" He kissed them one more time before breaking the hug and leaving.

Downstairs, his restrained daughter had wriggled to the door and was thrashing against it. His son, unused to the augmented strength, had kicked her back across the room, but the banging against the door had attracted new attention. In addition, a rat, infected by that same power as had taken those outside, had entered the room and was chewing on the binding hat.

With cleaver and club, Ghalen went after the rat even as another entered. This one sniffed the air and ran into the kitchen. Remembering how the beggar lady had grown as she ate the guard, Ghalen swore. At least he had smashed the rat. "Stay at the door," he said grimly.

It was as he had feared. The rat had already chewed into his wife's eye. The rat already looked noticeably larger than the other, and bigger than any rat he had ever seen.

Distracted by the feast provided by Terri's corpse, Ghalen killed the vermin easily. Ghalen tried to catch his breath and wished he were in better physical shape. He picked up Terri's head and put it into a clay pot. He started dragging the body to the side, just in case the girls came downstairs, when the ground trembled.

"Dad?" his son called to him. "What is that?"

The tremble felt different than when the volcano had erupted. Then, it happened again and they heard the sound as something large and heavy stepped down somewhere close by. A burning smell started to fill the air.

What now?, Ghalen thought. *Please Pha Rann, I'm doing my best here. I've lost my wife, maybe my daughter. Please bless and help me save the rest of my family!*

Another tremble shook the ground, and in that moment, Ghalen had a vision that broke his heart. His daughters lay dead and dying under the naked green sun. His roof shattered and tore apart. He ran back upstairs. "Come on!" he called to them. "Quickly!"

The girls ran to him and then he practically flew downstairs. As he rolled with them into the main room, a foul rot filled their air. The smell of fire grew. A building near them broke apart. The sound of snapping wood and tearing hinges and nail pop sounds punctuated the overall chaotic din.

"Daddy, hold you!" the three-year-old said to him. Normally a cute request, this one sounded like a command and it broke his heart. Tears and fright made wide her eyes.

"Stay with your sister. I can't hold you now, Chari," he whispered. "We need to stay very quiet."

Their house shook. Green light and shadows filled the stair well as their roof smashed to the side. Ghalen kicked the back door to the kitchen and stairs shut as a massive deformed head looked into the second floor bedroom. "Throw me the hat!" Ghalen mouthed. The boy nodded and tossed it to him.

Through small cracks in the door, it was not as well constructed as the outer doors, Ghalen watched the abomination look and sniff at Terri's blood. Small faces, he thought he recognized their local watchmen, pressed out of the creature's face and looked around too. Horse and livestock heads pressed out reaching for the blood.

Finding nothing, the undead monster continued to sniff. It then reached down the stairs and fished around until it grabbed Terri's headless corpse. It smashed her body against the door, but having just put the hat of strength on, Ghalen held the door closed. And, he prayed, pouring his soul out to Pha Rann for protection.

Miraculously, his children said nothing. His bound daughter's muffled cries proved quiet enough. Another miracle, nothing assailed their front door where only his son stood against the barricade. The youngest of his children, too terrified to move, made no sound – thankfully. Terrible sounds of tearing meat came from all around and above them. And then, for no reason Ghalen could determine, the abomination walked away. They felt the ground tremble. They heard another building smash to pieces. Another footfall, and then each one farther and farther away. Ghalen finally remembered to breathe.

Ghalen threw the hat back to his son. They waited. Ghalen took the girls over to his son and the four of them prayed together to Pha Rann, for a return of the golden sunlight, and for the return of their daughter. "And please, Sunshine," the three year old added to the prayer. "Please let mommy come back from her bye-bye."

"I'm so sorry, Charlotte," Ghalen said to her. "Mommy won't be coming back from her bye bye."

"Oh no, Daddy." She patted his chin. "This morning mommy went bye bye to get bread. She came right back!"

The outside had changed. Ghalen could not say what it was, but the whispering despair in his mind lifted. He did not know it, but the sceptre of Orcus had just been cut in half. A lot of his courage returned to him in that moment, and he peaked outside. The sick light continued to shine. He saw dead and dying following after the giant. One even looked at him, but compelled to feed on the largest food, the dead shambled after the abomination. All around them, Haven burned and he got a glimpse of several other abominations walking through Haven, peeling rooftops off houses. From the walls, someone launched a burning ball of pitch from a catapult into a cluster of homes. "It's hell," he whispered.

They returned to their prayers. Without warning, the green daylight ended. The despair lifted. With the suicidal voice whispering poison in his thoughts gone, it all came crashing in on Ghalen and his kids in an instant. Sorrow for his wife's loss filled him and he finally felt guilt, shame, and grief that he had not been able to save her. Struggling to not cry, fighting to look brave for his kids, he looked outside. The dead still walked, but golden sunlight filled the air. The dead moved out of the sun into shadows. Some tried to dig holes in the frozen ground. Others ran for the giant. They all began to burn in the sunlight.

"It's over," Ghalen said. "Well, almost over. We're going to win. Tania won."

Charlotte prayed, "Dear sunlight, will you have Tania bring mommy back?"

Ghalen walked over to his daughter bound with a sack over her head. She had gone quiet, calm. "Lani," he whispered. "Are you there?" The sack over her head nodded and he carefully pulled out the gag tied over the sack. "Say something, anything."

"I'm really tired," she said. "Why is there a sack over my head? Did you tie me up?" Her voice, tremulous and fatigued, was most certainly Lani.

Ghalen removed the sack while his son held the younger girls back. No evil light in her eyes, Ghalen anointed her with holy water. "Where's mom?" Lani asked.

* * *

The green sunlight continued to wash across the land. It poisoned animal and plant life alike. Monsters falling under its blighted eye rose up strengthened, emboldened, and hungry for slaughter.

As the light washed over Morilon, Mallaforax's world tree shuddered. Its roots strengthened the forest, which groaned under the unholy sun.

Morilon endured the green sun as the world tree's leaves withered and began falling one by one. The green dragon patriarch had insisted on total compliance and so the green light found no living elves in Morilon.

Morbatten received word from the magi fighting in Bloodstone. Dar Kell, sitting high in Alerius' mountain, touched the tower bloodstone by the Dragon Throne. "Morbattania, I speak to you. The war is joined in Bloodstone and a green sun comes to fill our souls with rage. Do not let the sun into your eyes, even a reflection. We have just minutes. Barricade your homes, cover your windows. Stay inside *no matter what* you hear outside. This command is absolute. Failure to obey, it is not by my command that you will die, but by the Jade God's. Comply now, or die."

Everywhere, the world that knew and obeyed shut themselves away from the light and endured. In Dock Side, Captain Calvin and his men ran through the streets for one final check. Completing his circuit, with many of the people calling out their thanks to him for his bravery, Calvin returned to his home. Ryvane greeted him and slammed the door shut just as the golden light at the end of the street sickened and died.

"There, there," Ryvane said while he caught his breath. "You did it. Dock Side is safe because of you."

Like in Haven, insects and missed remains of plant and animal material began its consumption. Tania had well-prepared itself for an eventual attack by the Jade God. Not ripe for necromancy, the jade sun found few servants in Tania. Those that did, were fought back by the citizens.

Calvin sat by the front door with Ryvane, while the old couple fidgeted in the kitchen. Every now and then, they heard the voice insistent in its demand for obedience. Calvin just laughed. "So this is the Jade God everyone is so afraid of?" He snickered.

Ryvane held his hand and added, "Well, it's a lot more powerful when you're actually in Bloodstone facing the undead."

"I don't believe it," Calvin snorted. "Don't tell me this is like the Khasran lich?" He referred to Malcor.

Malcor again, Ryvane noted. *Always Malcor.* She stroked his hand. "Be careful, Calvin. Tania has spent a long time being prepared for this. Our city would be a nightmare without the benefit of those preparations."

"I suppose. Still, I guess I expected more than this."

Chapter Sixty Seven – To Fell a God

Before Malcor's eyes, from where he stood on the Temple's roof, Screem hit the sceptre. It twisted and began to snap. The noise reminded him of a bone breaking. The Sceptre of Orcus, which controlled the sun, broke in half as the eldar dragons finally cut its neck. The concussive shock wave from it triggered another earthquake. Answering the quake, the volcano re-erupted as creatures from the plane of Fire burst from the lava to attack Orcus.

Once the noise died down enough, Daryx yelled, "Bloodstones respond to a user's command and must be in proximity to their target. Orcus is so large; we need to either be on it or, in it for this to work. We need a stealthy dragon. Oh come now, don't make that face, my King! Not all paladins are destined to march into battle. There is always advantage to be had through more deliberate and critical actions. You will fly with this to Orcus, find a secure location, and activate the stone."

A gold dragon landed near them and Dar Jeri stepped down from its back. "I will wield the stone," Jeri said.

Malcor saw the blood saturating her eye bandages and felt a deep twinge of sympathy for her. "Very well, my Dar," Malcor said. "I am honored to have you join me." He turned to Seline, Ayden, and Sofen. "You three shall be my riders." When he spoke it, something happened and he felt a deep and inexplicable connection open between himself and the three. He saw they felt it too. *So, I have three riders*, he thought. He dragonshifted, this time wrapping himself in shadowstuff as if armor plating.

Daryx had already walked away looking for the next strategic advantage, handsigning instructions and barking orders to the Fortress' defenders. "Good luck," he called back to Malcor. Two priestesses ran over carrying a wrapped bundle of long lances. Each lance glowed with magical runescript. Long as five men tall, Malcor read the lances' draconian names: *Godslayer*. They passed these up Malcor's back to Seline and Ayden.

Malcor dragonshifted and jumped off the causeway dragging the stone by its chains. The green daylight bathed everything here preventing shadows and forcing him to fly. He felt very small compared to the other dragons, who looked like hummingbirds compared to Orcus. One of the dread lords landed on and dropped the draco-lich into the poison mist filling the valley. Malcor saw Orcus turn in his direction and so he dove into the poison mist, hoping to avoid Orcus' attention. "Hold your breath!" he roared at them.

Below the mist, everything went twilight dark with a greenish cast. Everything battled, even the trees and plants, undead, and those still living or unable to fly moved in clusters of combat. Malcor turned to stay out of Orcus' view and saw a handful of heavily armored knights climbing Orcus' leg. As the group climbed, they cut and stabbed but undead from the valley absorbed from the ground into the wounds. The strange group caught their fascination and Malcor almost turned to join them.

Sofen smacked his neck and called him to focus. All around, as dead, dying and undying fell, they merged into Orcus. They passed low between two hills and noted a bright shining golden light, a cluster of holy paladins with the insignia of Cuthbert stood fighting atop one of the hills. Around them in the sea of undead, hellhounds began to open gates and bring demons and devils into the valley. Again, a fascination caught him but, where the other made him want to join in the fight, this one made him want to heroically charge Orcus' face and attempt to single-handedly slay the god himself. Sofen's reassurances helped.

At last, Malcor turned around the other cloven hoof and began to climb back up above the mist. "I need shadows," he screamed in draconian.

Far above them, Jeri's sisters dive bombed the base of Orcus' neck. One moved in front while the other two burst afire with golden light. Jeri leapt off Malcor's back. Dragonshifting, she similarly ignited her body in a golden sunburst of light. It flash-imprinted Malcor's dragon shadow on Orcus' leg. Malcor shadowstepped into his own shadow, leaping into it by the momentary flash of golden light. He reappeared through the shadow of Jeri's sister at Orcus' neck, beneath the curve of what appeared to be goat horns. Ayden's and Seline's ears popped with the sudden altitude change. Jeri held her light as long as she could, and then began to flap her wings, trying to climb and join them.

Turning to express his thanks, Malcor saw a tangle of dragon wings and spiked tails dripping venom where an aerial demon slammed into the dragon sisters. They fell away from Malcor in a tangle of yellow fire and abyssal fury. Meanwhile, Jeri struggled to fly up to them. *She'll make it*, he thought. Even though Orcus turned and moved, this spot seemed protected by the horns and proximity to Orcus' head. He carefully placed the bloodstone down on a hump of muscle covered by gray-tan quills. Each quill lay flat and nearly as long as a Tanian lance.

Orcus' skin had a translucent quality to it, beneath the quills, that reminded the Malcor of the polished soul tiles from the gate chamber. Whenever the raging battle all around them created shade, souls trapped under the god's skin would dart at them to the surface and rake their hands at them. Some of the souls held their hands out as if asking for aid. Only a few souls were recognizable as human. Most had an orcish quality to their features though still alien in the character of their forehead and form structure.

Ayden pointed to one trying to attack them from beneath the skin. "It looks like an orc crossed with a devil, doesn't it?" The phantasm suddenly vanished and an elf appeared. He opened his hands and signed to them: Please, save me. I can't endure this. He used recent sign language. "He must have died in the poison mist?" Ayden speculated.

Seline drew her sword moved to cut into the skin, but Sofen and Ayden both caught her. "No," Sofen said. "We cannot risk our mission for this. If the Jade God becomes aware of us, we fail."

Seline looked at Malcor, but the shadow dragon eyed the combat all around. He clearly looked for a chance to assist Jeri. The blinded dragon continued to climb, but every so often, the Necromancer would move and slam her. Unable to see, Malcor darted in and out of the River of Time, calling to her, encouraging her.

Seline and Ayden spiked the lances into Orcus' hide and began to coil the chains around them. If Orcus felt the lances, he gave no sign as a series of detonations from the other side knocked the god back a step. From a distance, Orcus' skin had looked covered with fur but up close, the fur became polearm long quills, barbed and oily. The stone compressed the quills making a flat area and his riders leapt down to secure the chains as best they could.

Fate favored them, as did the dragons overhead who intercepted or distracted any enemies that might have attacked Jeri. Whenever an enemy took an interest in them, and before Malcor had to jump or engage, Ynt'taris and Ora intercepted and pulled their attacker away. Protected in this manner, when Jeri at last arrived and humanshifted, the Ayden Stone sat as secure as they could make it. Elven cord and the chains themselves they had tied to multiple bundles of quills and spiked it all in place with lances. Ayden said, "It's not going anywhere, Dar Jeri. Give us a moment to clear the area. We'll guard you." Both she and Seline retained a lance each.

Malcor and Ayden leapt off Orcus and climbed in altitude to where Jeri's sisters fought against a winged creature of bladed tails and overly long arms. It had a metallic sheen and seemed immune to dragon fire. One of the two golds smashed into it biting and tearing to give the other distance. Both of the golds had been severely wounded. Ayden leapt from Malcor with her lance and pierced it clean through the demon's back. The surprise of pain and shock allowed the gold to leap back and Malcor struck it with his shadow breath.

The demon's head turned to him in the act of casting a spell when the other gold added her fire breath to Malcor's. Caught between Malcor's shadow attack and the gold's heavenly fire, it began to fall and then shattered. Malcor dove to catch Ayden in his claw and passed her back up to Seline and Sofen.

They did not have time to celebrate their victory because a gate opened above the gold dragons. A giant humanoid wreathed in brimstone and evil-looking chains wrapped one of Jeri's sisters in barbed hooks and landed on her back. Immediately, they joined battle. Malcor grabbed Seline and, as he flew upwards, he threw the paladin at the tangle of chains. Seline speared the lance into the devil and slid down to hack and sever an arm already morphing into a skeletal claw.

Dar Jeri meanwhile placed her hand on the Ayden Stone and activated it against Orcus. She did not know what to expect. Nothing seemed to change. However, for the mortals fighting all around, everything changed. The undead and those newly-dead transforming into undead, paused. More powerful undead grew confused and had to struggle for focus; the effect slowed them. The few sentient undead looked around in bewilderment. For the first time, they considered their enemies. As the hellhounds turned and fled.

A Soran knight saw the soldier right next to him die as fingers of choking vapor grabbed him. The monster, demon or devil or whatever laughed, waiting for the body to reanimate. When it did not, the creature reanimated it directly, but it seemed sluggish compared to the other undead. The green daylight bathing the valley flickered and then normal sunlight reasserted itself. Jeri could not see any of this but felt it as an up swell in the current of Time. Its flow, though still turbulent, cracked the stasis holding it in parts, and Time corrected itself. "For Rojo," Jeri whispered.

Chapter Sixty Eight - Domino

Ana dismounted from Crimson and floated in the air thousands of feet over Orcus. Red lines of energy pulsed from her to the dread lords and her swords still tearing Orcus' eye apart. In the middle of that vast web of red energy. She felt the tide turn and shouted, "All of you, attack now!" From all over the valley, bearers of bloodstones heard the command and shouted out orders.

The eldar dread lords fell like comets at Orcus. Feeling their unified will, Orcus looked up and smiled to speak a single command. "Burn!" Unlike other direct commands with immediate effects, this command did nothing.

For the first time, Orcus felt confusion. An unknown and strange force bound him. He tried to change it, but could not. All around him, he sensed something swirling over, around and through him. The shattered sceptre in his hand that he used as a club, the destroyed gate, the absence of his Bomoki, searing agony in his leg, the link of all these events finally connected in Orcus' mind. *I cannot change the sequence of these events*, Orcus realized.

Then, the dragons hit him. Each breathed and landed with claws and teeth open as they attached and began raking into his flesh. They attacked his head and neck most of all. Collectively, it hurt and Orcus struggled with this strange feeling of hurt.

A human, almost too tiny to bother noticing, appeared on Orcus' snout. Orcus recognized the red dragon that had thwarted him for so very long. Alerius raised his unbroken arm and said something. Orcus barely heard it because a dragon had delved into his ear and opened a gate to the elemental plane of Earth and Fire. Alerius raised his voice and spread his arms wide. "I wish for Orcus to become mortal."

Orcus' leg snapped, severed at last by the tiny soldiers of Kargoth. Falling to one knee again, Orcus felt the first twinge of agony in his other leg. His servants would not answer and the sunlight burned him. New gates opened all around Orcus as divine servants appeared from Creation and struck at him.

Though the titan thrashed about, Alerius stayed perfectly balanced on his nose. Another human appeared near his damaged eye. Orcus remembered to command his body to open new eyes, more eyes, everywhere. This human suddenly changed and everything went dark as Cor'tanos breathed anti-life into the now living Necromancer.

Not to be outdone, other gates opened and the forces of Hell joined the attack, for just a moment, before turning on the divine servants of Creation. In his mind, Orcus heard Alerius speak to him. "You'd think that Heaven and Hell fighting would save you. It will not. I bring you Takhissis' judgement. You are cut off and alone in Tehra. You are mortal. You are dying. How does it feel?"

Orcus tried to leave, but the way had closed. He tried again and again, wasting Time he was not used to having to use wisely or at all, for that matter. When it failed, he screamed for them all to die. "Pathetic," Alerius' voice answered.

A priest wearing a wolf skull helmet appeared adjacent to Alerius. The fire patriarch took the hand of the cleric and together, they opened a gate. The Slayer of Gods entered to stand on Orcus' nose. Appearing as a large armored wolf, the Slayer crouched down and then shot like an arrow into Orcus' forehead. "This is not the Endless Worlds," Alerius sneered. "You will not rise again, Orcus."

Orcus' body went limp and began, at last to topple over backwards. Alerius sent word, "Evacuate the Sixth Fortress now!" Orcus smashed backwards against the Sixth Fortress. Seeing it begin to happen, Malcor shadowstepped and caught Jeri before she would have died. So intent was her focus on the *Ayden Stone* that she did not notice Orcus' death.

Hovering in the air just in front of Orcus' face, Alerius gestured at the Destroying Stone. From within the Sixth Fortress, the tower stone there, fractured and exploded. The vortex of magical fire almost severed Orcus' head. Alerius touched it again. The tower stone decorating the minotaur ship Blade of Stars, also detonated from the center of Orcus' gut. The two vortexes of energy become tornadoes of fire dancing alongside Orcus' neck and another sawing through the dead god's middle. In spite of the damage to his shoulder, Alerius closed his eyes and lifted his arms to the sun. Blood streamed from his broken shoulder, but he smiled. "A gift for you, my love Takhissis."

As the body bounced and settled into the ruin of the Sixth, Orcus' body began to unravel into millions of undead and lost souls. They rose up like a hurricane. Calm in the center, the souls lashed out at any life they could take. Alerius remained in place, falling with the titan. He touched his bloodstone earing and said, "Ana, cleanse the valley."

Cradled behind the Third and Fourth Fortresses, a large dam detonated allowing a lake of water to flow into the valley. It cleansed the poisonous vapors, destroyed lower level undead, and began washing down into the tunnels and mine complexes. The river exiting Bloodstone to connect with the Cordabad was not large enough to hold the flow as it increased and then blocked with trees, rocks, and bodies. Like a bowl, Bloodstone began to fill with water. An explosion of steam detonated where the wall of water met the volcano.

* * *

Fighting still raged, but without Orcus to act as a focal point for divine intervention, the Cascade began to end. The divine servants stayed only long enough to protect and render aid to their chosen allies and then left. Soon, Bloodstone contained only the demonic and devilish. The devilish, seeing that many forces – many known to them – remained to take a few last stabs at plunder and murder before leaving. That left the undead and abyssal powers. A command came from Alerius to the Mage's Guild, "Remove the Cuthbert knights from stasis and let them know that even though they missed the battle, many nightmarish creatures of chaos and hellspawn remain."

Far down in the valley, the instant that Orcus ceased to move, two groups of very different gods faced each other. Kargoth, the Hell Saint, held dominion over all paladins not pledged to Creation's powers. His avatar stood on Orcus' leg as the first waters began rushing into the valley. Across the way, atop a hill, the winged avatar of Cuthbert stood amidst two deva guardians. Their wings sparkled in the day like rainbows but seemed dim to the bright white radiance of the God Saint to whom all paladins of Good bowed. Even with abyssal powers remaining to fight, and though Orucs had just been slain, the two gods' eyes met and a frown creased their faces. The two devas shook the filth of battle from their feathered wings as Kargoth's band of followers pulled up around him.

Off in the distance, the roar of a coming tidal wave sounded throughout the valley as the volcano continued to spew lava and fire. These two did not care about such mortal things. They had been brothers in life, and in ascension had each claimed a different destiny. Cuthbert claimed dominion based on the absolute truth of Creation's goodness in all forms. Kargoth claimed it for opposition to any and all powers that would twist Tehra towards any of the nexal gates. Like Day and Night, the two brothers stood worlds apart but in the same place. Cuthbert dismissed the devas back to Heaven. Kargoth ordered his men to seek out and bring him trophies of the chaos demons stalking Bloodstone.

Both vanished and reappeared with swords striking at the other. The force of the blow shattered their blades, but their wills held them in check as Kargoth spun and elbowed Cuthbert in the head. Cuthbert barely ducked and shield bashed Kargoth back. Then, the tidal wave hit and they continued their struggle under the water. For just a moment, it unbalanced

Cuthbert where Kargoth used its momentum to punch into Cuthbert's stomach. As he punched, another sword appeared and it stabbed Cuthbert through.

Retaliating, Cuthbert rammed his gauntlet into Kargoth's face as bladed spikes appeared around his fist. The punch blew them apart, sending up walls of mud around them. Without pause, they flew back at each other. Kargoth launched a dual spinning sword strike that, when it hit Cuthbert, the swords vanished. At the same moment, Kargoth's swords reappeared and hit the God Saint across his shoulders. The sword strikes cut through the armor and Cuthbert bled. Rolling with the strike, Cuthbert grabbed Kargoth's leg and threw him into the sky. His tumbling body rocketing up dragged a cyclone of water. Cuthbert blinked into being above Kargoth and dropped on him. His golden sword skewered Kargoth through. The force of the attack hurtled them both back into the raging waters below. Kargoth's hand found the blade still impaling the God Saint. Each avatar twisted the blade skewering the other.

"I slay you for Tehra," Kargoth said as blood splattered his lips.

"I slay only evil," Cuthbert spat into Kargoth's face.

Their bodies, striking the water, cratered the ground and left it dry for just a moment. Each rolled over to look at the sun, and the avatars died.

Chapter Sixty Nine – The Winter War in Bloodstone

When the avatars of the paladin gods died, paladins everywhere went insane. Tanian knights turned on the Pha Rannic Orders. Even similarly aligned paladins, working side by side as friends,b drew avenging blades and struck at each other.

"Vile murderer!" the Pha Rannic Orders cried out.

"Hypocritical liar!" the Tanians answered. Though Tania had suffered far more casualties in the war, they had far more paladins than the other nations combined. They also had the dragons.

The Mage's Guild had just finished freeing Golcir when Cuthbert fell like a golden star. Duke Golcir Able felt the God Saint's death as a fire kindled in his heart. He welcomed the madness as righteous retribution for centuries of Tanian mockery. He smashed Reznor aside and ignited his sword on the causeway. The Temple Fortress looked obscene and he vowed to destroy it.

A Tanian paladin guarding the mage fell to Golcir first. With near total surprise against the Tanians, Golcir harvested the Order of the Shield protecting mages, and moved on to the Order of Earth, which protected the siege machines.

Dar Kendra appeared before him and he saw her as an avatar of Takhissis. He bloodlusted for her death even as she signaled her unit to kill the other Cuthberic knights still in stasis. "Golcir," she sneered. "I'm not at all surprised to see you backstabbing the weak." Her voice oozed with murderous intent.

Golcir attacked. Dar Kendra outclassed Golcir in every manner imaginable and toyed with him, frequently signaling her battle priest to heal him while calling off any knights seeking to help her. Again and again they clashed and each time, Kendra sent him back with less armor and more wounds. When Golcir could hardly move, and the last piece of torso armor fell free, he spat at her. "You don't know the true power of my god."

"We killed a god today. I've an appetite for more," she taunted him. "Go ahead. Do it."

Golcir prayed to Cuthbert. Though he felt no response, still the bright white and gold feathered wings of his high station burst from his back. His size and stature increased as Golcir became an angelic deva. Kendra did not wait to marvel at and or appreciate his transformation. She ran her sword through his heart, and then sidestepped out through the River to repeat her attack five more times before Golcir could move.

Bloodied and near death, the deva struck and smashed Kendra with the edge of its holy blade. It almost cut through her, but Malcor stepped in and caught the sword on Coming Undone's anti-magic blade. The telltale shattering of glass sound heralded the end as Malcor shadowstepped behind the angel and decapitated it in a single blow. By the time the head bounced and rolled to a stop on the ground, Golcir's body had returned to its normal human form.

As the dragons found paladins warring with each other, they picked up the Tanian knights and removed them to the Temple. Fighter units under the command of Pember and Ayden fought the demons back. Their resistance inspired the other nations and within a day, reinforcements from dwarf, gnome, minotaur, elven, and Soran nations joined under Pember or Ayden's standard. With the paladins missing to take the initial brunt of combat, Tania began gating in mages from both Tania and Sora who had initially been left behind due to age or lack of battle skill. From a distance, these groups helped fill the gaps. Step by step, the Nineteenth Legion began to reclaim Bloodstone.

* * *

Seline shook her head through a wave of vertigo. Looking around, she realized she was in a Fortress dungeon. Wall markings told her she was beneath the Second Fortress. Her cell was not harsh and she had not been mistreated. In fact, good food and fresh clothes awaited her. She shook her head and turned towards sound nearby. Standing dizzily, she held on to the cell bars and and looked around. The dungeon was full of paladins. Attendant priestesses stood in the center and, seeing Seline, one stepped forward and asked if she needed anything.

"What happened? Why am I here?" she asked.

The priestess explained how the paladins had turned on each other at the culmination of Orcus' fall. Seline looked down at her hands and watched her fingers to see if they trembled. Nothing. "I feel fine," she stated. Suddenly, a flash of memory showed blood staining her hands as she pulled her holy sword out of an armored breastplate. Her body trembled with desire to resume combat.

The priestess nodded. She withdrew a Pha Rannic symbol from her robes. Another flash of vision and Seline spun decapitating a charger bearing Pha Rann's symbol. Blood spraying from the horse burned in her flame aura and she saw herself stand in a halo of blood ash. Seline shook her head again and pointed at it, "That's an odd thing for a cleric of Tiamat to carry."

"This one may leave. Mark her forehead. Lady Seline, you are allowed to move freely throughout the Second and the causeway to the First. You are forbidden to leave this area however until such time as we know all of you are doing better."

"What happened?" she asked while they unlocked her cell.

"There are two god saints in the paladin dominion. After Orcus fell, they turned on each other. Their mutual deaths triggered a bloodlust in all the paladins here." The priestess indicated the next cell, "See for yourself."

Seline walked out and noted Malcor sat alone in a cell, meditating with the other knights she had come to associate with the Order of Water. Their leader Dar Kendra also appeared to meditate. Malcor opened his eyes and she saw a strange silvery light in his eyes. The priestess pointed to it. "That's what you all looked like two days ago. If you see any knights like this, or seeking to combat any of the Pha Rannic Orders, report it to a cleric immediately."

Malcor smiled at her, but his smile reeked of berserker rage and bloodlust. Like Seline, Malcor shook his head and took a deep breath. "You have no idea how hard it is to stay in this cell," he said.

The priestess smiled and blessed him in Tiamat's name. "My king, you must resist. Tiamat commands it. Focus on your purpose and hear Her Words – do they tell you to war?"

"My heart tells me to tear this dungeon to pieces and march to battle." Seline saw his hands tremble as did the others in his Order. Dragonterror flooded the dungeon, but the priestess smiled and began praying for him, for them all. The terror receded and Malcor closed his eyes again. "Seline, tell Ora I want to see her, please."

When Seline entered the Temple's central chamber, Ayden waved and then turned back to a map. Noting that Ayden had been promoted to Legion Commander in Verit's place, Seline had to restrain herself from running up and congratulating her. Commander Pember and King Andrew pointed to different areas on the map and Seline heard words like, "Type Nine devil here", "Chaos fiend, not sure", and "a group of hellhounds escaped into a flooded mine shaft here."

Dar Ana sat on her throne. She looked gaunt and tired. Though not really wounded in the battle, healing could prove just as tiring as being healed and Ana had kept all of the dread lords alive except for one. Blade, Alerius' youngest son and head of the Order of Fire, had been the one turned by Orcus.

Seline had a brief glimpse of Kargoth sawing into Orcus' leg under the poison mist. She shook her head to clear it because the memory of Kargoth triggered vertigo. A priestess took her arm and then Dar Niss appeared at her side. "I'll take care of this one," her mentor said.

They walked to a bench and sat down. For Seline, her memories came in bursts that brought a disorientation she could not place. Dar Niss noticed her confusion and eventually said, "Let's step to a quieter place."

They found an alcove and Niss hugged her tightly. "I think you're ready, Seline. What you're feeling isn't the bloodlust. If that were still an issue, you'd be in the dungeon still. No, what you're feeling is the flow of Time. It changed direction so much during the Second Cascade that you had multiple moments where you accessed the ethereal. Well, and the paladin bloodlust." Niss pulled Seline down to a cushioned set of chairs by windows looking towards Haven.

"Seline, you are trying to reconnect these events in a linear way as Time tries to correct and reassert itself here. This is your chance. Listen to me. I want you to feel as much as you can about your current 'self'. Then, I want you to imagine you're rising up from under flowing water. Feel the air catch in your lungs as you take that first breath. Yes, do it. Good. Feel the floor, gravity, the air currents. Feel my hand holding your hand. Now, let yourself be underwater. You want to breathe but cannot. You can only breathe when you absolutely have to. You're a paladin so it may be a while before that urge, perfect. Hold it. When the time is right, imagine you're -"

Seline focused on Niss' words and tried to put herself out of the river, as she had with Malcor. Suddenly, her breathing stalled in her lungs and her body began to burn. She had done it!

Niss caught her hand and pulled her up from the River's flow. Like Malcor, like anyone else accessing it the first time on their own, Seline felt horror mingled with awe. Being Bloodstone, Niss explained that "It's not as lovely as it is in Tania, or in the naturally beautiful places of the world. I urge you to practice this. And, when opportunity arises, watch how Dar Shara dances in it. She is a master."

That was all Seline could withstand and she crashed back into the real world. Niss held her, stroking her hair and explained that she had been sent to assist the minotaurs. She told the story of how she argued and finally compelled them to take Tanian recall tokens before the Sceptre destroyed the Third Fortress. "It wasn't as bad as it could have been. We were overrun by hundreds of hellhounds. They swarmed up from the dungeon levels and the rampart walls. Orcus did more damage to them than us. I triggered all of their recall tokens before the Sceptre hit." Niss laughed. "You should have seen their faces when they appeared here at the Temple! They won't admit it, but they knew the Sceptre would kill them. Of course, having lived, they're all angry with me now."

Together, they shared their stories and only gradually did Seline become aware that a bard lurked nearby, eavesdropping on them. Seline almost confronted the bard before she realized that her mentor had arranged it and was essentially pumping Seline for stories. Niss smiled her confession and introduced them. "Lady Seline of Quattrain," Niss said. "A fire paladin who fought the real battle here. She stood alongside Dar Malcor when he ascended to Rojo's throne."

Seline's eyes widened and it dawned on her that Malcor had become king. Far away from them, the ground shook and an explosion sounded. "The battle still rages. The chaos and hell creatures just won't give up. Alerius thinks this place will be plagued by chaos monsters for many years to come." Niss waved over a priestess and requested food and drink.

The half-elf bard had a timeless look and he clearly had picked up the best traits from both parents. He smiled and introduced himself to Seline. His voice had a perfect tonal quality and before he even spoke, Seline found she liked him. More than that, she wanted him to like her. "Lady Seline, I cannot tell you how honored I am to be chosen to record your great deeds. I am Lars Jimen of the Artist's Guild."

Niss waved her hand dismissively and imitated him. "*I'm a member of the Guild.* He undersells himself. Lars is a master of drumming and sings a mean ballad. He's perfect for your story. Other bards will capture the songs of Tembri, Malcor, Ayden – yes, she'll have a song, Verit, Rojo, Jeri, Blade, and all the mighty heroes who fell and fought here. Once the god emperor is satisfied that their stories are codified, the tales of the survivors will be captured and sung throughout the Isles!" Niss paused in thought for a moment and at last conceded. "Though we do have to share Lars with Dar Ora. If you ever find yourself wondering if a Dar priestess can call rank on a dread lord, if that dread lord is Ynt'taris – the answer is no."

Food and drink arrived and Seline began to open up about her experiences. Lars pressed her to expound on the roles played by others in her group. "The best stories are told through those around the main character, after all. Seline, you have a knack for honing in on the best parts," Lars said. "I interviewed Malcor on the boats coming back from Khasra. He tends to get lost in his own philosophy that, frankly, I don't think most people even know exist let alone have memorized." He laughed. "A normal knight says, "I did this, then I did that." Not Malcor, he quotes a scripture and tells you that he wondered if the Queen meant this scripture to apply to the thing he ended up doing."

Niss punched his arm and, defensively, he said, "Seriously. Check this out." He pulled a book from his satchel and after leafing through it, began to quote Malcor quoting from the Book of Genesis. When he finished, he said, "In all fairness, my lady Niss, do you know of any cleric that has that particular passage memorized or who would relate it to the Second Paladin Rite?" He referred to the paladin rite to face and defeat a mighty foe.

During their long discussion, more battles raged in the valley and eventually, Seline asked if they could walk out on the causeway and watch the sunset. Holding hands, the two stepped out into the cold winter air. Enough time had passed, that the floods receded though the surface pools remained iced over due to winter cold.

"Tell me if you like this," Lars said. He picked up some drumming batons and tapped on the causeway stone. He found enough tonal variance that, after several tries, he began to drum a rhythm. It started slow as he experimented with different hits and taps on the battlements but once he had it, he sped up. "I call this, the *War Cry of the Battle Priestess* and dedicate it to Dar Jeri who grieves for our ascending King Rojo. This was written by a battle mage prodigy named Ithaca, but I've improved it with drums. If you like this, I can get my team over here with proper drums."

His words became a chanted song, harsh on every fifth beat.

> Fast strike a dread foe down
> Might notch an arrow to slay by bow
> Bodies flow by us; we reaping sow
> Heart song of battle only enemies know
>
> Pure love sustains Her child
> Tiamat goddess; our future chosen
> Healing and praying, a dark day wild
> My foe is there; I'll strike out so brazen
>
> Ever on watch for quick signal
> A hand flick, a boot stomp or a neck bent
> Heal the deep wound and bare the soul
> Health my friend, salve goddess sent
>
> Sweat in my armor and rage in feet
> Lost companions; foes lost to time

May chaos swarm to us; we can't be beat
We are Her love; they can't hear this rhyme

There's another day yet to battle
We're the tip of the spear in the fight
Another cold night in armored metal
It'll pay off tomorrow by Her might

Seline could imagine how this would sound with all the Tanian drums shaking her chest. During the draconian chorus, Lars made inhuman sounds resembling dragons breathing fire, lifted her spirit and warmed her against the cold sunset.

Fire giants standing nearby came over to listen and one placed his helmet near Lars, who instantly incorporated it into the drumming. Another, picking up the beat, began to clap and soon all the fire giants in their area joined in. It added a bass that enhanced the song. Lars threw his head and long blonde hair back and suddenly the volume of his drumming increased to match the fire giants. Seline found herself singing the chorus and clapping along with the Kerchki.

Dar Niss and others joined in and suddenly, Niss pushed Seline out into a cleared spot commanding her to "Dance!"

Turning with the shove, Seline began the traditional combat dance of the paladins. That most paladins remained in the dungeon did not cross her mind. Seeing her dance, Lars changed the tempo and began to improvise the words into a medley of other known songs, but he kept the beat.

Right at Seline's transition to the actual combat kata, Niss flamestruck her and everyone around laughed. The fire giants immediately joined in letting their hands drag through the tower of flame. Lars increased the tempo and other bards came out with actual drums and other instruments. Seline had never danced the combat kata with actual music. The clash of armor on armor created rhythm that Lars amplified. She almost lost her beat; she was not wearing her armor. Wearing a spidersilk wrap that Ana would have approved of, she became suddenly self-conscious. The fire felt so good though and Niss' approval carried her past caring.

Soon, the priestesses and mages assigned to the Orders joined the dance and then others, hearing the commotion, came to join. After all the fear and tension, the dance cleansed their spirits. Seline caught a glimpse of several minotaurs attempting to follow the kata. She heard one ask if the dance had religious meaning. When the priestess answered no, the Tauran leapt into the dance ritual.

Seline closed her eyes and threw her head towards the sky as she spun, kicking and smashing her arms against those nearby. After a minute or two, when she opened them, Niss and Jeri flanked her and she saw that she had accidentally broken the arm of a mage near her. "Sorry!" she called out to him.

Lars continued to improvise the music, adding syncopation that made everything suddenly feel faster but more ephemeral. Seline spread her arms and looked up the center of the tornado of fire to the stars overhead.

When the dance ended, Seline dropped to the combat dance kata's final pose. With the flames clearing she saw the Court of Dragons. The three had come to watch. Though his arm rested in a sling, Alerius smiled and bowed to her, as did the other two. Then, the young girl form of Ynt'taris spoke. "Brother, perhaps we should set this dance to music every time."

Not known for humor, Ynt'taris' words hung in the air and then the White Priestess – that's what the fighters had started calling Ora – began to laugh. Others followed and even Ynt'taris smiled. Ora stepped forward and said, "I've asked that your drums be brought here, Lars. If you could, give us a few minutes to retrieve them from Tania. Also, King Andrew and the other courts saw the lights and asked to join. They'll be arriving shortly. Might I suggest we move this back into the Temple?"

Chapter Seventy – Temple Requiem

"Here!" Ana pulled a garment of two sheer strips of cloth, cut and embroidered to resemble armor tassets. Her acolytes draped these over Seline's shoulders and began attaching gemmed white gold clasps to hold the strips over her breasts and drape them down her front and back. "Being in the Order of Fire, you've got the right look to pull off a transcendent priestess. Seline, my dear, you really should use your beauty to bully the other paladins around."

Seline looked at herself and seemed fine until an acolyte reminded her she would be dancing again soon. "Dar Ana, I can't go out there in this! I feel completely naked!"

The high priestess commanded her to be quiet. "I can't do this with the others, and my priestesses are too fragile to dance with the paladins. You're going to dance and you're going to look spectacular." As a finishing touch, Ana fastened a bracer to each of Seline's forearms. A small bloodstone glinted along the center of her forearm. "Hold still," Ana ordered. Ana summoned her sword and smashed it down at the bracer. An inch from it, a force barrier, like goddess armor, blocked the blade. It made a dissonant thunder sound. From there, they draped chains from Seline's knees to Imperic style slippers at her feet. Like the bracers, these had a similar protective effect. "There, perfect. Except for your hair."

Ana's attendants all helped fit Seline. Ana caught her eyes, looking serious, she said, "Remember, paladin. Tonight, you dance for us all – the victors, the fallen, the survivors." Her words carried a touch of divine and suddenly, the veil between the world frayed just enough that Seline could see the River. "Do not dance for Tiamat. Tonight, you dance for Takhissis." Down the corridor, a fast series of drum strikes reverberated through the halls. After a pause, it started again with the larger wagon-sized drums joining in. When Ana asked how she felt, Seline replied, "Sick with anxiety."

Ana laughed, "That's perfect. Don't mess up." The high priestess took her arm and they walked towards the main room of the Temple.

When Seline stepped out, Lars altered the drum beat so that she recognized the beginning of the combat dance. He had twelve musicians with him, plus all the others from the causeway. Ana gripped her hand and walked her to the center of the floor, squeezing it tight perhaps as a threat or maybe encouragement. Seline could not decide.

She scanned the room noticing the royal crowns of Taysor, Gnomsh, Tauran, Stone, and Gar Galad. Behind them, the imperial red furred minotaurs snorted and chomped. Around Ana's throne, the dread lords stood while Jeri's sisters perched on the open dome over Crimson looming in the back. King Andrew bowed to her when her eyes scanned over the Soran party.

The drums paused. Just as the fast drums ones started, Ana snapped her fingers and the raging inferno of a Dar flamestrike ignited Seline to the music. She put her anxiety aside and danced, helped by not being able to see well outside the twisting fire. Bordering the River's flow, she saw Shara and Ana and Kell rise over the River and pray. They enacted a ceremony that Seline did not recognize. She threw her head back and felt armor smash into her wrist bracer. All around the crowd cheered.

Her bracer smashed into another, muscled arm this time. With a phantom chill, she opened her eyes in the Temple room and saw. Tembri danced with her, his leg smashing against her own in perfect time. Around them, other fallen heroes appeared and joined the dance. Seline moved to Ayden and gestured for her to join the dance.

Reluctantly, Ayden started to say 'no' but then saw Tembri. She ran into his arms and they held each other tight in Seline's ring of fire. Seline danced around the two as they embraced and kissed. Seline saw Tembri's mouth speak words but she did not understand. Ayden responded and then dragon wings burst from Tembri's shoulders, uplifted into the flames. He took Ayden's hand and the two joined Seline's dance.

Tembri's strong arms and upswept wings held Ayden close. Despite the combat kata, their dance carried its own rhythm, its own kata. Adapting the music, Lars somehow captured the essence of their movements and gave them a song just for them. During one of the quiet moments where drum beats faded for effect, Ayden's voice rose out of the fires as a tearful whisper. "Save a place for me by your side."

Lars held the music so they could hear Tembri's reply, "My heart, I will hold a place for you in Tiamat's red skies." Boom! The drums came crashing in with the music starting all over again, but faster.

All around the chamber, phantoms appeared to say good-bye or to share one last moment with those they loved. The visitations were not limited to the Temple as all over Bloodstone, Orcus' residual will frayed and snapped enough to free those bound throughout the world. Free-will returned to those trapped in undeath.

A minotaur's leg smashed against Seline's arm as she ducked and caught the kick. The magical bracers saved her and the creature gave her a formal sign of respect before she realized it too had fallen in battle. It went on and on. But, Tembri and Ayden danced together, alone, lost in the moment. *Your love must be epic*, Seline remembered Ayden saying.

Above her, from out of the River, Seline saw Dar Shara step into the flow and begin her dance. Ana joined. Kell stepped away and returned the real world entirely. Niss had not lied. Shara's dance slowed Time to a crawl during an achingly sensual series of acrobatic movements, and then accelerated through complex kata movements that left after-images in Seline's eyes. When Shara connected with Seline, and the two began to dance together, Armageddon and Crimson breathed fire into the flames burning around Seline. Not to be outdone, the golds added their fire and then Blaze and Arminoth. At last, Alerius dragonshifted and breathed as well.

Seline choked, nearly losing her focus when she saw the oozing ruin of shattered bone where the god emperor's wing had been. She lost pace but Shara skipped sideways and somehow recovered Seline's pace for her. The air around them began to fuse and spark. Seline felt a growing torrent of power and, had she not been in this group, would have felt fear.

A sphere of energy rose up around her and Shara, burning hotter, shining brighter. Shara caught Seline's hands and whispered, "Take it. Embrace it."

Seline opened her arms and tried to hold the sphere. Instantly, it collapsed into a blindingly bright marble no larger than a pearl. Too bright to look at, Seline lifted it up and found words in her heart. "Takhissis, accept this trophy of your victory over The Necromancer. The Second Cascade is done!"

Tembri kissed Ayden one last time and then withdrew. His form wavered as he whispered to her, "I love you forever." Through his and the other ghosts' fading bodies, Takhissis entered the chamber.

All present dropped to their hands and knees in awe. Even the minotaurs fell to their hands and knees. Seline found herself caught by wonder, staring at Her Goddess. She wanted to bow, render obeisance, grovel, and worship but instead she walked into Takhissis' embrace. A small part of her mind registered that Takhissis looked an awful lot like she did.

From Seline's mouth, Takhissis spoke. "We knew The Necromancer in the aeon of the Dragon Wars. While we fought the All Father for dominion, Orcus set plans to devour this world and lock it eternally static and unchanging. Chaos ruled all, and by our will, undeath did not yet exist for there was no Death to be desecrated. The corruption of undeath only became what it is after Time moved. I remember the Necromancer coming to me with an offer to ally against the All Father."

Takhissis turned to Alerius, "Beloved, with the Necromancer, all dragons could have remained in our dominion forever. But, this one," she pointed to Alerius. "He forbade me and I was greatly angered. He said, *My Queen, do not create this union. We are who we are because we are here with you, not at the nexi of Chaos, Creation, or Warp.*"

Her eyes shot across the room and all present, even those serving other gods felt her dominion's touch. "We are glad we did not unify with the Necromancer. Seeing what that one's plan became in the poison of the River's torrent, I bless you, Alerius. I bless you all, assembled heroes."

Seline found herself walking forward to the Taysoran King Andrew. His kneeling form rose upright and Takhissis kissed his cheek. "Though Orcus is not the one intended for the spear and shield, we have felled the Necromancer and it gives us hope that the Mother of All Nightmares too shall fall."

She turned from Andrew to face the dragons. "The forge is hot and my children are refined, but there is more. You burn with passion, but are fragmented. I am greatly displeased with Morilon, Gar Galad, and Cuthbert." Takhissis spun to face Andrew's high priest of Pha Rann. "I am most displeased that the work of ages nearly fell due to the short-sighted and back-biting tactics of Cuthbert." Her eyes flashed golden in anger and said, "Forever after shall Cuthbert and its vain followers be forbidden in my holy places. *Forbidden*. Pray I do not change my mind and order their extermination."

Takhissis rotated in the air, her hands open to her sides as if welcoming all in the chamber. "You are known, counted, and loved," she said and then vanished. Seline dropped to the floor where Shara caught her.

Chapter Seventy One – Frayed Ends Retied

Golcir sat, biding his time. The righteous fury in his soul had yet to fade. He felt the Tanian knights out there and hungered for combat. He knew they hungered for him. "My cause is just and right," he prayed. Only three of all the knights Malcor had brought back along with Golcir, and their battle mage, had survived. He rubbed his neck. When the elven clerics had resurrected him, the wounds had yet to fade perfectly, but he knew they would. Cuthbert would not have recovered him through all these battles with the gate device intact, if not for great purpose. "The gate remains. The plan," he whispered. "The plan."

Vel Pajor asked the hospital cleric near him. "How long has he been like this?"

"A month now, King Vel. No sign of improving. Same for those in his order."

"Do you know why?" Vel sipped some wine from his goblet.

"The Lord High Priest of Pha Rann believes that until Cuthbert recovers his dominion in the blessed heavens, some of the knights will remain this way."

"Nonsense. My own paladins of Krentismar are recovered, as are the Tanian knights. Tell me cleric, where is Golcir's equipment?"

Vel walked over to a series of crates holding Golcir's armor. He quickly found Golcir's book and tore out the device pages. Vel walked to Golcir's holding cell. "Recover soon. The plan cannot continue without you. I'm taking your battle mage and priest back to Morilon. Come find us when you're better."

That night, the elves of Morilon left Bloodstone.

* * *

In hand and ankle chains, Malcor walked through the Temple. Ayden apologized again for the inconvenience, as did Sofen. The entire Temple remained tense as the paladins slowly recovered. About half had, but others like Malcor still struggled with it. Even now, Malcor trembled and shook his head side to side as if to clear water from his ears.

They turned the corner to enter the great hall. Malcor held his hands up and frowned at the shackles, "I wish I wasn't coming here looking like this."

Seline greeted them by the door and signaled for them to wait a bit. "You look like you're recovering well," she said to Malcor.

Being near Ayden had helped. Now joined with Seline, Malcor felt that strange rider-bond again and it calmed him. He realized he felt her calm and asked them both, "Tell me, do you feel it too?"

Seline answered, "I felt pretty good until you got here. Now, it's about all I can do to stand still and keep my composure. I don't know how you're doing it. Do you truly feel," she cocked her head, "like shadowstepping out of here to the Sixth and ensuring Golcir is dead?"

Ayden chuckled, "When I picked him up, he almost dragonshifted to fly out and find any Pha Rannic paladins left in the Seventh."

Malcor coughed and then it turned into a laugh. The story of Golcir and Kendra's combat had been retold to the point it had become epic legend. "Would it be bad if I said - Yes?"

Seline escorted them into the hall. Alerius sat in Ana's throne with Dar Shara and Ora standing to either side. Ora waved at Malcor. He tried to wave back but the chains prevented him. He signaled instead for reinforcements, a paladin gesture when not in combat that asked for extra strength and patience in the face of administrative challenge.

"Not funny," Alerius said noting the hand sign between them. "So, let's get to business. Malcor, you continue to impress. Like you, I wish we did not have you chained but the after effects of the Saints Battle, well, you know how it is. We all bear our wounds." He flexed his shoulder and winced. "The Circle has named you King, to succeed Rojo and take the military throne. You will accept the formal title of Rojo the Second, to honor our first king. I am told that you have concerns with this. I would like to hear them."

Malcor looked at Ora and drew strength from her calm and yet radiant demeanor. Shara also watched with a kindly expression. "God emperor, I have many concerns but I believe they are all known to the Circle. Rather than answer, I suppose I would like to understand why – with so many epic heroes in our midst – anyone would think that I would be a good king. I say this not to imply your judgement is flawed, but to humbly question – what is it that you all see in me? My liege, I do not see a king. When I think of myself as King Rojo the Second, it feels laughable."

From behind the throne, two small figures stepped out. One was Klara, who held hands with Kaia. The Halfling pointed to Malcor and said, "See? There he is. Go to him."

Klara clapped her hands and skipped down the dais' steps to Malcor where she tried to crush him with a hug. Kaia sat down on the top step and let his legs dangle down. Klara hugged him several times before taking his hand and turning to look at the god emperor.

Alerius said, "Malcor, besides the prophecy, your bringing the shadow dragon heretics back to Tiamat, who your father is, your meteoric rise through the Order of Water, and the pivotal role you have played in the six months since becoming a paladin, allow me to put this question back to you: Why do you think you would not be a good king?"

Klara said, "I think you'd be a great king, Malcor."

He brushed hair from her face and while looking at her said, "A king is responsible for so many things. Do you know what I'm best at doing, Klara?"

"Making scary swords?" she questioned him back. The innocent question hung in the air before everyone began to laugh.

"No, well – yes, I guess. Klara, I'm good at carrying out orders, pushing my boundaries past breaking, and just barely keeping my self-control intact enough to listen to the Queen. I would have died many times here without the intervention of Ora, and others." He looked up from Klara's wide eyes to the god emperor. "In spite of the prophecy, I've never heard the Queen tell me to be king. But, I have heard the calling to be Her knight."

Malcor looked to each of the other dread lords, "I have heard the Queen tell me to make things, where to find the lich's soul gem, and to step back through the gate for Bomoki when all others had left. I have also felt the Queen chastise me for foolish and vain recklessness that nearly ended me. I see now how my pride compromised my role against Fate. How are these kingly qualities?"

So focused on Ora and the god emperor, Malcor had not really noticed the others present. King Andrew of Taysor worked at a table covered with maps and messenger rolls of parchment. He said, "In Taysor, we have a saying. *Fear those who seek after power. Friend those who shun it.* I agree with your god emperor. You are perfect."

Alerius nodded. "Rojo the First did not seek to be king. In fact, like you, he was given a near impossible task. *Bring an end to the civil war,* I commanded him. So too, do I command you, Dar Malcor – you will serve as Rojo the Second, King of Morbattania. You obey the Mother. Tell me, will you obey me?"

It almost reminded him of R'Dar Tor trying to force him to stay at the Armory. At that thought, the berserker rage in his heart ignited. To hide it from his face, he dropped to his knees and hands before Alerius. "Do not ask me this command," he said.

A frown creased Alerius' face and he looked askance at Shara and Ora. "It is a question, not a command."

Malcor remained prostrate. "If a question, then my answer is No. If a command, then as a loyal knight, I live to serve."

"Get up Mal, what are you doing?" Klara asked. Her voice carried all the concern of a sister for her brother.

"Brothers," Alerius growled in draconian. "I would counsel with you."

Malcor found himself, along with Alerius, Spark, and Ynt'taris removed from the River. A stone table held the prophecy between them. Their titanic forms rose up and surrounded Malcor completely. He winced to see the raw wound where Alerius' wing had been torn and snapped off by Orcus.

Ynt'taris spoke first. "This paladin withstood me on the mountain with great self-control and divine focus. Also, my beloved Ora loves him. I would see him be king. But, I must remind you all, again, that the prophecy did not necessarily point to Malcor."

Malcor felt relief at the ice patriarch's words. Spark then declared, "Tania and its relations with other kingdoms has prospered with a human face in command of the military throne. Humans gravitate towards being ruled by one of their own. I regret we did not conduct this experiment ages ago. Like Rojo, Malcor has the raw talent and mindset to be successful. I am concerned with his self-imposed isolation. I recommend we consider that, while Malcor may be king tomorrow, he is not a king today."

Alerius looked at Malcor from several angles. "Point well taken, my brothers. Very well. I have reached a decision."

They fell back into the River where Malcor remained on the floor. "Malcor, stand." Alerius commanded. Ayden and Seline helped him to his feet. "You seem to have a sense that being king means being Rojo. This is not what we ask. Effective now, you are King of Morbatten. Your job is not to rule the empire. Your job, if you will accept it, is to prepare Klara to be your successor."

Klara's eyes went wide, as did Malcor's and Ora's. Klara spun to face the god emperor. "You want me to be king, with Malcor?"

A toothy dragon smile split Alerius' human face. "Yes Klara. You and your brother shall be king together."

Klara took Malcor's hand and squeezed it. "Mal, this means that you're a king! Wow! And," she looked coyly back at Alerius. "I'm a princess?"

Everyone burst into laughter. Nearby, a mage sketched the moment: Malcor in chains, Klara beaming at him, and Ora clapping her hands. Andrew stepped forward and took Malcor's hand. "When the god emperor comes to visit Taysor, I ask that you come too, King Malcor. I insist that you bring Princess Klara with you."

Malcor looked up at Alerius and said, "I will serve but do not understand your wishes in this regard."

Alerius stood and walked down the steps to Malcor. "Release the king to me," he said. "Come."

They walked to one of the many side rooms where a window looked down towards the plains of Haven on the other side. "I hope this isn't going to be a recurring thing with you, Dar Malcor. Right now, I'm willing to let this be that you're cut off from your divine purpose by the God Saints' battle."

"I have felt disconnected since that," Malcor acknowledged.

"But you have more to say? For thousands of years, I have worked to shape Tania. Do you really think you are the first human to doubt my judgement?" Alerius rubbed his shoulder and winced.

"Put that way, I'm sure I'm not the first but I am the first to succeed King Rojo. Rojo had gift -"

Alerius interrupted him. "Rojo did not have special training or genius to be king, rule, or even be a leader. He had a single-minded focus on the Goddess that has since taken him into ascension. As a king, like you, he behaved in a most paladin-like manner. There is a reason I select paladins to rule. You have an unflinching moral compass and an eye single to the Mother."

"So, tell me then about Klara. Please."

"At your Coming of Age ceremony, R'Dar Tor interrupted the prophecy. Klara also fulfills the conditions of the prophecy, but is obviously too young. We had hoped that Rojo would live a long and prosperous life as king so that either you or Klara would mature into this role." Alerius continued to rub his shoulder and when he pulled his hand back, blood covered his palm. He sighed and said, "Klara is not a literal daughter of Kell. Kell assisted Sai in creating her. She became your sister by her choice, by the acknowledgement of the people of Klenna to let you be her brother – in spirit. Truthfully, she is an experiment to fuse Sai's golemcraft with a living sentient being, that I created." Alerius wiped his hands on a cloth and took a deep, shuddering breath. This close to him, Malcor heard a wet rattling in the god emperor's lungs.

"I would render aid my king. Shall I call a healer?" Malcor offered.

"Sai has advanced his golem work to a point where he can imprint them on living beings. The imprints are virtually the same as the original. It's magic. With Klara, we worked to create a golem that could imprint on its own. Klara imprinted on you Malcor. Since you left Klenna, she has imprinted on Ora. If she stays with you and Ora, she will become either a powerful priestess or a powerful paladin. Either way, she will most likely eclipse you as she comes into her own power."

"Does she know she is a golem?" Malcor asked.

"Yes, and she has a deeply-rooted sense of her uniqueness. Either way, she fulfills the prophecy though most of the Circle, including me, felt you were the destined one." Alerius had started rubbing his shoulder again. "If an imprintable golem can choose its exemplar, will it evolve into having a soul? That is the experiment."

Malcor struggled to not call for a healer when blood oozed out around Alerius' armor plates. "I will need help, and patience," Malcor said as he resisted the urge to help or try to stop the bleeding.

"Let's go find Ana," Alerius commanded suddenly walking out of the alcove and down a passage Malcor had never noticed before. It entered into a small shrine.

* * *

Ana laid in repose on a stone slab set in the center of each colored dragon representation as a statue. She opened her eyes and sat up when they entered. "Any contact with Rojo?" Alerius asked.

"No, but my questions have been somewhat answered. Rojo accomplished the Second Rite and has proceeded to the Third." Without anything being said, Ana stood and laid her hands on Alerius' shoulder. "If this does not begin to make progress, I recommend amputation of the shattered wing bones."

Alerius hissed at her, "I would rather die than be cut off from flight."

"That may be what this comes to then, Alerius." Malcor had never heard anyone speak to a dread lord like this and it both amused and fascinated him. As if speaking to a hurt child, Ana continued. "All these ages and the mighty god emperor has never required attendance by the very clerics he created. I'm telling you. If we amputate the cursed flesh and bone, you'll be better off than these daily healings." The flow of blood stopped under her healing prayer, but Malcor saw it drain the color from her skin.

"I'll let you know," Alerius answered her. "You two have met already but since we are here, Ana. I want you to make time to share with Malcor all that you know about Bloodstone, Cascades, and the role of the Temples. Our next king needs a strong understanding of this before we introduce him to the political guild heads."

Ana nodded and smiled at Malcor. He could not help but notice how fatigued she looked after healing the god emperor. She went back to the stone table and laid down. "Did you know my king, that eldar dragons resist most mortal magic? Our stubborn god emperor resists even his Mother's will that he be healed." Her eyes closed and she fell unconscious before she started her next sentence.

* * *

Marcello found Khalla at last. About half of Rogue's Blade had died, or been lost in the cold fight against the remaining abyssal monsters. They had a lot to discuss, and it was hard to do so. Most of Rogue's Blade knew that someone named Marcello served as Guildmaster. But, no one knew what Marcello looked like. Thankfully, the group had been discreet and reverted to calling him by his alias, Ash. Still, it worried him.

One night, as they lay together talking, a gentle knock at their door sounded and Ynt'taris entered. The small girl child sat down at the table in their small room oblivious to their state of undress. Marcello pulled a blanket over him and sat up. "Dread Lord Ynt'taris, I hope you are pleased with my delivery of the diamond to Bomoki?"

"Yes. You did well. From what I can tell, you delivered it to Bomoki and it yielded maximum devastating effect. I am impressed. King Malcor executed on follow up. My revenge is complete. I am pleased."

"You've come here for a reason, great patriarch. I do not want to assume it is regarding compensation." Marcello said, desperately hoped it was about compensation.

"Yes, that. Also, I wish to know exactly what happened. To know this, would take more time than I have. As such, I have arranged for a mage to extract and deliver your sensory experience to me. Once I have that, I will decide your compensation. However, based solely on outcome, I am most impressed. I understand that you are enamored with Sai's metalloid golems. As a starter, I'm thinking of intervening on your behalf. Plus, the winter wolf cub was a most thoughtful gift to my beloved Ora. You will be contacted tomorrow morning."

Ynt'taris hopped down and left. Marcello pulled the mithril golem spider from behind his ear. It bobbed on the back of his hand. "Hard to believe that carrying this with me was one of the creepiest things I have ever had to do for the empire," he said. "It's so damn handy though. Hey," he whispered to it. "Go keep watch outside and alert me if anyone else comes to see us." The spider phase vanished, and Khalla pulled him over backwards.

* * *

Unter and Grito used tankards to hold the map down. Though the water level remained too high to access either Unter's Vein or Bomoki's Gate complex, they knew that with all the commotion and winter wars raging against the remnant undead and monsters, the tunnels would be, should be, clear. Moreover, since Orcus' fall, the undead all seem weaker. Reports had flooded in of priestesses and clerics turning with ease foes that before the fall, would have required a group to even stand a chance against.

"So, it's decided," Unter said. "We'll go back to the gate complex, to the wight hall and take all we can. That should be a fast in and out. From there, we'll head back to your mine and start a new excavation." Unter and Grito dumped out the thirty pounds of ore from the sepulcher tunnel. They squealed each time they found a flawless and optically-perfect bloodstone. "I count seven, possibly eight flawless tiny ones," Unter said.

"I count thirty flawed but potent ones," Grito answered. He raised his tankard and smashed it against Unter's. "Aye Unter, it will be glorious. We already have the dwarves itching for some more action. And the Gar clan, they have a chip on their shoulder after word got out that Alerius saw them as *reluctant*."

The two laughed. Though they both came from Stone, they had spent so much time around Tanians their own countrymen would consider them foreigners. With enough bloodstones, it would not matter. Unter raised his drink, "A brother with wealth is family indeed!" It was an old dwarven adage and they smashed their cups together. After a long drink, Unter raised his cup again. "To the dragon priestess: Thalian! She saved my life."

* * *

Dar Reznor and the Apprentice sat in the chamber beneath the Temple's Great Hall. Bloodstones worth all the world glittered around them in this safest sanctuary. The frozen bits of Bomoki captured by Malcor remained frozen. They had separated out the parts that might be worth considering: the head, eyes, and hands. The rest, they had spent days and days disintegrating with magic. "If anyone ever puts Bomoki back together, they'd have to be a god," Reznor said as he lifted the head up on a pedestal. "Is it weird that I look at this and wonder, what would Bomoki say to us right now?"

The frozen head with the ram's skull helmet atop it remained silent. The expression contained exactly what Marcello and Ynt'taris had hoped, exultant glee. The Apprentice placed the hands to the side of the pedestal. "No, not weird. Just human of you, Reznor. I'm actually wondering more about the ice patriarch. I'm sure father will seek him out about this, but did we know Ynt'taris could do this?"

Reznor placed the eyes each into their own crystal box and sealed them shut. "Of the three, Spark has always had the purest interest in magic. Ynt'taris though has a history of moments where he surprises. Consider the Sage Alaura. Until Ynt'taris took her as his disciple and began to teach her, who would have guessed that the ice patriarch knew so much? Still, I can't think of a single time that either have outclassed Alerius when it comes to magic skill. I would consider this Ynt'taris' greatest life achievement. Too bad he did not include the Mage's Guild in its crafting."

They sealed the head and hands in their own cases as well. The work took hours and when done, they called for Syliri. The eldar medusa, who tended to Alerius' menagerie, stepped through a magical doorway into the room at Reznor's invitation. "I remember Bomoki," she said with a tone of sadness in her voice. "That you have come to this," and she transmuted the frozen flesh to stone.

Reznor and Blaze looked away as she did this and then stepped with her through the gate, and back to Morbatten. Syliri had held an alcove empty with a carved placard on it for centuries. "Bomoki, the First Hellhound" it read.

Reznor and the Apprentice created an illusion of Bomoki, as he had been before being taken by the Jade God's sceptre. This human-sized illusion stood in an attitude relaxed and ready. They then created the giant-sized

Bomoki that had taken Jeri's eyesight. Around it, they superimposed the titanic hellhound Rojo had fought. The three images regarded each other and then the hellhound snapped at Reznor. Syliri said, "I believe Alerius will love it, Dar Reznor. Most illustrative."

* * *

In all, it took three weeks for the madness to fade from the Tanian knights. When Malcor could at last walk free of the dungeon holding block, he sought out Ora. He found her alone in her chambers, writing at a desk. Seeing him, she rose up and rushed to his arms. They held each other before they both began to talk at the same time. Speaking over each other, Malcor finally deferred, "The high priestess may go first."

"No, no. I bow to the King," she teased back. "But if you insist. Malcor, the god emperor has given me permission to step back from my cleric duties until the baby is born. I won't need it. You have no idea how easy birth is when you're surrounded by high priestesses and Sai's golems all day." She laughed. "And, Ynt'taris has asked if he might name our child. I wanted to ask you this."

"Ynt'taris, really?" Malcor rubbed his head. "I never saw Ynt'taris as being that interested in human life at this level."

Ora laughed and pulled him over to a sofa to sit down and lay back. "You don't give him enough credit. If you look back through the histories, Ynt'taris has been the source of mercy for more innocents than any of the dread lords. I'm okay with it, but only if you are."

"Yes, I am honored that the ice patriarch wishes to name our child. Please tell him so. Tell me, when I first met you, were you transcended? I've been struggling to remember and I find my memory is hazy in this regard."

He began to rub her feet, swollen from the pregnancy and she moaned. "Yes, but Ynt'taris did not wish it known he had chosen a rider. He and Sai created tokens that hid it, hazed it from people's memories. Once the war started, it didn't really matter and I felt it best to wield magic that had more purpose. The tokens could not hide it."

"So, Ora. How old are you?" Malcor looked at her a bit sheepishly. "Am I allowed to know?"

"How old do I look to you?" she countered.

"Twenty, maybe twenty-three? In my defense, I grew up with metal and fire, not beautiful ladies. I have no idea."

"You're close, Mal. I selected into the Temple when I was six years old. By the time I was fourteen, I served in the military. Ynt'taris noticed me the next year. I transcended when I was twenty-one. That was just four years ago." She kicked him. "You worried I would turn out to be a hundred-year-old crone?"

"It wouldn't matter, but when I was locked in the dungeon, I had a lot of time to think about it and talk with the other knights. Growing up the way I did, I never really paid attention to it but it seems that a priestess and paladin pairing is a story as old as Tania itself. Dar Tania and Sean started it, and I know that story. I just didn't realize it really happened."

Ora watched him and tried to hear what he really meant. "You're concerned that I may not love you, perhaps. That I took you – the strapping young knight – for either my own pleasure or for the empire? Don't be silly. How many of your fellow knights remained involved with their priestess afterwards? Only those truly in love. The dragons consider human love and passion like blowing air onto fire. It fans the fire brighter, makes the embers glow hotter.

"Yes, I was commanded. I already told you this. But, I was also given discretion to say no." She pulled him to her. "I said yes." She kissed his head. "You're so worried, perhaps I should ask you the same questions. You are king after all and I hear you had quite the adventures with any number of priestesses. Should I be worried about any of them, hmmm?" She started naming all the women he had fought alongside and he interrupted her.

"I know about Ana's advances, Malcor. It's a thing she does. I asked her not to, as a courtesy, but she outranks me," she began counting on her fingers. After a few moments counting, she finished. "Unimaginably outranks me. I also received word from Thalian, Sofen, and," she turned his head to look at her face. "Twenty other priestesses, including the old lady from Klenna. They all wanted to know if I objected to their being with you. I never replied."

"You should have just told them, no."

"Why? We are commanded to preserve the bloodlines of the heroes. It's a core function of the matriarchy for all time. Even Dar Tania had multiple children with heroes that were not Sean before at last marrying him. Malcor, it is not my place to say no, though I would appreciate it if you and I had time to know each other more before you said yes." She put his hand on her lower belly and they felt their child moving around. "He's very active right now. I think he recognizes your voice."

Jeri lay on an operating table. Not being able to see, it rather terrified her. Ana reassured her. "I've done this thousands of times. You're a dragon. You'll endure. It'll be fine. It'll work."

Her two surviving sisters held her hand and forehead. They also said reassuring things, but Jeri heard the concern in their voices. The eldest asked, "Dar Ana, how is this even possible? I always understood that even humans could not manipulate healing once natural healing occurred."

"True," Ana replied. "But Jeri's eyes have yet to heal at all. The cursed nature of the blade and being that took her eyes has prevented healing at any level. That's why this will work."

A door opened and several priestesses came in. Jeri could hear everything and did not like it at all. "Why do I need that much blood?" she called to them.

Ana swore at dragon hearing and came back to take her other hand. "Okay, let's go through this. Nothing has changed but there are some precautions I'm ordering. We're going to transfuse blood from your sisters to you. If you don't need it, no harm except for some pain. We have no drugs, poisons, or venoms that will render you unconscious, Jeri, I need you to hold absolutely still. I've asked Syliri to join us. She's going to petrify your entire body up to your neck. That'll allow us to do the transfusions, the required work, and prevent you from moving. There is a way to remove some of the pain, but your sisters have already said no. I'd like to ask you."

Jeri heard both her sisters hiss angrily at Ana. Ana caressd her hair and said, "A psionic creature could take your mind and thoughts far away from your body. Alerius himself has offered to oversee this in hopes you say yes, to spare you the pain. It gives us the best chance of succeeding." Ana paused and then squeezed her hand. "Jeri, the king Dar Malcor, he has requested you continue as his battle priestess. I hope this brings you joy."

"It is a bittersweet one, but joyful. Yes. I agree. How could I serve blind like this in continual pain?"

"No!" her sister said, but already a mind flayer and Alerius entered the room. Their presence silenced the two golds who shrank back but then, holding Jeri's hand, steeled their resolve and stayed.

The flayer stood at the head of the table and Jeri felt the first tentacle brush her hair back and tickle her neck. The creature made a series of trills and suddenly, Jeri could understand it. "Free your mind to me, golden one. I will take you where your heart most wishes to go."

Ana said, "We're going to start the transfusion. Jeri, once this begins we will be removing any and all tissue and bone that contacted the cursed blade. Regeneration and healing, in conjunction with your eye, will make this work. Please, relax and let your mind wander. Pretend you're daydreaming." Ana signaled and they started.

Guided by the flayer, Jeri found herself meeting Rojo for the first time. In her dragon form, she lounged on a rock in the hot desert sun. She had seen the dark armored figure riding at a leisurely gallop towards her for hours. One of her sisters had leapt to the sky to warn the rider off.

Her memories skipped to when Rojo had climbed the rocks to speak with them. Her sisters did not like him and breathed fire to chase him away. Only Jeri noticed that he ignored the flames as if they were not there. Only Jeri had noticed the speculative curiosity in his eyes when he stood before her and bowed. She could hear his words as if it were happening all over again.

"Daughter of Tiamat, I come to speak with you about your true calling in this world." He had seemed so dashing. One of her sisters landed behind him and bit forward. He turned and dropped to his hands and knees. "I am no threat to you, beautiful ones."

Her sister, the eldest holding her hand, had stopped just shy of biting him. Mentally, Jeri laughed. *Had she bit Rojo, what would have happened?*

An alien thought answered her. *Tiamat would have protected him until he had finished saying what She had driven him to say. I know this from interviewing paladins, at the god emperor's insistence.*

Jeri found herself agreeing and the memory continued as if she sat on the rock that bright day years ago. Rojo had been so brave and dashing, and utterly unconcerned about the hostile reception he received. She had said so. He replied, "If you stay here, you'll only ever be fallen dragons, victims of Fate, forever drowning in Time until at last you die as powerful Ancient Dragons. Or, you can let me stay with you and share a vision of this world as Tiamat's throneplane, where your glory increases and multiplies forever."

Her sisters had wanted to throw him off the cliffs. Jeri instead wrapped her body around him to protect him. "I want to hear about this. What do you mean when you say drowning in Time? Time does not drown."

"Imagine Time flowing like a river, from one moment to the next. Even now, you, me, these mountains are dying. It was not like this in the eldar times. Time is a sickness of this world but Tiamat has an answer for it in Her doctrine. If you'll take my hand, I may be able to show you."

Jeri placed her talon in Rojo's hand. For the first time, she humanshifted. She had not known that such a thing was even possible. That was the beginning of her conversion. Though her sisters humanshifted too, they remained convinced that Rojo had come to harvest their bodies for magical item and equipment components.

She laughed in her own memory when one said, "Jeri, you're quite naked. Is it this evil knight's purpose to have his way with you before our very eyes?"

"Such a thing," Rojo answered. "It is not possible. Draconians are a corruption of dragon eggs, not a mating of human and dragon. We view it as heresy. Tiamat forbids it. As Her paladin, I would fight regardless of colored or metallic. If you'll return with me to Morbatten, I can answer these questions you have."

Her sister had grown flustered. "I did not ask a question -"

"But you did," Rojo countered. "About impregnating dragons. While she is beautiful, I am a paladin and sworn to chastity. You are quite safe from me having my way with you."

"Then," the eldest interrupted. "Why do you come here armored and with weapons?"

Rojo had bowed and drew his sword. "It is my personal style and choice to travel this way. Might I also add, you are not exactly in safe and secure places, sisters. To get here, I had to travel many weeks through very dangerous lands to find you."

Something about his sword mesmerized Jeri. "Is your sword magic?" she asked.

In answer, Rojo's sword ignited burning through red flames, blue lightning, white ice, green vaporous mist, and purple dripping venom. "Tiamat holds the allegiance of these dragon types: red, blue, white, green, and black are sworn to Her dominion."

"Dominion," the eldest said. "At last the truth! So this is about dominion." The eldest spat at Rojo, "How many times must we endure these smug paladins climbing our mountain and demanding we serve as their holy steed? As if we were horses!"

Rojo laughed while sheathing his sword, such a genuine laugh. Jeri could not remember many times that Rojo had ever laughed that way. "Dominion, no. Not like that. Dominion has other meanings. As gold dragons, did you know that you each fall under the All Father Bahamut's dominion?" They shook their heads no. "Didn't you ever wonder why your natural tendency is to watch and protect, only rising up in combat to resist evil?"

The middle had bit at him then. "Evil like you."

The bite had not even fazed Rojo, who sat down still chuckling. "If you define evil as a certain disregard for mortal life, then perhaps I am. I prefer to see myself as a champion willing and ready to stand against evil in all places at all times. Tiamat's dominion is, after all, going to be this world. She, like me and Her worshippers, do not wish her throne plane contaminated by evil, same as you."

He proceeded to tell the story of his paladin rites, his greatest foes, his most fearsome battles. Even her sisters had fallen under the spell of his stories. He stayed with them for weeks before at last Jeri had said, "I will go with you, Rojo." She had fallen in love with the striking young knight, dark moods notwithstanding. She sensed great pain and anguish in his past, but his life's purpose could not have gleamed more brightly.

"Jeri, we're done." Ana said. "Can you see?"

Jeri opened her eyes and saw blurry shapes at first. Slowly, they began to focus. "The eye Malcor retrieved, it's perfect. I think. Tell me. The other eye, it did not work. It recovered but retained the scar across your eye's center. We have implanted a golem eye. It will serve you, in human form, like a normal eye. But it will not dragonshift with you."

Jeri looked around the room as faces, curious and concerned resolved to her view. She noted the golemsmith, Sai. He bowed to her. The mind flayer had already withdrawn and she could not sense him at all. Her sisters, when they saw her looking at them, burst into tears and hugged her.

"A golem eye?" Jeri asked.

Sai held out his hand and she lost her eye as a stream of silver flowed into it. "Yes. I'm working on a golem wing for the god emperor. It occurred to me that, if a golem could accept an instruction specific enough to mesh with your body, it could relay vision to your human brain." The silver flowed back to her eye and, without pain though she winced anticipating it, she could see perfectly. "The golem eye will become embedded jewelry when you dragonshift. Also, you are welcome to take it out. Removed, it will still work but be careful. Your mind will struggle with two unexpected images."

Through her sisters' hugs, she saw the new king and struggled to sit upright. Malcor stepped forward and bowed to her. In his hands, he held Twilight Fell and Rojo's holy symbol. He presented these to her. "Dar Jeri, I would have you continue as my battle priestess. Will you have me?"

Jeri tried to imagine Malcor as Rojo, and failed. But still, something majestic and endearingly humble about the young man struck a chord in her heart. "I will," she said. "You are no Rojo, not yet. But, you shall be my king!"

* * *

Spring came early and chased the snow out of the valleys and lower parts of Tania. Marcello stood before the entire Thieves Guild assembled at the front of Sai's estate on the East West Highway. The motley group fingered knives. As ordered, all had brought large tower shields that they would use to enter the estate before dropping them.

"Our honor and reputation is at stake. Your reputation! And, let me tell you. We have worked way too hard to recover it after Farant. The way I see it, with the Circle watching, we need to succeed. Even though Sai has spent months preparing his estate for our assault, even though Sai is golemsmith like unto a god, even though everyone expects us to fail – remember, they had the same expectation when Farant nearly killed Sai's priestess Ora. Our objective is this." He held up a rattle. "There is a baby boy in the central gardens. We need to give this rattle to the baby boy. That's how we win.

"Though the fighting we do will be real, and yes we will feel real pain; so will they! And the Temple will hold us in stasis so that we do not die. I've selected each of you because you hold something very special that is going to make us succeed."

Marcello continued talking to the Guild outlining in key detail how they would swarm across the bridge, dodge the guard golems, and enter the estate. It fired them up and they began chanting and applauding different parts of the plan.

Far away, the real Marcello and Khalla led the guild's cells against Sai's estate. Bribing and making bets with the estates neighboring Sai's had been easy enough. Marcello held the spider golem in his hand and said, "I trust you've honored my wishes and kept this from Sai?" The spider pulsed in his hand and phased back to his ear. They stepped through the wall of illusion that made Sai's estate look like a parkland in early summer. Instantly, the ravine moat, which dropped down hundreds of feet into a river of lava, appeared before them. They balanced on the perimeter waiting for the sign.

The other guild members, playing the role of the real guild, attacked across the narrow bridge. It was very flashy, and doomed to fail. Their role was to create a distraction that would last long enough for the real incursion. "It's time to go," Marcello said.

Ryvane cast a flight spell. This allowed Marcello, the cell leaders, and the fifty agents making up his best cells to fly across the ravine, turning invisible as they did so. A wall of force rose up in front of the actual wall surrounding Sai's estate. No doubt bad things would happen if they touched it. Six of the thieves held passwall wands, courtesy of Ryvane. They went under the forcewall, under the battlements.

Of the five cells, four had a role similar to the fake guild attacking the main gate off the East-West Road. They would create distractions wherever they happened to come up. Marcello thought Sai might not rearrange key areas and so sent Khalla to where Ora had first met Farant. That spot in the garden seemed to be where Sai conducted his official business. Marcello burst above ground in a building of some sort. Immediately, gargoyle statues and golems large and small of all materials animated to attack.

Khalla's group broke ground in a gleaming silvery garden. Marcello had sent Ryvane with Khalla at the last second. It made her wonder what the guildmaster was up to and she mentally swore at him, again. As Khalla's eyes adjusted to the bright daylight, a winter wolf pup howled nearby and filled their heads with terrible images of being bitten apart while alive. They shook it off and rose up, rolling and tumbling to the side. Khalla activated spheres of darkness that she threw all around the courtyard, same as her cell members. Once in place, they threw more hoping defenders would think thieves hid in them. The wolf howled again, closer than she liked. "Go get that wolf and silence it," she commanded.

She rolled under a bench and placed herself into a state near death. Still aware, she felt the dark spheres being dispelled as golems stomped all about. One, metallic, bent over and investigated her before it lumbered off. Only when all went quiet did Khalla return herself to full alertness. The shrine to Tiamat lay exactly where Marcello had described it. Apparently, he had been right. Sai had invested too much in the inner courtyard to rearrange it that much.

Khalla prayed to Tiamat and sprinted to the shrine. There inside, a small child lay on his back, asleep. She placed the child's rattle in a small baby boy's hands just as something grabbed her and lifted her into the air, shaking her violently. Against the pain, she exulted. "We did it! We won!" and then she blacked out.

They all came to in the shrine. Sai did not look pleased, but Marcello positively gloated. Seeing his cheerful mood, Khalla could not help but gloat a little too. "See?" Marcello yelled to no one in particular. "When the god emperor established our guild, he said – and I quote: *You will be a force contingency against my empire's elite. To keep them honest. To keep them in check.* And," Marcello continued to gloat, "we did not even use the most powerful tools entrusted to us to do this."

Khalla felt he may have pushed it a tad too much and stepped forward to take his hand. "I am Khalla, a lieutenant. This activity showed what a determined group trained and well-prepared, can do. If any of you," she felt silly speaking to no one and so focused her attention on Sai. "If you would like to test your security, we would be happy to oblige. For the right price of course."

Sai nodded and she felt suddenly the weight of a great many watchers. Marcello had told her the entire assault would be watched. Marcello then stepped forward and said to Khalla, "*Marcello*, I knew you would not lead us astray. Today is a good day for the Thieves Guild! Yes, yes. I know that many of you thought I might be Marcello. It's actually Khalla." Many of the thieves were eyeing the two incredulously. "Only the guildmaster could have pulled this off though," and he pointed to the small baby shaking the rattle and biting on it.

From behind the baby, Dar Ora walked out. The baby immediately reached up for her. Marcello and Khalla stammered for just a moment as they realized the child was Ora's son. "I did not realize the child would be the king's," Khalla said bowing. Khalla also understood that Marcello was retiring. He had hinted at it. He had just passed the guildmaster role to her.

Ora smiled at her. "My son was never in harm's way. It's one thing to assault an estate. To achieve a gentle outcome is what we wished to see." The child snuggled into her neck.

"No matter," Khalla said, continuing the play. "Maybe it is time that the guild come out a bit more into the open, yes?"

Sai bowed to Khalla. "I release any and all claims against your Guild, Marcello."

"May I ask," Khalla hesitated. "What is the child's name?"

Ora turned him so Khalla could see his face. "Malcor wanted to name him after Tembri. Tembri. It is a strong name for faith and unending conviction. The ice patriarch gave him his formal name, but we call him Tembri."

Khalla smiled at the child before she snapped her fingers and ordered the Guild to depart.

* * *

"So, tell me. What was the reward?" Halgrim asked Ash.

Ash withdrew a scroll and placed it on the table. He did not say anything, just pushed it to Halgrim.

"What is this?" Halgrim opened and read it. As he did so, his eyes grew bigger and bigger. "I never imagined."

Ash, formerly known as Marcello, sat down and kicked his feet up on the edge of the table. "The real question is, what do you want to do with this?"

Halgrim rolled it out on the table. It contained a letter of credit for a hundred thousand gold along with a charter for one of the Tauran world galleons. The actual scroll was a copy of a map of the ancient empire of Merakor. It showed the general surface holdings of the dark elves, but appeared to map out a safe route from the coast to the Arati Grasslands – Halgrim pointed. "Am I reading this right? A tower of sorcery?"

Ash nodded. "I asked the patriarch. He said that when they re-visited the Temple of Glass, they recovered some items. One was the original of this map. Not only a Tower of Sorcery, but one that was not common knowledge even at the time of Merakor. Ynt'taris says, and I quote: *You're welcome to go yourselves or sell this map for money. Whatever suits you. However, this Tower was known to the patriarchs and specialized in dragon-related magic.*"

Halgrim sat back rubbing his forehead and eyes. "I'm too old for such a quest, but I can see you're up for it."

"I would need a special kind of mage to attempt this," Ash pointed his finger at Halgrim. "I don't think you're too old for a grand adventure."

"I was hoping the reward would be more tangible than this. I have to pay my helpers." Halgrim tapped the letter of credit. "This barely covers the cost of the materials I put into making that wand work."

Ash smiled. That they had started haggling meant Halgrim could be won over. "Old friend, you yourself taught me that spell components and spellcraft in general do not cost that much. Sure, the material was exotic, but Marcello provided it through the guild. It was not your cost."

They went back and forth before settling on a payment to the helpers equal to a third of the credit. "The rest, we will split in half – you for your work and me for doing the dangerous part," Ash stated.

Halgrim almost continued the bargaining but nodded his head. "Ash, if we're going to do this, we'll need more than a clever thief and my tired bones. I'm not saying yes or no, but I think we need to be very deliberate about this. The Arati Grasslands were known back then for being the home to monsters that prevented settlement. We won't be able to just walk there, supposed safe route or no."

"We have time. Once we use this Tauran passage, it'll take months before the world galleon actually arrives. We have plenty of time. I have a few people in mind." Ash began writing names down on the edge of the parchment.

"Khalla, of course. Though won't it cause problems to take the guildmaster away?" Halgrim asked.

"Not at all. Since our success at Sai's estate, all of the Circle have contacted her to simulate their own security weaknesses. Well, not all. Daryx has not, and of course the god emperor. But, the others have. Meanwhile, the Merchant's Guild came crawling and begging that we declare them impenetrable. It's rather comical actually. Khalla must come. As an elf, she can help with the drow. Plus, we haven't been together very much of late. This will be a nice vacation."

Halgrim looked up and snorted. "Vacation. To Merakor. You need to reset your notion of what a holiday is."

* * *

Malcor sat in the command room of the Temple At Bloodstone. Throughout the valley where the fighting still raged, abyssal creatures continued to rise up, some summoning others. They also had a new problem. With each moment, Orcus' body rotted away revealing a skeleton bright with jade. Smugglers had come to Bloodstone hoping to dismember and claim parts of Orcus. Worse, those who had either been too far away to participate in the battle or who had allies outside of the valley, sent word. Every day, more and more profiteers arrived either by magic or by flying creatures.

The dam had exploded the river flowing out between the First and Eighth, compromising the road. With the Third through Sixth Fortresses damaged, perhaps beyond repair, Malcor had at last asked King Andrew to take command of the valley's forces. The Sixth Fortress sat as a gaping hole in the ground cradling Orcus' head.

Alerius had almost countermanded that order. "I am going to go and rally what Tanian forces are left. I humbly ask that the dread lords change their focus from fighting the abyssal fiends, to harvesting and removing the parts of Orcus we cannot afford to let fall out of our hands. I do not know what those are, but the Goddess tells me that we must secure the head and spine."

Alerius paused for a moment, and then with a roar, he sent the other dread lords to the sky. With Tania focused on the head and spine, Andrew had wondered if he should try to retrieve some parts for Taysor. Malcor put his hand on Andrew's shoulder. "I know you're wondering if Taysor should take some of this. Here is the thing. Help us and I will remove the Tanian marks on your bloodstones. I cannot promise for all Taysor, but I give you my word – those bloodstones held by the royal family, will be released of Tania's hold."

Andrew nodded. "Done, King Malcor."

The fighting from there had been a nightmarish task of Soran troops fighting on the frozen and toxic ash all around the valley floor. Above and behind them, the dragons tore flesh burrowing out the spine and neck of Orcus. Whenever they became aware of profiteers trying to teleport in and take anything, Malcor met them as a shadow dragon. With his riders and battle priestess on his back, he patrolled the dark places of Bloodstone. Though he could not be in multiple places at the same time, he could find them instantaneously as he moved through the shadows. It quickly ended the profiteering. As hours turned into days, larger chunks of the dead god decayed in blocks giving rise to undead that made it more and more dangerous.

He could not remember when or who, but there was a last chasing off of adventurers trying to harvest the jade bone. Almost two weeks later, the dread lords wrested the last strips of flesh from the skull and spine. Ripping it free, the entire corpse shimmered and burned away leaving only jade bones that lay stretched from the headless neck at the Sixth to the feet by what had been Valley Town.

The broken sceptre lay in parts by the Third. Jeri pointed and said that she saw a group of elves, in sunlight, sneaking towards the eyes of the sceptre. "They're wise. I can barely see in sunlight," Malcor hissed in draconian.

They almost attacked when Malcor noticed the elven King Vel Pajor among the group. Perhaps sensing the shadow dragon, a powerful mage in their group cast a spell that removed them from Malcor's sight. "Are they going for the sceptre's eyes?" Seline asked.

With no way to know, Malcor blasted the area around and in front of the eyes with shadow fire. When nothing happened, he hissed. "Maybe they retreated?"

Seline disagreed. "The king himself would not come this far without purpose. May I contact the dread lords for help?"

When Malcor agreed, Seline used her bloodstone and they saw Mallaforax rise up from the head of Orcus and begin flying their way. "I've never met that one," Seline said.

"Neither have I," Malcor added.

Mallaforax's body looked gnarled and bent, like a tree made up of many vines. A faint green trail of mist hung in the air behind the dragon who circled around the sceptre and then landed on the head. "Vel Pajor, you simpering worm. I am going to gas this area." Mallaforax took an exaggerated breath and then slowly began to breathe a poisonous vapor along the sceptre. An instant later, they felt magic and saw a doorway open and close in a flash.

Malcor landed on the neck below Mallaforax and waited. The green patriarch, the Dread Lord of Vapors, continued to expel gas until either he could not sustain it or he felt certain the elves had left. "Thank you, great lord Mallaforax," Malcor said.

The green turned his head ever so slightly towards them. "This sceptre is a priority. With Orcus decapitated, it is time to end this. I will disjoin its remaining magic. Leave."

Malcor bowed and shadowstepped away. They watched Mallaforax who bent over the sceptre as if praying. They saw a faint twinkle and then the green patriarch vanished a split second before the sceptre detonated. The blinding flash of light and energy pulled Malcor out of shadow entirely. Seline raised her hand and then felt Malcor pull them all out of the flow of Time. From the ethereal shore of time's current, they saw a vortex where the sceptre had been. Just upstream, they saw a glimmer of the elf king and his desire for it.

"I do not understand these who claim to worship Pha Rann and yet seek out such evil things," Malcor grumbled. "If their heart is so set on capturing or using evil, how are they not evil themselves?"

"They must rationalize it," Seline replied mockingly. "For the greater good, for Pha Rann, for heaven, we must destroy or hold this thing."

"Tania holds it for them. It must be that they do not trust us. After all this, it's offensive. I wonder why Alerius has never brought Morilon to bear under Tania's empire." Malcor watched as the vortex slowly filled and then faded away.

"With the green patriarch there, maybe they feel this is the best way to assert their independence?" Seline speculated.

Chapter Seventy Three - Court of Dragons

Alerius twisted his shoulder in the darkness of the Temple At Bloodstone. "How long until the golem wing is ready?" Spark asked.

"Sai has indicated that to create such a thing would require all of the mithril in Tania. As such, I have decided to not. When I fly, I will use human magic."

Ynt'taris hissed concern. "But the pain. Your wound has yet to heal, brother. Is there nothing?"

"Even dead, it seems the Jade God bothers me." Alerius laughed but his voice had an edge of pain to it. "I take this as a sign that too long have I lingered in Tehra. Though I do love to walk its gardens, the Mother calls me to ascend."

Spark and Ynt'taris bowed their heads. "So, the whisperings are true," Spark said slowly in an attitude of listening.

Alerius nodded. "This has been an expensive battle but one well worth it. The cost in valued lives, never have they shone as brilliantly as they did in that battle. I shall treasure the memory always."

Ynt'taris humanshifted and gave Alerius a hug. Her small girl form against his giant armored one seemed perfect. Spark moved his head down to them and said, "You have built a wonder here, Alerius. I am unsure it survives with the god emperor Alerius gone."

Already, Alerius triggered an illusionary copy of the moment and spun it to Ana's bloodstone sphere. "Yet, all things must end for that is how Tehra and Time march together. My second son is dead. My precious Rojo, and millions of others through the ages. Though I know it pulls at you both too, my brothers. Never before has Time pulled at me the way it does now. I feel it in the jagged pieces of my broken wing, and cannot stand my own sight in the River."

Spark and Ynt'taris looked at each other and the blue deferred to ice. "If you leave, Alerius, we have decided to let the humans rule." Ynt'taris' words surprised Alerius, who looked to Spark.

Seeing mutual agreement, Alerius bowed his head. "So, this will end the age of dragons."

Ynt'taris replied, "I choose to see it as the beginning of the age of dragon legends. The god emperor Alerius, the icy Ynt'taris, and the magical Spark.

We have watched over this land for ages, and like you, the weight of memory and nostalgia threatens to overwhelm. When the prophecy seemed about to be fulfilled, I thought, "Surely, my time has come to Ascend." But, then my Ora found love and a spark I had lost with the ancient Alaura rekindled with Ora's child. Malcor's sister Klara too. I would see a princess become Queen in Tania before I ascend."

Alerius stroked the hair of the girl at his side and answered. "You are wise and compassionate, ice patriarch. Tania is stronger for the sacrifice you made of old to join with us. And you, my brother in lightning?"

"My life's blood is the magic of the storm, the mighty clouds that spark and dance with fire. Tania's Magi are stronger than ever. In ancient times, you forced us to make a choice. You said that we must back off and not intervene if we would have the children become mighty and precious. You were correct then, and I see for ages now that the less we intervene, the stronger they become. For the spearhead to continue in strength, we must let the humans complete its forging. I shall not ascend, but will linger here in Tehra until my life's spark goes out. I would see what becomes of the children when you, Brother Alerius and Ynt'taris, have ascended. I would see what becomes of Tania when it slays Set without the dragons."

They held each other tight in silence. Dar Ana, Kell, and Shara found them standing in solemn brotherhood as fire, cold, and lightning slowly spun around them by Ana's throne. The three high clerics stopped and bowed, before retreating as quietly as they could. Once back outside, they stood by the central door and waited, praying. Tiamat's presence swirled throughout the Temple felt as chills, a lover's touch, whispered promises of future glory, and a sense that tomorrow would bring another day.

Ana closed her eyes and stepped from the River. The flow of Time progressed as it always did in Bloodstone. Its fits and starts stuttered along but there, just upstream from her, the Court of Dragons stood with broken winged Alerius in the center of ice and energy. From both sides of the flow, dragon heads reared up until Tiamat in her multi-headed glory could be seen looking down at the three patriarchs.

Alerius dropped to his knees and stretched his hands forwards and up to his Mother. "All this Time, Mother. So much Time! I have carried your banner through millennia and kneel here before you victorious against The Necromancer. The Heretics are home. Your children are stronger than ever. I have numbered the deaths of millions, many precious and dear to me. I would see, at last, an end to the deaths of those I love."

To her side, Kell and Shara joined to Ana to witness Alerius' ascension. The red dragon head of Takhissis looked down at him and spoke with a voice of passion and calm. "Alerius, patriarch of fire. As eldar, you served me and saved me from Time's execution. You rose up against My Consort. You have forged a Tehran construct I could not have imagined before Time. Speak your heart's desire and it shall be."

Alerius opened his eyes, wet with tears. "My love, the dominion of flames is my dream. I would fill it with the fire-breathers and ask that the Kerchki join in its dominion."

Tiamat withdrew and the other heads consulted with the flame breather. It returned and stated, "You have accomplished the Ascension Rites to allow this. Should the fire giants pledge to you, you shall have their dominion joined to yours."

"It shall be as you say, Mother," Alerius whispered. Alerius looked around seeming troubled. "I had hoped my precious Rojo would be here."

Tiamat answered. "Rojo fights for a greater dominion than required. The student emulates his teacher. Behold!"

An image rose up from the River where Rojo struggled against the Fifth Rite. Tiamat said, "This, for your children, may be the hardest Rite. To lay claim to a dominion against the endless time of eternal undying, it requires a degree of patience your children lack. You have taught your children to set plans, to execute strategies, to keep an eye single to the glory of My Cause. Coming through the middle rites, Rojo struggles with his dominion's natural drive to action."

"I do not understand," Alerius said. "He had completed the First. All he had to do was accept his role as the colorless dragon and claim the dominion shared by metallic and coloreds alike."

Tiamat considered it as well. "He has separated enough from my dominion that I cannot know. Something must have happened to drive him onwards. Should he succeed, like you Alerius, he will bring a much magnified dominion to us." The various dragon heads inspected Rojo from all directions. "He seeks to claim dominion over the breath weapons. How interesting, and imaginative!"

Ynt'taris and Spark joined and, for a time, they watched Rojo struggle with the very concept of eternity. Spark said, "For one born into the poison, to purge it and open their thoughts to something other than linear time. Though Tehrans can ascend, this is why so many fail. I would that we could help him."

One of Tiamat's heads turned to regard the high priestesses and Dar Kell. They fell to their knees. "How may we serve Goddess?" Ana asked.

"You already serve." The fire-breather aspect of Tiamat turned once again to Alerius. "Long have you chosen to stay in Tehra, beloved Alerius. See that your work is finished, and then come and join me in the endless skies of fire and flame." Tiamat leapt to the sky and flew away from the River.

Alerius summoned the clerics to join them. "My work is almost done. Dar Kell, you are to appoint a successor and hand over the Temple At Morbatten to one you deem worthy. Though I could ascend, I am inspired. I shall ascend in a manner befitting a red dragon. We shall quest, you and I, to the ends of the world until we are slain in mighty battle."

Dar Kell bowed, "I live to serve and obey, god emperor."

To Dar Shara and Ana, Alerius spoke next. "Malcor is young and secretly hopes that Klara will mature and take the crown from him. Shara, I task you to treat Malcor and Klara as if the Temple of Glass. Like Rojo, I prophesy that Malcor shall seek out a mighty deed as a way of proving his worth as king. With Ora and their child, Malcor is fragile. For the dragons to withdraw, there must be a strong unity between the Temple, the King, and the Innocents. Ana, you shall remain at Bloodstone but are commanded to ascend in the Third Cascade.

"For that shall be when the Nightmare awakens and attempts to devour the world. Though I cannot tell when this might occur or how, our defeat of the Necromancer reverberates throughout the Abyss even now. I see the Mother of Nightmares stirring in her prison of sleep. A yellow eye opens in the darkness. Set will come through Bloodstone."

www.ingramcontent.com/pod-product-compliance
Lightning Source LLC
Chambersburg PA
CBHW051054030726
47504CB00006B/1630